OUT OF THE IRON FURNACE

by

Homer W. Hunter

JMT Publications • Indiana

Out of the Iron Furnace
First Printing - August, 2000
Printed in USA

Library of Congress Catalog Number 00-106248

ISBN Number 0-9703045-1-X

DEDICATION

"Pete" Daugherty

MENTOR

Forward

The desire to "write a book" appears to be universal. Usually, this is an expression by persons who really have nothing to say and entirely lack the means even if they did. Fortunately, Homer Hunter is an exception to this rule. Over the years, particularly the past twenty, we have witnessed the growth and development of a mind, a method and a passion for the written word in the English language reminiscent of Larry McMurtry and Herman Melville.

Exhibitionism, tinged with just the right amount of narcissism, is the sine qua non of the writer. There is no lack of these in the general population, so something more must exist to mark the writer. The literary show and tell must contain the correct mixture of pathos, tragedy, humor and satire. There must be the substance, which is basic to the human condition melded by the discipline which comes only from obsessively writing, writing and writing more until the flask of composition is empty, followed by more writing.

Homer writes about real people and real life, not some copycat fantasy of the latest Hollywood or made-for-TV movie. Through Homer, we come to know these folks, their trials, triumphs and failures. We come to know ourselves better, too, through the eyes of a writer who is insightful, entertaining and painfully penetrating

Homer Hunter began his career in the Deep South, somewhere in Mississippi, Alabama, Georgia and South Carolina. His life is a mosaic of failed attempts to find himself and the part he must play in the game of life. He geed and hawed, floundered and stumbled, but never quit. He survived dissolution of family, poverty, ill health and the surgical evisceration of his worldly body guided, always, by his star of destiny.

Homer never met a stranger and was always gentle, genteel, softspoken and non-abrasive. Ultimately, fate brought him to a small steel mill in Georgetown, South Carolina. He gathered friends, found Karen, and the family he never had. Here his roots finally discovered the fertility and sustenance so necessary for his maturation. His fellow workers became his brethren and his progeny. Georgetown became the home and the cradle of his creativity. He produced this book and was fulfilled. Surely, he is one of God's noblemen.

Theodore E. Gagliano
May 30, 2000

PREFACE

The forty short stories, the three groups of poems, and the single poem, contained in this volume comprise a portion of the literary work of a man of sensibilities, perseverance, and the successful will to survive. I'm still here — seventy-three in January! There are novels I have written, and other poems, and bits of comment and opinion, which are not included. To reproduce it all would take, not a book, but a set of books.

I have in my life faced many of the challenges which are met daily by millions of poorer-than-rich, richer-than-poor working or hustling Americans, who must contrive to act out the instructions of Machiavelli in order to live. Or, as has been said, "Be wise as the serpent, gentle as the dove." When I have fallen into the snares and traps of life, I have written a story. This book might hold some small hints for members of the vast underclass — the near poor — which would guide them away from the cave of the bear, or show them that there is a road to prosperity and recognition, if they can find it. I believe that road lies within each person. It is not endowed and proffered by something outside. The benefit of age is that there comes with it a calm wisdom. This can help others.

During my lifetime, I have associated with the underdogs, the renegades, the radicals, and the down-and-outers. I have known the drunks, the whores, the addicts, the thieves, the great con-men, and those who wear the ever-existing, unerasable mark of being gay. I have gone into out-of-the-way places; humble homes, country barrooms, pool halls, street-corners and alleyways — the byways and the hedges. I prefer this company and these places. There is a gritty blue-collar world out here!

I invite the reader to come and find something here they have not known before. These are not the writings of the pride of some small college — the trumpeter of some church — a Rhodes Scholar — but the attempts of a man who has touched life in the U.S. of A. for sixty years and come out of it alive and happy, to tell it like it is. The DOW and the NASDAQ will never understand anything about this book. It is for the girl hitchhiking a ride, trying to get home to her children. She has with her enough money, which she has made (please don't embarrass her by asking her how) so that they can eat. She doesn't want to delay long, because they will become too hungry to bear and cry. The night lowers down cold on that sad highway.

This study must, to succeed in my purpose, breed some understanding among family members, members of communities, people in people-helping capacities, law-enforcement men and women, people in public office, and possibly between churches and those who need a church most — those who fight against redemption — The Rebel.

A careful reading of this book will reveal the evolution of various of my attitudes and beliefs — my developing philosophy. In the beginning, I was racially very paternalistic, seeing African-Americans as remarkable pets, to be cared for and loved. Later, an African-American boy is shown as becoming Messianic.

In the beginning, I believed that God was sitting up there in those "green pastures," watching every step that was taken, ready to reward or punish. God's Hand was everywhere. I believed what the preacher told me. In the end, I make apologies to no one, my philosophy as it touches religion is that everything we have we brought with us (lessons learned through millions of years of evolution) and carried in the genes, DNA, "the gospel is written on our inward parts." Whatever we get, we get from within. There is nobody out there waiting to hand it to us. There is no imaginary entity that will walk beside us and keep us company through life. In the beginning I was an "effete snob." I thought Spiro Agnew was a brutish beast. Now, I am almost an anti-intellectual. The heart and soul of America is in Nashville — not in the Ivy League mills of mind- and thought-control in the East, and not in very many of our public schools. I finally believe that everything that is to be learned is to be learned in the street. The thread of my problem with my father is woven on and on until suddenly it was gone. I do not understand why this string broke. Maybe it just wore out. My father is dead, and his picture hangs on my wall. What can it all mean? I don't know. In the beginning I was taught that sex outside marriage, practiced with someone of the opposite sex, someone of the same sex, or with one's self was a grievous sin. Now, I don't think so.

Now, I will answer the million dollar question. Am I gay? Forget heterosexual. Forget homosexual. Even, forget bisexual. I'm not going to say that I'm gay, but I will say that I am more gay than I am straight. I am one-hundred percent narcissus. I have always been in love with the man in the mirror. How many men can you get to admit that? I like men who look, dress, speak and move like me — mirror-images of myself. I like men who have the good taste and discernment to like me. Who cares about sex? What I have looked for is a twin, to "walk with me, and talk with me, and tell me I am his own."

What did Elvis Presley know? He had the little dead twin brother buried somewhere back in Mississippi, and he spent his life trying to glorify himself (and he succeeded in this), and when he got old and fat, he was so disappointed in the image his self had taken on that there was nothing for him to do but die. So, he did.

Homer W. Hunter
Georgetown, South Carolina
April 1, 2000

TABLE OF CONTENTS

THE 1940's

The 1940s were not good years for this writer. His town and his family failed to get ahead, and he was himself very poor. His health declined with debilitating illnesses which could not be diagnosed. He was 4-F, when every young man's self-worth was measured by his contribution to the war effort. He dropped out of college in his freshman year. He made a bad marriage. He was divorced. He lost a good friend. Yet, he wrote a three-volume family chronicle named "You Gotta Know How To Pray." He didn't. During this decade he and his father did not get along.

The stories written in 1944 approach the characters in a light which would have been unfavorable to many in that time and place, had they been circulated. They were not. The stories are about an ingenious and inventive Negro woman, a ghost of an Indian who carried over to the beyond a devotion to and responsibility for his dog, and a Chinese woman who gave her love forever and was able to be heroic.

The subject of interracial marriage is dealt with, illustrating white-male selfishness and arrogance.

Questions of race permeated society in that place at that time. People formed opinions about thes questions even when they were not aware of doing so. Racial perceptions and beliefs cropped up in every conversation and every written piece, sometimes a light lichen veneering the tree of conversation, sometimes kudzu, which can strangle an oak. Young minds were infused with all this. The subject was as much at home at table, and happy as Banquo's ghost. What should be done with it?

LYMAN, MISSISSIPPI

The town of Lyman, served by the Illinois Central Railroad and Highway 49, began the 40s having lost its role as a thriving sawmill town to become a ghost of a prosperous past which had died with the final destruction of the piney woods in Mississippi. No one who stayed on there had anything. The whites were poor, and the Negroes were poorer. The road and the railroad stretched away, almost untraveled, to places which for the people of Lyman were unknown.

"Jonah's Wife" proposed that even in the most unpromising surroundings a pearl of great price may be found. The story was written at Lyman in 1944. The writer was in eleventh grade. He heard the drumbeat of "a different drummer" than the one which led his father, who held a dark sense of having been cheated by life, and marched through Earth a pessimist. His peers were unknowing and unknowable. Thanks to the attitude of his mother, this writer was an eternal optimist, in those days, in this sad diminished village.

There was nothing material which taught this writer the view which is held by the narrator in "Jonah's Wife." He was an anomaly in his environment, clutching intangibles. Anyone he knew would have told him the premise of his story was preposterous. A Negro woman could not be this good.

"Jonah's Wife" shows that nobility, like lightning, may strike anywhere - and love may flow forth - early or late - expected or past anticipation - those vital cements which hold together the bricks of society.

JONAH'S WIFE

Somehow, I never could bring myself to believe all the things Jonah told me about the woman he had married. They were simply too farfetched.

Jonah was my negro handiman. I had given him a month's vacation not long before, and he had found himself a wife. She had come out of her native forest with him and was living in his shack down by the tracks. I had never seen her.

"Boss, my Tilda done writ a song."

"Really?"

"Yes suh. She say would you see as how you might sell it."

"Sure, Jo."

Jonah had brought me his wife's song. On pages of cheap white paper in neat straight lines, the notes spread. The aire was long and complicated.

"Tilda say fo' you to please write the words. See my wife can't write suh, an' ah can't do nothing with dem neither."

"But Jo, how can I write the words when your wife hasn't sent them?"

"She done made me remember them, boss. Ah can tell them to you."

Jo began to recite in perfect syllables a poem of such pagan loveliness and simple beauty that I listened with baited breath.

I wrote it down with trembling hand.

The publishers were exaltant, and when I first heard the music played and the words sung tears came to my eyes.

I went home to Jo. He was raking leaves in the back yard.

"They liked Tilda's song, Jo. Could she write more of them?"

"Yes suh. She can write 'em always, ah guess."

"Tell her to send them to me as fast as she gets done with them."

"Yas suh. Ah'll do that."

"All right. If you want, you may go home and tell her about her song and take her this money for it, tell her there will be more."

After that I sold six or eight songs for Tilda. All were amazingly original and all had the same simple beauty that had characterized the first.

One day, Jonah stood before me.

"Another song, Jo?"

"No suh. Wife say she tired of writing songs, but she writ a story for you."

"But Jo, she can't write."

"I have it here," Jonah tapped his forehead.

He sat down and slowly repeated the simple story Tilda had taught him word for word while I wrote it down.

The story was as beautiful as a quiet jungle river. It was so sincere and natural that like the songs, it almost brought tears.

"Jo," I said when I had written it all, "why doesn't Tilda come to me herself instead of making you memorize her work and tell it to me? It must be very hard for you."

"Yas suh, it is hard, but wife say ain't right fo' niggers to go bothering the white folk day don't know. She say you mah boss, an' ah de one to 'proach you."

"Well Jo, next time tell her to come herself."

The next day I opened the back door when someone knocked. A small colored woman stood outside.

"I am Tilda."

"Oh, come inside. Did you have something you wished me to write?"

"Yes sir. I have a story I would like to have written."

She spoke with no accent or defect of speech. Her English was perfect.

We sat in the kitchen and I wrote her story. She looked wistfully at the written pages.

"Why don't you learn to write?" I asked her.

"I've had no chance, sir. I should like to."

Then and there I began to teach Tilda to write. In two weeks she could put any common thought on paper. In two months she did not need me anymore. She quit coming to me, but almost every day Jo brought me something she had written for me to sell. Some days it would be one of her simple songs. Again it would be one of her stories full of the beautiful and natural wonders of life.

4

One day Jonah brought an especially long story. Then he said,

"Wife say she gonna leave me. Say ah no good. Boss, she'll go back to Carolina, back to the woods. Ah'll lose her."

"Don't worry Jo. I'll talk to Tilda."

I was beside myself. Tilda had to stay with Jonah where I could reach her. If she went back to her home her songs and stories would be lost to the world. She must stay.

My wife was ill but I would have to leave her alone in the house and go to Tilda at once. I hurried down the street.

My conscience assailed me. My wife was sick and I had promised her that I would tend to the house. Instead, I was out trying to patch the romance of my colored folks. Then a plan formed in my mind.

"Tilda, my wife is sick abed and there is no one to cook or clean the house. Won't you come and help me?"

I could see that there was a struggle in her mind. I had helped her, and she wanted to help me, but she had made her plans. She was ready to go home.

She looked at me for a long time.

"Yes sir. I'll stay and help you."

That afternoon she took over my house. My wife was soon well, but I arranged for her to remain helpless a while longer.

One day she approached Tilda.

"Can you sew, Tilda?"

Yes ma'am."

"Well, I wish you would make me a dress."

She gave Tilda a pattern and some money for the material. The pattern was for a simple house dress."

A few days later, Tilda presented my wife with the finished dress. It was made of green velvet. The collar was high and the sleeves long and slim. It was gathered at the waist and fell away in elaborate pleats to the floor. There was a wide sash and jacket to be worn over the rest cut from brown velvet and lined with silk. My wife sat down in the nearest chair.

"This is nothing like the pattern, Tilda."

"I'm sorry, ma'am, but I couldn't work with that thing. I just made it like I thought was suitable for a lady like you."

There were tears in my wife's eyes.

"Will you make me more, Tilda? I love the dress."

"No ma'am. I'm going back to my husband. Maybe when we're settled again I'll come back to you part of the time, but now my time is going to be for Jo."

I knew then we hadn't lost Tilda. She had fallen in love with her husband, and love would hold her here.

She strode down the road toward her home. My wife held her new dress on her lap. I was happy.

5

LYMAN, MISSISSIPPI

"The Indian's Dog" was written in 1944 at Lyman. The reader is taken for a walk on the mystical side of life. To this youthful writer the elements forming the natural and supernatural orders are interwoven. The world is corporeal and spiritual - as is man - as is God. This writer speaks for himself, not any prescribed orthodoxy. He views the creatures belonging to the supernatural side as being benevolent.

All dogs go to the Happy Hunting Ground. Who will want to go there if they don't?

THE INDIAN'S DOG

Outside, the dog looked at the moon and howled, and inside Jake Hansen sat at the door to his room and looked at the dog and was silent. It was his father's dog, and Jake cursed the dog silently.

The moon lay just above where the pine trees left off in the sky, and Jake could see that it was a big moon, and the next night it would be full, and Jake was afraid.

The dog sat on the bare ground and stared at the moon, and he pointed his nose at it and howled.

Jake spat.

The dog howled again.

Jake shivered. For generations, the Hansens had been men of the woods, and they had been close to nature, and had grown akin to nature. This kinship with nature had given them a warped idea of the supernatural, and they had gotten it all mixed up in their Christianity so they believed it.

Jake watched the dog and his heart sank. Jake thought of his sister, and a bird flew before the moon, and the moon sank, and Jake's heart sank as he thought of his sister.

He thought of his sister's illness, and he looked at the moon, and he decided to think things through from the start.

Mary Maud, that's Jake's sister, had been sixteen five years ago, and she had been in love. Now Jake hadn't known, and his father hadn't known, and there had been trouble.

Jake could remember how it all started. It had begun at church when Sadie Whitney, that was Jake's girl then, he was eighteen, had introduced him to Pete Hardlass.

This Hardlass fellow was from Texas, and he was tall and dark and handsome, and his muscles rippled when he walked. He carried two pistols, and Jake felt small beside him. He was doing some business with Sadie's father, and Sadie saw him lots, and Jake worried and began to think, and there was going to be trouble.

7

Now he thought of his little sister, and he hated himself, and knew himself for the low fellow he was, but he introduced Pete Hardlass to Maud Mary, and Pete begain to see less of Sadie. Jake wondered if he were meeting Maud Mary, and he hoped and then he thought Pete was not, but Pete was.

Then one day Maud Mary rode into the woods and came back with Pete and an old Indian and a dog. The Indian was sick and the dog was starved, and Maud Mary said she had ridden alone to a cave she knew, and had found the Indian and the dog there. Pete said he had been hunting nearby and had seen her and offered to help, and they said they had decided to bring the Indian to the Hansen's and they had.

The Indian was silent and Jake knew they were lying, but he kept silent, too, while they put the Indian to bed in the stable, and Pete left.

That night the dog howled, and the moon was full, and in the morning the Indian was dead, and the dog was quiet, but Maud Mary was gone, and in the town, Pete Hardlass was gone too, so Jake and his father and the dog lived on alone.

Now some of the folks said Pete and Maud Mary went to Texas, and some said they were nearby, but nobody knew and Jake and his father didn't try to find out.

Then, a week before, Jake had found Maud Mary unconscious on the front porch, and Jake's father had put her to bed in the stable, and would not let her be brought into the house. Every night since, the dog had howled and tomorrow night the moon would be full, and Maud Mary would die as the Indian had done. Jake wanted her to live, and he wanted to hear her story, and she would die if the dog howled.

Jake got a rifle from a rack on the wall, and stepped to the door. The moon was below the trees, but Jake could see the dog; he lifted the rifle, and he aimed it at the dog's head, and he pressed the trigger.

The dog died, and the last echo of his last howl died, and that was the end of the dog, but Jake wondered how he had died, because there had been no report from his gun. His gun had been empty.

Now the next night, the moon was full, and the dog did not howl, and at daybreak Maud Mary was well, and she told her story.

She and Pete had married and built a cabin about thirty miles away, and they had tilled the land and hunted and had children, and they were happy 'til Pete had shot himself in the leg. He had done it at hunting and she had come for help.

Jake and his father were sorry and went with Maud Mary to help Pete.

Now the story of the old Indian's dog got around and people talked. Some said the dog was hexed to death, and some less superstitious ones said Jake was lying. Nobody in town could explain how the dog died so everyone could believe he was right.

But Maud Mary knew. She knew the old Indian had come and got his dog, to keep him from being any trouble. She had seen him in a dream and he had told her so, and he had told her that all was well with Pete.

LYMAN, MISSISSIPPI

"Or In The Eye" was written at Lyman in 1944. This is a story about fancy - some good, intellectual fun - which took an unexpected turn. Shakespeare says that fancy (romantic delight) is born in the eyes. The writer of "Or In The Eye" sees fancy as any condition wherein things are not as they seem - a conterfeit vision. One such illusion is deliberately created here.

This writer as a child had always become cringingly afraid in horror movies, when permitted to go. A walk in the woods after dark - the shrouded figure of a quiet cow munching - would set him running - flying home sniveling. Yet he read many books of ghost stories in his teens.

"Or In The Eye" has a distinctly British flavor, picked up no doubt from British authors, or from writers like Poe, who tried to write British.

Apparently, the lesson to be learned here and from Shakespeare is that fancy is bad. Will said, "Let all ring fancy's knell. I'll begin it - Ding, dong bell." The protagonist in this story must have - after all - concurred in this.

"Bowwow," says Pal.

OR IN THE EYE

Howard involuntarily stepped around that spot there by the front door (on the floor, of course) when he came in at about eight o'clock this evening, but now that he has heard the spot's story, I'll bet he'll step around it on purpose.

This is the first time Howard has visited me here at Arthell Hall. He and I were friends at college and I have kept more or less in touch with him ever since, at dog races and so forth. Dog raising is my business, while dogs are just a hobby with Howard, but he knows a lot about dogs for an amateur, and I respect his ideas and opinions. Of course he is a Terrier man, and Spaniels are my choice any day. I keep one or two with me most of the time. I brought a little fellow (English type) with me here. He is very bright and I've taught him a good many tricks, not too many though, the wife says I play just like a child with my dogs.

The wife has disagreed from the first about my plan to frighten Howard. She claims it's childish and her intuition is against it. Of course as soon as I had heard the story of this house I could not resist.

When Howard came it was dark outdoors. The stars shone but dimly and the moon was still behind the trees over there toward Mayfield. There were no clouds, but Howard stumbled as he came up the steps, that goes to show how dark it was even without them.

"Watch out there, man!" cried I, giving him the use of my hand.

He stepped around the dull brown spot on the floor into the light.

I could hear his cab starting at the road and I wondered how the house had

9

looked to him, this his first time to see it. I could remember my first time to see the place after dark. My wife and I had been driven out in a rented car. The moon had been shining, and the house stood clean-cut and sharply defined against a background of moonlit sky. The knee-length grass in the yard was wafted back and forth in the breeze and its motion made me slightly sea-sick. We stood together (my wife and I) and looked at the place that was to be our home.

There is no tree near the house, but across the road, far to the other side of the field stands a gnarled cedar. This is all that remains of that long avenue of cedars which had led from this ancient plantation home to the road. This house was built before the Civil War, it had stood tall and white, the heart of a great plantation. It is not white now it has had little care and the weather has done away with much of the paint. The kitchen crouches to the back like some black animal, ready to spring up at the rest of the house.

The house wasn't damaged in the war because, of course, the Yankees never came as far south as Mayfield. Old David Arthell owned the place then. He was the third of the Arthells. He was too old to go to war, and he had no sons. He stayed at Arthell Hall and watched the place go to ruin after his slaves had run away, and his stock had been confiscated by the army. When the war was over, men from the front began to head south to their homes. All day long they passed by Arthell Hall, none of them stopping, none of them welcome.

The old man had grown queer toward the last and would not tolerate strangers. He stayed in his house, having contact with no man but his two old darky house servants who kept him fed and clothed and the house safe from returning soldiers, who, starved for food and shelter were turned on the mercies of the southern landowner.

One night when the negroes were in bed, a knock sounded at the front door. David went and opened it a crack. An emaciated man with a ragged beard and a faded and holey Confederate uniform stood outside.

"I'm sick, man," he said. "Could I have a night's rest?"

"Get away from where you ain't got no business," replied David.

The soldier flung the door open and clutched David. "Listen, Grampa, I been in a war. I been dirty, sick, and hungry for four years, in mud, lying in holes where it was so cold the grass had all died, and I didn't have no clothes or shoes or no warm house either. And it ain't been for me. I didn't have no slaves. You did, and I been fighting like hell so's you could keep 'em. Well I lost - is it my fault?"

"Get out!"

"Ungratefulness like yourn don't deserve to live. I'm going to kill you with my two bare hands."

He killed the old man and went upstairs to bed. The next morning, he buried David in a shallow grave a mile on down the road, and took the place over, house servants and all. Things went from bad to worse for Arthell Hall.

Harris Greenburg was no farmer, the crop failed and the house became more desolate. One year after David Arthell had died, it stood grey and weathered against a clouded sky. The wind roamed about it moaning and tearing at loosened shutters. Harris sat in the dining room disconsolately going over his accounts. The furniture emitted peculiar sounds and the windows shook. His single candle waivered. Suddenly, there was a knock at the door. He arose and opened it.

* * * *

In the morning the negroes found a pool of blood there by the open front door.

Harris was gone.

Legend ran that David Arthell had after one year arisen from his untimely grave and come back to seek revenge.

There were night travelers who swore that they had seen him in rotten torn clothing, an ugly wound at his throat, wandering about. Clay from the grave was on his face the color of blood.

The negroes could not be persuaded to stay about the place, so it was sold at auction. An old officer from the Confederate Army bought it and planned to fix it up, but he was called to New Orleans on busines, and left the place with a caretaker. One year from the night of Harris' disappearance he came back to Mayfield with plans to go out to the place in the morning.

When he got there he found the front door open and a fresh pool of blood just inside.

The caretaker was gone.

No one would live in the house after this, so it had stood vacant until last month when I came. Everyone says that once a year on the night of his death, old David returns, to knock on the front door and kill whomever answers.

Of course I don't believe this, but I decided to get Howard out here on the night old David is supposed to knock and see if he would. Everything is in readiness. I have told Howard the story of the house, and my little Spaniel is outside trained to make a sound against the door like a person knocking when he wants to come in. It took some training but I know dogs and they learn quickly from me. He has done it perfectly every night for a week.

The wind has sprung up outside. How it moans down the chimney. Howard is uneasy. Poor Howard, I would put more wood on the fire but the gloom suits my purpose better. It is cold in here, but then it is about time for Pal to want to come in.

Lord, how that scared me! It was Pal's knock.

"There Howard, you laughed at my story, go open the door." How pale he is! "Go on, you don't believe David Arthell can rise from the grave."

My voice sounds very natural. He's going to open the door. How silly he will feel when he finds only a dog.

* * * *

Why - there's the wife on the stairs. "What is it dear?" What's that she's saying? Not Pal at the door! She has Pal in her room! She didn't want Pal to frighten Howard! "Not Pal, but who ..?"

* * * *

The door is open. There is blood on the floor. Howard is gone.
"My God! What have I done?"

LYMAN, MISSISSIPPI

"Death In Oil" was written in 1944, when the writer was studying at Perkinston Junior College in Perkinston, Mississippi. The second world war was becoming real to this writer, who was seventeen.

In the story, telepathic knowledge of the destruction of a way of life, in which the protagonist had found beauty, and of the death of a talented, loved woman, demonstrates to him in terms which are real the tragedy of war.

Revelation to himself of his motives in the matter lead the protagonist to see his own seamy side. This he cannot bear. As has been said by Jack Bickham, "Preservation of the symbolic self is our number one priority."

Any threat to a person's self-concept means fight or flight - war or capitulation. The identity of southern white males would soon take many batterings, reel away from the battleground changed forever. What worse could happen? The black race fought for a new self-concept, one of pride for its own intrinsic value and virtue, and its ancient culture.

The protagonist in "Death in Oil" fled the war in China and in the end he fled again. Never did he stand and fight. The women he knew were stronger than he. Is this a reflection of the women who must cope alone in this writer's real world?

DEATH IN OIL

A Japanese dive bomber fell across a blood red sky. From out its almost severed tail, a spiral of black smoke followed it on its ever shortening journey toward complete destruction on the barren soil of China.

An ancient anti-aircraft gun stood idle after having feebly resisted the end that was inevitable for the frail city now being battered into obscurity by the Japs.

Buildings burned all about; walls were smoked black, and windows were gaping jaws revealing the flaming interiors of the once prosperous public buildings and business houses of the city.

In the foreground a statue stood of some noble Chinese, a solid statue which had resisted the trial, but now stood minus an arm and melting.

Across the feet of the statue lay the relaxed figure of a dead Chinese girl. On her face was a look of great content.

She was very beautiful although her hair was bloody and torn and her face was black with the ashes of her city.

The clothes she wore were dirty and in rags, but she lay with dignified repose, and the glow of the fire on her complexion made her seem more a statue than the melting copper thing above her.

She was one alone, a dead girl in her dying city.

* * * *

13

The little man in grey looked away from the painting to Mrs. Murdock.

"This is superb! Of infinite worth! I was in Paris and London so I know how an authentic bombing should look. This is the best thing I have found on canvas"

"I wonder how David did it."

"There is genius here."

The little grey man and Mrs. Murdock stood in David Murdock's studio above his luxurious Fifth Avenue apartment. David's painting sat in the light from the skylight.

The brushes lay on a table as David always carelessly dropped them after a day's work. Paints too were there.

David Murdock was gone.

"Queer, a man should do a thing like this and then calmly go off and leave it."

Mrs. Murdock became uneasy.

"You don't suppose..."

The door opened and David Murdock was inside.

"I'm sorry dear, I didn't know you had company."

"He came to see your painting, dear."

David looked at the painting on the easel.

"I painted that," he said.

"We know. It's ingenious."

"But, I painted it! I! Oh, Cindra! Is it true?" he shouted. He raised his voice. "Oh, can it be true?"

Mrs. Murdock tried to quiet her excited husband.

"Of course you painted it, dear. It's yours."

The little grey man talked to Mrs. Murdock in an undertone, which was quite unnecessary for David was no longer aware of anything in the room but the painting.

"He did not know it was his at first. He looked at it as though he had never seen it. And then, suddenly, he knew it was his."

"Maybe it isn't his."

"Oh yes, and the realization that he has painted it has shaken him."

David sat on a chair, staring at the painting, mumbling.

"Cindra - Cindra, is it true?"

The little grey man turned to Mrs. Murdock. "Who is Cindra?"

"I've never heard of her."

"Go down and call a doctor. Tell him to come at once, your husband is on the verge of a nervous collapse."

The little grey man turned to David Murdock. "You must get to bed, old man, at once."

David submitted meekly when the little grey man put him to bed. He still mumbled, and shook in every limb.

"Try to be quiet."

"Cindra - is it true? Is it true? Cindra?"

Suddenly he was still.

The doctor came, prescribed and went - over-work, nervous tension and so forth. A few day's rest; quiet. David was in no danger.

"You've been most kind." Mrs. Murdock held the little grey man's hand as he was leaving.

"I want David's painting, Mrs. Murdock. As soon as he is able send him to me. I will pay him well for this."

Then the little grey man was gone. Mrs. Murdock stood alone in her house. Her husband slept. Soon she did, too.

* * * *

About half past four in the morning, Mrs. Murdock awoke. Sleepily, she saw that the moon's reflection in the mirror had wakened her. The sun's twice reflected light had brought her out of sleep and she marveled at the brightness.

Suddenly, it was gone.

Someone stood between her and the mirror. She wanted to scream, but an icy terror prevented this. The light - she must turn on the light! There.

David Murdock stood looking at her, and spoke.

"It's all your fault, you know."

Mrs. Murdock could not speak.

"You were so beautiful."

"You shouldn't be up David, you're sick."

"Oh no! I'm all right." He drew close to her. "I was so mean, so poor, so beneath you, and you were so beautiful. I was almost insane."

"You're insane now. You're mad."

David seized Mrs. Murdock's head in his hands.

"Don't ever say that again. I'll kill you, whom I left the most faithful little woman in the world for. It is your fault she had to die alone."

"Don't talk like that, David. Don't! I didn't know. How could I have known there was another woman? Don't say it was my fault."

"I have come a long way, my dear. I lifted myself out of the filth of the gutter. You remember how inferior I felt and was? It was very hard. I worked to get away from all that and I did it, did it for you."

"I loved you, even then."

The sun was rising in the east. Mrs. Murdock sat as though she might never move. She was smothering, she wanted to breathe but her lungs felt as if they were held in the icy fingers of some iron hand.

She was horribly cold.

* * * *

15

David's bitter, insane voice droned on. He told Mrs. Murdock of how he had attended college in the hope of someday becoming an artist for her and how the faculty of the college had recognized his talent and sent him to China to paint.

When his ship had docked at Shanghai, David Murdock had gone at once to the interior and set up his studio in the little city of Shang Ho, by the Yellow River.

He went into the hinterlands of Shang Ho and painted natural scenes and paintings of the common people at their mean tasks or at play.

Each night he had spent at the bar in the Hotel St. Louis (for Americans) through the earlier part, and later on these nights had stayed in his room there.

His room was small and could have been a room in any of the milliions of hotels in our larger American cities. The view was good and he was in good company, for his own people were the only ones who lived there.

Next door, a young reporter battled daily with a badly crippled Royal typewriter. Sometimes he would come to see David and they would have long talks together.

"Have you ever been down in the native quarter?"

David was made to feel as if going down in the native quarter were a thing he should have done while still an infant.

"No," he apologized.

"Oh. You must see Cindra."

"What is Cindra?" David could have kicked himself.

"A girl - a fortune-teller, she's great." Arty Cook's contempt grew tangible.

David squirmed. "I might try her."

And he did. The very next day he and Arty sat in her small booth on a quaint street in the native quarter.

"These curtains came from the mountains - made in some monastery, I think."

"Who told you?"

"Cindra did, took me all through the place." Arty Cook swelled with importance.

"Did she tell your fortune?"

"Yes."

"Has it come true?"

"Part of it."

The brown hair curtains that David Murdick and Arty Cook had been scrutinizing parted and a tall, lithe Chinese stood in the deep carpet of the room. She was the most beautiful girl either of the men had seen. She wore a dress of green silk that shed some of its color onto the shiny floor when it crossed it. Over her face was a veil.

"What do you wish?" Cindra's voice came to David Murdock and Arty Cook as a bell from the steeple of some Asiatic holy place.

"This is one of my friends, Cindra. Tell him his fortune, won't you?"

The girl turned and looked at David. "Love. A devoted woman, a beautiful woman, one whom he should like to paint."

"When?" prompted Arty.

"Tomorrow." Cindra turned and was gone.

"Well, let's go," said Arty.

David was silent. There was something about the woman that attracted him.

"I wish I might see her without that veil. I want to see her face," he said softly. "I'd come here tomorrow, but I have a busy day."

He had been invited to the home of one of the nearby wealthy men to paint his house and fields.

The next day on his way to keep the appointment he saw her.

The girl wore a brown business suit and stood applying powder to her face beneath a statue in the square.

David Murdock looked at her. She must be waiting for someone. The girl turned and stared at David.

"Do you paint?"

"Yes."

"Your hands..." she pointed, "I love to paint."

"I am going over on the left bank to get some scenes there, will you ride with me?"

David looked up and saw a huge car standing before him.

"My car," said the girl. A friendly chauffeur looked out.

It took half an hour to cross the river, because they had to use a hand-ferry and several cars were ahead of them.

"My uncle may someday build a bridge here. I hope so."

David had spent many long hours at the ferry landing painting the workers, so the scene about him did not interest him. He yearned to know the girl better. They talked of life and love and the fate of nations and about painting and religion. He took dinner with her uncle (for he was the man he was supposed to visit) and painted her uncle's friends.

That night, Arty Cook met David in the bar. "Did you find the beautiful, devoted woman whom you should like to paint?"

"I found her."

David met the girl many times. They had long talks together. She told him her philosophy. "There is no such thing as a marriage of bodies without a marriage of souls. A man's personality leaves him when he dies and becomes his after-being or soul. When a man and woman share a lifetime together, their personalities are so intertwined as for each to become interdependent with, and incomplete without, the other."

17

""When one of a couple dies, his soul is earthbound until his mate's is released and may joined his. Then this complete product may enter heaven."

"Then might it not be best for the remaining mate to end his existence here on Earth as quickly as possible so that his soul-partner might be at rest?"

"Oh, no! The earthbound soul will not be unhappy, but spend this period in traveling about this Earth and who can say but it may go to the more remote planets?"

"And the other soul misses this?"

"That is the price paid for a few years of life, but then, they will have this to discuss through eternity."

The girl say that David understood and smiled.

"A tragic thing happened to many of the girls of China. Americans and Europeans are marrying them every day and when their time here in China is spent, they leave and go back to their own women and the girl is left with an unhappy old age and broken eternity to look forward to."

"It's a pity."

The girl eyed David closely. "I have devoted my life to the prevention of these marriages. I am Cindra."

A few weeks after this talk with the woman who was Cindra, David asked her to marry him.

"I love you, David Murdock," she told him sweetly. "When that fool, Arty, brought you to me, I knew that you would understand my philosophy and help me in my work. You won't go home to your own women like the rest because you are my lover - and my disciple!"

That night when David was moving his belongings away from the hotel to Cindra's home on the river, the city stood silent. China had received a terrible blow. Japanese troops were on the march on her soil. She was at war. David had received the news with incredulity.

"The Japanese are in China! They wouldn't dare! Why Japan is only a dot in the Pacific, and China covers a fourth of the continent. They'll be stopped in a month."

But they weren't stopped. The Japanese pushed on. Cities were bombed, armies destroyed, ships sunk. Asia was aflame. Shang Ho was in peril.

But while China was being battered and tortured, Cindra and David painted together and furthered their belief in the immortality of the personality. They had fun, but all the time a shadow was crossing Cindra's face. She knew that soon she must send David away. One morning she spoke to him.

"You have got to go, David, home to your own country. The Japanese will take Shang Ho and you must not be here. A truck is waiting with my paintings, it will take you to Shanghai. Get away with my pictures, and when it's over, you can come back, and we will have the story of our first year together in my paintings. Please, please don't let anything happen to you!"

"If anything happens to me, I'll come to you. We'll have a second meeting there at the statue. Good-bye, Cindra."

"Good-bye."

* * * *

Mrs. Murdock looked at David, horror in her face.

"David."

"I stole her pictures, they made me famous. It was through her that I got to where I am and got you."

"Do you love her?"

"She's dead."

"Oh no!"

"It was her hand that guided the brush that painted the scene of her death."

"She was a lonely figure."

"Cindra won't be alone much longer. I'll go to her."

David Murdock seized his painting and rushed to the window. Mrs. Murdock thrust herself between him and the window and clung to him desperately.

An old Chinese clock hung on the wall and David struck his head on this while escaping Mrs. Murdock. He fell unconscious at her feet.

She rushed to the phone. "Hello, police? This is Mrs. David Murdock, 470 Fifth Avenue. My husband has become insane. Come immediately."

* * * *

Later, a psychiatrist talked to Mrs. Murdock about her husband.

"Your husband seems to think that some girl whom he may or may not have known is dead and he should be with her."

"Yes, Cindra." Mrs. Murdock looked at the funny little psychiatrist in white clothes and glasses.

"We have to guard him very carefully as we do all suicidal maniacs. He becomes violent, and shouts, 'I'm coming, Cindra,' over and over while he tries to kill himself."

"Can't you do something, prove that Cindra is alive, even find her, or at least prove the city is different?"

"You might try."

The refugee board helped and finally an ancient evacuee from Shang Ho was found who had been present at the city's destruction.

Mrs. Murdock looked hopefully at the aged Chinese. He examined the painting closely. The little man in white clothes and glasses, and the little grey man, were there.

"It was exactly thus."

"Your husband is hopelessly insane. He will resist us until in the end he will join Cindra."

"Then," Mrs. Murdock turned to the little grey man, "You may have the picture." The two men were gone. "Dear Lord, what's to become of me?"

THE 1950s

The 1950s - not a good decade in the life of the writer. He was persuaded that he had "a call to preach," entered Mississippi College, stayed a year and left - his life altered forever - but not in the manner it had been hoped. Roy Alton Nicholas, Jr. was the bright moment. Idyllic love for a student nurse did not hold up. The writer disappointed many people before he gave up and went home (to Lyman, MS.)

The writer went to work for a truck line - moved himself and his parents to a house in Gulfport, MS. He engaged in freelance philanthropies. Then he married for the second time, a dreadful coup launched against himself by himself. Roy had died. During this time the writer had one friend. Then that friend left the city.

The writer then developed ulcerative colitis. He was continually sick. His employment was terminated. That's the way life was in 1959. Unable to work properly, one lost job and insurance. The employee had no recourse. As Hemingway said, "Let him that does no work not eat." The ulcerative colitis was finally corrected by a colonectomy.

The writer worked tirelessly through it all gathering research data about Gen. Earn Van Dorn of Port Gibson, MS. Van Dorn's father was a judge. The writer wished to write an historical novel which would juxtapose the father's life, wherein he sought to order society by the law, against the life of the son who believed Gordian Knots are best cut with a lightninglike stroke of the sword.

At the end of the 1950s, the South was about to catch fire. Meredith would soon seek to enter the University of Mississippi. Then, men would converge on Oxford, MS, with ax handles in the trunks of cars. And shotguns. It was all coming. But, no one where the writer was could see these things yet - or that they had to be. The writer imagined a Little Italy in a local pool room and sought a haven in the Catholic Church.

It was time to move on. The writer needed a new place. What he had until now almost destroyed him. He began to dream of finding a new people, people as mercurial as showbiz folks, who pranced to a different flute's song. People with new faces, new numbers, and all new gowns. And, always good lines.

CLINTON, MISSISSIPPI

"Of Mice And Such" was written in Clinton, Mississippi in 1950. The writer was at Mississippi College to study for the Baptist ministry. The shoe did not fit.

During the year spent there,, many deep impressions were made upon the writer. The events that are depicted in "What the Earth Knew" are loosely based on happenings observed by the writer "in the field " that year.

"Of Mice And Such" was written when madness had not yet been made manageable by the development of the new psychoactive drugs. Dementia was thought to be a permanent state. One man was taken to the state mental hospital, evidently in a state of paranoia (the Communists were infiltrating the churches.) It was said he would never be out. He was the writer's faculty advisor and the writer would never see him again!

In this story, the pathetic sin of vagrancy is punished by death. The writer had once taken this ride in a paddy wagon. Can good people, with purposes, die because they infringe some small ordinance? What of the young boy in for his first offense, a nonviolent crime, who is raped in his cell and hangs himself at the shame of it? What of the young mother, a pretty embezzler, who contracts AIDS in the jail from forced contact with a guard? What of all the slaps on the hand which take on lives of their own and balloon up to death sentences? We may, all unplanned for, punish too much..

Mississippi College defended the justness which lies in exacting "the wages of sin" from sinners. The school believed in the efficacy of punishment, and they would say who had the duty and responsibility to punish. The Divine Right of Kings was alive and well.

The writer loved the sinner and he found it difficult, while loving the sinner, to hate the sin. He was an amoral son of an amoral father. His softness on wrongdoing was incompatible with his "call to preach." Many young men arrived at ministerial colleges to become preachers, but left as caring social-workers - full-fledged, left-wing liberals. This writer just gave up. After a period of debilitating illness which defied diagnosis, he went to work for a truck line.

"Of Mice And Such" mentions nepotism in state government, even at the lower levels. It is critical of the handling of vagrants in New Orleans. The writer describes favorably a pantheistic gospel (inspiration for the protagonist.) Where was the innocent young boy who, six years before had written "Jonah's Wife" and "The Indian's Dog"? Gone. Gone! The remaining husk of that young man, an outsider at Mississippi College. The kernel was altered. Moloch was eating up the brains of Pericles, as was to be howled by Allen Ginsberg.

It was the 1950s now. The Rev. Martin Luther King, Jr. would boycott, and he would write, and he would speak, and the people would get ready to march, singing "We Shall Not Be Moved." Kerouac would come. People would mourn the whole decade over the death of Hank Williams. The old things were slipping away. It was a new day - the ecstacy was coming - everybody was young and hopeful of a new turn in society in America - during this prelude to the coming of the iconoclastic 50s.

Thank you, John Steinbeck, for all you did for us.

23

OF MICE AND SUCH

The strangeness of the world surrounding Joe Laurie of late was only exceeded by the singular nature of the world which existed on the inside of his troubled mind. Joe Laurie dwelt in a place of strange sights and strange sounds, inside, outside, scrambled so that he couldn't tell. Since that day on the river, everything had taken on an air of unreality for Joe. Perhaps, things would never be the same again.

Joe was puzzled by the peculiar place where they had brought him. Everything here was white or grey. He wondered what they had done with red and blue and green and orange. There had been other colors, too, colors that he had forgotten. The river had been brown, and the truck black. Everything had been some color, but now there was only white, and grey.

Joe seemed to see the little mice looking up at him out of the brown waters. Their noses were shiny, shoe-button black. Their eyes were pinpoints of black, too; afraid, questioning, panicked, dying. Joe put his white hands before his face. His shoulders began to shake. His hands were dry. He did not shed tears into his hands. Only his shoulders shook.

"Hello, Joe."

Big Lou looked in at Joe through the little window. His beefy face was genial, smiling. His eyes were blank and blue, expressionless. He did not care about Joe. His geniality was an act. His smile was false. He had had to put down his Little Lulu comic-book to come and see about Joe. He wanted to get back to his reading. He wanted to escape from Joe and from all the Joes on this ward. He wanted to escape from the sobs and the giggles, the curses and the explanations; people talking endlessly and emphatically, whining and moaning out details, all trying to tell Big Lou why they happened to be here. It seemed so necessary, so important. Big Lou must know how they all had come here. Big Lou didn't care.

"What's the matter, Joe?" Big Lou's lips spoke softly and caressingly. "What's the matter with you? Is it your rats again?"

Joe looked up guiltily. He could see Big Lou's mouth and his eyes. He could see his flat, ugly nose. He couldn't see his hair, or his chin. The window was too small.

"I saw brown a moment ago," he said.

"Goody," Big Lou said, thinking about Little Lulu.

"The river was brown, and the mice were swimming around in the cage. They could have gotten away, if they had not been in the cage, but it was locked up. It sank, pulling them down. They didn't have a chance to save themselves. If you could have seen the look in their little black eyes, you'd know how I feel. Their noses went down last. Little black pointed noses, fighting for air. It was terrible, Big Lou."

"Sure it was," Big Lou comforted. "It was a rough deal to have to go through. Let's not think about it any more. Let's think about something nice. I'll let you have my Little Lulu comic book when I get through with it."

"Will you, Big Lou?"

"Sure. I will if you'll be real quiet." Big Lou began to back away from the little window. In a moment he was gone. Joe hunched down on the narrow cot and put his head in his hands again. He did not want to look at the grey floor. He did not want to look at the white walls. He wanted to see the color. In a little while, Big Lou would bring him the Little Lulu comic book, and he'd look at all the pretty colors, and things would be better.

The administration did not like for Big Lou to give comic books to patients. One time he had given Joe a Mickey Mouse comic book by mistake, and Joe had to be placed in a straight jacket for three whole days. They had called Big Lou on the carpet about it, but Big Lou didn't worry. Big Lou's sister was employed as a secretary by a big man in the State Capitol, and once when he had seen fit to do her a big favor, he had given Big Lou this job at the hospital. Big Lou didn't need to worry about losing it.

Joe Laurie sat in his cell, engaged in his own personal nightmare, watching the cage with the mice inside sink again and once again into the swirling, brown, devouring waters.

* * * *

Solum Osborne had come from the west. He had come out from the places of wide prairies and spacious plains. He had come from the places where there was room for everyone, room for a man to move about, to flex his muscles, to make noise, to feel free because he was free. Solum Osborne had come from a strong, clean land which lay in the shadow of a great mountain.

Solum Osborne was a silent, thoughtful man. His face was the face of a dreamer, a man of deep, silent thoughts, a man of broad and profound philosophies, a shepherd-thinker.

He was a slight, wiry, blond-haired man, young and clean-cut in appearance. His eyes, large and clear and blue, held in them the look of a man who had a purpose, a mission. He seemed to wear the air of a chosen-being, a called-out one. His eyes burned with a fervency and a passion which bespoke a man who had special knowledges, wisdoms and truths, which must be imparted to others.

Out of the silent, wide places, he had come, and his feet bore him eastward, toward the land of the sunrise, carrying the light to the place of darkness; going home.

Solum Osborne had never been east of the Mississippi, but his genes could remember Georgia. Generations before, his ancestors had inhabited the lowland, the land of dense swamps and somber marshes which lie along the coast of Georgia. And now, the memory of the old home was strong inside him, and he was going back, going home to take the things which had been spoken to him out of the land and the sky in the great West where he had been given birth.

25

* * * *

Lafayette Square was silent this morning. It was springtime, and the traffic on Camp Street was slight. An occasional bird sang. Silent, lonely, empty men sat about, grateful for the sunshine. An atmosphere of hopelessness pervaded the place. The faces of the men were hopeless. Old and young, worldly and innocent, they were lost. Lost and empty.

But, the park was beautiful.

There was a great statue, and a bench, and on the bench a man, and a man, and a man, and Solum Osborne. His face was different. His eyes were full of the gospel which he had taken from the earth and the sky and the great silent mountain, and the passion to tell it. God in all things, and that something deep within the bowels of Solum Osborne which drove him eastward to tell it.

The police came. The dull, lifeless eyes of the men, old and young, worldly and innocent, filled with fear. The drooping, lazy bodies of the men alerted, and straightened. Faces twisted with fright and hate and dismay. The fate of the vagrant is jail, with the guilty and the innocent, the weak and the victim, the parasite and the fool. They took them away: a man, and a man, and a man, and Solum Osborne.

As they walked from the car into the station, Solum Osborne saw the St. Louis Cathedral standing tall, and cool, and grey against the sky, a little way down the street.

* * * *

The hard, cracked voice of the woman came from somewhere on the other side of the room.

"Yeah, I'm a Christian." Her tone was belligerent. "I'm a Christian. I was in church Wednesday night."

"Then what are you doing in jail?" This voice was a man's, smooth and mocking. "Why are you here, locked up like a criminal?"

"I'm not a criminal. I'm an alcoholic. That's a disease, like they explained in Alcoholics Anonymous. It don't stop me from being a Christian. You got to believe in Christ to be a Christian. Paul said, 'Believe on the Lord Jesus Christ, and thou shalt be saved.' I'm a Christian. I just slipped the other night, and they picked me up."

"You're nuts!"

The Negroes in the center row of cells had begun to moan and to sigh. In a few moments, they began to chant, and to sway back and forth. A slender, sensitive-appearing white youth broke into song.

"Just a closer walk with Thee. Grant it, Jesus. It's my plea..."

His voice was high and clear, a tenor. His long hair fell down on his forehead. His face was smudged with black. In a few minutes, the spell broke, and he began to sing another song.

"Though it's cost me a lot, There's one thing I have got, It's my gal..."

He crooned and swayed on his feet. Sinatra, Damone, Russell ... he was all

26

of those and more. He sang on, enjoying himself, but across the aisle, alone in his cell, another youngster buried his face in his arms and sobbed.

"Nine years. Nine years. Nine years."

Solum was silent in his cell. He looked down at the floor, thinking about the tale to be told, his own tale.

* * * *

There in the West was the woman. She sat alone in the midst of her prairie, and her eyes were turned eastward where her man had gone.

He loved something more than me. He loved his dream more than he loved me.

She would have turned then and cursed the ground and the sky which had spoken strange things to him. She would have poured out her hurt and her anguish upon them, but the lethargy of her spirit would not let her. Her loneliness and emptiness and despair made her numb. She could not speak her sorrow. Only her eyes could tell of her broken heart.

Such things as she felt, were the things felt by the dove who has seen her mate shot down, or the lioness who has seen the lion captured and carried away. It was the universal pain and ache and soreness felt by the female when the male is taken from her.

The woman followed her sheep, there in the shadow of the great mountain, but her eyes were turned eastward where her man was gone.

* * * *

Joe Laurie came into the cellblock, proud, confident, and cocky in his policeman's uniform. He was happy with the peculiar masculine happiness which comes from being placed in a position of authority over other men. He swung his shoulders jauntily, and looked at the motley crowd of men in the cells with a sparkle in his eye. He was immaculate, close-shaven, smoothly-combed. The men before him sat with forlorn eyes, tousle-headed, unshaven and unclean. Joe Laurie's uniform was pressed with all the practiced perfection of the cleaning man's art. His shoes shone brightly. His voice was hearty and satisfied.

"You folks are going to the line-up," he said.

Other policemen were in the place. They began to unlock doors, letting people out of the cells. They herded them out the front of the station and loaded them into the black trucks. Men and women, colored and white, and Solum Osborne, locked in together.

"Don't cry, Louise," a strong Negro man comforted, "Don't do no good to cry."

The frail colored woman - white dress and pearls - looked up at him with her suffering eyes.

"You know what selling dope means," she moaned. "They ain't going to let us off. We're going to Angola. Angola, Angola." She let her head drop forward,

27

and wept into her fingers. The man put his arm around her, drew her close to him, trying to make her feel safe, the male comforting the female.

The sensitive boy who had sung in the jail looked at her bowed head with his large, brown eyes. His friend, sitting beside him, smoked a cigarette, rapidly, very much afraid.

"Where are we going?" he asked.

"To the line-up," one of the Negroes said. "They'll question us. Don't worry none. They won't hurt you unless you talk smart to them. They don't much hurt the white-folks, anyhow. It's us niggers they treat rough."

It was oppressively hot in the panel-body truck. One of the prisoners knocked on the little window into the cab and asked the policeman to open it and let them have some air. Joe Laurie slid back the window, so that a little air came in.

The truck boarded the ferry and stopped. One of the Negroes peered out the rear windows.

"We're going to Algiers to pick up some more guys at the precinct over there."

In a few moments, the ferry began to move away from the dock.

Joe Laurie and the other cop sweated in the cab of the truck. Joe Laurie smoked a cigarette indifferently. He was thinking about the date he had had the night before. He wasn't sure that he wanted to see Marcia again.

Dick was sitting beside him, separately without a care in the world. Dick never seemed to have any trouble. Joe thought of asking him for advice.

"Let's get out of here and stand in the breeze," Dick said.

Joe opened the door and stepped down to the deck of the ferry.

"Come over here by the rail," he said. "I want to talk to you about something."

The two men stood beside the rail, looking down into the brown water, smoking cigarettes. Joe Laurie told Dick all about his problem.

Behind them there was a cry. Joe Laurie turned around in time to see the truck roll slowly against the rail of the ferry, and through it, into the brown water. The prisoners, locked in and unable to help themselves, screamed frantically for help.

Slowly, Joe Laurie raised his hands and covered his ears so that he could not hear the sound of the screams of the prisoners. His eyes were fixed on the truck and the water. Slowly, the water swallowed the truck and it was gone.

Then, Joe Laurie began to scream.

* * * *

"Drowned like rats in a cage," Joe Laurie whimpered.

Big Lou came and looked in at the window.

"You were a right guy," he said. "Here's the Little Lulu comic book, like I promised." He thrust his beefy hand in at the window, holding out the brightly colored book to Joe. "Come get it, Joe. It's a good one."

"I don't want it," Joe said.

"Don't want it! What's the matter with you, Joe? You're not going to be like that, are you?"

"I don't want it."

"Have your own way." Big Lou's feelings were hurt. He began to withdraw his hand.

"Don't you understand?" Joe shouted. "A man is more than a rat is. A man is more!"

Big Lou walked away slowly. No one paid any attention to Joe. He was insane.

LYMAN, MISSISSIPPI

Living again with mom and dad at Lyman, Mississippi, this writer decided to try his hand at producing some publishable fiction. It seemed to him the women's magazines were the most plentiful and would present the easiest market.

"Uninteresting" is a story about a woman who is an antiheroine. It was thought this was a novel idea which would catch some editor's fancy. Surely, women's magazine staffs were jaded by the myriads of attractive, thinking, active, vital, self-determining women constantly seen and written about in their synthetic environment.

The heroine (?) in "Uninteresting" did not act. She reached. She needed to have a man define her. She did not reach out and grasp. She expected the good things of life to be dropped in her lap without effort. Her planning was a formula to fail.

Yet, she won out.

The writer, in the early '50s, could not desert his optimism. He could not show a loser losing. He was writing in America - the land of fair play. Was life fair? Life was more than fair, granting people richer bounties than what they deserved. Ernest Hemingway might preach, "Let him who does not work not eat." This writer was steeped in the social philosophy of Steinbeck.

This female protagonist won out because a man believed against odds that she would be good for him if he kept believing in her. She would react to his confidence because reaction was the way she knew.

The theme of an indifferent father who thinks more of the land and less of his family appears. That oft-seen southern character, the rural lad who despises work for another for wages is also introduced here.

UNINTERESTING

The moment I got inside my shabby third-story room, I set the bottled Coke I was carrying on the table, and sat down and took off my shoes. My feet ached and my back hurt. I was tired. I settled back in the uncomfortable chair and looked up at the ceiling.

A pretty picture, I thought. This was my home. The sight of it almost made me sick. I lived in an ugly old smoke-blackened house down near the railroad. There was a wide, unscreened front porch with its draggled rockers and the weathered old sign which read, Rooms, a sign which had been white with bold black letters once, but which was now grey, the word barely distinguishable. This horror was Mrs. Barnes' boarding house. This horror was my home in Middleridge. And I couldn't afford one of the nicer rooms on the second floor. Oh, no! I lived here in the attic, my single window overlooking the back yard, a yard where old automobile bodies and assorted junk were kept. Down the street I could hear the sounds from a taxi-dance hall each night, and

31

the music and scraping of feet against the floor would almost drive me mad.

I looked about me at the sagging old iron bed and the scarred and scuffed dresser with its cracked mirror, and I hated this room. I hated it with passion and fierce personal loathing. I held a contempt for it, and for myself.

This afternoon I had quit my job. Now, I didn't know what I was going to do. I had been working as a waitress at a small cafe where railroad men came to eat. It was a smelly, smoky, dingy place, and the men who were customers there were all bearded and grimy and coarse. I had been appalled when I had gone there to apply for the job. The employment office had sent me, and I had gone in clutching the white card of introduction in my hand, wishing that I was back home on pa's farm.

Mr. Chuck, as everyone called him, had looked me over, and said that he didn't think I'd last long, but he'd take me on. I had bridled angrily under his words and determined that I'd last as long as the next one, and I had stayed with the place for two months, but now, it was all over. This afternoon I had quit.

Well, I wouldn't think of Mr. Chuck or his hash-house anymore. I'd thrust all thought of them out of my mind. But, I had to think of how I was going to make a living. Mr. Chuck had paid me off, and I could pay for this horrible room for one more week, and I could eat on the little money I'd saved, but I had to find a job almost at once. Early the next day, I'd have to go back to the employment agency and tell them I wanted a job.

I distrusted the old man that ran the employment service. His job was to find workers for the employers that applied to him for labor', and he did his best to do just that. Naturally, he had a lot of unpopular jobs that no one wanted, and he palmed these off on his most desperate cases. He would remember me, and he'd know that I had been working for Mr. Chuck for two months, and he'd know how desperate I was. He'd send me out to interview for the seediest spots in his file. I dug my heel into the ragged rug with hate. I realized that I was full of hatred for almost everyone.

But, there was no help for it. I didn't know anyone in town. I didn't have a single friend. Of course, there had been Jacob Johnson. He was a country man who had come and lived for about two weeks at Mrs. Barnes' boardinghouse. He had moved out and I didn't know where he had gone. It didn't matter. He really hadn't been a friend of mine. We had sat together on the dusty porch in the evenings and talked sometimes, but he really didn't interest me, and I was sure that I couldn't have interested him greatly. I never interested men. I knew that I was classified by all men as "uninteresting."

I knew that I was unattractive - tall and big-boned and scrawny. I had scraggly washed-out blond hair, and I knew that my sisters at home (and there were plenty of them) all had pale, peaked, rabbity little faces with faded blue eyes. I knew that I looked like my sisters, only lately, since I had been in the city, I had noticed in the mirror that my face had taken on a hard, brittle set which drove away the scared, rabbity look, although I felt rabbity enough. I was terrified of the city and my insecure place here.

Jacob Johnson had been friendly, but it was because he didn't know anyone, and we were both from the country. I could remember things he'd said to me sitting in the old rockers on the porch.

"We're a lot alike, Martha Jane. We're from the same sort of people. Sometimes I guess that the city ain't any place for us, 'cause we don't understand city ways. Reckon I'd have done better to keep the farm, but after pa and ma was gone, I couldn't see the use of it. Someday, I'm going to set me up a little store here in the city, a place for poor folks to trade at. My granddad owned a store back home once. He was sure a slick trader, too. Of course, pa didn't know nothing about anything but the land."

Yes, and my pa, too, I'd think when he talked like this. Pa had clung to our old farm, even when our neighbors were selling out, back during the war, moving away to the cities to do defense work where they made lots of money and could buy their families luxuries like I was forever looking at in the mail-order catalogs. We never had anything, barely enough to eat, never rugs and curtains and plumbing and modem kitchens. Pa couldn't have known how much his woman-folks longed for these things. Just having the land was enough for him.

So, here I was in the city, and I wasn't much better off.

"There's something about us country people," Jacob had told me once. "We hate to work for the other fellow. We set a high price on independence."

"I could do with a lot less independence and a lot more to wear and eat," I'd said.

He had smiled his warm, hesitant smile. He was a bashful man, despite his hulking frame and his huge shoulders. He weighed more than two hundred pounds, and I judged his age to be about thirty, but still, I sensed that he was timid and backward about getting acquainted. His country background, I supposed.

Well, there was no use thinking about him now. I had no idea where he had gone after he left the boarding house, and he was nothing to me anyhow. I was all alone, and I had my own battles to fight. I'd find another 'ob somewhere, and the old grind would begin again and where it would all end, I had no way of knowing.

The Coke I had brought with me when I came in was sitting at my elbow, making a circle in the scarred varnish of the old table. I could see tiny bubbles rising in it toward the surface. It was getting warm. I'd have to drink it.

I picked it up and raised it high above my head, looking at the bottom of the bottle. Middleridge. It was made right here in town. I was annoyed with myself for allowing myself to engage in that childish old habit of looking at the bottom of every bottle to see where it was made. It brought back memories.

I could remember how, at home, when I was younger, I would go down to the country store whenever I had a nickel and buy a Coke. Every time I got one in a bottle from some other part of the country, it would thrill me, and all sorts of visions would flood through my mind. I could remember getting bottles from places like Birmingham, Alabama and Jackson, Mississippi, and Tallulah, Louisiana. These places were all near to home, and not particularly exciting, but once when I had gotten a bottle all the way from Los Angeles, California I had held it close to my thin chest, not even feeling the cold of it, and it had seemed like the most wonderful thing in the world that I had in my hand a bottle that had come all the way from Los Angeles, California. I tried to imagine what great movie stars might have drunk out of this very bottle before it had come south, and the thrill was almost as great as a trip to the west coast would have been.

After this, there was no longer any doubt that I would leave home. Home was a place of poverty. There was no beauty there anymore. Never had been much. My only brother had married a girl as uneducated and unattractive as his many sisters, and moved away. I was the oldest of the girls, and it seemed that my mother took out her dissatisfaction with life on me. The town could offer nothing but the country store with its Cokes and smokes, and the church which dispensed a type of emotional religion that I couldn't understand and didn't like. I couldn't stay there after I'd actually had in my own hand a bottle which had found its way here from Los Angeles. Possession of that bottle had opened too many roads of thought for my excited mind to wander up and down. Life could never be the same after that.

I would go to Middleridge and find a job, and when I had saved a little money, I'd head west, working my way, maybe, but one day, I'd wind up in Los Angeles, too. I'd pull myself up out of the poverty I'd been born to and brought up in.

But, I hadn't. I was as poor now as I had been when I'd come into town from the country. I had a few more dresses, and an extra pair of shoes now, but outside of this, I hadn't done much for myself.

I drank the warm Coke. I felt like an animal caught in a vicious trap. What would happen to a woman like me? Men didn't like me. I didn't know anything about men. They never tipped me at the places I worked. It wasn't only that I was homely. Some of the girls who looked much worse than I did made good tips. They had a way with men, I didn't, and I couldn't learn. No men ever made fresh remarks to me, or tried to find out where I lived, or hung around until I got off work to take me out, like I'd seen them do with other girls. I was afraid that I'd never get a husband, not that I wanted one, but that means of security seemed out for me.

How good to be able to marry some man who would work hard and spend his money making me secure and comfortable. But, I wouldn't think things like this. It was hopeless.

Being a waitress was no good for me. I hated the work, and I wasn't successful at it. A waitress couldn't make any money if her customers wouldn't tip. I knew that I had a good head for figures, and I could have worked as a cashier and learned something about business if I had a chance, but as long as I was hampered by that terrible old man at the employment agency, I'd never have a good job. I was certain he didn't like me.

Every time I changed jobs it turned out the same. He always found some miserable job for me that I didn't want, and I always snapped it up without losing a moment's time. I was afraid to refuse a job and wait for a better one. That better one might not come along, and then, I'd be left with no job at all, and that would mean starvation. If only sometime I'd have enough money ahead not to have to be in a hurry about getting a job, I'd rather refuse the jobs I didn't like, and bide my time until a good job with a future came along.

I could see why Middleridge was a big place. People came there, and they never again had money enough to leave. They had to stay. That was my case, and me with all my big dreams of the west coast. I'd never see the west bank of the Mississippi, much let alone the Pacific.

If only I had a hundred dollars.

The Coke was gone, and I was hungry, and in a minute I was going to be crying in self-pity, so I decided that I'd go out and walk around town. I wanted to go to a movie and forget it all, but I didn't dare spend the twenty-six cents that would require. I might need it later to eat on.

I went out into the dimly lit hall and locked the door of my room. The narrow stairs were as cluttered as always. Someday, someone would be killed falling down these stairs. Let them. Anyone who had to live in this house would be better off to fall and break his neck.

Several men were smoking on the front porch. One of them tipped his hat to me. I spoke to him absently and went down the steps to the irregular brick walk. I hurried up the street toward a brighter and more cheerful part of town.

I don't know how long I walked that night, but I was right in front of Jeff's Toggery when I saw a ladies' red billfold in the street. I took a hasty look up and down the street to see if anyone was looking, and stepped into the gutter and picked it up, my heart racing wildly.

I walked casually along until I came to a dark doorway. I went in this and hid, opening the wallet with nervous fingers. There was a great deal of money inside. There was a lady's name and address on a card, too, but I tore this up in a hurry and scattered the pieces on the sidewalk. Then, I threw the billfold back into the shadows and tied the money into my handkerchief.

Hope, my heart sang. Hope at last!

The next morning I woke up early. I counted the money again, making certain that there was really sixty dollars tied in the comer of my handkerchief. Sixty dollars. It was a fortune. It almost meant the difference between life and death to me.

Happily I went to the employment agency. Impatiently I waited my turn. I was going to apply for work, and then, I was going to wait just as long as need be until old man Meadows provided me with the kind of job that would give me a chance in this world. I wasn't going to remain one of the downtrodden masses all my life. I'd climb up in the world, somehow, if it took everything I had.

After a while, Mr. Meadows called to me, and I went back to his desk. He smiled up at me.

I was almost gay.

"Good morning," I said. "How are you today?"

"Fine, Martha Jane. Looking for work?"

"Yes," I said. "I quit Chuck. I couldn't cut it any longer."

"I don't blame you much," he said. "It wasn't much of a job. It was the best I could do for you at the time, but lots of good jobs are opening up all the time now. I'll have you something before you know it."

"I want a decent job with a future," I said. "No more sixteen dollar a week stuff either. I know that I don't have any experience, but I want a break. You find me something worthwhile."

He smiled with more interest.

"Martha Jane, you're improving. You've got more self-confidence than you had before. It's a good thing. The thing that worried me about you was the fact that you didn't seem to be sold on yourself. You gave yourself a mighty bad advertisement. You've got to push yourself forward in this life."

"That's good advice," I said. "I'll be up to see you every morning. I'll see you tomorrow."

He smiled as I stood up, and his smile seemed almost kind.

"I'll do my best for you," he said. "I'm here to help you."

Walking up the street afterward, I told myself that everything and everybody seemed nicer when a person had a nice sum of money in his pocket. Mr. Meadows would still bear watching, and I mustn't be taken in by his friendly ways or anyone's. I had to hold out for a good job with security. Playing my cards right was more important to me right at this time than it had ever been, or might ever be again.

Several days passed and nothing important happened. I went to see Mr. Meadows at the employment agency each morning but he had no prospective employers for me to go to interview.

After I left his office each morning, I'd walk around town for a while, looking in store windows and imagining all the things I'd buy when I had a good job making lots of money. I'd eat dinner somewhere uptown, or I'd buy some food at one of the stores and take it home to my room and eat. The first thing I was going to do when I got a better job, was to move out of Mrs. Barnes' boardinghouse, and out of this part of town forever. This part of town meant poverty and hunger and fear to me.

Mr. Meadows smiled heartily the next time I went to see him, and motioned for me to sit down. Something had opened up, I could see, and he was enthusiastic about it.

"How do you think you'd like the grocery business?" he asked.

Grocery business. Well, I told myself, that would be easier than waitress work, but people in that business worked terribly long hours. Probably, I'd like it just so-so.

"All right, I guess," I mumbled.

Mr. Meadows looked at me sharply. He said, "I want you to go and see this man. His address is here on this card. If I were you, I'd go over there this morning."

I took the card and looked at it. Clear across town, and I'd have to walk. Thank goodness! It was nowhere close to my old neighborhood. I thanked Mr. Meadows and left the office.

All the way over there, I walked rapidly and told myself over and over how I must act and what I must do. If I didn't like the looks of the place, I mustn't accept the job no matter what kind of persuasions or promises they made me. I wouldn't be fooled by a lot of talk of big things to come. Employers had used that scheme on me before, and no big things had ever developed. I was going to be hard, hard as nails. No one was going to put anything over on me while I had better than seventy-five dollars in my pocket.

Later on, I'd feel guilty about not returning the money to its rightful owner, knowing the lady's name and address was right on a card in the wallet, but now, I could only be thankful that I had this backlog of security and didn't have to snap up the first little job that I was offered.

Well, the moment I saw the store where Mr. Meadows had sent me, I knew that this would never do. I stood across the street and looked at it, amazed that Mr. Meadows would send me to a place like this. It was a shabby place in a shabby neighborhood, but worse than that, it looked as if it was not even in business. There was no sign, and the show-windows were empty. I couldn't believe that this was an operating grocery store which was open for business.

I would have turned and gone back to my drab room at Mrs. Barnes' but I was curious to see just what kind of place this might be. The outside of the old building was unpainted, and the roof sagged sadly and I felt sure that it must leak. I had been raised in the land of patched tar paper roofs, and I could tell a no-good roof when I saw one. One of the big show-windows was cracked, and the front door seemed about to fall off its hinges, and the screen was the rustiest I had ever seen. Someone was crazy, I thought.

I crossed the street and pushed my way into the dark and dusty interior of the store. Sure enough, there were no goods on the shelves. The store had not been in use for years. The place seemed to be completely deserted.

Sudden fear clutched at my heart. I staggered back with the thoughts that rushed into my mind. Could this be a careful trap that someone had laid for me? Could it be that some man had arranged for me to come to this deserted old building so that I'd be in his power? Surely, men did such things, men that were not quite right in their minds. I knew nothing of men, and I could believe anything about them. I could remember terrifying tales which I had heard girls whisper about women who had been attacked by men in solitary places. What if such a thing should happen to me? And worse than that, what if he should find the money I had hidden in the front of my blouse? Oh, to have such a thing happen to one, and be robbed besides. I had to get out of here.

I gave a little cry and began backing to the door.

A huge man stood up at the back of the dimly lit building and looked toward me. He was the largest man I had ever seen, and in the semidarkness, his eyes glowed in the dark. I put my hand to my throat and groped, blind with fear, for the latch of the sagging door.

"Why, Martha Jane!" said a familiar voice. "I'm glad you've come."

I stared at the huge man, unbelieving.

"Can it be? Why, it's Jacob Johnson! Jacob, I'm so glad it's you. I was afraid.

"I should have waited for you out on the sidewalk," he apologized. "I forgot how gloomy the store would look to a woman the first time she came into it. It looks mighty good to me."

"Is this your store, Jacob Johnson?" I asked. "Why didn't Mr. Meadows tell me I had no idea you had a store."

He had come through the darkness and stood close to me. His great presence overpowered and smothered me. I needed to get out in the air.

"It's all mine," he said proudly. "I bought it with the money I got for pa's farm. I'll have it cleaned up in a day or two, and then put the stock in, and I'll be open for business."

"I see," I said.

"Martha Jane, I've got a mighty good deal here," he said earnestly. "There's not another store closer than twelve long blocks from here. Most of the folks in this neighborhood have been catching the bus uptown to buy their groceries. I don't have any capital, but I figure the wholesale houses will give me credit, and in a year or two, I'll get ahead."

He was talking with a note of enthusiasm in his voice that I had never heard before. He was not shy or bashful now, while he talked about his store and his plans. He seemed younger and more alive than I had ever seen him.

"Let's go out on the steps," I said. "You can tell me how I fit into this picture."

"I want you to go to work for me," he said when we were outside in the sunshine. "I've counted on it all along. I'll need a clerk, someone to keep the counter and the cash register. I'm going to spend a lot of time out of the store. I know all there is to know about farms and stock. I'm going to get out and look for good vegetables that I can buy cheap, and I'm going to find meat that's fresh and not expensive. You'll stay here and run things while I'm out. I know it's not what a grocer usually does, but I say, why wait for the farmers to bring in whatever they choose? I can take the truck and go and pick up what we need, and I'll bet I can get it cheaper."

I looked at him doubtfully. Something in his manner was contagious. I almost felt myself swept up by his spirit of enthusiasm, but I had to remember that I was looking for a good thing for myself. This sounded like a fine arrangement from Jacob Johnson's viewpoint, but it didn't look so good to me. What if all his harebrained schemes didn't work out? Where would I be then? Probably, all my money would be gone, and I'd be looking for work again, panicked into taking the first thing that was offered to me.

"So you think you can carry all that?" I asked. "You'll have to make payments to the wholesalers, and keep up the truck, put some back for taxes, and pay my salary. Will this little store bring in that kind of money?"

He smiled. "Sure it will."

"I don't know," I said. "I'd doubt it. I'm looking for a job that's going to offer me security. I'd hoped for a job with an old and established firm that would be steady and certain. I'm afraid to take this job."

His face fell. He looked terribly disappointed.

"You don't believe in me," he said.

"Heavens!" I said. "It isn't a case of that. I believe in you enough, but I've got to be careful."

He looked at me miserably, and I felt a little sad about it myself.

"I had no idea you'd refuse."

"No," I said, beginning to be angry. "When you heard I was out of a job, you probably thought I'd be so hard up I'd snap up any job that was offered me. You thought I'd be delighted to come and work for you here in this store. Anything at all to pay the rent and buy food for my mouth. Well, I'm not as hard up as you thought. I've got some money, and I don't have to go to work for weeks if I don't want to. I'm going to hold out until something good comes along, something worthwhile."

"I'm sorry," he said. "I didn't think you'd feel this way about it."

I turned on my heel to go. I held my head as high as I could and took a step away from him.

"Good-bye, Jacob," I said.

"I'd hoped that working with you would lead to other things," he said, "Maybe later we'd ... "

He stopped in the middle of his sentence, and I pretended that I hadn't heard, but as I walked up the street, an angry pain was gnawing at my heart. Could he have meant that he was interested in me as a woman? My heart fluttered and my breath came excitedly. He must have meant that. A man actually had shown an interest in me. I smiled and my step was light.

Then, I became angry with myself. What was I going to do? Surely not what so many unattractive girls did, jump at the chance to snare the first male who showed an interest in them. I might never have another chance, it was true, but I would hold onto dignity and pride. I wouldn't make a fool of myself, leaping into the arms of Jacob Johnson. Probably, he hadn't meant his words to sound as they did, anyhow.

I went home, and that afternoon, I lay in bed and cried and wished that I were miles away from Middleridge and Mr. Meadows and Jacob Johnson and everything.

The next morning I went back to the employment agency.

Mr. Meadows was surprised to see me.

"Mr. Johnson asked for you special," he said. "I thought sure you'd take the job."

"Well, I didn't," I said peevishly. "You find me another one."

Day after day passed, and Mr. Meadows didn't find me another job. The money, which I was spending so carefully, dribbled rapidly away, and I didn't have the good job that I had expected to have by now. I shuddered to think what would happen if I didn't get a job. I began to think that I had been a fool not to take the job Jacob Johnson had offered me. It was as good as I could expect to find.

Finally, one morning I paid Mrs. Barnes the rent for one week in advance, and I knew that this would be the last time I could pay the rent if I didn't find work. All that money was gone. The adventure I had started out on with such high hopes was at an end. I had played every card wrong and lost.

I knew that I had to give up. Pride and dignity and everything must be sacrificed and I had to give in to Jacob Johnson. I'd go out to his store, and beg him to take me on. I'd tell him that I was desperate and had to have work. He'd have to give me the job.

I dressed hastily, icy fear clutching at my heart. What if he had given the job to some other woman? What if he was no longer interested in me? Oh, it was too awful to think about. I hurried out of the house and down the street, very much afraid.

I was panting when I came in sight of the shabby building. But, I was almost there, and inside would be Jacob, and he was so big and strong and protecting. He'd work out something. My worries were almost over.

How deserted this building looked! With a feeling of cold dread, I said to myself, "He must be here! Surely, he is here!" But there was a chain and padlock on the door, and the dusty windows were dark. I sat down on the step and cried.

"Someone must know where he is," I thought. I stood up in a few minutes and dried my eyes and looked around. There was an old house next door to the store. I pushed my way through the rickety gate and went up the narrow brick walk to the door. An old woman came out and stood on the porch to talk to me.

"Mr. Johnson?" she said, "He didn't stay here but about a week. Seems he closed up the store and went to sea, shipped out on a tanker. He told one of the neighbors that he didn't have money enough to open the store, really, but that he was going to try because of some lady-friend of his. He wanted to give her a job so she could quit her waitress job. He was sweet on her, but she turned him down, someway, so he gave up the idea of opening right now and went off to sea. He'll make some money there and when he comes home in about a year, he'll be able to start into business without a big debt. He seemed like a mighty nice man."

"Thank you," I said. "I guess I'd better go."

"You don't look too well," she said. "Won't you come in and sit down for a few minutes?"

"No, that's all right," I said. "I have to go."

I hurried out of the yard, not even shutting the gate. The old lady stood looking after me in surprise. I could hardly see where I was walking. "When he comes back in about a year," I kept thinking. About a year! What a long time. And me about to starve. He had really cared about me.

I could remember all the talks we had, and the way he was always saying that we were alike, and we came from the same kind of people. I wasn't like him, though. There was something strong and capable about him, and I was helpless and weak. Right now, I felt weaker and more afraid than I ever had in my life.

I wished passionately that I had never seen the money that I had found in the street that night. I had stolen that money, there was no other word for it. And this was what it had led to. Because of that stolen money, I had turned down Jacob Johnson when he had offered me a job and much more, and now, I'd lost him.

I didn't even go back to my room. I hurried straight to the employment agency and went up to Mr. Meadows' desk.

"I've got to have a job," I said. "This is desperate. I can't wait any longer. You've got to find me something."

"I've done my best," he said. "There's just nothing opening up. Jobs for inexperienced women are scarce."

"I'll be on relief in another week," I said. "I can't pay my room rent any longer, and pretty soon, I won't be able to eat."

He looked a little sad and very tired.

"Chuck was in here yesterday," he said. "You can get your old job back at Chuck's. That's all 1 have for you."

"Thank on," I said. I went wearily home. The next day, I took my old job back, working down in that little railroad cafe for Chuck. It was the old grind that I'd hated, and this time, I knew there was no escape.

Never a day passed that I didn't wish that I had been more responsive to Jacob Johnson. If only I'd have accepted the work he so kindly offered me. Why, by now, I might even have been Mrs. Jacob Johnson. We might be making lots of money. I might have all the security I'd always dreamed of, so I'd never have to be hungry or cold or afraid again. But, there was no use thinking about that now. People were always saying that opportunity doesn't knock twice. The next time it did knock, though, I'd have sense enough to accept it.

There was a little shifty-eyed, nervous, black-haired man who came into Chuck's every day in his overalls, greasy from his work down in the railroad yards. Secretly, I despised him. He was everything that Jacob had not been. He was weak and unstable and, I feared, dishonest. His name was Morris Strong, and he couldn't get any of the other girls to have anything to do with him. He was very friendly with me.

One day, after I had been back at Chuck's for about three months, Mr. Chuck called me back in the kitchen, and talked earnestly to me.

"Martha Jane," he said. "I've never had any trouble with you about men. You come here and do your work, and you don't cause me any worry. I'm going to raise your pay to twenty dollars a week. Don't say anything about it, because that's more than I pay the other girls. Now, I want to give you a piece of advice. If that Strong fellow says anything to you about a date, or tries to get friendly with you in any manner at all, you give him the cold shoulder. He's no good. He's a heavy drinker, and worse things. You discourage him, even if you have to be rude to him. I don't care if he gets mad and quits coming in here. He's not worth anything to me or anyone else."

I went back to work wondering why Mr. Chuck had said these things about Morris Strong. Surely, he wasn't doing it just to help me. Everyone knew that Mr. Chuck was hard as nails, and didn't help anyone out. For everything he did, he got something in return. I had felt a little sorry for Morris Strong and now, I felt more like I should defend him than before. When he came in the cafe that afternoon, while Mr. Chuck was out for his rest, I was especially nice to him.

He asked me for a date. I remembered that I had lost one man by trying to use dignity and pride, and putting on airs, and I wouldn't lose this one. Not that I wanted Morris Strong, but I wasn't going to make a fool of myself again.

I told him that I'd go out with him on Saturday night. I told him to meet me at a place down the street, because I was afraid Mr. Chuck wouldn't like it at all if he came by the cafe for me. He had grinned his silly grin and reached across the counter and pinched me in a way that I didn't like at all. Then, he sidled out. I tossed my head, and began to clean the counter with more energy than usual.

On Friday afternoon I was sitting on the high stool behind the counter when the door swung open and Jacob Johnson came in. I was so surprised that I couldn't believe my eyes for a moment. There he was, tall and broad and clean-cut. He smiled at me with a new air of confidence. I could tell that he'd learned things where he'd been. I stood up shakily and looked up at him.

"Jacob," I said. "Jacob, I'm glad to see you. How are you?"

"Wonderful," he said. "I'm home between trips. How are you?"

"Oh, all right," I said. I was afraid he was going to point out that this surely wasn't the fine job I'd told him I was going to wait for, but Jacob was too much of a gentleman to do that.

"When can I see you?" he asked. "I'm going to run out to the country to see my sister this evening, but I'll be back in town tomorrow. Can we go out somewhere tomorrow night?"

My heart leaped up at the prospect of going out with him, but then, I remembered Morris Strong.

"I have a date," I said.

His firm face fell.

"Oh," he said. "I didn't think you would have. I have to get back to ship on Sunday afternoon. Can I come by Mrs. Barnes' on Sunday morning? I'll want to talk to you before I go back to sea. Shall I see you then?"

"That would be nice," I said. I was feeling angry with him because he didn't think I'd have a date on Saturday night. Did he think I was such a wallflower that I'd never have any dates at all, but just wait for him to come along once in three months and take me out? Then, I remembered that this was the first date I'd had since he'd been away, and Morris was no prize. I looked at him rather unhappily. "That would be very nice."

"Well," he said, looking a little uneasy. "I'll come by to see you on Sunday morning, then." He got up and went out. I noticed how his broad back almost filled the door as he passed through, and for a moment, I wanted to shout to him that I would break my date with Morris Strong, that I would do anything only to be with him. I wanted to run after him and beg him to come back and talk to me, but I sat still on the high stool feeling very, very unhappy.

Morris Strong had tried to get dressed up for our date. He was cleaner looking than usual, and he had on a loud plaid shirt and a pair of dress blue trousers instead of his overall work clothes. His hair was combed and he had shaved, but he looked sillier than ever if that was possible. I couldn't help but think of Jacob, and it was hard for me to smile and act like I was glad to see him. If only I hadn't suggested Saturday night for our date!

He took my arm, and we walked up the street together. I could smell beer on his breath. He had been drinking already. This was going to be an evening for the books. I was so angry with myself I could have cried. However, I didn't know how to get out of my predicament.

It was late, because I didn't get off from work until ten. I thought maybe Morris would take me to the midnight show, but instead we turned down a street that I had never been on in all my life, and he took me inside a little backstreet bar which looked to me like an ideal setting for a murder. Only a few men and one or two women were sitting about the place, I was glad to see, but there was lots of noise. A jukebox blared loudly, and everyone was talking in loud tones to get above the sound of it. We sat down in a booth against the wall, and a man in a dirty white apron came to wait on us.

"Two beers," Morris Strong said. I started to object, but I knew Morris wouldn't like it.

"Morris," I began, "I'd like to go to the midnight show. I think it would be fun."

"Midnight shows is for the birds," he said.

"There's a new Esther Williams picture on. I'd like to see it." I tried to make my voice sound very enthusiastic. I tried to act as though I'd be awfully disappointed if I didn't see this show. Of course, I wasn't really interested in the picture. I only wanted to get away from this place with its frightening noises and its disagreeable smells.

"Drink your beer," he said bluntly.

I took a swallow and then sat looking around at the unfamiliar sights, and listening to the jukebox. He continued to drink from his, and began to smile stupidly across the table at me, and to make fumbling attempts to pat my knee under the table.

I drank about half of my beer, thinking maybe I wouldn't be so frightened if I could drink enough of it. He ordered another bottle for himself, and I knew that I was going to have a drunk man on my hands in this strange part of town and I was all alone and anything might happen to me. I was so exasperated with myself that I could have cried about it.

I finished most of the bottle, and Morris ordered me another one. When he excused himself for a few minutes after a while, I had the bartender pour most of it out. I didn't drink any from the second bottle.

Morris Strong had had about five or six.

After midnight, the crowd began to grow. People seemed to come in from everywhere. The noise was deafening. I felt confused and mixed up. The beer was making me slightly sick. Morris had insisted that I smoke a cigarette with him. I sat holding it in my fingers, wondering what I was going to do.

A group at one of the back tables had been getting louder and louder, and I could see that there was going to be a fight. One of the men stood up and looked down on one of the others threateningly.

"Morris, get me out of here!" I cried in terror. "I'm going. You get up and get me out of here."

He looked at me vaguely and then his eyes seemed to brighten.

"Sure, baby," he said. "I know a quiet little place on the other side of the tracks. This place is too noisy for you. I should have known you wouldn't like it here."

We got up and went out on the street. The fresh air was like medicine. I took a deep breath of it.

"I want to go home," I said.

He looked up at me with his stupid eyes. Somehow, they were like a begging dog's.

"The evening's young, Martha Jane. Let me get ahold of myself. We'll go over there and have some fun."

We headed down to the railroad tracks. He started into the gates of the railroad yard. It was very dark inside.

"I'm not going in there," I said.

"What's there to be scared of?" he asked. "I work down here every day. It's a short cut. The night watchman's around some place. Nothing's going to get you."

I still would have refused, but he gripped my hand very tightly and pulled on me. When he had led me behind a great shed we stopped in the shadow of a boxcar.

"Now, give me a little kiss," he said.

So! This was all a trap. He had led me in here and now this was the turn things were going to take. An ice-cold anger gripped my heart.

"You dirty little dog!" I cried. "Let go of my arm. I'm going home. If you try to stop me, I'll scream for help."

He laughed an ugly laugh and pulled my body against his. I leaped back from him and slapped him with all my might. I heard him draw in an angry breath and felt his fingers dig into my arm.

"You shouldn't have done that," he said.

There was a note like steel in his voice. I began to tremble and my knees grew weak. I was terribly afraid of him.

"I'll scream," I said. "I'll scream as loud as I can."

"No, you won't!" He put one hand over my mouth and pulled me roughly up against him again. There was an insane roaring in my head. I felt myself losing consciousness. I felt myself sinking into a deep black pit.

Then, there was a sound in the darkness. I heard hurrying footsteps and a muffled oath. Someone seized Morris Strong by the shoulders and threw him roughly away from me, so that he crumbled in a limp heap on the railroad track.

I looked up at the man in the darkness.

"Jacob! Jacob Johnson!" I began to cry. He took me in his arms and let my head rest on his shoulder. "How did you find us?" I asked.

"Chuck knew who you were with. He told me. I've been following you. I didn't intend to let you get hurt."

"I almost did," I said. "I've been such a fool. What must you think of me, Jacob?"

"I think you're all right," he said. "I think you're a fine girl. You come on with us. Everything's going to be all right."

The next morning we were married.

I had thought maybe we should have waited, as Jacob had to go back to his ship that afternoon, and we had only the morning to spend together, but Jacob insisted that I was always doing foolish things because I was afraid, and if I became Mrs. Jacob Johnson, I would never need to be afraid again, so everything would be all right. He had talked to Mr. Meadows and Mrs. Barnes and Mr. Chuck and found out all about me.

When he had come into the cafe on Friday and I had told him I had a date, he had thought that maybe I was going with someone else, but as soon as he found out the truth, he'd come looking for me that dreadful Saturday night. I still tremble with fright every time I think of that awful time with Morris Strong, but I know that will never happen again.

I'm fixing up our apartment now, and doing some work down at the store. Jacob said that he would be home for good in about six months, and I want to have things ready for him. I think that our apartment will be very nice, and I'll do everything for the store I can. When Jacob comes home, things will begin to hum.

Now, I write to him, and remember the few delicious hours I had in his arms, and look forward to the time when he'll be home for good, and I'll never be alone. I'm doing everything I can in preparation for that day, learning things and trying to improve myself, so that my husband will never find me uninteresting.

GULFPORT, MISSISSIPPI

"Narcissus Rex" was begun at Gulfport, Mississippi in 1956, and never completed. What it was to have been is not now fully remembered. The theme of the father who cared more about the land than for his family is central. Dualism is discussed. The narrator's sense of his solitary destiny contributes to the melancholy atmosphere.

This writer's "advertisement for himself" would supposedly be found funny. A friend, upon reading this fragment, said, "I don't have the words to tell you how unfunny and depressing this is!" The writer wrote still remembering Mississippi College. Soon there would be other things to worry about.

The "Roy" who is addressed several times in the work was Roy Alton Nicholas, Jr., who was deceased. The writer was seemingly in denial about Roy's death. Roy was a school chum of the writer's with him at Clinton. Roy had been a kindred soul when there was no other.

The memory of Mississippi College must fade. Elvis Presley, with his angry guitar, had moved into Heartbreak Hotel. Nothing outside that edifice would ever be the same.

The writer invests himself with iconoclasm, anti-clericalism, dissidence, insurgency, and the will to power, all of which he felt - more or less.

The Old South - "that ideal society," the writer's father always said, "where everyone was happy" - lay in ruin in parallel non-existence with the burnt-out manor house acquired by the family of the writer. It was restoration of this symbolic world and the talisman house which had represented it which was desired by the father. Their revivification would restore life to his own emasculated self-concept, which could not survive without the shoring prop of his own image of himself as Country Gentleman.

And Hungerford itself was sacked by a poverty brought upon it by imprudent men. How restore that? When a government fails, the nation suffers. When the city fathers are slack, the town suffers. When a father is lax, his family suffers. Where are men who are strong? Not those, such as the poor artist in "Death in Oil" - but alive!

Ichabod! The glory has departed. The writer probably saw those who lost the Old South, those not managing the piney woods allowing poverty to come, and his own father - that dreamer - that Don Quixote - as all being part of the same problem.

The writer's rhapsodic rendering of the strong father was hogwash. The father may have appeared strong to the writer - a habit born in babyhood - but to no one else. His strength was as nonexistent as the presence in reality of a restored Melville House, or a return to power of the Old South.

NARCISSUS REX

To Dear Roy: Freud has taught us, and I believe that it is true, that black is

47

black, but black is also white. This is one of the foundation axioms of Freudian doctrine, and one which, I believe, has never been disputed.

Freud was never too concerned with the grays of the world, but with the absolutes, the goods and the evils, the clean and the impure, the whites and the blacks of things.

To draw an analogy in the realm of sex - and most Freudian thought came sooner or later to the sexual aspect of things - one might believe that a man who was basically unsure of his ability to perform sexually, adequately - there is abundant talk of sexual adequacy these days - would manifest his unsureness in this regard in one of two ways. Either he would indulge in abundant sex activity, seeking to prove to himself and to others that no inadequacy existed, or he would withdraw from the world of sex and live as a celibate, gratifying himself in daydreaming or more positive auto-erotic behavior.

We might say that celibacy and fear to take part would be the logical or positive reaction or a feeling of sex-inadequacy, whereas the converse, promiscuity, would be the alternate, negative reaction.

It would be most difficult for the analyst, upon cursory examination, to discover if the patient - over-active in bedroom and haystack episodes - might be troubled with defective, hormone-secreting glands, or harboring some deep-seated fear of his own romantic inadequacy.

I really wonder if there is such a thing as the person who is (as the layman would say) over-sexed. Your comments upon this would be appreciated.

Other analogies might be drawn, proving that black (as Freud has said) is black, but also white. However, this must be short, and I will skip these, as I am positive you grasp the point. You know so much more about such things than I, anyhow.

What I am getting at is, I am beginning to believe that this is the trouble with the twins. My mother is terribly worried about the twins.

It seems that since they came here, there has been no peace for anyone, especially me, and my mother and father. You know that I have written you that it is seemingly getting worse all the time, and really it does seem so.

Do you think it possible that two human beings of identical appearance, who have been subjected to identical experience could grow up reacting exactly opposite to their so-similar beginnings, so that when they reach maturity, they will go to make up, complete mirrors of each other?

I am very much surprised to see how different the twins have become, one from the other.

My job goes tediously along the way. It is really more than I had ever bargained for. The hours are too long, and no time is left for indulgence in the finer things. Life has become a desert. But, what is one to do? I can only afford to live in the fine manner to which I should like to become accustomed by keeping the job, so there you are.

I am thinking that I will have the ceiling of my bedroom paneled with mirrors. I have furnished the room with solid mahogany, and the decor is deep burgundy wine and gold. The carpet is deep wine, and the chandelier is gorgeous. A ceiling reflecting that splendor, would add magnificence upon magnificence. Of course, nothing but a pure white spread will ever grace my bed. That is the color of purity, you know.

I have sat here and imagined how nice it would be to lie abed, and stare up into a mirrored ceiling. I would see myself revealed in a dazzling setting indeed.

My idea of complete happiness would be to have a room fitted out, exactly as I would like, and then, to stay in it. More and more, I am becoming averse to venturing out into the world. Contact with people is seldom pleasant, and the business world is becoming more and more horrible to me.

I do envy you your financial independence. Your ability to follow your studies without monetary worry must be a source of unending delight to you.

I would like to return to the University, but never under such circumstances as when I attended it before. Dormitory living is not for me. If I ever return to school, it will be when I can take a small apartment, away from the campus, where I may live quietly and, to some extent, alone.

Getting back to the twins. There has been a quiet time with them, but I am not fooled. It is the quiet which precedes the storm. I do not know what to think of them.

I could almost believe there is only one of them.

I have noted that while one of them is most active, the other will lie (as we might say) dormant. And, when that dorman one asserts himself, the other one, apparently, goes to sleep. It is a very great mystery, and I try to think back to the time when they first came, and to remember if there was one or two, but it is all vague. I can't recall with surety when they came, but it must have been when I was between the ages of fifteen and eighteen.

It was surely after I had seen "Gone With The Wind." I could almost believe they came that day.

Bob, you know, is the good one, and Tom is the bad one. I have always believed that Bob is a little older, although I don't know why I believe that. It merely seems so.

Bob has been about home a lot of late. We haven't seen much of Tom, and a certain excitement has gone with him, wherever he may be. I think I miss Tom, when he goes away, perhaps because Bob is silent much of the time when he was here, so that he is scarcely missed during the time he goes away.

Bob has been very good of late, but still my mother and father wear a concerned and anxious look. I think they are wondering where Tom is.

I know that he will be back soon.

I think back on the time when we were together, Roy. It seems so long ago. I wonder if I did the right thing to give it up and come home. It was my second attempt at college, my second failure in that direction. There have been so many failures. Educational, financial, spiritual. And, no success in the field where I most desire it.

Roy, do say some words of encouragement to me in your next letter, even if you don't mean any of them. I have worked so long, so tirelessly - with no encouragement. No hope of success. Try to be kind to me. Be a friend and tell me that there is a chance that someday I will have everything, just as I have always planned that it should be. Tell me that I may believe in my eventual success.

I feel that I am so gifted, and so cursed, so extremely blessed and damned! It is only exquisite.

The words are inside, beautiful, lofty and musical sounds and phrases, tumbling about. And, my mind is peopled with the shadows of characters, gigantic, noisy, powerful people who come feebly forth to people the pages of weak literature. The words and the stories and the people, all God-given and godlike, needing only the proper blending, the welding into that perfect whole which shall unleash the ability in me to create - Oh, to create what mighty and enthralling tales of wonder and enchantment. But, when I reach out for the glory it fades before my baffled eyes, and turns to mist in my fingers.

But, it is nearer, and there is a breathless stirring inside. Someday, I will succeed!

Today has just been too much!

There is no one whom I can talk to. I remember our talks so well, when we were at college together. We cold have been great friends, but as soon as I began to know you, I went away. I should have stayed, if only for the happiness of knowing you better.

One day, we sat on a bench together outside the museum and talked of poetry. You had a theory then, about beauty in ugliness. There is a certain beauty in the ugliest and most hideous things, a hue of white in the deepest blackness, and a shade of jet black in the most gleaming whiteness. Is there not a measure of humor in horror!

Someone has said that you may tell most about a man by discovering what it is which makes him laugh. Poe was said to have possessed a warped sense of humor, finding humor in the miseries of men. But, a phrenologist has stated that "the bump of reverence" was completely lacking in Poe. We must judge that he was lacking in charity, empathy, and compassion. Doubtless, he was least charitable to himself.

Your theory of beauty in ugliness. It appeals to me. And, my own derivation - humor in horror. I like the whole idea. Perhaps, we might do something with it.

I recall the first time I ever saw Darnley.

It was the fall of the year, and the grasses of the fields were brown, and the sun shone on them with yellow dimness. The hill sloped away toward the west, and further on lay the swamp. Where the crops would be, there was an unkempt field of brambles and tall dead grasses, dotted with thickets of gallberry bushes. The nut trees were tall, and shaped well enough, but the winds of autumn had driven away their thin leaves, and their thin grey arms stretched starkly up before the tarnished sky of Hungerford.

The cedars were green, and the pines.

Range cattle, which belonged to the neighbors, stood about, emaciated and dull. Weary cuds were chewn.

Here and there, a rotting fence post still stood. And, brown, rusty wire stretched along the dusty ground. (For it was not a rainy fall.) The earth sent up an odor of mustiness, and the bark of the trees peeled off in places, revealing the powdery grindings of bugs. Bugs which should have died ere this, with the first frost, but winter was late that year.

It seemed then that winter would never come.

A dead leaf, skeletal, in the process of dissolution, would roll along the earth before the fitful wind, or one would notice that the coats of the cows were thick, but still, one could not believe that winter would come.

It was breathless and humid. There was a hush upon the face of the air.

Evil biting flies droned or darted above the cattle.

A spindly calf ran behind the mother to take suck. Too young, as yet, to know the pain of being what it was ... a small animal in a land where there were too many animals for the earth to support. The mother's eyes were calm and wise. There was resignation and the chewing. The chewing must go on, rhythmic and slow,

The cattle seemed to wait. They were patient.

The house stood waiting, too. I looked at it, and I sensed, but did not yet know, that it waited - waited for the glory to return.

The yard was filled with trees. There were magnolias with dark, waxed leaves. These looked less real than artificial ones made by florists for funerals. There was not the perfection in the real ones.

The cedars lent a heavy odor to the air. The ground beneath them was bare. There was an old superstition - if a man plants a cedar tree, he will die when it attains size enough for its shadow to shade his whole grave at noontime.

Someone had planted dogwood. Once there was a crucifixion, and the cross was hewn from the wood of the dogwood.

The grass was not green.

The sky turned ashen, and clouds scudded before the rising wind. Some of the humidity, the heat, lifted. The earth seemed to sigh with relief. There was a whispering in the grasses and the leaves.

Not all life is fled.

The house at Darnley had been built upon a rise of ground on the eastern edge of the property.

Now, I let my eyes drift down from the tumultuous heavens, and they slid down the majestic, stately cast-iron columns which graced the front of the place. The front veranda was wide and spacious, made from crushed stone. The width of the veranda was sixty feet.

Behind the porch and the columns lay nothing. Many years before, the house had burned.

The place had belonged to a family named Melville. They had been a proud and aristocratic people, cultured and learned.

There had been troubles, however, and the family and the name had died out. Today, there were none of them left. Some of them lay in an ancient graveyard on a hill behind the ruin of the old house, under the trees.

We were to live in a small shotgun house which had been built for the over-seer or caretaker of the old place, after the big house had burned, and the family had moved away. There were four rooms, set one behind the other, with chimneys for wood fires, and no conveniences.

I was eleven at the time and used to something better.

Our furnishings arrived in one small truck. I ran about, playing come imaginative game of my own devising in the tangled, out-of-hand shrubbery. There was a gnarled bush which was to bear blue roses. That would be in the spring.

After a while, I drew near the ancient porch, and the noble columns, I approached down the concrete walk, and stood at the foot of the steps. The columns were exceedingly high.

I felt small and over-awed by them.

My father approached.

"It's a beautiful sight, isn't it?" he said.

I gaped. I had been almost afraid to walk up the steps to the porch. My father took my hand.

"Come."

Together, we walked up the steps, and stood on the smooth, rock floor. My father turned about slowly, and stood peering off down the hillside toward the swamp. "Standing here like this," he said, "You can almost believe that the house is still there. You can almost imagine that you might turn around and walk inside, into the wide entrance hall, with polished floors and curving stair. A chandelier hanging high."

I looked up at his face. "It must have been beautiful," I said.

"Yes." He walked a few steps apart. Naughty boys had written some words on one of the pillars in red crayon. My father looked at them for a moment. His face became angry and red. "A profanation," he muttered. He strode down the steps and gathered up a handful of soft, sweet-smelling earth. He came back with it in his hands, and rubbed it against the words. I took them away. "The soil is good," he said. He let it slip through his fingers and fall to the ground. He released it slowly, as though reluctant to see it go. "A cleanness comes up out of the earth to us," he said.

Roy, I cannot tell you now what my father meant to me in those early days. I suppose that my reactions, today, are the same. He is something I have never outgrown. However, I cannot begin to portray, in a letter, the worshipping awe and the reverence I formerly ascribed to him. He was the central reality of all life in those days.

And now, there is a ghost which follows me.

In his personal appearance he was tall, rather dark, and more handsome than average. He was still youthful looking, although in his forties.

He wore overalls and heavy work shoes. The overalls were the two-strap, blue-denim kind. They ill-suited him. He had been made to wear a black suit, with white shirt, and broad-brimmed hat. His face and bearing did not go with workingman's clothes.

He went away from me, leaving me standing on the porch. He carried himself proud, walking straight and tall on the land.

And, I turned my back upon the emptiness which lay behind the porch and (as my father had said), I could imagine that the great house was there. I felt that I had only to turn about and take a few steps to be inside. I could feel that great house behind me, that house which had belonged to a great people called Melville. I moved to one of the peeling pillars and lay my face against it. I could smell the clean, rich earth my father had rubbed there, and the odor was good.

I stood there for a long time, with my eyes closed, and the sights and smells of the old days crept back to astonish me.

The spirit of that first day will follow me forever.

There were many times when I hated Darnley; the poverty, the privation, and the unavailing work, but whenever I stood at the foot of those so lofty pillars on that gracious porch, I was swept upward - exalted. I was caught up in the dream. Once Darnley had been peopled by Melvilles, a great people, and we after.

But now, Roy! Strangers walk there. Or not strangers, for Rochelle is no stranger. But, it is not we who dwell there. The family is divided in fact, as it was ever divided in spirit. And, I miss it so ...

But, you will laugh at me for saying these things. You know me better than most, and you will feel that I do not mean what I am saying.

But, love and hate stand back to back and are one. You can understand my love - hate for Darnley, and for Hungerford, and my father.

Love is love, but love is also hatred, and hatred is both its self and opposite. But, I can say no more to you this time. I will write to you again when I can. Please, please let me hear from you.

* * * *

Your kind letter came. Thank you so much for the nice things you said. There is no one here who understands. There is no one who knows what I feel and suffer and endure. But, I do endure, and endure, and last.

I feel that I am most strong to bear all which I must bear. I have the strength within to continue.

How frustrating the study of history is! For it shows us, more and more certainly, that the ancients were our equals (or our betters) in most things. Only in mechanical proficiency do we excel them, and still, we build nothing which they have not imagined. And artistically we are so far behind them. Who today, without the experience of two thousand years to draw upon, could conceive works of art such as the mind of man created during the era of Pericles?

Today, where is art for art's sake? Everything must be (pardon the expression) commercial. The craftsmen of the arts of this era are cursed with a Midas touch. Never has there been so much money to reward the appearance of talent. Never have so many shared so much for so little, but the gift is itself a curse. Like Midas experienced the starvation of the body, and the death of his daughter, the artist of today is experiencing the starvation of his soul, and death of his talent.

To allow one's talent to die is an unforgivable sin, for a talent is the gift of God, and must be permitted to grow and be fruitful.

But, where Oh where shall I find contemporaries?

When we moved to Hungerford, a great loneliness settled down upon me. It was then that I began to feel acutely that I was a person set apart, one who did not belong to the pack. I had little in common with anyone there. My family had little in common with them.

My father was an aristocratic man. More and more, I came to understand what Darnley meant to him. It was a link to the past. We are Southerners. The memory of what was still burns with us. We recall a land, not exactly a democracy, which did exist with its aristocracy, its peasant classes, and its slaves. We recall hills templed with houses constructed in the best tradition of Grecian architecture. We recall that people read and studied and sent their sons to Europe for culture. We recall that life was more (for a few) than making a living and begetting sons and daughters.

But, where today is that life to be found?

The South is poor, and there has been little opportunity to cling to culture and refinement. The old civilization toppled, and the years have been spent in sweeping up the pieces and surviving. There has been little time for the arts.

Yet, an occasional voice is heard. Not all the glory is departed.

Jeremy Tolbert had Darnley. The lofty facade of columns (eight in all) stood as a symbol of departed greatness, a greatness which might rise again.

It was his dream that he might build, once again, the mighty house which would stand behind the columns and the porch. It was his dream that the fields might bloom, and sleek cattle stand about in the pastures. It was his dream that a way of life might return which had been swept away in bloody upheaval.

He felt that he could do this ... Or his son.

Like David gathered materials for the temple which Solomon built.

How many times have I described Hungerford? It was a town which came to be, because there was there a great sawmill. So long as the sawmill stood, the town stood with it. It had been a place of riches and consequence. But, for many years before we went there, it had been a ghost. Its significance was no more.

I recall that, from the school yard, we could see the tall ruin which was what was left of the mill. It was maroon and black against the sky, and even then I sensed that, with former splendor of this relic, had passed the greatness which was Hungerford's.

It was strange being in a new school, when I had been accustomed to one city school all the days of my life. The school in Hungerford was different, inferior, weaker, and poorer. It was a tribute to the character of part of the faculty that there existed any chance for education in Hungerford at all.

There was a lady who took it into her head to ride the crocodile. "You see," said she, "He's as tame as he can be. I'll speed him down the Nile." The croc

54

winked his eye, as she bade them all good-bye, wearing a happy smile. At the end of the ride, the lady was inside and the smile was on the crocodile.

So you see, there is humor in horror!

I do not know what kind of political views my father possessed, but to me, it seemed that they were to some extent similar to those fostered by Machiavelli. Of course, I always saw everything connected with my father in exaggerated, gargantuan proportions, and probably all out of reason when compared to actual fact. It is true that my father was a born aristocrat. (I have said that we were Southerners - members of an old family which had once belonged to the landed gentry, possessors, now, of the estates of another proud family, steeped in tradition, imbued with pride of heritage.) My father did not feel that the people were fit to rule. Like Machiavelli, he felt that an absolute monarchy was the most practical, efficient, and economical form of government for a given race of people. Also, there must be a dual standard of morality. The Leader must not be governed by those rules governing common man. He must be left free to do that which would do the most good for the whole - the State. Regardless of what hardship this might work upon any given individual. In these respects, at least, he must be compared in his political belief to Machiavelli. As for Machiavelli's art of duplicity and deceit, Jeremy Tolbert was an admirer of these things, if not a practitioner. He recognized a certain strength in evil.

In my earlier life, and especially after we moved to Hungerford, I always persisted in the belief - no, the simple hope - that I was a royal personage, the missing prince of some small principality, in hiding, in the care of Jeremy Tolbert and his wife, but a personage royal born, one who should one day come into his own, to discover that I was heir to some glorious greatness, and my father was really a servant - a trusted and faithful servant - but, a servant.

I frequently had a dream, or was it a waking vision? I saw myself stealing out of the mouth of an underground passageway in the company of several men who wore dark capes and moved with an air of secrecy. This would have been when I was fleeing some grave danger in my own land. This would have been when they brought me away from that country to America where I could be safe until the time was right for my true identity to be made known, and for me to come into my Kingdom.

I was fond of reading "The Lost Prince" in those days.

My father was vehemently opposed to the New Deal and everything it stood for. I think now, I understand a little of what made him find the Roosevelt Administration so hateful. In Roosevelt's plans and actions, there was a "leveling down" of society. Perhaps, it was for the common good, but something in it detracted from the individual. Jeremy Tolbert believed that a man should strive toward the goals he had set for himself, in the environment which was thrust upon him, alone. It was the aloneness which was important. Acceptance of aid was a sign of weakness, and weakness in a man was unforgivable.

I remember what Pin, an old Negress about the place, used to say.

"Jeremy Tolbert strong! Good God, he strong! He like the black stud horses what see de little mares on de other side of the fence. He such a man as could walk on de clouds. He fight on de side of de good angels atop de clouds. He chasten de bad angels what done go wid Lucifer wid de sword, 'til de blood run down out of de clouds at midday so it look like sunset. He breathe out heat, and the fresh rain skip up from de ground and rise into de clouds it just come from. De grasses grow ill and die if he want dem to, but he got heart and will, and things listen to him. He make de plants want to live and grow. He make de crops raise day haids and look up. He make de fields green, because he want dem green."

That was my father. At the height of the great depression, he took over the old Melville place, and set about to carve out a kingdom for himself and his son. He wrenched the trees from the earth, and plied them up and burned them. He terraced the lands and repaired the fences.

He altered the face of the land.

He did not ask for any New Deal handout. He asked only to be allowed to make his own place honorably.

He began early to mold and to teach me. By the time I was twelve, and we had moved to Hungerford, I thought a little like Machiavelli, too.

GULFPORT, MISSISSIPPI

"A Gift From Aeolus " was written at Gulfport in 1959. This is your academic life, and welcome to it. The writer constructed a satirized portrayal of a twisted and kaleidoscopic scholastic world. It was such as he found in 1944 and 1950, their homespun goods, his embroidery. This may seem like a romp among the zanies, but this is not camp. The writer was dead serious! The play is a tragedy.

It is admitted it was a mistake for the writer to go to "Perk" that summer he was too young. But the war was pushing. It was a mistake for this "original " to go to Mississippi College. A bird in a vacuum - no air to fly on. Nothing nontraditional had happened at Mississippi College since the night Grant's horses slept in the chapel.

The writer was beginning to find out about Jack Kerouac. John Steinbeck's book, "East of Eden, " was made into a movie in 1955, and how about that Leslie Fiedler? There were places in the world beyond Lyman, and Perkinston, and Clinton.

A more global vista did not benefit Harrison Nix, the protagonist in "A Gift From Aeolus." Nix was turned from flesh and blood into gold for the establishment which would pick his brains. He wasn't "beat. " He was tired. He quit fighting the enemy and joined then. Warts and all? How did this happen?

A GIFT FROM AEOLUS

Professor Harrison Nix, who instructed the students at The Isaac Walton Junior College in Classical Literature and English, was wearing a stiffly starched shirt, and his necktie, and his suit coat.

The big windows were open, but the room was stifling hot. He sat on the Victorian sofa beside Miss Gazelle (Rocky) Bound. The lamp had a thick paper shade with long fringe, so, although it was a big one, the light in the room was muted. This was the old-fashioned living room in the house of Rocky's father, Mr. Laban Bound.

The professor had met Rocky Bound at church, and now he had come to call. Already, she had passed him six pieces of candy and he was feeling a little sick.

"I took a course in painting china," Rocky said. "I really didn't have anything else to do. I'm not smart enough to do something really creative like doing oils or writing a book. When I was younger, I think my father wanted to make another Eudora Welty out of me, but he's given up."

"Uh, yes," Harrison said. He had his feet close together, and he made a conscious effort to keep his hands still on his lap, except when he was eating the candy she offered him. He was conscious that he had his best side toward her. He had a good profile. He felt he should lift his hand and smooth his hair, but he did not.

"Yes, what?" Rocky asked.

"I was agreeing."

"Agreeing that I'm too dumb to do something really creative?"

"No. No. I thought you said your father felt you had it in you to be another Eudora Welty. I was agreeing with him."

"Oh, Professor! You're joking." Rocky patted his hand.

Harrison had turned slightly so that he was looking at her. He looked at her face giving her his full attention. He had come here, so he must be polite.

There was nothing at all about Rocky which was disagreeable. She had nice grey eyes, and a rather aristocratic nose which was Straight and dignified, and lips that had just the right fullness. She had a moderate tan. Even so, her cheeks bloomed with a healthy pink which showed through. Her body was young and firm. She was an active woman who kept herself in trim. But, her hair was cut ridiculously short.

Her hair was light brown, and would have formed a perfect frame for her classic face, if she had let it grow.

Harrison looked down at her well-tended hands which lay in her lap. She was a relaxed person.

Harrison was tense. This room looked like something out of Great Expectations, and an aura of the out-of-date pervaded the place. The Bounds seemed to have permissively been bypassed by progress. Harrison almost wondered that they did not light this great barn of a house with gas.

The carpet had faded until it was a dingy grey.

"I painted an entire set of china; the cups and saucers, plates, soup bowls, occasional pieces, everything. I tried an oriental design on the white china. After the first few, I could do it quite nicely. I'll show them to you sometime. I wish I could do something really worthwhile."

"Believers in metaphysics feel that if we do all we can to equip ourselves - to educate ourselves, to make our characters what they should be - and then remove any obstructions which might be, presenting ourselves to the power of inspiration like a blank canvas to the artist, we will be used." Harrison spoke with his classroom tone and voice pitch. "If I were you, I wouldn't give myself up to a life of mediocrity. We don't know what is in store for us. We are being tried every day. The way that we behave in small matters is the means the source of the power of inspiration will use to determine if we may be permitted to do greater things."

He would have quoted directly from the Parable of the Talents, but he did not want to sound like a minister.

"Do you really think so?" Rocky asked. "Do you really think my poor efforts are noticed?"

Harrison had said his speech by rote. He had not considered whether he believed it or not. He said that he did believe it, though.

Rocky beamed.

"Isaac Walton is so lucky to have you," she said. "I wish that I could sit in your classes. I would just like to sit at your feet forever and listen to you talk. I'll bet you'll develop into another Socrates one day."

"Yes, Socrates," Harrison said.

"I'm going to read some good books, and I think maybe I will try to paint simple watercolors. I did a very pretty job on some of the pieces of china, and there's a woman in town who gives lessons in watercolors. I'm going to start going to her."

Harrison wished that someone would come walking through the room carrying Miss Haversham's mouse-bitten wedding cake, and would let a loud fart right in front of where they sat on the sofa. And, not a quick explosive one, but a long, drawn-out one like wind gradually escaping from a large balloon.

But, there was no one else in the house. Mr. Bound was out on business of his own, and the cook always went home after she washed and put away the supper dishes.

"Would you help me select some good books to read?" Rocky asked him.

"Oh, yes. I'll get you some from the college library," he said. "May I use your bathroom?"

She stood up and he felt the presence of her and smelled her cologne. She was a woman, and a desirable one. Only she couldn't stop talking, and all the chatter made Harrison so nervous he couldn't get his mind in the right state to think of her that way. Now, he was so nervous his kidneys were going to start giving him trouble unless he could calm down.

She was a good hostess. She went with him to the head of the stairs, pointing at the doors, saying this was her room, and that was her father's and that was a spare room, and that was a spare room they never used. They had thought about renting it to someone, perhaps a faculty member from the college, a woman of course, but they never had, as they actually didn't need the money, and a woman in the house would be company for her, but a nuisance, too. You just couldn't be at home when someone else is in your home, no matter how congenial that person might be. She was sure anyone from the college would be a decent and considerate paying guest, but the college had ample space for its teachers in the teachers' dormitory, so they wouldn't be performing any service by putting their spare bedroom up for rent.

She hoped that there were clean towels out on the racks, but if for any reason there were none, there were some in the little cabinet above the foot of the bathtub.

She went back down the stairs, thinking to herself that she would have let him use the half-bath, which was in back of the kitchen, but Cook used that one, and she wasn't too careful, so Rocky never knew how neat it was going to be.

She went to the kitchen, now, and when she heard Harrison coming downstairs, she called to him to join her there.

She had the electric coffee pot perking, and had set two of the painted cups and two of the saucers out on the table.

"I had time to get them out," she said. "We never use them. I don't think they look too bad, do you?"

Harrison studied the cup which was sitting before him. Very daintily, a pair of Chinese lanterns had been painted on the round cheek of the cup. It was done in orange and black. This made an unpainted dime-store cup look like a painted dime-store cup.

It's very nice," he said. The saucer was similar. At least she had been restrained. She didn't overdo it, trying to crowd a number of designs on the small area. It would have been easy to have gone too far, so that the china would have appeared cluttered and crowded with all the painting.

"If I'm going to take watercolor lessons," she said, "I think I'd like to read upon the lives of some of the painters. Would you get me some books that deal in biographies of some of the artists?'

"Oh, yes," Harrison said. "I can get you any number of those."

She got up to pour the coffee, and Harrison ran his finger around the inside of his collar and looked at the big back door, wishing that it was open so the night air could come inside.

Rocky was dressed in the sheerest of lightweight summer dresses. It had no sleeves, and her bare arms were very smooth, and evenly tanned. A light powder lay on her throat. Harrison would have liked to have laid his face there.

They drank their coffee. Rocky was silent for a few minutes. Harrison felt himself relaxing. He leaned back in his chair, letting his stiff back relax for the first time that evening.

He smiled.

Rocky thought to herself that when Professor Nix smiled, he looked Just like a little boy, appealing out of little-boy loneliness to be loved, cradled against some gentle feminine bosom.

Harrison was not yet thirty. He had really not been a professor for very long, and sometimes he was terribly unsure of himself, but he would not let anyone know. He hid behind an oratorical manner which he put on like an actor assumes his costume. When he put on this manner and let his voice wander on and on, drawing on the great wealth of material he had stored in his mind, residue of a lifetime of arduous reading, he was not really himself. The self was far away, cloistered, and very safe.

"Could that door be opened?" he asked.

Rocky leaped up as though she had suddenly seen a ghost. She moved hastily to the back door and opened it all the way back, letting a refreshing breath of cool night air into the kitchen.

"Let me take your coat," she said. "I know you must be too warm."

But, Harrison declined because by now, his shirt was wet and wilted, and he would look a sight if he took his coat off.

His suit was new, and he cut a very neat figure in it. He had been a collegiate tennis champion not many years before, and he still had a slim athletic figure. It was necessary for him to teach one class in Physical Education at Isaac Walton, and this helped him keep in shape. Further, he was not a person who would easily put on fat. No one in his family had ever been fat.

Rocky suddenly suggested that they go outside and sit down on the back steps, so he stood up, and they went out and although the steps were probably dusty and her dress would be soiled, Rocky sat down, and Harrison sat next to her.

Harrison felt that it was expected that he put his arm around Rocky's shoulder, so he did, and she immediately rested her head on his shoulder so that her hair brushed against his face.

Rocky's perfumed hair felt soft and caressing against Harrison's cheek. He felt his face grow hot, and his breath began to come rapidly. He whirled Rocky around and began to kiss her.

He kissed her roughly, searching for her lips, and when he found these he pulled her violently up against him and kissed her with passion, trying to force her lips apart with his own.

Rocky disentangled herself from him and leaped up, standing a few steps away from him.

"Mercy," she said.

Harrison became frightfully embarrassed. He took out his handkerchief and wiped his face.

By mutual but silent agreement, they went back into the house. They returned to the grim parlor and sat down again on the high-backed sofa.

"I'll bring you a life of Audubon," Harrison said. "And, I think I can get you some material on Sargent."

Rocky smoothed her skirts.

"Audubon will be nice," she said. "All those birds."

The conversation lagged. Rocky passed the box of confectionery to Harrison. He took two pieces.

Harrison would have excused himself and walked back to the school, but she would have thought that he was leaving because of what had happened on the back steps.

Rocky said to herself, "Oh God, if only poppa would come home."

And Harrison thought, "Oh God, if Mr. Bound would only come home."

Mr. Bound, with his western type hat, came affably into the house shortly. They had heard his car drive up. He sat in a large comfortable looking chair which was across from the sofa, and for a few minutes, he and Harrison talked together of inconsequential things.

The conversation pertained to the simplest of everyday things, but nonetheless, Harrison felt that he was on trial.

Mr. Bound was a bank president because he had made a fortune in cattle, and he was not impressed by either Classical Literature or college professors who taught it. He was more interested in discovering the man - the man whom Rocky had brought home.

Harrison was too slender and too ready to please to suit Mr. Bound. Mr. Bound's estimate of Harrison's manhood was nil, and Harrison thought of his own father, and that finished ruining his evening.

He got up to his feet, and in spite of everything, he began to stammer, and he felt sure that his face was growing red.

He said his good nights very quickly and darted for the door. Rocky accompanied him, but her father called after her not to be but a minute as there was something he had to discuss with her before she went up to bed.

He began to fix himself a drink before Harrison had even gotten out of the room, and he had not offered Harrison one, because, as Harrison thought, he felt Harrison too immature to need a drink of liquor.

At the door, Harrison said that he had enjoyed the evening, and stepped out into the darkness.

He hurried along the path to the gate.

Nix did not, however, leave the yard. He stationed himself under a large oak tree which grew by the fence, and watched the house for a few minutes. He could see the shadow of Mr. Bound on the window shade in the front parlor. He was standing up and talking to someone. Every now and then, he waved his arm in some emphatic gesture.

Nix moved furtively around to the back of the house and entered it through the still open kitchen door.

In a few minutes, he came out and walked leisurely along the road toward the college.

Mr. Bound had forgotten all about him. He was talking to Gazelle about a business matter which had come up which made it necessary for them to entertain a couple whom neither he nor Rocky cared about in the least. It was something which could not be avoided, and he wanted Gazelle to take complete charge of the evening, making certain that the event was a perfect social success.

Mr. Bound had a contempt for cocktails, taking his whiskey neat. He rolled it in his mouth and swallowed it slowly. After this, he smacked his lips.

Rocky was annoyed by her father's drinking on this particular night, although it did not ordinarily bother her. She excused herself as quickly as she could, and went upstairs to her room.

Mr. Bound was actually feeling tired this evening, so he went upstairs almost at once.

Rocky was borrowing in the linen closet, mumbling to herself.

"What's the matter?" Mr. Bound asked. He tilted on his feet and grabbed the stair rail to support himself.

"I turned back my counterpane and there were no pillow-cases on my bed," Rocky said. "Cook must have forgotten them."

"She's getting old," Mr. Bound said.

"We are going to have to get her an assistant," Rocky told him.

"I suppose so," he agreed. "She has been with us for almost thirty years. We can't just turn her out into the world."

A pension for Cook was another possibility, but they wouldn't think about that until a successor had been trained in Cook's work. It was no small matter to keep up a big house such as the Bounds had, especially as the Bounds were always entertaining.

Rocky took two embroidered pillow slips in her hand and kissed her father good night, and went into her ever-so-conventional bedroom.

She closed her door, and began to stuff the pillows into the cases, thinking all the time about Mr. Audubon and his watercolor paintings of birds.

* * * *

Nix walked along the road thinking that Mr. Bound was a big bag of wind. Rocky was a sad-sack, square-type, conventional broad if there ever was one. He would not go back to call on her again if he could help it. He could always say that he had been given some extra work to do at the college so that he would not have any evenings free for awhile.

He had forgotten that he had promised to bring her some books.

The pillowcases which were neatly folded and placed on the inside of his shirt were so comfortably placed that Nix did not feel them, and no one could have told by looking at him that he had any such thing under his coat.

It was a good thing, too, as he met the night watchman making his rounds, and if this worthy old man had noticed a bulge of any sort under Harrison's clothing, he would have taken it for granted that it was a bottle of whiskey which Harrison was smuggling into the teachers' dormitory, and he would probably have said something about it, and then Harrison would have had to make all sorts of explanations.

Harrison walked a little way with the old man up the center of the campus and past the flagpole. Isaac Walton had been one of the first colleges in the area to obtain a 50 star flag. Every morning a different freshman boy had to get up early and come out with a helper and put up the flag. It was a beautiful little ceremony with the sun coming up and the air crisp above dew-laden grass, but Harrison had never gotten up early enough to witness it.

The steps up to the teachers' dormitory were steep and high. Harrison climbed them lithely. He was very graceful and very light on his feet. He had excelled on the tennis court, and was a good dancer. People had often told him that he would make a good boxer because his weight would probably cause him to be classed as a welterweight. Yet, he had a long reach and was exceedingly agile. But, Harrison would never consider such a thing. He did not want to go through life with a flattened nose, and a cauliflowered ear, and perhaps an angry red scar over one eye.

Harrison had a corner room. He was not assigned this room to begin with, but had made a swap with the professor who was to have occupied it, enabling himself to have it. He had traded his old set of The Golden Bough in 12 volumes for the privilege of living in this room all year. So he had cross-ventilation and a two-way view of the campus, which most of the teachers did not.

His professor friend, Red, inherited the room next door which was to have been his. If Red had less of a view of the campus, he had twelve volumes of comparative beginnings in human thought about magic and religion. Perhaps there were items here of greater interest than were to be observed on the college campus.

Harrison had kept the thirteenth volume, titled Aftermath, because Red did not seem to be aware of its existence, and some perverted streak in Harrison made him gloat over having withheld it.

Harrison and Red shared a bathroom which was between their rooms, and usually left their doors unlocked so that they might go and come freely between each other's rooms. Red was always coming into Harrison's room for help on some problem which arose in regard to one of the courses he was teaching.

Red was a relatively young professor, too.

Now, when Nix got inside his own room, he locked the door to the hall, and the door which gave into the big bathroom, and when he was assured that no one could come in, he took off his coat and unbuttoned his shirt and took out the two pillowcases.

He took all the contents out of his pants pockets, placing them carefully on the dresser. He had a frog-gigging knife which he always carried, which no one knew about. The blade was four inches long.

He undressed carefully, putting his clothes on racks and hanging them away in the closet. Then, he picked up the two pillowcases and sat down crosslegged on an oval braided rug which was on the floor, and began to fold and unfold the pillowcases, lifting them to his nose, smelling them, smelling Rocky's perfume, holding the smooth material against his face. He crumpled them and buried his face in them. Then he rose to his knees and reached the knife which lay on the dresser, and opening the blade, he began to cut the material of the pillowcases roughly. When he had made many little cuts around the edge of the cases, he began tearing them with his hands, and the sound of the cloth tearing excited him so that he became unaware of anything except the ripping cotton, and his own mounting passion.

The moon shown in at the large windows, and Nix crouched on the rug, white in the moonlight, crouched like a dog, and the only sounds in the room were the sounds of the tearing cloth and his panting breath.

Finally, this tearing of the cloth was at an end, and his excitement began to ebb away. He threw himself at full length on the floor among the mutilated bits of white cotton, and his breathing became easier, and he slept.

His hair was tousled and his face was slack and troubled. He turned himself on his back, in his sleep, and began to dream.

It was a dream, but it was a dream he had many times before. Sometimes he felt that it was not a dream, but that he was half awake, and remembering something which had actually happened. It had the unreal, other-worldly aspect of a dream, but it was so real to Nix that he could hardly believe that it was all a nightmare.

He saw himself as a little boy. He had a beautiful mother, full-figured, fair of skin, with long curling hair that fell below her shoulders. She was very vain of this head of brown hair which she spent hours each night brushing and arranging, and whenever she went outside she covered her head with something, as she believed that the sun would fade the rich, chestnut brown color of this crowning glory.

Nix was playing in the mud beneath the clothesline which had been in the backyard of their house, and his mother was hanging clothes on the line. She had put her long hair inside a pillowcase and had pinned the mouth of this tight around her forehead so that the case bagged out and fell behind her head protecting her neck from the sun.

She was telling Nix a story.

"Once when there were nothing but Indians in the land, the Indians were without fire because they had never heard of it. They called all the creatures of the forest together and said, 'We must have heat to warm ourselves by, and something to cook our food over.' Someone who was very wise had spoken up and said that the Great Spirit had knowledge of something called fire-sticks which would bring them the warmth and light they needed, if only they might steal these from Him. The Indians thought to send one of the wild creatures after this, and Raven was the first to volunteer to go."

Raven had started out on his long journey, and Nix's eyes were gleaming with anticipation to hear the end of the story, when Nix's father, black-browed and big, came bursting out the back door of the house with his usual energy.

Nix's mother looked up and smiled, taking up her clothes basket and leaving Nix sitting in the mud.

"You're home early," she said.

"And I caught you looking like a colored washer-woman," the father laughed. "With that thing on your head, you look just like some of the colored girls I've seen."

He slapped her on the buttocks with great exuberance and familiarity, and they laughed and hugged each other and ran up the steps to the house.

Inside the kitchen, the mother fixed her tired husband a glass of iced tea, and when she looked around for Nix, he was nowhere to be seen.

Nix had run up the stairs, and thrown himself in his mother's bed, burying his face in her pillow. He sobbed and sobbed, not knowing why, but feeling that his heart would break without fail.

Now, the dream went away, and Nix awoke on the floor of his room at Isaac Walton. His face was buried in the torn pieces of white cotton cloth on the rug, and he was sobbing, now, as hard as the little boy Nix had cried in the dream. His fingers worked among the pieces of pillowcase, and his whole body convulsed and relaxed with the spasm of his crying.

He sat up, and put his face between his hands, and slowly controlled his sobbing. He walked to the window and looked outside, and then he went and got in bed.

But, he did not sleep until it was almost daybreak.

* * * *

At seven o'clock in the morning, Harrison heard a loud pounding at the door which led to the bathroom. It was Red, realizing that Harrison was about to oversleep.

"Knock it off!" he shouted. "I'm awake."

But, Red kept up his pounding, so that Harrison pulled himself up out of bed and rummaged in a dresser until he found a pair of clean undershorts. He put these on and hastily picked up the pieces of pillowcase from the floor, which he placed in a paper bag he happened to have. He stuffed this in a drawer, and put his knife away. Then, he opened the door.

"What took you so long?" Red asked loudly. He was fully dressed, and looking neat and fresh as a daisy except for the brush of red hair which he had, and which no comb or brush had ever been able to control.

"I had to get myself awake," Harrison said crossly. "I was out late last night."

"Where were you?" Red asked. "I came over here looking for you. I needed to ask you something about William James. You ought to be pretty well up on him."

"Well, I'm not. I went to Gazelle Bound's house."

"Well, no wonder you were out late. It's not often you find a girl who is attractive and has a rich old man, too."

"Let me get in the bathroom," Harrison said. "There's a copy of William James over there among my books. You can read him for yourself."

Red always got up at five o'clock and went down to the football field and ran around the track three or four times, and then came back to the dormitory and dressed, and usually he and Harrison went to breakfast together.

He dug about in Harrison's books which were in a wooden crate in a corner, and it wasn't long before he found the copy of the thirteenth volume of The Golden Bough. He looked at it for a long time until he was sure of what it was, and then, he sat on the bed with this on his knee until Harrison came out of the bathroom.

Harrison was feeling so completely let-down and tired-out that he could not argue. He told Red to take the book to his own room and to keep it as it was part of his set which Harrison had neglected to give him. He pulled his copy of William James off the bottom and handed it to Red.

"I don't need it," he said. "Keep it as long as you want to."

Red asked him if he was going with him for breakfast. Harrison told him no, that they were late already, and he had to pass by the incinerator on the way to the dining hall.

Red took the two books and disappeared into his room.

* * * *

Harrison had to take something for his head, and when he finally dressed he took an armful of books and the paper bag with the torn pieces of cloth in it and left the room.

It was too nearly time for his first class for him to go to the dining hall for breakfast, so he walked briskly down the campus past the tennis courts and the oleander thicket to the heating plant. The student who slept here with the boilers was nowhere about, so Harrison threw his paper bag into the furnace and continued on to the foot of the campus.

Crossing the road, he went to a small off-campus restaurant which was there, and ordered coffee and doughnuts to eat. His first class was in Classical Lit, and he opened his book now to brush up on what the day's lesson was to be about.

They would begin the third book of the Aenead. Harrison looked it over hurriedly, trying to fix the details of the action in his mind.

He enjoyed the first-period class in Classical Lit. The year before, he had frequently let the class wander from the subject, spending more time in a discussion of what was bad in the classical tradition of literature, than learning the material furnished by the textbook.

Somehow, word had gotten around that this was a real live class, and now he had about six students who represented the independent thinking, rebellious minded faction on the campus.

They had some rousing discussions, and the classics suffered greatly at their hands. He never went further in the text than Goethe, for hadn't someone stated that Goethe was the end product of classicism?

After Goethe, a new day was ushered in with Dostoevsky, and some of the French writers and Americans.

There was actually one young man in the class who lived off-campus and wore a beard, and there was a flat-chested girl who didn't seem to have many friends, who wore dark-rimmed glasses and combed her hair very severely and had a bad complexion.

Harrison hoped that both of them would be present this morning, and would have read over the text of the lesson, and would have some good, caustic comments to get an argument started. If they did, he would only have to sit, and act as monitor, and perhaps he wouldn't have to lecture or ask questions at all.

After Harrison had paid for his coffee and left the restaurant, he walked along the cindered path to his classroom, preoccupied and whistling to himself. He was thinking about the girl in his class who was so unattractive, but such a literary firebrand.

Her name was Ruby Persia. Harrison almost laughed every time he thought about it, because she was such a plain girl, and the name did not suit her at all.

It was warm in the classroom, and Harrison stifled a yawn. He dispensed with calling the roll as he could see who was there and who was not there. He would mark it down later.

Bob Barley came in late, but this was not unusual.

The day before, they had gone thoroughly into the matter of the Aenead's being centered completely around the idea that life was controlled by Fate in the person of Jupiter, and that man was predestined and preordained to the will of destiny. Empty lands must be settled. Empires must be established, and persons who were in the way killed or otherwise disposed of without consideration for personal desires or rights. History must be fulfilled.

Bob Barley had vehemently opposed the whole construction of the Aenead and was ready to consign it to the flames as an obscene thought through and through, but the end of the period had come before he could fully make his point.

Ruby Persia had been especially icy and nasty and had compared the manner of writing of the Aenead to that of the Old Testament, a telling of history after the fact in the prophetic manner, so that everything is patly explained, and she had said that the Romans justified their conquering of the known world in the same manner that the Hebrews justified their rape of the Promised Land, claiming they had a Call to do this. She said that whenever someone began to tell people that he had a call, it meant that that person was arranging in advance a justification for some particularly horrible thing he planned to do.

Mae Grace Rein, who was a fundamentalist, had been shocked by what Ruby Persia said, and began to argue in a manner which was unintelligible to Harrison, so he had said that they had better get back on the subject, and had spent a few minutes discussing the actual facts of the Aenead as laid down in the second book..

This morning, Bob Barley rudely took the floor, and took exception with the idea that the town-site in Thrace could be accursed because of the murder of

Polydorus. By some reasoning of his own, he connected this with the Mark of Cain, quoting Frazer as saying that Cain was not cursed, but that the mark was placed on him as a protection, so that no one would harm him. He felt that Steinbeck's delving into the life of Cain as set forth in East of Eden was applicable to the issue, and told the class at length about the search by the Chinese for the exact nature of God's remarks to Cain after his murder of Abel, and clinched his argument by stating that the Chinese in East of Eden had found out that the Lord sent Cain away, telling him that "Thou mayest do well." Cain had a choice.

"Cain was the first existentialist," Bob Barley said. "He was abandoned in the existentialist sense, in that he was left with no excuse, no one else was responsible for him. He knew the existentialist anguish in that he was left to choose for himself and all his race, as if the eyes of the world were upon him. He knew the existentialist despair, for he had no other which he might count upon, only himself to rely upon, and no illusion was left to him. He had very little hope. His life was cut off from natural foundation or supernatural guarantee. He was in a state of dreadful freedom, and total responsibility. Standing completely alone."

Ruby Persia said that Cain entered the new land even as Aeneas entered the land of Italy or the colonists settled the New World.

"However," she said, "Cain could enter his Land of Nod without the subsequent guilt which the Protestant white element has always felt for the rape of the wilderness of America, as Nod was probably populated but thinly, and Cain was only one arrival. Contrasting the overthrow of the old order in Italy and the creation there of a civilization in the wilderness, with the similar events in North America, we see that Aeneas and his followers justified their actions as being the Will of Jupiter and Venus, whereas the American Colonists had no excuse. Even the South American Latin invaders felt that they had a calling to bring the Catholic faith to the heathen, but the North American colonists make no excuse. Everywhere in our literature is the guilt which is felt at the mistreatment of the Indian and the Negro, and the rape of Nature on this continent. And, the woman suffered, for the appeal to being which is the emptiness of woman was so drowned in the greater appeal of the emptiness of the continent that she was neglected. Man turned his creative impulses to creating great cities, and to linking them together with transportation facilities and communications, and filling the sharing buildings of the metropolises with material luxuries. There is something sexual in the building of a civilization, otherwise why the inherent desire on the part of the people to refer to the Empire State Building as 'Al Smith's last erection'?"

With this the bell rang, ending the period, and Harrison closed his books and picked them up and hurried out of the room. He hoped that no one would tell anyone of what had been said in his classroom this morning, but he was too tired and sleepy to worry.

He had the next period free, and he determined to hurry across the campus to his room and lie down.

He stopped at the bulletin board and noticed that there was to be a meeting of the faculty that afternoon. Tiredly, he left the building and went down the steps.

* * * *

The President of Isaac Walton Junior College was a tall, stately white-haired gentleman of the old school. He always spoke softly and courteously no matter how diabolical the content of his utterance.

Harrison and Red took seats on the back row as befitted apprentice professors. The faculty seemed wilted and tired. They yawned and looked out the windows with frank boredom.

Dr. N. S. Noel was called Old Never Satisfied by the majority of the student body and part of the faculty. Only in their private thoughts or among the most trusted of friends, of course. However, the lower the position of the individual on the campus, the more daring he was about using this appellation. The cruddiest of Freshmen used this designation entirely when speaking of Dr. Noel except when he was present, whereas the faculty members nearest the President hardly dared think it.

Dr. Noel had dreamed of owning his own publishing house.

"As you know," he said, "Each year we have every member of the faculty submit an essay to the Office of the President which is appraised for merit in research, composition, choice of subject matter, originality of thought, etc. etc." He smiled expansively. "The time is coming for this again. This is my own little venture, and you know that at my expense, one or several of the best manuscripts are printed in pamphlet form and kept as a permanent part of our library, and this year the Board of Trustees is going to sponsor the winner at two all-expense paid weeks at the Bethel Writers' Conference. With this added inducement, I am sure that you are all going to work very hard on your papers. We only have about three weeks, you know."

Dr. Noel was terribly pleased with himself over his little contest, and he smiled in a fatherly way on the faculty for a moment or two after making the announcement. Then, a cloud crossed his face, and he looked very distressed.

"Some of you may have heard that a carnival is coming to town," he intoned. "I have heard of this for some time, and have been to see the Mayor and the City Commissioners in order to try to find out if there were not some way of preventing this, but they say that there is none. The carnival will be set up just outside the city limits next week. I know that there is no use for us to hope that the student body will not find its way to this parody on the theatre, where I am sure they will see and hear things which I am certain the parents who have entrusted them to us would not want them to see and hear." He looked the room over, letting his eyes rest on first one of his faculty and then another. It seemed that his eyes dwelled extra long on Red and then Harrison. "I am going to ask that the professors do all that they can, subtly of course, to discourage the students from going to this cheap and unsatisfying place of entertainment, and that they set an example by not going to the carnival themselves."

A note of harshness and threat almost crept into his voice at this last remark. The teachers shifted about in horror, thinking of what the punishment might be if they accidentally should stray onto this unhallowed earth of hanky-panky and hokum..

69

"Alas," said Dr. Noel. "There is going to be a huge balloon set up in the very center of the carnival lot which shall be visible all over our fair little valley. It will stand as a constant source of temptation to the unwary to investigate this emporium of Satan, and I am afraid that no signs stating 'Let the buyer beware,' which we may erect will be of any avail."

Hurrying on from this distasteful subject, Dr. Noel announced that Professor Trotter, who was head of the English Department, had handed in his resignation and would be leaving Isaac Walton at the end of the semester.

It immediately occurred to Harrison that a promotion for someone might be forthcoming due to Professor Trotter's decision to leave. He looked sidewise at Red to see if Red had entertained a similar thought, but Red's eyes were quite glazed, and Harrison doubted that he had heard anything which Dr. Noel had said.

The meeting adjourned soon after this, and Harrison and Red walked slowly to the teachers' dormitory. Harrison lay down for a nap, but asked Red to wake him up for supper.

* * * *

One day not long after this, Harrison and Red sat on one of the benches out on the campus under a large oak tree, enjoying the late evening breeze.

A group of Freshman students had come over to talk with them, and they lay sprawled about on the ground or hung onto the ends of the benches, and Red talked with them about softball. Red had been a better than average baseball player when he had been in high school, but one summer he had broken his ankle, and he had lost out with his home team, and after that he had not seriously tried to excel in the game.

Harrison was not called upon to say anything, so he relaxed and looked down the long sloping campus, thinking what a pleasant place this was. The college was I like home, with the protection and guidance of Father and Mother, and Harrison felt very safe here and removed from the world, but he longed for adventure, too. This summer, he would go to New Orleans and spend the whole season in the French Quarter walking about bearded and barefoot, but come September he would come home to Alma Mater like a penitent and prodigal son.

Red was explaining to the boys of the group that you could not possibly win at baseball without cheating, and was instructing them in the sleight-of-hand that made it possible to use perspiration in the manufacture of the "spit ball."

Everyone was giggly, self-conscious at the audacity of a professor to talk so frankly of something which everyone knew went on, but no one talked about.

He hinted at other things such as the use of the elbow in an opposing man's ribs, the subtle kick, and the belt-hold, and in basketball, the opposing man might be rattled if one stood close behind and surreptitiously pulled the hair on his legs, if he had such.

Of course, the umpire must not be looking!

"Sportsmanship is one of the cardinal principles of our American Way of

Life," Harrison said absently. He was studying a Freshman girl who knelt on the grass at his feet, staring intently at Red with blank uncomprehending eyes.

She was a very pretty girl, blond, pink-cheeked and plump. Harrison had seen her at dances, where she was always in great demand, doing an animated cha-cha and a wild swing. She liked to dance in the center of the floor, and she wore very full skirts which she hiked up with her left hand on the turns to reveal a great show of petticoats.

She was called High Gear.

She was in Harrison's afternoon class in Freshman English, and he doubted that she would ever be able to learn the difference between an appositive and a predicate noun, but perhaps she would live to grow old without this knowledge.

Even now, the Freshman class was midway through the writing of the research paper for the year, and Harrison supposed that High Gear had some boy helping her with hers. Otherwise, he saw little hope of her having one.

High Gear suddenly became aware of Harrison, and smiled up at him.

Maybe her eyes were a little weak and watery appearing, now that he was up close. Sometimes in class, she put on a pair of glasses which she had that had transparent blue frames, and were shaped in the cat's eye styling.

"I guess you think I'm terribly stupid," she said. "I know some of the things I say in class sound like I just don't know anything."

Harrison thought that she was about as stupid as Arachne

"Did you have a weak English Department in the high school you attended?" Harrison asked.

High Gear seized eagerly upon this proffered excuse, and leaned a little closer to Harrison's knee. She turned her face up to his and smiled with earnestness and sincerity.

"Two years, I had a teacher that I just couldn't understand," she said. "What she said never made any sense to me. I just didn't get a thing out of her classes."

"Quite often, when a student is having trouble with a subject in college, it is because he had a weak teacher in that subject in high school. He doesn't have the foundation, you know. A student like that must try extra hard, studying a little harder than others, work and master whatever it is that is creating a problem for him."

"Oh, I will do that," High Gear breathed, using her diaphragm to speak. "I'm going to try ever so hard."

"I'll help you in any way I can," Harrison said.

"Oh, I get a lot out of your classes," High Gear said. "You make everything very clear. I just couldn't get anything out of my high school teacher's classes." She grimaced. "Well, she was kind of old."

"Perhaps her language was a little out of date, and she may have been too academic in her discussions."

"Oh, that's it exactly," High Gear said. She drew her feet up under herself and curled at his feet, purring and stretching like an adorable, roly-poly, soft, lovable kitten. She stretched her full mouth in a lazy yawn, and a far-away, dreamy look came into her eyes. Harrison thought that, in another moment, she would be asleep.

71

He looked at his watch.

"It's only a few minutes until supper time," he said.

Red was explaining that a baseball which has been kept in the refrigerator right up until it is pitched, when struck by the bat, will fall to the ground like a ball of soft cotton. When supper was mentioned, he leaped up, saying that he must go to his room for a minute beforehand.

Harrison and Red hurried to the teachers' dormitory.

"The campus is so restful at this time of day," Harrison said. "I was thinking a few minutes ago, how much like home this is for us."

"You don't know anything," Red said. "You were an only child. I had eight brothers and sisters. You don't know what it means to me to have a room all to myself where I can read and study, and think. This is the first time in my life I've ever had a bathroom I have to share with only one person. All I ever had at home was a bunch of screaming, fighting brats climbing over me, and someone always in the bathroom. My father and I never got along. I was a match for him and he hated me. We stood like two stags with our horns locked together for three or four years. Then, I decided to end the deadlock and I dropped my own horns and retreated. The only trouble is, I've never been horny since."

"You've never been anything else."

"That's not so," Red said good-naturedly. "If I was horny, I'd be in a terrible place for it. A college campus in a small town is no place for a man with aggressive notions toward women."

"This town's not so small," Harrison said. "You've heard boys' dormitory gossip the same as I have. You know where the little bad boys go. You could go there the same as anyone else."

"I don't like the idea of commercial sex," Red said. "I feel like it removes the chase and the conquest. You only have the consummation, and the consummation is merchandise you buy and pay for. It doesn't prove anything."

"You're a romantic!" Harrison said.

"I guess so."

Harrison sat down and thought about this.

"I don't think I'll go to supper," he said.

"What's the matter with you?" Red asked. "You know it will be a long time 'til breakfast. You'll get hungry."

"If I do, I'll walk down to the restaurant. I've thought of something I want to do."

"You're not going to town, are you'?" Red asked suspiciously.

"No."

"Well, I hope not. I'm trying to work up a lecture on the psychologist's view of Edgar A. Poe. I want you to help me out. I'm too normal to be trying to teach psychology. I hope they don't give me this course to teach next year. The only reason I got a minor in psychology was that I liked the teacher. I wish I'd got one in economics or history instead."

Harrison dug about in his box of books until he found a thin volume of poetry he had borrowed from the Dean of Women. He took this, and hurried over to the girls' dormitory.

The Dean of Women was just about to leave her office for the dining hall. Harrison gave her the book, which he had for a long time, and thanked her for it. She stepped into her apartment to put it away, and he flipped through an alphabetical file which was on her desk and found out the number of High Gear's room.

"I thought that was a lovely little book of poetry," the Dean said when she returned to the office. "I hope you enjoyed it."

"Oh," Harrison said. "I did. Your poet had something of the tone of Emily Dickinson."

"She was a girl I was in college with a long time ago," the Dean said. "She passed away some time ago."

"I'm sorry."

"Well," the Dean said crisply. "It's that time. Are you going to the dining hall?"

Harrison apologized.

"I must go to my room first," he said. "I have to pick up something there."

The Dean of Women looked at her watch and moved briskly to the door. Some of the girls came running down the stairs, and hurried out of the building.

"We're going to be late," they told each other excitedly.

Harrison doubted that they would be able to eat a thing when they got to the dining hall, they were so upset.

The Dean of Women forgot all about Harrison and began to stride up the sidewalk after the girls, snapping her fingers.

"Girls! Deport yourselves as ladies! You know it is not dignified to run across the lobby of the dorm like that."

When she was gone, Nix glided noiselessly up the stairs. His heart beat wildly for fear he would meet some tardy girl in the hallway. Any college man would as soon desecrate the Holy of Holies as be found out of place in a girls' dormitory.

The building was ghostly silent. Even his most careful footsteps echoed up and down the corridor. He found High Gear's room and carefully stole inside.

It was easy for him to tell which was her bed. Her roommate's was much neater.

Quickly, he stripped her pillowcase off her pillow and thrust it under his coat. He replaced the spread over the pillow and went to the door and peeked up and down the hall.

Everything had happened so quickly that he was able to go to his room, hide the pillowcase in a drawer, and get to the dining room in time not to miss any part of the meal except Grace.

The teachers' table was full, and he had to eat with some students among whom was Mae Grace Rein. She looked at him coldly all through the meal, and he knew that in her room at night, she was praying for him.

* * * *

Harrison walked all the way uptown to pick up a paperback copy of Advertisements for Myself. When he got back to the dormitory, Red was sitting in his room idly fingering a copy of The Narrative of Arthur Gordon Pym.

"I don't understand Poe at all," Red told Harrison despondently. "I think I had better give up this whole idea and use someone else."

"You'll never find anyone as good as Poe for the lecture," Harrison said shortly. He lay down on his bed and began thumbing through Advertisements for Myself, ignoring Red.

"What've you got that book for?" Red asked.

"Bob Barley was telling me about it. He's one of my students in my Classical Lit class."

"I know who he is. He flatly refused to take part in Physical Education classes. The big sissy!" Red said contemptuously. "He weighs 180 pounds if he weighs an ounce. He should be out for football."

"It's a little late to go out for football this year," Harrison said.

Well, he should have gone. I don't know what he's going to do when he comes to graduate. He said he was against being coerced into taking Physical Education, on principle, and if they try to withhold his diploma from him because he has not taken it, he will take the school to court."

Harrison lowered his voice appropriately.

"I wouldn't be surprised if old Never Satisfied doesn't meet his match when Bob ties into him."

"It's a damned disgrace. Wearing that beard as a symbol of his superior manhood, and then won't take part in P. E.! Why, I've got beardless little boys that don't weigh 90 pounds in that class."

"Bob Barley is not going to do anything he doesn't want to," Harrison said.

"What's he getting an education for?" Red asked. "As soon as he's through here, he'll run out West and flop in some Beat community, boozing and smoking peyote and associating with Beat women and queers and making a problem for honest, hardworking policemen."

"He's a poet"

"My God!"

"You should sympathize with him. He's rebelling against Isaac Walton, which is old Never Satisfied Noel, the never satisfied father, and when he leaves here he'll be rebelling against never satisfied law and never satisfied society. It's all the father, all authority represented in chains and jails and hangman's ropes and the attrition of fear that bleeds a man's soul until it's white. You said today you didn't get along with your father."

"I didn't," Red said. "But, I can't transfer the feeling I had for him to every person or thing which represents authority and order."

"Well, some people can."

Harrison turned his attention to his book.

"Another damned poet like Poe for someone to sweat about in a hundred years. I want you to tell me where any of Poe's writing made any sense."

"You've got to unravel it psychologically. Have you studied your Jung?"

"I think I know quite a bit about Jung."

"Well it all deals with the eternal triangle which exists between the father, the mother, and the son."

"The Oedipus complex."

"The Oedipus complex and more," Harrison said.

"I know what you're about to say," Red said. "And, don't say it. I'll throw up.

"Well, you've got the key right there in your own hand."

"I know there's supposed to be something symbolic in the ending of the Narrative of Arthur Gordon Pym, but all I can see is that he met his indescribable Eternal Woman or White Goddess or whatever in the form of a mist, and that was that."

"It's not the incestuous guilt-ridden meeting which he had with the mother image, but his death which is important. That death occurred with his finally achieving union with his mother which he had striven for all his life. People of his day believed that there was a dark pit running from pole to pole through the center of the earth like it says in Invictus, the Earthwomb. The Earth is our Great Mother. Poe, like they say of Miller, was always dreaming of making that Journey to the End of the Night, the trip back to the womb. As Pym, he did it. But, the horror of this unnatural and incestuous return is disclosed in the actions of Nu-nu. Nu-nu, crazed with fear, raised 'with his forefinger the upper lip, and displayed the teeth which lay beneath it.' This was the speechless warning. The aperture which led into the dark womb of the earth was toothed! Therein, the horror which Poe had all his life of the nubile woman. Woman of the vagina dentata. Woman, toothed so that she might castrate. Woman who, transformed into Mother Earth, gaped open her hungry mouth, the grave, to devour and smother, to rend in the suffocating darkness. Any trip to woman was a premature burial, a trip leading to the grave. Therefore, his fear of the teeth of Berenice. Therefore, his aggression against the body of the undead Berenice, his visit to Berenice in the grave, his removal of her teeth. His imagined triumph over her. He was representing his own person, the archetypal hero of the Jicarilla Apache Indians, called Killer-of-Enemies, who outwitted the murderous father, Kicking Monster, and deprived his four daughters of their unnatural teeth so that they were forced to stop devouring men, playing the role of the Black Widow, who mates and kills, the phallic mother believed by Freud to be the origin of power of the spider as a fear-releasing sign. But, Poe did not conquer the Oedipal Father or the devouring mother, or his own fear of them. He carried it with him until the last when he cried out on his deathbed for 'Reynolds,' who had been the man great in his mind at the time he was composing the nightmare, The Narrative of Arthur Gordon Pym."

"If you think," Red said, "that I am going to get up before a classroom of boys and girls at Isaac Walton Junior College and give a lecture on any such thing, you are crazier than I think you are. I grew up in this area, and was a student in this very college, and I know that I would be lynched before morning if I voiced such obscene thoughts in the ears of the pure daughters of this county. The good fathers would not permit it."

"There you go," Harrison said. "You do feel the threat of the punishing, vengeful, destroying father as an almost material presence the same as Poe probably did. You've just repressed your fear."

"I'm going back to my room and prepare a lecture on Thomas Bailey Aldrich."

"Listen," Harrison said. "It's true that the subject of Poe's inner nightmare is something that you can't use in a lecture to Sophomores, but why don't you build up the theme and add some other significant facts to what I've told you, and turn it in as your research paper for old Never Satisfied's contest? He called for something original, and he might be struck with your daring. You'd know how to slant it to his viewpoint."

"I don't know", Red said. "I don't think he'd like it."

"It'll be a relief to him after reading all the papers on insipid, milk-sop material, which the others will gather. I'm going to do a paper on The American Existentialist. It will be subtitled: Hophead as Hero. I'm going to draw heavily on Mailer's description of the Hipster in his role as the American Existentialist. This will be something out of the ordinary, too."

Red was doubtful, but he took his book and went to his room to scan A Story of a Bad Boy hurriedly, trying to think if there might be some significance here, but the powerful thoughts which Harrison had set in motion with his talk of Poe had Red strangely fascinated so that he could not keep his mind on anything else.

When Red was gone, Nix hurriedly locked all his doors and turned out all his lights except a very small lamp, and took out High Gear's pillowcase and his knife, and sat down with them upon the floor.

* * * *

Ruby Persia had obtained a copy of Tropic of Cancer, and was very much impressed with the notion that obscenity is definable by the way the individual feels inside after the fact. Obscenity is a matter which must be defined by every person according to the physical revulsion or lack of revulsion he may feel after seeing, hearing, reading or doing some act which could possibly be defined as obscene.

Bob Barley agreed that much of what is attributed to psychic trauma is really physical conditioning, citing a passage from the unlikely Wuthering Heights of Emily Bronte, wherein Catherine the Younger receives a physical reprimand from the diabolical Heathcliff in the form of a shower of slaps upon the side of the face. When Heathcliff reentered the room after making tea, Catherine instinctively raised her hand to her cheek. His neighborhood revived a painful sensation. Heathcliff mistook her action for fear, but it was not fear of the spirit but a physical reaction to which the flesh had quickly habituated itself.

The spirit was able to dominate the fleshly fear which the presence of the black father-image Heathcliff inspired. Emily Bronte made her women strong, as contrasted with the weak and ethereal Edgar Linton and the cowardly Linton Heathcliff who felt moral terror for his father. Even as the second Catherine was too brave to give in to the fleshly fear she felt for the dark and sensual, physically powerful and manly Heathcliff, the first Catherine had been strong enough to resist her passion for this same lusty being so that it was only after her denial and her will had killed her, and she had lain for many years in the grave, that Heathcliff was to know his night of love with her, invading her coffin and holding her in his arms through a night of sleet and rain and darkness.

And, he did not feel that he had committed an obscenity, but was glorified. So great was his preoccupation with the transfiguration he had known, that he died of his preoccupation with the event and the unnatural excitement it engendered. All his thoughts of earthly revenge eluded him at the last, and he moved up to a higher sphere, plummeted there by the mad act of his cold night of necrophilic love.

Mae Grace Rein looked terribly distressed. She determined that if she ever finished this course, she would never take a class with Professor Nix again. And, yet something about him compelled her to think of him. She spent long hours alone, dreaming of how she, in her purity, might somehow bring about a reformation of Harrison's character. There was no sacrifice which she would not make to save his erring soul, even to compromising herself as Hester Prynne had been compromised, wearing Hester's "A" in silence and suffering, or even like Joan of Arc being burned for Harrison as Joan had been burned for France.

When Harrison had reached the seclusion of his room during the second period, which was free, he sat in his rocking chair with his head in his hands. His fetish with the pillowcases was an obscenity by Ruby Persia's definition. The act was always followed by the sobbing, the remorse, the guilt, and the sleepless night. His day following the event was always a day tread in terror.

Yet, even now, he felt an irresistible impulse to go to the girls' dormitory, find out where Ruby's room was, and take her pillowcases, so that tonight, the madness might be repeated.

But, he knew that to do so would mean the suicide of his career. He had successfully invaded the girls' dormitory once, where no masculine foot may ever tread, but the next time he would fall. Some harried girl with studying to do would be in her room when the rest were gone, or some girl with a headache would be lying down resting, and the guilty footsteps of Nix would be heard. There would be a start of terror, and then an outcry. People would come running - the Dean of Women, other faculty members, male students ready to do or die to protect pure womanhood, even old Never Satisfied himself. Nix would be seen and captured. Questions would be asked. The disappearance of High Gear's pillowcase would be recalled. There would be an investigation. Strange things which had been taught in his classroom would be remembered. Vengeful students would testify. He would be fired, and he would be barred from ever working again. He would have to lose himself in a big city somewhere and go to work in the clerical end of the transportation business.

He could imagine himself in some faraway place, working as a menial in the dirty office of some motor freight line, when news would come to him that Gazelle Bound, having suffered from the humiliation and disgust that his acts had brought about, had died, now he would hitchhike back to Isaac Walton, throw himself on the perfect body of Rocky, white and angelic in death, sobbing, disarranging her aphrodisiac hair, disordering the corpse, leaving the marks of his fingernails and bruises on the frail white arms. And Laban Bound with his western hat would be standing by, grinding his teeth in anger, his face blackened with a wrath so great that he seemed choking with it, and when Harrison had been drawn away from the casket, there would be the invitation for him to meet Laban outside where, on watery knees, Harrison would receive a terrible beating and finally die at the hands of the irate father.

Harrison became so upset with this line of daydreaming that he leaped up trembling and hurried to the restaurant at the foot of campus, where he drank two cups of coffee and stayed so long that he was late for his third period class.

* * * *

Harrison threw himself into hard work, because if he did not keep himself incessantly busy, incessantly tired, he would give himself up to the doing of no telling what terrible deeds.

He made an exhaustive study of the existentialist philosophers from Kant to Kierkegaard through Kafka to Sartre and Becket and Camus, and crossing the ocean to America, he read Mailer's say on the subject three or four times. He wrote a long research paper glorifying the Hipster, the Cat, the jive-talking, dope-taking, jazz-oriented, disaffiliated American; the prototype of Cain, the isolated, the anguished, the abandoned and the despairing.

He looked at American life with the eyes of those who have developed a morality of the bottom which is the antithesis of moral, conventional, normal society, splashing the paper with quotes from Mailer and Ginsberg and backing them up with the more orthodox studies of such people as Harold Finestone of Chicago.

He did not write one searing paragraph, or one bitter line of this work without showing it to Red and consulting him about it. Red was amazed at Harrison's daring, and a little afraid, too, for Harrison was loosing hounds of literature which snapped ravenously at every facet of the American Way of Life.

By comparison, Red's account of the psychological side of Mr. Edgar Allen Poe seemed rather tame, almost orthodox. Harrison gave him a lot of help, for really, Harrison had read much more than Red and had a wider grasp of American literature, and his natural instinct for problems in abnormal psychology seemed to be greater than Red's too. Harrison was able to see things as a whole, which Red only saw as bits and pieces.

Many of the best lines in Red's paper were direct quotes of things which Harrison had told him. After the long weeks had passed which were taken up with the writing of the paper, Harrison volunteered to type Red's for him, as Red was atrociously slow on the typewriter. When Harrison had the scrawled manuscript in hand, he edited it carefully, changing a word here and there, and in some places whole phrases and sentences, which Red would never notice, making the work more necrophilic, sadistic, grave-oriented, Oedipal, and beclouded with the overall fear of castration than it already was, Like a master artist, he painted in black and red a vivid portrait of sick sex.

He set aside his own paper on the American Existentialist, and wrote a very academic and conventional paper entitled The Oresteia, Hamlet, and The Files: A Comparison. He showed how one theme had been handled dramatically by the pagan Sophocles, the Christian Shakespeare, and the atheist Sartre. This allowed him to utilize some of the material he had gathered on Sartre, and to manifest his horror at matricide (which emotion would be understandable to anyone), to exalt Shakespeare, and do all the things which would be acceptable to a conservative school administration, and did it with a great show of erudition, yet with a seeming modesty and gentlemanly virtue, too.

When President Noel and the group he had selected to help him had judged the papers, they found themselves appalled by the piece of work which Red had done. They looked upon it as being either a hoax, or a rank piece of insubordination. President Noel set the paper aside until he might think of what reprimand to give Red for having turned in such a degenerate thought, and more especially, for having such a mind as could conceive such a thing.

On the other hand, Professor Harrison Nix's work was beautifully done, and revealed the spirit of a fine and sensitive young scholar who should have the benefit of every word or material show of encouragement which it was possible for the school administration to give him.

It was unanimously decided that Harrison should receive first prize, including the publication of his research paper, the expense-paid trip to the writers' conference, a raise in salary, and he would be made head of his department in place of the retiring Professor Trotter. He would be counseled to take a special interest in Red who would be beneath him in the English Department, acting toward him as a big brother who would lead him away from his dark thoughts and seek to help him establish his feet upon that road which is traveled by civilized and cultured gentlemen who have the good of their students, the school, the town, the country, and their God at heart.

When President Noel called Harrison in to tell him that he had won, he discussed Red with Harrison with a great deal of concern.

"I have heard," he said, "that you have called upon Miss Gazelle Bound. An estimable woman. Might you and Gazelle not enter into a little conspiracy with me to introduce Professor Edom to some nice women also. The purifying touch of a decent woman would do more to help that confused young man than all that you or I could ever do for him." President Noel believed in Richardson's theory of the pure virgin as Redeemer. "I am grieved to tell you that if Professor Edom has not shown marked improvement in his - what I must call his Inner Life - by the end of the next school year, we will be forced to release him from his contract. The school board and I feel that we must give him another year at Isaac Walton during which time he may mature and gain stature and stability, but if he does not develop as we hope, pray I will seriously say, then he will have to go. It is lamentable, for we had thought from his work in the classroom and from his enthusiasm upon the field of clean sport that he was a well-adjusted young man, but no one has the power to see the workings of the human heart. For some reason he has chosen to reveal the picture of his warped soul to us, and believe me, it came to us as a shock. Everyone who is part of the administration at Isaac Walton is distressed to death about this."

"I believe that he is sick," Harrison said. "What he has done is his cry for help. In the name of charity, we must help him."

The President congratulated Harrison again, and begged him to keep all that he had said about Red in strictest confidence.

They shook hands warmly and Harrison left the building.

"Someone is going to get sacked for sure," he said to himself.

* * * *

Red was duly called in and notified of the outcome of the contest, and President Noel gave him a long lecture in which, in veiled terms, he said to Red almost the same thing which he had said to Harrison about Red.

Just such a thing as this had caused Edom to spawn the Herods.

"When you so desire," President Noel said, "you may build for yourself a good reputation and place of honor on Isaac Walton campus, for the sword of your intelligence is sharp, and you are well thought of, even loved here, for you are one of our own sons, a native of this county, a student of this school not too many years ago, a young man of good, yes, clean record. You are not held to be in any fault even now, we are only sorry that some inner flaw has prompted you to write a paper which reveals the somber, even the ill note of your secret thoughts."

"Professor Nix came to us from another school, another state. We tried to give you every favor which we could without feeling that we were being partial to you over him. I recall that the Dean of Men assigned you to a large comer room in the teachers' dormitory, because we felt that it was like a birthright. We did it as a little extra regard for you because we felt that we were welcoming you home. This is your home. I want you to look upon Isaac Walton as your mother, and the rest of the administration and myself as your father."

"I feel that I've lost both my birthright and your blessing," Red said. Sportsmanship in the True American Spirit demanded that he not make any accusation against Harrison, for although Harrison had cheated at the game, it was a game, and next year there would be another inning.

"You will earn my blessings again," President Noel said confidently.

* * * *

Harrison looked through the window which he would not have had he not traded with Red for possession of the room, and through the trees, he could see the night sky lit by the lights of the town.

Red did not come in to see Harrison any more, but sat in his room looking dejectedly at the pages of his Golden Bough. He realized that he had given up more than the use of a room to obtain these books. This room was a symbol of the thoughtfulness of the administration of the college, their love for him as a native son, the recognition of his birth, his belonging, his place in the school family. It was a sincere act of kindness on the part of scholars and gentlemen; his birthright. And he had thrown it away for a set of books, and a set of books which had led his mind along dark corridors which had finally brought him to the disapproval of that part of the college which desired to be to him a loving and helpful father, he who had no father. He had grown up with eight other children belonging to a man who did not care for them, and who came to hate them when they were grown to manhood. The competitive, angry, jealous father. Red would not shy away from the word, now that he had been through so much on account of: the castrating father.

How opposite kindly President Noel.

Thinking of old Never Satisfied, he put his head down and cried.

* * * *

Harrison looked at the sky behind the town, and there he could see outlined the twirling lights of the ferris wheel at the carnival which had arrived at last.

The great man-carrying balloon was there, and right on top of it was a red light. It was enormously high. On the last day that the carnival was in town, a man would get in the little basket which hung down under the balloon and they would release the ropes and let him be carried away into the air.

President Noel had said that students and teachers could be excused from their classes to view the balloon ascension, but he strongly advised that otherwise, they remain away from the carnival.

Harrison decided that he would quietly walk over to the carnival lot and see what was taking place, as he would probably not meet anyone he knew, or if he did, they would not mention that they had seen him there. No one with a code of honor would ever get anyone in trouble, or do anything to embarrass one.

Just in case, Harrison put on a plaid sport shirt and left his white shirt and necktie at home, He felt he would blend into the crowd better if he did this.

The walk to town was very pleasant, as a breeze had come up and the night was cool. Harrison walked briskly along, for the first time in weeks pushing aside thoughts of the classroom and books.

He kept his eye on the little red light which was on top of the large balloon which seemed to be beckoning to him, luring him on.

When he was a block away from the carnival, he could hear the rasping music which came from the loudspeakers, and a droning murmur which must have been made up of the voices of patrons, and the shouts of barkers, all trying to be heard above the din. The racing wheels of the rides made a steady metallic rattle, and the screams of girls could be heard intermittently. Whenever something especially jolting would happen to them, the girls would scream.

When Harrison walked onto the carnival lot, he smelled the odor of sawdust and peanuts and popcorn, and the sour smell of beer.

Right away, he saw some boys from the school standing in a little group, but he ignored them, and they only looked at him, not saying anything.

He stood for a time watching one of the simpler rides. A father had his little son there, encouraging him to have a good time. Harrison wondered how it felt to be a father. The man looked as if he was hardly more than a boy himself. The little boy was enjoying the frightening ride, which he would not have been doing had he not had the confidence inspired by having his father with him.

Harrison recalled one time his mother had taken him to the circus. She had taken him to ride on the Pop the Whip because he had wanted to go, but she had been scared to death, and therefore Harrison had been, too. His father had never taken him anywhere.

The man left the whirling car after a time and stood talking with some men that he seemed to know, all the while tossing the boy up into the air and catching him in the most absent manner. Every time the little boy left his father's hands and sailed up into the air, he would catch his breath and twist the corners of his mouth.

Harrison started thinking about his father and mother, and the dream he had about them. His father had always been a hardy, robust man, but Harrison had never seen his ribaldry with his wife go so far as it had gone that day when he had come home and found her dressed up in washer-woman's garb.

Harrison hated the washday clothes of his mother. Hated the pillowcase tied about her head. Hated the things which gave his father license to treat her like a servant girl, she who was usually so beautiful, so dignified, and so prim.

He walked idly toward the balloon. This seemed to be the center of attention.

A young man with need for a haircut, wearing high-topped shoes, was there with a girl who might not have been bad looking if her teeth had been perfect, but her teeth were brown and filled with cavities. She was wearing a cotton dress and no hose.

"I wouldn't want to be that man that's going to get in that little basket and ride that thing away from here," the man said.

"Me neither," the girl replied with a little shiver.

They stared at the basket under the great balloon with a horrid fascination.

Harrison looked at it for a moment. Then, his eyes traveled up to the balloon itself. The balloon seemed to be made of canvas strips which were sewn together. It was wonderful to Harrison that anything so large, and yet so fragile, was going to bear a man away from the earth.

Harrison was familiar with aircraft of all kinds, jets and even rockets, heavier than air ships, and these seemed natural to him, sturdily made, motor driven, powerful, with all sorts of scientific controls, but this balloon was a trip into the past. The balloon was a marvel of the century before, which due to its long disuse and the unfamiliarity of the general public with it had become a wonder again.

The carnival ground was filling up. The rides, which had been running with only a smattering of people, were now almost full. A crowd of noisy children raced past Harrison, shouting with an incredible energy.

Harrison was recalled from his lost inspection of the balloon. He walked slowly about among the stalls, his head thrust forward, his hands in his pockets. He looked at the plaster of paris images and the stuffed animals intently, as though their form and makeup meant something important to him. He listened to the barkers and the music. He passed the tent of the fortune teller, Gypsy Joan. A rough picture of the zodiac was painted on a piece of canvas which was stretched up before her tent. Harrison was an Aquarian.

"Unstable as water," he told himself.

A man in a blue suit with wide lapels and wide cuffs told Harrison that at ten o'clock there was going to be a good show in the tent which stood in the shadows behind the ferris wheel. The carnival had a group of interpretive dancers called, Queen Xanthus and Her Beginner Browns.

"They got busted in the last town we were in," the man said. "The boss had to go down to the jail the next morning and ball them all out."

"They must put on some show," Harrison said.

"I'll say," the man said. "I've seen it a hundred times, and I still can't take it without getting stirred up."

Harrison waited at the hot-dog stand, eating the mustard-drenched hotdogs they served, and waiting for it to be ten o'clock.

A few minutes before ten, the barker came out in front of the tent and turned on the lights and began to make his pitch. A few men and boys sauntered up and stood looking up at the fat, red-faced barker with black eyes, betraying no flicker of interest, waiting to be sold.

The portly barker leaned back and raised his hands.

"This show is for men only," he said. "Men only. We wouldn't dare let you bring the little woman or the girlfriend inside. This show engenders too much excitement. Why men, when Xanthus and her girls start to do their stuff, men go wild. It's all we can do to restrain them from climbing up on the stage after the performers. That's why we wouldn't dare let you bring the lady-folks inside and have them sit right out front with the men. The management just couldn't be responsible. There'd be trouble sure, because some poor man wouldn't be able to contain himself, and he'd do something that'd be right embarrassing, if not downright criminal. We tried letting the lady-folks in to see this show a time or two, and there was always fights. I tried to get the boss to let the little ladies come in and see Xanthus, because in her own way she's a real artist, but he said the risk was just too great, and he didn't want any trouble, and especially, he didn't want any of his patrons to be put in jail. Good people, he appreciates your business too much,"

Harrison had walked up to the crowd. Now, a group of young men had joined the group. He recognized them as being from Isaac Walton. They looked up at the barker with glistening eyes, taking in every word he said. Harrison stood back in the shadows. The barker noticed the arrival of the group from the college, and he began to talk directly to them.

"What's the matter, with this country today?" he asked. "We have drifted too far away from the Pagan. Now, I am not knocking anyone's church, but the Pagans had a good method all their own. Where did their boy children live? Why, in the lodge with the women of the tribe. I say they lived there until they reached a certain age, and then they went to the camp where the men were, and they were trained in all the manly arts and responsibilities, and the work of men, hunting, fishing, war, and after this instruction they underwent a puberty ritual. Good young men, if I should tell you the details of the awful practices which took place when these young Pagan boys were submitted to the rites of the puberty ritual, some of you would throw up and others would faint. They lived on the blood of their men relations, and they endured pain. They endured more terrible pain than any of us will ever endure, we that run for the iodine when we scratch our finger with a pin, but there was a reason for the pain and for the eating of the caked blood and for everything that went on - the frightening roaring noises and the trips alone into the darkness. They were enacting a ritual which meant something, and when it was all over these boys knew that they had made a transition. They bore in their own bodies the marks which told them that they were not boys any more, would never go back to the lodge of the women, but would go with the men, now men themselves. They would hunt and fish and fight in wars and become fathers, because they had been instructed in these things and the puberty ritual had set their feet firmly in that direction. You'd never see one of those boys that had endured that ordeal doing embroidery. It was the makings of real he-men."

The barker stopped and wiped his face with a big white handkerchief.

"But, what do we do in our namby-pamby civilization? What signposts have we stationed along the road to let a boy know that it's time for him to become a man? What instruction do we give a boy to help him understand what he is and what his duty is in life? I'm ashamed to say that most parents do nothing. And the schools don't help either. It's not enough for a boy to learn how to read books and how to dribble a ball. His character has got to be firmed up by something concrete. Somebody's got to take him in hand and put steel in him. Somebody's got to put horns on him."

The fat little barker had to make a quick gasp. He was almost out of breath.

"I hate to say it, but sometimes a young boy has to turn to the rough, wrong element of society to learn anything about a man's place in the world. Boys that live on the wrong side of the tracks, so to speak, or have kin or friends who do, usually get informally broken in on the ways of being a man, and mind you, I'm not in favor of this. But, the boy who doesn't know any but what we call nice men, gentlemen, has no one to lead him at all. My Lord, would we send a man into a lion's den to engage the lion who had never been trained? We teach man a trade, how to run his machine in a machine shop, how to do his bookkeeping if he's a bookkeeper, but when it comes to performing his duties as a man, we hope that nature will take its course, and figure that his glands will assert themselves. The answer is unhappy men and women, wrecked marriages, marriages that last just long enough for a child to be conceived, so that children grow up in broken homes, orphaned because of the neglect of society, probably half-fed, half-clothed, and half-educated, and growing up with no father to guide them, they are worse off than he was."

"Imagine the beauty of the island paradises that dot the beautiful blue southern Pacific. Why, those islands are just like water-bound Gardens of Eden, every one of them. Think of the beautiful brown-skinned natives who live such idyllic lives there. What is the secret of this paradise on earth where love is pure and clean and fresh? The kiss of the man and the maiden is like a breath of the crisp flower-scented air of the little mountained islands themselves. I'll tell you what the answer is. They are taught the roles of love as carefully as we are taught geometry, and the subject is out in the open, discussed. There's no strain, no nervousness, no fear. None of the things that go to make sick sex. That's the trouble with this country! Sex is sick. It's sick of being a topic that must be shunned, and a bugbear that must hide in darkness. I feel sorry for the young men of this Country. They must all suffer for the guilty blot of Puritanism which still clings to us. Puritanism was a horrid black sickness. A putrefaction! A disease that came to these shores from England and spread out across the Edenic wonders of this great continent, stifling and choking everything that it touched."

The fat little man looked down at the skinny-faced boys and the pink-cheeked boys who stood in the sawdust beneath his stand.

"I'll bet there are young men here tonight who have all sorts of doubts and questions about their manhood, but of course they wouldn't let anyone know. We've been taught to be ashamed of our fears and weaknesses. We've been taught not to speak of these things. If we speak up about them, we might embarrass someone. Well, I've never found that pushing a problem into the dark and turning my back on it made it go away. It just made it bigger."

"Now, my employer would laugh out loud if I was to say that we are doing a public service here by putting on this show, because he is not interested in being the Welfare Department, that is for the Government to worry about, and they collect the taxes to do it, but my employer is here to make money. I'm frank and truthful about it, but Queen Xanthus is a wonderful woman. She's almost a white woman. I figure she's got just a drop of Negro blood in her veins.

The barker stopped and looked all around in mock anxiety.

"I know that I am down here in a part of the country where such a remark might not go over too big, but I will say without apology that Queen Xanthus is a LADY."

He paused for a minute and everyone was very quiet, waiting to hear what he would say next.

"Queen Xanthus has got a big understanding heart that is always just busting to help anybody. After the stage show, she will be back in the rear portion of the tent, and she will reveal things that will put a lot of people straight about a lot of things they may have been worrying about for a long time. I guess maybe it's her race, but she's a passionate woman who's all woman and she knows more about love and sex and love and romance than all the experts in the country. You may have read Havelock Ellis, but that's no good. You may have read Kinsey, but that's no good. You may have heard your teacher teach about it, and your preacher preach about it, but there's nothing like having a bighearted, unassuming, compassionate individual sit down and tell you what the score is. Ask her any question in strictest privacy, only one of our own people will be standing by out of hearing to chaperone. Queen Xanthus is an artist, and we like to show her the respect that her great talent deserves. She's coming out on the platform in a few moments to say hello and to let you see what she looks like, and what her colored girls - yes, they're colored girls, but they make a black harem fit for Solomon - they're coming out on the platform in a few moments and give you a sample of what's going on inside."

"Let's see them," someone shouted, and others took up the cry. The college boys edged in closer and closer. They kept pushing on one another and laughing at things they were saying to each other.

The loudspeaker began to blare Ravel's Bolero, and the tent curtains parted and Queen Xanthus led her Beginner Browns out into the light of the platform.

Queen Xanthus walked with regal dignity, her shoulders thrown back and her head high. She wore a gold colored dress and her long jet black hair fell down about her shoulders in a neat puff. She could have been one of the old queens of Egypt or even Sheba herself. The brown-skinned girls of her troop walked behind her, as dignified as she was herself.

They stood together on the platform with Queen Xanthus ahead, and the dusky beauties in a straight line parallel to her back. They did not smile, but stood demurely still, tall and stately and icy and dignified like so many shadowy trees.

"Show us something," someone shouted, but they ignored the audience and just stood looking out over the heads of the men, aloof and beautiful.

In a few moments, they walked back inside the tent, lithe and tiger-like, to the pulsating beat of the music of Ravel.

The barker bowed his head and kept it bowed until the last one of them was gone, and the music had reached its climax and become still.

"Who'll buy a ticket to go inside?" he asked quietly. The group of waiting men moved to his box as one man and began to lay money up on the little rail.

"Don't crowd," he said softly and kindly. "There's room for everyone."

Harrison waited until the students had gotten inside before he moved up to the group. Furtively he bought a ticket. Inside he found a seat on the opposite side of the tent from the one the boys had entered. It had cost a dollar to get in.

This included taxes.

When everyone was inside, an orchestra appeared, and they began to play The Song of the Islands, the way Louis Armstrong used to play it, and Queen Xanthus and her girls danced onto the stage in grass skirts.

They danced for a few moments and then did some sort of pantomime which no one could interpret, but no one cared as they showed plenty of leg and shoulder, and their dignity was gone.

"That's doing it, Coon-gal!" someone shouted when she began to undulate to the music again. Her dance became more and more orgiastic. She leaned back, bending her knees and letting shoulder-blades gradually work down toward the floor.

"That's the kind of nigger-gal we like to see," someone else yelled.

"Jesus Christ! Be quiet!"

Queen Xanthus calmly finished her number. When the dance was done, there was a good hand of applause and the orchestra started to go into another number, but she motioined to the leader to wait, and she stood down center on the stage and looked out at the men in the hot tent.

"I didn't come here tonight claiming to be but one thing," she said. "I'm a colored girl that's trying to entertain people, maybe help a few people out, and to make a dollar for myself and my girls. I'm a hard-working colored girl that don't want to be nothing else. I'm a woman that knows how to be a mighty good woman. What else would I want to be?"

Suddenly, she threw back her head and laughed, opening her mouth wide, revealing the marble whiteness of her teeth and her red tongue. Harrison could not tell if she was a great actress, or if she really wasn't angry. She seemed to take the whole thing as a huge joke.

She moved among her girls touching one here and one there. She whispered a word or two to several of them. She looked out at the audience apologetically as if this was something which she had to do to restore the girls' morale, and she was sorry for the interruption.

"Some of them had a rather bad time before I got them," she said by way of explanation.

The band went into another chorus of Song of the Islands.

Queen Xanthus did part of her dance again, and this time when they finished there was positive, enthusiastic applause.

They left the stage, and a white man in black suit, black top hat, and string tie made an entrance carrying a whip. He also carried a large sign which read, "Alchemist Extraordinary! I turn base human flesh into gold." He stood in the middle of the stage and twirled the end of his Simon Legree mustache.

Queen Xanthus and her girls ran onto the stage with hoes, and began to go through the motions of chopping cotton while they gyrated their hips inside tight silk dresses that were split up the sides. They did not move their feet, but worked the hoes and writhed and twisted their hips so that they looked like so many tangled serpents standing together in the cardboard cotton patch. The music rolled and blared, accentuating the motions of the women.

On her head, each of the women had a white cloth which looked almost like a clean cotton pillowcase tied there.

Harrison began to notice sweat in the palms of his hands.

The man with the sign turned on the group and singling one girl out, he raised his whip against her. All the girls rolled their great white eyes so that they looked like raw oysters on brown plates.

The girl began to run from the man with the whip. He thrashed it in the air a few times and then threw it aside and cornering the poor girl in what seemed to represent a fence-corner, he approached her with drooling lips and a vicious sneer of lust.

The girl threw her head and shoulders back, arching her body, showing the audience the wonderful line of her breast.

When the villain laid his grasping fingers in the midst of that sacred precinct, and began to tear away the thin cloth of her low-cut dress, she began to tremble and to whimper and to writhe orgiastically, working her body suggestively and taking on a look of terror in her dark eyes.

Harrison grasped the back of the wooden bench in front of him.

Queen Xanthus cast aside her hoe, and made a great leap, worthy of the Imperial Ballet, landing on the villain's shoulders. He ran with her to the center of the stage where the entire group attacked him, tossing him into the air, swinging him from one to the other, standing him on his feet and twirling him about, pulling and pushing him in deadly earnest.

They were smoky Bacchantes. Through some horrid device of the theatre, they caused something in the semblance of blood to spill from the man which they frantically tore between them. Their hands became covered with the red liquid. They dashed him to the floor and trod upon him.

He leaped up and ran up on the top of a post that was set against the fence, but they pulled the post down and took him up in their hands again, tearing at his clothes until a wig that he was wearing was torn off, revealing a mangled and bloody scalp, and his clothing began to fall apart. In his madness and the pain of his ordeal, he reached out wildly and tore at the clothing of the women which came apart easily and the red on his hands came off giving the aspect of blood smeared on their breasts and stomachs.

All was disorder, but yet there was order too, for the whole fantastic ballet, if it was a ballet, managed to be enacted in the rhythm of the jazz orchestra which played for dear life on the sawdust floor of the hot tent.

When the man seemed subdued, the girls moved back to the rear of the stage and began to dance in an orderly fashion some conventional steps, and Queen Xanthus moved in for the kill.

The man stood cowering and bloody in what remained of his shorts. His pants and shirt were completely torn away, and he had lost his shoes. One arm seemed to hang down useless, and when he tried to take a step, he could not.

Queen Xanthus pulled her tattered dress about her and contemptuously brushed the blood off her arms. With the power and grace of a sleek panther, she circled him, and then leaped upon him, grasping him by the throat. He arched his back and rolled his head toward the audience. A ghastly darkness suffused his face, his eyes seemed to pop, and his tongue lolled out.

Xanthus stood proudly, like a queen indeed, her slanted eyes glittered, her lips drawn back from her teeth, her neck bursting with great blue veins that stood out beneath the yellow skin of it.

As the villain sank lower to the floor, she tossed her long black hair from side to side and crouched down over him. and as he almost came to the floor and seemed to expire, she bent even further over him and sank her angry teeth into his neck.

The audience was so moved at this piece of melodrama that they sat stunned and silent for a minute looking at the dreadful charade which was disappearing behind a closing curtain.

"That's how she does it," Harrison said. "She puts everything she feels into her act. She sublimates it. But, my God, what violence. What hatred!"

There was an empty feeling at the pit of his stomach, and now a trembling took possession of his legs, so that he could not have walked if he had desired. He turned icy cold and the trembling spread to his entire body.

In a moment, the curtain parted and the white man who had played the part of the villain came out in a bathrobe of the type boxers and wrestlers use for entering the ring. It was a rich blue, and somehow he had a full head of hair, and was smiling. There was polite applause.

Xanthus had gone to take a quick shower.

He began making a spiel telling the crowd that for another dollar, they might go back into the back room of the tent where there would be another little show each man the privilege of going up to Queen Xanthus where she would be sitting out of earshot of all, and the sight of any but the barker who had been out front at the beginning of the show, to ask her one question, any question about any problem of life and love one might wish to ask.

Almost every man in the tent rushed forward to get a ticket, but Harrison got up and crept outside.

He had just walked around the corner of the tent which housed the freaks, when he came face to face with Gazelle Bound and two other women. He was so dishevelled looking and he darted so quickly behind the corner of the tent again that Rocky didn't recognize him.

He tried to find his way around another way and ran head-on into the tattooed lady, who glared at him with undisguised hatred, but didn't bother to pull her coat about herself any more tightly. She had ponderous, dangling breasts tattooed entirely blue.

Harrison darted away and found himself looking in the door of a trailer which was the costumer's. All sorts of masks and wigs and theatrical clothing hung along the walls.

He whirled about, running out of the park past the balloon. Looking back over his shoulder he saw the balloon standing tall and firm, and it looked to him like a huge inflated pillowcase.

When this comparison came into his mind, he increased his speed, running and running until he was breathless and lost, and he lay down at the side of the road saying over and over,

"Oh, my God! Oh, my God!"

Harrison beheld a vision.

There was a lush grapevine which intertwined itself about itself in such a way as to make itself rigid so that it might stand, and in this fashion it grew taller and taller and seemed as though it would reach Heaven. However, a pine tree, having no cones but being very large, spread its arms over the grapevine so that the grapevine became tangled in its branches and could grow no higher. The vine and the tree were overhung with glistening spiders' webs which entrapped the dew, sparkling in the moonlight. And all the while, a procession of dancing top hats left the ground and went spinning up the vine, but when they struck the limbs of the pine tree, they collapsed and in the form of discs they sailed away into the darkness. The pine tree was ornamented with plump ripe figs which had been tied to its limbs, and the whole was interlaced with bunches of bearded heads of barley.

Sitting in the road, Harrison looked at the tree with wonder.

Then, a voice was heard which spoke to him.

"Man has a choice. You may inherit all that your heart would desire, if you so choose. There is nothing which you may not possess. Nothing in all this land."

The vision disappeared and Harrison arose and walked back to the school, not aware of himself, or of the way he had come.

* * * *

Red was writing a poem entitled The Lay of the Belle. He never came over to talk with Harrison any more. Harrison wished that Red would sometimes come and sit and talk with him as before. Isaac Walton had become a lonely place since Red was angry.

Red shut himself away from everyone like a brooding bucolic Brutus, despising Harrison's ambition.

Harrison spent a restless night, and in the morning he overslept and Red did not awaken him. It was almost time to go to class when Harrison woke up.

He gathered his books together quickly and went to the off-campus restaurant for coffee.

Bob Barley, with very red eyes and uncombed hair, was having coffee, too. He had evidently been out late the night before.

Harrison sat down beside him.

"Have a rough night?" he asked. There was no point in his not being familiar with Bob.

"Man!" Bob said.

"Me too."

"You go out on the town?"

"Carnival."

"Crazy."

"Listen Bob," Harrison said, "we may be late for class, but I've got to ask you something. I've got a problem that bothers me and I haven't ever talked with anyone about it."

"Like I've always known you were hung up over something," Bob said. He picked up his cup without using the handle.

Harrison colored a deep red.

"I tear up pillowcases," he said.

Bob looked at him out of the corner of his eye.

"Like, Man ... why?"

"It's what they call a fetish."

Bob thought about this.

"You don't mean you think God lives in a pillowcase."

"Not God, but a woman."

"Yes," Bob said. "Yes, man. I dig you. The connecting link to God. You're trying to make the connection and you can't. You need that connection to God which is woman, and you can't make out, so it's like you substitute. But Man, a pillowcase! That's from Crazyville."

"It's crazy all right," Harrison said. "And, I'm afraid."

Bob was silently thoughtful.

"This gig," he began, "I mean the school-teaching bit. It's probably important to you. Like, it's your bread, and you wouldn't like to be bugged by a gig where you couldn't come on big. I mean like Elijah and Socrates. You could lose your gig if anybody found out about this pillowcase bit.

"It's like you hear the Mills Brothers singing Making Believe and they say they'll 'turn out the light, go to bed, and kiss my pillow, making believe it's you,' and at the same time Paper Doll was popular, because there was a war on, and the studs were separated from the chicks. And, nobody ever thought that these songs were auto-erotic, and large obscenities, like blaring on the Hit Parade every Saturday night, and coming out of every Jukebox. And here people are making it with their pillows, and having to imagine the opposite role. I mean create, Man. Two in a bed, and both the same person, and pretty soon it's such a habit the person's bisexual, and no ordinary kick is going to bring on that connection with the universe that we all got to have. Like, I say Man, you're sick and you'd better do something about it."

"I want to know if I can do anything," Harrison said.

"Like Freud would say, 'No'," Bob said. "But, Sartre would say, 'You got to choose.' Somewhere down the line, Man, something made you choose to make out with yourself by tearing up pillowcases instead of shacking up right with something REAL. You can unmake that choice, and make a new choice. Can't no cat help you out. It's your life, Man. Dig?"

"Yes. I dig," Harrison said.

They heard the bell ringing to announce the beginning of the first period.

"You go on," Bob said. "If you don't want to walk across the campus with me. I'd never fink on you, you know. I hate to see you so bugged."

Harrison walked away and Bob was cursing softly to himself about the tyranny of Tin Pan Alley and Hollywood.

"The next thing we'll see will be Doris Day in blackface making the screen version of 'The Life of Billie Holliday,'" he said. "And, that will be the real obscenity."

His face and pose became messianic, and he muttered to himself, making horrid faces and wild gestures. His beard waggled with each movement of his chin, and his eyes were afire and apocalyptic.

* * * *

Harrison was so annoyed that when he got to class, he began by reading Milton's On His Blindness all the way through, and then launched into a diatribe against the blind poet.

"Milton alas, was a Protestant poet, sidestepping the Great Goddess and writing religious verse, and meddling in politics. His remarks about himself were self-righteous and full of self-pity.

"Milton was warned of his impending blindness," Harrison told the class petulantly. "He was given the choice by the physicians of reducing his workload or losing his eyesight, and he CHOSE to accept blindness, if that should be the penalty for continuing to do that work which he flattered himself he was called to do. His blindness was not an irrational punishment from God. If the light was 'denied' him, he denied it to himself, and when he began to realize that he was not called to do that work which he had set himself, he verbally confessed that 'God does not need either man's work or his own gifts,' and made a show of choosing patience in his calamity above other emotions. 'The choice lay before me between dereliction of a supreme duty and loss of eyesight ... I could not OBEY the inward monitor that spoke to me from ABOVE.. If my affliction is incurable, I prepare and compose myself accordingly.' It was his choice and his responsibility. He chose to obey a feeling he had which led him to believe that he was called to do a certain work, and this choice denied him his eyesight and ruined the lives of a number of the members of his family. He enslaved his daughters as amanuenses and readers. (Who can conceive of the horror of reading aloud phonetically from great tomes in languages which one does not understand?) But, out of his darkness was born Paradise Lost, for better or worse."

Mae Grace Rein had never read any thing that Milton wrote, but she had been reared to believe that he was one of the great sacred cows of literature.

"Paradise Lost is one of our greatest examples of Christian literature," she said.

"It has done more to breed confusion concerning the first four chapters of Genesis than anything else. People would do better to study the Cabalah. The Jews have a right to interpret their own," Harrison said.

Mae Grace Rein hung her head down and her face grew very red.

"We bring our misfortune upon ourselves," Harrison said. "God does not expect us to do works which shall blind us or cause us to get burned at the stake. We bring these things upon ourselves by our own free choice, and we are not compelled to make these choices by some traumatic hangover from an unhappy childhood, as Freud would try to tell us, either. Man is free. He is awfully burdened with freedom. And, he is responsible."

Harrison walked to the window and stood looking outside.

"He's going to wig out," Bob Barley thought.

But, Harrison remembered that he had prepared a pop test for that day, so he asked one of the boys to pass out the mimeographed questions, and while the class struggled with these, he sat at his desk and drew little hieroglyphics on paper. The hieroglyph for the womb looked exactly like symbolic drawings the ancients made of figs. This was ent menath, and if there was a tab across it, it indicated that the womb was virgin. Harrison had seen pictures of figs which had the same tab across the stem.

"Like Buddha took a symbolic trip back inside the womb when he had his period of isolation and silence and thought under the Bodhi tree, and he came forth from this interval reborn," Harrison thought, falling into Bob Barley's jargon.

When the period was over, Harrison stood at the door and took in the papers for the test, and then, he hurried to his room in the dormitory to get a little rest.

* * * *

That night, as soon as the evening meal was over, Harrison walked slowly toward the town, thrusting his hands deep into his pockets while he walked, because this attitude always helped him to reason.

The only way he could see out of his dilemma was to win over the thing which troubled him by what Kierkegaard has termed the virtue of a triumph of the absurd.

For even as the disgusting and bloody and absurd puberty rites of the aboriginal Australians and probably of all primitive peoples were a triumph over childhood by manhood, and also a triumph over the Mother, so Harrison must commit some absurd but impressive act which would indelibly impress upon his mind that a transition had taken place in his own sexuality destroying the fetish and freeing him to know access to the real love object.

The act, when chosen, would be an act which he was responsible for.

The balloon stood tall and brooding like a great, gestating egg against the purple sky. The little red light on the top of it burned merrily.

Harrison walked toward the carnival with a pervading fascination. He could hear the sounds and see the sights of the park, familiar to him now because he had been there the night before.

He thought of Queen Xanthus and wondered what questions she had been asked on the night before, and what answers she had given. She was that new phenomenon, the stripteaser with a social message. The undressing which Harriet Beecher Stowe had done of her mind, Queen Xanthus performed in the flesh and preached the same message: the war of the classes.

The park was already filled with people who moved about in little groups, staring and whispering, and eating big handsful of cotton candy.

Harrison stood in the shadow of the balloon.

Rocky Bound was there again. She was looking at him from behind the hotdog stand. She had a stout, older woman with her. The older woman was eating a hotdog. Harrison looked at her, and she looked at him.

This Delilah seemed annoyed that he did not come over and speak to her. She was looking at him with a big question written upon her face. This female was making an appeal to being. She wanted to come into existence; that existence she would take upon herself when she was infused with the male principle. She was hungry. She wanted to devour Harrison.

Nix ran and leapt the little fence and stood upon the platform that was under the balloon. He felt his knife in his pocket.

A group of curious people came up to the fence. Rocky and her friend hurried that way.

Nix took out his knife and opened the blade. It glittered in the artificial light.

Like Samson, he would destroy all of them. Men with long hair like Samson's had their hair tied to the bedpost while they slept after a successful intercourse with the priestess of the Great Goddess. They were awakened to find themselves unable to escape so that they had to lie helpless, a witness to their own deaths by a sword in the hands of the woman.

The spider struck using the web of the victim's own hair to help her: - Evil Arachne who competed with the Goddess.

Nix could stick the blade of his knife into the taut canvas of the balloon, just above his head, so that it would rip and burst, and the gas would blow away in a great puff, and the great weight of the yards and yards of canvas would come tumbling down to enfold Nix and the group of bystanders which stood about. They would all be crushed, and would smother and would die.

Nix touched the tip of his blade to the canvas, and a smile of triumph played at his lips.

Suddenly, there was a burst of sound from a police whistle, and people began to shout.

"There's a maniac trying to do something to the balloon !"

Two policemen and several other men who must have been members of the carnival came running across the lot toward the balloon.

The police blew their whistles desperately. The very note of this sound of authority paralyzed Nix with fear. Furtive and with eyes flashing with craft, he leaped down from the platform and waving the open knife, he jumped over the fence, and ran through the scattering crowd.

He ran behind the freak tent, and hid in the shadows for a second, but he could hear men running everywhere, waving flashlights, cursing, trying to find him.

He looked for someplace to hide. Suddenly, he was thinking of Edgar Allen Poe, and he remembered The Purloined Letter which, disguised, had been hidden in plain view.

He ran to the trailer he had blundered into on the night before, where the costumes were. Hurriedly, he put on a beard and a mustache and a wild wig. He threw a brown robe about himself which completely covered him. He walked slowly across the lot to Queen Xanthus' tent.

He knew that it was much to early for her performance, so her tent would not be in use. He turned on the lights on the outside platform, and the microphone, and began a harangue.

"Tekeli-li; Tekeli-li!"he shouted. " It is I ,the son of Agdestis, from Mount Yaanek, near that boreal pole which is our ultimate destiny who speaks to you. Oh, Father Agdestis, your folly did I inherit. How great my unhappiness! Little did I know that I did not have to imitate your foolishness. No one told me 'til now."

Several men in overalls came and stood at his feet, and looked up at his flashing eyes and sparkling teeth, and asked each other what he was and what he was talking about.

Nix, seeing this encouragement, beat himself upon his chest and worked his hands open and shut convulsively, all the while turning his eyes up to the night sky.

"Oh, the green almond tree!" he said huskily. "We can change. I didn't know what you meant, Norman, when you said that we can try to build a new nervous system, but I see. Jean Paul Sartre is our Christ, and you are his prophet." A policeman came up and looked at the gathering crowd, which now consisted of a dozen people, and came up the steps onto the platform and looked in through the tent flap at the inside of the empty tent. Nix threw himself on the floor and holding himself up with his hands and bent elbows, he groaned and ground his teeth and continued, "Oh, Norman, how could you so far have lost control of yourself as to have chosen to do violence, you who are Hip to everything?" The policeman walked past Nix, to go down the steps on the other side.

"Parasite!" he said. He would have liked to have spit on Nix. "The fakir."

As soon as the policeman was out of earshot, Nix stood up and extended his arm in front of himself and began to chant,

"Bust the Fuzz. Bust the Fuzz. Bust the Fuzz."

The group was growing larger, and Nix saw Rocky Bound and her lady friend stumble across the rough ground, coming that way.

"Great is Mother Nana. Great is Cvbele. Great is responsibility. Oh, anguish! At night we go to bed with you, oh, anguish, and in the morning we rise up to see you sitting there watching. For we must choose. We have the freedom to choose. And, we must choose as though the eyes of the whole world were upon us we must choose for all, for we are part of the all, and what we choose affects everyone. Is there crime and murder in the land? We choose it. Is there war? We choose it. Is there financial panic? It is our choice. We bring it all about by what we choose to do, or choose not to do. All of mankind equally sharing in the responsibility. And the eyes looking at us."

Rocky was looking at him. He couldn't tell if she recognized him or not.

"Oh,abandoned!" he shouted, trying to lower the pitch of his voice. "Abandoned by the dim lake of Auber. Set loose to drift through the world like a haunted vessel on the high seas, from the very instant of birth. A clean page. A scroll to be filled. A canvas to be painted. And we the hand which must write, or paint, or otherwise make our essence. Set free without excuse. Without any excuse at all.

"Oh, dreadful freedom of choice. Dreadful freedom. No wonder men fled into the safety of Calvinism where there is a safety in chains. Chains that say we do what is ordained and predestined. An excuse in chains. Leadership in chains. Guideposts in chains. Just follow the map. There is no need to choose. No responsibility. Everything is excused. It is God's will. I have a Call."

The crowd had gathered until there were forty or fifty people crowded in front of the platform. They looked up at Nix with wide, uncomprehending eyes. There was no sign on the platform telling them what he was supposed to be.

Rocky and her friend had gotten pushed back to the rear of the crowd. Nix didn't think she could see him very well. He looked about over as much of the lot as he could see, looking for the policeman who had chased him.

"The despair of life," he murmured in a low tone. "I, Reynolds the Seer, son of Agdestis, tell it. Who can we rely upon? Who can know us? Who can we count on? There is no one. There is no one we may count upon. What illusion may we entertain? What hope may we know'? We may not entertain illusion, and only little hope. We walk alone. We find our life cut off from natural foundation, and from supernatural guarantee. In our freedom and our responsibility, we stand alone. Completely alone! Like Prometheus, who on that awful rock did daily receive an awful visitation from that carrion bird, evil black bird incarnate in Poe's Raven, torturer of the masochist, but the masochist who could not be defeated. Unstable as water! Who can fight water? Freeze it, and it melts and returns to itself. Heat it so that it turns to steam, and it will condense and return to itself. Dirty it, and it will flow along over sand and become clean. Pour it into the Earth, and it will rise again. Oh, Nix, the water monster of central-European folklore. I am an Aquarian and unstable as water, but like Prometheus, I may not he destroyed. I am of this essence, created since being.

95

"Raven went to get us fire, and while he flew about with the fire sticks, he was swallowed by a whale. Lucky for him, he was able to kill the whale and get out. Lucky for us. Raven did his work even as Prometheus did. He brought fire to man; fire which complements water; fire which purifies. Fire which melts away the dross."

Nix took a step back and bowed.

"Tekeli-li!" he said. "Tekeli-li!" He backed to the slit in the tent and went insi de.

Queen Xanthus was standing just inside, where she had been listening to him, and watching him through the flap.

"White boy," she said, "you and this carnival better split." She helped him get out of his costume, and folded the robe up and laid it over her arm.

He stood looking at her dumbly.

"Well, go haid on," she said. "Fuzz going to get you if you don't."

He ran out the back of the tent, and as he went outside, he heard Queen Xanthus laugh in the loud, mirthless way she had laughed on the stage the night before.

She went out on the platform and talked to the crowd, which was beginning to get restless.

"My friend, Reynolds, will be back in a little while," she said. "Now, in just a few moments, my barker will be coming along to tell you people a little something about the show that my girls and I put on. I think, seeing how so many of you ladies are already here, that we will let the ladies in tonight to share in our little show. Girls, it will be something that you can tell your grandchildren about."

Nix, with his good suit on and a new pair of shoes, climbed a fence and slipped into the woods and headed for the swamp.

* * * *

He sat down by a little stream and picked the beggar lice of his trousers leg. He took his knife out of his pocket and looked at it. He opened the blade. It gleamed murderously in the moonlight.

"I ought to throw this thing into the creek," he said.

But, he decided not to. He put it into his pocket. He carefully arranged his mussed clothing. He smoothed his hair.

"It is my choice, and right or wrong, I am going to cure things for all time. I can commit that absurd act, and then we will see."

He crossed the stream on some stepping stones which someone had put there for that purpose. He walked through the woods until he came out on a road which was in one of the more thinly-populated parts of town. He knew where he was. He turned his feet in the direction of the town's red-light district.

He came to a street of pawn shops and cheap clothing stores. The streetlights were dim. Far down the street, a new blue convertible was drawn up to the curb, and a well-dressed, attractive woman was struggling with the top of it, trying either to get it to go up or down. She gave up and stood looking at it helplessly.

Nix felt to see if his knife was still there. He approached the woman. She was very pretty, and dressed to kill. She had on a rich, blue satin dress, and wore a shoulder-length furpiece. She had on several tasteful pieces of costume jewelry.

"You need help?" Nix asked.

"This car is brand new," she said. "I don't know why I can't get the top to work."

"Do you want me to try?"

"Don't just try," she said, "come on and do it."

Nix got into the car. She came around to the driver's side and sat down beside him. He fumbled with a knob or two on the dash. The woman reached over and turned a knob efficiently and the top rose up and settled into place above their heads.

"There's nothing wrong with it," she said. "I use that gimmick in case the cops come along. They wonder what I'm doing parked on this street."

"I wonder, too," Nix said.

"I like money. I work in an office making forty dollars a week after taxes. You see this dress? Eighty dollars. This stole? A hundred and seventy five. I hope to get a really good one someday. This car is over half paid for. Like I said, I like money. I don't care what you like."

"I need something a little bit special. I've got fifty dollars on me. I'll give you fifty dollars if you'll do exactly what I say."

"Listen," the woman said. "My name's Thursday. That's because Thursday is waiting for Friday. I'm always waiting for Friday, because Friday is payday. A payday like you suggest means I'll do anything. I'm also named Thursday because that's the fourth day of the week, and the fourth is waiting for the fifth. I like the fifth. I drink one every weekend, and that takes money, too. Someday, when I have everything I want, I'm going to quit this life and quit drinking, and get married real cozy and rich, and have a house full of kids, but right now, I'm going to live."

She glided away from the curb and sped through the streets until she came to a nice house in a fashionable neighborhood. She drove up to the garage, which was in the rear, and led Nix up a flight of stairs to an apartment which was above.

"Do you want me to fix you a drink'?" she asked.

"No."

"Well, what""

"You have a fireplace, I see. Does it work?"

"Yes."

"Would you get undressed and sit on the couch over by the fireplace?"

Thursday shrugged, and went into another room. In a few minutes she came out without her clothes, and sat down on the gold-upholstered sofa. She folded her hands and smiled at Nix.

"Was that your bedroom where you undressed?"

"Yes."

"Then, I need to go in there." He went into the bedroom, and in an instant was back with one of her pillowcases. "Would you put this on your head, over your hair, making a sort of turban out of it?"

Thursday smiled amiably, as though Nix was a little boy who must be placated.

Nix got down on his knees and built a fire in the fireplace. He waited a few minutes until it was burning briskly. Then, he went and stood over Thursday, and taking hold of the pillowcase, he pulled it violently off her head. He took the pillowcase to the rug in front of the fireplace,and sat down on the floor, and smelled it carefully to see if Thursday's perfume was on it, and lay it on the floor, and took the knife out of his pocket.

Thursday asked herself what this crazy man might be going to do.

He opened the blade slowly, and the firelight caught it so that it flashed red, looking like blood. He slashed the pillowcase once, and lifted it up to his face. He lay down on the floor and the spasms of his mounting passion rocked him, and his heart pounded, and he began to breathe heavily.

Thursday saw that he was going to do by himself, that thing which she should have been helping him to do and she said, "Well, I'll be damned."

Nix rose up on his knees and taking the knife, he slashed his thigh with a long shallow wound, and the blood poured out on the pillowcase, and his face went white and broke out in a sweat.

He took the bloody pillowcase and the knife, and threw them into the fire.

The odor of burning cloth filled the apartment.

When the pillowcase was consumed, he leapt up and without a word, ran to the door and down the stairs, leaving a trail of blood on Thursday's carpet.

Thursday got up and put on a robe, and locked the door, and began to clean up the blood with clear cold water before it ruined something.

"What a hell of a way to make fifty dollars," she said.

* * * *

The next morning, Harrison Nix got up and limped to the dining hall for breakfast. He was ready for his Classical Lit class ten minutes ahead of time.

The weather was crisp and sunny. The day would be hot.

Professor Harrison Nix decided to give the students a little pep talk.

"It's my responsibility," he said, "to see that you students understand the material in our textbook. After all, the success of this school year, here at Isaac Walton, starts with each one of us individually, our daily habits, and our attention to detail. If Isaac Walton does not have a year which we may be proud of, it is the responsibility of each of us. We must each of us put his shoulder to the wheel."

The class looked bored, and some of the students repressed yawns.

"In the past, we have frequently wandered from the subject, and I don't think the purpose of this class has been fulfilled as it should have been. I don't make any excuse for this. It is something I just let happen. Now, we must mend our fences. I graded your test papers yesterday afternoon before supper, and I could see that many of you have not been getting very much out of this class.

Especially, you seemed to have missed the function of Socrates in world philosophy. I think we will take the whole period today to talk about Socrates .

Mae Grace Rein smiled contentedly, and Ruby Persia looked at him with wide, blank eyes.

Bob Barley groaned and put his head in his hands.

"Socrates, yet!" he exclaimed to himself. "The next thing he'll choose to emphasize will be Goethe and his Werther. And, this course runs for seven more weeks!" But, he brightened and lifted his head, "I bid my hideous progeny go forth and prosper," he said.

1960s

For three and a half years after the inception o 'the '60s, the writer lived in turmoil. As did everyone around him. Despite critical illness, periods of unemployment, legal entanglements, and dire.financial woes, he wrote "Wind Flower" and "Make Port At Samarkand" and suffered the rejection of these stories. He worked assiduouslv gathering research material for a biography of Gen. Earl Van Dorn, C.S.A. He made a disastrous trip to Port Gibson, MS, the town Grant found "too beautiful to burn, " to gather background material for his book. Van Dorn was from Port Gibson. The writer carried on a voluminous correspondence with several friends.

Two bright moments at this time were his discovery of a group of the world's unnoticed (swept-under-the-carpet) voung men, at a local pool hall, and an introduction to the pageanty and dra,ma of the Catholic Church. Freelance charities a work took up his time.

Then, rather late in Julv of '1963, he determined to escape - to go and find a better life - Gulfport like a once-trusted watch,, had now broken its main spring. So, thanks to God and Greyhound, he was gone. He went by circuitous route to Charlotte, NC, the town of Harrv Golden. He saw beauty and met kindness on every hand.

In Charlotte the writer soon met roominghouse habitues, Chinese laundry workers, a Jewish boss, clowns, a painter of portraits of Stonehenge, a man cared for bv Vocational Rehabilitation, Baptists, Catholics, black people who were different from any he had seen, and he lived three blocks from the library! He met drunks, and people performing every hustle. He did not meet Harry Golden.

A Monsignor got him a job in an ice-cream plant. This lasted until the weather became cold.

He got another job. It was a job where he would be traveling in all the states of the southeast. He worked in Andalusia, AL, Weston, WV and Richmond, VA, and wrote in Gastonia, NC, Augusta, GA, and Columbia, SC. He loved Charleston, WV, except for the weather in winter. In a barber shop in Augusta, he heard a wonderful story about a storm, that went through, where the wind blew so hard "It blowed a rooster into a jug."

August 17, 1969, Camille decimated the Mississippi Gulf coast. The writer's parents joined him in Columbia, SC to escape the hurricane's aftermath. The writer and his.father were constitutionally estranged one from the other. It would not fix. The parents did not tarry long, but returned to Mississippi to live on their own.

Thev were both eighty years old.

GULFPORT, MISSISSIPPI

For this writer, the '60s began with production of a short story named ,,Wind Flower " The anemone, the flower of Attis. This story is a modern rendering of the Orpheus and Eurydice legend. It warns how unsubstantial and temporary, inherently, are any hoped-for results from planned activities which might have accrued, when the planner takes a look backward.

The writer, understandably, did not wish to look back at the '50s, as the latter portion of the decade had been a time for him of broken marriage, estrangement from loved ones, legal mnbroilments, and woeful illness.

"Wind Flower" was offered to several.fbr consideration in 1961, and was not well-received. The story was written in Gulfport, but its locale is New Orleans.

The habitual optimism of this writer is weakly reflected in the protagonist when he tenaciously clings to a new-fuind and vagrant promise he sees embodied in an old phonograph recording. Any straw to grasp could cause him to hope.

For the character in the story, hope is quickly shattered. The past is too strong - the hope too frail. The dream of the past was shattered. Could never be fixed.

The writer passed this story around among his doctors, attempting to show them why he was depressed.

WIND FLOWER

The French Quarter walkthrough where Old Shep lived was a narrow, dimly lit alley, which ran between Bourbon Street and Royal. The back doors of bars and stores opened there, and the door which led down a short hall to the foot of the stairs Old Shep must climb to reach his third-floor apartment.

There was in Old Shep's building always a harsh whisper, a rumble like the sounds of distant battle. These were the muffled thrill and pulse of Dixieland.

In New Orleans, jazz was endemic. It was omnipresent. Old Shep did not with any awareness hear it, any more than he heard his heartbeat.

A stranger walking in Old Shep's alley would smell the brewery, but Old Shep was impervious to the stink of mash.

Beer was abundant - Jax, Falstaff, Dixie and Regal. Who did not know someone who worked in the breweries, drove the beer-laden trucks, or sold the golden lager across the bar? Beer presided at marriages, getting pregnant, in political life, and at death.

Death - Old Shep thought about death a lot. Death he did battle with. Death had beaten him once - taken something from him. Now, death, with greedy bloodless fingers, was back - wanting Old Shep himself.

It was early evening. Tourist-attracting sounds were becoming more noticeable - demanding attention. Hospitable bar doors were thrown open; music rolled out into the dark grey of coming night. There was the shriek of jazz combos, the quavering cries and the moans of torch singers, the drums which were behind everything. The lights shown brightly up onto the blacked face of a man who was a perfect imitator of Al Jolson. Old Shep smiled at him and waved as he passed the doorway. The man knelt, singing on top of the bar. Barkers stood outside the open doors, pounded out their metered inducement to the emerging sidewalk crowd to "see the pretty girls."

A billowing excited buzz, like a sound from the sea, grew louder and louder as the darkness settled beyond Bourbon Street's brave circle of Napoleonic street lamps and the light which flooded out of the doors. Excited visitors to the city screamed with delight at shop windows, making a sound like shore birds scavenging the beaches of Lake Ponchartrain, dividing with glistening eyes treasure from carrion. Old Shep saw, as he saw each evening, his quiescent world come alive.

He knew it was artificial, a hollow, a shadowy realm of dream-matter which could, in a thrice, turn into nightmare. The firm ground of reality under his feet could save him, but Old Shep had not fared well in the real world. He was drawn to a world more fanciful. It was his weakness to spin evanescent imaginings. These could drive his tangible opportunities away. Alas for Old Shep!

Old Shep walked carefully along the street, hurrying home. He carried a package, lovingly and tenderly cradled in his arms.

And he limped.

He always limped because he had a stiff leg. His chest, against which he held his package, was bony and thin, and his shoulders were not quite straight. A rip in his trousers had been sewn up in the laundry, and they had not done a very neat job.

He had his limp and worry creases in his forehead, and he had snow white hair. People had been calling him "Old Shep" for a long time.

The sidewalk was narrow and rough.

A crowd of boisterous young boys jostled along getting in each other's way and laughing. They pushed past Old Shep with carefree disregard, not even seeing him as he stood uneasily in the shadows, afraid of them.

They pushed by, and Old Shep still could feel the animal vigor of them. It was like a slap on his face.

He had turned to the wall of the building and hunched his thin shoulders over his precious burden, standing still, waiting until they had passed.

"Drinking." He said the word wryly, but he was not annoyed. Once he had been young.

Perhaps these were college boys. They were dressed neatly, and were about the right age. They were in that period of complete unselfconsciousness and utter selfishness which comes to men once in a lifetime, and passes. Filled, they were, with a great immediacy, an awareness of nothing but their own private goals of the moment, transient wishes and images. Life would never for them be this self-oriented, so uncomplicated again.

"Youth is like that," Old Shep sighed. He limped on again, not even seeing where he as going because he had been there a thousand times. He saw, nostalgically, himself as the youth he had been. Once he had not been Old Shep, but plain Shep Anubis, and he had enjoyed this city; enjoyed it as these boys were doing.

Now, he was tired (it was Friday evening) after the week's work, and he looked forward to the two days of rest he would have. But he would have looked forward more if there were someone to spend the free time with.

He sighed weakly as he paused at the door to his building, checked his mail-box, and began to climb the stairs. The building was shabby and his apartment was up too many stairs - stairs unlit and steep.

He made his way painfully up the two narrow flights, feeling very frail and very old. But he was not old. He was alive physically, vital and strong, and in years he was a young man.

After the accident which had caused his leg to be rigid, he had walked for a long time with a cane, and this, coupled with the fact that his hair had turned grey very early, had led people to begin calling him "Old Shep" and he was "Old Shep" to everyone who knew him, whether this saddened him or not. He did not even think about it any more. He accepted it like the whiteness of his hair.

He could not recall when his hair had begun to grow grey.

Two girls lived in the apartment at the head of the stairs on the second floor. Their door was open, and Old Shep could see that they were entertaining some boys tonight. They were all standing around the room listening to one of the boys who was talking excitedly about something which seemed to interest all of them.

Old Shep lowered his eyes and hurried past. He didn't want to seem to be spying on them.

The staircase was dark. Old Shep made his way up to the second flight very carefully as he was afraid he might stumble and this would cause him to drop his package. He placed his package carefully on the floor while he fumbled with his keys and opened the door to the room which was his kitchen.

A slender young girl in pedal pushers and a bright red blouse had come out of the second floor apartment into the hall. She was laughing and looking back into the apartment over her shoulder. Old Shep caught a glimpse of her upturned face. She had wide, honest eyes and a good chin. She seemed to Old Shep to be a wholesome girl. He looked down at her for a moment, enjoying her.

She wasn't aware of him.

"Do you want mustard on yours?" she called.

Another girl came to the door.

"Sammy says he wants mustard and onions. I want mayonnaise, and Roger wants mustard but no onions."

Old Shep went into his hot and stuffy kitchen and closed the door. He opened the little window which gave on the back patio.

In a few moments, he would open a can of beans.

He lit one of the top burners on the old gas range and set his granite coffee pot over it. He would heat this morning's coffee again and drink some of it, although he knew it wouldn't be good.

He placed his package on the oilcloth top of the kitchen table and sat down in one of the unsteady wooden chairs. He filled his pipe, tamping the tobacco carefully. He]it it with a large kitchen match.

His library was on the kitchen shelf; his cookbook which he never used, his Baudelaire, his Rimbaud, his volumes of Beckett, and his Kafka. Others.

When the stale coffee was hot, he slopped some into a cup and immediately forgot about it. Having gone through the motions of making and pouring the coffee, he was satisfied.

Old Shep liked to see his books there on the shelf. He had read all of them, and now they seemed like company to him. Old friends.

There was a little shop, just a block and a half from his place, where used books were sold.

Several weeks before, he had gone there to spend a few idle moments, and among a pile of old phonograph records, he had come across an old 78 rpm recording by Sherman Carter, a trumpet solo with a six man background, a long rendition of "She's Funny That Way."

The record was twenty or more years old, and Old Shep felt himself very fortunate in finding it, and had bought it at once.

Old Shep often stopped at the shop when he passed on his way home from work. The proprietor was a thin, scar-faced man who wore dirty grey workingman's clothing and used peroxide to make his hair blond. He sat in a battered old chair in his shop listening to far-out progressive jazz, or talking with dykes.

He ignored the customers who came Iin to browse, and when he made a sale, he collected the money without a word, keeping all the while, ninety-nine per-cent of his attention trained on his music.

Old Shep had brought the record carefully home and placed it in a box where it could not get broken, as Sherman Carter was one of his favorites.

Sherman Carter was not to be confused with Benny Carter, who was playing great jazz at about the same time as Sherman, that is to say in the late thirties and early forties, just before the world of jazz was turned topsy-turvy by Dizzy Gillespie and Charlie Parker - the days of Coleman Hawkins, Roy Eldridge, Jo Jones and Lester Young, not to slight Buck Clayton, Ben Webster, J. C. Higgenbotham, Pete Brown, Buster Bailey and Benny Morton. Harry Edison and Stuff Smith were around in those days, too.

They grabbed off their piece of the millennium. Old Shep wondered where they were now. Somewhere talking the blues. Sounds like theirs don't die. Somebody remembers.

It had been about twenty-five years before when an orchestra had come to town featuring Sherman Carter and his trumpet. They had played in a tavern out on the lake front all summer. Shep Anubts had danced there every weekend, listening to the beat of the drum and the plaintive passionate sound of Sherman Carter's horn. Sherman could play a trumpet solo like Harry James had never heard of, but now Sherman Carter was somewhere forgotten, and Harry James was still up there. Something in Sherman's personal life, or a flaw in the man himself, had probably kept him from sustaining. The summer when Shep Anubis had heard him at the lake front must have been the time when he reached his apogee. It was something Old Shep would not try to explain.

Maybe Sherman had been lost in one of the wars.

Old Shep set his pipe down and turned his attention to the package which he had brought in with him. It was an electric phonograph which he had bought at the secondhand store for seven dollars and fifty cents.

Ever since he had first discovered the recording by Sherman Carter of "She's Funny That Way" at the book shop, he had been able to hear the dim, ghostly echo of the great solo trumpet parts in his head, but he had not played the record because he did not have a player.

He had friends whose players he might have used, but the playing of this record was to Old Shep like a happy trip to the empty tomb and he wanted to be alone when he first heard it. He didn't take it to any of their places.

He knew that the exultant voice of the trumpet would carry him up to heights which he had known of old, but had not tasted for a long time. He couldn't experience this in the company of others. This was something to enjoy alone.

He wanted the full impact. No distractions. He would play the record when it could evoke its spell, and he could savor what was brought forth.

He took the player carefully out of the package and plugged it into the plug which screwed into the drop cord above the kitchen table and also held a naked light bulb.

He got the dusty old record out of the box where he had been keeping it and placed it on the player.

He did not turn the player on.

He forced himself to cook something, to heat a can of beans, to make a small lettuce salad, to get out bread and margarine and jam. He found that he had two potatoes so he decided to have French fries.

In the apartment beneath him, he could hear laughter and talk, and someone was singing.

Old Shep sat down and ate, not even looking at his new phonograph, and when he was through he washed every dish.

At last, when all his chores were finished, he turned on the switch and let the player warm up, and then set the needle in the groove.

Immediately, the room was filled with a loud, strangely out of date, yet eternal pattern of jazz. The introduction was played by a six piece combo.

Old Shep leaned near to the machine. He narrowed his eyes and listened.

In a moment, Sherman Carter and his trumpet took the solo lead. Old Shep felt the flesh of his forearm crawl, felt the root of each hair tingle.

In back of Old Shep's eyes, the melody began to unfold and spread out. It grew exceedingly red, a flower blown out on the soloist's hot wind.

Shep saw another day, when he had worked on the river, done a man's work, had a man's fun, been a young vital man. He had scurried about the ship then, climbing, jumping, able to run. He had been straight and strong, and loved to dance.

But now, there was no ship, and no place to run, and no one to dance with.

The trumpet burned through the air in the little kitchen. The soloist knew the ecstasy of being loved, and the sorrow and guilt of knowing that he did not deserve love, and he mingled the joy and sadness into blast after blast on his horn. Shep felt every vibrant quiver of Sherman Carter's breath , every split second's hesitation as he let the sweetness and power of the story he was telling on the trumpet take effect. To Shep it seemed that all the passion and lusty vitality of life, and all the tragedy too, were wrapped up in the wailing rendition of this simple song by the trumpet.

Shep closed his eyes and he saw the flowers; acres and acres and acres of them, bloody red in hue like the pomegranate, and swaying on, oh, such delicate stems.

And out of the red came a blackness, and out of the blackness came a light. It was the light which burned in the roadhouse out by Lake Ponchartrain where Sherman Carter had played.

Shep could see the blackish-green of the night-darkened oak leaves, and see the Spanish moss that hung mustily in the humid summer air, and see the silver grey of the starlit lake, and the thin strip of white sand which was the beach.

An area of marsh with waist-high grasses and dwarfed shrubs lay between the roadhouse and the sand.

Shep saw himself with Aggie, caught up in the distant spell of the music, running with her over the sand, laughing - saw them swimming naked in the lake, saw himself lying with her on the dry sand which was still warm from that day's sun.

All he had known had been Aggie, as they lay close together, lost in each other's beauty, and the passionate cry of the instruments of the band as it floated out upon the night air and lost itself somewhere on the lake.

It was a hot reverie that Shep was having, but the chill was there, too. There was an iciness about the picture which Shep was seeing because of the fear.

There was something in the damp, green-black darkness of the lakefront which could kill.

Shep abruptly stood up and walked about the room shaking off the vision not wishing to see the end of it.

He grew restless and became aware of his aloneness. He needed someone to come in and talk with him. He wished one of the men he knew would drop by. He would turn the music down, and make a fresh pot of coffee, and they would sit and talk of inconsequential things.

He felt the sand in his shoes, smelled the water, recalled again how he had felt with Aggie, began to lose himself again in Sherman Carter's music.

"Those were the good days," he said to himself.

A wildness took possession of Shep. He felt an urgency in the heavy stroke of his heartbeat.

He went into his bathroom and shaved. Then he put on a clean shirt. He chuckled to himself, limping quickly about the apartment. He was almost strutting.

"I'm not dead yet," he thought. He thought how surprised all his many acquaintances would be if they could know how vital he was feeling all at once.

He had a third of a bottle of vodka put away in a cupboard somewhere, which he had since the previous Christmas, Now, he got stiffly down on his knees and opened the little door under the kitchen sink and sought it out. He fixed himself a drink and began to have a party all by himself, letting his record play over and over.

Through the window which gave on the back patio, he could hear the young people in the apartment below. They made a happy buzz like the underbrush sounds of crickets and locusts and tree toads.

They were like happy insects, and if one day something big and awful should crush them, they would simply be gone, with only other simple bug-folk to stand around and weep.

Shep recalled that one of his books said that when the Egyptians of old would die, the other Egyptians would take out the dead man's heart and place a tumblebug inside.

Between drinks of vodka, Shep felt sorrow for the insect-hearted corpses who walked around the face of the Earth, not realizing they were dead.

They were happy because they were part of the hive or the anthill.

Shep, when he thought of his daily occupation which he performed to live, and his state of living solipsismatically, felt that he was more like the lonely tumblebug, forever trying to roll his burden of manure (a source of heat even as the sun is) uphill - tireless, plodding, ever with eyes turned inward, thinking his way deeper into self, more than he was like the gregarious, regimented ant or the bee with their castes and preordained destinies.

But, the faint chirrup from the apartment below was a pleasant sound. The young ones were happy.

Shep wished that he knew them better. He saw the girls often, and they spoke to him politely when they met him on the stairs, but their interest in him was impersonal, and most of the time they ignored him.

Now, it would have been a pleasant thing if he could have called to them all to come up to his apartment, and he could have fixed them drinks and let them listen to his record.

He would say, "That's the kind of music we enjoyed when I was your age," and if they seemed surprised at his interest in old jazz, he would say, "Oh yes, was young once. I enjoyed dancing and the company of women the same as any man."

But, he didn't know them well enough to invite them up.

It would be good, though to have company, someone to see his elation of spirits, share his sudden feeling of adventurousness with him, someone to laugh like Aggie had laughed with him so many years ago.

"Adventurous," he said. "That's the way I feel. Like I could do and dare. Like I haven't done or dared in a long time."

He had drunk more than he intended to.

He checked off in his mind various friends he might go out and look for, but they were a dull lot, dull like himself; old, perhaps, too old to be thrilled by anything.

Shep wanted to feel one more thrill.

All alone, he would go into the city. He would look for adventure, even danger, turn things over until he found life underneath, and he would see what happened when life came to grips with him.

He filled the ice trays with water and returned them to the refrigerator, and carefully turned off the record player, and put out the light.

Out in the hall, he could hear the buzz from downstairs more plainly, but the sound did not make him sad and lonely now. He was going to go out and have a good time, too.

It was always harder for him to climb downstairs than up. His stiff leg made it very hard for him to go down the stairs, and now, he was tipsy with vodka,

In the hall, outside the door of the second floor apartment, he was upset to find a half-eaten hamburger lying right on the floor. Evidently, someone had not wanted to finish his and had tossed it out into the hall with no regard for the fact that it would attract roaches, and perhaps even mice, into the building.

Shep had a roach problem already, and could not do away with them.

He looked at the hamburger with the crescent bites bitten out of it for a long moment, not knowing what to do about it.

Finally, he picked it up and put it in his pocket, thinking that he would throw it away later.

He held carefully to the rail and made his way slowly down to the street.

His old riverboat days called him toward the river. There were noisy little bars only a few blocks away which catered to seafaring men of all nationalities, where he could have a good time, and have it cheaply.

He didn't want to spend any more money having this adventure than he could help.

He hailed a taxicab when he got to the corner and asked the driver if a place called Tortuga's was still open for business. Shep had been there before and he recalled that it stayed open all night.

"Oh, yes," the driver said, "Tortuga is busier than ever. He's enlarged the place. They have three separate bars now."

Shep was sitting in the front seat beside the driver to show that he was democratic.

"It's a very warm night," Shep said.

"There aren't many people around. You're the third fare I've picked up since I went to work." The cab driver said this by way of commenting on Shep's remark. He said it as if the one thing caused the other. He was having a hard time getting the car to go into gear. "I see this hack goes into the shop tomorrow," he said.

"It acts like your clutch is slipping," Shep said, but he didn't know.

The driver nodded, showing respect for Shep's opinion. He was a middle-aged man with a great bay window and a worried expression which would leave his face momentarily when he smiled, but only momentarily.

"You live in the Quarter?" he asked.

"I've lived around here on first one street and then another for almost twenty years."

" I thought I'd seen you around. You're the kind of fellow someone would remember, walking with a limp, you know." He apologized hastily. "Not intending to get personal."

"I almost lost my leg," Shep said. "It happened a long time ago. I was lucky I didn't die."

"Was it an accident?"

"A snake bit Me."

"No kidding?" the driver exclaimed. "You were lucky. I had a brother in-law bit by a snake once, and he died Just like that." He raised his big hand and snapped his fingers.

"Some man I didn't know saved my life," Shep said. "I was out by Lake Ponchartrain when it happened. It was nighttime and my friends could never have got me to a doctor in time to do any good. This stranger thought fast and put a tourniquet on my leg and cut the bite open so the poison could drain out. The tourniquet kept the poison that was left from spreading, so I didn't die, but that kind of treatment did something to my leg that left it stiff. I saw the doctor later and he wanted Me to take a course of exercises that would have given me the use of my leg back, but I didn't do it."

"It might have been the best thing if you would have," the driver said sympathetically.

Shep haltingly told the cab driver what he could almost never bring himself to tell people.

"I didn't have the heart to be bothered with it," he said. "I was out at the lake with a woman, She stumbled into the snake den first. She was bitten before I got there, and she didn't live."

The taxi driver felt Shep's emotion more than he perceived it. He gripped the steering wheel tensely wishing he hadn't brought the talk around to this turn.

"What kind of snakes were they?" he asked.

"Moccasins."

They rode along in silence for a few moments.

"I didn't mean to ask you a lot of questions about your personal business," the driver said. "I was just making talk, you know. I hope you don't mind that we talked about this."

"It doesn't matter," Shep said. "It was a long time ago."

"We're almost to Tortuga's place, and I've come up from the wrong direction. I'm going to hit the one-way street if I go this way. I'll have to backtrack and go around the long way."

" You can let me off on the next corner," Shep said. "It's only a block from here, isn't it?"

"That's all."

"Well, I can walk a block and save you from going way out of the way."

"If you don't mind, I'd appreciate it. I think I'm going to take this cab in. The gear shift is giving me too much trouble."

They stopped on the corner, and from a block away Shep could hear the beat of the music which was being played in Tortuga's.

He told the cab driver that he hoped he would get his taxi home with no trouble, and paid him, giving him a twenty cent tip.

He turned and gave the appearance of being almost jaunty as he walked up the block.

A glowering and massive-chested dog with a great wide mouth sat on the curb and looked at Shep. The rims of his eyes were red, and a deep growl rolled out of his chest.

Shep's first thought was to be angry with the cab man who had put him down a block from his destination.

"If he had been paying attention to where he was driving instead of making me talk about Aggie's death, he could have put me out where he was supposed to.

But, in a moment, he shrugged his shoulders, realizing that things like this happened and were no one's fault.

He recalled the partly-eaten hamburger which he had put in his pocket, and he took this out and tossed it to the dog, and while the dog gulped this morsel down with one ravenous swallow, Shep scurried past him on his stiff leg and hurried to the door of Tortuga's.

The dog had a collar on and identifying tags. He obviously belonged to someone. Shep could not imagine people letting a vicious animal like that roam the street.

But, the sound of the music was compelling him onward, so he put all thought of the dog out of his mind, and hurried under the illuminated beer sign and pushed his way inside Tortuga's.

The first room which Shep entered contained a long bar of an antique de-sign, mahogany elbow-rest with neat grooving, and a polished top.

The light was very dim. This was partly intentional, and partly because the walls were a dirty grey which could not reflect light. There was no decoration except for a huge oil painting of a turtle which hung next to a cracked mirror above the cash register. There were signs about which said, "$ 1.00 deposit on Maracas" and things like that.

The 'jukebox played a merengue, blaring with a powerful burst of volume, while various young men added to the din by shaking the maracas and beating sets of bongo drums with rapt enthusiasm.

One very nice looking fellow, who looked like a football player dressed up in his Sunday best, sat upon a high stool with a sort of an Americanized tom-tom thrust between his knees. He patted the end of this, keeping perfect time with the jukebox.

There were men about who wore beards, and seemed to belong to the Beat generation, or who wished to give the impression they did. They were, most of them, serious-expressioned people who did not smiile, but drank their beer and talked together in low, muted voices.

There were dancers. These strove erotically in the crowd of standing drink-ers, making the best of things in the cramped space. Everyone who danced tried to dance as near to the jukebox and the bongo drums as possible. Most of the dancers seemed to be South or Central American seamen who had found their way into the place.

These were the men. The women -

Shep looked at the women silently, musing and wondering. He did not know if they worked in this place, or were just persons who for various reasons came here for kicks. It could be that these women were Daughters of Jezebel plying their trade among the foreign sailors, but they didn't look like Daughters of Jezebel.

They really looked like country women ready to do their housework, except they all had hairdos which burlesqued every forlorn Beat hair arrangement which had ever been.

They carried on multilingual conversations between dances, speaking fluently in English, French, and Spanish, Shep felt they had drifted into town from the bayou country. People born on Bayou Lafourche could all speak six different dialects of the three languages from childhood.

A group of dark men stood along the walls, or sat on the tall stools, talking together intermittently, but for the most part keeping silent. They did not understand English.

The gay kids who lived in the Quarter had found out about the place, and some of them were always here, trying to figure how they might communicate with the Spanish-speaking seamen, or staring tensely at the Beat fellows, who carefully ignored them. Most of these were the type who did not look like what they were.

The square out-of-town tourist was not seen here, except by accident.

When Shep came inside, he made his way through the crowd to the second bar (there were three) and stood looking about for some place to sit down. There was none. The bar, here in this second unadorned grey room, was not as crowded as the first had been, but even so, the stools at the long bar were all occupied.

Shep pushed his way up to the bar and ordered a beer,, and then stood waiting.

Some young boys hurriedly drained their glasses, deciding to go outside where a man was stationed with a hotdog pushcart, so, that they might have something to eat.

Shep and several other standing men immediately took their stools, and Shep drank his beer too rapidly, all the time knowing it would not mix well with the vodka he had already drunk. But, he was anxious to save his money, and mixed drinks would have cost him a little more.

There were tables in this room, and more women were in here than had been in the front bar. Evidently, these women did not care for dancing. They did not look like the dark Latin women who danced in the front bar, but were very plain, sad-eyed girls, with their hair long and parted in the middle, falling carelessly down to their shoulders, and no makeup on.

Shep had happened to be placed so that he faced a group of four of them, which was made up of a tired-faced younger woman and three old crones.

He stared at them unblinking, and without apology, looking from one to the

113

other, but most often at the younger woman.

The trio of old hags boldly returned his gaze, but the young woman seemed to be in some awful reverie of her own, detached, sorrowing, almost despairing and hopeless.

Her woe did not seem to Shep to be a fluid, urgent sorrow of the moment, derived from a personal calamity, but was more a pervading weltschmerz. The emotion could have been more lethargy than woe, a melancholy weariness about everything.

The music in the next room beat upon her I Ike some hot and pitiless ocean, pounding everything inside her into softness - the earth of her becoming a dank marshland, the sky of her weeping, tear-laden slate grey, the air of her a murky, fogged, green mistiness charged with heat lightning.

She sat alone in this barren scenery.

When Shep finished his first bottle of beer, he asked the barmaid to go over to the table where the four sat, and ask foir permission for him to send them drinks, and to ask them if he might join them, as he wanted someone to talk to.

The barmaid could not speak English very plainly, and the noise made it hard for her to hear him, but she grasped his meaning in a little while, and went away on this errand.

She came back smiling and said he might go and sit at the table with the women.

Shep got up and went and sat on a chair which no one was using at the table with the women. The three older ones said they were called Myra, Lillian and Beth. The younger woman was called Eula.

Shep gave them all cigarettes and then he sat and looked at Eula foolishly while the ladies babbled on about something, without his even hearing them.

Suddenly, a woman on the other side of the room jumped up from her place at a dark corner table, and came to the center of the room. She was a stout, blond, Germanic-looking woman with severe braids of hair coiled on top of her head. She had on a pair of dark blue slacks, and a man's shirt which she wore with the sleeves rolled up and the collar open. Her pale blue eyes looked particularly blank and somehow lashless.

"I have something to recite," she cried in a loud voice.

By some telepathy, the bongo drums and maracas in the next room became still, and the jukebox was turned down.

"She comes here every night," Myra said. "She's writing a long poem. She must have some more of it finished. Whenever she finishes another section of it, she reads it here, to all of us. It's awful for her to do. She's very bashful and sensitive."

"One night, some young boys got kind of drunk," Beth said. "And started yelling for her to shut up and go on back down to the pier and start unloading the banana boats. She went back in the ladies' room and cried and cried."

"None of us would do anything to hurt her," Lillian said firmly. "She's a beautiful person."

The Brunhilde had been working industriously on her poem for eighteen months. It seemed possible that the gradually evolving and rambling piece might someday have a total of 23,000 lines like the Kalevala.

"It's a beautiful thing," Lillian said. "She calls it "My Tears Have Been My Bread.""

Eula raised her head and looked sadly at the poetess's face.

The woman folded her hands and began to recite in a large expressionless voice. A number of the bearded men had come from the other room, and stood crowded in the doorway to listen to her.

"The shivering, winter-tired Lady Venus - Vamp-Tramp - spreads
    love's musky perfume
and dons her huntress garb
    decollette dress,
cinchers, stays,
    rouge red as anemones-
corners Adonis under the trees,
    gives eviction papers warning
she will put out
    of him his virginity
but butt
    and chest she lost (a bust?)
to a bore and / or pig
    (while her head was turned
in her yellow Cadillac)
some old whore
    came
in first -
Miss Death.

* * * *

    Pomegranate seed, blood drop, an
Anemone on the side of Mt. Lebanon
    at Eastertime
Resurrection - Impregnator
    of women,
alas, Cybele, see it is also the symbol of death.
    Warm and ready fruit fairly split open,
bare bears
    semblance
of a wound -
    How oft has they blood flown, Attis -
for so easily can Core
    become Persephone, and
Persephone black Hecate?
    Thy May Day purple violet draped around
thy pole
    of pine

is thy funeral wreath.
    Weep, Apollo, as
Zepherus blows
    Hyacinthus
out of this world -
Blows open the eight scarlet petals of
    the anemone,
and most destructively
    blows them away."

There was a moment of silence while the poetess stood still and looked at everyone sadly, and then the music in the next room was turned up, and the bongo drums and maracas began again.

Some of the bearded men followed the poetess to her table and clustered about her, congratulating her on what she had done, and offering criticism and advice about the poem.

Eula looked up at Shep and smiled weakly.

Shep went to the bar to order some more drinks for them all.

"He wants me to go with him when he leaves here," Eula said. "I can tell. I thought I was past that. I thought no one would ever want me again." She let her head sink down until her chin rested on her chest. "I'm going to go with him, if he asks."

Myra and Lillian and Beth looked at one another with hard anger, and with regret, but with understanding too. They did not say anything but turned away, thinking of other days.

"I don't think there's any harm in him," Myra said at last.

Shep came back to the table. He sat down in the crowded little space that was left to him, having to hold his knees close together so that he could squeeze into his place.

The barmaid brought them drinks.

"You don't say much, do you?" Shep asked Eula.

She smiled. The smile was wan, but Shep didn't notice. He was feeling bold and alive. The beer was doing this to him. He had never felt more reckless. He had spent almost all of his next month's rent money, which he had been saving so carefully in a certain division of his billfold.

"I don't see many men I want to talk to," she said. "I don't find many men who seem sincere."

"Men get in the habit of shooting a woman a line of bull. I don't think they can help it, or even know, they are doing it, after a while."

"I don't think you're that kind," Eula said.

"We could talk better if we went somewhere it is quieter," Shep said nervously. He laughed a little snickering laugh. "I can't even hear what I'm saying myself, the music is so loud in here."

"I'd like that," Eula said.

Myra and Lillian and Beth sat looking into their glasses, between the chips of ice, down through the liquid, into the depths. In the cold liquid, their separate dreams should have been swimming, but their dreams had drowned in glasses like these a long time ago. Somewhere their blighted, cindered, hopeless dreams swirled about on the bottom of a stale ocean of old liquor.

The three old ladies made a studied effort to appear to mind their own business, to be indifferent, to ignore what was building up between Shep and Eula.

"Should we go out and walk?" Shep asked hesitantly.

"I think that would be nice," Euta replied. "It's probably cooler outside than it is in here. I find it awful hot in here."

Shep asked Myra and Lillian and Beth if they minded if he took Eula away with him for a walk in the fresh air.

They turned faces which were polite masks on him and nodded and smiled, and all spoke at once assuring him that they would not be hurt if he and Eula left them for a little while.

When they were outside, Shep noticed that the hotdog man was still on the comer with his cart. He asked Eula if she would like to have a hotdog, which she declined, but she said she would not mind if he had one.

Shep bought himself a hotdog and walked up the sidewalk eating it.

The vicious dog was not there any more.

Eula walked very close to him, because she liked the picture they made walking along - the picture of a man and woman who wanted and needed each other.

"We could walk up to the French Market," Shep said. "Or, would you like to walk down to the river'?"

The pervading odor of the brewery penetrated everywhere.

"I don't think we should go near the river," she said. "It's dangerous to go down there."

Shep remembered Aggie, who had died a long time ago.

"You're right," he said. "Something terrible happened to me once, out by the shores of Lake Ponchartrain. I guess you've noticed I limp. I was out by the lake with a girl. We were walking together on the beach, and a man ran toward us out of the darkness and attacked her. He knocked me down and attacked her, tearing her dress and trying to push her down on the sand. When I was able to get up and started to wrestle with him, she ran away into the underbrush and a snake bit her, and she died. I went to help her and one of the den of snakes bit me. That's why I limp."

"You were very brave," Eula said.

"I took her there. We went there, night after night, and danced in the roadhouse, and walked on the beach, and made love. I took her there, and she was attacked and bitten by a snake and died. And, I can't forget. All my life since then, I have borne in my own body the evidence, a positive mark of Cain, to remind me of what I did. Every limping step I've taken has brought to my mind the fact that if I hadn't taken her there, had not asked her to leave the others and go with me to the beach, she would not have died. Died so frightfully."

Eula slipped her arm through his.

"You did all you could to save her," she said. "She must have been proud to have someone like you who wanted to take her off to be alone with him." Wistfully. "You wanted her. That must have meant a lot to her."

"I wanted us to play at making life together," he said. "We found death."

She cuddled against him.

"I'm so glad you want to tell me these things. You need for me to hear these things. You can't guess what it means to a woman to be needed."

"We were at a dance. An orchestra was playing out there that featured Sherman Carter. Did you ever hear of him?"

"No."

"He played the greatest trumpet you ever heard," Shep said. "You'll think it's a silly thing, but I found one of his old recordings in a secondhand shop over in the Quarter, and tonight I played it and it's because of that I came out looking for a good time, looking for you, I guess you'd say."

"I'm sure glad you got it, if that made you come over to Tortuga's. You should have come there before. I liked you when I first saw you. I think your hair makes you look awful distinguished."

"After what happened at the lake, I got old. I've been an old man all these years. Old and useless until tonight."

Eula was so delighted with having Shep walking beside her that she could not keep a glow off her shiny face. She lifted a hand and pushed the long straight hair back from her forehead. For the first time in a long time she regretted that she did not look like a woi-naii. She had let her sex ebb away because it was scorned. She lay her hand with her unpainted, close cropped nails on his arm.

"Maybe you'd take me to your place and let me hear this record," she said. She would make it easy for him. She made the suggestion she knew he wanted to make, knew he wanted to have her alone with himself in his apartment. When they got there. she would show him how much it meant to her to have found him.

They walked away from the area of the breweries and the river.

Shep stopped at a quiet bar and used the last of his money to purchase a bottle of wine. Then, he walked silently along, not speaking again, with Eula walking a few steps behind him.

He made the clumsy ascent to the third floor of his building, and went inside his apartment, and turned on the light. Roaches had been clustered on the top of the oilcloth covered table in the darkness, and the sudden light frightened them so that thev ran away in all directions.

Shep set the bottle he had bought on the table and got ice trays from the refrigerator.

He fixed himself and Eula drinks. She scarcely looked at hers. He bent and carefully set his phonograph in motion, starting the record.

Eula smiled and began to snap her fingers and sway her hips.

"You want to dance?" she asked.

Shep didn't but he did.

They danced crazily about the kitchen, scuffling their feet on the worn lino-leum of the floor. Eula pushed her hips tight up against Shep, and her left hand on his shoulder pinched him.

Shep shrugged her away from himself, and on the pretext of taking another drink, he sat down and picked up his glass.

He let the record play three times while Eula fidgeted, and drummed her fingers on her arm, and shook the ice in the bottom of her glass nervously.

Shep closed his eyes and saw the red flowers that the sound produced, and felt his youth and vitality return to him - felt that once again he was a carefree boy in his early twenties, out looking for a good time, untouched by the tragedy of this world.

He stood up and took a step toward Eula. She smiled up at him and set her glass aside. He limped when he stepped on his bad leg. He stopped and stood still for a moment, looking down at Eula foolishly. Abruptly, he turned and sat down again, and stared at the cracked oilcloth on the table, and he let the record play.

"Honey, I'm still here," Eula said feebly. She looked at him blankly. Her lips began to form a pout.

Sherman Carter on the trumpet was great.

Eula's slender chest began to rise and fall rapidly. She pulled at the fringe of her dress with her rough fingernails. Her fingers were cracked with working. Her face reddened and her eyes grew damp.

Suddenly, she jumped up from her chair and took up the record from the spinning turntable and hurled it on the floor so that it broke.

Immediately, she blanched ghastly white and turned aside from Shep.

Old Shep looked at the broken pieces of the record on the floor for a moment without comprehending. Then, a white rim appeared around his lips, and he moved lithely toward Eula, and took her frail throat in his hands, and squeezed it until her blank face grew blanker still and her head lolled backward so that her plain hair hung down in two forlorn mops behind her head.

He let her body slowly settle to the floor and sat on the chair. Absently, he pushed the switch which turned the record player off. He sat still for a long time.

At last, he picked up a piece of the record and looked at it solemnly. He would have to gather up all the pieces and throw them away.

He looked down at Eula. He would have to do something about her, too.

But right now, he was too tired. He turned out the light. and walking to a corner of the room, he rested his back against the wall, and let himself slip down the wall until he was sitting on the floor.

Old Shep rubbed his eyes and put his head down on his crossed arms on his knees, and slept.

GULFPORT, MISSISSIPPI

"Make Port In Samarkand" was written in Gulfport in 1960. Samarkand is the place where bad things first ever began to happen to Alexander the Great, and a fictional Gulfport was shown as a place where bad things began to happen to the protagonist of this story

The protagonist arrives at the assumption that homosexuality motivates the actions of a new-found friend. Whether or not this supposition is correct, it is acted upon. Tragedy ensues.

The writer had here a pessimistic view of individuals' abilities to understand one another There is a loss of communication between various characters in the story.. This is fostered by a lack of trust for one another.

One character trusts too much.

MAKE PORT AT SAMARKAND

The chief of detectives had been a seafaring man himself many years before, that was the only good thing. He was going to conduct the questioning himself. The prosecuting attorney and his assistant were both there. They had told the captain from the David's Nathan that he might be present. Also fortunate, the chief of detectives and the captain had taken an instant liking to each other.

The captain, in his full dress, smoked a pipe quietly while the others smoked cigarettes and listened to the muffled sound of street noises outside the jail. His hair was snow-white. He had followed the sea since he was fifteen years old. That was forty six years. His face was almost unlined. It was burned a deep manly brown by the sun and the salt wind.

The chief of detectives had just come from the barber shop. He was a portly man of consummate girth. His bulk would increase no more. He wore a white shirt, especially tailored, and a dark blue suit. Once in a while, he took a handkerchief from his pocket and swiped it across his face. He attended his church regularly and worked as superintendent of the Sunday school. He was a family man, and petit politician. Even now, though, he sometimes remembered his days at sea. Chief Steward he was for a time, and for one voyage, Second Mate.

This was going to be a big case. It would be one of the biggest criminal cases the town had seen. Antinoe Harbor was not accustomed to large cases. Disorderly conduct and fighting were the usual fare. Now, what seemed to be a cowardly and senseless crime had been committed, and the newspapers were voicing a public outrage, and demanding punishment for the guilty. The very nature of the crime made it loathsome to the people of the city. Would have done so, even if J. Wolfgang Brown, II had not been involved.

J. Wolfgang Brown, II was a rich man, owning a factory which did much to support Antinoe Harbor. Almost every family in town had at least one person on his payroll. Mr. Brown controlled the newspapers and lots of votes.

He would have been here with chief of detectives and the others, but his minister had persuaded him that this was not the place for him to go, at this time. He was sitting alone at his large old house, far up the hill, his face ashen and grey, and his thin lips pressed into a grimace of hatred and vengeance wished-for.

He clutched his Cuban cigar, thinking that his family tree was down. His hands shook a little. His dry sorrow burned but did not melt. No tears.

A male stenographer, ready to take down the testimony, sat and chewed his pencils and doodled aimlessly from time to time on his pad. Twice, he had yawned. The office was air conditioned, but it was warm after someone had sat there a while.

A deputy had gone to bring Bucknell from his cell. Any moment, they would hear foot tread on the iron stairs, and Bucknell would be brought in.

In a moment the clatter came, and the deputy came through the door with Bucknell walking in front of him.

Bucknell wore a dark blue and white striped tee shirt and a pair of workman's dungarees. He had a long mop of black hair which was completely unruly and needed cutting. He was a big man, wrestler type, not slim and hard but thickset and beefy. He sat down wearily where they told him to, and looked about at the captain, and then at the chief of detectives, who seemed to be in charge. He did not try to simulate sailors' bravado, but looked troubled and sad. At the corners of his eyes, there was almost a wrinkle of fear.

He was not in very good physical condition. There were little paunches beginning to form under his eyes, and he was much too heavy.

We were told that you are ready to make a statement," the chief of detectives said in an impersonal voice. "That's what we're here for. You just tell us everything that happened in your own words, and later we may want to ask you some question

Bucknell looked from one to the other.

"I know what you think," he said. "But, I didn't do it."

"We don't think anything," the chief of detectives said "It looks like it's possible you did it for the little money you thought that kid might have been carrying, but we don't know. You were there. Three men saw you talking with him. But, we won't know what happened until we investigate."

"He had an ugly mark on his face," the prosecutor told the captain. "A brutal blow caused it."

Bucknell's face clouded. He looked at the chief of detectives appealingly.

"Just go ahead and tell your story," the big man said.

Bucknell had come into port on the David's Nathan out of Norfolk. They had sailed down coastwise and around the tip of Florida, and he had worked like the sea-dog he was all the way. When the ship docked, Bucknell had been the last to quit the ship for the shore. Everyone else had gone down the gangplank and away to town an hour and a half before he could wind up his duties and get dressed for shore leave.

He had come off the pier and followed a foot path through the marsh grasses to a tavern which occupied a place on the waterfront. There were no customers there. It was early afternoon. While Bucknell had a beer to drink, the proprietor of the tavern told him that a crowd would gather after dark. Bucknell must come back.

Bucknell did not go back to the paved street which led away from the pier, but continued along the foot path toward some distant buildings which looked as though they might have been places of entertainment. Bucknell didn't relish the idea of going to the downtown business district and looking in store windows. And, as for movies, he never attended them.

He needed another beer to go with the one he had at the tavern.

He pushed through a dense screen of grasses and reeds and burst out upon a little cleared place where there were rocks scattered about, and some small fishing boats were tied up.

A young boy was sitting on top of an old grey piling, looking down into one of the shrimp boats where some men were working. They had a truck backed up to an improvised wharf. It was loaded with ice, and they were unloading this into the boat. They put the blocks of ice into a hand-cranked crusher, and the crushed ice poured down into the hold of the boat.

"Buddy Boy," Bucknell said pleasantly. "I am a stranger in this port. Never been here before. I just docked on the David's Nathan and I don't know my way about. Are those buildings I see ahead a place where a man could get a bottle of beer?"

"Yes, sir," the boy said. He looked like he was about fifteen years old, but he was probably older. He was one of those slender and pale beardless boys who always look younger than they are.

"Well now, Sonny," Bucknell said. "You don't have to call me 'Sir' unless you just want to. I wonder if those places over there are nice places that would welcome a seafaring man like myself?"

"Oh, I'm sure they would," the boy said earnestly.

"Which one would you say is the best?" Bucknell asked, giving the boy a broad wink. "Man to man."

"I really don't know," the boy stammered. He colored a deep red and seemed to be greatly concerned that he could not give the information which was asked for. He dropped his eyes and looked at the ground near his feet. "My father would never let me go in one of those places."

"Your old man won't let you'?" Bucknell snorted. "I never asked my old man where I could go after I got to be your age. How old are you?"

"Seventeen." The boy looked up at Bucknell with undisguised admiration. "I wish I could be like that," he said. "I'm afraid of my father. I wouldn't dare go any place he'd disapprove. He thinks I'm at band practice at the school now. Band practice let out early and I slipped off to watch the men work in the shrimp boats. I'd like to go out on a shrimp boat once."

Bucknell stood with his feet apart. He always stood as if he was trying to anchor himself to the deck of a patching ship. He wore a seaman's cap which covered his tangle of black hair at a rakish angle.

"You'll get to go one day, Buddy," he said. "Old Bucknell has been going anyplace he wants for a long time."

"Is your name Bucknell?"

"I am J. Wolfgang Brown the Third."

"The third! I never did believe in ships named after other ships what's had bad luck and ain't about no more. It gives people ideas about the vessel before she's even out of the shipyard. They expect her to be Just like the ship she's christened after. Every ship has her own personality. You got to be yourself, Buddy. You're the first you. You're not the third image of someone else. What do they call you?"

"Wolfgang."

"A damned square-head appellation. The Nazis shot two shops out from under me during the war. Both good ships and true. I got a bad scar right now come from a piece of flying debris struck me on the leg. The Nazi submarine surfaced right there and watched the Beth Sadye go down, and we heard them singing some hellish song of theirs in that language they got. They didn't machine-gun us in the water like I've heard they would do sometimes."

Bucknell pulled up his pantsteg and showed Wolfgang a long jagged fishbelly-white scar which darted down through the black hair of his calf. His leg looked like the trunk of a young pine tree, rough and black with hair, and the white scar looked like the sap-coated scar on a pine which has been turpentined.

"The war must have been terrible," Wolfgang said.

"I was in the Merchant Marines," Buckiiell said. "I didn't fight like some of the poor devils."

"Do you think the Germans would really shoot men that were swimming in the water trying to save themselves after their ship was sunk?"

There was appeal in Wolfgang's voice. Bucknell took a quick look at his face. He smiled and his voice softened.

"No," he said. "You hear those things in wartime. It ain't natural for people to hate. If thev didn't tell things like that about the enemy, the people wouldn't want to fight."

The shrimp boat was now loaded with the last block of ice, and the rickety old truck which had brought it started up with a loud clammer and moved slowly away down a rutted road which had been made through the reeds and grasses by trucks going back and forth.

The engine of the shrimp boat had been running slowly all the while. Now, the men started the boat moving and made slowly out of the harbor.

"That's a poor craft," Bucknell said.

"I guess you've been everywhere," Wolfgang said.

"I been around. I was born in New England. Always followed the sea, except for two years I drove a truck across country. I didn't like the push and the crowding on the roads, people trying to get ahead of each other. The sea's a calm place at times. Sometimes when the weather is good and the work's all caught up, you just steam along, and it's as peaceful as heaven. I got tired of eating at truck stops and sleeping in cheap hotels and pushing those big diesels across the mountains and through the low places. I just had to get back to salt water."

"I've never been anywhere," Wolfgang said.

Bucknell laughed.

"You're young. You'll get to go places. Get you a good ship like the David's Nathan. That's a clean ship. Captain gets up on the bridge every Sunday and preaches to us. It's always the same sermon, about how Nathan the Prophet watched out for King David, kind of led him out of shoal water when he got himself in danger. Captain says the Good Book today is like Nathan of Old was himself. He tells us we ought to use the Bible for a guide. It reminds me of my old mother. She was a Bible-reading Christian. I was raised on Simon Peter and all them fisherfolk and Jonah that was lost in the whale. We went to church every Sunday, but I was looking at the lasses, I guess. I don't remember too much about it. But, when the Beth Sadye was shot out from under me, and my leg was ripped open, and sometimes I thought I'd lose my pin, and sometimes I thought I'd croak, I know I sure prayed."

"Would you tell me something?" Wolfgang asked. "You must have an opinion since you've been all over the world, and seen so many people. Are people good?"

Bucknell was tolerantly amused by Wolfgang's seriousness. He sat down on the ground at Wolfgang's feet and leaned back against a timber. He pulled a piece of grass loose and chewed it.

"Most times," he said. "I think they are."

"I'm so glad you said that," Wolfgang said excitedly. "You see, my father talks all the nine like people are evil. I hear him talking to other people about how they try to cheat him, and how he has to watch them every minute because they steal from him, and lie to him, and how they're always trying to organize under a labor union, so that they can take advantage of him. He says the average man would sell his own grandmother for a dollar."

"He said that""

"I don't know what he meant. The worst is what he tells me. He tells me I'll inherit the factory someday, and it'll be mine to run, and I'll have to watch people all the time and learn how not to let them get the best of me. He wants me to believe that people are not to be trusted."

"The man must be a fool," Bucknell snorted. "I've seen bad sea captains that held those views. They'd have a ship in near mutiny before she'd made her maiden voyage. You can't deal with men that way anvmore. Long time ago, a man could be hard, and the people couldn't help themselves. The people won't take that kind of stuff from the bridge anymore."

"My father thinks everything is corrupt," Wolfgang said. "He thinks the government is out to get him, and the unions, and this whole town. He doesn't believe in the police force. He has told me terrible things about what goes on in prisons. He tells me how they beat prisoners with hoses because they don't leave any marks, and cheat on their food, and sometimes even kill a man. I get scared to death every time I see a policeman in uniform. If I ever got arrested, I'd die of fright."

Bucknell spat out the grass he had chewed.

125

"I ain't ever been in irons on land," he said. "Or at sea, either. Long time ago they used to flog men on shipboard. I don't know much about that kind of discipline. I never saw any of it practiced."

"I just want somebody to tell me the world is not bad," Wolfgang said. His lower lip began to tremble. "I want somebody to tell me that people are good."

"There, there Buddy," Bucknell said uncomfortably, "don't get yourself all worked up. You'll be a little older soon, and you can leave this town and your old man, and you'll find the world is whatever kind of place you believe it is."

"I've always tried to think that the innocent will be safe in the world. The cynical meet cynicism. People like that devour one another. Like wolves. But, I'm afraid I'll be devoured. I don't know anything about how to protect myself. And, sometimes I have dreams. I have terrible dreams."

"You're almost sick," Bucknell said. "You've heard things that you don't understand. You'll be all right when you get away from here and find out they aren't so."

"I wish you'd take me away," Wolfgang said sadly. "I wish you'd take me away on the David's Nathan."

"I couldn't do that," Bucknell said. His face clouded. He suddenly became very wa4y and uneasy. "I'd get in trouble with your old man. Besides, I don't have any say about who ships out on the David's Nathan."

You're the first friend I've ever had," Wolfgang said. His eyes misted full, and he looked at Bucknell imploringly.

"Oh, you must have plenty of friends. You're a smart boy, still in school, in the town you were born in, with a wealthy father. You must have hundreds of friends."

No one has ever understood how it is," Wolfgang murmured.

"I understand how it is." Comment was futile. "There's nothing I can do to help. No one can help you. You've got to find your own way."

"You could kind of show me where the reefs are hidden," Wolfgang said. "Like Nathan did David. I like you better than anyone I've ever met."

"Kid, I've got to be going," Bucknell said nervously. "I was on my way to get a bottle of beer. A seafaring man needs to have a little something to make him feel comfortable when he hits port. A coupleof beers will start me feeling a lot better."

"Don't go"' Wolfgang said. He almost screamed the words in his excitement. "I never had anyone I could talk to that knew anything about life. I've always been so afraid of everything."

He threw himself down off the post and caught Bucknell around the legs with his arms and burrowed his head into him.

"What the hell?" Bucknell growled in surprise.

"You can't leave yet," Wolfgang cried. He clung to Bucknell tightly, his arms about Bucknell's thighs and his face in his groin.

"Damn! Let go," Bucknell said. His face clouded suspiciously, all at once. "Say, is that what you're after? I've run across your kind before. I don't like anything like this. Get away from me."

126

Wolfgang held him tighter. Bucknell looked anxiously up and down the path to see if anyone was coming.

"Get up off me, kid, before I hurt you. You and your line of crap almost won me over. I should have known what you were working up to."

"Don't talk to me like that," Wolfgang said in a muffled voice. "I don't know what you're talking about. I only know you can't leave me."

"You know!" Bucknell shouted. "You know! You think you could get me to do something like that. Goddamn you!"

Wolfgang sat up at the terrible violence in his voice.

"What's the matter," he whispered. He reached out a thin hand toward Bucknell.

Bucknell lifted his great hairy fist and struck Wolfgang full in the face. Blood popped out of a cut above Wolfgang's eye and he looked at Bucknell unbelievingly for a moment.

"It's true," he screamed. "It's true. Everything my father says is true. People are bad. They're evil." He turned aside, rubbing his face, with his back to Bucknell. "All evil."

After striking the blow, Bucknell had turned white and sat completely stunned for a moment. Now, he groped his way to his feet and stood looking down at Wolfgang for a moment. He started to speak, but then turned away and went crashing through the reeds to a road that ran nearby, and walked rapidly away toward the town.

* * * *

"We found that boy's body in the harbor, three days after the afternoon you've told us about," the chief of detectives said. "If your story is true, Wolfgang drowned himself after you left him. Whatever you did to him must have been pretty bad to make him do that."

"I did what I said I did."

"You didn't knock him out and search his pockets, maybe, and then throw him into the water?"

"No. He was sitting on the ground sort of holding his head when I left him," Bucknell said. "I wished I hadn't hit him. Now that he's drowned, I can't help thinking it was not like I thought. I guess I've got an evil mind. I jumped at conclusions. I'd never get over it, if the kid was on the level."

"Well, we'll see," the chief of detectives said. "We're going to send you back to the cell, now. The deputy will take you back."

After Bucknell left the room, everyone was silent for a few moments. The chief of detectives looked at the rest of them doubtfully.

"I don't think he could have made the story up," the prosecutor said.

"I'm going to check up on that kid a little. I'm going to go around and see some of his school buddies," the chief of detectives said. "I'll find out if anything odd's been going on. Mainly, I want to find out how he felt about his father. I want to find out if Old Man Brown had really scared him about life the way it seems. The old bastard is hard. He's not going to like the way this case is going."

"I'd vouch for it we'll find that kid on the level," the prosecutor said.

"Bucknell won't be able to I've with himself if the boy was all he claimed to be," the captain of the David's Nathan said. "I know him pretty well, New England conscience and all. He'll never be the same man."

"Granting, of course, that he's on the level, too," the chief of detectives said softly.

"Yes. Granting," the prosecutor said doubtfully.

CHARLOTTE, NORTH CAROLINA

"Battle Lost Battle Won " was written in 1964 at Charlotte. The writer had, in the summer of 1963, caught a Greyhound bus out of Gulfport, MS, saying "Good-bye To All That." The change was frightening. Human relationships were broken and left behind - a never-before felt freedom lay ahead with its fearful responsibilities.

"Battle Lost Battle Won " begins as a short story and becomes an essay. The protagonist, realizing he is alone, allows his mind to turn inward where he assuages his loss of kindred companionship, finding satisfaction in a seductive inner dream.

Man will find within himself whatsoever answers he shall ever find. He must be impelled to look inward. There is nothing "out there" to help him. Alone, man must teach himself to survive. In all, he must be a realist.

The sentimentalist, with all his sensitivities bared, seeks to unite with something or someone he can blend into, become part of, lose his selfhood in. He will not find this perfect union - this escape .from self. The quest is futile.

The conquest of many women in affairs of the flesh validates a man's maleness. A champion such as James Bond makes many women submit thereby proving his prowess. It is for his self-concept. It is not for them - the ladies.

It is best to learn and to accept that man must be alone. In loneliness. What is lost in human warmth and fellowship is redeemed in self-realization.

BATTLE LOST BATTLE WON

Sleep had become a time not of rest but of struggle. The issues were vague. Peter Fillmore had come to know the terrain, the awesome atmosphere of the place. It was desolate and wild. The only life in the place was the wind. And Peter walked there, night after night, all alone. The moon was a full moon, and colored chartreuse, and it tinted the grey clouds with its color, and the wind made the whole landscape cold and filled with turbulence. He kept to the roads. Shuddering and sweating, and hunching his shoulders against the chill, but she ran at random on the marshes so that he constantly feared for her that she would sink. He knew that he was going to lose her.

She ran on the sick puce mud in her white gown with her long hair black and inky, a blot on the wind, and Peter could see her face, but the lines of her body, her pitiably frail and bloodless body, were etched upon his eyes so that he saw her vulnerability even when he could not see her. Her feet were bare, and she ran on the rough ground so carelessly that her legs were empurpled with this hostile and treacherous earth, almost to her knees, so that she looked like some peasant of Italy who had spent the day squeezing the grape for wine.

Peter would call her by many different names, but she did not heed him and he would cry out to be brought back from this place, and always just as he awoke and left the dread dreamscape behind, he would see her sink with an incredible sucking noise into the devouring fatal mud.

"I've lost her again," he'd say.

* * * *

He put on his bathrobe and went and sat in his deep chair beside the window where he could look down at his yard and part of the street. The city was dark. It was after three o'clock. Everywhere, people were sleeping, but Peter could not sleep now. Peter was afraid to sleep again.

The moon, the real moon, was at about the first quarter and the yard was shadowy and dim. In the daylight Peter could have seen his shrubs and picked out each japonica from among the azaleas and the evergreens, but tonight they were all one huge shadow, blurred and inseparable. The sidewalk to the front door was straight and grey. Peter looked at the solid line of substantial houses which stood across the street and a feeling of security and confidence tried to assert itself in him. At least Peter was safe. He had done everything which could be done to insure his own safety and his daughter's. Everything which the wise investment of money could do for the future had been done. If they had any worries at all, they were not money worries.

Peter leaned forward and looked down into the drive. He had seen a sudden flash as of the glint of light on metal. A car was parked near the corner of the house. It was a small sporty red model and Peter knew at once that it was Bobby Morris's new Mustang which his father had given him as a reward for his good record at the college which he and Patricia Fillmore attended. It was a good, small school which the Presbyterians operated. Bobby was well thought of at this good college and he seemed a good boy, so Peter did not worry about his daughter. She had a strength of character which made him feel safe about her. Anyway, Peter was now past fifty, and fortunate enough to have learned that worries, that mental torments, did not emanate from circumstances surrounding other persons or from external conditions, but are born within. In his philosophy, there was no opportunity for him to say, "If circumstances were altered, or if only so-and-so would act otherwise, I could know peace of mind," for he judged that some inner unrest, some maladjustment of the soul itself, caused all suffering and the remedy to heal lay only in the possession of the sufferer. To himself he must minister.

"When Pat goes to school tomorrow." Peter thought, "I've got to get a hold on myself."

He heard the car door slain and Pat skipped to the front of the house and let herself inside. Could her skip be too jaunty? Was there bravado in it? Peter heard a warning bell ring out in his mind. He knew how greatly young people hate to be intruded upon, and he was afraid that she might take offense if she knew that he was up and had observed the hour when she came inside, but still - instinct warned that she might need him. Something could be amiss, for it was very unusual for her to stay out so late. If there were trouble, perhaps there would be something that he might say.

He pulled on his trousers and went and stood in the hallway at the head of the stairs. Patricia came up slowly, holding to the rail. Peter felt guilty about being there, and concerned for her, and a little foolish.

"Is anything the matter?" he asked, and as soon as he could see her face, he knew there was.

Sometimes Pat could be very poised and confident appearing, putting on a brave face for the grandstands (she had been like that on the day of her mother's funeral), but now she was all open to her father. He read her distress.

Most of the time, she dressed herself in the best of taste and carried herself with dignity, and bore her head with its crown of dark hair with a certain regal air which made one expect that at any moment, she would issue some firm command in the manner of a budding queen, but tonight her shoulders drooped and she seemed very tiny and she moved with the tired fear of a frightened and lost little girl.

"Come in my room and let's sit for a few minutes," Peter said. "I had a bad dream and I've been awake for hours."

"Okay," Pat said.

After his wife's funeral, Peter Fillmore had a decorator in and all the ruffles and the lawn curtains and the delicate furnishings of the room had been taken away, and the wallpaper had been replaced with a dark blue which bore a geometric design. The furniture had been replaced by solid mahogany pieces with sturdy square framed mirrors, and heavy plain drapes had been hung. It was now a man's room, with books against the walls and huge square burgundy ash trays, and a reproduction of an ancient Egyptian sistrum on the apex of which a Sacred Cat sat enthroned. He had other curios lying about.

He still felt guilty and foolish talking to his daughter about her personal affairs, of which he knew but very little. He tried to study her face to see if she was annoyed or not.

"Could I get you something from the kitchen?" he asked. "Do you want anything to drink?"

"No thank you, Daddy."

"Is something the matter tonight?" he asked. "Are you troubled about something?"

Oh Daddy, this room is so square and heavy! If there weren't a bed in here it could be a sitting room at a gentlemen's club. It looks like one of those places you see in English movies."

"It lacks the odor of cigars," Peter said.

"Yes. That's what it lacks. Only that."

Peter wondered if subconsciously she was not resentful of the way that he had uprooted her mother and swept her out. He had wanted no ghosts. But, the dreams came. He still dreamed the dreams.

"When you come home again, we'll go shopping and buy some new paintings for the walls. We'll get something softer that will relieve the stodginess. You look around in the library for some ideas while you're at school. Maybe something French would help. Perhaps, a 'White Clown' by Picasso, or a 'Bird Catcher' by Klee."

You wouldn't really like something like that, Daddy," Pat said, with a tone of authority. "Daddy, Bobby and I are not going to go together any more."

"And, you're unhappy about this?"

Pat sat very straight and stiff in her chair. She toyed with the hem of her skirt and looked down at the rug at her feet. It was a burgundy rug splashed with irregular blobs of color. She got up in a moment and turned on the overhead light to supplement the lamps.

"It's going to leave an emptiness. It's half my life being cut away, and so soon after I just have to face it. But, living's going to be strange without him. We've gone together since we were thirteen. That's almost ten years. I've spent all those years going with him and being a good girl, and I don't know how I'm going to live any other way."

"Well Pat, maybe he'll come back to you after he tries being without you for a while. He's got a lot invested, too."

"He feels deprived," Pat said. She was not the frightened little girl now, but a tired woman, old-feeling and disappointed. She heaved a sigh. "He feels that he has never had the chance to date a variety of girls, or to experience the things that other boys have experienced by the time they reach his age, or even to think for himself. I've been there while he formed opinions about human history and religion and the politics and sociology of today. He feels that he has never been free (especially) intellectually. He thinks that the only way he can really be a man is to live and act and think on his own for a while, and then to experiment and try everything that there is to be tried, to see strange places and to do everything. Suddenly, after all these years, I stand in his way. I stand in the way of his self-development."

"He has been influenced at school. Either some professor or some student who is presently inspired with the ideas of individual freedom and intellectual self-determination has influenced him. It could be only a passing fad."

"I don't, think so," Pat said sadly. "We talked a long time. He's thought it out very carefully. I agree with him. Oh, I agree with him! Only I can't see why we can't finish school and marry and then have these experiences together. I'd go with him to Easter Island, or to Tierra del Fuego, or to Terre Haute, if he asked me. I feel that I'm a modern woman, and an adventurous sort. I wouldn't hold him back."

"I'm sure you wouldn't, baby."

Pat settled back in the chair and looked completely miserable. "I'm sort of whipped, Daddy."

"If there's such a thing as the battle of the sexes." Peter said, "it's a battle that none of us ever wins or loses. Whenever we engage in it, we both win and lose. If Stoutheart wins Fairlady, Stoutheart loses his freedom and part of his right to be himself. If he loses Fairlady, he gains his freedom and his right to be completely himself. It is debatable whether the winning or the losing were nobler. If Shymaid wins Bonnielad, she loses herself into his subjugation, and if she loses Bonnielad, she wins a life for the self of her which she could not have had. She would probably be happier and more content winning Bonnielad, but her life might be richer in experience if she lost him. In any case, I think it is always the woman who loses most and is hurt most deeply by the losing."

Pat felt that she was going to be crying in a few minutes. "You've got your adjustment to make, too," she said. "What will you do, Daddy?"

"I still haven't made up my mind."

"I've thought about it," Pat said, "and that's one thing that Bobby and I agreed about completely. You love your books and intellectual conversation, and quiet, old ordered places. We think you should take some special courses and bring yourself up to date and then teach. You'd make a wonderful professor. You're so much wiser than some of the men we sit under."

"I don't know," Peter said. "It's a good idea, but ... I don't know,"

"Well, don't wait too long to make up your mind. You could sit here waiting to make a decision and your whole life could pass by ... What's left of it."

Peter wanted to smile with amusement. Pat seemed to think that he was very aged, and that his time was short.

"I might come up with something tomorrow," he said. "Or, I should say 'today.' It's almost morning."

"Would you excuse me?" Pat asked. "I have to take the train back to school. Bobby said he would take me in the car, but if we've broken off, we've broken off. I'll go back to school on the train." She stood up and squared her shoulders bravely.

Peter stood up and she kissed him. Then, she slipped quietly away.

Peter turned out his lights and went downstairs. In the large sitting room there was a sign which he had caused to be printed and framed. It said, 'And if thou gaze long into an abyss, the abyss will also gaze into thee..' - Friedrich Nietzsche. This sign hung over the television set, which was seldom turned on.

Peter sat down beside the French doors which led onto the terrace and began to imagine himself as a Professor of English at a small privately endowed college somewhere in the rural south. He could see himself, his hair just a little greyer, his dress impeccably precise and neat, and his manner dignified and commanding of respect, standing before a small earnest class, guiding their minds along serious and important intellectual paths.

The picture was so satisfying that he stretched himself luxuriously in his chair and relaxed completely. In a moment or two, he could hear his own voice teaching.

"The basic conflict," he was saying, "is an old one. It is the conflict between sentimentality and realism. It is the conflict between Gertrude, the mother of Hamlet, and Lady Macbeth. Contrast the two: Queen Gertrude, well-meaning and superficial, with quick but shallow emotions, desirous of being happy and seeing those about her happy, touched by the distress of others, but unequal to personal sacrifices, a total picture of a weak character. She does not see any unpleasantness which she does not wish to see. She is capable of forgetting any past misdeeds of her own which might trouble her in remembrance. She was a completely self-complacent person.

"But Lady Macbeth!" Peter saw himself giving a little flourish of the wrist while an impish twinkle came into the corner of his eyes. "'Ah' you will say, 'an entirely different cup of tea!' Here was a woman who meant well for no one but herself and her husband, a deep and complex woman in whom the fires of passion and emotions built slowly until they kindled into a seething inferno. She did not care if those about her were happy or not, not even her husband, not even herself, so long as her overpowering ambition was satisfied. Her heart was hardened against the plights of others. She could look upon the most loathsome sights and never flinch. She recalled her misdeeds as a soldier might recall his cherished victories. She did not consider whether or not she was satisfied with herself, but whether or not she was satisfied with the results of her scheming. Lady Macbeth was a woman of action whose ambition fed upon itself and could not be satisfied, so that frustration turned in upon frustration so that she died. Always gratified, never sated."

Perhaps Pat was right. Peter was half a mind to submit a schedule of his college credits to the board of education so that he might find out what courses he would be required to take in order to qualify himself to teach.

"The basic conflict is between the sentimentalist, who clings to the belief that 'no man is an island' - 'that two can be one' - 'We live heart to heart all day long, and every day the same' - and the realist who knows that man is doomed to stand alone.

"The realist, walking alone, like some character from Beckett, like some figment conjured up by the imagination of Sartre, lives in his isolation - Cain cast out of the land of his parents and Abel, into Nod. He is the American Existentialist, the hipster, Mailer's White Negro, absurd with the absurdity of Camus. He has learned how to live in the world which there is today to be lived in. He has learned to protect himself from hurt. He has learned how to live in this - the New Jungle.

The sentimentalist of whatever species will not give up the idea that it is possible to man to be not alone any longer. He seeks his mate and even the most ridiculous encouragement will fire him with enthusiasm again, believing that he has found an escape from his loneliness. He will cling to the new object of his attention as to the support of his life itself, never relinquishing his delusion that the two of them are not indeed separate and strange entities one to the other. He invests this beautiful Phoenix which has suddenly appeared upon the lifelong ashes of his loneliness with a plumage like unto that of his own idealized image of himself, and he worships and marvels at and loves this image of his own making. Svengali talking to Svengali, and if the truth begins to assert itself and the marvelous plumage to fall away, one feather at a time, he goes through all the agonies of a Midas who sees his fortune diminish one coin at a time, clink, clink, clink down the rathole."

Peter rose up and stood with his back to a fireplace which was in the room, turning his head so that his profile showed in the mirror which was above the mantle. A villa in ancient Rome would have held him.

"The sentimentalist is doomed to a life of pain and hurt because he clings and he clings and he clings to the delusion that he will find someone to blend himself with. The solitariness and the singleness and the oneness can be dispelled. And, no repetition of disappointment can crush the belief out of him. Somewhere there is a perfect union, and the perfect union can be achieved.

"I am speaking to a realistic generation. Perhaps, I was born in a sentimental age, before the First War, when people gathered around the campfires to sing 'There's a Long, Long Trail A-Winding Into the Land of My Dreams,' every doughboy dreaming of the time that he would reach the end of that long, long trail where he and his girl would be one. We read The Rosary and believed that it was possible for two people to become permanently one flesh. But, I am getting old.

"Today's wiser, harder, more knowing generation is the Generation, not of George Primrose, but of James Bond. James Bond takes it so totally for granted that he is alone that he does not even think about it. He plays the game of detecting crime with no feeling for the other pawns on the board except that they must rightly play their prescribed roles in the drama which is built as a lonely showcase for his charms and talents demanding as they are of stooges. He is isolated in his role. The others are merely the machinery which makes it able for him to play his role efficiently. He does not break through any wall to approach his adversaries. He does not know the ones he kills - is licensed to kill. He does not have any feeling for or against those he brutally beats. The physical contact makes no genuine meeting with foes. There is not learning to know and to respect the enemy, as it was with more sentimental heroes of yesteryear. It is all cold and clinical and without feeling. This sort of thing is reserved for pop records like 'Ringo.' How juvenile!

"James Bond's beautiful women are merely the INSTRUMENTS of his solitary passions, an assertion that he is virile and male, more playing of the game, proving something to himself, satisfying himself that he can win, a simple seeking after selfish pleasure. He is pure narcissus. It is in his lovemaking that he stands most alone. Most completely given over to realism. Farthest from sentimentality. And this is the tragedy of James Bond and all his generation of hard thinking realists. Lovemaking for the realist is not one tenth the pleasure it is for the sentimentalist. The sentimentalist suffers to the pinnacle of passion, and then endures the slow agonizing misery of seeing love subside, and then dares hope once more and begins the ascent to the spires of the glory of it again. The sentimentalist is wracked and wracked and wracked by love, but to the realists it is just another ball thrown through the basket, just another baseball struck over the fence.

"Try to fan awake the drowsing sentimentalist which lurks in you all. The sentimentalist could savor one affair so that it would rend the emotions for half a lifetime. Today, love endures for half an hour. This is why there is promiscuity. There is a rush to make up in quantity for what is lacking in quality. In all the haste and fury, it is feared that there will be many who never shall 'have loved at all.' This is a tragic waste for all our people.

"We must hope that it is possible for there to be a rapture of souls, we must hope this. We must hope. But deep inside, we are all tinged by the atmosphere which prevails around this generation, and a voice tells us 'Man is alone.'" Peter Fillmore was tired now and he would sleep. He had lost a wife but gained realization of himself. He had lost much, but there was much he had won.

Pat's troubles would turn out the same - a winning after the losing.

CHARLOTTE, NORTH CAROLINA

When "Why Grievest Achilles?" was written in 1964, the writer, gone from Gulfport, MS, supposed the door to his life there was closed. He was busy in Charlotte opening ways into new vistas. Yet the deadening, overweening, familial construction built by the archetypes of his youth still held him. Now, for the first time, the writer would, for a long duration, be separated from his mother in fact, if perhaps not in spirit.

This is a "back to the womb " story, the tale of a good, striving man with a fatal flaw.

The players in this story should prance with new faces, new masks, perform all new numbers, wear this year's gowns, a new season in a new theater, but the outcropping protagonist is the same man we have before seen - the writer's alter ego. The revolutionary change offsetting has not changed anything but itself. The circle has come back to its beginning. A snake swallowing its tail.

Sorry, Thomas Wolfe, we do go home again. Rather, we never leave there. We frequent forever the old places, among the old things. The old places and things never leave us. We bear our own spiritually symbolic homes along with us like gingerly turtles move about carrying their covering shells. The same sense of place and self is in us wherever we go. You, Thomas Wolfe, should have known that!

"Why Grievest Achilles? " is by many definitions a tragedy. A man flawed into helplessness, caught in the web of Lady Spider and her to-be-eaten Consort. A man who must be led by the hand out of a steaming marshland of the mind. A man who will never be as happy as he once could have been. A man to pity in the classic sense.

WHY GRIEVEST ACHILLES?

When I knew Phillip Bright a few years ago, he was a policeman in Charlotte, North Carolina. He had been for two years, and he was proud of that.

He was a young man, living alone.

"What I need," he would tell me, "is someone who will believe in me. I need someone who will stay with me, through good times and bad, and be proud to have me, in spite of anything that comes. I try to believe in myself, but it would come easier if someone else would believe, too." He always spoke shyly, bashfully, as if he were ashamed of desiring the things he wanted. He blushed, even in these modern times when men don't blush. He was too modest, too self-effacing, and too lacking in assertiveness.

I heard him talk about getting himself a supportive-type mate but, sadly, I knew he didn't know how to begin to go about it. But, I'd always say, "I'm sure you will find what you need, one of these days." I even said this to him, much later, when I visited him outside Charlotte, where he was trying to get well.

It wasn't only the fact he had come to Charlotte from a poor and rural section of North Carolina which made him seem so unsure. Many young people

137

came from the old towns and the country places and fit right in the city. Phillip had been marred by his parents. From time to time he talked with me about them. The way they had raised him had made him different. "I know I'm not like other people," he'd say regretfully. He didn't know yet, being different can be either the greatest gift or the greatest curse a person can inherit. He hadn't begun to learn how to use the way he was.

He had accomplished much, studying and working until he had made a police officer of himself, but he always ran scared. There would have been less anxiety, less fear of failure, if he had someone to stand with him, encouraging him, telling him that he would be able to do it. He had heart, so he had not failed, although he was obliged entirely to fortify and strengthen himself.

He had always been alone. Maybe he never bonded with his parents. His father was an autocrat and his mother was his father's sycophant. Where Phillip grew up, a man's wife and his children were his chattels. He got no bolstering or buttressing from his parents. "I was a child who wondered if it would survive in the world," he once told me.

When he did something good, he was told he had merely lived up to normal expectations. No one praised him. Now, he told me, "If I decided to train myself to be a police officer, normal expectations demanded I successfully accomplish this, and normal expectations compel me to maintain my place. These are the things I worry about, living up to normal expectations." He was afraid he would one day feel what he had made for himself slip away.

"But, I am not unhappy," he said. I knew that he counted himself as being powerless. He was that scared little boy with a stem father and a mother too frightened to be his ally. He possessed only the small power that his employment gave him, the authority vested in him, his gun and his stick.

Because he was so much alone, he read a lot. He read about power and the powerful, specifically the Nazis of World War Two. He didn't want to be a Nazi. He had lots of books in a cabinet in his room, along with his bedding and towels. He had biographies of Goebbels, Goering, Hess, Himmler and of course, Hitler. He had read all these books at least twice. He opposed Naziism, as he opposed much of what his father had taught him. "My father always told me that Hitler was right." He looked guilty when he said, "I don't believe this any more." He never had believed it, but he was fascinated with Nazi Germany. He bought every book on the subject he could find. He didn't, however, keep memorabilia of the Nazis hanging and lying about as some people did. His reminiscences of the Nazis were all inside his head, where his father had put them. "I guess it's all right to say that, now, I don't believe what my father told me about Hitler and the Nazis," he explained. "But, I wouldn't say I didn't believe it then. Then, I was living under his roof."

He went to the library often. He read the German writers, trying to understand how there could have been, in the modern world, a phenomenon like Nazi Germany. It seemed impossible that there could have been a Third Reich, or that his father could have admired it. Somewhere there was a clue. There was evidence all along of the sleeping giant who would one day awaken in Germany and cause the Nazis. Phillip studied German history and literature looking for him.

He imagined himself trapped in the condition of man which Schiller described as being that of "a ball tossed betwixt the wind and the billows," In his childhood, he had been thrown out between the father and his mother who were constantly at war.

He felt himself a part of mankind since all men are uncertain and he was uncertain, but he knew he was different from all others because his life was precarious in its own way, so he was unique, and consequently mysterious. He was a mystery, as the Nazis had been a mystery, and his father had been a mystery. "I thought about these things, but I didn't let thinking about them consume my whole life," he said.

He had applied himself to his purpose, which had been to come to the city and find work and get ahead in the world, leave the past behind him. "I needed to work where I would have authority," he told me. " I respect authority. I want to be respected. I want a position where others will look up to me." He needed to work where there were guidelines, rigid rules, a structure which would protect him from making any mistakes. "I was never allowed to make my own decisions," he said.

Now, he was a policeman. He had done well. He had much. He could have more. The world saw, each day, that he had made for himself a measure of success.

Every day when he wore his pistol and stick he found that every door was open to him. "I like it when I talk with waitresses and drug store clerks and they laugh and joke with me. I feel good when men defer to me and young boys show they admire me and my uniform."

Yet, he came in for some criticism. Down at the station, his superiors looked at him as though they were somehow uneasy about him. They told him that he continued to take things personally. "As long as you do this, you are going to have trouble with your 'ob," they said. Small things which happened irritated him. Frequently, he found himself upset by trivial occurrences, when they took the form of slurs upon his uniform or his position. These things hurt him. He seemed to cry out, "Why are they saying these things to me?" or "Why are they doing these things to me'?" He couldn't think, "Some people simply don't like cops." Everything was personally directed at him.

He came to me, very upset, on one occasion. A car had passed him as he walked, and a boy had shouted with a hate-filled voice from the open window, "Fuck all cops.'" It was the raw anger, the scorn and the contempt in the tone which had lacerated Phillips' sensibilities. "It is so unfair to me," he told me. "I have nothing but the best of intentions toward every citizen whom I am here to protect and to serve. Yet, some of them will torment me." It shook his entire inner security when an individual didn't show him the approval he felt his position merited him. "My father couldn't stand it when people didn't agree with him; dishonored what he was or what he thought." I wondered if he was revealing to himself the ominous admission that he still bore with him some traits of his father which harried him.

There were other, more immediate things which bothered him. For two years he had been a scrupulous police officer, yet he still had a walking beat downtown, keeping an eye on such trouble spots as the bus station and bowling alley. This didn't seem right. This failure to advance was the most real of his worries. He thought again that his superiors held some foreboding about him.

"I don't believe my fellow officers like or respect me. The others laugh together and play together and go to each other's houses. They go out together in their boats on the lake. They go hunting. They help each other with their wives and children. I don't know why they don't like me. I am surely as dedicated a policeman as they."

He had passed all his examinations in the beginning with good scores and since then, he had studied hard. He was obedient, courteous, and hard working.

Contributing to his unhappiness, there was in the city one man whose simple presence there bothered Phillip more than all the other things put together. The man was a stranger to him. Whenever their paths crossed, which was almost every day, they were careful not to speak or give to each other any sign of recognition, but the stranger would look at Phillip with a deep, steady gaze which seemed not to see, and Phillip would feel ill at east and get angry. But, he never showed this. The stranger's face was always empty, but it was a poker player's blank countenance, concealing something, some knowledge that he had. "I can never guess what the stranger is thinking of me," he confided.

Phillip would stop for a cup of coffee in one of the cafes in the deteriorating portion of the town where his beat was, and there the stranger would be, and he would step Into a barber shop where it was air conditioned and the stranger would be there.

The stranger would always look at Phillip boldly and impersonally like he might look at a parking meter or a post, and sometimes Phillip seemed to sense that a faint grin of amusement was about to play about the stranger's lips, and always he had the feeling that the stranger had weighed him and he had somehow come up wanting.

"I believe he is some sort of bad person," Phillip told me. "He is, somehow, on a nefarious mission. Someday, he will tip his hand and do the overt thing and then when he's caught all his conceit and wry amusement and rejection will be gone." Phillip would be ready to catch him. Then, it would be the stranger who had lost his self-possession and Phillip who was in command.

I knew Phillip's landlady. That is how I came to know him. Our mutual friend was a motherly Irish woman named Mrs. O'Flynn. She related to Phillip as one who needs to mother relates to one who needs mothering. "He is, indeed, a nice young man," she would say, "who has worked and studied hard to make himself a policeman." She declared to her other boarders and to the neighbors that someday we would all be proud to have known him.

Mrs. O'Flynn told me his room was always neat as a pin. He had furnished it himself, every piece but one bought out of his wages. Everything had been purchased since he moved in her rooming house, except for a cabinet which he had brought with him when he came. This he had even in the furnished place where he had lived before.

This was a rather old cabinet, a very sturdy one, which was really a chest mounted on legs with a door on one side that folded down and made a writing board. The cavity of the chest was quite roomy and Phillip kept his extra bedding and off-season clothing packed away in it. His books were there. Little chains held fast the board which formed the door so that the writing surface was level. Sometimes, Phillip took out one or two of the books he kept there under the bedding, and he would study.

All of this was very marvelous to Mrs. O'Flynn. Once she asked him about the cabinet and he told her it had been his mother's.

One day, Phillip arrested a man at the bus station who was drunk and had broken a bottle on the men's room floor. The man wore a shirt with long sleeves, although it was summer. When the shirt was removed because the man had fallen in the glass and was bleeding, everyone saw that the man's arms and chest were covered with jailhouse tattoos.

"Jailhouse tattoos," Phillip explained to me, "are very different from regular tattoos, since they are clandestinely applied to men in prison by other inmates as a means of alleviating boredom." I gathered there might be, perhaps, other more exotic reasons for the presence of these decorations, which Phillip was not able to imagine. He seemed excited by the subject and continued to explain that men who have been in and out of jail over a number of years wear their jailhouse tattoos proudly, painting to them and accounting for them, saying, "I got this one in Parchman, I let a man put this one on in Angola. And, this one was done by an Italian in a county jail down in Georgia." Each tattoo had its own story.

"Who knows," Phillip wondered, "why anyone would do this. It is an odd ritual which occurs between incarcerated men. I feel it means something significant to both the participants, but the motivation is a mystery to me. One man permits himself to be adorned. The other engages in a labor of love. It is something which is socially acceptable under the conditions of prison living, but which none of us would practice in free society."

The man Phillip had arrested was tattooed extensively. The workmanship was poor. No one would have paid to see him in a side show.

"The ink that was used had all been blue, and the pictures were from Anglo-Saxon mythology; knights, and castles and serpents searching for symmetry, and Gothic recollections of the Crusades," Phillip said.

Phillip Bright felt very sorry for the man. "How many jails, how many chains, how many hours under the sun at hard labor must this man have known? And, for what crimes? Why had a totalitarian system continuously held possession of him?" He seemed to Phillip one of those confused, untrained, helpless individuals who is always blundering into trouble, getting locked up as a result of chance. This was not professional thinking. Phillip's face grew hot telling me about this.

Later, I learned that when Phillip got home that day, he stood for a long time and looked at his shirts which hung neatly in his closet. All of his shirts had long sleeves, even though Phillip's arms were white and clean and bore no tattoos or other disfigurations.

"The tattoos are imprinted on the soul," Phillip thought. "Pricked there with needles during the jail time of my childhood."

And, he could remember a voice saying, "Look at his spindly arms," and "He's got pipestem wrists," and "His shoulder blades stick out sharp as knife blades."

Phillip wanted to cry out, "It wasn't my fault. It was because we were half starving."

He heard the sneering voice say, "You can count every one of his ribs."

So, Phillip Bright wore only long-sleeved shirts until that day.

He looked at the carefully placed objects in his room.

"This is the home I have made for myself," he said.

He looked at the old cabinet up on its sturdy legs, and for the first time it occurred to him that it was large enough for him to get inside.

The next day, he candidly told me he was particularly annoyed when he saw the stranger going into a movie, as the man gave him a casual sweeping glance which seemed insolent and smirking, although his face was as blank as ever.

Phillip asked the girl who sold tickets who the stranger was, and she said she did not know, but that he attended the movies often as he worked somewhere at night and had a lot of free time in the daytime. This explained why Phillip was always encountering him.

In appearance, the stranger was what Phillip called - having read the phrase in one of his Nazi books - the pure Aryan type. He was a blond German. His eyes were blue, and the whites of his eyes were remarkably white, so that he had the appearance of a great sharpness of vision.

"He looks like he can see right through you."

He was above medium height and well-proportioned. His complexion was white and clear and there was no blemish upon him, or so it appeared to Phillip.

Phillip had never thought about it before, but the stranger always wore white clothes. Phillip became preoccupied with him, and he would tell me about it each time that their paths crossed.

After the day at the movie theater, the stranger did not come to Phillip's attention for three days but on the fourth day, Phillip came upon him in one of the drugstores. The stranger stepped back with seeming politeness to let Phillip pass, but it seemed to Phillip that the man made too great a show of avoiding any physical contact with Phillip, as if Phillip's very touch might draw off some of the stranger's elemental virtue.

Phillip was angered by the snub and arrived at home in a depressed state of mind. He busied himself with putting his room in order, and to make use of the time he took everything out of the cabinet and stored it on the shelves in his big closet.

He sat on his bed and thought about Jesus and how He had known when someone had touched the hem of His garment in a great crowd. It had taken something away from Him.

One day, the old man who sold papers fell down in front of the hotel door and struck his head against the pavement. He was a crippled man who dragged one foot and his toe had caught on the concrete and tripped him.

The old man was bleeding and his eyes were closed. Several people pretended not to notice and hurried away, while several others stopped and stood looking, not knowing what to do.

Phillip was about to act when the white-clad stranger hurried up, dropped to one knee, examined the old man briefly and, asking a bystander to help him, lifted the old man up and took him into the drugstore where he got a few necessary items and administered first aid.

"All this time," Phillip said, "I stood with my back against the hotel wall. I can still feel the pressure of the bricks. He made me incapable of doing anything."

He had never been secretive with me about anything before, but now he became guarded about what he would tell me. Much of what happened to him during the next weeks I would learn of later, during my many trips to see him.

That evening he felt very depressed taking his shower and when he came out, he moved without dressing to the old cabinet and crawled inside. He found that by lying on his side and pulling his knees under his chin, he could get completely inside and close the door. He felt warm and comfortable and safe.

An ancient odor remained in the wood of the cabinet, reminding him of his mother.

Phillip only stayed within the cabinet for a moment. He climbed right out and stood looking at himself in the mirror, thinking what a sad excuse for a man he was. He was nothing like the other policemen, who were proud of their bodies and proud to be what they were. His gun and stick lay on the bed. He went over and touched them. Stripped of these, he was not real. He did not exist at all.

He put on his clothes and went out to walk about in the night. The streets were his home, who had never had a home, who had been permitted to live in someone else's home, but never had a home, the streets were his home, and the warm, comforting womb of the darkness his safety.

After this, Phillip began to act in so bizarre a manner that he was alarmed for himself, but he felt powerless to help himself. He told me nothing. Something had begun which he couldn't stop.

Having once gotten inside the old cabinet, he seemed possessed by a passion to get in it over and over again. He would come home from work, take his shower, and curl up as he was, naked, in the cabinet, remaining there sometimes for as much as two hours. One night, he fell asleep there and slept the whole night through. The next day, his muscles were so sore he could hardly walk his beat.

Now, he began to neglect things. He would forego eating in order to hurry home and get in the cabinet. He went without a haircut. His shoes were not shined. He was called on the carpet at the station on account of his appearance.

He was reminded that he was due for a promotion before vacation time. He needed to be especially on his toes.

Phillip was saddened by the interview, but he only hurried home and got into the cabinet, not even taking time for his shower.

I did not see him.

After this he spent all his time, when he was not actually working, inside the cabinet. He had found that he could lie in there, on his side, indefinitely. He had lost a lot of weight. There was more room for him in the cabinet now.

"In the cabinet, the hours slid by, liquid and dark and hot, and my mind rested and rested and rested," he told me much later.

One day, when he had a day off, Mrs. O'Flynn came into the room while he was in the cabinet and never guessed he was in there. She went out again and Phillip felt a small thrill of triumph.

Just before his two week vacation began, he was called in and told that he had not merited the promotion which should have come to him after his time of service, and that, in addition, he was being suspended for two weeks right after his vacation ended. It was hoped that he would use these four weeks as a time to take stock, to energize himself, to study, to procure a new burst of enthusiasm for his job, to become the policeman he had once been, etc., etc., etc.

When Phillip left the station, the white-clad stranger was standing across the street in the sunshine. Perhaps, it was the sun which did it, but the stranger seemed surrounded by a glory. His blond hair shimmered. His strong regular face seemed cast from some precious metal. His body was supple, straight, strong and radiating - a "blond and naked angel." Who looked to Phillip like pictures he had seen of Harald Quandt, stepson of Goebbels, who, Aryan and proud, lost Mama and Papa, five sisters and a small brother, by his father's will, in a Gotterdammerung.

Today, the stranger bore in his eyes a look of deep sadness when he looked at Phillip.

"It is at an end," Phillip thought. "The finish grows near."

In the cabinet, Phillip found he need almost never get out. It was possible for him to spend a whole twenty four-hour period in there, perhaps coming out only twice for a few minutes. There he remained, taking no thought as to what he should eat, or what he should drink, or what he should wear. He asked himself in his father's estimate, was he not more than the larks?

Mrs. O'Flynn became worried. She talked to me about it. She was sure that he was up there, in his room. There were certain signs, but on Fridays when she went to change his linen, even so, his bed had not been slept in.

Finding this to be the case on the second Friday, she sat down to give the matter enough thought to try to solve the mystery. Phillip's pistol and stick were lying on the bed, and it was this that bothered her. Wherever he was, he had abandoned his pistol and stick.

That night, following a blind impulse, Mrs. O'Flynn went up to Phillip's room and performed a spur-of-the-moment, reasonless act which was to be very important in the life of Phillip Bright. She stooped down and swung open the door of the old cabinet.

She gasped for breath to tell me about it. How could her amazement be measured? Mere inches from the tip of her nose was the haggard, emaciated face of Phillip, his strained, starving limbs gaunt and white. He seemed to be dead, but his eyes were open and staring. They were huge, deep, black pools revealing what humanness he still owned, chiefly the possession of his own boundless misery. This look of unlimited suffering reminded Mrs. O'Flynn of only one thing, the expression in the sorrowing eyes of the statue of the crucified Christ at her church.

She realized that he was naked, so she quickly closed the door of the cabinet and stood erect.

"My!" she said.

"My"' they said all up and down the block. "One of Mrs. O'Flynn's roomers, the one who's a policeman has got naked and crawled into a cupboard." Men came to help and a group of ladies gathered downstairs. The police arrived and the ambulance. I was there.

"I thought he was such a good roomer," Mrs. O'Flynn exclaimed. "Oh, it's the damned, damned, damned luck of the Irish!" She recalled herself and crossed herself and did not say more. She stood back quietly, stoic and dignified.

Some of the men pulled Phillip out of the cabinet and stood him on his feet. In spite of his long inactivity and his fasting, he seemed to possess muscles of steel. He slashed bystanders with his long nails and tried to bite them.

"It's my right to stay in there," he cried.

The white-clad ambulance driver had come near to Phillip. His calm voice was heard above the turmoil.

"Handle him easy, men. Look at his spindly arms." And then, "He's got pipestem wrists," and then, "His shoulder blades stick out sharp as knife blades." And finally, "You can count every one of his ribs"

This voice arrested Phillip's attention. He stopped and looked at the speaker. Phillip recognized him because he was bright, enhaloed, the Young Siegfried setting out on his Rhine journey, a perfect example of the Aryan type. He was Sleeping Barbarossa now awakened, the father within, whose snoring and rumbling foreboding, but whose appearing at last, finally brought with it the total defeat, more desired than a partial victory, the Hero's sought for and embraced Gotterdammerung, the death-wish fulfilled. And, it is strange that anyone would feel this way, for did not the dead Achilles tell Odysseus that it is better to be alive?

"You must come with us."

It was he, the man in white unknown, and the man who had been with Phillip forever.   It was he, shining and white, coming in power and glory, pomp and circumstance, to claim Phillip. As it had ever been, his nobility, his strength, his calm assurance and his command were supreme.

"It's my father, come to draw me out of my safety," Phillip said. He let his head sink forward in submission, and they took him away.

CHARLOTTE, NORTH CAROLINA

"Willard" was written in Charlotte in 1964. The protagonist seeks to improve himself. His efforts lead him through perilous adventures and finally into a dangerous realm.

This writer was deserting the simplistic and paternalistic view of Negroes he evinced in "Jonah's Wife" and moving toward a perception of black people which was more in line with their actual abilities and attainments. He depicts the friend of Willard's mother and Willard as educated, knowledgeable, and self-confident, upwardly mobile Charlotte denizens.

The name "Willard" was taken from Willard Motley, author of "Knock on Any Door" and "Let No Man Write My Epitaph." Motley's literary milieu was the slums of Chicago, where he found many injustices practiced by society to the disadvantage of the poor. He spent his last twelve years in Mexico where he also did not find economic or social equity.

A compulsion to become a crusader will sometimes lead to broad travel and chancy exigencies. Willard would do what he had to do. What would happen to him? Something not good? Perhaps, it is better not to try to be a Messiah.

WILLARD

Vesta Portell had always thought deeply about things, and she had worked out exactly her own idea of the place in the world where she stood. She was one of those Colored people who had made something worthwhile of herself, and she was proud of her accomplishment and rather confident of herself and her future and the future of her children. It had been hard, but she had made progress.

Vesta's husband had a very good job at the city's very best private club, and they lived comfortably. She had a good start in life, as her mother had been a school teacher, and she had educated herself and learned all that she could by trying always to associate with the very best people she could come into contact with. She realized that economic plenty was not the final goal in life, but that a person must also acquire culture and social position.

The problem of acquiring and keeping social position bothered her a little. In the Negro community she had reached the highest pinnacle and this gratified her, but she knew of course there were doors which would be closed to her forever, and this seemed unjust and was a sorrow to her. She strove always to do the correct thing, and everything which she ever did in the social realm was perfectly right. Much of her time and energy went toward the accomplishment of this end.

Only once in a while did she relax her grip on her social conduct and do something wrong, and when she did she would be very much disappointed in herself and would say to herself, "Why ANY colored girl might have done THAT!" and she would usually have to lie down in her upstairs sitting room with a cold towel on her head and drink a little toddy to cool her dismay.

Vesta was perfectly willing to work. Her best friend worked for a Greek who owned a catering service, and Vesta was called upon quite often to serve at parties which different clubs and individuals would have: weddings, merchandise shows, and school functions. She was very much in demand because her deportment was always exemplary and her appearance was so right. She was a beautiful, stately, strong-featured dark woman.

Vesta had a girl working in her kitchen who was a slut, as the British would use the word, and this morning Vesta had become so out of patience with her that she had abused the girl vocally in a common and coarse barrage of language which was entirely out of character with her and now she was so appalled in the face of the shattered image of the idealized self she had built up that she was lying down with the curtains drawn and a pitcher of toddy on the small marble-topped table beside her couch.

Just the other day, Vesta had been reading a book which dealt with the history of religion and she had felt her attention arrested by a ritual in which the king of Babylon had been forced to take part, in the shrine of Marduk. The king was made to posture himself upon his knees and to make a confession in which he stated, "I have not rained blows on the cheek of a subordinate; I have not humiliated them."

Vesta had thought at the time of reading that it was amazing to realize that one of the most important tenets of a religion considered pagan, which held sway five hundred years before the birth of her Presbyterian Christ and was based upon even earlier religious, was a check by the priesthood upon the power of the king, limiting his right to treat his underlings inhumanely even to the degree of mental cruelty. Now, Vesta had fallen into a grave fault and had said cutting and hateful, humiliating things to her slattern of a kitchen girl and she was totally disillusioned with herself. For all the talk of "the American sense of fair-play" somehow inherited from the Anglo-Saxon culture and assimilated into the consciousness of the upper-class Negro by a sort of osmosis, Vesta was not able to handle power any better after 2400 years of progress than the barbaric kings who went to the observance of the Annual Festival in Mesopotamia each year way back then.

Well, the "people of Babylon" were called "dependents of Bel" which meant that Bel would take care of them, and no doubt the kitchen girl was a dependent of the Presbyterian God and He would take care of her, and He would show Vesta how to make it up to the kitchen girl for her injustice.

Vesta's telephone rang loudly and insistently. She was so startled that she threw the wet towel to the carpet and leaped up all at once. She answered the phone and it was Mr. Tauropolus (his ancestors had been butchers) and he wanted her to attend a small private dinner for him that night.

A Passover Seder was to be held at a Jewish home and the Jewish family wished a refined and educated colored woman.

Vesta could show a bit of temperament like a Great Star who did not deign to perform, and this was an occasion where she would do so. She told Mr. Tauropolus that she was not feeling well and could not leave the house. Mr. Tauropolus was insistent. He did not want to disappoint these Jewish people who were actually his personal friends. Vesta posed herself in a stance like a mule, which digs its feet into the warm earth and arches its mane in stubbornness and she told Mr. Tauropolus that she could not arrange for a sitter for her children in time, which was not true, and that her husband would be out that evening, which was not true, but the lies would not hurt anything.

Mr. Tauropolus was getting angry and excited. He asked her about various of her friends who sometimes went out to dinner parties and the like, and she told him she would call around and try to find him someone.

Suddenly a thought came to her. One of her friends from church had a nineteen year old son who had finished high school the year before. He had been on the football I team and he made a very good appearance. He was gentle and soft spoken and refined and cultivated, and would blend into a prosperous and festive background quite nicely. He was everyone's darling, and right now he happened to be available. He had not been working since school was out. His family was making arrangements to get him into a college as soon as they might, but in the meantime he was loafing about and putting on unsightly weight.

He was not the sort of boy one would send into the turpentine camps, and yet so many occupations were barred to him. What was one to do? Mostly, he ran errands and his family prayed that his idleness would not get him into trouble. Doubtless their prayers had been answered as he had survived these many months with only some speeding tickets to show.

"What about a young boy?" Vesta asked.

Mr. Tauropolus was not sure.

But, Vesta became very insistent. She persuaded Mr. Tauropolus that Willard (the boy was named for Willard Motley) was his ideal solution to the problem. She would see that he was dressed in a tuxedo and present at the appointed time at the home of Mr. and Mrs. Kaufmann.

Well, after all, Mr. Tauropolus had other matters of business to think about. He could not spend all day worrying about this one thing. He consented for Willard to go.

The home of the Kaufmann's was perfectly appointed, and a quietly festive atmosphere reigned there that night.

Willard was immaculate in a freshly pressed tuxedo, and he moved with lithe grace about the kitchen and dining room, as much at home as though he had been there forever. He had gotten his early training working for an undertaker.

He held himself rather aloof from the other help and took every opportunity to observe the strange ritual which the Kaufmanns and their guests took part in this night.

Willard was more serious-minded than anyone supposed. He delighted in strange and interesting experiences and he fully enjoyed this one in which he now took part.

He spent a lot of his time in thought and usually his thoughts hovered upon one subject and that one was that he was not truly and genuinely free, nor were any of his people. If he were totally free, why was he not working toward becoming a teller at one of the banks even now, like many other qualified high school graduates, with a future membership in the country club in view?

Willard had heard the cheers of the people when he performed on the athletic field the seasons before, and he enjoyed the adulation. He had in mind that he could be something special, and he did not intend to end his life as a delivery boy on some small truck for some second-rate business.

No matter what.

No one seemed to be noticing him after a while, so he went and stood in the doorway and listened to the phrases and prayers which continued at the table.

Suddenly, he heard the host make a thrilling pronouncement.

"Now we are here, but next year may we be in the land of Israel! Now we are slaves, but next year may we be free men!"

Willard was so amazed that he went back into the kitchen and sat down on a chair and he began to repeat the words over and over so that he would not forget them.

"Now we are here, but next year may we be in the land of Israel! Now we are slaves, but next year may we be free men!"

Willard might have forgotten about the Passover Seder, but it seemed to be going to be the last good and pleasant thing which was to happen to him. After this, he did not get anywhere. He took a job at a service station but he only kept that a short time. He was too good for the job. He recalled the Seder as a marvelous dream sandwiched between acrid stretches of desert. His life was pointless. He would seethe with anger and unhappiness as he drove the family car to the drug store to pick up a package for his mother.

One time he went over to Vesta Portell's house to see if she couldn't arrange other jobs for him, and she had said she would try, but Vesta's husband was gambling these days and she was having her own troubles. Nothing came of it.

Finally one day, Willard left home and went to New York.

Right away, everything began to be better. He met some young men who knew their way around and they got him a job on Long Island as a chauffeur for a gentleman. This man saw right away that Willard was a superior type fellow and enrolled him in a school that was nearby and took a very paternal interest in him, but Willard almost never saw any money of his own. He had a lovely room with a fireplace and a private bath and he ate his meals in the kitchen where anything would be prepared which he chose, but his pay was very small. He felt many times that he would be better off to receive more cash and less advantages. It would have been kinder of his employer to pay him enough for him to have bought himself one suit of clothing, rather than have his employer take him to the store and buy him five outfits, this seemed like patronage and made him feel something less than a man.

He would have been very much interested in the school he was attending had it not been his employer's idea. He did not give it his best efforts, however, as he was annoyed that his benefactor had chosen it for him, and when his employer and family went away on an ocean voyage leaving Willard at home, he quit working at his studies at all and just dawdled his time away and became a drinker of beer and a watcher of television, his hours spend in idleness.

When his employer came back and received a report of his conduct while he had been away, he was very disappointed and took Willard into a room alone and told him of his displeasure. Willard was angry and said that he would quit the job and leave the house, and the employer was grieved and said that he might go. He said that he loved Willard as a son and meant only what was best for him, and Willard had not played square, but there was nothing that he could do but quote Mazzini who had said, "It is a serious fault to receive money from others and make a bad use of it; it is a more serious fault to hesitate before a financial sacrifice when there is a probability that it will help a good cause."

Willard went away then and his employer's wife cried at the door when he went.

Next, Willard fell in with some jazz musicians in the city and they got him a job as bartender in a dreadfully sordid place. Willard did not like this very well, but evil companions taught him first one hustle and then another so that he was able to save some money, as he had no costly habit of his own to support. For the first time in his whole life he began to feel like a man. Just having his own money in his pocket did this for him.

One day, some of his musician friends said that they were going to Paris and they began to tell him that the Negro got very good treatment over there, so Willard decided to go to Paris with them. He quit his job and drew his money out of the bank, and the arrangements were made so that they all sailed for Europe.

They did not find exactly the Paris which Henry Miller left behind when he returned to this country, but what they did find was good enough.

But, Paris was soon to divide the little group. Each of the Americans was to find a niche for himself in the pied underworld of the French capitol, and they began to see less and less of each other.

Willard was a great favorite among the habitues of the fleshpots and he began for the first time to live a life of real debauchery. But, he was young and he had not experienced living before, so who could blame him for being caught up and carried away among all the temptations.

Finally, a perfectly dreadful woman who had an immense amount of money asked him to move in to her home, and it must be confessed that the offer turned Willard's head so that he went to live with her.

After this, he had his closet filled with the best clothing which money can buy and his own automobile. The woman did not bother him much of the time, and he spent his days strolling about the grounds of her estate, and in a wood which was across the way. The woman had a very large library, but only a few of her books were in English.

She made Willard go to the gymnasium and she watched his diet, and indeed took the same precautions with him that she took with her horses, which she had a large number of. She had doctors and dentists come in to look at him whenever she suspected the least thing might be the matter.

It was all nice enough but aimless, and such arrangements do not bear the same elated happiness after a time which they hold in the beginning, but they do not collapse all at once, as a general thing.

Jeanne Lerner became bored after a time and wanted to leave her Paris estate, so she got Willard ready and they traveled to Rome. Willard had been fond of looking at the Cathedral of Notre Dame in Paris, but he had to admit that it was as nothing when compared to the things he saw in Rome. Saint Peter's in Rome was the most perfect thing which Willard had seen. Something of the sanctity of the atmosphere reached him, and he began to examine his status in life. He did not like the picture which was presented to him as he made this examination, but he thought that he had little chance of starting out anew for he did not know how to help himself. He did not even know how he might get back to the United States should he be left to his own resources.

Jeanne bought him some cuff links made of Roman coins which were nothing exceptional, but he thought they were, and he tried to forget about his position.

More and more, Jeanne was displaying Willard to her friends like any of the works of art which abounded in her apartment, and Willard was tired of being stared at and having people say how beautiful he was.

At last, Jeanne crossed back from Rome into France and at a port on the Riviera, she took Willard and a small party of people and embarked on her yacht on the Mediterranean -

As soon as she was at sea, she was like a madwoman. She pushed her way around the island of Sicily and around the heel of the boot of Italy and skirted the Grecian Islands. She sighted the Island of' Byblus off the coast of Syria where the coffer of Osirus had floated, but she did not pause at this Mecca of the Phoenicians. She drank heavily and was rude to her guests and to Willard and she spent long hours tanning her wrinkling dry skin in the strengthening sun. Willard wished he could have been back in the United States, even in the rural south.

One night he was sitting alone on the deck when he heard Jeanne come outside with a middle-aged man called the Jing. The Jing had long flowing hair and wore Japanese kimonos and strap sandals. He plucked his eyebrows and he waved his hands in elaborate gestures when he talked. Willard could see them standing in the moonlight.

"Wherever did you get Willard?" the Jing asked Jeanne.

"He showed up in Paris," she said. "He came over with some friends from New York. His money was running out."

"He is one gorgeous nigger," the Jing said breathlessly.

"I'm getting tired of him," Jeanne said indifferently. "If you can make headway with him, I won't be mad. You may have him if you can get him."

Willard's head dropped forward and he crept back to the very stern of the boat and sat on the deck with his head resting on his knees. He looked out over the waters of the Mediterranean.

"I have come into a terrible bondage," he said.

Later that night, Jeanne led her friends ill a party of drunken reveling. Willard had slipped away from them and was sleeping in his compartment. At the height of the orgy, a storm arose and the yacht began to be tossed about as though it would break to pieces. The drunken revelers did not become frightened. They laughed and one of them wrapped a silken tablecloth about her head and taking up a deck of cards, said that she would reveal upon whose head it was this storm was sent by Providence.

With great ceremony she picked a card, and it was the King of Spades.

Screaming and laughing and pushing each other out of the way, the group ran down the hatch and dragged Willard from the bunk, they stripped off his shorts and, lifting him up naked, they tossed him over the rail of the yacht into the tossing sea.

The Jing stood on the foredeck with his hair and kimono blowing wildly in the wind and his arms outstretched and shouted, "What luxury in being able to throw something that choice away! What utter luxury!"

In a few minutes, he began to cry.

Fortunately, they were near land and both the wind and the current were moving landward. Willard came ashore, but it SEEMED that he was in the deep for three days.

Now, he stood naked on the sand. It was morning. There on the side of the mountain, were not those the marks of the chains of Andromeda? Andromeda left for the monster to get? Well, Andromeda had escaped her monster with the help of Perseus, and Willard was now free from his. From all the monsters on the yacht.

Andromeda who was the daughter of Cepheus, Ethiopian king of Joppa, was she not now in the heavens adorning space?

Willard had broken free.

He realized that he was, for the first time in his life, moreso than most men can ever be, entirely free. Naked and standing on the sand he could choose his fate. There was nothing binding upon him. He could go in any direction, turn his hand to anything, be or have or know anything.

"Look, I have come through!"

He ran and leaped in his freedom, climbing the rocks like a madman, shouting and singing. This was a freedom to become drunk on.

But, he ran into the shadow of Andromeda's mountain.

He sat down.

With the freedom had come an awful responsibility. He could no longer say, "I am powerless to choose. I cannot help myself. My hands are tied. I am not my own man."

Whatever step, no matter how small or insignificant which he might take would be totally his own choice, and the result of that step taken would be his own self-earned punishment or reward.

Willard trembled and the sweat ran down his ribs and he cupped his shinbones in his hands and squeezed his eyes tightly closed.

"Oh God!" he said. "It's too great a burden to place on a man."

"Why are you resentful, and why has your countenance fallen? Surely, if you act right, it should mean exaltation. But if you do not, sin is the demon at the door, whose urge is toward you; yet, you can be his master."

He had to move. He could not sit still upon the earth.

He found a shepherd who took him in and gave him an old robe and fed him, and he worked for this man for three weeks because he felt he must repay him. They did not talk because they could not speak each other's language, but sometimes they would look into each other's eyes and that which was between them was known.

Willard made the man understand that he must go, and the man gave him food to carry, and Willard took a strong staff and in the ragged robe and sandals, he began to walk across Israel toward Jerusalem.

Once he came to a farm and two sisters stood at the fence and they called to him and told him that their brother lay ill at the house and their crop was not planted and they would make no yield that year unless the crop was put in. Willard stopped to work with them and stayed for a fortnight and he was happy there as the two sisters and the brother spoke a little English, having known many Americans. They gave him a huge supper on the night before his departure from them, and the man claimed that he had been the same as the dead man when Willard came, but now he was alive again and happy in the hope of a harvest because of Wlllard's kindness. Many of the neighbors came in for the supper, and they paid Willard all honor which could be paid.

This was on the sixth day before the Passover.

Willard found a mule colt that was lost and he named her Razzala and took her with him toward Jerusalem.

"Last year we were there, but this year we are in the land of Israel! Then we were slaves, but this year we are free men!"

Jesus had said, "You shall know this truth and the truth will make you free." He had known the truth first, and he had been free, and being free he had chosen to enter Jerusalem and to face Pilate. To become free is to begin to be crucified.

Willard climbed onto Razzala's back and rode down toward Jerusalem.

"I am the Omega and the Alpha," he said. "The Omega - the end of the old enslaved Willard. The Alpha - the beginning of the new Willard which shall be. A prophet is an end of the old dispensation and a beginning of the new. The ending comes before the beginning. He is the Omega and the Alpha. He is not the Alpha and the Omega. That is something else. That is the One Who was in the beginning, and shall be in the end. A mere prophet is different."

Willard, in his beard and with the staff and the old robe, on the back of Razzala, made an impressive sight, and the people came out and lay the fronds of palms in his path, and now and then he could stop and preach to them about things he could remember from his Presbyterian upbringing and about things which life had taught him. The people stared at him and the ones who could understand English listened.

Some of the people heard and thought this must be some sort of publicity stunt, perhaps plugging some epic religious movie, but there were many who went away and believed.

And already, anger began to be stirred up against him.

CHARLOTTE, NORTH CAROLINA

"Declining the Tutor" was written at Charlotte in 1964. Visionary. This story teaches that love of learning in an applicant is a better indication that he will be a good tutor than are many other obvious advantages.

For a long time, this writer had placed a high value upon that quality which is now called "soul." Soul is not conventional wisdom, but something deeper It is a wisdom developed in jungle places of America (urban streets, remote farms) by persons who understand the jungle, including its simple natural laws and the penalties for the breaking of these. They understand play, mating, parenting young, and surviving against odds. Soul is not a road map telling where to go or what to do, but is a guide to how to adapt and cope while going and doing.

Since 1957, when the writer read "The White Negro" by Norman Mailer, he had sought out in story and in life examples of the American existentialist, the phenomenon come to be called "the Beatnik."

Beatniks come in all guises..

In this story, a capitalist - a man of wealth - an educated man - discerns in a lad a fervor for learning and the stirrings of a passionate zeal for teaching. This youth embodies the ideal found in the Chinese proverb: "To be fond of learning is to be at the gate of knowledge. "

DECLINING THE TUTOR

Now that middle age and his most successful years had come, Joel Burnhardt was usually able to arrange his days so that he could slip away from the mill for a while in the afternoon and so have a little quiet time to himself. Today, however, he had to remain at his office. Today, he must decline the tutor.

The mill whistle had blown, calling the men back from their lunch, and now the millyard was cleared and all the men were inside the plant. The automobiles, including Joel's black Lincoln, stood in the bright sunlight and all was still. No breeze tossed any paper about in the yard, nor was there any probing dog within the gates. Joel required order and system and method in everything.

He looked very much like a German shopkeeper now, and he fidgeted about drying his moist fingertips on his trousers. His eyes were very blue behind his gold-rimmed glasses, and his hair was grey. His eyes were ever ready to crinkle into good-natured wrinkles at the corners as his face lit up in a smile. When he was about his business, dealing with his men, he walked about, stubby and compact, looking very much like a starched and polished Heidelberg schoolmaster.

He looked out of his window and saw Emmett Ewell asking admission at the gate. Emmett was driving his powerful European sportscar which Joel kept forgetting the name of, and he would be impeccably groomed, and his manner would be perfect.

Joel looked at his gold pocket watch. Emmett was exactly on time. He would arrive in Joel's office at precisely the moment for which his interview had been set.

Joel was almost weak enough to wish that he were tramping somewhere in the Woods instead of seeing to this hiring of a tutor for his son, but the thought passed. If one were a man, one had to do unpleasant things upon occasion.

In 1944, when there was tragedy in the World due to the war, the Burnhardts had been made happy by the birth of a son and now, Winston Bumhardt, was nineteen years old.

In the philosophy of Joel Burnhardt and his wife: from those to whom much had been given, much was required. The Burnhardts saw for their son an education at the state university with, perhaps, graduate work abroad, and a life lived for the benefit of humanity. The obligation of man lay in unending self-improvement, and the developed self used for the benefit of the world. There was no place in the scheme of things for those who were out of step with mankind, but each must be part of that procession which moved through the world steadily onward and upward toward the fulfilling of man's God-granted destiny.

Now, Winston Burnhardt imagined himself to be in love with a girl of seventeen who had a background very different from his own, and he seemed now to be opposed to all the alms and purposes his father and mother had told him he must strive toward.

Ever a man of decision and action, Joel Burnhardt had talked with his wife about the problem and they had decided to hire a proper tutor for Winston and to send the two young men to Europe for an entire summer of study in preparation for Winston's entrance into college.

Amid the sights and sounds of Rome and Paris and Berlin, Winston would forget all about his ill-timed and ill-advised high school romance. This unpleasant impediment which lay in the way of the fulfillment of Joel's plan would disappear.

Joel was aware of the tremendous importance which was attached to his finding the proper tutor, and he knew that a man can never be absolutely certain he is making the right decision in any matter of this nature, but he was convinced that Emmett Ewell was not the proper tutor.

Emmett Ewell had been sent to Joel with excellent recommendations. At his high school, he had held top scholastic ratings and had been active on the debating team and in dramatics and had won a medal on the track, although this latter indicated that he was too individualistic for group sport, but had chosen to pit himself as an individual against other individuals. The fact that he was a lone wolf did not detract from his ability to tutor, it was felt, as no group cooperation would be required in this profession.

His university record was almost perfect, and he belonged to the same Protestant denomination as the Burnhardts, and had always taken an active part in the affairs of his church.

No whisper about his personal life had ever been heard.

Now, he came into Joel's office and took the offered chair, a perfect young man without spot or blemish.

Emmett was completely self-assured, completely self-confident, anxious to be about the job which he felt sure was about to be given him. He was already thinking of days spent above the canals of Venice, and nights filled with great music of Strasbourg.

"I am a little humble before all your accomplishments," Joel began slowly. His color had heightened a degree, and his shoulders stooped a little. "I have decided against giving you the chance to tutor my son. I am engaging Harry Meyers for the place."

For an instant, shock and unbelief flickered across Emmett's face, but he mastered everything that rose up to possess him and managed a polite smile.

"Oh," he said. "I had hoped you would choose me. I wanted the position."

"I wanted to call you in for a private talk," Joel said, "rather than just phoning you with my decision. I wanted to tell you why I have decided to decline your offer to serve the Burnhardt family in this way. I felt it was right to do this."

"I hope that you will tell me," Emmett said. A little of his sureness and strength seemed to slip away from him.

"I don't know if you approve of what I am trying to do for my son," Joel said. "Maybe you think that I'm wrong to speed him from the country to get him away from a little girl who has not enough to give him, and who cannot accept all he has to give. I hope that you don't think that Mrs. Burnhardt and I are parents who will give life and then try to deprive the one life is given of the privilege of living it. We don't think that we are like that, but we take parenthood very seriously, and feel that we are older and more educated, and wiser and more understanding, and more experienced in life than our son is, and for as long as it is possible, we will prevent him from making any serious mistakes by whatever means we may. We only thank God that we have the means to do this for him this summer."

"I feel that you're exactly right," Emmett said.

"Harry Meyers didn't go to as fine a school as you," Joel continued. "He never went out for track, and he wasn't on any debating teams, and he wasn't in plays. Many of the courses of instruction which you've had he never had. But, I talked with him, and he is the one to tutor my son."

Joel could hear the machinery of the mill. If one individual machine had been running badly, he would have been aware of it. He was always subconsciously aware of the state of the mill. He knew the rhythm of it like he knew his own heartbeat.

All was well.

"What was it that impressed you?" Emmett asked. He was still trying not to show his hurt and disappointment. He was trying to appear objective, to play the stoic.

"We talked." Joel said, and his voice took on the tone of one recalling a profoundly inspiring event. "We talked, and the great men of history and of literature and the arts were mentioned, and when Harry spoke of them, he held their names in his mouth with a quality like reverence, and he spoke of them as though he were speaking of gods, of titans, of giants like those who once dwelt in the Earth. He loves them all: Homer and Socrates, Aristotle and the tragedians of Greece, Alexander and Julius Caesar and Seneca, and the great Italians of the Renaissance, and the Elizabethans. He talked of Melville and Hawthorne and Poe like they were some sort of literary saints. He is hungry to know about them all, and to help others to know about them. Intellectuality with him is completely genuine and sincere because with him learning is a passion. It consumes with heat and fills to bursting. He seems to throb and pulse and his whole being to be taut with the energy of the feeling he has about knowledge and understanding."

Joel paused for a moment, but Emmett did not say anything.

"I took him into my little library there," Joel said, pointing to a door which was in one wall of his office. "You saw it, too. I took him in there, and he just stood still for a minute or two and looked at the books, and then he began to pick them up and lay them down, one by one. He picked up A Tale of Two Cities like it was an old friend, and he touched the binding of Jane Eyre with a casual forefinger in simple recognition. He lifted them at random and put them back down, and some of them he straightened in their places on the shelves like a tender shepherd minding his sheep, and for a few minutes, I think he forgot that I was there. He did not say anything. He never said a word while we were in the library. He just handled the books and looked at them."

"You have a good selection in there," Emmett said.

"A man who loves learning and loves books in the way that Harry Meyers does could not do less than communicate a part of this feeling to anyone he came into prolonged contact with. It must be contagious. He will give this to my son. If my son spends three months with him in Europe, he will come back to this state and enter the university with a new vision, a new will to learn, a new purpose and desire, and hope, something of Harry Meyers' passion. I will stake everything that has become part of me and made me a success that he will."

Emmett Ewell was a paler, more ill-composed young man. He sensed that he had lost something. He had lost the position, surely, but he had lost a grip on something within himself. Suddenly lie was insecure and frightened, and very much alone.

"Perhaps so," he said, because he didn't know what else to say.

"The Burnhardts have always been churchgoing people," Joel said. "We have always been fond of quoting from the Bible. I recall a verse that strikes me as applying to the general subject of education, but I'm not sure I recall it exactly. Perhaps you remember it. 'He who follows after words only shall have nothing, but he who possesses a mind loves his own soul, and he that keeps prudence shall find good things.' Do you remember the exact wording?"

Emmett shook his head and looked bewildered.

"No," he said. "No, I'm sorry. I'm not familiar with it."

GASTONIA, NORTH CAROLINA

The poem, "The Great House" was written when the writer was working in Gastonia, creating the city directory for a company which was then known as "The French Foreign Legion of American Business." This was in 1965, shortly after Rev. Martin Luther King, Jr's march on Selma.

This writer's basic objection to the existing structure of American society lay in its economic divides, which were so cruelly present - evident to anyone who cared to see. Like his father before him, he saw greater injustice in matters of the purse than in affairs related to one's innate sexual election or the inevitability of one's skin color.

Later, in Georgetown, South, Carolina, "The Great House " was read with approval by the writer's fellow union members. It revealed something about the writer which led workers to accept him as being one like themselves. In Georgetown, he would be called a "good old boy" by whites, and a "friend" by black people.

THE GREAT HOUSE

The house of John White stood tall, clean and wide.
It had been built of red brick and heart pine.
The windows had come from far 'cross the tide.
In the county, there was nothing so fine.
The grounds were quite neat,
All the way to the street,
And the hedges were trimmed with great pride,
And each shaded bower
Each shy blushing flower
Perfected family nobility's shrine.

Everything that was here was completely right,
Everything which was built or was planted.
To do this had been for Boss John quite a fight,
But his children took it all quite for granted.
And the people passed by
Never wondering why
Boss John should have this show of his might.
For they never once thought
How this house had been bought
By the sweat poor people had granted.

Yes, the sweat of the poor
Had been wrung from them more..
Thus saith Pharoah, "I will not give you straw,"
But the bricks were still made

159

And the pyramids laid
Along the Nile to stand evermore.

Oh, what has become of the once straight back
Of the tenant farmer they call "Old Jack" ?
All that manly strength which once stood so tall
Is lost forever in the strong west wall.
And the brightness of eye of a maid named Jill?
She works as a spinner in Boss John's mill
Why is her eye not so bright as before?
The gleam's in the knocker on the big front door.
Boss John's Lady examined each brick
Made sure it was perfect, uncracked and thick,
Gave it to a nigger who put it in place -
He never dared once look her full in the face.

But he built her house,
This poor human louse,
All the work he never did mind it.
She sat there in her chair,
In her garden so fair -
"Go ye, get you straw where you find it."

And the people who worked on John White's farm,
And kept his cattle and minded his sheep
And worked in his mills, and bore all his arms,
And did without food and did without sleep,
Never questioned why, for a minute
For them there was almost nothing in it.
All the work and all the pain
Was theirs, and all the gain
Was Massa John's who owned a great house
They had built for him.

Sometimes in their houses was an empty bed;
Some little baby of theirs was dead.
But because of the needs of which it was deprived
Some child in the manor house had survived.
So another great room up there was filled
And this is what Massa John would have willed.
Up there there lived one White more
To grind down the faces of the poor
Who tolled back from the burying that way
And passing the great house hadn't wit to say:
Why have we worked?
And why have we sweat?

What have we to show?
What did we get?
All we can show is what we have lost.
We, we built Massa's great house at awful cost.

But they plodded along and questioned not
The hardness of their empty lot,
Every man a worker and breeder,
Until some day a thinking leader
Would come and bring a whole new day,
"Men, the Red Sea is over this way."
Go up and say to Old Pharoah
"God said, 'Let My people go!'"
So Pharoah got into a state,
His great great house wouldn't be so great,
Without the working multitudes.
And Pharoah said, "Who is the Lord that I
Should obey His voice, and let Israel go?
I know not the Lord, and neither will I
Let Israel go."

But death came for Pharoah. He had been Moses' old Massa.
And the Nile and the Pyramids belong to Nasser.
And the John Whites too, have known their day.
The world they built has crumbled away.
Their great houses stand side by side
With the bold pyramids which ever abide,
Symbols of man's love of power and man's stubborn pride,
And monuments forever more
To the patient suffering of God's Holy Poor.

AUGUSTA, GEORGIA

"Subtle Ways I Keep" was written at Augusta in 1965. Idyllic! Rustic simplicity in Japan.

This story demonstrated the good results which may come unawares from the open practice of righteous living.

This writer, once again, finds goodness - excellence - in nonwhite people.

SUBTLE WAYS I KEEP

When all the children of Hajime and Himiko were grown up, the two old people complied with what had been for them a prompting of many years duration, going to live in a small house upon what, in Japan, would pass for a mountain.

By now their bones were as brittle as ancient porcelain, and their skins had begun to look like faded and wrinkled parchment, so they continually cautioned one another as they walked about.

"Hajime, please to be careful as you ascend," or "Himiko, please to be careful as you descend," or whatever was fitting for whichever to say as the other went up or down on the mountain as the case might be.

Much of the time, they knew great peace and contentment sitting together through the long afternoons in their sweet-scented garden.

A careless bumblebee in full flight would heedlessly bump the stem of a rich, red poppy so that the mature petals of the flower would scatter to the earth. There would come into fleeting existence a sigh in the garden, and the old couple would be aware of it and they would sigh too, but they did not feel sadness.

Whenever a flower died, the couple would feel the sigh which was given in parting, so great was the harmony between Hajime and Himiko and the garden.

The spring where Hajime and Himiko went for water was outside their garden, and higher up on the side of the mountain. In the late afternoon, Himiko would go up to the spring for fresh water, and returning, she would make tea for Hajime.

For a husband and wife to drink tea together is most commonplace. But Himiko, in the Japanese way, would be most extravagant with the care with which she prepared the tea for Hajime. She used her most appropriate bowls, making them conform to the surroundings whether they were inside or out. She would set them down in the most artful way so that everything was in proportion. She had many pots and Hajime might never guess which she would use on any given day. He always had to agree that the one she had chosen was exactly right for that particular day and place.

Close to the tea things would rest several of their familiar treasures; a carved box of teakwood, an elaborate fan, flowers cut and brought in from the woods in Himiko's best basket.

Himiko would see to it that the tea was prepared, served and drunk in the most graceful manner possible, so that each day after the tea, Hajime would say to her,

"Today, in preparing and serving the tea, you have created a poem."

They would sit in the twilight and feel a great gratitude for the privilege of living their lives graciously and with dignity, for what more could be desired on earth?

Hajime and Himiko knew complete freedom, and freedom by its Oriental definition is simply the right of self-motivation.

One day Himiko had walked in the wood, and upon nearing the humble house which was her dwelling, she felt a catch in her side, and then a burning under her ribs, and she knew that she was going to die. She seated herself on the grass in a shady place, and removing her sash, bound it about her knees because she feared that if her agonies grew worse, she might thrash about and become disheveled so as to present an improper appearance to whomever might find her.

Hajime felt a great sigh go up from the trees of the woodland, and felt a quiver of pity in the flowers of the garden, and heard the whispered sympathy of the grasses, so he set out to look for Himiko.

He found her resting on her side, composed and at peace, her basket of flowers beside her.

How transient indeed is life.

Hajime would not be consoled. He was very angry with God for having taken away the delicate and beautiful Himiko. When he fixed his tea now, he made it in their ugliest pot, and drank it from a cracked cup, and after drinking he would belch loudly.

He did not tend the garden and, one by one, the flowers died. First the annuals, then the perennials, and finally, the large flowering shrubs began to wither.

But, man cannot always mourn.

When spring came, Hajime began to feel a new feeling. He began to seek a reason for the tragedy which had overtaken him. Undoubtedly, Himiko had been taken away and he had been permitted to live on alone because he was going to have the opportunity, even yet, to be of service to someone on Earth. Otherwise, the wise and orderly God would have done the more seemly and reasonable thing - taken Hajime and Himiko to Heaven together.

As soon as Hajime became convinced that he was, after all, to be useful once more in his life, that he was alive for some purpose, he became filled with gratitude so that he once again began to observe the pleasant ceremonies of living, and he began to repair the garden.

Several years went by and the garden became, once more, beautiful.

Hajime thought that he was alone on the little mountain, but the truth was that a wicked, violent man named Kumagai had come to hide in the great boulders that were strewn about on the steep slopes above Hajime's house.

Kumagai lived in a cave and did not dare show his face because he had made all men hate him. There was a price on his head.

Kumagai sat high up in his rocks and looked down on Hajime who worked in his garden and walked to and from the spring. Kumagai used the same spring, but he only went down to it by night. Hajime always went to sleep as soon as the sun set, and he got up very early.

Several times Kumagai thought of murdering the old man for whatever he might steal from the small house to eat and to make his cave more comfortable, but something in the frail old man's bearing dissuaded him. He noted how Hajime devoted himself to his work, and looked about himself always with gratitude at the world he lived in.

Hajime was patient, but at last he began to doubt that he would ever be useful to anyone again. The world, at the foot of his mountain, hurried this way and that and seemed totally self-sufficient. A new sadness engulfed Hajime, for he felt himself completely unneeded.

The beauty of his world brought him less joy.

One night, when Hajime was very old, there arose a terrible storm. Never had the ground shaken so with thunder. Never had the trees bent and creaked so before the wind. Never had the river tossed so in its bed at the foot of the mountain.

Now was the busy life at the foot of the mountain disrupted. The self-sufficiency of worldly men and women would be broken. Now, if ever, the people in the town would need Hajime. He put on his cloak and began to descend. He was going to help.

The path was inky black, but Hajime made his way to the foot of the mountain and to the bridge which crossed the river to the town. It was on the bridge that a great crest of water engulfed him so that he was swept back toward the mountain, cast up upon the foot of the mountain, drowned.

The next morning, the sun shone brightly, and the activity of the world went forward.

Kumagai crept out of his cave and walked to the foot of the mountain. He found the body of Hajime sprawled in an undignified tangle on the bank of the river. When he recognized the old man, a sadness came over him. It did not seem seemly to Kumagai for Hajime to appear in this disordered fashion. He recalled that Hajime had always borne himself with dignity and decorum when he busied himself in his garden.

Kumagai straightened Hajime's limbs and ordered his clothes. He unsnarled his long hair and folded his hands and closed his eyes.

It would not have been fitting for a stranger to Hajime to have seen him as Kumagai had found him.

Kumagai did not stop to wonder why he, who had lived as a stranger to all men, had felt himself to be the one person not a stranger to Hajime. Nor did he analyze why he had concerned himself to be of service to Hajime, preserving Hajime's dignity when Hajime was powerless to help himself. He only knew that he felt and did these things.

He went upward past the house of Hajime and Hajime's garden to his place in the rocks, and from that day he began to reform.

COLUMBIA, SOUTH CAROLINA

*"just call me edom " is a group of sonnets written in Columbia, while the
60's was stumbling along the last mile, under the weight of its own cross.*

*Lyndon Johnson was gone, and Richard Nixon had inherited the White House.
America was reeling. Support of the war and opposition to the war split the
nation. The writer was about to experience one of his undiagnosed illnesses.
People said that with Lyndon Johnson gone, he had no one to hate! After Hurricane Camille destroyed the Gulfport, Mississippi home and almost carried his
parents away, the writer decided to try to bury the hatchet with his father*

*Gone was the time of psychedelic green and eye-burning orange for the
writer. The grey-flannel suit would come. He went to work in a steel mill at the
dawn of the decade of the '70s, and began to become a pillar of the community,
to contribute time to charities, and to keep cats. He gave hospitality to stray
cats and stray humans.*

*These poems are poems written to the writer's father, expressing his grief at
his separation from home - the sorrow he feels for all individuals who find themself
alienated from supportive families and the laughing faces of the friends of childhood.*

just call me edom

CAIN'S UNACCEPTABILITY

Some plow the fields, while others herds lead forth,
   and others prophesy and preach and sing
   Some are blessed to work at a better thing
But Cain found his portion a bitter draught.
The Lord came by and smelled Abel's lamb broth;
   The air with praises for Abel did ring
   But unto Cain, and unto his offering,
Had He not respect. So Cain was quite wroth.
"I am what I am. I give what I can."
   He envied his brother's greater reward.
Envy became hate - Cain a violent man.
   Violence possessed him, exiled him abroad
But God made him safe there before he ran.
   Cain went out from the presence of the Lord.

December 10, 1969.

JOB'S SEARCH

In his pain, Job came like a youth to be
   Uncertain, afraid, his life all gone sour;
   He searched for his God - his father - that tower
Of strength Who could from Satan Job set free.
Anguished, Job turned to his God naturally -
   The sun is turned to in trust by the flower.
   "Will he plead against me with His great power?
No, never! But he would put strength in me."
Every budding flower is granted the air.
   The rain's not withheld through wisdom or whim.
But, Job called his God and sought everywhere,
   Moaned in a world where the sky had gone dim,
"Lo, I go forward, but he is not there;
   And backward, but I cannot perceive him."

December 6, 1969

ISMAEL'S REJECTION

Ruled by women, Abram let himself be-
   What Sari asked was immediately done.
   She had no child, yet she'd see Abram get one.
As she bid, to bear offspring, Hagar used he.
Sarai's plan had been hasty, regret it did she!
   But, spoke an angel to Hagar, "Don't run;
   For thou shalt bear a wild man for a son,
And against every man his hand shall be."
Sarah, become a mother, took a stand -
   Against Ismael made declaration.
Abraham drove Hagar out of the land.
   God brought water to be her salvation.
"Lift up the lad, and hold him in thy hand,
   For I will make of him a great nation."

December 13, 1969

ESAU'S DISAPPOINTMENT

Rebekah had helped, and Jacob could say
  He held Esau's birthright with title clear -
  What if Esau raged? Isaac's eyes did not tear?
Jacob had everything going his way.
Poor Isaac with eyes dim and hair gone grey
  Had to tell that thing - terrible to hear -
  "Thy brother with subtlety has come here,
And he hath taken thy blessings away."
Esau, who e'er had enjoyed his life,
  Made regret for loss of his place to be,
Thought of his children and thought of his wife,
  The land - his blood - the vow God gave them free.
"All lost!" he cried, as though cut with a knife
  "Hast thou not reserved a blessing for me?"

December 14, 1969

JACOB'S NAMING

He wrestled with what in the dark did dwell,
  From this thing seeking his mystery to rob,
  Thing of no face (who could know what his job?)
Whose blessings given would make Jacob's soul well,
Jacob was maimed as the sun came to tell
  Who there alone stood by a rocky knob -
  Said, "Thy name shall be called no more Jacob,
Henceforth thy name shall be called Israel."
Jacob fiercely held on and Jacob won.
  His blessing and what he wanted to know.
With everyone gone, he stood with that one -
  That father, priest or God and said, "It's so.
'Til I know you, and my naming's been done,
  So I'll know myself- I won't let you go."

December 2, 1969

169

JACOB'S DEATH

Jacob aged in Egypt - Tired there was he,
 He dozed and his brain knew confused dreams then
 Of the Promised Land which was to have been -
That land over Jordan he'd never see.
"In that broad field near Mamre, you put me,"
 He said to Joseph, and told all the men.
 "In my grave which I have digged for me in
The land of Canaan, there shalt thou bury me."
Gray he was and shaggy - gnarled crafty ram.
 He gave advice and warned and blessed - death near
Said, "Here's who you are, and here's who I am."
 In the land God promised, rests Jacob's bier,
At peace there with Sarah and Abraham,
 And with Isaac and Rebekah and Leah.

December 7, 1969

ISRAEL'S ESCAPE

The dark time had come. Death was coming too.
 For in Egypt, the Lord God had spoken.
 "You fathers had best be all awoken;
Your sons shall live, or die by what you do.
It is yours live to bring them this night through.
 Your sign to me shall see my curse broken
 The blood shall be to you a token.
When I see the blood, I will pass over you."
Strong against every danger and hardship
 Which beset the first born with woe and tears
the older and wiser man gets his grip -
 Pharoah goes, and Death's Angel disappears.
That night Israel went out of Egypt.
 They'd worked there four hundred and thirty years.

December 11, 1969

DAVID'S SORROW

Most women adored brave King David it's said.
   He begat children on the high and low.
   His armies and kingdom dealt him less woe,
Than his affairs of the heart and the bed.
Amnon, his son, did an act full of dread,
   In violence, his brother revenged him so.
   "And the soul of King David longed to go
To Absalom." (For was not Amnon dead?)
For three years then David saw not his face.
   And for two years more missed the absent one.
Planned Absalom to take his father's place
   Battle came. It was David who won.
David's sorrow was great. His victory base.
   He cried, "O Absalom, my son, my son!"

December 2, 1969

SOLOMON'S TEACHING

Solomon! King! Not much more than a boy
   Asked God that he be given as his part
   In life a wise and understanding heart,
So that Justice and right he might employ,
He was David's son and his good envoy.
   He finished the work his father did start,
   Had sons of his own who made him impart
That "the father of a fool hath no joy."
All useful he was, this wisest of men -
   God's Temple he built of cedar and stones,
Truth engraved he in the hearts of his kin -
   "A merry heart," preached he in earnest tones
"Doeth good," he said. "Like a medicine:
   But a broken spirit drieth the bones."

December 8, 1969

171

JESUS'S RECOGNITION

Healer to be for a world sin-diseased,
   Power of revival for souls seeming dead-,
   Terrible mission and it all ahead
He walked that day with his mind all uneased.
His Father Who makes all divine decrees
   Boomed approbation from over his head
   "Man, thou art my beloved Son," He said.
"My beloved Son in whom I am well pleased."
In Jordan's water, bathed in holy light,
   The Father's mandate, and the Father's Dove,
Gave him the reason and gave him the might
   To teach the deaf world God's meaning of love.
What he was born for, he'd fulfill just right -
   With the strength given him by his Father above.

December 1, 1969

PRODIGAL ACCEPTANCE

No thrift - no judgment - in this son was ground -
   His education from birth was amiss.
   To his father, he seemed no son of his
So he was set free-, advised to abound.
Abound he did not. How might good come around?
   He found his way home to his father's kiss.
   "We should be glad: dead he was, but is
Live again; lost once he was, but is found."
Self-exiled from home, cut off from his roots,
   Lone in a world of alien bother,
The gods he had worshipped revealed clay boots -
   Be a servant at home, he knew that he'd rather
Than this. He had decided, no disputes -
   "I will arise and go to my father."

December 7, 1969

172

JESUS' AGONY

To alter man's lot Jesus held the power,
   He'd void Adam's Fall, not make mark less -
   Mark of his Father's high calling - dark guess
Of things coming so salvation might flower.
The guess became real. The cup it was sour.
   Jesus' death then did all who live in dark bless,
   "When was come the sixth hour there was darkness
O'er all the whole land until the ninth hour."
Worst of all suffering he endured that day,
   (He willingly bore - made salvation free -
the Will of His Father Who must look away
   While Christ bore all sin, in dark, on that tree)
Was God's desertion which caused him to pray
   "God, my God, why hast thou forsaken me?"

December 7, 1969

1970s

The decade of the '70s was a time which brought a change in many lifelong conventions and attitudes of the writer. He was hired to an hourly position at the steel mill built by Georgetown Steel Corporation, at Georgetown, South Carolina. He became clerk in the plant in October of 1970. From that day forward until his retirement in 1992, the steel mill held the center of his attention and benefitted from the lion's share of his motivation and performance. He did his company work, worked on the company's newspaper, held union office, wrote a union newsletter, and engaged in many charitable and political activities which were steel mill or union related. The writer's guiding principle was and is: " What's good for General Motors is good for the USA." He had no ideological attachment with organized labor. A labor union is to keep things orderly: make employee benefits and responsibilities consistent, one individual to another. Where there is orderliness and peace the work may flourish. This benefits the company and this benefit trickles down to the workers. The writer always saw the company, the union, the management team, and the workers as all being part of one entity. Do harm to one segment of that entity and all are weakened.

The writer was forty-three years old when he went to work at the steel mill, and something had been amiss with his growing up. Georgetown Steel Corporation was a brand-new company, the plant completed the year before. The majority of workers were young. Many came straight out of high school. They came to learn and to grow, to mature and become men and women. The writer began to grow along with them. He put away many of his old hang-ups, his perpetual doubts and fears, his prejudices, and learned to live with other people. The writer made great strides during the '70s, rooted out faults and weaknesses, but there were still traumas which were so painful, so bruising - so strong - they would not die. More troubles lay ahead. The father was still there, troubling him, as is evident in the stories the writer wrote during the decade.

In 1975, a companion of the writer's (a woman who was greatly supportive of him when he needed a champion) died, and also in 1975 his father died. His mother came to live with him. There was also a house guest who came and stayed for about ten years - well into the '80s. The death of the father did not end the father's influence upon the writer. But, this would one day turn positive and diminish.

During these years, the writer permitted cats to live with him.

To this day, the writer's debt to Georgetown Steel Corporation and its employees cannot be overestimated. His years spent there, working, exemplify the best years at work this writer ever had.

CHARLESTON, SOUTH CAROLINA

"A Man, His Ax, His Woman, and His God" is a group of poems written in Charleston in 1970. At the beginning of the new decade, the writer turns to the old values, the virtues his father felt were the marks of a man. This poetry was duly sent to the writer's father

In the poems, the writer expresses the hope he has found the essence of his father's heroic view in his own calling - authorship.

Can becoming a writer substitute for being a woodsman?

The writer is still not satisfied that he has his father's approbation. The journey of this hero is not completed.

The writer saw his father's hero - his own hero - as a lean man stripped down for action. Self-sufficiency, rightly exercised, will win the day.

A MAN, HIS AX, HIS WOMAN, AND HIS GOD

I

Whenever it chances the untroubled air
    Stretches from earth to sky
    Horizons empty lie -
Man will build a city there.
    The vacuum -Nature hates it!
    The man who is worth his spit
    Defeats the void dark a bit -
Fills and fulfills, brings life, and light and heat,
Makes a thoroughfare of an empty street.
    There is a river. It must be spanned.
On the other side a new civilization's planned.
    Man goes forth with foot that's shod
    Walks where bare native foot has trod.
    Soon the land belongs to him.
    His smoke floats so the sky grows dim.
    Nothing's the same as before.
    The changeless peace is no more.
    There's come to fight this frontier
A man - his ax, his woman, and his God.

Charleston, South Carolina - 1970

II

In Pennsylvania, now settled and bored,
  German, watched the land bloom.
  Jacob Fager needed room -
Set out River Yadkin to ford.
  Cabarrus County was new,
  A man was free to do
  All his ax and arm could hew -
Cutting out a homestead under the trees.
Bringing down the forest to its knees.
  This was the way of men. They build -
But destroy as they progress toward what they had
willed.
  The earth was rich - every clod.
  The man who didn't dream or nod
  By day, knew hours just as fine
  As those spent near the River Rhine.
  The Lutheran Faith severe,
  Hard work, and a lack of fear
  Carved a land created by
A man - his ax, his woman and his God.

Charleston, South Carolina - 1970

III

From Jacob Fager came a race of men
  Who'd do what lie had done -
  Grasp a place in the sun -
Modest gentility win.
  Life's source is within the earth.
  Man's labor brings forth its worth.
  His sweat and hands give life birth.
And he has even as a god become
Creative and generative in sum.
  Rock upon rock - no rock alone.
He constructs his walls and towers. All of them of
stone.
  Then sank the plow in the sod.
  Fagers tolled and Fagers plod.
  Set to work with hand and tool
  To build a home and church and school
  Patterned the road to success
  Set a life-style all to bless.
  Life's fight is simple fought by
A man - his ax, his woman, and his God.

Charleston, South Carolina - 1970

IV

Technology came. The world seemed to change.
>   There seemed to come a dearth
>   Of individual worth.
Old verities now seemed strange.
>   Women wished to share the lead.
>   Steam saws filled the woodman's need.
>   Forgotten were tenet and creed.
Gone was the need for a brave pioneer.
Mass production and Henry Ford were here.
>   Oh! for the days when men were men,
When black was black, white was white, and sin was
scarlet sin!
>   How endures a caged Nimrod?
>   Hard necessity must prod.
>   Man must stand upon the land;
>   Challenging spaces be at hand.
>   Futility he'll feel less
>   Pushing back the emptiness.
>   But more seems needed today than
A man - his ax, his woman and his God.

Charleston, South Carolina - 1970

V

I know how it is. I know how it felt.
>   I'm from Jacob Fager too -
>   Cabarrus earth through and through -
 Born out of time is misery dealt!
>   My people, in another age,
>   To people a land did engage,
>   I must write full the empty page!
In this writing of words I find my frontier.
The challenge, the goal, the glory is here.
>   Where paper is - empty and white -
I'm less than a man if I don't write, write, write and
write.
>   Wedded to Scheherezade -
>   Zeus's thunderbolt my rod -
>   I'll strike the solid World Oak
>   So free the mistletoe is broke.
>   I'll then have immortality
>   Like builders building before me.
>   At best, I'm just like all the rest,
A man - his ax, his woman, and his God.

Charleston, South Carolina   1970

VI

John F. Kennedy came to change the scene,
　Sought out the best of men,
　Like astronaut John Glenn,
To move Earth and Moon between.
　Science made the best of tools.
　Established undreamed of schools,
　Let the wives know all the rules.
It was the same as it has ever been.
A new frontier had been given to men.
　The human spirit moves on still.
Space lies beyond space, as on Earth hill lies beyond
hill.
　'Til the galaxies are trod.
　Unriddled is each mystery odd.
　All Gordian Knots untied,
　And everything imagined tried.
　Man's pattern he will not change.
　There's nothing new - no idea strange.
　Mind or hand, the quest's same for
A man - his ax, his woman and his God.

Charleston, South Carolina - 1970

VII

Whatever the journey we start out on -
　Our own self's depth to plumb,
　Add up life - find its sum,
Men of spirit we were born.
　Men or spirit that won't die -
　We must try and try and try -
　Reach the sky beyond the sky.
With zeal each new experience embrace,
Stand up - meet the worst of it face to face.
　The eternal part remains strong.
We plow our furrow, write our sonnet, or sing our
song.
　Fagers strip seed from the pod
　Cast seed under the Piedmont sod,
　Watch with love the things they sow -
　Or watch with love a novel grow.
　When the cornstalk's old and brown,
　And the corn ear has turned down,
　They know it all can be done by
A man - his ax, his woman and his God.

Charleston, South Carolina - 1970
180

GEORGETOWN, SOUTH CAROLINA

"Benjamin" is a fragment written in Georgetown in 1970. It paints a picture showing how sad it can sometimes be to be a boy moving up into a man's world -filled with reluctance - very anxious - but compelled onward.

The boy, Benjamin, does not know that there is a reward at the end of every hero's journey. This is the first item in this volume which was written in Georgetown. The writer's arrival in Georgetown heralded a sea change in him.

BENJAMIN

I guess I've known him all his life. He had good parents, and he was a good child, and a pretty child, and when he was about seventeen years old he began to look like a man, and he was a good man, then, and a clean man.

Some boys - you can see the hell in them. It crackles out of their eyes, and you see it in the slope of their shoulders and in the way they carry themselves sort of swinging along wicked, but he was not like this.

He was smooth and fair and the glow in his face was healthy and his smile was open, and he carried an air of freshness along with him, because he was youth and innocence and something unspoiled, and to be these things is good.

His mother raised him to be good.

His father was a pious man who sang in church on Sundays, although his face would grow red because he was embarrassed for singing out. But, it is a good thing to sing out with rejoicing, because God has brought Salvation to us.

They called him Benjamin, for is it not true that many men shall receive once, but Benjamin shall receive five times?

Benjamin was like someone sleepwalking, whose eyes have never been opened to the presence of evil in the world, and when he was seventeen, he had done nothing in his life that was wrong.

At this time, there was a woman living in town who had no husband. She had been married to a policeman, and one night he and one of his policeman friends had been sitting in a small cafe drinking coffee, and he was telling his friend about how well his hens were laying. When the two men had gone outside, a desperado had shot at them, and the woman's husband was hit and had fallen down on the sidewalk and died.

She had been a tattoo artist with a carnival before the policeman had married her, and before hardly any time had passed after the death of her husband, it began to be rumored about town that she would tattoo men and boys for free up at her house of an evening if the man or boy would venture up there alone. Now, she had become a little mad.

The boys used to gather together behind the gymnasium at school and smoke cigarettes and talk about her, and it was a test of bravery to have been up to her house and to have been tattooed. Some of the older and braver boys were forever showing off tattoos on hidden portions of their bodies and bragging about the things which had happened to them at the woman's house and what they had done.

Benjamin did not really WANT to do the things the other boys were doing, but he felt these were things he SHOULD do.

Many times he thought of this - of going up to the woman's house, and always he turned away from the thought, but finally one night he made his way with quaking heart and trembling nerves to her door, and when he left her, he bore a small tattoo, so insignificant one could hardly see it, hidden away where it would never be noticed, and he knew that life would be different for him after this.

Walking home, he saw little children playing in the moonlight and he could hear them singing:

"Spoony-spoony-Spogh,
Why'd ja do it now?
You gave your precious jewel
To a gotch-gutted cow.
Guffin-Guffin-Shack,
You'll never get it back.
What you had now none can own,
Gone - it's everybody's lack."

The children rhymed other verses that night, which went back even to the Celts, and Benjamin could not drown out their voices chanting:

"So many pretties. So many nice things. All the pretty, pretty, beauty."
Under a smug and brazen moon, a sad breeze coughed and sighed. Sweet innocence had whispered softly, given weak good-bye and died.

GEORGETOWN, SOUTH CAROLINA

"Necklace of Figs" was written in Georgetown in 1970. A Cajun patriarch imagines he bodes within himself only good for his family. Could it turn out that it is a flaw in his character is harming them? These trusting people?

This story is based on an actual happening which took place in "the bayou country, " west of New Orleans. The writer had read of it daily in the Times Picayune, but on the sidewalks of the French Quarter, he found a very different telling. This is the street version.

A family's welfare is weighed against the entitlements of established law. The patriarch must make a choice. Many will be hurt either way he chooses. What is a patriarch to do?

NECKLACE OF FIGS

In a town of antique Norman houses, Jean Jacques Plauchet's was more Norman than the rest. It was distinctly French it its architecture, and notable in its furnishings because of an old armoire which had been brought by ship, by Plauchets from Nova Scotia in 1755, when the people had come to Louisiana. Still to be seen, after almost two hundred years, were the stains the water made in the wood while the armoire stood on the wet earth beside Bayou Teche, before it was hauled a little inland to Petit-partout; Petit-partout, which Plauchets built in a bend of Bayou La Chevre, a town come into existence under Capricorn. Still, too, in Petit-partout, were to be felt the French ways, the Napoleonic Code, the Canadian survivals, the strong guiding hand of the Church of Rome.

The house of Jean-Jacques was weathered and old, and the man was likewise, as washed-gray, as slack-beamed, as roughened, and out of square. Alone, now, with Edith dead and soils grown, lie drank his morning coffee in his bedroom. The ancient armoire was before him, symbol of the perseverance of the Plauchets, a statement of the family's excellence at survival.

Long had the man, the house, and the town seemed blessed, and the blessing a single blessing which if removed from one would be denied all. Jean Jacques' family must continue to survive, and Petit-partout. It was the strong families which held the town together, and each family was held together by its patriarch.

"What have I to help me maintain this continuity of life?" Jean Jacques sighed, coughing, and giving a groan, "except the Napoleonic Code and the Church? I have myself. Yes, but whom besides?"

He sat his coffee cup down heavily. A little of the liquid splashed out and Jean Jacques wiped it up with the side of his brown hand, his skin like old autumn leaves, and the bristling hair on his arms long ago turned white. Jean Jacques felt, this morning, like a seared October leaf clinging to its tree. If the coming wind should blow violently, he would flutter downward, his state of blessedness at last at an end, and woe to Plauchets and Petit-partout!

So many had died; his own wife, Edith; his brother and sister-in-law, Grandet and Henriette; and his brother, Beuregard, who had left the widow, Berthe Marie.

Jean Jacques and Berthe Marie were the only Plauchets remaining of their generation, and he feared she was not in agreement with him, now, when a crisis had come and a man was in danger.

Jean Jacques could not die yet. Everything must happen in orderly process. First he must step down and another take over the leadership of the family with his blessing. Then he must rest in the background, calm and certain, lending stability to the new order of things, and finally there would be no need for him. Then he might die, but not yet. At present, no one must die.

Now, the war with Germany and Japan had come and many of the able-bodied men of Petit-partout were taken away. To survive, the town must not lose another of its men. Each must be in his place, trapping, shrimping, tending the fields, hunting for meat, for the sake of the old, and the women, and the children.

A few days before, in the afternoon, late, a monster had loosed himself in Petit-partout for a short time to ravage and to kill. As a result, this morning, Plauchets were called to a meeting at the home of Jean Henri, son of Grandet, and already Jean Jacques had a vague feeling things were being arrayed against him. Why had not the people chosen for the meeting to be held in his home? He was the patriarch. Or in the home of one of his sons, Felix or Celestine? Why this suspicion of himself and his heirs? He was not even certain that Berthe Marie would show him the respect of walking with him to the gathering when he called to take her. She had looked at him with suspicious, red eyes and made no answer when he asked her.

Jean Jacques took a last look around the familiar room, seeking to draw some warmth, some encouragement from the dusty remembrances of Edith which were strewn about. He jammed a broad-brimmed hat onto his head and made his way down the steep steps at the back of the house, which was built high off the ground, as many of the houses in Petit-partout were, with room for a man of average height like Jean Jacques to walk about upright underneath. Where the floor was scattered with straw lived Leh-leh, the greedy goat. Jean Jacques stopped to feed her a handful of yellow grain.

"Poor goat," he said, She tottered on nervous legs, but Jean Jacques stood firm. He stooped down and peered through the shadows toward the rutted street. Two young people were sitting on the front steps. They were Berthe Marie's grandson, Jean Nicholas Arthur, and Barbe, daughter of Jean Henri and Catherine Marie. At sight of Jean-Nicholas-Arthur, Jean Jacques gave a guilty start and sweat began to form across his brow.

"Rosy in the sunlight are their timid blushes," Jean Jacques thought. "As they whisper together in the sweetness of innocence. There is no innocence to compare to that which is between an untouched boy and a girl who is a virgin. They can wait a little time for the full love. Life is far off for them."

But life, Jean Jacques knew, had a way of sweeping one on, bearing one forward, engulfing one as the bayou had been known to sweep over the levee and engulf Petit-partout. Present things might not always stand, but must be grasped while at hand or lost on the face of the flood. One could not forever escape the surge of events. The levee had begun to breach for Jean-Nicholas-Arthur and Barbe the day the men had discovered the little grandson of Jean Jacques, Suhlay, just five, torn and beaten, ravished and murdered, and tossed aside.

"Son of Felix. Son of Vitalie. He has met with a monster," Jean Jacques sobbed, burying his face in his arm so that Jean-Nicholas-Arthur and Barbe would not hear. He must postpone having his nightmare intrude upon their childish dreams.

"Poor goat," he said aloud. "I shape events which move you. I manage your simple world. Would I hurt you'?" He caught a sunlit glimpse of the drooping lashes, the curling black hair, the pinkened cheeks of Jean-Nicholas-Arthur. He gave Leh-leh a pat. "Poor goat," he said again.

He left his place under the house, walking heavily, one shoulder lower than the other, his body all out of line as if from some overburdening load. He sloshed indifferently up the muddy street to the house of Berthe Marie.

Berthe Marie came to the door looking like a broken bundle of kindling which was tied with old string and held in a black sack. Jean Jacques held the rusting screen door open for her and she moved carefully onto the porch.

"Will you go with me, Berthe Marie?" Jean Jacques asked pleadingly. "Will you walk with me to Jean Henri's'?"

"Since we are going to the same place," she said coldly, "we may as well walk the same road together. I do not care about anything. Since Suhlay is abused and murdered, what have I to care about?"

Jean Jacques bowed slightly and gave his arm to help her down the steps. In the street, Berthe Marie began to move rapidly along, as if to shorten the journey, as if to make her time with Jean Jacques as brief as possible.

"I hate to see you not feeling well," he said to her cautiously. "Is all this too much for you?"

She looked back at him with her reddened, piercing eyes. They were like the eyes of an angry bird. She did not speak, so he continued.

"I must ask you quickly, do you think that it is possible for a good man to become, for one little moment, a monster; a monster which he has never before been, and one which he could never be again'"

She stared at his face as though she thought him mad.

"Do you remember how, long ago, the people believed in Loup-garou, the werewolf?"

"Yes, I know Loup-garou," Berthe Marie whispered. She was walking slowly and beginning to pant.

"We used to frighten the children with tales about the werewolf. When Celestine was little, he freed a valuable mink from the cage because he fell in love with it, and it was afraid. He always loved beauty. He was afraid I would punish him. He ran and hid in the tall grass at the edge of the swamp. It was after dark when I found him. He didn't recognize me. He was beside himself. He kept crying that Loup-garou had him."

"I remember," Berthe Marie said. "He was sick for days."

"He thought that I was Loup-garou come to punish him. He thought that beautiful things had to be set free, but he learned the truth that beautiful things must be used and must die."

"Celestine has been a good provider," Berthe Marie said dryly. "A trapper and a killer."

Jean Jacques winced at her tone. He must defend his firstborn. "He is the Oldest son of an oldest son," he said proudly. "I always expected that he would head the family. I always expected that he would take my place."

They stopped for a moment and Berthe Marie took hold of the fence which stood at the front of the church with its cemetery guarded by the statue of St. Eulalie.

"That is where they have put Suhley," Berthe Marie said bitterly. "His face was always like sunshine, and now he is in the dark. He was always singing, but now he is silent. See his little grave; I am afraid now. I am afraid that there is a monster which will break out and destroy all our children."

Jean Jacques' heart beat excitedly. "The werewolf will not strike again," he said. "He is a man again and sorry. He is feeling most guilty. Even now he probably feels like running, like an animal in danger, looking for a place to hide."

Who will hide him?" Berthe Marie asked sharply. "Who will hide him?"

"I am patriarch of the Plauchets. Plauchets come to me for safety."

Berthe Marie began to walk on.

"You have governed this village always," she said. "You hold the people in your grizzled fist, and you have your way. You have always been able to make matters which are your personal desire seem necessary to the public good. I know your secret. Beauregard told me this about you before he died. You have not failed before. You certainly will not fall now. The people will do what you want them to do, just as soon as you can convince them that doing this is necessary to their joint survival and the survival of Petit-partout."

"Men will come from the parish seat, and perhaps from Baton Rouge. We will not surrender them one of our working men to take away forever. If one of our married men, a worker, a head of a household, has done this, we will not surrender him. A substitute must be offered."

"What substitute?" she cried out, full of anxiety. Jean Jacques did not answer. His neck was firm and his head up. Berthe Marie knew that he meant to have his way. "Celestine and Felix and theirs will be safe," she said in a dull voice heavy with disagreement.

"Celestine will go to the traps, as only he knows to go, and Felix will operate the boat and net the shrimp. It is necessary."

"Wasn't it necessary for Suhlay to have life?"

"He was Felix's son, my grandson. You know what I feel for him."

They had reached Jean Henri's gate. Several of the men came forward and greeted them.

"Is Father Gautier to be here?" Berthe Marie asked.

"No. He was not told to come."

She looked at Jean Jacques with her reddened eyes. Her lips were thin and pale. "I'll go inside alone," she said.

The men came and stood about Jean Jacques. "Celestine and Felix are already here," one said. "And they have let Jojo Enfantin stay. He is sitting in there with his aunt, Catherine Marie, and Jean Henri.

"It's Jean Henri's house. He gave his wife's nephew permission to stay," another said .

"This is an affair for Plauchets," Jean Jacques said, but he did not care if Jojo stayed. Jean Jacques had never concerned himself with this boisterous family connection, Jojo. Jojo was no Plauchet and Jean Jacques almost never spent any time thinking about anyone who was not a Plauchet except for Father Gautier.

Jojo always strode when he walked, bringing with him a scent of strong tobacco and old leather and fish. He bore himself as though he were his own man. Plauchet men belonged to the patriarch. Jojo would try to reach out and take whatever he wanted, and what he could not take he would crush and throw down. His hands and wrists were made for grasping, and his biceps for drawing things to himself. His chest was deep and hairy for hiding things away. His legs were lean and long for dancing and making love, or for running away if there was trouble. He did not use his hands and arms for striking out, only for possessing.

"What does Jojo want here," Jean Jacques asked, for he knew Jojo's greedy character. "What does he want of us?"

"He wants Jean Henri's girl," one man said. "He wants Barbe."

"That innocence - That sweet child?" Jean Jacques exclaimed.

"She is promised to Jean-Nicholas-Arthur," the man continued. "That could save her. But, if something should happen to Jean-Nicholas-Arthur there would be no excuse. Jean Henri would give her to Jojo."

Another man, old, appealing worried, one of Jean Jacques oldest friends, spoke up in a quavering tone of voice, "We hear rumors that something might happen to Jean-Nicholas-Arthur. We are afraid for him."

Jean Jacques did not reply.

A younger man began to laugh. "We all know for sure that Jojo is a horse with the women. He could break a girl in right. We hear that lots of women like him. They wait for him with their doors unlocked. He is well known in Morgan City and Lafayette, too."

"I want to be alone for a minute or two," Jean Jacques told them. "Then I must go inside." He walked to the steps arid stood for a moment with bowed head.

The sun was high above the cypress trees. All trace of dawn was swept away. The birds had risen up and were flying about tentatively. In a few minutes they would sweep away to the swampland. Already the water of the bayou had taken on a solemn stillness. There was no breeze to stir it. The sun reigned.

In this heat, Jean Jacques wiped his forehead and fanned himself for a second with his misshapen hat.

"This is a new trouble," he thought. "I did not think, when I made plans for Jean-Nicholas-Arthur, that it would hurt Barbe in this way. She will be a child, gentlest of angels, going to a rough master, that Satan, but what is to be done? Men will come from the outside to investigate the murder of Suhlay, and I cannot let them take away one of our working men to kill him!"

The old man roused himself from his thinking and made his bent way up the steps, almost crawling.

Some time later, when he came out of the house of Jean Henri, after the meeting of the family, he walked almost on all fours, more like a beast than a man, and a terrible woe bore heavy on his brow casting his face down in an expression of suffering. He did not stop to talk with the people at Jean Henri's steps where they gathered. Perhaps, he should have, but he could not. The sights and the words he had seen and heard inside the house were too fresh in his mind. He would never be able to erase the image stamped there of his daughter-in-law, Vitalie, who was so ready to accuse Celestine, the brother of her husband.

The family believed about Celestine as Vitalie did, but Celestine had not confessed.

"I can still hope," Jean Jacques sighed to himself. "I can still hope, but almost, I don't hope, because the hope will be broken. Vitalie is the mother. She knows. Like the doe when the scent of the hunter is smelled, any mother knows how to fear for her child, and what to fear, and who."

The family knew Jean Jacques' mind. They knew that he was on the prowl, was already stalking, and was ready to entrap the scapegoat. The family, even Vitalie and Berthe Marie, believed they must follow this leader, this patriarch who had always wisely ruled them. But, it would never be easy for Jean Jacques again because the support of the people was no longer wholehearted.

Jean Henri was already assuming a place of leadership which would have been impossible before the death of Suhlay. He had spoken for the family.

"It can be as you say, Uncle. You can have this your way, but the boy must be willing. He must offer himself and go because he chooses. Otherwise, we will tell the truth and the real murderer will die."

Now, as Jean Jacques walked away slowly along the bayou, past the few shrimp boats, the pirogues, and through the crates and old drums stacked all about, he asked himself what right he had to ask so much of Jean-Nicholas-Arthur.

"We will think up a story," Jean Jacques said to himself. Something like self-confidence, even optimism, began to sweep over him. He sat on an old box in the shade of a chinaberry tree. "We will make it look like an accident which happened at play. It will be innocent; a big boy playing too roughly with a little one. Jean-Nicholas-Arthur is good. Men can see that. They will keep him a few years, maybe only three or four, then he can come home. That is the way it is when it is a matter of an accident at childish play. When it is a matter of child rape and murder and the attempt to hide these crimes ..." Jean Jacques wanted to change the subject in his own mind, "It may even save his life. Jean-Nicholas-Arthur will be old enough to go to the war next year. At Angola he will escape this fatal trap."

Celestine would continue to work the traps which he had set in a great circle around Petit-partout, where only he knew. He would bring in the furs and dry them in the sun and Felix would take them away on the boat. Celestine did not take the furs to sell them. Petit-partout was surrounded by a network of bayous forming a maze in which a boat could stay lost forever. It was Felix who knew his way through this ring of traps set by Nature to confuse man. And beyond this circle was another ring of traps, set by man, and then another, and another, and another, each circle set with greater power to maim and hold. About these rings or traps, Celestine and Felix knew nothing. These must the patriarch try to battle. One of these was the law. The law would not have Celestine or Felix.

"Or any of my people!" Jean Jacques said aloud. "The law will have Jean-Nicholas-Arthur, but only for a little while. And, in giving him to the law he'll be saved from the ring of traps which is next farther out, and most merciless and cruel, war."

Jean Jacques' blue eyes squinted under the limp brim of his old hat. He looked out across the marsh toward the cypress woods. A steam seemed to rise from the marsh, before the green and brown of the swamp, quivering in the air. The landscape seemed to shimmer. Then, Jean Jacques saw the orphan, grandson of Berthe Marie, Jean-Nicholas-Arthur. The boy walked solitarily along the bayou, his head thrust down and forward, thinking his solemn thoughts, watching the ground, seeming ever hopeful that he might find some treasure hidden in the limp grass. Jean Jacques played at the game of conversing with himself about the kind of boy Jean-Nicholas-Arthur had grown to be. He was seventeen, slender, a gentle boy, becoming a man, but still possessed with the ethereal quality of all the Plauchet children. Still a child, with soft curling black hair and trusting eyes and a touch of pink in his cheeks, Jean-Nicholas-Arthur had all this beauty, overspread with a grey mantle of melancholy. He bore the mark upon himself of his loneliness.

"It could have happened," Jean Jacques thought. "The same thing could have happened to Jean-Nicholas-Arthur as happened to Suhlay."

Jean-Nicholas-Arthur saw Jean Jacques sitting in the shade and ran over to him. He immediately sat down on the ground. "Is the heat bothering you, Great-uncle?" he asked with a show of cheerful interest.

"Why do you say that?" Jean Jacques sparred warily.

"You look worried, or unhappy, or both. Is something wrong?"

"You know this town is full of trouble. Suhlay is dead. The meeting today in Jean Henri's house was about that."

"What will happen?" Jean-Nicholas-Arthur asked, turning solemn, revealing his true self.

"Someone must pay for the death of Suhlay. That is the law. Men will lay their nets carefully to lure us into their grasp and, like turtles which have ventured in with the shrimp, we will be caught up, innocents with the guilty."

"But, who is guilty'?" Jean-Nicholas-Arthur asked.

"Who is not?" Jean Jacques replied. He was silent for a long time. Jean-Nicholas-Arthur felt the old man's mood communicated to himself, felt himself more dejected and saddened. He did not feign joy in the day. That had left him.

Jean Jacques seemed to change the subject. "Celestine was always nice to you," he stated. "Wasn't he always nice to you?" he asked.

"Yes. Always," Jean-Nicholas-Arthur, replied.

"And, he was good to Suhlay, too, because he loved him." Jean Jacques spoke very gently, looking out across the shimmering marsh, seeing the heat rise. "His brother's child, grandson of his father. How he used to talk about Suhlay! It seemed that he must have spent his days following the traps, thinking up pretty things to say about him. Celestine is the type of man who is touched by beauty. He has told me that he feels a pain in his heart when he looks into the eyes of the creatures caught in his traps. The fear in their eyes wounds him, and he hurries to kill them so that they won't continue to be afraid and suffer. Suhlay was a child with such a fresh beauty in his face. Suhlay had the softest, gentlest eyes of any creature in the world. Celestine could not escape being affected by these eyes."

"I don't see why anyone would kill Suhlay," Jean-Nicholas-Arthur said wondering.

"It is easy to kill when you kill every day," Jean Jacques said aside. Then, he returned to the subject of Suhlay. "We always saw him, loud in his play, singing, his face as bright as the sun, always happy, too beautiful for the world, standing only a little higher than a man's knee, and soft and pretty as a girl. He was as happy in Petit-partout as a baby muskrat is in its swamp."

" Celestine told some of us that a stranger did it," Jean-Nicholas-Arthur said "He said the man docked his pirogue at the foot of the street and walked through Petit-partout behind the houses. He found Suhlay playing alone with his cypress knees, and Celestine said, 'The man reached out his horned hand and ...' Great-uncle, I thought things like that only happened to little girls. I thought boys were safe."

"No one is safe who is beautiful," Jean Jacques said sadly.

"But, did the stranger really try to love him like he would a girl, and kill him, like Celestine said?" Jean-Nicholas-Arthur asked in amazement.

"No," Jean Jacques said. "It was a Plauchet who did that."

What Plauchet?"

I am not sure yet. It is hard for me to believe it of anyone, especially one. If it should turn out that Celestine did do it, or any of our grown men, they would take him to Baton Rouge and kill him. If it should turn out some young fellow about your age did it, accidentally at play, with no evil motive, in fun, then he would hardly be punished at all."

"Would he be sent to prison?" Jean-Nicholas-Arthur asked with seeming indifference.

"Perhaps, for a little while."

Jean-Nicholas-Arthur looked sideways up at Jean Jacques' stony profile.

His eyes were narrowed and hid under long lashes. "Pity me," Jean Jacques read in them, but he could not think now of pity for anyone.

They saw Celestine approaching, slowly, across the low land at the edge of the marsh. He walked on legs big from much walking, with shoulders and arms made large from carrying the pelts from the traps. His hair was long and black and straight, curling only a little at the ends. His face was dark with sun and a heavy beard, but his eyes were like the eyes of all the Plauchets. Today he carried two hides, suspended by a cord, in his large hand. He did not see Jean Jacques and Jean-Nicholas-Arthur watching him. When he was about to pass them, Jean Jacques stood up and stepped out into the path before him.

Celestine dropped the hides he carried and stood rooted to the ground.

Then he turned and bolted down the path, running, not looking back, sweating

with heat and panic. Jean Jacques ran after him and Jean-Nicholas-Arthur

trailed behind. Jean Jacques could still see in his mind's eye the look on Celestine's face when he first saw his father. He had looked upon Jean Jacques with an expression of horror. He ran on board Felix's shrimp boat and scurried down below deck, closing the square hatch-cover above himself.

"You're Loup-garou!" he cried. "You're the werewolf. I'll kill you!" But, he did the old man no harm other than to shout at him. He pulled himself up out of the boat and ran away toward the swamp.

"Are you hurt, Great-uncle'?" Jean-Nicholas-Arthur asked Jean Jacques.

Jean Jacques did not hear him. "He did do it," he said. "Only when he is

very guilty and frightened could he think that I am Loup-garou. It is like it was

the first time when he let the lady mink out because she was frightened in her cage. He will always try to release helpless things from their fear. His is the single quick blow that releases from fear. Then there comes for him guilt and he finds the fear is now his. He becomes afraid of me, believing that I am the werewolf come to punish him."

"What will you do?" Jean-Nicholas-Arthur asked.

"I must try to save his life."

"I see," Jean-Nicholas-Arthur said in a serious tone. "Only it was he who made Suhlay afraid in the first place."

"That is the catch," Jean Jacques admitted. He studied the boy's face with it's expression of beginning distrust and disagreement with his great-uncle. "Jean-Nicholas-Arthur will probably not help me," he said tiredly to himself. "And, if he will not, no one will make him. That was made clear today."

In the weeks following the disclosure to Jean Jacques of the guilt of Celestine, Jean Jacques moved about Petit-Partout in a state of excitement brought on by his concern for his son, the awesome ever-present thing which hung over him; his responsibility to protect and move forward his family and the town; and the empty feeling he had that everyone had forsaken him, turned away from him and set their hands against his plan for saving Celestine and the family and Petit-partout.

He had heard them talking. One day, one of his oldest friends had stated that Jean Jacques was wrong to encourage Jean-Nicholas-Arthur to take the blame for the death of Suhlay. "You are sending this soft boy-flesh to be the bride of Angola," the man had said. Comments like this made Jean Jacques hesitate in his determination, but after wavering his resolve would grow firm. He would see Jean-Nicholas-Arthur go away a surrogate for Celestine. Since the day when Celestine had run from Jean Jacques, seeing him a hungry werewolf out to punish him, Jean Jacques purpose had been fixed. He would not see Celestine taken away from Petit-Partout to die.

"But what am I saving?" he moaned on the morning of the trial. "Is he worth it, this man who lusted after a little boy, and frightened him, and killed him because he was afraid? Is this man worth saving for the town's sake?" He pulled himself together and told himself carefully that Celestine was a man who had a wolf which hid within him, and that wolf had sprung up and walked in Celestine and taken possession of him and lusted after the child and killed the child. Celestine was possessed by the wolf which had long slept within him, and this wolf of Celestine's was a wolf who only walks once. Somewhere, now, the wolf lay dormant: no, dead. Celestine would do no more wrong.

So, in this frame of mind, Jean Jacques went to the trial of Jean-Nicholas-Arthur. The trial, with its dour judge and its handful of strangers to Petit-partout, was a duplicate of the hearing, which had been held earlier, where it was determined a crime had been committed. The same witnesses got up to say the same things; Jojo Enfantin accusing, Berthe Marie defending, Jean Henri helping Jojo along with his accusations, the brothers, Celestine and Felix, playing their roles of bereaved uncle and father, the women with despairing eyes, sorrowing and silent.

The only notable additions to the testimony were the testimonies of the children of the town and that of Jean-Nicholas-Arthur himself.

Into the court had come the children of Petit-partout. Obedient and polite, with doting parents watching, they marched. It was like a Christmas pageant. "Rachel weeping for her children, and she would not be comforted, because they are no more." Every woman was a Rachel in Petit-partout that day. But, the children were Angels. They talked freely, many of them still clinging to the French which was their first language. They came forward to testify.

"We were playing and Jean-Nicholas-Arthur hurt Suhlay."

"Jean-Nicholas-Arthur took a chair like they do in the movies and began to wave it. He hit Suhlay."

He broke Suhlay's head."

"Jean-Nicholas-Arthur was always scaring us. He would jump out at us from behind a bush and yell. He would throw things at us. He would hit us if we said we'd tell. On this day, he wanted to play Lash Larue, and he picked up a chair off Aunt Berthe Marie's porch and hit Suhlay on the head with it, and Suhlay fell down the steps. Jean-Nicholas-Arthur got scared and tried to make Suhlay stand up, but Suhlay couldn't. Jean-Nicholas-Arthur picked him up and ran with him toward the swamp."

Jean Jacques looked at the tiny girl's face, prim and righteous. She was dressed in blue and white, the image of a proper Christian child. He looked at all the children who paraded with the transparent luminous quality of cherubs through the drabness of the courtroom.

"I have never seen such beauty," Jean Jacques thought. "How is it these can be turned to falsehood? These innocents?"

The judge listened to the children with great attention. Something about the case seemed to bother him. He was not sure and this was not a jury case. This was a case where the verdict would be rendered by the judge. The children almost convinced him, but he was determined to hear Jean-Nicholas-Arthur testify. He wanted to hear from the boy that he had done this thing for which he was accused. The actuality of Jean-Nicholas-Arthur's guilt was not written on his face nor in his actions. The judge wanted to see him take on the appearance of a guilty man if the judge must convict and sentence him.

Jean-Nicholas-Arthur had sat passively through most of the trial, listening to the witnesses, hanging his head, not looking up, with his natural shyness. Only when Jean Henri stated that Barbe was promised to Jojo to wed had he shown interest. Then, he looked up at Jojo; Jojo who said he had gone to the spot where the dead Suhlay lay, where his dogs had taken up the scent and led him to Jean-Nicholas-Arthur. A deep expression of guilt settled over the boy's face. He felt the inadequacy of youth and inexperience and passivity. His inability to assemble his borning, dying manhood was condemning Barbe to the arms of Jojo, the hunter and destroyer, the one who would uproot the flowers and leave wounds upon the earth. This weakness deserved any punishment it brought upon itself. He must hurry the approach of whatever his fate might be.

"He consigns her over to Jojo gladly," Jean Jacques thought, reading his face. "He believes he is not worthy of her, but that seething hero is.

The judge looked at Jean-Nicholas-Arthur, searching him with a new intensity, from this briefest of moments. For the first time, he could see guilt written on the boy. What had worried him from the start of the trial had been Jean-Nicholas-Arthur's lack of any show of liability. Now, accountability was there in his face.

Jean-Nicholas-Arthur was called to the stand. As he went, he passed close to Jojo, and for a moment he hesitated and looked into Jojo's face as though he expected some trace of recognition from the other young man, as if he felt Jojo would acknowledge him, making him sure of his acceptance of him. But, Jojo's face became a closed mask. He shut Jean-Nicholas-Arthur out. Disappointment settled down upon the younger lad, and hurt, and a sense of injustice. He walked slowly on and took the stand.

Jean Jacques bowed his head and stared at the floor. He had seen that Jean-Nicholas-Arthur sat so that he could see his great uncle. For a terrible moment, he became alarmed that Jean-Nicholas-Arthur might show fear and Celestine become so anxious he would confess. Or, if the boy broke under the judge's questioning and denied his guilt, the people of Petit-partout would rise up and recant their testimony. Celestine would die. Jean Jacques felt his heart beat in panic. There was no reason that Jean-Nicholas-Arthur should make this sacrifice.

"Doubtless," Jean Jacques thought, "he will protest his innocence."

But, Jean-Nicholas-Arthur could only think of the scorn which Jojo had shown for him, could only think of Jojo's worthiness and his own shortcoming. He felt shut out and frozen, that accursed thing which better men would not accept. His was the way of selfless service. He was a poor thing, but he could win acceptance from Celestine, and Jean Jacques, and even from Jojo. These thoughts raced through his mind, as he woodenly answered the questions which were asked him before the court.

"We have been told how this killing happened," it was said. "You were at play with the little children. You swung a chair. You struck Suhlay on the head with a chair at play, and then you took him away and hid him. This is what they say happened. Is this what happened? Is this what you did?"

Jean-Nicholas-Arthur looked full at Jean Jacques. Jean Jacques raised his head and looked deep into Jean-Nicholas-Arthur's eyes. Jean-Nicholas-Arthur gazed back, looking deep, trying to see the old man's innermost soul.

" I offer you the most important gift I can give, but I want to be sure that you really ask for it. It would be a shame to give so much, if it were despised."

He continued to let his eyes bore into those of the older man. Then, he smiled slightly.

"You're pleading. I see the need you have for this. I see that you do want it. Oh, you do want it so much!"

He let his head sink forward a little. Out loud he said, "Yes sir, that is what happened. Yes sir, that is what I did."

So, Jean Jacques had won.

"I know there is some terrible trap set for me," he told himself. "I have saved Celestine at the cost of that sweet boy and that girl. I have leagued myself with that devil, Jojo, to ruin them. I know that there is a trap prepared for me to punish me." He did not tarry at the scene of the trial, but hurried away, ashamed for his face to be seen by his peers, the old and respectable people of Petit-partout. "It is the wolf who fears the trap," Jean Jacques thought to himself, and he felt the hair rise arid prickle on the back of his neck. A chill swept over him, although it was very hot, and he staggered along the rutted street to his house.

Jean Jacques began, after this, to avoid the people of the town. He who had felt himself a father to everyone had come to feel like an outsider. He let the government of the village slip away from him and from his sons to his nephew, Jean Henri. Jean Henri kept Jojo ever at his side, and already the banns were published and the wedding of Jojo and Barbe was at hand. Celestine and Felix's inheritance was divided. The townspeople knew that half of Jean Jacques' estate was to go to Jean-Nicholas-Arthur, and Berthe Marie would leave nothing to the sons of Jean Jacques. Her property would go to Jean-Nicholas-Arthur. The people of Petit-partout insisted upon this.

On the morning of the wedding, Jean Jacques poured himself a large glass of wine. His stomach was sick. He felt a pain near his heart and his head reeled.

The day would be long and lonely, spent in dozing in the empty house, drinking the wine and trying not to think.

"Tonight there will be celebration. Tonight there will be shivaree." He thought of Leh-leh who must be fed and milked before he could leave the house. "The goat won't be able to go." He thought of Jean-Nicholas-Arthur, as he did a hundred times each day. "The goat cannot go."

Night came, and he put on a necktie and coat as befitted the patriarch, and pulled an old comb through his hair. He looked deeply into the mirror, studying his face, studying his expression, tracing out the character of the face there as though it were the face of a stranger. He looked at the shaggy grey hair and the grey whiskers on his chin. He looked at the small, flattened ears and the long jaw. He whipped his tongue out and his eyes became fierce. He felt something grasp his heart, so that it seemed for a moment to stop beating. He felt that he would reel and fall, But, he took not his eyes from his face in the mirror.

"I am the werewolf!" he cried. "It is I who has ravished and eaten the beautiful young of Petit-partout! It is I in whom the wolf has walked continually. Always. These poor men, like my poor Celestine, have felt the wolf walk in themselves once. The wolf has walked in me so constantly that I did not even recognize him, because daily he was part of myself. He is myself. This wolf that I am has ruled the forest, not permitting anyone else to bring forth the deeds of whatever wolf might be within him. I have not ever let the men of Petit-partout be men. The wolf in Jojo Enfantin is happy, because it can frolic free. Jojo's wolf is happy and controlled, almost a playful dog. But, the wolves of the Plauchets cower deep away from my sight; they have ravened and maddened, and in these men, at least once, the angry wolf has broken out to commit terrible crime. There has been a curse on the house of Plauchet, and the curse is me! I never let the wolf-part of anyone under my grim hand carouse. And so, they have turned sick and bitter and the family is wrecked. I am Loup-garou!"

When Jean Jacques arrived at the wedding feast, held in Jean Henri's yard, Jean Henri was acting as host and was already more drunk than Jean Jacques could approve of.

"See how this great horse wears the bridle?" Jean Henri cried out as Barbe led Jojo through the crowd to a place near the music. "How is it that this wild one can be so tamed"'

"He is ready to be tamed," Jean Jacques said to himself. "But, the rest of us will never be."

He looked up at the full moon, and deep within him was an almost uncontrollable desire to howl and howl and howl.

GEORGETOWN, SOUTH CAROLINA

"What The Earth Knew " was written in Georgetown in 1970, but it harks back to an event which took place when the writer was at Mississippi College in 1951, visiting with preachers a nearby church field. He saw again (as Steinbeck taught) that the tragedies of the dispossessed reach out to humble us all! We feel small and helpless in the face of their misery.

This story touches again on the theme of non-communication between individuals. A preacher's wife leaves him because she can see only his criticism of her and not his need for her.

Is it better to do what is expedient but not sanctioned, or to scrupulously follow the dictates of established custom?

WHAT THE EARTH KNEW

Henry Graft, half-time pastor of Bright Hill Church for Everybody, and half-time pastor of Crooked Branch Church for Everybody, always, his wife observed, saved exactly one third of his orange juice to wash down his breakfast after he had eaten it.

This morning was no different. He swished the juice in his mouth and swallowed it. Gloria felt that he would be put out all day if a toast crumb remained between his cheek and teeth after he left the breakfast table.

He pushed his chair back and sat looking like the very serious young preacher, with only one more year at seminary, which he was.

Friends, brother preachers, had politicked very hard to get him a chance with these two churches. Sure enough, God had called him to preach at both of them, right here in Judson County. This had happened after another young preacher, just out of the seminary, who was pastor at First Church for Everybody in Carey, the county seat, had taken Henry around and introduced him to the members of the pulpit committees in their homes. They had seen right away that God wanted this man in Judson County because of his education, his serious purpose, his obvious sanctification and too, because of a certain tough stubbornness he had.

Henry and Gloria had been on the field about four months. They lived in a house the Bright Hill church paid rent on, which was nearer the Bright Hill church than the church at Crooked Branch. The house was pretty bad. But, the Bright Hill church had a pastor's study in the church building and this was where Henry liked to go and stay.

"I'm going to work on my sermon for Sunday," he told Gloria. "I will take my text from Hosea." His last remark was said with solemn intonation.

There was a long silence. Henry did not look at her, but she was looking at him, hard.

"Forgive me for staring," Gloria said, "but I'm about looking a hole through you trying to see what you mean. Is that a threat you just made?"

Henry was cold and stiff. "I see you know something about Hosea," he said.

"I guess you'd say his wife was a whore," she said in a flat tone. "Yes. I know something about the Bible." She spoke as though this were news which would surprise him.

He put on what Gloria recognized as his professional air, something he had practiced for a long time which he used with people he had to deal with in his calling. He had one approach for sinners and another for troublesome Christians. Both of these ploys placed him in control of the situation, leaving the adversary person at a disadvantage.

He let his lips smile at Gloria, but she saw that his eyes were remote. "I believe you do know a lot about the Bible," he paused, and then said, "In your mind. I wonder how much knowledge of God you have in your heart."

"I know that I am a preacher's wife," she told him. "I try to do what I'm supposed to do."

"It's something you learned with your worldly intellect, I think," he said. "If this is the case, it's not going to hold up. It's not Spirit fed. It's not a blood bought change of your life you've got. I doubt you've changed at all. I believe you're still in sin, and separated from the Lord's church."

"Which includes you," she said.

"I'm a part of the body of Christ," he was happy to admit. "The church is called out, a separate people, separate from the world. I'm wedded to Christ along with other born-again believers. I had believed, in the beginning, that you were one of us."

"But now you believe I'm not."

"God let Hosea's wife be a whore so Hosea could learn how much it hurt a man for his wife to be a whore, so Hosea would understand how much it hurt God for Israel to play the whore with Him. God always has a reason for letting things happen as they do."

Gloria did not argue with him. It was no use. She knew that Henry demanded, above everything else, obedience to his standard.

Henry arose with his air of professional dignity and went out of the house and headed toward the church. Gloria continued to sit at the table.

Gloria believed there was an Earth-wisdom apart from divine revelation, things the Earth knew and would tell. Sometimes she had this. Henry never did.

She saw an old lady pass the windows and go around to the back of the house, and then she heard a knock on the back door. She got up and went and asked the old lady in, glad that someone had come, that something had happened to get her mind off Henry and Hosea.

The old lady said that she was Maud Spinet and she lived down in Crooked. No one called the section Crooked Branch. They said Crooked. Maud Spinet said she had caught a ride up to Bright Hill to visit her niece, but her niece had gone to Carey for the day. Since Reverend Graft was the pastor at Crooked, she felt like she could get something to eat at his house.

Gloria was pleased having the chance to be of service to Maud and she had her sit down at her table and she fixed her a nice breakfast. Maud Spinet went on and on about some sermon Henry had preached on Job which had impressed Maud and everyone a lot.

"I hope you haven't disfurnished yourself none, giving me this breakfast to eat," Maud said.

Gloria was thinking about the one time she and Henry had really quarreled, when she had been able to scratch his veneer of pompous dignity. She had never been satisfied about their marriage in that area which she felt was the most important part. What she thought of was sex. The time they had quarreled in earnest, she had heard his affectations and airs of superiority until she couldn't stand them, and then she had said, "You think you know so much, Henry. You think you know so much, and you don't even know how to take a woman to bed!" After that, he didn't even try anymore, and he suspected her of straying away with other men, but she hadn't ever. She never had one time.

"I'm disfurnished," she told Maud. "But, you didn't disfurnish me. I disfurnished myself."

"There's a young couple down at Crooked," Maud said. "I think Reverend Graft ought to know, they lost their baby. It only lived a day and a half. It was their third child. Thank God they have the other two healthy ones. They don't go to our church, but I thought Reverend Graft would want to go and visit."

"I'm sure he will," Gloria said. "I'll tell him when he comes back. He's down at the church."

Maud Spinet was a very polite woman and she did not want to stay longer if she was in Gloria's way, so she said she must go, but she would be glad to clean up the breakfast dishes first if Gloria would let her.

Gloria started to say no, but then, on the spur of the moment, she said yes and she and Maud carried all the dishes out to the kitchen and Gloria put on a kettle of water to get hot so they could wash things up. Leaning against the counter, Gloria looked Maud in the eye. She decided she could trust her because she was obviously a good woman.

"I don't have any friends here," she began. "I don't have anyone to talk with. Let's sit down while the kettle bolls. I want to tell you about my husband. He is a good man and he wants to be a good preacher. People hereabouts are lucky to have him."

"He's an educated preacher," Maud said. "We've had lots that weren't. He's good looking, too. All the young girls are crazy over him."

Gloria smiled to herself. "He came from a well-to-do family," she said. "All his uncles own factories and mills up in West Virginia. Henry's father owned a gun factory that made all kinds of hunting rifles and pistols and shotguns. Everyone in Henry's family is successful. They run their businesses honest, but one time Henry's father did some things wrong and he lost a lot of money and was about to go bankrupt. He thought about all the thousands of guns he had manufactured and sold and he couldn't believe that he was really losing everything."

Maud Spinet sat with her back very straight and smiled her pleasant old person's smile. Her eyes were very kind.

"Henry's daddy got an idea," Gloria continued. "He remembered that one particular model rifle had been their best seller and there were thousands of them in the world. He put ads in all the sportsmen's magazines saying that the rifle had a defect and could be dangerous and all of them should be sent in for correction and return. He advised sportsmen to send their rifles in at the manufacturer's expense and they would be sent back, after repair, postpaid . He rented a warehouse where they could be delivered and the rifles began to pour in. He had a warehouse full of them in a short time and sold them through a fence so they found their way into Central America. When people began to look for their repaired rifles, he denied having placed the ads or having any knowledge of what went on. The business was saved, but Henry's daddy had become head of what was called the crooked branch of the family and Henry was ashamed."

"Yes ma'am," Maud said. "He's such a strong Christian, I can see he would have been."

"Oh, he wasn't a Christian then," Gloria told her. "He was away at school. He was embarrassed in front of his cousins. He would never keep any of the family money. He gave his share away. He said his daddy stole it and he wouldn't have any part of it."

"It takes a lot of strength to do that," Maud said. "And, if he wasn't a Christian then, that made it twice as hard."

"He's strong, all right," Gloria said aloud, "strong in action and stronger in self-denial." To herself, she added, "The trouble is, he drags others along to practice self-denial with him, while he is doing it."

When Henry came home for lunch, Maud was still there. Gloria told Henry about the baby that had died out at Crooked, so they decided to give Maud a ride home and go to see the people who had lost the baby.

Crooked Branch Church for Everybody was built down in a hollow, by the branch, with a place to park cars up on high ground. Someone had given the land for the church building. It was a low strip beneath hardwoods which was no good for farming. The church had been there for about seventy five years. Few people farmed in Judson County any more. Natural gas had been discovered in the area. Everyone sat at home and waited for their monthly checks to come from the oil company for their leases.

Jezra and Yoorah Kindler were victims of the way things were. They did not own land. They and their forebears before them had always tilled the land of others. They were sharecroppers. With the discovery of gas, landowners had found it easier not to bother with having sharecropper families on their land. Sharecroppers found it more and more difficult to find someone to give them land to live on and work or to have a stake on. The Kindler's lived in a very poor shack on flat, exhausted land, with their two small children and the baby which was dead.

Maud Spinet showed Henry and Gloria where it was. Henry offered to drive her home, but she said it was not far. She stood behind the car, at the side of the road, watching while Henry and Gloria walked up to the house.

Gloria knew that they were being watched from inside the house. She knew that Maud knew it, too. Maud's being with them would make the Kindlers less hesitant about meeting them. When they knocked, Yoorah Kindler, pale and unsmiling, her lips thin, her cheeks hollow, her hair in wisps, asked them to come in.

"The baby is in there with my mother," she said. She pointed to a room where the windows were covered. "You can go in and see him if you want to."

Henry and Gloria got the impression of an old, old woman, tiny and the color of leather, bones covered with yellowish-tan skin, wrinkled and bent. The baby was in the crib that had been prepared for him before he had been born and died. It was too dark to see, but Henry and Gloria, once again, got an impression. There seemed to be wild flowers in the crib with him.

Yoorah came and stood in the door behind them. The old woman did not look up or speak.

"Brother Luther Clegg is here." she said. "He's our preacher. He'd like to talk with you all."

Brother Clegg had come out of a room where there seemed to be a number of people. He motioned to Henry to go outside with him. They left the shadowy house and stood together in the glare of the afternoon sunlight. This brighter place where men of God could meet and talk had to be the real world, not that dark hopeless place inside. The real world was in the sunshine, circled by corn. In front of the house, the poor grass on the flat land looked bleached and wispy yellow like Yoorah's hair.

Gloria stood with Yoorah by the open door, just inside, and the silence grew deeper and deeper and deeper. She felt that Yoorah was measuring her, probing to see if Gloria would act like a preacher's wife should act. And, Gloria told herself desperately, "I don't know how!"

They had not seen Jezra Kindler, but Gloria sensed that he was in the room where they knew some people were sitting. This was the inner circle. She and Henry didn't belong in there. She could understand that, but Henry never could.

In a minute, he came for her and they went to the car.

"They haven't made any arrangements for the funeral," he said. "Brother Clegg is very concerned about it. I like Brother Clegg. I don't know what they will do. They are Brother Clegg's people. I can only do so much about it."

Riding beside Henry, Gloria thought how it should be.

"I do want to be a good preacher's wife," she blurted out. "The kind my mother could have been."

"That is between you and Jesus," Henry said. "He is the way you can be that. You will be that if you're right with Him."

"But, I don't want Him," Gloria thought wildly, "I want my husband." She said, "I thought I was right, but you make me have doubts. You make me doubt it all: that I am saved, that I am born again, that I can lead others to do anything. You seem to doubt me. That makes me doubt myself. You said this morning that I don't have a blood-bought change of heart. When you say things like that, it makes me afraid. I feel I'm all right with the Lord, in spite of everything, until you say things like that."

"If you really know the Lord, nothing can shake you. You know that He has saved you and He can keep you." His voice was professional. Then, his voice changed and became intensely personal. "I suppose you mean by 'in spite of everything' that before we met you were promiscuous. Wanton. You haven't let go of that. You haven't relinquished it. You're still fascinated by it. You are a marred Christian, a very weak Christian, if you are a Christian at all."

"I didn't get to be a Christian the way you did," she told him. "I sort of eased into it. My family were all good. Every one of them was good. It came natural that I should be good, because my family is good. Are good. My parents are so glad their daughter is a preacher's wife. The Christian faith was never anything new to me. I didn't find it suddenly like you. It was always there. I was raised up in it."

"It looks like you were the only crooked branch on your family tree."

"And, you're the only straight shoot that grew out of the crooked branch of your family."

"I'm a graft on the family tree of Jesus Christ. My family is made up of other like-minded Christians who believe with me as I do. What can I have to do with the Devil's bastards?"

Gloria wanted to run. "I have total admiration for you," she said. "You are, actually, like Hosea. He was alone and he did what the Lord told him to do. He demanded obedience to God's standards. He demanded, for forty years, and he didn't succeed in what he tried to do, but he never retreated."

"There is no possibility for retreat with a Christian," Henry said. "From the moment when I came to Jesus in Charleston, West Virginia, my future was assured, sealed, and held in the possessive Hand of God. He won't let go of me. I see His purpose and will in everything I do, and I don't do anything that is not in accordance with His will and purposes. And, I have to win others over to Him. There is no passion like the passion for saving souls!"

"But, haven't you ever regretted giving away your money?" Gloria asked. She was going to be brave today. She was going to ask things she had never asked. "Was giving away your money God's will? You could put it to good use, now. When we see people like the Kindlers, or even Maud Spinet, don't you wish you could help them'"

"I take them the message of salvation, just as the word of salvation was given to me. I never had a moment's peace from the day I found out my father stole money until the day I got rid of it and found Jesus." He had taken on again the voice he used when he preached. "I felt that the family money was a curse. Unclean. Something kept turning in my heart and it led me to give the money away to the mission in Charleston, but I still didn't know peace, and they knew this at the mission, and they led me to Christ, and this was more being given to me than being given everything in the world would have been." His voice was husky, emotion-filled. "I want you, too, to give yourself wholly to Jesus."

"I just don't understand it the way you do," she screamed.

"Oh, let's pray," he shouted. "Let's stop the car and pray!" She nodded her head. He stopped the car beside the road and he prayed out loud, excitedly, wildly, clinging to her. And, she became caught up in his fervor so that she prayed aloud, too.

The next afternoon they rode out to see the Kindlers again. It was Saturday. Once again, Henry talked with Brother Clegg. Gloria did not go inside.

When they started back home, Henry told her that Brother Clegg did not believe the Kindlers would have a funeral for the baby.

"What will they do?" she asked, but she already knew.

"If everyone would leave," Henry said, "If Brother Clegg would go, and everyone else, they would take the baby out in the field and bury it between the corn rows. They don't have any money for a funeral."

Gloria was silent for a time. "I can't stand Saturday night," she cried. She felt too unhappy to care if he approved. "Saturday night was the time I used to have fun."

"Saturday night belongs to the Devil," he said. "Your heart still yearns and hungers for that kind of life." He was shouting. "The hog has returned to her wallow. The dog has returned to his vomit." He paused, paying attention to driving. Then, his voice softened. "The world is calling you back. The world and the flesh want to take you away from me. Please don't go, Gloria."

"I don't want to go."

"I need you to stay and help me care for my spiritual family," he said softly. "You care about them. You understand that they do need more than the gift of salvation. I don't understand this. You can give them what they need, apart from what my ministry gives them."

"Let's go back, in the morning, to see the Kindlers one more time," Gloria said. "You and Brother Clegg have been urging them to do something they really feel they can't do and that they may not be able to see the reason for. You need to get it across to them why certain things must be done, and we need to help them to be able to do these things. We can help them. We'll find a way." She felt excited, warm and alive, She and Henry were doing something together. "We'll go there in the morning and offer to help Brother Clegg. Between all of us, we can stop things from being so terrible."

"Yes," Henry said slowly. "I think we should do something. I feel led of the Lord to try."

That night, Gloria didn't feel empty and alone. She knew hope.

When she woke up in the morning, she had passed a happy night. Henry had not done or said anything more to indicate that things had changed between them, but still, she knew hope.

After they ate, they got in the car and drove over to Crooked. Henry parked in front of the Kindlers' house. They hurried up to the door.

After they knocked, the house remained still for a few minutes. Then, they heard movement inside. A child came and peered out a window and was drawn hastily away. Then, the door was jerked open. A man stood in the doorway, whom they guessed was Jezra Kindler.

"Is Brother Clegg here'?" Henry asked. "We've come to see how we can help with arrangements for the baby."

Jezra fixed his eyes on a clump of brush out in the middle of the cornfield. The corn was about knee high, and did not have a good color.

"There is no baby," Jezra said. Slowly he closed the door.

They drove back to Bright Hill in silence. The voice of despair had risen up for Gloria to hear, as that pale corn preached its own sermon, telling what it knew.

The congregation had already gathered at the church when they drove up.

Henry picked up his Bible off the seat of the car and hurried inside. Gloria followed only as far as the vestibule. She stood with the door half opened, listening to the preliminaries of the service, the hymns, the prayers, the offertory, the announcements. Then, there was a rustling as people settled down for the sermon. Without looking, Gloria could tell that Henry had walked to the pulpit and was opening his Bible. Then, she heard him.

"My text today is from the Book of Hosea," he said. He began to read loudly, angrily, preaching harder than he had ever preached. "'Behold, I will hedge up their way with thorns, and make a wall, that you shall not find your paths. And you shall follow after your lovers, but you shall not overtake them, and you shall seek them, but shall not find them.'" His voice was harsh and loud. Gloria heard the anger. She let the door close and turned away. The next thing he said, he said softly, sorrowfully, fearful, hoping: "'Then shall you say, I will go and return to my first husband: for then was it better with me than now.'" Gloria had heard the anger, but she did not stay to hear the need.

By the time Henry closed his Bible and began to preach about God's sorrow at the defection of his people, Gloria was walking up the big road, heading toward Carey.

GEORGETOWN, SOUTH CAROLINA

"Home Again, Home Again, Jiggerty Jig" was written in Georgetown in 1971. Will a woman who needs a strong man at the helm reconcile with her husband after he asserts himself?

HOME AGAIN, HOME AGAIN, JIGGERTY JIG

Mallet Motherwell had been sitting on his heel in the sawdust at the rear of the carnival tent for almost an hour - since seven-thirty, and had listened to a scratchy recording of "The Tennessee Waltz" played over and over so often he developed a headache. He took another long drink from the Coca Cola bottle he held in his hand, and wished that he had never heard "The Tennessee Waltz," or set foot in Tennessee, or consented to leave his home in Georgia when his wife went to work for the show.

Mallet was beginning to feel a little dizzy and confused. Nowadays, he stayed slightly drunk most of the time. He had a gallon of white lightning in the motor home which was provided his wife by the show, and he was forever refilling the Coca Cola bottle he constantly carried about in his hand, so that he might sip along and forget how really useless he was.

Almira, his wife, did not need him. She was in solid with Mr. Pendul, who owned the show, and Mr. Pendul had made things cozy and secure for her, for Mallet too, only Mallet didn't want it like that. Mallet wanted for it to be like it had been back home in Georgia when he had worked in the log woods and Almira had stayed home and depended on him to see after her. She had showed him respect in those days.

Mallet looked so small, huddled down behind the tent flap that he might have passed for a fourteen year old boy, although he was over thirty. His face was pinched and he wore a worried, strained expression. His skinny arms were coated with heavy black hair, and his hands were bony, with large knobby knuckles.

In a few moments, Mr. Pendul would walk out on the stage and introduce Almira's act, and Mallet would groan and say to himself, "Anyone told me I'd marry a woman'd get that fat, I'da called him a liar."

Tonight, Almira was wearing a dress of light blue which was printed with flowers. The neck was very low-cut and Almira usually kept it pinned with a safety pin. Now that she was on the stage, she had taken the pin out. Standing on the platform above the men in the audience, her skirt looked to Mallet as if it was plumb up to her ass.

Mallet shifted his foot about on the ground and felt his cheeks begin to burn.

Right away, Almira began to captivate the audience, saying "shit" a few times, getting them to really feel at ease with her. She knew an audience of men can be as skittish as a field of spooked horses if they get approached in the wrong way. She tried to be brassy while remaining coy, prancing about on her red high-heeled shoes, fluttering her hands daintily in the air.

205

She really showed all the grease mechanics and the sharecroppers, sitting on the wooden benches, she could be a good sport and, with a little coaxing, a barrel of fun.

She began to tell them about a tornado which had once devastated the area around Hawsehole, Georgia, where she said she lived before beginning to travel with the show.

Mallet always hung his head when she began to talk about Hawsehole, Georgia. He doubted there was such a place. Mr. Pendul had told her to say they were from there because it sounded funny and got a horselaugh or two from the men.

"Right off," Mr. Pendul bragged about her, "Almira liked to see her audience as galvanized as a feed bucket that were still setting in the hardware store."

"They was a fierce tornado hit Hawsehole, several summers back, in which they was a couple of women pulverized so they was never found." She kept moving around, light-footed on her high heels, and swinging her arms. "They was an old man, all doubled up with arthritis, tumbled in his wheelchair down a long hill, with his bulldog. One house was left undisturbed inside when the wind took the roof away."

"After the wind, it rained like an elephant passing," she said, building toward a climax. "Cats was all up in the trees, and dogs was swimming up to their butt-holes in water. It weren't nothing happy but the green tree frogs and they was just whizzing everywhere, croaking and running their tongues out to catch bugs!"

She paused to see what effect her talk had made. It was time to pause dramatically and make a grave announcement.

"That wind blowed so hard, right there in Hawsehole, Georgia, that it blowed a rooster into a jug."

"Are you shittin' us?" someone shouted.

Almira laughed and slapped her thighs and her fat face flushed prettily because she was enjoying all the attention. The men were responding the way they were supposed to. They were supposed to doubt her word. She had been naughty and baiting. Now, she turned proud.

"I've got that selfsame rooster right here!"

It was always the same. Mallet could hardly stand it, and yet he always witnessed his wife's performances. She teased the men and enjoyed herself until she was tired, and then she would motion to a man backstage who would bring the rooster, covered with a large black cloth, onto the stage.

"Show us something. Show it to us!" someone would yell, and then all the men would begin to shout, "Show it to us! Show it to us!"

Almira would bounce and bubble. Her chubby hands would wander slightly toward her dress hem. But, they would stop before she actually lifted her skirt. She possessed a bawdy laugh, and she would laugh with the men.

Mallet had always hated the rooster. Almira named him Hogbean, and he slept at the foot of their bed. When Mallet was cleaning out his jug each morning, he and the rooster would glare at each other, filled with hatred. Mallet could not stand to see the poor thing stupidly trapped and imprisoned. Almira had stripped all the rooster's pride away from him. "The poor critter couldn't help himself, neither," Mallet would say. It seemed Almira just had the means to overpower things and people, whether they wanted to be controlled or not.

Now, she jerked the cloth away, and Hogbean gazed foolishly out at the people in the tent. His head dangled out of the mouth of the jug, appearing to roll on his neck, giving him the appearance of being addled, confused by the sudden light.

The men howled and bent nearer. Some jumped out of their seats and moved closer. The place was getting hot. It smelled of smoke and sawdust and sweat.

"She weren't shittin' us. That rooster really were blowed into that jar."

Mallet left the men to marvel and Almira to preen with pride. He shuffled outside and went and sat down on the steps of her motor home. He hoped that Almira would come home, when her show was over, and the two of them could go and have a hot dog together.

However, in a few minutes, he saw her come out of the tent with Mr. Pendul. They got in his big black Buick together and drove off toward town, probably going to have a steak. Mr. Pendul's Buick, with its brilliant white sidewall tires and its lavish chrome trim, was a businessman's car, and everyone knew that Mr. Pendul was a businessman who meant business. He used the car to advertise who he was. Mallet hated the car.

One of the men came, carrying Hogbean home. Mallet was so angry he didn't even speak to the man. He waited impatiently for him to leave so that he could take a slavering nip from his bottle.

He didn't drink as much as usual, though, but kept himself sober so that he would be awake when Almira came back. It was past one thirty when she did.

"I wanted you to go with me for a hot dog," he said.

She lit the lamp.

"You didn't tell me. You should have told me you wanted me to go with you. Me and Mr. Pendul rode over to town to get a sandwich and some coffee."

"Mr. Pendul treats you mighty good, like you was something handed down," Mallet said bitterly. "I wonder how much he'd think of your act, or how much it would mean to those men that squall at you every night if they knowed what I know."

"They don't know," Almira said.

"How would it fucking be if I told people that Hogbean never got blowed into that jug? How'd it be if I told men that's put down their good money to see you put him in there when he was a biddy and he growed up in that jug? How'd it be if I told people I watched you try to do it with five or six other chickens before him, but they all died? Hogbean was the first one that was asshole enough to live, in spite of being shut up in a glass jug. Ain't no wind blowed Hogbean nowhere!"

Almira sneered at Mallet, showing him she couldn't bother answering. It was old ground. When Mallet started to threaten her like this, she'd get so nervous she'd grind her teeth against each other. She hated it. She had explained to Mallet a thousand times how miserable their life had been back home, and how hard she had worked, and how she had sacrificed to make things better.

Almira had very white and very thin skin, and whenever she became irritated she began to itch. Now, she scratched herself along her ribs and inside her forearms. She stood beside Mallet, lowering over him.

"You're not going to tell nobody nothing," she said. Her voice had begun to rasp. "Your scrawny ass has everything it wants or needs now. You've got it too good to spoil things."

"Look at how you talk to me! I don't have respect," Mallet said. But, she didn't hear him. He sat down and stared at the floor and turned his Coca Cola bottle around in his fingers. "I don't believe you ate a sandwich and drunk fucking coffee."

"What!"

"I think you had a steak."

Almira kicked off her shoes. "What if we did have steaks?" she asked. "What of it?"

"You're a hog, Almira," he told her. "The trouble is you crave for the fancy meat Mr. Pendul can give you. I'm the one as has meat where it counts."

Almira leaned back on the bed, scratching her left ankle with the toenails of her right foot. She looked at Mallet blankly for a moment. Then an incredulous look came to her face and she reddened and sat up straight. "If you're talking about that little thing you carry around with you, it wouldn't take much of nobody to produce better than that."

A flicker of panic darted into Almira's eyes. She looked at Mallet sidewise. He was staring at the bottom of his bottle, trying to make out where it was from. Almira slid out a chubby hand and caressed his arm and lay her hand on his shoulder. Mallet did not move. Under her fingers he felt lifeless, in spite of his bravado, like a side of dead meat with all the blood drained out. They had meat like that, for Almira to cut up, in the smokehouse back in Georgia.

"It were better," he said very softly, "back when I worked in the log woods and you stayed home, and on weekends I had pleasure like a man should, spending my own earned money. During those times, I felt like a man."

A glint of happy remembrance crept into Almira's eyes, but she turned away from Mallet, drawing her lips together in a grimace that mocked Mr. Pendul's businessman's grin.

"We had to start thinking about getting ahead," she said. "You can cry for the old times, but they were bad times. I don't want to go back! I wasted my whole life hanging around the company store and sitting on the fence watching the men work at the sawmill. In those days, the most exciting thing that ever happened was when some new fellow drove up to the mill with a load of logs, like you did one day. We thought the men who drove the trucks were straight out of the movies." She burst out with her bawdy laugh which she usually saved for the stage. "Well, I've seen plenty guys can drive trucks since then, and they ain't that special. I was a girl with girl's hopes. Now, I got a woman's hopes. I hope for a fuller life, and that means a life lived somewhere besides on the edge of the log woods."

When the lights were turned out, Mallet stretched himself in the darkness, staring up above himself, thinking and worrying for a long time.

He slept and, almost before it seemed possible, he woke again. It was still dark and he felt cold sober.

"I don't have to fucking stay and put up with this kind of shit," he thought. "I'll go back to Georgia. I'll catch me a truck, hitchhike me a ride back home." He had not taken off his clothes. He got quietly up off the bed and moved silently toward the door. When he was almost there, a thought struck him so that he bent down and picked up Hogbean's jug.

The sun was rising on the carnival lot. Dew was on the grass, and the tents and ropes were moist and smelled of damp canvas and creosote.

No one was about. Mallet took the jug some distance from the motor home, and seizing a hammer lie knocked the bottom out of it. Hogbean was frightened by all the noise and the fresh air rushing in about him. He pushed his beak out of the mouth of the jug and frantically tried to escape.

Mallet grabbed him by the tall feathers and jerked him out of the jug and tossed him a few feet away.

Hogbean, who had never been free before, floundered around on unsteady legs, frightened half out of his wits not to have the protecting walls of the jug to shield him. He began clucking, and squawking, and staggering drunkenly about among the trailers and tents, flapping his wings, and weaving his neck, choking and wobbling, until finally he half-flew and half-rolled under a trailer and hid.

"Getting loose so quick and unexpected has scared him," Mallet said. He sat down against the wheel of a truck and let his head hang down between his knees. "I reckon I wouldn't know what to do either if I was plumb shet of Almira right off."

An awful quaking and trembling took possession of Mallet. "I'm shaking like a dog shittin' peach seeds," he thought. His arms bounced on his knees. His legs felt so weak he was afraid to get up.

At last, he staggered up and went inside the motor home. Almira was still sleeping. She lay flat on her back and her stomach arched up, round as an inverted washpot under the sheet. Mallet took his foot and kicked the bed roughly.

Almira opened her eyes and stared at him angrily.

"What do you mean, waking me up"" she demanded. "You know I got to get my sleep. I got a show to put on tonight."

"You ain't got no show to put on."

"What to you mean"" A suspicious squint formed around her eyes. "What have you done?"

"I've broke Hogbean's jug. He's a-loose."

Almira clutched the skin under her throat with one hand and pushed herself up to a half-sitting position with the other. "You piss-ant!" she cried. "You limber-dick piss-head." She began to make a sound like the whining of a dog that's been run over by a farm tractor. At last, she sat straight up and quieted herself down for a minute. "Hogbean's a-loose?"

"That's right."

She sank back on the bed. "What are we going to do?" Mallet could recognize raw resentment. He had never seen that in Almira's face before. But, he could see fear there, too. Almira was afraid.

He clamped his jaws together and drew a deep breath. He forced a look of courage to spread across his face for Almira to see. "We're going home," he said. "You get up, right now, and pack up everything we've got in Tennessee, and get out of here and make a settlement with Mr. Pendul. Turn this motor home back over to him. We won't need it. I'll get us a home when we get to Georgia. We're going to take what's ours and get out of here. You hurry up, too. I want to be home afore dark."

Almira sat on the edge of the bed. Mallet held his breath. He was afraid she was going to throw herself back on the bed and work herself up to one of those states where she would howl and curse and try to claw Mallet to pieces if he went near her. She rose, slowly and wearily, picked up a handkerchief, and blew her nose. She found a suitcase and opened it. She dropped the handkerchief in.

"Yes," she said. "Let's go home. I'm tired being man, woman and mule in this family. I'm ready to quit."

She stood in front of him with her head slightly bowed. She spoke softly. "Mallet, if you get another log truck when we get back, could we paint a rooster head on the door and name it Hogbean? Just so I could remember?"

Mallet took a long time to answer. He spoke calmly and with authority. "I don't know," he said. "I guess I'll must have to study about that a little."

GEORGETOWN, SOUTH CAROLINA

"Restoration at Gull Tree " was written in Georgetown in 1971. A woman who is damaged by her father's denial of her, and her husband's absence, is threatened by a ghost.

This writer had seen his father for the first time in six years when the older man took refuge from Hurricane Camille's aftermath in 1969. Obvious had been how wide the gap between then still remained.

The woman in the story tries to cause the somber, silent, ominous ghost to pity her by revealing the emptiness of her life to him - and the need she has for her recherche husband, whom the ghost is about to take away.

RESTORATION AT GULL TREE

The house which was called Gull Tree stood far out on a marshy point of land. It was the only house in view. The highway, which ran coastwise through South Carolina, lay approximately a mile west of it, and the ocean, now blindingly blue and dancing onto the sand, now sullen and grey, lay in front of it. The gravel road from the highway was little traveled and Gull Tree saw few wayfarers. A mile away, the living sped onward in frenetic procession toward Myrtle Beach or Charleston. This was just as well since Vita Sash Ebony, the occupant of the house, was not eager for companionship.

A sandy track, just wide enough for one car, ran through palmettos and reeds from the gravel road to the door of the house. Where this track began, there was an old country store. Several rural mail boxes, supported by gnarled posts which leaned at tortured angles, were at the side of the road. Sharecropping farmers of the area made small purchases at the store, buying soft drinks and candy, some canned goods, sugar and flour, cigarettes and chewing tobacco.

Furbish, housekeeper at Gull Tree, visited the store each day, but Vita was seldom seen there. She spent her days in her house and her nights there. Sometimes she went to the house of one of her few sharecroppers, or to Pashtown Point, to attend to business.

Mrs. Vita Ebony had been given, at birth, the name Vita Sash. She was Newt Sash's natural daughter, which he was willing to admit. He had given Gull Tree to her so she could be independent and safe, but he hadn't married her mother.

Newt Sash owned everything, animal, vegetable, and mineral, which was above ground or in the waters, for miles around, and Vita took a certain bitter pride in her relationship to him, and even now always referred to herself as Vita Sash Ebony.

Newt had not valued her mother, so the community had not valued her, and Vita's mother had not valued herself. But, Vita knew her mother had value. She was a puritanical Roman Catholic with an innate work ethic. She served Newt well. She filled a chink in his life with an obstinate strength. Vita recalled, as quaint, her mother's blind belief. The older woman spoke of events which took place in Heaven, and Hell, and Purgatory, and Limbo (where babies who died before the age of accountability went), with a certainty of the existence of these places which was more manifest to her than the actuality of areas shown on maps of the United States which she had seen. She believed that travel between all these realms and the Earth, went on with the same purpose and energy as that on the Pee Dee and Cooper Rivers, as God willed.

Vita was thirty two years old and her poet husband was gone. Somewhere, he might be experiencing hard times. The thought gave Vita no pleasure. In the 1950's, America was not as accepting of poets as it would become a decade later.

The tin roof of her house was rusty and warped, and the pillars at the front porch bowed, preparing to fall. Without a man to tinker with it, Vita did not know how much longer the house would stand. The sand-laden, salty wind had long since ground all the paint off the pine boards. Night after night, Vita lay in her uneasy bed, listening to the shriek of this same wind, while she thought of how her mother had lived out her life alone, after Newt, and how she was living out her life after Sad Ebony.

The sea lay to the south of the house, and to the east of it, and to the north of it. Her land was just a sandbar tossed up in a heap by some great disturbance of the Atlantic. The only thing which was closer to the ocean than her house was a wizened, whitened, time worn tree, which was dead and served as a perch for seagulls and gave the property its name.

"Mr. Sad always say dis plac'd be a lot cleaner if we'd hack dat old tree down," Furbish said.

"The gulls would only come and roost on the ridgepole of the house itself," Vita told her shortly. It was hotter that day than anyone could tolerate, and Vita didn't feel like talking.

Furbish immediately sensed the mood Vita was in, so she said, "If you don't care, I'll take Mite and walk down to the store."

Mite was Furbish's granddaughter, whom Furbish was raising. The little girl was all the family Furbish had left. All her many children had gone north. They never came into the region or were heard from any more. Mite was the only thing her grandmother had to care about and her only responsibility.

Furbish was very old and her teeth were gone and her hair was thin and she was lean as a clothes pole. She wore gold-rimmed glasses. She was forgetful about many things, but she never forgot to give Mite the care she needed.

"Bring me back something cold," Vita told her absently. Furbish put on her broad-brimmed bonnet and Mite put her tiny hand in hers. They walked slowly through the sand toward the store.

Vita watched them go, and the heat shimmered up from the ground, wavering in the air. The sky was an unblemished blue, like some great inverted bowl of glazed ceramic.

A shiver teased up Vita's back, as though a 'possum had trotted across her grave. The quiet, the emptiness of the scene made Vita shiver. She hoped the day would hurry and pass before something bad could happen. In the evening, she would feel reassured. The evening would be cool.

It was a fierce country. No one but Newt Sash could have carved out an empire here. Newt, the Salamander, equally at home on land or sea. Newt, capable of dwelling in fire.

And, Vita was his daughter.

But, Vita didn't love the country any more. When she had been younger and had attended college using Newt Sash's money, and had brought carloads of madcap friends home for holidays, so the house had always been loud with fun and crowded with life, it had been good. The moss-draped trees on the highway to the college, the somber graveyards, the tail red brick houses held an atmosphere of age and charm and enduring social structure which was beautiful and comforting to Vita, then, but now, such things seemed merely dusty and decaying, when she thought of them, and she took no pleasure from them.

The good times when there had been swing music on the Victrola, and dancing, and booze stashed away under the porch, were gone. The young men who had laughed in her yard and run along her beaches, right before and during the Second World War, were gone - scattered - scattered so widely she could never find them any more.

And, after all that, there had been Sad Ebony, the poet. Sad Distich Ebony. And, he was gone too.

When Furbish came back she gave Vita a Big Orange drink in a glass of ice.

"Dey say down at de store dat Mr. Newt have gone up to his place at Myrtle Beach, and he may not be back all summer unless something goes wrong."

"Is that so?" Vita said without interest. She knew Newt didn't place any value upon her or her doings. People who had nothing to do talked about Newt. Her own sharecroppers would be idle until crop gathering time. There was now nothing for anyone to do but sit out the hot season.

Furbish and Mite went and sat down in the back yard in the shade. They could sit for hours together without speaking or showing any sign of life.

Vita gazed out across the stilly standing reeds to where she could see the waveless ocean.

Slowly the afternoon wore away.

When it began to be twilight, a small breeze stirred to life and Vita came down off her porch and walked out onto the sand of the beach north of the house. She stood and contemplated the curve of the shoreline and thought how restful and serene this familiar scene sometimes was at this time of a summer's evening. But, she didn't want it restful. She didn't want to rest. She wanted something to happen.

Feeling a warning tug, a mere tingle of apprehension, she observed that she was not alone on the beach. A man was walking slowly in her direction. He was not one of the black sharecroppers from the vicinity. Vita could see he was a white man dressed in dark clothes. He plodded. There was an air of weariness about him. His passage was labored but soon he was close enough for Vita to see that something like a small dog walked at his feet.

Vita could not imagine who he might be. No stranger ever came to the beach. She stood frozen and watched the man and the animal approach. Her face prickled. Her chest moved with a growing staccato rhythm. She wiped her palms against her skirt. She had wished that something would happen, but now she was afraid.

Before reaching her, the man stopped and stood still, but the animal continued to walk directly toward her.

The animal proved to be a large cat. This was a matter of wonderment to Vita. He was a proud, robust cat with fur of swarthy black. Without hesitation, he stalked up to Vita's feet. Vita was more interested in the man, but the sun was setting so she could hardly make out his form in the dusk. He stood looking at her, and she felt a chill, although the evening was still warm. She turned and hurried toward the house.

The cat accompanied her.

When they arrived in the yard, the cat went up to the rusty old hand pump, which was not used since an electric pump had been installed. After the war, Newt Sash had electricity put in the house. Vita had a radio and refrigeration now. She had an electric pump which provided running water, but the old hand pump still stood in the yard. The cat looked up at it, and gave a loud cry.

"That's a smart cat," Vita said. "He knows what a pump is."

She led him inside and gave him water to drink. Then she took him out on the back porch and fed him bread and milk and hamburger.

The cat did not arch his back with satisfaction and rub himself against her legs. He did not purr. Even for a cat, he was aloof, his pleasure subdued. Vita could see he disdained friendship.

"I wish he'd stay with us," she thought.

But, Furbish looked at him with suspicion, and he viewed her with particular scorn.

After he ate, he sat perfectly still in a solemn and melancholy study and Furbish remarked that he was a Gib-cat for sure.

But, Vita's thoughts were with the man on the beach. She had quickly noted, in the glowering twilight, that he was young appearing, sturdily made, and masculine. There was a strange conflict in his bearing, a near-defeated self-assurance, a tired, proud man who was attempting with difficulty to be confident and stable.

"He could be a firm and durable man," Vita told herself. That would be a relief after Sad Ebony.

Sad was only twenty seven, even now. He had been one of the younger and more helpless Bohemians who had shared in Vita's festivities during the old days. His weakness had touched Vita. He possessed a certain sweetness of nature, and he was endowed with a look of eternal innocence although he was not innocent.

Vita felt sorry for him now. Wherever he might be, he probably didn't know what to do to help himself.

The visitor on the beach was a different matter. Vita put on one of her prettiest dresses and arranged her hair in the most attractive style she knew. She made Furbish tidy up the living room so that Furbish grew suspicious and asked,

"You expecting someone to come here?"

Vita laughed self-consciously and asked who could possibly come. No one ever came. She just wanted things set in order for a change.

She turned on the bright light in the living room and went out and sat on the porch.

"I'm foolish to think he might come here," she thought. "He probably lives up the beach toward Pashtown Point with a wife and five children. He'd never come down here at night looking for his cat."

The cat, knowing that she had come outside, came around from behind the house and sat on the top step near her feet, staring out into the dark yard. They heard the rustle of the reeds, and they smelled the salt.

"Even if he did come," Vita thought, "what would I do?" A little feeling of panic stirred up a tumult inside her. "What would I do?"

The moon would be full on the following night. Vita could see the sparkling of the water on the face of the ocean,

"But, I would like to talk with him," she thought. "I'd just like to talk to a man like that."

The man did not come, and when Vita finally decided to go inside and go to bed, she tried to pick up the cat and take him in with her, but he bolted from her arms and went and sat down at a distance in the yard, where she could see his eyes flashing.

Vita got in bed and felt the emptiness stretching away from her out into the endless darkness. She lay very still. There was no need to reach out, for there was nothing there to be reached. She slid her soft hands along the sides of her body. She felt herself grow hot, heard her own panting. She began to feel herself, moist and open.

"I wish I had two fingers, each as large as a hoe handle, to put inside me," she thought.

The next morning the cat had gone away.

Vita was looking for him in the tall weeds which grew around the old pump when Furbish came to tell her that Mite was sick. Mite had always been a sickly child, and Vita did not think she was quite bright.

Now, however, she helped Furbish dress her and put her in the car, and they drove to the clinic in Pashtown Point to see a doctor.

Mite was in a high fever, and the doctor used every method to save her, as her situation was desperate, but even so, at sundown that evening the tiny child died.

Furbish was inconsolable and Vita was unable to reason with her, so finally she let her alone. With Furbish's pastor and some of the sharecropper women, the funeral arrangements were made. The funeral was a grim ceremony. A child had died. The community was deeply moved.

The funeral over, Vita settled down as before in her bleak home which was made more desolate due to the presence of the mourning and sorrowful Furbish.

Furbish rarely spoke now and she did not attend to her work. Vita had to do all of the menial tasks connected with their living. Furbish could hardly be prevailed upon to go to the store. Vita would take the car and go bumping down through the scorching field whenever they needed something.

"It's all de same to me if I live or die," Furbish would say. "I was only trying to stay here to raise dat baby. Now, I got nothing left to do. I wish de Lord would take me."

Vita wept in despair about her life. She lived in a punitive and progressive state of frustration. In her mirror, she could see that her appearance had become disheveled. She had developed a tic. She would sit, moodily jerking her head from side to side, trying to clear her mind.

"What am I being punished for?" she would ask herself. "And, who is punishing me? I should leave Gull Tree. Perhaps, in a new place, things would change for the better."

But, walking outside, she would take up a handful of warm sand from the earth at her feet, and let it trickle through her fingers. "This sand is Newt Sash," she would think. "This is the part of himself that he gave me. This sand is his body, and these familiar waters are his blood. He never gave himself to me when I was a child because I was not his legitimate daughter. I never had a father, and now I've got no man of my own, and if I leave this ground, then I'll have nothing. I have to stay on this soil which is Newt Sash."

Furbish had been acting as if she had something which was an increasing burden in her mind; something which she wanted to say, a complaint, or a grievance of some sort.

"Miss Vita," she said, "I've got to tell you why Mite ain't here no more. I got to tell you why she died. All of us knows why. We knows why, down at the store, and out on de farms, and up de beach to Pashtown Point. Ain't no use not to tell you."

"Tell me what?" Vita asked. "Mite got a fever that the doctor couldn't break and she died."

"It was you caused it," Furbish said.

"I?" Vita shouted sharply. "I? How?"

"You brought dat cat up to de house."

"I what?"

"Dat black, silent cat. You found him on de beach, and brought him in."

"But, he didn't go near Mite," Vita said. "She didn't touch him."

"Dat cat been coming to visit folks up and down dese Georgia and Carolina beaches for over a hundred years," Furbish said. "Dat cat is an omen of death."

Vita was completely out of patience with Furbish, whose imagination, she felt, was running away with her. Furbish was merely, superstitiously, associating the fact of the cat's visit with the fact of Mite's death, where in reality no connection existed.

Vita talked about the matter with her sharecroppers, out on her farms, and although they were reluctant to talk about it, she was able to determine that there was an old legend along these coasts concerning some man who had been wronged by a woman. He had drowned in the Atlantic, and was said to return from time to time, to the beaches, in the company of a black cat. He never approached a dwelling or spoke to anyone, but the cat would go up to particular houses hoping to be invited to eat, and whenever he could enter in, death would always follow within twenty four hours. Residents along these shores never showed hospitality to a cat they didn't know.

Vita felt that it was a mere stroke of bad luck for her that the events surrounding the death of Mite should coincide with the details of some old legend and thereby further complicate her exasperating existence.

A month passed, and the moon was almost full again, when Vita walked on the beach once more, picking up shells and interesting pieces of driftwood. As she often did, she toyed with the idea that she should move to town and open a small shop which offered souvenirs of the region for sale, suitable for gifts. She had a large pile of shells and driftwood accumulated under her porch, and assorted cypress knees.

Around the curve of the beach, she saw the man and the cat.

"If he's flesh and blood," she said, "I want to know it."

She walked resolutely toward the pair, tossing aside her trophies of the sands. When she was about ten paces from the pair, she stopped and stood looking at the man. He was dressed in fisherman's clothing of a bygone time, and in his eyes was a look of hopelessness and fatigue so intense it could only have been born out of ages of being goaded by some monstrous obsession which led to the monotonous performance of some compelling but repugnant endeavor.

"He is not a living man," Vita thought sadly. "Please don't make more trouble for me," she said. "Is there anything I can say? I've heard it was a woman who hurt you and wronged you. Can this woman do anything to even things? Make restitution? In any manner make you easy? What can I do?"

He looked at her with deep desolate eyes, and a sudden thought penetrated Vita's mind.

"There is nothing which the living may do for the dead. We cannot apologize, or gain their forgiveness, or atone to them. Once they are dead, the bond between is severed and we cannot right wrongs, or pay debts, or give warmth and companionship. These things must be done while the person lives, or it will be too late."

"I'm sorry," she told him. "I'm sorry. I'm so sorry." She could feel his fury, was aware of his singleness of purpose. She knew his motivating force was vengeance, and this was directed toward all women. Turning, she saw the proud, black cat marching with the stately tread of an executioner toward her door.

"Furbish," she whispered. "Furbish."

She stumbled on the rough ground, and the roots of the palmettos. The twilight thickened, and she became tangled in a network of reeds. For all her effort and hurry, the cat arrived at the house well ahead of her.

She went around back and flung open the door of the kitchen. The cat was eating from a large bowl in the middle of the floor. Furbish was standing over him with glittering eyes, muttering and talking excitedly.

"You nice black kitty cat. You come to take old Furbish out of her misery. You come so old Furbish can die at last. You eat good, kitty cat. You eat and satisfy yourself. Soon old Furbish will be satisfied."

"Furbish, you'll drive yourself crazy." Vita shouted. "Get that cat out of here!"

She took up the broom and drove the cat out of the door. He had eaten his last mouthful of food, and he walked before the threat of the broom with haughty air. He climbed a chinaberry tree which grew beside the unused hand pump, and seated himself on a low limb where he waited, brooding and somber, for the moon to rise.

Furbish ran inside her cabin behind the house and locked the door.

Vita stole close to the door and she could hear Furbish chanting and wailing dismally, talking to the good Lord and Mite.

Vita went inside and closed her doors and did not bother to light the lights. She would not sit up and wait for the man to visit on this night.

When the sun rose the next morning, Vita went immediately to Furbish's cabin, where she found that Furbish had died. She had probably died of apoplexy.

Vita could do nothing but attend to the burying, which was even more depressing than Mite's funeral had been - old people frightened that Death would come for each of them because He had come for Furbish.

After this, Vita lived alone. She would go down to the beach and sit down on a great log that lay near the spot where she had talked to the man who brought the cat.

"He was such a nice man," she would preface her cogitations with. "I don't see how any woman who had a man like that could mistreat him. If I had a man like that, I'd be good to him forever." She felt she needed a man like that, a man who was different from Sad Ebony.

The thought occurred to her that, perhaps, somewhere, some woman was looking at Sad, thinking that he was a nice boy, wondering how the woman he belonged to could not have fulfilled him, could have failed to make him happy. But that woman did not know Sad Ebony as Vita did, and Vita did not know the man on the beach as his wife had known him.

Yet, in her life, Vita had failed in everything. She had failed Newt Sash, who had educated her and given her a start in life, so that she might do more for herself than become a recluse, a hermit, some sort of developing eccentric, and she had failed Sad Distich Ebony, the recherche.

"Oh, what am I to do"' she sighed. "What can I do?"

She recalled her mother's Catholicism, and that she had herself been baptized into the Church.

She got in her car and drive to Pashtown Point, where she sought out the priest, Father Scarlatti. They sat down in his garden to talk.

"I am Vita Sash Ebony," she said. "My mother named me Vita because she felt, when I was born, life had come into her existence, but I wasn't allowed to stay with her very long. She was Newt Sash's mistress. She ran a saloon and dance hall for him and made him money. I have been told his wife was an aristocrat from Savannah who gave him aristocratic sons. Newt Sash had many women, and many sons, and many daughters, and much land, and he's the strongest man who ever lived. He's powerful enough to give someone a life, or to take someone else's life away. He educated me and gave me two small tracts of land which can support two families of sharecroppers and me. When I married, I didn't go to my husband empty-handed. I had the land. I enjoyed the life Newt Sash gave me, but I never had a mother, and I never had a father. This did something to me. And now, I don't have a husband."

"Oh." Father Scarlatti sounded sympathetic. "Did he die, then?"

"No," Vita said, "he left me."

"Then you have a husband. He is just not with you."

"You're right. I believe you marry only once. My mother taught me that. I wish I could be loyal to him. In truth, he is the weakest person you could imagine. He is a poet and a writer of plays, sensitive, lyrical. He is, simply, endearingly helpless."

"There are strengths and there are weaknesses," Father Scarlatti told her kindly. "Every man is not strong in the same way. Every man is different. No other man is exactly like Newt Sash."

"I know," Vita said.

"You have never forgiven your husband for not being a copy of Newt Sash, and yet it was you yourself selected Sad Ebony to wed, knowing that he was exactly opposite of your father on every point."

"I don't know why I married him," Vita said. "There were plenty of others."

"You are the one who needs to be strong," Father Scarlatti said. "Your blood is Newt Sash's blood. In this world, we are made to complement one another. A person who is compelled to be strong needs the weak of the world. It is for them that he is strong. You need a person like your husband, like Sad Ebony, although you may have much more admiration for a man like Newt Sash."

"I don't know if I will ever see Sad again," she said. "He may have made a life for himself where he is."

"You could try to find him. You could seek him out and ask him to come back."

"Where must I start? What should I do?"

"Begin a little at a time, a newspaper ad here, an inquiry there. You'll be getting used to the idea that he is coming back. Maybe he won't. You'll never know if you sit and wait for him and do nothing. If you do nothing, nothing is going to happen." Father Scarlatti stood up. "Come in my study. There's something I'd like you to read - a bit of history pertaining to this church. This is a very old church as North American churches go. We have many bits of regional history which should be interesting to people living hereabouts. What I want you to see is a statement which was written over a hundred years ago by a woman who lived, perhaps, in the very area where you live. Quite often the written legacies of the very old help the young. You are young. Those who are about to die write, when they have a completed experience to tell of. It is their seeing things whole which makes their perception different." He looked out across the graveyard which lay, with its brickwork and its aged shrubs, behind the church. On his face was the expression of one who has made his peace with dying and death. "It is meant for the dead to be of service to the living through the example of their finished lives. Surely, the one tale which all the dead speak is that life is short and fragile and should not be misused or wasted. It is for the dead to help the living, and not the living the dead."

"The dead do speak to the living?" Vita asked.

"Through their lives and their works while living, I would say," Father Scarlatti said. "In the Middle Ages, the Church believed that souls in Purgatory could come back and visit the living. They believed that souls out of Purgatory who restrained themselves from doing evil to ones they had come back to make reprisal against, would receive a reward. Their days of punishment would be shortened."

"Is that true?" Vita asked.

Father Scarlatti laughed. "No one believes that any more," he said. "The woman who wrote the statement I would have you read was named Betsy Brierwood. Her husband was named Roach Brierwood. He worked as a fisherman and he robbed the bees. Once while out looking for blackfish, he was drowned. His widow came to this church, in a somewhat irrational state of mind. She is buried here. There is a stone back there in the comer of the cemetery." He removed a paper from an old file box. "We have copied this over from time to time. The original is put away.

Vita touched the paper tenderly. She read it slowly, letting the words sink in. "I, Betsy Brierwood, widow of Roach Brierwood, at the Church of St. Theodore, this 27th day of July, 1913, do write herein my confession and repentance for the evil I have done on Earth, being now at the age of eighty-seven and feeling Death to be imminent -

"At the age of twenty seven, I married Roach Brierwood, a man of the Hatteras region, who was a man good and true, but I did not think so because he was flirtatious with other girls, and violent of disposition, and jealous by nature. When we had been married less than two years, I locked him out, and he took my pet cat (which I loved and which seemed to have more love for me than he had), out of his fierce jealousy, and flung it into the ocean where it drowned. So I told him what a cruel brute I considered him, and bid him go be with the cat. Now, he went out with the fleet with me cursing him and wishing him dead, and somehow, he was lost overboard out there at sea, so's I never saw him again.

"Now, I have lived twice as long a widow as I lived in my whole life before I drove my husband out. I know now that every person has faults and Roach Brierwood's were no worse than the next man's and might have been eased if he had lived, but even with his faults, it was better living with him than being alone. All my life, since Roach, I have kept this church clean and waited on the Fathers, but it would have been better tending my own house and waiting on my children.

"If any young woman reads this, she had better stay with the husband she has got herself; whether she thinks he is exactly the kind of man she wants or not. She might be like me and find out, when he is gone, she had what she wanted all along.

"I don't know why my husband died, but maybe it was because, after he heard me curse him, his life didn't matter enough for him to take care in the boat. Anyway, he died thinking I hated him - may God have mercy on my soul."

* * * *

Vita Ebony had a crop to gather in. Suddenly, she was busy again and the heat declined and her days were filled with business affairs. She hurried about, to the bank, to the gin, to the farms, noting that her crop was good and her profit would be satisfyingly great this year.

She found a small poem by her husband in a quarterly magazine and obtained his address from the publishers. When the farm business was ended, she went for him.

"I want you to come home, Sad Distich," she said. "The house at Gull Tree is empty, and I need you there with me."

Sad sat down and his fine, fair hair fell down onto his forehead and his lip trembled and the tears rolled out of his eyes.

"I haven't done anything since I left you," he said. "I want to write a rhymed drama. 1 have the whole plan of it in my head, but I haven't been able to write it down."

"At Gull Tree, you will be able."

That fall, Sad Ebony wrote on his scraps of paper, and Vita walked about the yard and the beaches.

She talked aloud to herself. "I don't know what he's doing, or if it's worth anything. He may never amount to anything. He's full of anxiety and secrecy. He probably only came home with me because he was tired of being hungry, and insecure, and of working to exist. I can't be sure he cares anything for me, or even for Poetry."

Then, she would stop and pick up a handful of sand.

"There may be no strength in my husband, but Newt Sash's strength is here in the land for me to draw upon. As long as it is here, I can be strong, and maybe I can help Sad achieve his dreams."

She was afraid that Sad was sick. He appeared sick.

Late in the season, when the reeds on the dunes were brittle and dry, and the wind was crisp, Vita walked on the beach looking at the various shells which lay scattered about. The sun as setting and the world was totally quiet.

Vita felt that someone was looking at her. She turned slowly and looked down the beach to where the great log lay. Just beyond it, Roach Brierwood was standing, and the black cat sat on the sand at his heel. Roach watched her intently. He stared at Vita with sorrowful countenance.

Vita felt her heart begin to pound. She ran immediately up to the apparition and spoke to it.

"Why have you come here'" she demanded. "Are you so bitter and unhappy that you can't bear to see anyone else have even normal satisfaction? Betsy regretted what she said to you. All her life she regretted. I have read what she said. She knew every minute for almost sixty years that she was wrong. She did not forgive, because she learned that there was nothing to forgive. Can't you forgive her and know peace? Forgive her and quit punishing her through every woman in the world. She punished herself for sixty years. It was enough." Tears showed her misery and desperation streamed down Vita's face. "Haven't you had enough of loneliness in over a hundred years of this, you and that cat? Have I got to be lonely, too, to satisfy you? Must I be lonely for all the rest of my life?

"I can see that you were a vital, handsome man, and a nice man," Vita told him, and his face grimaced in an expression of terrible loss and despair. "I would like you if we could be two people knowing each other. I would do anything for you. We'd get along. But, there is nothing that I can give you. The dead have no need of the living or the things which the living possess. It will do you no good to take my husband from me. Neither you nor your eerie cat need him.

"I need my husband. You can help me, rather than taking revenge on me. Sad Ebony is all I have, and what I can help him to make of himself is all I can ever hope to have. If he's taken away, I'll have nothing, and I'm too crippled to find myself someone else." Suddenly, she knew that Sad was the most important thing in the world to her.

Roach Brierwood stared at her with a blank expression. He seemed to be thinking.

"You'll never have peace until your hatred for Betsy Brierwood and all women is burned out of you."

The black cat left Roach's heel and started to walk away toward the house. Roach looked down at him and seemed to communicate with him.

"Oh, stop him! Stop him!" Vita screamed. She felt heavy tears fall on the bib of her blouse. A sharp breeze rose from the sea. She heard it buzz, making a sound like that made by insects. The sound seemed to craze Roach. His face contorted even more.

The cat stopped and looked up at Roach angrily. For a moment, their eyes locked in a look of hatred and abhorrence, a battle of their wills. The intensity of their rage and determination was so strong that Vita was terrified and began to cry aloud. The three of them grappled in wordless battle.

Roach seemed to grow taller and broader, and the cat seemed to swell and darken. They stood gripped in that terrible mental duel for several minutes while the frightful buzz continued. Then, the cat seemed to deflate and to soften a little. The arch of his neck was not so regal. His eyes did not burn so bright. For a moment, Vita thought he would fall over and die of frustration, but he got command of himself and began to walk away, back up the beach to the north, in the direction from which they had come. The buzzing stopped.

The man turned and slowly followed the cat.

Sad Ebony had come out onto the dunes. He ran down to meet Vita.

"I've finished one act," he said. "The play is going to be good."

Vita put her hand in his. She felt comforted that their shoulders touched, as they walked to the house. In the settling night, under a moon which was almost full, she could see around the curve of the beach, Roach Brierwood and Betsy's cat, walking slowly out of her life.

"Find peace," she whispered. "Oh, both of you, find peace."

GEORGETOWN, SOUTH CAROLINA

"Marais, Marais, How Does Your Garden?" was written in Georgetown in 1971. Is it possible a wealthy, embittered widowed actress (now retired from the stage) can bury the lifelong hatred she has borne for her father, through the gentle admonitions of a slow of speech and dusty of person Italian stonecutter?

The writer is again writing about the negligent, uncaring father. See "Restoration at Gull Tree. " Now, the father is dead. The writer depicts in this story the emotional chaos that is left to reside in the offspring, by a failed parent. Presenting himself as female, the writer can express the hurt he feels at his father's indifference toward him. The male in him cannot be hurt, only angry. It is not manly to feel hurt. See forthcoming "When Circles Run Backwards."

A bastard that is denied is a serpent which will turn about to bite and kill.

MARAIS, MARAIS, HOW DOES YOUR GARDEN?

Marais ran instinctively to the spot in her ugly garden where the copy of Ossip Zadkine's statue of Rimbaud, she had erected, stood in the place of the St. Francis her father had originally had there. She did not even see the late spring flowers which were blooming against her will, flowers which, flowerlike, bloomed in spite of their possessor's desires - when the sun called them proclaiming life. Marais was not thinking of life this morning.

If only she had not been compelled to give Fenny a ride out to San Simeon to look at a copy of Michelangelo's David, which she had removed from its pedestal in her headlong effort to render Hardy San Simeon's garden hideous! The statue had been put away in a shed, and was for sale.

If only Fenny hadn't gotten her off balance!

She had stopped her car in the drive in front of the large house on the Gulf called San Simeon, a house, grey and Spanish in architectural style, her house. She had sent Fenny at once to the barn where she had stored the David. If he wanted it, he could have it for nothing for all she cared. She only hoped he would be off the place by noon.

Her full breasts rose and fell, and her dark eyes flashed dramatically. He had no right to talk to her as he had! She hardly knew him - dumb college kid! He was not dry behind the ears! But, he considered himself one of the now generation, and perhaps he was what passed for "mod" in Waveland, Mississippi, in 1969.

"I am Marais Eau d'Amont," she thought angrily. "I couldn't be in love with Pumo Juvarro. I've got too much pride to let myself love that handyman. Let his father protest that they are artisans. It is all the same. What is a stonecutter, anyhow? Someone who works with his hands, and walks around with his clothes covered in marble dust."

But, Fenny had said she was afraid.

Marais beat her fists against the statue of Rimbaud. It could not be true.

223

Fenny said that Marais sought older men and avoided young men because she was afraid of them, that she had no experience with young men - she had never known her father, and she sought him in grey heads, behind gentle, almost senile smiles.

Talking with Fenny had made her feel like something dirty and unclean. She felt an awful guilt. Now, as she thought of it, she was angry with herself.

"He talked about me as though I am sick," she thought. "I'm not sick. I don't have some inner flaw that I should be ashamed of. I've done some wrong things in life. I ..."

She never let herself think about any wrong she had ever done. She was her own woman. She made her own decisions, and paid for her own mistakes.

"I'm thirty years old," Marais told herself. She was a ripe, mature woman. Her body was full and firm. She carried herself well, a learned habit from the days when she had been an actress. "I don't have any interest in the conversation of boys like Fenny (he's almost a girl), or for the charms of a man like Pomo. He is a perfect animal. I could admire him the way I'd admire a blooded horse."

At the thought of pure bloodlines, a look of despair crossed her face. That was the center of the whole problem. She recalled that she was a bastard.

Whenever she thought of this, the ground under her feet seemed to turn to sawdust so that she became afraid that she would sink down in it and flounder there until she was smothered.

There was the screech of tires on the pavement at her front gate. Marais was thrown into full panic to note Pomo's dusty truck coming up the drive. There was the almost illegible sign painted on the door - Melus Juvarra & Son - Stonecutters - Lawn Statuary & Funeral Monuments. Marais wished she had never contracted with them, of all people, to remove the statuary her father had placed at San Simeon, and to replace it all with pieces she had chosen.

That might have been a mistake. But, she had gone a long way toward making Hardy San Simeon's beautiful garden a horror. This was her driving purpose. She could handle any annoying personal difficulties with the Juvarras!

Pomo had parked his truck behind her car and leapt out. Marais tried to cower behind a brick wall on which was displayed a stone death's head with shawl, the hands crossed on its bony rib cage.

Pomo was looking all about. Marais shook her mane of chestnut brown hair. She had covered it with a silk scarf, and now, soft strands of it spilled out on her shoulders.

Pomo was coming along the path. He had caught sight of her. She noticed, now, how a look of near adoration had come into his soft, friendly grey eyes, as if he were beholding a Madonna.

She was half Spanish and half French. Maybe this slow, dusty Dago could see something in her of the Blessed Mother. Her eyes held a deep enough look of patient suffering!

"I'm not afraid of you," she said.

"I didn't come here to make you afraid," he told her.

She walked a few steps, and looked down at her reflection in a clear pool. Flowers bordered the pool and framed the image of herself in sunlit color. Now, she became aware of them, optimistic, determined, "smiling through" here in the midst of foreboding and dismal statuary which she had brought to the garden - changeless and timeless before the terrible change she had wrought. Well, she'd fix that! Already, she had a contract with a landscape gardener from Bay St. Louis. He would follow her instructions to the last violet. She'd uproot everything Hardy San Simeon had done! She knew what kind of plants would grow there when she was through!

"I've got to get rid of the flowers here, and the shrubs. I won't be through until this whole garden is barren and repulsive." She tread on a row of narcissus. She especially hated them - their odor. "And, the house." she said.

"You have strange ideas," Pomo said. "I had made up my mind to leave you alone, but I've found out I care too much about you. I've got to find out what I can do to help you to be happy."

"How did you arrive at the conclusion you care for me?" Marais asked sarcastically. "Where did this marvelous insight come from?"

Pomo sat down on a bench by the pool. He put one foot up on the bench. His pants leg rose up so that an inch of his sturdy, hairy leg showed above his heavy work shoe. The hair, like that on his chest, was very thick and black.

Marais looked at his leg for a moment and looked away.

"I found myself wanting to defend you," Pomo said, choosing his words carefully like one who isn't used to talking much.

"Oh, you felt defensive of me," Marais said. "You saw yourself as my knight in shining armor. Well, I'm no lady in distress. I'm handling my own affairs all right. I think I've done pretty well for myself. I had no father. You know that." Her face hardened. "You do know that, don't you?"

"Yes. I know that," Pomo said. He blushed so that his fair face became slightly pink. Marais noted how dark and coarse his beard was. By late afternoon, he would badly need a shave.

"My mother was a great actress. Rosalind Eau d'Amont possessed something which made her great - a quality of the soul. People said I was like her, but with me it was a practiced, learned, contrived sort of thing. It wasn't real. But, it passed for the real thing. I was successful on the stage."

"But, your heart wasn't in it," Pomo said softly.

"What heart'" Marais shouted. "I have no heart. I'm incomplete - crippled. I have no heart. Hardy San Simeon did that!"

Marais knew that Zarathustra realized that if there were no men for the sun to shine for, the sun would take no joy in shining. Marais had never been permitted to shine for her father, and so did not know how to shine for any man.

"And, are you lonely?" There was deep sympathy in Pomo's voice.

Marais looked for a moment as though she would fling herself against the hideous wall out of frustration and anger.

"I manage to fill the hours," she said with scathing sarcasm. She wondered if the sarcasm was directed more toward herself or Pomo. "I married a man. You know that I am a widow."

"Yes," Pomo said.

"An old man. I inherited wealth."

"You have done well."

"I bought the estate called San Simeon after Hardy San Simeon was dead. I am going to totally deface it. I am going on to destroy every work he ever did. I will get my revenge against his name, the name he never gave me."

"If you do this destruction," Pomo told her sadly, "you may destroy yourself, too."

"There is no place in my life for love!" Marais cried. "I have chosen hate and revenge over love. If that means I have also chosen death over life, then so it shall be."

Pomo looked her full in the eyes so that Marais drew back feeling an unpleasant confusion. His eyes seemed about to fill with tears.

"It is so much waste," he said. "You are so beautiful." He extended one hand and touched her pale forearm with his fingertips. How rough his hands were, square and large and work worn. The backs of his hands and his wrists were coated with coarse hair, but his skin was light. He did not tan, although he spent many hours working in the sun. "The townspeople are hurt by what you are doing here. Seven years ago, the library burned. Hardy San Simeon had given that library to the people. It was taken from them. Now, you are taking away the beauty of this great house. The people have always shared in the joy that this house has brought; they do not understand how you can do this. The people say things about you. Even my father..."

"Especially your father, I should judge," Marais said meanly,

"Whenever my father says things about you, I defend you. On the way here this morning, Hewett Manus said things about you. I stopped at his lumberyard for a two by four. He said things."

"What kind of things."

Dirty things."

Marais was irritated almost beyond bearing. She didn't care what people like Hewett J. Manus said about her. She didn't want to hear about it. "So what did you do?" she asked in a cold tone of voice.

"I wanted to hit him," Pomo said. "I might have, only I picked up an ax and swung it into a block of wood. The block split in two the first stroke. It was then I knew for sure that I cared something for you. I couldn't hit Manus in his own place of business. When I split the block, I felt better. You couldn't hit Hardy San Simeon because he was dead. Doing this to his house has made you feel better - but, it is enough. I can't see you going to waste. I want to defend you. I want to lead you out of the tangle you've made of your life."

"Well, you can't!" Marais said shortly. "I am going to do what I set out to do." She raised her chin and set her lips firmly. But, she wondered if she could be strong enough to hold to her purpose. "Oh," she said to herself, "how could this impossible situation between Pomo and me have come about?"

It was the incredible arrogance of the Juvarras.

Only the day before yesterday, Marais had been of one mind. She had been satisfyingly busy, finishing up the removal of the sculpture from San Simeon, and already her attention was turning to what would be the next step in her alteration of the old estate. She had no idea that anything could happen to set her in conflict with herself or with anyone else.

Then, yesterday, she had waked up to look off her balcony and see Melus Juvarra striding about in her garden. The St. Francis had been in place and cement birds were set about on the ground at the feet of the statue as though St. Francis were feeding them.

Melus was walking briskly about as though he owned the place! His feet brushed the dew from the drooping flowers, and the spiders of the place scuttled away in panic at his approach. He stood right under the St. Francis and arched his back and threw his head back and looked around as though he were lord of all he surveyed.

"There are live birds down there, and he's talking to them!" Marais said. She hurried down to the chill garden to meet him.

The older Juvarra, steel headed and wrinkled, greeted her with a broad smile.

I hope you will forgive me for intruding here," he said, "but I wanted to see the work that my son is doing. We Juvarras are simple people, plain artisans. We have little to take pride in except our work. We take pride in the creations of our hands. Although, we are of a good family. I can assure you that in sixteen generations there has been no bastard in our house - not in our direct line."

There it was again! Marais was furious with him. He had done it on purpose. She colored a deep red. "You've got a lot of nerve!" she said angrily.

Melus bowed his head.

"I did not mean to boast," he said softly. "But, we must take pride in our labor and our lineage, when that is all we have. I feel that my son is a fine man fit for anyone."

That was what he had come to say.

Now, a day had passed, Marais looked at Pomo and her face took on a look of contempt. How had Melus Juvarra dared plant the notion in her mind that Pomo could be interested in her" It was ridiculous that he would have the audacity, and it was more ridiculous to suppose that she could have any use for him at all.

"Your father advertises you highly," she said. "It is strange he would so oversell such merchandise."

"I don't understand some of the things you say," Pomo said.

"That is evident. I tried to tell you yesterday afternoon, when you and Jebus Jimma were setting up the Rimbaud, that I didn't want you to come back to San Simeon. I told you your work was finished, but you chose not to hear me.

"The statue is not safe. The foundation has to be reinforced. I couldn't leave without making everything right. It is a matter of honor with us The Juvarras take pride in their .."

"Don't tell me," Marais cited. "I know what you take pride in. Just do what you have to do and come by the house and let me pay you off. That will close our contract."

"Yes. I guess that will."

Marais drew in a little breath of relief'. Maybe he was going to listen to reason. That morning she had gotten up early and gone to their shop and attempted to close out the contract she had made with the Juvarras, but Pomo had refused to accept the money, and Melus had been insulting. The wily Machiavelli had not said anything to her directly, but he had poured out his opinions to do anything. And, Pomo had the insolence to try to protect her, and then, after all that they had told Fenny that she had a David which she might sell, and she had to drive him back to San Simeon, listening to his philosophies about life and his suppositions about herself, every step of the way. Then, before she could recover her equilibrium, Pomo had arrived to torment her.

She wanted to sit down, but Pomo continued to relax on the bench with his foot up on the seat. He swung his knee back and forth. Marais looked at it for a moment, fascinated by the pendulum motion of it.

"I wish you would come into the house right now," she said. "I'll pay you whatever I owe you. Then, I won't have to see you again. Do you have a record of the contract, your hours, money you have spent on expenses? Is it all ready? Do you have it with you? Perhaps in your truck?"

"I have everything right here in my coat pocket," Pomo said.

"Will you come in and let us get this settled? I have other things to do."

"Yes, ma'am," Pomo said. He put his foot down and started getting up. A spider, warming itself near the bench, ambled uneasily away when Pomo stood up. It went under the narcissus clusters.

Marais walked briskly up the path, onto the porch, and into the wide entrance hall. Pomo walked a step or two behind her.

"We can go in here," Marais said. She indicated a formal room to the right of the hall. "There is a desk here."

All the furnishings of the house were Spanish.

"I can add this up and give you the exact figure in just a moment," Pomo said. He sat on a chair and spread a handful of papers out on the desk.

"I am very anxious to begin work on the inside of the house," Marais told him. "The heart - the very heart of Hardy San Simeon is here. I already have ideas about the paintings I'll use to replace the old ones. Heavy, dark drapes will do a lot to create the mood I want, too."

There was not, in the house, any traditional painting of the Spanish bullfighter as is usually found in houses of Spanish decor. Hardy San Simeon had not believed in violence.

"I'm not putting down any time for today," Pomo said. "We won't count this."

Marais stood looking through a tall door into an adjoining room. "I'll replace all the pottery and the brassware and the tapestries. And, of course, I'll get rid of his books." She was looking into the library. It was lined with high shelves of expensively bound books. A look of anxiety and fatigue crossed her face. She shut the door and came back to sit near Pomo. It was almost as though she drew close to him for comfort.

"Something bothering you?" Pomo asked.

She glared back at him. He gave her the figure she owed him, so she took out her big checkbook and wrote him a check with quick, nervous gestures. She tore it out and handed it to him without smiling. "Now, if you will do whatever it is you have to do to make the statue of Rimbaud stand firm, you may leave San Simeon forever, and I won't have to see you or your father again."

Pomo leaned back in his chair. He folded the check in the center and put it in his shirt pocket.

"I'll be back," he said.

"What?"

"I'll be back. Our business is a small business. I have my father to take charge of things when I'm not there. Now that school will soon be out, we are thinking of hiring Fenny to help us. He hopes to be a sculptor. It would help him to work with us. I am going to have a lot of free time."

"Well, don't plan to spend it here," Marais said with a hard set to her jaw.

"I guess I'll have to," Pomo said. "I'm going to be working for Johnny Forza. He's going to do your landscaping for you, I hear."

Marais leaped up. "You knew this all the time! You knew this when you were talking to me yesterday afternoon, and when I came to your shop this morning. You let me make a fool of myself."

"I wouldn't put it that way."

"No wonder you were so ready to accept the money! You let me believe that I had seen the last of you. Well, maybe I have. I'll see Mr. Johnny Forza about this. I'll tell him I don't want you here."

"There's nothing in your contract with him that says you can select his helpers."

"No," Marais said, "but he'll do what I ask. He's a nice man. He seems very fair. I'll tell him I don't want you here."

"He's my cousin," Pomo told her.

Marais ran to the big front door and threw it open. "Get out!" she screamed. "Get out of my house! Get out and don't come back."

Fenny was standing at the foot of the steps. Pomo took long strides across the hall and onto the porch.

"Fenny, you go get in the truck," he said. There was real authority in his voice. Marais looked up at him and a weak feeling spread at the pit of her stomach. "Go get in the truck, I'll be there in just a minute and take you home."

Fenny, slender as a girl, bedecked in medals, ran across the drive to the truck. His long blond hair floated on the breeze. He got in the truck and slammed the door. He sat there, peering toward the house through his dark rimmed glasses.

Hot Mississippi sun drenched the porch.

Pomo grasped Marais by the arm. He jerked her around so that she had to look at him. "I've got something I'm going to tell you," he shouted.

"What!"

"I love you."

He let her arm go. Marais went and sat down on the porch floor with her feet on the top step.

"You can't."

Pomo stood over her. "Why can't I'?" He looked about at the extensive grounds of San Simeon, the horseshoe drive, the huge trees. In the distance, he could see the Gulf of Mexico and San Simeon's private pier. "You're a woman with property," Pomo said sadly. "You let this property own you, the property and what it stands for. You think you could never give yourself to a working man like me."

"It's not that I'm well-to-do," Marais said. "I don't take pride in that! You know how I got this money."

"Yes."

I want to destroy Hardy San Simeon! I want to destroy him in the minds of those who remember him. I want to destroy everything he left to the world. He worked all his life to make a name for himself, and I want to destroy it."

"Have you always felt like this'?" Pomo asked. "Have you felt this way since birth?"

"I guess always. I think always. I must have had a passive hatred for him from the beginning. The active plan to damage his memory only came to me about ..." Marais tried to think. How long had it been? All these years, it had been as though she were in a sleep - a living death. "Seven years," she said.

Pomo took her arm again. "I do love you," he said.

At the touch of his hand, Marais was seized with feelings which she had never experienced before. She began to breathe rapidly. Her stomach turned in panic. She leaped up and took a step back toward the door of the house. "You can't!" she screamed.

Pomo's hand dropped. "I do."

"You don't know what kind of woman I am," she screamed. She was laughing and crying at the same time. "I burned down the library!"

"The library?"

"The library that belonged to the people of Waveland. I set fire to it, and burned it to the ground!"

Pomo stepped down to the first step. He looked up at her. "The people's library? Hardy San Simeon gave that to all the people. Many people contributed books. My family gave a number of books in Italian which came over from the Old Country - Dante, St. Augustine, Horace. He thought they would be safe and useful. They were lost. How could you do it?"

Marais backed into a narrow window niche which was next to the door as though she wished to hide from the strong sunlight which revealed the guilt in her face so glaringly. "I have the sun," she thought. "What is it good for except to make flowers grow" The sun, flowers, love and life." Aloud she said, "I was performing as an actress. We had a long run in New Orleans. I had spent my whole life thinking of how my father had cast my mother aside - how he had refused to own me. I made several trips to Waveland. No one knew me. I found out that he had given the library to the town, and that it was the cornerstone of the good memory the people here had for him. One night, I don't know why or how, I drove over here and set it on fire."

"And then?"

"And, then I began to make plans as to how I would destroy his name and memory completely. I have not thought of anything else since. You can't love me. I have nothing for you. I have nothing for anyone. I have hate for Hardy San Simeon, and plans for revenge."

"And guilt."

"Guilt?"

"You have to cling to the idea that he wronged you so greatly that it is worth wasting a lifetime   vengeance. Otherwise, you would not be able to justify to yourself the burning of the library."

A shudder shook Marais from feet to shoulders. She had become deathly pale. "I was his beautiful daughter," she said, "and he threw me away."

"I had better go," Pomo said. He turned around and swung himself up into his truck. The truck did not start on his first attempt to start it, but in a moment the starter caught, and he drove away with Fenny beside him.

Marais turned, then, and ran into the house closing and locking the big front door. She ran up the stairs and slammed the door of her bedroom. She kicked the stone statue of the Aztec Fire Serpent which she used as a doorstop against it.

It was as if she were throwing up a series of barricades to keep all thought of Pomo Juvarra out - all thought of him and the horrible picture of herself he had begun to paint of her, a picture which was beginning to be etched into her mind, detail by detail, so that she could not face herself.

"I guess I've won," she said to herself. But, she burst into tears and lying face down on the bed, her body shook with nervous and exhausted sobs.

She slept, or she fell into some sort of swoon. She was still until about four o'clock in the afternoon. She saw Pomo's truck in the drive. Cautiously, she made her way down the stairs and outside. Pomo must be working with the foundation of the statue of Rimbaud. She stood beside a large Cape jasmine bush that grew in the shade of a huge oak tree to the left of her walk. A large spider had a web there. The spider was shiny black and had yellow stripes on her. She was much bigger than a silver dollar. She liked the shade.

Marais never knew how it happened, but suddenly, Pomo was standing in front of her. The spider made such haste to escape his presence that she fell down tearing her web, in complete panic and confusion. Marais watched her frantic struggles to get away. But, for a moment, Marais could not even try to escape. Finally, she got possession of herself and ran. She ran into the house and bolted herself in her bedroom. She could hear Pomo coming up the stairs. He tried the door. Marais buried her head in the silken counterpane. She could hear Pomo's footsteps. He went down the hall and onto the balcony. In a moment, he burst in one of the tall windows which led from her bedroom to the balcony.

"You get out of here!" Marais said, sitting upright.

Pomo looked about the room. He picked up the Aztec Fire Serpent and tossed it through the window so that it cleared the balcony rail and landed on the grass near an althea bush.

"I've come to tell you what we are going to do," he said. "I have found the words." He sat down on the edge of her bed.

She lay down, too weak to sit erect.

"We are going to restore San Simeon to the condition it was when you bought it. I can find most of the statuary. You will buy it all back. Then, you will sell San Simeon, and with the money you will build back the people's library. You will stock it with books. You will bring the light of learning to Waveland."

"You're out of your mind," Marais said weakly.

You will bring the light of learning to Waveland, and then you will be free of the thing you have done, and you can come out into the light and bloom. I want you to unfold like a rose opening, and become the woman you can be."

"Don't sit there spouting Italian romanticisms to me!" Marais snapped. "If I were to do as you say, I would be destitute. I didn't inherit that much money. What will I do then'?"

Pomo had taken hold of her. His strong, supple hands massaged her body. He leaned over her. She felt the heat of him and the will.

"You'll marry me," he said. "In the church. I'll support you and our children. That's what a man is for."

Marais twisted about on the bed. She took her hands and tried to push his hands away.

"You know my hatred for Hardy San Simeon! You know about my need to get revenge. What will happen to all that?"

Pomo gathered her up against himself. She was helpless in his grip.

"You've gone at it all wrong," he told her. "You've tried to erase him from memory by burning libraries and defacing houses and gardens. What good is all this if you let the ruined woman he brought into existence remain whole? It is that ruined woman that you must remove. Houses and libraries don't matter. It is the woman which must be made a new woman, a different person. You are the chief thing Hardy San Simeon left. You must become someone other than his ruined daughter. Then, you will have your revenge on him."

Marais became still. "This slow, dumb Dago has learned to talk," she thought to herself.

His hands were talking. On her body, they sent her messages which caused her to feel herself coming open like a jonquil coming open to let in the light.

"I'll go right to work to restore San Simeon," he said insistently. His hands moved over her. "I'll put the place up for sale." He bent his head and kissed her. "I'll go with you and we'll see what must be done to build the library."

Marais found herself kissing him back.

"For seven years, I've lived with guilt," she said. "I never even let myself know."

"I'm going to get rid of that woman," Pomo said. "I'm going to help a new woman come into being, and I'm going to marry her, and take care of her."

Marais felt his hands and his lips and his hot breath all over her. She felt the strength of his will. Something inside her gave way. She threw herself back on the bed in an overwhelming excitement.

"Oh, do it!" she screamed. "Do it! Do it! Do it!"

GEORGETOWN, SOUTH CAROLINA

"When Circles Run Backwards" was written in Georgetown in 1971. A young man is caught in a net cast by the spell of his father. Does he realize, at the last, that he is not in life a predator but has forever been the prey?

The incident of the killing of the doe was told the writer by Julius Lee Dennis in the steel mill in Georgetown. This is the first story with the steel mill flavor. The plant and the workers held a strong influence upon the writer. Most of his stories, beginning here, will display a certain type of rural, Southern blue-collar hero - such as those with whom he associated every day.

WHEN CIRCLES RUN BACKWARDS

Congaree, in the heat of late May, in his worn shirt and faded work pants, stood almost at the end of the road. The street had turned to an unpaved road, and the road had narrowed to a pair of crusty ruts leading into the marsh. "Shit," he said. "I'm so screwed up I don't know who I am." He could not put the city behind him for even a few minutes, as he had come here to do. The Delaware River was not a river of his native South Carolina. There he could sit dreaming of peace and rest for himself. He was here, living this reality, the heat on his thin shoulders and the anxious feeling in his gut. "I figure the hunter has got to keep hunting until, finally, someone comes to hunt for the hunter," he told himself. A heron rose up from the marsh, afraid of the man. "I wish I had my rifle," he thought.

He sat down on broken concrete, not comfortable, in the late afternoon sun. Absently, he took his long knife out of his pocket and opened it. The bone handle was solid in his hand. He caressed the weapon out of idle habit, and looked down the river toward the south. "A man's got to have something with him that makes him strong. I might be a weak son-of-a-bitch," he said to himself, "but it would be worse if I didn't have things like my knife and the memory of home."

Congaree was short and hungry looking, with a broad forehead. He liked to wear several days' growth of beard and to go with his shirt unbuttoned part way down the front to display the hair on his chest. Girls seemed to like that. He had been troubled by the thought of girls ever since he had reached the age of fourteen, ten years before.

He had never before been up north. When he had gotten off the bus and walked up the main street of the city, he had noticed that the town looked as if there had been a war. The stores had been burned out and windows were broken. Merchandise lay ruined and strewn about. Right away, he saw the National Guard trucks, and all these conditions amazed him. He dared approach a man who looked like a good old boy from the south, and asked him what the matter was.

"It's like this because Martin Luther King was murdered," the man said.

Congaree shook his head. "I figured there must be a reason," he said. "I sure thank you for telling me."

Now, Congaree laughed to himself. "There's going to be a little more violence here in Delaware. I'm going to find out whether I've got any balls."

The buildings of the city stood drab and dusty, outlined against the sky. He almost felt that they might fall on him and bury him, so brittle and so much a prey of gravity did they seem. They had been thrust up so high only that some day they might fall.

Congaree remembered the swamps of home, the swamp grass, slender trees with fresh leaves, and old trees with moss. He could see the sweet stream which flowed rippling through the woodland of his daddy. Thought of home made him almost unbearably unhappy so that even his grip on the good stout fish knife did not comfort him. "I thought when I left home, I'd discover what, and who, I am. But, it didn't work out. I figure I'll never know this until I get finished here and go back to South Carolina."

Congaree was living in a Main Street hotel. He had followed his adversary, Mr. Racso, here, all the way from Charlotte, and now he had Mr. Racso in a snare. It was only necessary for him to meet Mr. Racso face to face, and he would cut Mr. Racso's throat.

He had already seen Mr. Racso's shadow, Jay Bob, who was also staying at Congaree's hotel. Mr. Racso must be there too. Congaree would search them out like weasels in their burrow. Then, he would free himself of the terrible affliction which Mr. Racso had brought upon him.

Congaree folded his knife and put in back in his pocket. He started back through the low flat part of the city with its housing projects and its streets full of children. Congaree knew that it was not safe for him to walk in this area after dark, or any area here. He returned to his hotel with its false face making it seem, at street front, a decent enough place. There was a bar and a place to eat. The elevator was to the right. The ride up was quick. The hall, on his floor, was shabby. His room was dirty. It was on an air shaft. Congaree took off his shirt and put it in his canvas bag. He had very few clothes. He kept with him a light jacket that had been his daddy's. It had the name "Oscar" embroidered on the pocket. Congaree did not know when he would need this, but he would not part with it.

Congaree made himself go to sleep. In a short time, he awakened suddenly. It was the voice awakened him. Ever since he had been at the hotel, he had been bothered by the sobbing, cursing, hysterical voice of a disappointed woman, somewhere high up the air shaft. Half a dozen times, he had heard her chanting. She always recited the same thing. "You're afraid. Just because you've got hair on your chest don't make you a man. You'll never be a man as long as you keep on letting everything scare you. "

Congaree felt the bone handle of the knife with his sweaty hand through his pants. The room had become dark. Women always protested when men left them. He thought of his own wife, Doretha, somewhere back in Carolina, married again. He had not gotten out of the marriage what he expected. All his life, he was a bashful boy people liked. They trusted his big sensitive eyes, and his winning quickness to be of service.

People had always liked Congaree's daddy, Oscar, too. His hair had been grey ever since Congaree had first known him. Oscar's farm had been a place from which people went to church each Sunday, and a place where kinfolk came. Sometimes, on Sunday, the men would gather at the barn with a captured young rooster. Oscar would draw a circle on the clean, smooth ground, and lay the rooster flat inside it. He would trace a line from the tip of the rooster's back to join the Circle. All this would place the rooster in a cataleptic trance so that he was powerless to get up and escape.

Oscar had explained that when he charmed the rooster the spell would only hold for as long as he kept his eye on the bird. Whenever Oscar took his eye off an entranced chicken, it would invariably jump up and run away, all in a panic.

Congaree had seen his daddy perform this ritual many times, but he always remained afraid of the rooster. It seemed a possessed, selfless thing to him, something completely unnatural and dangerous. The last time Congaree had seen his daddy do this, he had been fifteen, and his daddy had given him a playful push in his shirt front. "Just because you've got hair on your chest don't make you a man. You'll I never be a man as long as you keep on letting everything scare you."

Congaree found early that he had less things to be afraid of when he was alone. He started taking his old sleeping bag out alone nights onto the bank of the river to sleep there. Some small animal would run along a limb of the water oak he was resting under, and Congaree would wish that he could catch him and sleep with him in his sleeping bag so he wouldn't be so totally alone. But, there was no way to catch creatures like that. Out of school, he was a solitary hunter, and fisherman, and trapper. The beasts of the field could he kill, but he could not make pets of them.

Then, he had discovered Doretha. She was fifteen and had never left home except to go to the schoolhouse or church. Congaree wanted to catch her and for the first time in his life, he had found a gentle adversary who seemed to want to be caught. Slowly, carefully, so as not to frighten the quarry, he spread his net, and the fluttering bird, the velvety squirrel, came into his hand.

"Now," Congaree thought, "I will find I am no different from the rest of these bastards that seem to get so much fun out of life. I will like what they like." But, when Congaree and Doretha married, it changed nothing. He was still alone. And, he still felt Oscar's eye upon him.

Congaree could successfully perform the husband's role in marriage. But, there was something about sex which troubled him so deeply that it took away the joy of it, so he wasn't much interested in it.

Doretha seemed bored, and when they went to church, she would show an undue interest in the other boys. He spent his time on the creek banks and in the woods. By Christmas, he knew that she despised him and he was exasperated by her crying. She gave him the knife for Christmas because he had said that was what he wanted. He never went anywhere without it thereafter.

On an intensely cold day in January, he took his skiff and made his way slowly upstream, bundled in boots and mackinaw, wearing a hat with earflaps. His rifle was in the bottom of the boat. A mile or two from Oscar's farm, Congaree tied his boat to a stump and went ashore. He wore heavy gloves, his breath floating in a white cloud on the crisp air. Then, he startled a little doe; a doe, the most female of all creatures in the forest.

The doe became alert suddenly. Instant fear of the man swept over her. Her stubby body was shaped like a keg and her legs seemed too small to carry the weight of her. She jerked her head up and turning, dove gracefully into the underbrush. Congaree threw off his right glove and took the safety off the rifle. He plunged into the bushes after her.

She hopped along easily, staying a little ahead of the running man, her head high, and turned to one side so that she might see and hear her pursuer. She tantalized him, seemed seducing him. Congaree panted in excitement. The doe made for the river and leaped into the icy water. Rapidly, she swam away.

Congaree ran to the boat. Like a man on a horse would drive a lone cow, he herded the doe along in the river. He forced her away from the shore. Then, he took out his knife and opened it. He let the boat drift alongside the deer. Carefully, he reached over the side and with his left hand caught the doe under the chin. In the cold water, the hair on her jaw was soft and silky. He raised his right arm and stabbed the doe in the neck vein. Holding the doe by the chin, he felt her last struggles and watched the flow of her blood as it spread away behind them in the sparkling water of the stream. The water dispersed it, and in a few minutes, there was none. The area was clean.

Congaree let the boat drift to shore. He had to get the doe into the boat, but he was so satisfied, so relaxed, and so content after the victory over her he could only sit in a pleasant warmth which was deeper and more fulfilling than any emotional satisfaction he had ever felt in making love to a woman.

He lifted the doe into the boat. Going back, he began to feel black about it all and almost to wish he had not killed the doe.

"I figure I'm a born killer," he thought.

Congaree felt the circle of domination Oscar had kept tight around him loosening by will of the knife, which had a mind of its own, an incestuous, murderous lust for Oscar.

"If I stay at home, the knife will kill him."

Soon after this, Congaree left home and went to Charlotte, North Carolina.

Without trouble, he went to work for an outlet for phonograph recordings. He started as a helper on the delivery truck, riding around Charlotte with a man named Jay Bob. Jay Bob would go inside the record stores and juke box supply places and find out what records were wanted, and then Congaree would carry them inside.

Jay Bob bothered him. He was much taller than Congaree, and he walked with a swagger, and talked in a loud confident voice. He talked constantly about his conquests of women, and Congaree felt himself growing smaller and smaller and more withdrawn in the other man's company. "You getting plenty?" Jay Bob would sometimes ask him, and Congaree would bristle angrily and say, "I can get anything I want. I just don't want nothing." He never told Jay Bob anything which he had done because Jay Bob might sneer at it.

Congaree liked his boss, Mr. Racso. Congaree had the same build as his daddy. In contrast, Mr. Racso was soft and round appearing with a bulging stomach from drinking beer. He waved a strong cigar in his left hand when he talked, laughing out of magnified eyes which made him look like an owl. He laughed a lot, even when he was angry, and Congaree had been immediately taken with him. He would compare Mr. Racso to Oscar, who was so white, so Anglo-Saxon, so Protestant, and so Rural Southern, while Mr. Racso was Mediterranean, Catholic, and from somewhere up north. Congaree felt at ease with Mr. Racso because he was opposite of Oscar. Congaree had never felt at ease with his daddy.

They had written Congaree from home that Oscar had died on the same day that Congaree had taken the job with Mr. Racso. Congaree had not gone to the funeral. Doretha had written to him, "He died of a heart attack, just like your grandfather and your Uncle Henry. Your mother told me to write to you. She is afraid that unless you change your way of living, you will not live long." Congaree was angry at this threat. He crumpled the letter and threw it away. That night, he went out and got drunk.

Jay Bob learned that Congaree had been married. "Seems like you didn't like what your wife, give you. You don't seem to ever want no more."

"She gave me this knife," Congaree said, taking it out.

Mr. Racso had a lot of money, and owned a big house up on the Catawba River. He went up there every weekend with Jay Bob. They would spend the weekend making pornographic movies. This was where Mr. Racso's money actually came from.

"I put Jay Bob in a room with three girls and let him go," Mr. Racso would laugh. "He can keep going all weekend, and the cameras keep grinding. He is very professional!"

Congaree stood more in awe of Jay Bob than ever. Jay Bob taught Congaree everything he could. When Congaree learned how to handle the truck and to make sales, Jay Bob started taking Mondays off, because he was all worn out on Mondays and needed to stay home and get some sleep.

It was more pleasant for Congaree, now that Jay Bob seemed ready to accept him.

One day Jay Bob took hold of Congaree and began massaging his ribs and kneading his shoulders. "How would you like to go with us this weekend?" he asked. "Racso says you can go, and he'll let you be in one of the movies. He'll pay you fifty dollars. I told him you needed a little extra money."

Congaree walked around the warehouse elated and optimistic. Mr. Racso made him get a short haircut.

The three girls who went with them were new ones. Mr. Racso had found that Jay Bob lost interest if they kept the same girls too long. They did not pay much attention to Congaree after their first look at him. Jay Bob studied each of them in turn. He seemed satisfied with them, but he did not say much to them yet.

Mr. Racso told Congaree that he could go to the pier and fish. He took the prettiest of the girls and a camera into a studio to take some stills of her.

Mr. Racso had the best of fishing tackle, and Congaree took a rod and left Jay Bob sitting quietly with the other two girls. He found that the pier was shaded. He sat down in the oncoming twilight to try to catch a fish before dark, but no fish came to his line. He was about to go to the house, when he heard footsteps on the boards of the wharf. It was Jay Bob.

"Mr. Racso thought maybe you were worried about what you are going to do tomorrow," he said. "It'll be simple. We know you wouldn't be the best fellow to take part with one of the girls, especially being new to this and all. We don't want to ask too much of you. It's just fifty dollars you're getting. We've got a small thing for you to do. It'll be easy. You'll be the only one on camera."

Congaree reeled the line in. "Jay Bob," he said, "I sure thank you for being a good friend to me. I figure you're about the best friend I got."

"You're a hard working boy," Jay Bob said. "You deserve something." But Congaree knew that he didn't deserve anything.

The next day, picture making began in earnest. They let Congaree watch Jay Bob work. The girls had taken to Jay Bob naturally and he seemed to be permitting himself to have a restrained good time. Mr. Racso kept shouting excited instructions from behind the camera. Finally, Jay Bob was tired so he put on a bathrobe and sat down for a drink. They told the girls to go into the next room.

Mr. Racso spoke to Congaree very gently. He showed him, behind a screen, where they had set up a long corridor of mirrors. It was possible to set the camera on a tripod at such an angle that the figure of a man standing in front of the first mirror would be caught, reflected over and over in all the mirrors, repeated again and again dozens of times from a hundred angles.

"We have something very artistic here for you," Mr. Racso said. "There will be nothing vulgar or in bad taste about this. This will be something which could be shown in any art movie house anywhere. You are very fortunate that we thought of you for it."

"What do you want me to do?" Congaree asked in a very weak voice.

"I am going to draw a circle on the floor," Mr. Racso said in his businesslike tone of voice. "Where's the damned chalk?" He found the chalk and got down on his hands and knees. He laughed good-naturedly. With his left hand, he carefully made the circle. "We want you to take off your clothes and stand here inside the circle I've drawn," he said, "and commit your sex act."

"What kind of sex act?" Congaree asked.

"Oh, you know what kind of sex act," Mr. Racso said in mock indignation. "Just do it, and don't stand too still. Move about a little so it won't be monotonous. But, don't go outside the circle. The camera won't pick you up if you do."

Congaree stood looking at the circle on the floor. He didn't move. Jay Bob brought him a drink. "Take it easy and think about it for a minute," Jay Bob said. "It isn't going to do any harm. No one you know will ever see it."

Congaree's eyes moved up from the floor and he looked into Jay Bob's face. He began to unbutton his shirt.

Mr. Racso smiled and went to the camera. "He's going to do exactly what Jay Bob tells him to," he said to himself. "Jay Bob's got him eating out of his hand." Then, he shouted aloud to Congaree, "Make it last as long as you can. I want to get some good footage on this."

Jay Bob sat on a stool and offered soft-spoken instructions and encourage-ment. The camera made a buzzing sound. Congaree pretended that he was all alone with only the soft urging voice of Jay Bob leading him on.

"Put some life in it," Mr. Racso shouted once, and almost spoiled things, but Jay Bob talked to Congaree in his soothing voice so that everything went well.

Mr. Racso had reason to be enormously pleased. He and Jay Bob were very nice to Congaree all the rest of the weekend. Congaree spent most of his time sitting on the pier with a fishing rod feeling embarrassed and ashamed. He could imagine the picture being shown before a great circle of people, all laugh-ing at him and ridiculing him.

Several weeks later, Mr. Racso took Congaree home with him to see the finished movie. In the darkened game room at Mr. Racso's apartment, Congaree saw himself enacting a fragmented, solipsismic ritual of loneliness, endlessly repeated down a gaudy corridor of glass and artificially bright lighting. He was quiet until it was time for him to leave for home. He thanked Mr. Racso for having him and went away. The next day, he did not go to work. He moved to another part of the city, and went out to look for another job.

"I know now what I am," he told himself. "I am alone. Other people can get close, but I can't. There is no bridge between. I am all shut up, and divided in pieces. If it hadn't been for Mr. Racso, I never would have seen this."

With a new job and small apartment, Congaree began to feel better about himself, and to get ahead. Then, on one terrible night he was suddenly taken with a shattering series of impressions. All over again, he felt himself standing, naked and ashamed, an object of ridicule, the pawn of the caressing voice of Jay Bob. He felt himself torn apart, the rise of his passion, and its final decline into fatigue and despairing surrender. He was all alone, and he threw himself down shaking and crying. "I thought I could get away," he said, "but I can't. I'm caught. I am Jay Bob's thing. Mr. Racso is using him to hold me."

Some sympathetic magic had been worked upon him. The web of his life had become entangled with the life of the film. Each time that the movie was run, Congaree would experience again what he had experienced in the hour of its making. It would all be repeated over again for so long as Mr. Racso had the film.

Congaree remembered the circle which Mr. Racso had drawn, using his left hand. Mr. Racso had made the circle with a counterclockwise motion. This is black magic, a potent voodoo. "We all know the power of voodoo in the Low Country," Congaree thought sadly. Idly, he ran his fingers into his pockets. His hand touched his knife. He took it out and opened the blade. "This is my man-hood, if I have any. I will kill Racso." He grew cold and a horror passed through him. "That will complete everything."

But, Congaree was afraid because he knew in his heart what Mr. Racso had been to him. "You have the same feeling," he said to the knife, "that you had for Oscar; lustful, incestuous, murderous. It was Doretha who put this sin in you."

As the weeks went by, the attacks that Congaree had, which he believed to be the result of Racso's showing of the film, increased in frequency. His eve-nings were a torment to him. He was terrified that the movie might be shown in the daytime when he was at work so that he would be seized with his affliction right before everyone. It all became unbearable to him. He stroked his knife, caressing it, whispering to it. "I will give you satisfaction," he'd say. "You shall have him."

Finally, he convinced himself that, in spite of the aversion he felt for the killing of a man who had almost been a father to him, Mr. Racso must die. The next day he set out to find Mr. Racso. The warehouse was closed. A man told Congaree that Mr. Racso had left Charlotte. He was somewhere in Delaware. Congaree caught the bus north.

Lying in the steaming darkness in the Delaware hotel, he heard the woman's heavy, hoarse voice muttering and cursing out of the airshaft. "You're afraid," she said.

Congaree pulled on his shirt and started to go out, but he met Jay Bob in the elevator. Jay Bob smiled at him pleasantly. "What the hell are you doing up here?" he said.

"I thought I might go to work here," Congaree told him.

"Racso has a new thing going up here." Jay Bob said. "We could use you."

"They want to hold on to me," Congaree told himself. "They don't want to let me go." To Jay Bob he said, "That might be nice. It was fun in Charlotte."

"Racso was all pissed when you walked out on us," Jay Bob said. "We never have shown that picture you were in. Racso is saving it for a rich collector he knows. He may sell it to him."

Congaree looked at Jay Bob suspiciously. He knew that the film had been shown, how often, and when. This was another trick. They had used their voodoo magic to try to bind him to them. Well, he, Congaree, could break the spell of that magic with his knife.

"It was a stupid thing to make, I figure," Congaree said.

"Racso was happy with it. We're in Room 406. I'll tell him you're here. You come up to see us after a while."

"Okay," Congaree said. "I'll be up there in about thirty minutes."

Congaree went. Jay Bob let him in the room. Mr. Racso was friendly in his usual preoccupied way. He fixed himself and Congaree a drink with the last of the whiskey. Jay Bob hurried off to get another bottle at the bar downstairs.

As soon as Jay Bob had left the room, Congaree whipped out his knife and stabbed Mr. Racso with it. Mr. Racso's blood spurted out of the wounds in his chest and ran up Congaree's arm. Congaree shook his hand violently and threw the knife aside. Mr. Racso died quickly without really being aware of what had happened. Congaree went down the stairs to his own room.

He heard the voice from the air shaft again, guttural and incoherent. He tore off his bloody shirt and ran water on his arm. The voice in the air shaft became deeper. Now, it sounded like Jay Bob sobbing. Congaree laughed. "See how the big man snivels when his master is dead?" He looked for another shirt to put on. In his bag, his hand fell on the old jacket which had been Oscar's. He would wear this. It had a zippered front. He pulled the zipper up to his chin. He left the hotel by the back stairs.

On the street, he walked slowly. There was no one about. There was a curfew in the city. On the corner, there was a man's clothing store with a full mirror. He wanted to make sure his hair was all right and there was no blood splattered on his face. He would check his appearance, and would walk to the bus station and buy a ticket back to Carolina.

In front of the mirror, he straightened his trousers and brushed his hair down with his hands. He moved close to the reflection of himself and examined his face carefully. The jacket which had been Oscar's was a little too large for him. He brushed at it, examining it closely. The name "Oscar" embroidered on the pocket showed up clear and stark in the mirror, "R-A-C-S-O". Congaree gave a gasp. It all came back to him, everything he had ever known about Mr. Racso. Mr. Racso was nothing more than the mirror image of his daddy, Oscar. When Congaree had quit the one and gone to the other, it was the same being he was with. Mr. Racso had never been anything except Congaree's image of Oscar passed through the mirror.

"Then, I have killed my father," Congaree thought. "My knife lusted to know him, and I sent it home in him, and he is killed. Is this what I am?"

He heard a National Guard truck on patrol moving slowly along the street. He cowered into the shadows for a moment. Above the narrow avenue of lights on the street, the sky was dark. The city seemed covered with a smoky inverted bowl. Congaree could not breathe. He put his hand to his throat and opened the jacket. He moved back to the mirror and looked at himself. His hairy chest rose and fell excitedly. He put his fingers out to touch the reflection of himself.

"I am a killer," he thought. "I will never know the love of woman, but will go on killing my father forever." Looking deeply into the mirror, he seemed to see there some sort of truth about himself. "If Oscar could step through the mirror and become his opposite, I can do it too. I can step into the mirror a killer, and step out on the other side killed, no longer the hunter, but the victim." He moved forward imperceptibly.

Suddenly, he was walking very fast down the street. He turned at the corner and went along a darker side street. He was stumbling, half running. He felt his chest heave. When he passed the telephone building, he felt a change come into himself. His body became heavy and round. He seemed to become solid and compact with a body shaped like a keg. His little legs beneath him felt wobbly and clumsy. But, he moved with speed and grace. His head was forward, and he ran more with the stance of an animal than a man.

"I know who I am!" he cited. "I am the doe!" He knew the instinctual terror of the doe at bay. He ran on with his head forward and raised, watching the street behind himself, Out of the side of his eye, listening to the sounds made by the pursuer. Then, the street vanished away and he was in the river at home, swimming in the icy water. For a few moments, he thought he had escaped, but he heard the sound of the motor. Someone in an outboard was coming after him, and he knew that he could not escape the machine.

So, Congaree swam in the icy water, in the darkness, feeling that everything in his chest must burst. The sound of the motor became louder and louder and throbbed above him. He smelled the gasoline. It was Jay Bob come to claim him. He heard Jay Bob say, "Come, my pretty! That's a nice boy. Let me get ahold of you," and he felt Jay Bob's large hand slip under his chin, and he felt the warmth of it and the life in it, and the self-possession and self-knowing of the man. He wanted to slow down and surrender to the caressing hand of Jay Bob, but he was afraid. Then, he felt Jay Bob lift his chin so that his neck stretched, and deftly Jay Bob plunged his knife home. There was a moment of piercing pain, and then it was all over.

The street was empty except for Congaree lying on the pavement and the National Guard truck standing with its motor softly purring in the light of the street lights. The guardsmen jumped down out of the truck and came over to where Congaree lay.

"There's not a mark on him," one of them said. "He acted like something was chasing him. I thought when he saw our truck he'd know nothing was going to happen to him. He must have heard us coming. This truck's motor is pretty loud, but he never acted like he saw us. He just kept running until he fell."

GEORGETOWN, SOUTH CAROLINA

"Heather and the Wuzzy Fuzzies," was written in Georgetown in 1972. Heather is paranoid. Her past is replicated (in disguised mode) in her fantasies and acting out, and will eventually merge with the present to become her ultimate reality. There is a culmination here. The writer has reached a point where the commanding preoccupation of four decades is finished.

In this story, the dysfunctional relationship between family members is widened and found among a larger cast of characters. Everyone becomes the enemy. The affliction results in outright madness, or the madness may be spent and the sufferer pronounced cured. One cannot go on forever crying over lost treasures. Guffin-Guffin-Shack, You All!

At this time, many new interests began to occupy this writer and there were no more short stories until 1980.

HEATHER AND THE WUZZY FUZZIES

Heather Bard, spinsterish, thirty four, slender, almost frail, and not used to running, was running as if for her life. The wedge heels of her shoes beat out on the pavement a staccato of' panic which echoed against the trunks of the moss-laden oaks along the low lying boulevard. To her right lay the marsh, and beyond it the bay. On her left stood the dike, protection against floods, massive and over-brooding.

She had never been in this part of town before, and she swore, now, never to come here again. At the end of the street, where the streetlight was, she would hall a cab and in a few minutes she would be at home at Mead Hall. "How can I expect Mead Hall to hide me, to make me safe, for it is within Mead Hall itself that the very beginning of evil is."

Under the streetlight, Heather's blond hair shone against the background of summer foliage, lush and tropical, the kind of underbrush often seen in low places in South Carolina. Her face was white. She would be easy to see if a taxi came.

"At least I have escaped from Moss House with its terrors," she told herself, her almost flat chest rising and falling excitedly. "I won't think about the things that happened there, things which Aunt Dame and Dana caused to happen. I will think about what I am going to do to them." Her body grew tense and her face hardened. "I will protect myself from them. I have my rightful place. They will not trick me and drive me away.

Heather was not very familiar with the town of Liten Overallt, although she had lived there, part of the time, as a child. She had, however, seen taxis cruising about when she had been on her night walks. She knew a taxi would come. The time had come for her to settle with her aunt and cousin, and the settlement would come, just as soon as the taxicab got her home. A showdown had been due. Heather had seen it coming ever since the morning when the box of stiff and twisted caterpillars was found in the freezer compartment of the refrigerator

243

at Mead Hall. They had crawled over each other, trying to get out, but the cold had killed them at last. Aunt Dame and Dana had given little shrieks and pretended to be surprised when they found the grisly box, but they were not surprised.

Heather's father had been Aunt Dame's brother, who, due to his choice of a wife, had with Heather's two brothers, been excluded from the family, and from inheritance by his father's will. Aunt Dame and her daughter, Dana Geater, after the death of Dana's father, lived always at Mead Hall with Heather's grandfather. When he died, it was found that Mead Hall had been left to Dana and Heather, jointly, forever. Heather had come there to live, but she had felt like an intruder who must be driven away.

"They have always been quick to say that my mother was an immoral woman, a strange woman," Heather said to herself. "But, it was Aunt Dame who was immoral, and Dana who learned all her immorality and strangeness to use it." She felt a chill, damp and terrible, borne out of the marsh on the salt wind. "Now, they have compromised me," Heather thought hopelessly. "They can ruin me."

The lights of a slow moving car reflected on the pavement made damp by the mist. Heather saw the taxi sign on top of the cab. "I will find a way to feel that I really own Mead Hall. They won't succeed in putting me to shame and making me retreat. I am as good a person as Dana; maybe not as pretty, but decent, maybe not as smart in business, but a lady. I have my own value. I will be accepted because of the good things I am. It is my role to cleanse it of any evil which may reside there."

She got into the taxi. "Mead Hall," she told the driver, but he didn't know what she meant, so she had to tell him very carefully where she wanted to go.

Heather had lived at Mead Hall for a few years as a school girl. After her mother died, although Heather had never understood how he could do this, her grandfather had taken her away from her father and her two brothers, but later when she was a little older, he send her back to them. She knew that he had taken her away to show them he could, and then sent her back to show his contempt for her father's daughter. He had never wanted her. Her father wanted her. Her grandfather wanted to hurt her father through her. His affair was with her father, whom he never forgive for his marriage and his style of living.

Secretly, Heather nursed the idea that since her grandfather's adversary, her father, was dead, the old man had decided to make amends to her for the way he had used her by leaving her part of Mead Hall. The legacy was payment of a debt. She was to be satisfied like the other creditors. Then, too, he had always tried to separate her from her brothers. This inheritance had driven them apart. Her grandfather felt nothing for her. He had always been icy cold toward her.

She had come to Mead Hall handicapped, feeling that she played the role of a mortgage holder who has foreclosed. She did not possess through the sanction of love as Dana did.

In the beginning, Heather left Dana and Aunt Dame and their routines scrupulously alone. Then, she noticed that, at Mead Hall, little attention was paid to the grounds which surrounded the house, and which were spacious. She began to work each day with the flowers, Sweet William and Narcissus and Dog Tooth Violet. Around their roots, she would caress the loose brown soil with a hand cultivator, the witch's claw.

Under her care, the gardens and the lawn, the shrubs and the trees became beautiful. Dana and Aunt Dame seemed not to notice at first, but later they cautioned Heather about spending money on the enterprise.

The family lumber business was still in operation and Dana spent all her days down at the office where she was acting as manager since her grandfather died. Every night she came home stating that the business was not doing well, but Heather did not believe this. She began to spy on Dana and her aunt and she came to believe that they were engaged in a second business which was more important than the lumber yard. The phone would ring in the evening, sometimes rather late, and Dana would dress hastily and go out.

"There's been an emergency out at the mill," Aunt Dame would say, or "down at the railroad yards," or wherever.

"I wish I could help," Heather would say, and her aunt would give her an icy look and remark, "This is not within your area of experience. You couldn't help with this."

Once, Heather overheard Dana say, "If that phone rings tonight, I don't think I can stand it." Aunt Dame had only laughed and replied, "You know you love it. It gives you something to do with yourself. You never found a husband, so without this, what would you give yourself to?"

Dana Geater was full-figured and chic. She always dressed stylishly and used makeup to good advantage. She walked with assurance, carrying her breasts high and remembering to smile. Heather felt eclipsed by her, had always felt this way, even when they were children.

Only the garden made Heather feel capable and productive. Here the cold loneliness she so often felt ebbed away, and the sunshine warmed her body and spirit.

Some days, Dana would come home ill the middle of the day, and on many summer afternoons young men would call. Dana and her guest would appear in the yard in swim suits, and Heather would watch as they played in the water of the pool, splashing and laughing, their bodies brown in the sunlight. Dana liked the men. She looked at all of them as if they looked to her like something good enough to eat. They would disappear when the swim was done and Heather was curious as to where they might be and what might be going on.

One day a man had spent an hour or two romping with Dana at poolside, but had finally left, and Dana had come to where Aunt Dame stood talking with Heather, who was trimming an Althea bush. She was drying her hair with a large towel.

"What a way to make a living," she laughed.

"Who was that man?" Heather asked.

"A contractor," Aunt Dame said quickly. "A very good customer for the lumber yard." Heather decided not to believe her. "I am beginning to suspect something terrible about my cousin," she said to herself.

Soon after this, Heather was in the back hall when she heard several short shrieks and a commotion in the kitchen.

Something is really going to have to be done about this!" Dana said in a loud angry tone. Aunt Dame answered quietly, with a note of annoyance in her voice, "I'm going to ask Heather about this."

Heather entered the kitchen to find Dana and Aunt Dame examining a box of frozen caterpillars which they had taken from the frostless top freezer of the refrigerator. The box lay open on the kitchen table. The black, woolly creatures were twisted grotesquely together, their fur limp and stained with some clear sticky liquid which was now frozen. Heather could even see their open mouths and their angry eyes. She made a little murmur of disgust.

"What is the meaning of this"" Aunt Dame asked. Heather knew that it was expected of her that she should answers "I guess that someone felt they had no right to live, so woolly and so warm. They were eating beautiful things. They put them in the freezer to take the heat and appetite out of them." Aunt Dame closed the box angrily. She took it outside and threw it in the trash can.

Heather hurried to her room. The incident had upset her. Dana and Aunt Dame were not above talking about the occurrence. They would surely tell people that Heather had put the caterpillars in the freezer. They might have already told people this. They would tell this in advance to head off any idea which Heather might have for revealing the fact that Dana was a high-priced call girl operating right out of Mead Hall, with Aunt Dame receiving the telephoned orders for her services.

"They have some plan to get rid of me," Heather thought. "Because, they know that I know what they are doing."

Heather knew that she could not show fear, but that she must push herself forward. She had her way in the yard. Now, it was time to move her campaign into the house. She began to busy herself in the kitchen.

Without asking anyone, she selected and put up new drapes in the kitchen. Dana seemed preoccupied and hardly noticed, but Aunt Dame remarked coldly that the pattern was stripes and did not blend with the rest of the decor. "They will spoil this for me, too," Heather thought. "They will make me feel that this is not mine and I intrude here."

In only a few days, Dana brought a young man home one night, introducing him as "Gob."

"He will be in charge of the kitchen," Dana said. "He just got out of the Navy, where he was a cook."

Gob seemed to leer at Heather. His eyes were very dark, and his thin hands and arms were coated with black hair. Heather quickly noted a tangle of black hair which peeked out where the collar of his shirt was unbuttoned. She hurried into another room. When she was alone with Dana she asked how long Gob would stay.

"Oh, I don't know," Dana replied. "I may be able to use him in business. I'll have to work with him and find out what he's good for."

"I wonder if I should warn that boy what Dana is planning to lead him into," Heather asked herself'. "But, surely he knows what he's here for. He's probably a born hustler. They'll be giving what they call exhibitions now, for the trade." Heather retreated to the garden. "But, what can I say about this corruption of my grandfather's house! Aunt Dame and Dana can both say that I put the caterpillars in the refrigerator!"

The next day there was a call on the phone and Aunt Dame had a hurried conversation with Gob who took the car and drove away. "She's called for him to help her at one of her assignations," Heather thought. "She's already put him to work." Aunt Dame paced the house anxiously all afternoon. At twilight, the phone rang again. "There's been an accident," Aunt Dame told Heather. "Dana will be in the hospital until later tonight. When she comes home, her leg will be in a cast. She will have a rolling chair, but most of her time will be will be spent in bed."

"Somebody played too rough," Heather told herself. She went into the sun room to sit down alone.

"It will interfere with business," Aunt Dame said, standing in the doorway. She went upstairs.

"I guess we're in terrible financial trouble," Heather thought. "When the phone rings, Dana won't be able to go. In order to save Mead Hall, would I dare answer that phone? Would I dare to go to the places that Dana goes, do the things which she does! Aunt Dame said this life is not within the area of my experience. She had contempt for me. I could prove, once and for all, that I am as acceptable as Dana, if I answered one of her calls and the client was satisfied. If I step in and pick up the reins here and save Mead Hall, I will show everyone that I am as good as Dana and as worthy to own this house."

She heard Gob drive up and pretty soon she heard Aunt Dame go down to the kitchen. Then she heard Aunt Dame's footsteps in the hall, coming, looking for her.

Always before, she had been a little afraid of Aunt Dame, but tonight she was relaxed and at ease. Looking back on the encounter a little later, when she was dressed and going out, she was quite proud of the way she had presented her plan to the older woman. She could see the way Aunt Dame had grasped at Heather's idea that she would work for Mead Hall in Dana's place. For the first time, Aunt Dame really wanted her to do something! She had become important to Aunt Dame. Right after Aunt Dame and Gob had gone to get Dana, the phone had ring. Now, Heather knew exactly where she must go, and what she must do there. She took a taxi to the foot of the street where Moss House stood.

Samuel Ben Franklin Moss was getting old. He lived alone with his servants in a two-story, red brick house, on a low piece of land not far from downtown Liton Overallt. A boulevard, oak lined and dark, led along his massive wooden fence with its two gates. An artificial lake had been dug. The yard was crowded with water oaks, dismal with moss, and a pair of dying pine trees, strangled to death by twisting wisteria. A horseshoe drive led up to the white fan-lighted door.

Heather walked along the drive uncertainty. Here and there the concrete was raised an inch where the roots of trees had grown under it. At last, she knocked on the great door. The biggest man she had ever seen let her inside.

She as afraid to look up at him. He led her into a very large room where Sam Moss was. The room was dark except for a settled fire burning in the huge fireplace. Sam Moss was small, wrinkled, with thinning brown hair. He had the bluest and the coldest eyes Heather had ever seen. His lips were thin and he seemed to look at her with disapproval.

"He doesn't want me," Heather thought. "Already, I displease him." But, she knew that if she didn't satisfy him, he could call Aunt Dame on the telephone and tell her what a failure she had been, She moved uncertainly toward him. He lifted a skinny and bare arm, and extended his fingers in her direction. Heather shuddered and began to cringe away from him.

"You're not ready yet, I see," he said in a voice, flat and lifeless. "I guess you need a little encouragement." Two of his men appeared out of the shadows. They took hold of her roughly. In a moment, she found herself standing without clothes in a room which was pitch black and icy cold. She heard the heavy door slam and the latch click home. Currents of cold air swept around her, and the dark made her dizzy so that she was afraid she would fall to the stone floor which she could feel, damp and clammy, under her bare feet. She began to shiver and to shake out of loneliness and terror and cold. She heard a noise like the whimpering of a puppy. It was herself. The sounds were coming from her.

A dim light appeared at the other end of this long room. It gradually brightened until she could see three huge shaggy creatures standing together, looking at her. They were men, hairy and hot. She could hear them laughing and whispering together. They seemed warm and comfortable enough. Their blood was alive and racing, and they were covered with a grand fuzz. Heather crept toward them. She wanted to roll herself up between them as in the folds of a bear rug.

"These want me," she thought. "This is where I belong." She felt a peace she had not felt for more than twenty years.

They passed her from one to the other, touching her tenderly, lending her warmth. Just when she was satisfied to stay with them forever, Sam Moss came into the room. He whipped the three men away from her with a mean riding crop. They crept off in a corner and let Heather go. Sam Moss took her into the other room by the fire where he could have her all for himself.

Later, he took her to the door and threw her back to the three who still waited.

"He didn't want me," Heather thought despairingly. "He took me away from his servants to show that he could, and now he has given me back to them to prove his contempt for me. I was not important to him. His men are important; what he can do to control them, and what he can appear to them to be. He is a little man trying to have a large image before large men."

Heather was ready to give up. She let the three men do to her whatever they wanted. When she was at last in the street again, she ran away from Moss House as fast as she could run. "I did this for Mead Hall," she thought. "I did everything Dana could have done and more."

In the taxi going home, a new thought presented itself to her. "What if it was not for Mead Hall? What if Mead Hall is safe and needs nothing? What if Aunt Dame and Dana have let me believe that Mead Hall was in financial trouble just so they could get me to do this?" An awful truth began to develop in her mind. What if everything had been a plot? Aunt Dame and Dana had let her believe in Dana's immoral behavior? Let her believe that the money derived from this was necessary to Mead Hall's continued existence? Let her believe that she would be acting heroically to step in and fill the breach when Dana was hurt? They had known who would call and what the results would be. Now, she had been to Moss House, and her aunt and cousin must know this. Already, they had a full report on everything which happened, and who knew what secret microphones and cameras were there! "They've got the goods on me," Heather thought desperately. "They can use the evidence they have to turn me out. This time, I'll lose Mead Hall forever." Riding in the slow taxi, a smile came over her face. "I can do things Dana never thought of doing. I can do things that make Dana ashamed." She hardened. "There is one way to keep them from taking Mead Hall away from me. I can kill them. I can do anything. I'll kill them."

When the taxi stopped, she ran lightly up the steps and into Mead Hall. Aunt Dame was sitting alone in the parlor. "We got Dana home," she said. "She's upstairs. Why don't you go up and speak to her?"

Heather went upstairs. Dana was in bed, her leg in a cast on top of the cover. "Dana, I want to talk with you," Heather said.

"All right," Dana answered smiling.

Heather asked her, "You are not a promiscuous woman, are you?" A look of astonishment appeared on Dana's face. "No, I'm not," she said coldly. "What brought this up?"

"You're not a call girl here in Liton Overallt, are you? You and Aunt Dame don't have a business like that."

"Of course we don't. Now listen, we've put up with your strange ways and ideas, but I draw the line somewhere. "

Heather told herself, "She's going to threaten me. They are going to use what they know to throw me out. They're going to take Mead Hall!" Aloud, she said, "Mead Hall is not in danger, is it?"

"Things aren't that bad," Dana said in an irritated tone of voice.

"Then, why did you and Aunt Dame let me believe all these things? Why did you let me do what I did tonight?"

"What did you do tonight?" Dana asked tiredly.

"You know."

"No, I don't know," Dana told her, out of patience. "I don't know anything you do. You have been so secretive and strange ever since you came here, neither Mother nor I know what to think of you."

"You know what happened tonight. The phone rang. It was Samuel Ben Franklin Moss. He asked for you. He said you were supposed to go to him. I went in your place. You know what happened there, because you set it up."

"Samuel Ben Franklin Moss!" Dana shouted. She threw her head back and laughed. "I never heard of such a person." She laughed and laughed, while Heather seized a heavy letter opener with which she began to stab Dana in the shoulder and arm. Dana cried out, "She's killed me," and fainted. Heather ran downstairs to the kitchen for a better knife to finish the job.

Aunt Dame had heard the screams. She was sending Gob away to get help, while she herself was running to the phone. Heather got the butcher knife and drove Aunt Dame into the kitchen. She killed her and threw one of the new drapes over her, although it did not match the color of Aunt Dame's blood. Then, Heather ran upstairs and finished killing Dana who had revived and cried piteously in her big bed.

Even at the last, they devoured Gob as they had done so many men. They had no right to live, so warm, always eating pretty things. Heather went out into the garden with a flashlight. In the dark, she busily tried to find any caterpillars which might be damaging the flowers.

At the preliminary hearing, she did not speak except for one time when she said in a loud, clear voice, "I wand cremation. I want the fire." The excellent character of the two murdered women was presented. Gob made it absolutely clear that there was no disorderliness or immorality at Mead Hall. "The old dragon got to him good," Heather thought. "He lies for her even now that she is dead."

Earlier, she had told her attorney about the events at Moss House. Now, she heard him saying that the house she called Moss House was a vacant one, locked up, dusty inside with no evidence that it had been entered in many months.

"There is no Samuel Ben Franklin Moss in Liton Overallt," he said.

"He belongs to Dana," Heather thought in desperation. "They are all against me." She would not look up at him when he talked to her after it was all over. He explained that she was going to take some examinations. "They do this because it is the law," she thought. "But, I read their faces. In the faces was praise. I have killed monsters. " She stared straight ahead and did not speak. There was no need to answer anyone in a world which was all enemies.

They led her down a corridor and pushed her into a room which she had never seen before. A chill came over her. She heard the heavy door slam and the latch click home. Currents of cold air swept around her, and the dark made her dizzy so that she was afraid she would fall to the stone floor which she could feel, damp and clammy, under her feet. She began to shiver and to shake out of loneliness and terror and cold. But, she didn't despair. She knew that, in a few moments, she would see a dim light at the end of the room, and her three hot, hairy friends would be there for her to cuddle with and lie next to, making her feel warm and protected and wanted forever.

1980s

By the time the 1980s came in, the writer's mother had lived at his house for five years. She was feeble and would become homebound. And, someone close to the writer and very important to him was dying of alcoholism, a day to day process. The writer's life was taken up with housework, caregiving, company work, and union activities. The press of minutia prevented him from writing and, since writing was the thing he did, he was, in his estimation, doing nothing. And very deeply but unconsciously resentful. See "The Ruined Cat."

The friend died.

Then, there was a strike at the steel mill. It was short of duration, but the writer's belief in the cohesiveness of the two integral parts of the total manufacturing operation was shattered. So, he was lost somewhere between adversaries - out of the loop, as they say. His port for all storms was closed to him. It had not in actuality ever really existed. It was a dream.

The writer fell into debilitating illness, similar to those sick periods in his life which had before been deemed undiagnosable, only this time it was much more severe, The winter of 1983, to use a cliche, was for this artist truly a "winter of the soul.

But, spring came, as it always does. The writer found a good doctor who understood about the death of the friend, and the significance of the strike, and the stultification which came with the writer's lifestyle.

The writer accepted a new duty with the union, and more activities with the company, and, as the decade wound down, joined a compatible writers' group and attended classes at several local colleges.

In December of 1989, the writer's mother died at age 100. She was buried in Biloxi, Mississippi.

So the end of the '80s found the writer alone. Even the ghost of the father was not there. Was he Norman Mailer's dreamed of American Existentialist? Philosophically? No, he was too straight, too square, too conventional, and too conservative for that. He would try to work both sides of the street, as he did in everything. In this case he would try to be the Wise Old Sage on the one hand, and a Bad Little Boy on the other. Great fun!

251

GEORGETOWN, SOUTH CAROLINA

"The Final Season" was written in Georgetown in 1983. A noticeable change had taken place in America between the years of the writer's childhood and those of his present. When the writer was a boy, young people hung around in Dickensian aspiration praying that the old folks might hurry and die, thus removing the expense of their keep and permitting the young to inherit. After FDR, the aged had incomes which were worthwhile to keep coming. The old peoples' income could be used to pay down any small mortgages which might exist limiting the size of the young people's anticipated inheritance.

It was now a common prayer that the old folks would live forever - keep the income coming - pay down their pesky mortgages and all other debts. The old took on the determination to become very old. This was often accomplished with great suffering by many of the aged who were ill and lamed and would be more comfortable just to give up and die..

Kudos to the pain-worn and the bored - the immobile and the confused of mind. This writer has seen examples of these.

The Roman Catholics have a name for everything. The determination of the old to survive and contribute is a facet of "dedicated suffering." Of course, those who will live after may be benefitted by these acts of dedication, but the practice (primarily through the constant offering of prayers) is efficacious in the spiritual realm, adding to God's Glory.

THE FINAL SEASON

The three men stood outside. One was obviously very much older than the other two. He looked to be ill to Lilly, and seemed vaguely familiar to her. There was about him a resemblance to someone she knew.

"Is Mr. Horace Whittaker at home?" one of the younger ones asked.

Lilly squared her shoulders and said, "He is at home, but there is trouble here this morning. He can't see anyone. He can't possibly."

"It is most important," the older man said weakly. "We have come a long way. We will come back at three o'clock this afternoon. Please try to have him see us."

"But, who are you"" she asked. Lilly was sure everything was all right, but her anxiety showed.

"He knows who we are, " one of the younger ones said.

They went down the steps through the damp and chill of the morning while Lilly watched how feebly the older man moved about.

With the door reclosed, the house was warm.

Horace came in from the kitchen where he had tried to understand what the voices at the front door were saying.

"Oh, Horace," Lilly asked in an outraged tone. "What have you done?"

"Lilly," Horace spoke in a voice almost inaudible. "That man is my older brother. His name is Virgil. Those two young men are the sons of my dead sister, Beatrice. Our mother was Pia."

Lilly sat down with the shock of it. Horace had always told her he had no family!

Horace, in spite of all his weakness and fear, had to tell Lilly everything. He had to take the risk that she would follow her usual pattern and take the matter out of his hands and manage and manipulate him in her cheerful way leaving him feeling that he was not a man at all, but a puppet - no, a zombie, walking in some living death.

It had to come out. He began by telling her how it had been during the war. In 1941, he was with the Army in the Philippines. In December there was Pearl Harbor. In 1942, even before spring arrived, he was wounded and malaria-ridden and sent home. The war, for him, was over. But, he had had time to see his friends die, and the dying was not pretty nor edifying and inspiring. The dying was just - sickening. He missed Bataan, and he missed Corregidor, to his shame!

But, what came next was worse," he told Lilly. "The worst came when I got home."

"Oh, surely not so bad as all that," Lilly chirped.

Horace almost hated her for her refusal to face anything unpleasant.

"My family was in terrible trouble," Horace said doggedly. "You see, our mother Pia had everything. Our father had nothing. When I was in high school, she set him up in business. When I came home from the Pacific, he had almost ruined the business, had given in to heavy drinking and was dead."

"My mother and Virgil were fighting to save the business and they told me my mother was dying of some wasting and painful illness."

"Her money was squandered away, except for a monthly stipend which came from money in trust, money which would revert to a university alumnus fund upon her death, leaving her children penniless with a sinking business which could only go bankrupt."

They needed my help, especially our sister, Beatrice, who was only fifteen, but none of this looked good to me after the dying and the pain and the sickness of war, so just left."

"Oh, Horace," Lilly whispered. "How could you have'?"

"It turned out all right for you!" he told her. "I came here, got a job, and when I met you I told you I had no family. You got to play Cinderella. You got to go to the ball. We were married, and we have lived happily ever after."

Lilly wanted to cry because of his tone of sarcasm. She had been Cinderella. She had lived so, so happily forever after!

"There was something strange about my mother's dying. Somehow, she lived for ten more years. They had found out where I was, my brother and sister. They let me know when she cited. It was 1952 and I didn't go. In 1974, 1 got word my sister, Beatrice, had died leaving two sons. I wasn't part of that family which had somehow stayed in the same place and survived with members who gave birth and lived and died. It has all passed me by."

"But, what is your brother doing here now"" Lilly asked. "He must be here because he loves you and wants to see you at last."

"No doubt he is here to forgive me," Horace said bitterly. "I don't want it. He is here to talk of death, his own which is not far off, and Beatrice's, and our mother's which came first."

"He wrote to me care of the office a few weeks ago. He spoke of his failing health and forgiveness for me and the family property which he says our mother wished for me to share in."

"That's very nice," Lilly said, dabbing away a tear. "After all this time!"

"There's more," Horace continued. "He sent a package. It contains things that used to be mine which my mother saved for me. Trivial boyhood things. Every time I would think of it in a locker down there at the office, I would only wish I would hear that Virgil had died so I could dispose of the box and no one would have to know about these things."

"I want to know about them," Lilly said.

"There is a scrap of wrinkled paper in the box. My mother had written upon it, 'Remember me, who am Pia.'"

"Please stay at home and meet your brother this afternoon," Lilly began. Horace could see her squaring her shoulders getting ready to manage the situation, to work hard at manipulating him.

"I'll do as I please," he said. "You don't tell me what to do."

"Oh no, dear," Lilly protested, but Horace had already stomped angrily out of the house.

When Horace returned it was after one o'clock and he looked somewhat sheepish. Lilly tried to act as though nothing had happened. She was almost more cheerful than usual,

She would have fallen at once into her criticizing, managing role, but she sensed something new in Horace, born that morning, which deterred her. She allowed him to move first.

"I brought the box with me," he said.

Together, like broken children struggling to enjoy a macabre Christmas, they took the items from the box, one by one. They were things Pia had saved because Horace had once attached importance to them: "Tom Sawyer" and "Penrod," a dirty tennis ball, a 78 rpm recording of "Once In A While" by Tommy Dorsey. There were gloves which Pia had knitted for him, school pictures, a report he had written senior English, a spinning top and marbles.

Horace folded and refolded the gloves.

"Do you remember how different music was then?"

"Of course I remember."

Horace put the record on the player and turned the needle over. He listened self-consciously, not looking at Lilly. She was enraptured at once, by the music and all it evoked.

When the record had played, Horace said, "Then, the music made us move. We couldn't listen to it and hold still."

"Oh yes," Lilly exclaimed. "And remember how much we danced, how much of the time we were dancing together?" They had been joyously and eagerly loving then.

"You let me be in control," Horace told her. "My left hand holding your right hand steered you like a rudder steers a ship, and my right hand just beneath your left shoulder blade and my body pressed against yours let me guide you steadily into any path I wanted you to take."

Lilly remembered Horace's air of firm and gentle, masterful command. "I felt safe then," she said, "and content."

"I wonder that things like that can be lost."

"Mislaid," Lilly said, her brightness getting the upper hand.

"I'll put on a clean shirt before Virgil comes," Horace said resignedly.

Lilly moved quickly to get him one. Then (his own idea) he even put on a necktie and splashed his face with cologne before they heard Virgil's knock at the door.

Virgil and Beatrice's two sons came inside. When the introductions were completed and the first self-consciousness began to go away, Virgil explained why they had come.

"We told the truth, Horace," he began. "In 1942, we found out that our mother was dying. Our father had just died of alcoholism, and she was our mainstay. Her income from her inheritance was the only hope of the struggling business which she had established for our father."

"Her uncle had left her a large sum in trust," Horace explained to Lilly. "He couldn't stand our father, so income from the trust would be paid to her in her lifetime and then be diverted to his old alma mater. He didn't want our father or our father's children to come into control of the money. We would get secondary benefits from it only for so long as she lived and received it."

"Our father had already gone through the legacy she had received from her father by the time this arrangement as made," Virgil continued. "News that she was to die was a financial disaster for the family business, as well as a bitter tragedy for the family."

"But, our mother felt that she would be leaving us in the lurch, to die and deprive our business or income. She felt guilty about losing a fortune on our father. Somehow, despite the predictions of medical science, she kept herself alive for ten more years!"

The poor, sweet lady," Lilly exclaimed.

"She lived in an earthly purgatory, always in pain, always the victim of a crushing weakness which depressed her mind and feelings, as well as made her body helpless, but she lived. She lived because she wanted us to have something."

"I deserted this lady," Horace said. "For ten years I never sent any word, any token to her."

"She always said you loved her so much," Virgil said. "You could not stay there to see her suffering,"

"Well, I didn't deserve that much kindness."

"She continued to draw breath, to stay alive. Her income came and we built up the business. It is a very valuable business today. She felt that she did it for all three of her children, for me and for Beatrice and for you."

"Oh, no," Horace protested. "I shouldn't have anything."

"That's what I thought, too," Virgil admitted. "I suppressed her wishes after she died. I didn't tell you. I might have, if you had come at the last minute or come to the funeral, but you didn't come. I didn't tell you anything about our circumstances."

One of the younger men spoke up,

"Uncle Virgil was terribly sick last year. He was sure to have died, but

thought of you began to prey on his mind. He felt he had wronged you. He wanted to live long enough to come here and tell you what he had done so that he could make amends. He remembered Pia and the way she had kept herself alive through all those desolate years, and he brought himself back. That's how it happened we were able to come here."

"We have drawn up all the necessary papers to divide the family properties in accordance with our mother's wishes. We have been scrupulous in our efforts to do things fairly," Virgil said. "If you will accept what is yours, everything in this family will be attended."

"I can never mend what I have done. I have cut myself off from love for forty years, and I am dried up inside."

"One spark remains," Lilly told him. "I saw the spark trying to burst into flame earlier today." But Lilly did not continue. She did not want to be manipulative, to pontificate, she just smiled.

"We want you to come back into the family and be one with us and bring your sweet wife with you. The exile you have imposed upon yourself must be ended."

Virgil and his two nephews rose to go, but before they left they gave Horace the papers which would explain to him what his financial holdings were. Horace walked them to their car.

Horace and Lilly looked at each other like strangers. Their life together had to be reassessed. All the pieces seemed scattered about like pieces of a jigsaw puzzle on a table top. The pieces must be gathered together in a new configuration.

"I guess things haven't always been as bright and happy as I thought," Lilly said. "You've had such deep sorrows on your mind all these years and I didn't see them because I didn't look. I was content to see the world through rose-tinted glasses. You must have thought me a giddy fool so many times."

"I had my own way of running away from things. I wouldn't admit that anything is inevitable. I believed anything at all could be run away from. I was a specialist at running away.

"For people who let it be, the inevitable is ugly," Lilly said.

"When I have to face anything which is inevitable," Horace said, "I will remember Pia and the way she drew the inevitable out over ten years. She thwarted death. And, I will remember Virgil who was able to postpone death so that he could come and make things right with me and so later die in peace. I shall remember these through all the autumn of my life."

Horace lifted the box with its boyhood possessions, with the scrap of paper with the words, "Remember me, who am Pia," the school report quoting a poem, "Grow old along with me. The best is yet to be," and the recording. It all moved Horace beyond words.

Horace started the record. He drew Lilly to him. He held her right hand in a firm grip. His fingers under her shoulder blade pulled her tightly against him. Her left hand lay lightly on his shoulder. He had complete charge of her. She was relaxed, waiting for his signal. He moved his left leg forward. Her right leg had to slide back. In smooth, graceful motion, in time with the music, they did a fox-trot around the floor.

GEORGETOWN, SOUTH CAROLINA

"The Ruined Cat" was written in Georgetown in 1984. A man and his sister come to grips with an emotional problem he suddenly manifests which endangers their livelihood. They reason that his approach to weak people and other strays is to take them under his wing - adopt them - thereby making them into idle, helpless, "ruined cats." He considers his sister to be one of these. Being strong for her has lost him his chance for a successful life. She blames him for creating the plight they find themselves in.

Study of a new painting which he has produced shows them that the brother's response to life enables him to escape planning for the future or outlining any new positive actions. He can drift as he used to when his mother would take charge of things and make the decisions. It is he who is the "ruined cat, " they surmise.

The sense in which he sees his life as ruined is in the fact that he has never had the time to create the great works which he feels himself capable of. He is too mired down in day-to-day routine. The writer was depressed at this time and much of his problem was that he was giving over his life to a daily, run-of-the-mill schedule when he could have been erecting masterpieces instead.

There is no father here. The father is gone. The conflict is between the brother and sister and within the brother's self. He feels his sister has deprived him of life. She, on the other hand, is reinforced in her belief in the rightness of her actions toward him by memory of a "martyred" mother's example and the presence of a mercenary gentleman caller.

THE RUINED CAT

Laura stood in the midst of a perfect South Carolina spring morning, on the second floor sundeck of the old house which she and her brother Tom had inherited from their mother. She could see Mr. Jim O'Connor striding along the sandy shoulder of the road which ran in front of the house. He was heading her way, looking up, smiling as usual, always cheerful, a born salesman.

Laura usually spent part of each morning out on the sundeck. The air here was warm and fresh. Here, she escaped the paint smell. Her brother, Tom, painted souvenir china (various bric-a-brac, including ash trays, pill boxes, and demitasses with saucers), which Mr. Jim took down to Charleston where he sold it to retail shops and independent vendors.

Laura and Tom had to live very simply because almost the only money they had came back to them from Mr. Jim when he disposed of the china. Their house was old, but there was a mortgage. Sometimes they rented one or two of the spare bedrooms to paying guests and Laura cooked meals, but Crayville, South Carolina was out of the way. There was not much chance of outsiders coming to Crayville to stay overnight or for several days. Any business a stranger might need to transact in Crayville could almost always be completed in one day.

Laura repeated to herself, once again, the old hope that Tom would someday find time and the inspiration to work at what Laura called "real art." Success in this would enable them to get some money ahead, sell their old house, and move away to some promised land where Tom would have contemporaries to associate with and she would meet and interest someone eligible.

The only remotely eligible man she knew in Crayville was Mr. Jim O'Connor himself, and the very thought of a social understanding with him bored her, as she phrased it, to extinction.

Drab as existence was, they did have some comforts. Tom had built the sundeck at the rear of the house after their mother's death. There had still been a little money. Laura enjoyed it every day. Of course, it did not fit in architecturally with the rest of the old house, which was impoverished Victorian, but it stood, sturdy and utilitarian and plain, a hint of the present grafted on an eroded, carved dream symbol from a wistful and impractical past. It was like Laura pictured her own life and Tom's. They lived in the past, with one foot in 1984 reality, she felt.

Mr. Jim would stop in and visit with them. He did this daily. He begged belief in his explanation that he did so in order to check on how Tom's work was going, but Laura guessed with only mild interest that he called so often so that he could visit with her.

Now, Mr. Jim walked with shoulders back, bouncing on the balls of his feet, like a young man walking. Laura knew that he was fifty-two if he was a day, perhaps older. He had many of the small flaws of body and habit which come with aging. Laura was Conscious of every one of them. She was herself thirty years old. Her brother Tom was thirty six.

Mr. Jim waved his hand as he approached the foot of the outside stairs.

Tom's dog, Roderick, lifted his head when he heard Mr. Jim's foot on the board, but upon recognition of the frequent guest he lowered it slowly to the rough boards where it had lain, his eyes closing in unison with the gentle downward movement of his head. Laura looked at her round-bellied dog who seemed already to accept Mr. Jim as part of the household. Everyone told her that Roderick was too fat for a dog. It was because his master fed him cookies and tidbits from his own plate. Tom did this every day.

There were plastic and aluminum chairs on the deck. Laura and Mr. Jim sat down, as they did every morning. Tom's smoke grey cat, Quint, was stretched on the table in the shade of the big sun umbrella. He opened one eye and then slept again.

Mr. Jim did not like cats. He had told Laura long before, that Tom would ruin a good cat (if there were any such thing as a good cat) by spoiling it. He believed a hypothetical good cat would be one that was self-sufficient and could, for the most part, forage for itself. Tom fed cats so well and pampered them so continually that they lost all initiative and became overweight and lazy.

"I have some good news," Mr. Jim began.

"The day portends good news," Laura said. "It's such a perfect day." She continued for some minutes to enumerate all the beauties of the day.

The day did appear, they both agreed, to be one in which nothing but good could happen.

"I've made a contract with the central office of a chain of novelty and gift shops to furnish them with all their painted china. They use thousands of pieces each season. They will take those pine and cedar plaques with mottoes lettered on them, too, and painted kerchiefs and scarves, if Tom can find the time," Jim told her excitedly. "We'll still have our old customers to satisfy, too. This will be the best year we've ever had."

"It shall be a good year," Laura exclaimed. She rubbed her hand unconsciously along Quint's side. The cat curled his paws into balls and stretched his front legs. "A good year at last."

"We'd better go in and tell Tom. He's probably working already," Mr. Jim said.

They heard Tom call Laura's name. There was an urgency in his tone. He called again and again from within his workroom. Laura and Mr. Jim ran to him.

Tom sat at the work table where he painted china. His face was deathly pale. There was an expression of horror on his face. He had broken a partially decorated demitasse saucer.

"Tom," Laura cried in a shocked voice, "what's the matter?"

Softly, very calmly, he said, "I can't see!"

"What do you mean, you can't see?" Mr. Jim shouted.

"It's like I've been struck blind," Tom said. "I was listening to you talking. I could hear what you were saying. Through the open window. And the, suddenly, I couldn't see."

Laura sat down. Her shoulders slumped forward and her chest seemed to cave in.

"What will we do"" she asked. "You have to see. You must see, in order for us to live."

"And me!" Mr. Jim cried. "I'm getting older. It's not easy. I need the commissions I get on your work. Your work is the backbone of my operation. The other merchandise wouldn't make it worthwhile for me to stay in business if your volume was gone."

"I'm sorry," Tom said. "But, I can't at all see."

Laura lifted her head and looked at Mr. Jim. Mr. Jim was in a panic. She dug her fingers in his arm. "We can't think about ourselves," she said. "We have to do something for him."

"You're right," Mr. Jim said quickly. "Tom, we'll call a doctor for you."

Crayville's Dr. Cukro was summoned. When he arrived and had examined Tom, he told Laura that he could not, with his available resources, find any reason for Tom's inability to see. He recommended that Tom be taken by ambulance of in Mr. Jim's car to a hospital in Charleston. Laura relayed this idea to Tom. Tom bluntly told her that he would not go.

"I don't want any other doctors to see me," he said.

Outside, on the deck, Laura and Mr. Jim and Dr. Cukro stood together talking over what to do.

"He should have a complete checkup," Dr. Cukro said. "Delay could possibly cause a temporary and treatable condition to become permanent. We need to know what's wrong with him to see if it can be treated."

"What do you think it is?" Laura asked anxiously.

"I can't see any reason why he can't see," Dr. Cukro told her. "I know he believes he cannot. It's possible that, in spite of what he believes, he can."

"You mean he's faking?" Mr. Jim demanded.

"Not faking," Dr. Cukro said. "Something's really keeping him from seeing. What that is is what we need to find out. When we know what it is, we can eliminate it." He thought for a moment. "Let him alone for a few hours. Maybe this afternoon he will decide to go for help."

When Dr. Cukro was gone, Laura and Mr. Jun sat down and began to speak in unconsciously conspiratorial whispers.

"What do you suppose the doctor meant?" Laura asked. "He didn't seem to be sure whether Tom can see or not."

"He seems to think there's nothing wrong with Tom's eyes," Mr. Jim explained. "But, Tom is being prevented from seeing with them by something else."

"Something else?"

"Something in his mind."

Tom had gotten up and come outside. Laura and Mr. Jim watched him closely, trying to tell if he felt his way around the doorjamb or if he saw how to step around Roderick.

"We're over here," Laura said.

He came and dropped into a chair beside them. "I'm sorry," he said, "I guess I've ruined everything for all of us. Maybe you two had better make plans for yourselves. Forget about me. You can have some sort of life. How can I survive, if I can't see'?"

"Are you giving up so easily?" Laura asked. "Are you really blind or just pretending to be and using that as an excuse to give up'?"

"I can't see," Tom shouted, showing the first display of emotion he had shown since it had happened. "I can't see!"

"Tom," Mr. Jim said, "you should take Dr. Cukro's advice. You should go see other doctors. You should go and see as many as it takes."

"I won't go and see any more doctors," Tom said.

Laura began to cry. She went down the stairs to the ground. She knew Tom heard the screen door slam when she went inside. He would know where to find her if he needed her.

When she was gone, Mr. Jim put his hand on Tom's arm. "I want you to tell me why," he said. "I want you to tell me why you don't want help to get you out of this."

"It's not worth bothering with," Tom said.

"Your sight, your ability to function in the world are not worth bothering with?" Mr. Jim exclaimed. "You are down."

"It's me," Tom spat out. "I'm not worth it."

"Why do you feel that way about yourself?"

"I'm all used up. There's nothing left of me any more. I'm no good to anyone. It's all spent."

"Tom," Mr. Jim said. "I do believe that you can't see. You can't see, can you Tom?"

"I can't see."

"Do you think it's a punishment that God has sent upon you? You do so much for other people, but I've always felt as if you feel you never do enough. It must keep you under a strain. I wish I could take away from your responsibilities and make things easier for you and happier for myself, but you know that won't work at present. She doesn't want to let me take care of her. She wants things to go on as they always have."

Tom thought for a long time. Then, he said, "If I have a fault in this world, it's that I am just too good."

Mr. Jim looked at Tom curiously. He got up and went down the steps and stood in the yard. In a few moments, Tom followed him, not hesitating, not feeling his way, but walking certainly out.

Mr. Jim talked with Laura through the kitchen screen door. "I'm going to leave for a few minutes," he told her. "You talk to him alone. Maybe you can find out what's the matter with him."

Laura was completely spent. Her attempts to talk with Tom were merely frustrating. After a few tries, they fell silent and this was the way they spent the rest of the day and evening. Tom did not eat any lunch or supper or anything for breakfast the next morning. Laura ate very little.

Tom walked aimlessly about or lay on his bed during the entire time. Laura noticed that he turned on the lights in the bathroom and his room after it got dark. He needed the lights to be on in order that he might move around the house. However, he still stated to Laura that he could not see.

When morning did come, they sat on the sundeck and Laura looked at the beautiful day and told herself that probably it was true that Tom could not see.

"I don't know why this has happened," she said. "I know that you took care of our mother and me for years, and since Mother had died you have taken care of me. I know there were other things you wanted to do with your life."

"Yes," Tom said, "other things."

"I guess you've worn yourself out helping us," Laura said. "Now that Mother's gone, it doesn't matter about me. If, after you can see again, you just want to leave, I'll understand. I'll get along somehow. If need be, I can marry Mr. Jim O'Connor. He'll take care of us."

"Don't play your martyr role with me," Tom said sharply. "You learned that ploy from our mother. She was always a master at playing the martyr while pretending to believe that I was one."

"I don't believe you are a martyr on my account," Laura said in a voice heavy with sarcasm. "Or on account of our mother either. You didn't make enough of a sacrifice to be a martyr for us."

"I feel that I gave up my whole life. If that's a small sacrifice in your view,what would it take to be a big one?" Tom asked huskily.

"Did you give up your life or did you throw it away? And, if you gave it up, what did you give It up for?" Laura screamed. "You have always, since you were a little boy, picked up every stray person, stray dog and stray cat that came along and you've done everything for them, and given everything to them, the whole world, and you've never kept back any time or money or energy for yourself. Mother and I were just a small part of that voracious army that has eaten away at you and eaten away at you until you're empty and dry; drunks, young men, old men, old ladies, organizations, churches, labor groups..." Laura gasped for breath. "I've seen your tired, your poor, your huddled masses.." She had to stop.

"I needed those things to fill the void you made. I felt there was no chance of my ever doing what I wanted to do, because of our mother and you, so something or someone should benefit. I wanted someone to get something out of it or else it was none of it worthwhile. Otherwise, it was all for nothing."

"We benefited, Mother and me, we got something out of it. This should have satisfied you, but the fact that your mother and your sister were happy counted as nothing. You had to have all those others as a sort of validation. What you did was for our family. Your sacrifice, as you seem to think of it, was to keep our family's good name intact," Laura said. "We have a good name to maintain. Our family stands for certain things. We're not like most of the people in Crayville. We're not like Mr. Jim O'Connor and his mercantile thinking. Mr. Jim O'Connor is merely crass."

"You can really spread it on just like our mother, chapter and verse! If we'd had a little more crass materialism in our makeup, we might not be in the fix we're in now," Tom told her.

"What kind of fix is it, Tom?" Laura asked. "Tell me just what kind of fix we're in."

"I can't see," Tom shouted, "and we'll probably starve because I can't paint any more demitasses with saucers."

"I know that I'm useless when it comes to taking care of you or myself," Laura said sadly. "Mr. Jim was right when he said you'd ruin any good cat that you took in. I know, Tom, what you've made of me. I am just another of your ruined cats."

"Do you think pampered cats can ever be taught to catch mice?" Tom asked her.

"No," she answered desperately. "If you can break them in that way, you have to nurture them for life or someone else has to take over the task. They can never fend for themselves."

"I don't know if that is correct when it comes to cats," Tom said. "But, it applies to sisters."

Laura looked terribly distressed. "I know you feel trapped," she said.

"Shut up in a box."

"Do you think you can stand it?" Laura asked. "It's so terrible for you."

"It's only that I hoped for so much," Tom told her. "I didn't ask for anything. It was just there. I felt that I could see more than anyone else had ever seen and know more about what I had seen that anyone had ever known. I felt

264

that I could paint it all on canvas. Everything I could see. I could see into the souls of people and depict what was there for others to see. I felt that I could see well enough to capture the essence of' landscapes, the spirits in buildings, the life of towns, the romance of the sea. I felt I could put it all down for people to see. My vision."

"I remember how you loved to paint," Laura said. "How much imagination you had. I remember how proud mother and I were."

"It used to well up inside me, like some surging glory. It was a passion which required being expelled."

"Is it still there?" Laura asked him.

"Yes. It's still there, in spite of everything. It still wants to come out."

"You've got to go and talk to someone and get this settled," Laura said. "It's your life you'll be settling. It's your whole life at stake. You've got to see again. You've got to decide what you are going to do."

"I'll decide," Tom said. "And, I'll see. I'm going to see more than I've ever seen and, because I see, others will see, too. That's important. Somehow, nothing else seems important now. There's nothing else that I can even think of."

"A sister is pretty unimportant, I guess."

Mr. Jim O'Connor approached along the road. He crossed the yard and started up the stairs. "How is he?" he shouted.

"He still can't see," Laura shouted back. "He still can't see."

Tom put his head down on the table beside Quint and drummed his forehead lightly on the table. "I'm so angry!" he said.

* * * *

So far as Laura was able to see, things did not change in any notable way while Tom remained unseeing for three days and nights. During this period, Tom had a feeling that something was about to happen. He listened for a knock at the door or a shout from down in the back yard. He felt that something good was coming to him, a sign lighting his way to the future. When he told Laura about this, she found herself trying to believe, too, that something they needed was coming to them. Neither of them could define what it was that they expected.

When Tom had been unseeing for three days and nights, the thought came to him with the morning of the fourth day, that he should paint a picture. He still believed that he could not see, but he also believed that he could paint a picture on a canvas. He resumed eating. He had not eaten anything for three days. Laura fixed breakfast for him, which he ate without assistance.

Laura took the dishes away when he had finished. He shut himself in and she did not see him again until the following afternoon. He had been without sleep for most of the time he was shut in the workshop. He had painted. When he came out the painting was done.

The painting was all in various shades of yellow with some areas outlined in black. It depicted a chair placed on a bare board floor. There was no other item of furniture near it. The chair was a straight wooden chair with a woven straw bottom.

"This is very carefully done," Laura said, noting that each board in the floor was outlined. The grain of the boards could be clearly seen. The woven seat of the chair was detailed. Several broken straws could be seen. "This is an accurate depiction of an old chair we used to have," she said.

"It's a sunlit room," Tom noticed. "It's like I used all that yellow paint in an attempt to capture the whole light of the sun. The canvas was not big enough to contain all the light that I tried to squeeze into it."

"Do you know what it is?" Laura asked.

"No. I don't know what it is," Tom said testily. "Do you?"

"Mother used to take a chair like that, when you were bad, and set it on the bare floor like that away from everything else, and she'd make you sit in it for punishment," Laura remembered.

"She'd make me sit there," Tom said. "She'd say, 'Don't you move or do anything until I come back and tell you what to do.'"

"You remember it," Laura cried. "She did that a lot."

"I'd just sit there knowing that I didn't have to plan or to get ready to act. I only had to wait passively until she came for me."

"That's what you want now," Laura told him. "You want someone to come and tell you what to do."

"I wish I could be given a large work to do, like a great mural, that would take a lifetime to complete. So that every day it would be there and I would have to add to it and I wouldn't have to think what I was going to do in a day. It would be all projected. Each day, I would go in like Proust when he had begun to work on 'Remembrance of Things Past,' knowing the grand design and having only to add in the details which the grand design required each day."

"Would that be enough for you," Laura asked him.

"I would never think of anything else."

"I would want more than that," Laura said. "I don't feel that I have, within my own self, everything in the world that I can ever need. You do feel that self-sufficient, don't you?"

"Yes."

"What would happen to you when the mural was done?"

"God," Tom said, "would have a defective electric fan waiting for me."

* * * *

Tom ate and he slept a little and then Laura did not see him again until several days had passed and another painting was completed.

The new painting, Laura saw, was still yellow, for the most part, but now there were brown shadows encroaching from the sides and a gloom pervaded the entire thing. The chair was now in the center of a circus animal cage. The cage was round. The bars ran vertically. The trainer's whip lay on the floor. On the chair, in the center of the cage, sat an old lion.

"What a terrible picture," Laura gasped. "That's you, that lion. The lion is you, and you don't sit in the chair now, because our mother is here and tells you to, but you sit there because there is a cage all around you which you can't come out of. You've built the cage yourself. You built it to protect yourself from others who might want to get in to you; you sit there anxious and afraid and hoping to be safe. The result is that although the cage fails to keep others out for you, it does succeed in keeping you in."

" Yes," Tom said. "That is me. That is me, that old lion, that great ruined cat. That is me." He looked at Lilly sadly. "Remember what we read in the Bible one time?" he asked her. "'The roaring of the lion and voice of the fierce lion, and the teeth of the young lions are broken. The old lion perisheth for lack of prey.'"

He went out onto the sundeck and sat down.

"That lion in that cage is me," he said. "Defanged, tranquilized, old, sightless, fur-frayed and ear-torn, with no one my kind to talk with."

* * * *

When the sun was almost setting, Tom got up from his seat and went inside the workshop. He picked up a demitasse and he could see it in his hand. He picked up an ashtray and placed it on the table before him. He could see his brushes and his paints arranged neatly before him. He took the brush and painted a circle of flowers on the ashtray. Inside the circle he painted "Souvenir of Crayville, South Carolina." It was as neat and as craftsmanlike as anything he had ever done.

"I can work again," he said to himself. "That's a victory."

But, it felt like a defeat.

He had demonstrated that he could still paint an interesting canvas. The urge was still there. In those minutes when he could lay the souvenirs aside and do what he wanted, he would work on a canvas here and a canvas there, leading up to the day when he could create his mural, his remembrance of things past. This accomplished, he would have brought victory out of defeat, this not accomplished, he would have purchased despair.

GEORGETOWN, SOUTH CAROLINA

"Willie D. Pry" was written in Georgetown in 1984. Both this story and the preceding one were written while the writer was on sick leave, being treated for depression. The protagonist, carrying always feelings of guilt over his avaricious killing of an innocent animal many years before, regrets any obligation he may have today which demands he be mean. (His people trust him. He is dedicated to doing them no harm.) In line with his calling, demands for guile and aggressiveness toward the adversary come often.

He tried to live in such a way as to exclude no trusting person from himself, or ever to bring hurt upon one of these. Trust is the factor. The trusting he won't harm but will champion.

But, can he define harm? Can he recognize trust? He can define champion. That is what he is.

He has problems common to those who would do good. He will learn that working through these is the way that labor leaders and other bestowers of selective righteous wrath interspersed with frequent social kindness are made! And, he will walk humbly.

WILLIE D. PRY

It seemed to Willie D. Pry, president of the local union, that the union hall had emptied almost instantaneously. One moment, it had been full of smoking, talking, excited members and their friends, and the next almost all of these had gone outside into the night and scattered in separate ways.

Willie D. smelled the cigarette smoke and listened to the revved up engines of the cars and pickup trucks taking off into the darkness.

When the guest of honor had gone, everyone else but two or three had followed. The guest of honor was Sidney E. McManus, called Mac. With the help of Willie D.'s union and the district farmers and the black people, he had won election to the office of Congressman from the seventh congressional district. He had dropped by to thank the union for its support and to visit with the men.

The evening had been a great success. Alcoholic beverages were not served, but were allowed. There must have been plentiful supplies in the cars and trucks outside. This was evident in the dramatic changes in demeanor which took place in the men each time a group of them went outside and then returned to the hall. They went out quietly and cool, and returned laughing, sweaty and loud.

Willie D. had his share to drink and he felt sleepy and light. He felt light, as if he could float away. He walked around, straightening a metal chair here and there and turning out some of the lights. The union hall grew almost dark and outside it was quiet. No more cars or pickups were starting up.

Mabin Wheatley was one of the men who had stayed behind. He came to the front of the hall and sat on one of the tables.

"It made me feel good to see how happy Mac was and how good he got along with everyone," Mabin said. "I believe he will do a lot of good for us when he gets to Washington."

Mabin was a bigger man than Willie D. Most men were bigger than Willie D. Willie D. was small and trim. His hands and feet were small, as was his lower face. He had a rather prominent forehead, topped by a burst of light brown, curly hair.

His eyes were active and blue and his skin was fair. He was an energetic man. His vigorous and forceful presence could be felt the moment he entered a room.

Now, he was subdued because the evening was over and he had been drinking.

" He won't forget us," Willie D. said.

Mabin said that it would seem strangely quiet, now that there would be no campaign work to be done, now the election was over. Even though their side had won, there was an emptiness at the loss of the stimulating activity of the last few months.

"It won't be the same," Willie D. mused. "It's been a nightly thing, going to meetings and speaking around and about. There's been something to do every day. I know I'll miss it." Willie D. did not often go home early at night, although he had a wife there and two children.

"You might go into politics full time," Mabin told him. "You're good at it, and you seem to like it a lot."

"I wish I'd learned more," Willie D. said. "I wish I'd started younger. I didn't realize 'til I was grown that I needed to learn anything. I didn't learn what I should have when I was young."

"I'll bet, if you asked him, Mac would get you a job helping him in Washington. He could probably use you up there on his staff doing something."

"I'm not an educated person," Willie D. said. "I know that there are a lot of things I can do. I do a lot of these things very well, but I don't think I'd fit in in Washington. Mac will have the kind of people he needs up there. We'll only see him when he comes to Crayville. When he needs us, we'll hear from him, and when we need him, he'll help us out, but it won't be like it has been, any more. Or, maybe it won't until next election and then he'll come back and we'll work together again. I'll miss him. He's such a smart man. I just like being with him. I like to hear him talk. There are so many things to learn from him."

Already, Willie D. could sometimes feel the presence of Mac, when Mac was not there. It was like feeling the tingle in a hand or foot which had been amputated. For a second, the lost limb would seem to be there, and then the shattering truth would come down that it was, indeed, gone. Willie D. would took into the shadows of a darkened room and almost see Mac sitting there gazing at him, or he would drive along the highway in his small red car and imagine Mac there in the seat beside him. He would ask Mac questions about things which bothered him and figure out in his own mind what Mac would reply to these questions.

Willie D. could answer his own questions for himself by thinking what Mac would say in reply to his inquiries. He could not have answered them without using this means of doing it.

"I reckon I'd better go home," Mabin said. "I'm on evening shift tomorrow, You need any help locking up or anything ?"

"No," Willie D. said. "I'm going to stay here tonight. It's late and I've been drinking. I'll just get some sleep in the office. I've got a lot to do here tomorrow."

"Your old lady won't worry, will she?" Mabin asked.

"I told her I might not come home tonight," he said. This would just be one of the many nights that he did not go home at all. Lately, his wife wasn't able to expect him until she actually saw him. Sometimes, three or four days would go by when Willie D. did not see his wife or children.

Willie D. listened as Mabin Wheatley drove away. There was the same noisy start up, the same roar as the engine came to full power. Then the quiet, resonant purr as the truck moved away from the hall and, then, whirred down the street toward out of town.

The high-backed chair at Willie D's desk was padded and had just the right contours to fit Willie D. comfortably. Tilted back, it made an ideal place to rest. Willie D. had thick carpeting installed on the office floor, and he would stretch out there and rest in complete comfort, sleeping the night through with just the floor and a cushion for his head to rest on.

He sat in his chair and swung around a time or two. He was president of the local union and this made him feel good. He got the chance to help people every day and this was what he liked to do.

He tilted the chair back and put his feet up on his desk. He lit a cigarette. The room was dark, but a glow came in from the dim lights he had left burning out in the meeting hall. He could see the outline of the filing cabinets and the other chairs which were in the room. Even though he could not see them, he knew where the clock on the wall hung and, also, various plaques which had been presented to the union from time to time. His hand went unhesitating to the ashtray on the desk. He knew every inch of the office as though he had placed every object there himself. Many of them, he had.

Now, as he looked at what should have been a bare expanse of wall, he seemed to see a dark outline there where there should have been nothing. There was a small lamp on the desk. He turned it on. A young girl, one Willie D. had seen around the union hall a few times, was sitting on the floor with her knees drawn up under her chin. She was wearing jeans and a tan T-shirt. He had seen her sitting in the audience earlier that evening when Sidney K. McManus was speaking.

"Where'd you come from?" he asked.

"I hope you're not mad, Mr. Pry," she said. "I just wanted to stay here a while longer. I don't feel like I ever want to leave here. Mr. Pry, I think this is just the most exciting place. I wish I could be part of what goes on at a place like this."

"Who are you'"'

"I'm Urtha Lee Shore, Mr. Pry," she said. "My brother knows you."

"Get up and sit in a chair," Willie D. said.

Urtha Lee slid up into a chair and looked at Willie D. with undisguised interest. She had never seen anyone like him this close before. "You sure can talk, can't you?" she asked. "You talked something wonderful out there tonight in the meeting. You talked as good as Mr. McManus."

"Mac," Willie D. began, proud that he was on a nickname basis with a Congressman elect, "Mac says that he never saw anyone without training that was as good a speaker as I am in front of a crowd. I can move a crowd more than lots of people that are in politics. I spoke to a meeting of black people a couple of weeks ago and I had them agreeing with every word I said. One of the leaders at a rally said that he had never seen a white speaker hold a black audience like I held that one. Speaking to a crowd is one of the things I do very well."

"You must really be someone who can lead people," Urtha Lee said.

"I don't think that I lead them as much as I just take them along with me," Willie D. told her. "I get so excited by ideas that I think are good ideas, and the kind of ideas I believe will help people, I take off on new paths, following these ideas, almost running, and I talk about them and the people get excited, too, and run along with me, keeping up, and staying with me. We grow together, toward a common goal. That's what we do. We grow together, toward a common goal."

"I used to get excited about ideas that would come in my head when I was younger," Urtha Lee said. "I don't as much any more."

"How old are you now?" Willie D. asked. She really looked too young.

"I'm nineteen," she said. "I've got a baby at home. My brother and his wife are raising her."

"I'll bet you grew up the same way I did," he said. "Did you live out in the country?"

"We lived at San Savor."

"I still live at Cherry Park."

"I know where you live. You're married."

"Yes. I'm married."

"When I was a child," Urtha Lee told him, "I thought living was a lot of fun. I thought we had a good life, but now I can see that we were just poor. That was all. Just poor."

"We were poor, too," Willie D. said. He stood up. "I made you get up off the floor," he told her. He took a step forward. "Let's sit on the floor again, both of us. This is a special carpet I had put in here. It's soft and gives under you. They clean it with something that gives it a clean smell. We can sit down, side by side, there by the filing cabinet."

Urtha Lee reclined on the floor and stroked the nap of the carpet with her hand.

"This floor's as soft as a lot of beds," she said. "It's wonderful carpet."

"I had something in mind when I did this," Willie said as he settled beside Urtha Lee on the floor.

"George," she said, speaking of her brother, "says you sure have done a lot for this union. He's always talking about it. He says you've just remade this union hall."

"I can do some things very well," Willie D. said, repeating what he had told her earlier. "I can help people and I can hurt people. The difference is, I don't like to hurt people."

"Mr. Sidney McManus talked like you had really helped him. He said in his speech tonight that you nearly ran his whole campaign for him."

"I guess I did do a lot. I can get people to follow me. That's one of the things I do best," Willie D. admitted.

"You wouldn't ever really hurt anyone, would you?" Urtha Lee asked in an unbelieving tone of voice. "I can't believe you would ever be mean."

"I would," Willie D. said, "if that person was doing something to hurt someone else. That's what a union and union officials are for. When they see the company of anyone else trying to hurt a member, the union is there to defend that member."

"I'll bet that's when you really get mad and have it out with them."

"I can be a real adversary in an adversarial situation."

"They make you be like that," Urtha Lee said, snuggling against him. "I'm not afraid of you."

Willie D. poked the carpet with his fingers. He sighed. All at once, a feeling of fatigue came over him.

"It says in the Bible that parents should provoke not their children to wrath. There are too many parents, wives, employers and law enforcement people provoking other people to wrath. That's what makes broken marriages and wars."

"Life gets real complicated when you're grown up," Urtha lee said.

"Childhood has its heartaches, too," Willie D. told her. "One time when I was about ten years old I shot a dog. The man who owned the dog didn't want him any more. He told me he would give me a dollar to shoot him. A dollar was big money, then. I didn't think much about it. I had my gun with me, so I took the dollar and got the dog to follow me on down the road. The dog ran along beside me just as happy as he could be. When we had gone a little way, I led him under some trees and we stopped and very quickly I shot him. In just a few seconds, he was dead. But, in one instant before he died, he realized what I had done and he looked up at me with a look in his eyes that asked me why I had done it, and I wondered myself why I had done such a thing. Even for a dollar."

"Poor dog," Urtha Lee said. "That's really a sad thing. That's a sad thing you're telling me."

"I thought about it for a long time after that," Willie D. told her. "For a long time after that the thought would come back to me about that trusting and happy dog that was so glad to walk along with me which I killed."

Urtha Lee tried to think of something to say, some comfort to give. At last, she said, "You aren't like that now, Willie D. Now, you're tender and kind. I know you are. You wouldn't hurt anyone who wanted to be with you."

"I won't hurt you," he said. He gave a little pull to her arm and she crept nearer to him. He put his arms around her. There was no need to hurt her in any way. Others require that lie hurt them, but she came to him in innocence. She belonged there beside him because she wanted to be there.

"I want it so much, much, much," she said.

They, the two of them, could have been running together along a sandy country road, she asking nothing but to be with him and he under no obligation to do her any harm.

Willie D. was never happier than at a time like this when life was uncomplicated.

He made a move toward her, and then he moved closer, and closer, and closer, and closer.

AMERICAN SOUTHEAST

"Various Highlights in the Life of 'Thaddeus Crazy Hat" (1965-1987) -
These poems were written in various searing or freezing, poor rented rooms
hidden in the declining portions of towns and cities scattered across the Ameri-
can Southeast. They were composed over a span of twenty-two years for the
writer's mother. She - born in New England - a staunch Unitarian - a reader - a
lover of cats - took great delight in them.

Amy M. Faggart died in Georgetown, South Carolina, in 1989 at the age of
100. Thad Crazy Hat's meowing outcries, his guttural snarls and his hissing,
have been silent, but don't sell him short! Thad Crazy Hat may rise again.

In poetry, anything is possible and justified of belief.

VARIOUS HIGHLIGHTS IN THE LIFE OF
THADDEUS CRAZY HAT

AN ANTIC PASTORAL

Take notice of that!
   Old Thad Crazy Hat
Is a bad lazy cat.
   Thad Crazy Hat always woke slow,
Stretched and yawned, not ready to go,
   Looked all around this way and that,
Recalling he was a marvelous cat.
   All jet black and sleek,
There was never a squeak
   In the bones of fat
Old Thad Crazy Hat
   Sometimes his muscles came all uncoiled
And he dashed about completely spoiled
   All order in the best white bedroom,
'Til Ann screamed, "Turn him out with the broom!"
   Old Thad would spit and curse,
And then do things even worse,
   Jump up right inside a hearse,
Knock the flowers all about,
   "Kill that cat" you'd hear the shout.
But, Thad always would go too far
   At funeral or gathering of D.A.R.
Baptist and Catholic were the same to him
   For Thad was a bright Unitarian
He wasn't concerned with the life to come
   (As an annual he was far from dumb.)
He spent his endeavor and kept up all the buzz
   Attempting to be the best cat there was.

And a marvelous cat he was - said some.
Once when Thad woke up he saw before
A lilac mass that billowed more
On the breeze than all the plumes for
The horse heads of the Sultan's Corps
And he smelled the smell.
Now, all Thad's senses reeled,
He ranted and he spieled.
How his mighty voice pealed!
He was caught up in a mad hysteria!
It had been so long since he smelled wisteria.
Round the flower beds he lapped
Many the tulip stems that snapped
Bees and fuzzy worms and slugs
And funny yellow flying bugs,
All gazed in wonder at all that
This out of control, disordered cat.
This bolt of energy and sound
Which ran the garden round
Ran and ran but finally sat,
This damp-nosed, panting, Crazy Hat.
Now, he noticed the sand on his paws,
Began with his tongue to clean his claws.
All day long his games he played,
Now in this or that charade.
Up that bank! Across that lea
There he is half up a tree.
Awake to every cry of bird
He's eaten mice up by the herd.
Waits 'til night to be absurd,
He is, in a single word,
Marvelous, that Thad Crazy Hat.
But after a night of orgy and a day of fun
Thaddeus Crazy Hat comes quite undone
And throws himself down on the earth to rest
For by now to curl up and sleep is best,
And no matter what anyone might suggest,
Thad Crazy Hat is having none.
Little Ann comes home from school and no one's there
She seeks out Thad in his rosebush lair,
She stoops and pulls him by the ear.
He won't wake up, no not near.
Now he's a stranger to action and din.
She doesn't know how busy he's been.
She doesn't know how much he needs rest.
She doesn't know that sleep is best.
She only knows she wants to play,

But her sturdy friend has gone away
With a gentle pout, she has to say,
"Take notice of that!
Old Thad Crazy Hat
    Is a bad lazy cat!"

April 24, 1965
Charlotte, North Carolina

NO ONE EATS THE HORSE
They said, "Knock on any door and you may find him..."
    "Nick Romano"
And, so
    Lo!
There he is again.
    Tony and Joey and Benny and Slick,
Mickey and Pete..
    They are all Nick.
Leonard now.
    His pants are black and tight enough,
And show excessive wear -
    Cheaply made of quite shabby stuff,
They've shrunk clear up to there,
    Leaving ankles bare
With thick black hair,
    And frayed greying socks,
Far beyond repair.
    No detergent
Will make them white again.
    See him in his own environs with fear at bay-
In safe haven -
    The street.
Here
    He prowls in safety.
Poolroom and alley and corner and bar,
    Cafe and movie,
A refuge they are,
    An escape.
He's heard the sounds and breathed the air,
Seen life bathed with neon light.
    He's smelled the smoke and sat up where
Men played at cards all night.
    Women come and go,
Here on Skid Row,
    And men are the same-
All on the go.

Great Salvation
Can't make him pure again.
   Thad Crazy Hat went down to the zoo,
Stared at the monkeys a moment or two,
   Glided away somewhat in a stew,
He found the apes -
   Sad jack-a-napes.
Went near the camels and how his spirits fell,
   When he smelled the awful smell.
What doth make the heathern rage?
   Living in dirt all of his age.
Thad liked things clean
   As well
As warm and dry.
   Wet filthy things
Made him
   Raise a hue and cry.
Thad ran about, this way and that,
   Looked for a thing folks called The Big Cat,
Got there in time to see the steak feasts
   They give to that lion, King of the Beasts.
And the lion roared.
   Thad saw his teeth and his great hairy head.
The other animals almost fell dead
   When they heard whatever it was the lion had said.
But Thad just stared with unblinking eye,
   Said he would never fly,
No matter how or why -
   The lion roared.
"The lion's kinship is just a sham,
   He's not half the king that I am."
Said Thad.
   "No one keeps me locked in a pen,
From my native jungle keeps me locked in
   Takes me from the choice of mate,
Makes me depend for food on their grudging plate,
No one has set bars all about me,
   Every night and every day I'm free.
I'm free," said Thad.
   The lion had vigor and the lion had vim,
But what good are muscles when you can't use them?
   To instill fear leaves one quite bored,
If one can't reap the terrorist's reward,
   And prowess with the female gets nowhere
When every day no lioness is there.
   Being King of the Beasts was a job Thad would scuttle.
He was a small frog-duke in a very small puddle -

And happy to be there.
And Leonard on his corner downtown on Skid Row
    Had gone just as high as he wanted to go.
He saw a rich man   - Yes, it's a fact
    He owned a Lincoln and a Cadillac
Drive by. And this man blew his horn
    And the horn seemed to sing,
"In all this town, I am the king."
    But what kept the blood of this man at a boil,
Was he was owned in turn
    By Standard Oil.
"No one keeps me shut in a trap,
    Tells me where to go on the map,
Keeps me away from the girls I know,
    Makes me crawl to them when I need dough,
No one has set bars all about me.
    Every night and every day I'm free
I'm free," said Leonard.
    So he stood with neon in his hair,
And the wind in his clothes,
    And the world was fair,
For he liked his free place there among the dregs,
    The feel of a bad lazy cat at his legs,
The errant Thad
    This Leonard lad
A pair
    Of incubating eggs.

NOTE: Good eggs, like good horses, are to be set, not eaten.

November 20, 1965
Augusta, Georgia

THAD CRAZY HAT'S CHRISTMAS VIGIL

Thad Crazy Hat had frost on his feet,
    Came in the house to get something to eat,
Saw the bright light and felt the steam heat,
    Left mud on the cloth when he rubbed the loveseat.
Halfway down the hall he took great pause
    He smelled an outdoors odor here in the indoors.
Right in the parlor there stood a great tree,
    As scented of pine as a tree e'er could be.
It was covered all over with stars, bells and balls.
    It stretched to the ceiling and two of the walls.
And packages beneath

And at the window a wreath.
Thad emitted some excited cries.
　　The lights reflected in his eyes -
Red was seen,
　　And green,
Purple hue,
　　And blue.
Yellow too.
　　And the silver tinsel was nothing remote.
And the mud on the street
　　Was on his feet,
Earthy and good, if not too neat.
　　Like the tree -
It was earthy and good.
　　Little Ann Could hardly stand still.
She danced a swift dance and sang with a trill,
　　"Up on the rooftops the reindeer pause,
Out jumps good old Santa Claus."
　　Knowing he would
She had been good.
　　Ah, visions of sugarplums leaped with a will!
After they'd eaten,
　　And after Thad ate,
They all sat down
　　In the parlor to wait
For any Christmas Eve guest who might care to call.
　　The music played as a record twirled.
"God's in His Heaven, all's right with the world."
　　Declared Ann's father, drowning out Ethel Merman.
This was the text and the end of his sermon.
But, Thad was happy just to nudge a pine burr
　　And then to sit and contentedly purr,
Here among the things and people held dear,
　　In this wonderful Christmas atmosphere,
'Til sleep overcame
　　It was a shame,
but the happy game
　　Made Thad ready to sleep for a year.
Thad knew of God's peace much better than Ann,
　　And they both knew it better than her father, the man,
For with Thad, a stranger to civilized arts,
　　The Gospel was written on his inward parts,
As it had in the beginning been for man,
　　And even the child, Little Ann,
Recalled a paradise which is lost somehow,
　　While her father, the man, took a prideful bow -
After they ate,

To pontificate,
Standing ready to give, at his whim,
    The Holy Gospel according to him!
With no sham or pride and no caprice,
    His sleep demonstrated Thad Crazy Hat's peace.
And Little Ann with faith and trust
    Started to bed but first she must
have a word with Thad.
    She shook him roughly and woke him up.
Said if he wasn't good she'd get a pup,
    Looked him in the eye, said she waked him because,
"I want you to sit and watch for Santa Claus.
    You must sit by the fireplace in the big soft chair,
When Santa comes down, you'll be there.
    You run up the stairs. Come straight to me.
I'll come and catch Santa at work 'neath the tree.
    No one will ever forget my name,
I'll have long life and endless fame.
    I'll have a title that will ever stick,
'The Girl Whose Eyes Beheld St. Nick.'"
    See, Gentle Reader, in her ego's need,
The gradual unfolding
    Of that bad, Bad Seed
Which comes from Adam
    And comes from Eve -
Nothing can disguise it,
How humanity doth grieve!
    But, Thad was a Unitarian and couldn't recognize it.
To whatever Ann said, he didn't attend,
    but slept once again as if sleep had no end.
And if Santa came with all of his elves,
    they had the house all to themselves.
And when morning came and Ann saw what she'd got,
    She forgot all about the wicked plot,
Which she'd hatched out so terribly quick
    To be "The Girl Whose Eyes Beheld St. Nick."

December 12, 1965
Richmond, Virginia

THE BISHOP'S PRAYER
In Thaddeus Hat's town stands a cathedral tall,
    With an elaborate spire and a very thick wall,
And a rich red carpet the length of the hall.
    And the altar rail is wide.

Statues abide,
    And the elements are defied
by a grey slate roof of very steep pitch.
    And all who go to this church are rich
And live pleasant lives without a hitch,
    And they manage to hide,
A great emptiness inside,
    That emptiness which
Solomon once decried -
    Vanity and pride
And all.
    Certain poor people felt unwelcome there.
They're tolerated, but some will stare,
    And there is a chill upon the air,
So the needy and the friendless are preached elsewhere;
    Preached and prayed and forgiven and wed,
Given the Last Rites when they are dead,
    For them the Gospel is solemnly said,
As a matter of course,
    Way down across,
The town's Railroad
    And if it's snowed
The cold is hard to bear.
    As for the great cathedral, all men know,
it is a place of wondrous show
    And here the poor aren't worthy to go,
By passing it by they quite confess
    To low estate and unworthiness
And question never - they question not -
    The right of those of more fortunate lot
To worship there.
    But, Thad Crazy Hat was built of sterner stuff,
He couldn't recognize the world's rebuff,
    Had never been cowed nor had to bluff.
His will never faltered no matter how rough.
    He looked back at the world with a calm eye,
Wouldn't cry
    Or heave a sigh,
Or admit he wasn't just as tough
    As the next one,
And he had faith enough
    In Thad.
It happened as the sun was setting one day
    that he caught a bird but it got away
And flew up and made its way
    To a high windowsill of the church, to stay
Thad thought, so he ran up a limb

But when he leaped to the sill the bird left him
And took to the air
   So Thad sat there
And lashed his taut tall with vim.
   The bird must have known just where he had headed
For colored glass was carefully leaded
   Into a great window in which was embedded
The image of St. Francis.
   And glass birds fluttered near his shoulders and head,
And he helped them be safe and saw they were fed,
   And his famous Mass to the birds was said,
In that wood so airy
   the first Bird Sanctuary.
Across the sill Thad did glide,
   And found the way to get inside,
Looked all about for a place to hide
   and, when he found one, hid.
He smelled the incense now grown stale
   And forgot the bird, so quieted his tail,
Saw the candles burning with glow so pale
   through red glass.
It came to Pass
   Their light began to fail.
The church grew dark
   And out in the park
A cicada began to wail.
   Thad went up and found a throne
With a pillow there as soft as his own,
   The most comfortable place he'd lately known,
So he curled in a curve -
   He had the nerve -
And relaxed in every bone.
   A peaceful steep Thad had found
When he was wakened by a lot of sound
   As people came in and gathered round
Kneeling to pray and to come unwound
   For a period of worship.
Thad left the throne and hurried to go
   Up on a beam where he wouldn't show
So no one there would ever know
   That Thad had been there,
In that Bishop's chair,
   Watching the candles go.
Now the church was all alight,
   Never was any place so bright
As the cathedral was that important night
   When the best people and the people called "right"

had come out with great show -
    The organ was playing all apace
And the only shadow, in the place
    Was the one Thad threw on the statue below.
The Bishop marched in as they played a triumphal hymn.
    The throne and the cushion were set for him.
He was the only man in town
    Supposed to sit on that cushion down.
He marched and turned and then he sat,
    And sat upon his excess fat,
And sat where Thaddeus Hat had sat,
    That arrogant, cocky, impious cat,
And he quietly bowed his head
    This prayer was said
"Oh Father, Who reads each heart here best,
    Tonight I put You to this test,
That some heart in this church be supremely blest,
    Some life he completely turned about
Some erring one be made devout,
    By Thy Grace,
In this place,
    Tonight."
The organ drummed and they preached with a will.
    the cold congregation sat quite still,
And made their responses and sang their hymns,
    And gave of their money stifled any whims,
They might have to nonconform.
    The Bishop did his very best.
But, God didn't deign to pass the test.
    No heart that night was supremely blest.
No brand from the burning did the Bishop wrest.
    His heart weighed heavy in him.
When the people left and the church grew still,
    The Bishop sat in a kind of chill,
And felt dismay
    For baiting God that way,
And finally went away
    Quite ill.
And something had happened that never happened before.
    The custodian forgot to lock the front door,
So it wasn't long 'til a man who was poor
    Came wandering hopefully in.
He went up to the Virgin and down he knelt.
    Above him an odor of whiskey Thad smelt.
Thad looked down and the man looked ahead.
    And in a hopeless voice the man said,
"If there is still a God,

284

And He is mine,
Give me a sign
  Give me a sign.
I'll tell you, Virgin
  I'd tell the Pope
I'm down and out and out of hope."
  The man had come to the end of his rope.
The Virgin's face in a shadow laid,
  The man grew more and more dismayed.
His faith and trust began to fade,
  And he wished that he outside had stayed.
And Thad,
  Felt sad,
And was somewhat afraid.
  So he got up and crept away,
And when he moved a light like day
  Burst liberated from fluorescent light,
And took away the gloom of night
  From off the Virgin's Holy Face.
A radiant glow suffused the place,
  Which seemed to center on Mary's head,
To emanate therefrom and about Her spread,
  and Her eyes so sorrowful a moment ago,
Seemed now with joy and hope to glow,
  So the errant man without a moment's rest
Ran to tell his friends he'd been supremely blest,
  His life from that moment was full and fair.
He had a new direction when he left there.
  The Bishop's prayer was answered so,
But the poor tried Bishop was not to know,
  And Thad was not to care.

February 12, 1966
Sanatorium, Mississippi

THAD'S INDISPOSITION
Thad Crazy Hat spurned his milk,
  Said he was the saddest of his ilk -
and kind.
  Lay in the sun and pined and pined,
Even on a nesting martin would not have dined
  he felt too low.
All bowed down with woe.
  Imagine just that! A nervous, sick, neurotic cat!
Full of bad dreams - Dog growl and cat screams.

285

He twitched in his sleep,
Awoke to leap - stretched all his fibers deep-
    right down to the seams.
Trying to shake off the terror
    Thad had felt this way before.
Maybe less or maybe more
Found being just a cat bore-
    and shook.
Deep within, cat-nerves vibrated and throbbed.
    Breath was short. Lungs were robbed.
Tall was taut and paws were barbed.
    He spoiled for a fight.
He would delight
    To test his might,
Out of sheer bad disposition.
    Always before the spoil had passed.
Thad had seen the flowers massed -
    At last.
His spirit had lifted.
    He had taken note how great he was gifted.
What a marvelous sort he was,
    All strong sinew and sweet-smelling fuzz,
Long pink tongue and keen cat brain,
    Cool hard head which would not wane
In good sense.
    He'd leap to the air and sit on the fence -
and yowl out loud in the face of the skies
    That he was amorous, strong and wise,
And, suddenly he'd realize
    How hungry he was.

September 22, 1968
Wilmington, Delaware

THE COMING OF THADDEUS HAT
Tasteless and flat
    The world was like that
To the lonely lost cat
    Who was not yet become Thaddeus Crazy Hat,
And not yet a cat,
    But a dank soggy kitten,
A little frost barren
    Hunger smitten
All alone -

286

Fur, skin and bone
Needing a place to call his own.
   Where did he come from?
   No one could tell.
Like Melchizedek
   he came to dwell
Without a beginning
   Nor an ending as well
A timeless mystery of a cat,
   As black as coal dust,
As quiet as as a bat
   He purred
And arched his back,
   Found the place where Little Ann sat.
Little Ann picked him up,
   Made in her dress front a little cup,
Lay him to rest 'til he was dry,
   Said she'd feed him by and by,
and when she'd fed him
   And made him a bed,
A feline prayer of thanksgiving he said.
   (Don't be dismayed -
It was the last time he consciously prayed.)
   And thirty minutes after he'd come,
He'd already made himself at home.
   Thad, in his darkest hour, had known
He'd made for himself
   A place of his own
His plaintiveness and weakness had done their part,
   But of most help to him
Had been Little Ann's kind heart.
   She named him Thaddeus just like that
And put him to bed in a crazy old hat
   So he was called Thad Crazy Hat
He was never cold or hungry again -
   He'd come in forever out of the rain
(With soft pillows ever to lie on
   Didn't he take his ease in Zion?)
He rapidly became a bad lazy cat,
   But everyone loved
Thad Crazy Hat.

November 4, 1968
Lynchburg, Virginia

THAD: A BEE HAVING GATHERED
TOO MUCH HONEY

Thad Crazy Hat had been quiet for so long -
   never a pointed story, nor a blatant song,
He thought finally he had lost his mighty voice.
   It wasn't his choice.
It was the times and his age.
It was the age and his times.
The bellowing chimes
   of his anger and rage
   had stilled
   for a time of times.
Everything turned inward, heavy as lead.
   Thad stayed abed,
   and the rapid tick-tock
   of his mind's racing clock
   slow it was
   and tolled a knell now;
   did not buzz
   to awaken
He never thought what a marvelous cat he was
   at the dawn's alarm -
All his swashbuckling pride had been mistaken.
He mourned he'd lost his grace and his charm.
He was down, and his glistening
   black hair turned brown,
   and he was too fat
   for such a cat
   as that
   Thad Crazy Hat.
The life of the bon vivant and the boulevardier
   had at last become
   the sort of life which Thad was from.
He'd redirected the surge of his so great elation,
   now gracefully sought
   the meed of cool contemplation -
   and he waited each evening for the paper to come.
Little Ann who was now a teen
   would read aloud the news
   and say all it all did mean
   and her mother would recap it between
   giving her slant
   and Little Ann's father would spread out his cant
   and Thad would get excited
   and Thad would pant
The epicenter of the day

was when the paper came 'round their way.
Late in October, near Halloween,
 right there in their paper
 a real life horror was seen.
Little Ann and her parents read with dismay
 of what things transpire in Detroit today.
Some Davis girl, name of Greta had a baby boy
 said she didn't know better
 didn't know she was pregnant,
 the paper said
 anyhow, she wished her baby dead.
She threw him away
 on a late fall day
 and the cold had come
 and left him alone on an alley floor
 motherly kindness not a crumb.
What good Good Samaritan would come?
 She didn't care.
 What for?
Reading made Little Ann sigh a prayer,
 her mother brushed at a tear and
 her father did swear
Thad could not hide
 the rage inside
His emotion stood up all his hair,
 and he spit
 because of it,
 was fit
 to be tied.
The paper went on to say,
 a German dog came around that way
 and licked the baby and in its dog's mind
 knew this was a terrible thing to find
 and soemthing to keep alive,
 And the dog lay down and lent its heat
 to warm the baby, now blue its feet,
 and lay with their bodies all entwined
 until someone came along to find
 the precious outcast.
Help came at last.
The baby was alive
The dog waited for no reward she'd won.
 She went away pronto
 Into the night on the run.
 She had come and gone like the Lone Ranger and Tonto.
She'd fought with death and won.
About the dog, it is a pity

she disappeared into Detroit City.
"I want to go home," she seemed to say.
But, did she have one?
Or didn't she
have one where to stay?
it must be part of the Devil's plan:
On the streets of Detroit, dogs have more humanity
than man.
And the desperate women live to see the day
fear makes them throw
their innocent babies away.
There they go, as it were, to the dogs,
and better off for it
In Detroit.
There is bad in the world.
Tonto's horse can never be tethered.
And the Lone Ranger must ride into town,
Jimmy Swaggart's word must go down,
and some he tarred and feathered.
We have forgotten how to punish.
Thad, no friend to dogs, gave credit where credit was due.
His keen mind could discern.
He knew which was which,
the dog was the saint,
the woman the bitch.
And Thad growled out what her streets made him learn,
"Vengeance Is sure, so burn baby, burn."
Oh, what power will redeem us?
It's hell to be Romulus or Remus.
Thad is awake now.
The paper is laid down.
He had opened his eyes to what's wrong in his town.
With woeful countenance this feline knight
full of spit and full of fight
screams he would make it very clear,
"We won't have Detroit here!"
This is the quest
as you may have guessed
that Thad has sung in his cat songs
to right unrightable wrongs, just to right unrightable
wrongs
A large order for Thad, you would say that.
But, remember, he's a marvelous cat
A cat who won't give up,or give in, or give under,
but, one who will roar and spark and thunder,
and mix the fires of lightning with his spit.
And most of all,

never quit.
but carry on.
Little Ann put the paper away, and her folks said they
   would "call it a day."
And, a day it had been;
   for them not much of a day,
   but the dav and the news had set Thad on his way.
Some people lose, some people win.
And Thad was heard to meow
   "I call do well
   now
   The dog showed me how."

Georgetown, South Carolina
November 2, 1986

Lo! I am weary of my wisdom like the bee that hath gathered
too much honey. I need hands outstretched to take it.
   THUS SPAKE ZARATHUSTRA
   Nietzsche

THAD CRAZY HAT DOES DIETRICH

On finished romances
   and times like that.
that marvelous cat,
   Thad Crazy Hat,
would not dwell.
Of his amorous exploits,
   he never would tell
Even when he'd sleep and dream,
   erotic memories
were not the theme
   weaving themselves,
in the gleam
   of his imagining.
Thad slept a lot.
And if and when
   he dreamed,
he pictured how he'd get ahead,
   grow wise, instead
of recalling
   old loves
which were dead.
He would never love again
Thad felt,
   in his cat's brain

that his old encounters
 had all been in vain,
were best forgot
Even those most hot
 had not
been worth the strain.
Thad switched his tail,
 up and down paraded,
he was sedate
 and very jaded.
And sure.
But, Thad would soon find
 to his surprise
a part of himself would
 heave up cries.
This deep inner part
 heard from before
would make itself heard,
 aloud, once more.
For Thad bore in his body -
 Image that!
The genetic pool which went
 with this cat,
and it was supreme
 business for him
to preserve this gene pool
 with veniality
and vim.
And it chanced one day as Thad walked the world by,
 he saw, like himself, such an other
as caused his genes to all shout and decry
 as brother greets recognized brother.
As, with Marlene Dietrich,
 fate had taken a hand.
he was "Falling in love again,"
 though he'd never planned.
And the other's gene's heard
 and they purred
and purred -
 said not a word -
but the two of them loved one another.
But, lest Thad exalt,
 say "Look what I am."
It is possible with God
 (But, spare us this cup)
for Him
 to from stones raise up

children of Abraham
It was easy to see
    What the outcome would be
For both of them were single.
    They said "What the hell?"
Aand did things quite well,
    which caused their gene pools to mingle.
And, in a few weeks -
    which wasn't half bad -
there were kittens born
    in the image of Thad.

Georgetown, South Carolina
August 23, 1987

1990's

In the 1990s the new cast of characters came:

1. *Young people living in the country, very clean - pastoral.*
2. *Earnest persons of middle age, each striving to capture a private elusive dream, at the cost of losing a chance for real happiness.*
3. *A young man who begins to face the inevitable surrender he must make to social conformity, due to past commitments he has made.*
4. *Sad ex-athletes who have no inner resources that may take the place in their lives of their waning physical prowesses.*
5. *A woman who has made mistakes and must pay for them.*
6. *A man who arranges for God to protect his beloved mule - from him.*
7. *A man whose self-concept is not actualized because of the dominant role played in him by the built-in parent image.*
8. *A woman and a ghost who cooperate to save yet another woman from making a terrible mistake.*
9. *A young man, following his mother's example, is heedless of the destructiveness of his behavior with others.*
10. *A strange woman, found on the subway, brings a man happiness, although he does not completely understand her.*
11. *A young woman experiences the sorrow of growing up.*
12. *A woman who has given up on life and wishes only to hide herself is pleasantly surprised when a strange young man talks with her husband and her life begins to change.*

The 1990s brought in a new day for this writer. The decade began with devastating illness and financial troubles - being alone except for the gentle dog, Karen - but right away new thoughts developed with this write pertaining to his experiences in the past, his present place in the world, his calling, his contribution in life (what it should be.) The things that must come.

In short, his self-concept was defined and fine-tuned. He saw that he was what he had always thought he was: A man with a mission to look at life, see what he would see, and "go tell it on the mountain."

John Steinbeck had his "dispossessed." This writer is a watchful eagle stretching warming wings above his own fledglings. They find with him, momentarily, a rostrum - a stage. They are only figments - shadow - faint hints of real persons. But, alive on the page. Read here! Take an hour to move among them; See them; Listen as they speak; Know them! They are each a piece of humanity - as much as any. Perhaps they are not as skilled as some in coping. But, their vision is tempered hope. Happiness will come into their lives, or the fortitude to bear the bad. Sometimes there is bad which must be told. Mainly, this writer speaks of the good news.

It has been said, "How beautiful upon the mountains are the feet of him that bringeth good tidings, that publisheth peace." Isaiah 52:7

Peace!

GEORGETOWN, SOUTH CAROLINA

"Harvey and Byron" was written in Georgetown in 1990. Tough love is superseded by gentle love. Gone are the old ways depicted in this story. This is sheer nostalgia. On the threshold of the '90s, it is time for the writer to finally find a new breed of character for his stories, men and women with new faces, dancers who writhe to fresh-writ numbers, and people who move about in earthy, working class costumes.

Now, will come a new alter ego of the sentimental dreamer, the recherche, the pedantic bore, the father-ridden, fearful, ever-child, the pseudo-Beatnik, the babbling one who is angry with established religion. This new alter ego will not now be a suffering female, who being rejected by her father, desperately seeks as substitute for him someone or something outside herself.

Twenty years at the steel mill could cause this to be.

At the time of this writing, the air was rent with the squalls and flashes of television. It was a time of computer literacy and street-smarts, a time of the tired and the threadbare in the arts and entertainment, of four-letter words, and a woeful lack of delicacy or propriety in all. Amid all this, the writer wrote lovingly of "Harvey and Byron, " a quiet story of gentle days now gone.

HARVEY AND BYRON

Harvey and Byron decided that they would not work the late cornfield like their daddy had told them before he went off to town that morning, but instead they would go down to the creek and go skinny-dipping. Harvey was a year older than Byron and he felt like he could figure out someway to make their daddy believe, when he came home, that it was Byron's fault they had not done the work he had told them to do.

Byron did not think very far ahead. He only thought of how hot it would be in the cornfield where the breeze could hardly get in to hit them because of the corn's being so tall now. Neither of the boys believed that the late corn needed to be worked. It would only be a waste of time to take hoes in there and spend the whole day getting every last little weed out.

Harvey and Byron looked at their poor dogs, Samuel and Gideon and Eli, and they knew how much the dogs would like to go with them to the creek where they could swim out in the water and get cooled off and cleaned up and maybe wash away some of their fleas. Samuel and Eli were quiet dogs who never bothered anyone and Harvey and Byron wanted to do something good for them like taking them for a swim. Gideon was a fighting dog and it was good to have him go along in case they ran into trouble. Old Gideon could take care of anything that might come up including meeting a wildcat.

Harvey and Byron left the hoes hanging in the barn and didn't even go near the field of late corn. They walked, with the dogs, to the creek which was about a mile from their house. They stripped off their clothes and leaped in the water and called the dogs to come in with them. Gideon and Eli jumped right in, but Samuel thought about it a little. Finally, he came with the rest of them. Harvey was swimming a deep hole in the river which was in the place where the river had a sharp bend. The water was black and he couldn't see the bottom. His foot struck against something in the water and he called Byron and the two of them began to dive for whatever it was Harvey had found. It was a beautiful piece of driftwood. It was the nicest hunk of driftwood either of them had ever seen.

"We'll carry it home," they said. They laid it out on the sandy bank, and when they got ready to go they took the driftwood with them. It was a big piece and heavy. They carried it all the way home.

Their mother was very happy with it, and that night she talked their daddy out of punishing them for not having worked the late cornfield like he had told them to do. They had to do it the next day.

"God must have put that piece of driftwood there," Harvey told Byron, before they slept. "You know, to get us out of the trouble we had put ourselves in."

GEORGETOWN, SOUTH CAROLINA

"Barbie June" was written at Georgetown in 1990. This story and the equally short "Harvey and Byron" were written while the writer was attending Horry-Georgetown Technical College. This is about more doings in an imaginary place, where it would be in bad taste to say "sweat" or "stink" and "belly " would be okay if it belonged to an animal, but no one would mention a human belly.

In the story, a lonely, young girl is dismayed when her pride is pricked and her dreams waylaid.

The reader suspects that this strong, resourceful girl will be able to bear her disappointment with aplomb.

BARBIE JUNE

Barbie June decided there was nothing for her to do but go horseback riding. She had tried to get Fred to go with her, but he was too lazy to saddle up the horses and ride across the fields and into the woods with her. She was sure he had the least energy of any boy she knew. She liked him enough, but his lack of ambition made her believe that there would never be anything between them. She was sure that he really didn't care either. He just wanted people to leave him alone.

Now, she decided that she would get Harry to go riding with her. Harry Plovic was not thought of by anyone as being a good companion. Barbie June knew that he was ignorant about most things and slow to speak and awkward of movement, but he would be better than nothing when she was riding across the wide sedge field at the back of her grandaddy's house, where there might be snakes to contend with, or her horse might step in a hole. She decided to wait until she saw him coming down the road in his daddy's old truck, and then she would hail him down and ask him to go riding with her. The way she felt about it, they might not come back until after the sun set.

Barbie June's grandaddy had two horses, named Brutus and Cassius. Brutus was a real brute and Barbie June was afraid of him. She would make Harry ride him. She would ride Cassius. Cassius was a lean and hungry-looking horse and very gentle in his manner and actions. However, he had a deep mind and would sneak up on humans with mean tricks if he got the chance. Barbie June liked this kind of give and take and she could think right along with Cassius and outsmart him when he would try to put one over on her. She got to thinking about Harry Plovic and the more she thought of him the more good things about him would come up in her mind. She could remember how strong he had always been in high school and how much at home he was on the basketball court, where his awkwardness miraculously left him. There he could be pure grace. Fred, on the other hand, was hopeless on the gym floor. All the worst came out in him. But, he hadn't cared. He had been too lazy to really try to play ball. He spent most of his time in high school smoking behind the gym.

Barbie June went out to the gate in front of her grandaddy's house to watch for Harry's truck. It came in sight a few minutes later and at once Barbie June's heart sank. There was Dorathea Jane sitting up right beside Harry on the front seat!

Barbie June realized Harry wasn't going to be going any place with her! Not any time soon!

GEORGETOWN, SOUTH CAROLINA

"The Date" was written in Georgetown in 1990. People do not listen. In a couple on a first date, each is unable to see the viewpoint of the other. The writer has returned to the theme of noncommunication between individuals. People do not respond to each other and develop friendships.

A man or a woman, in today's world, is likely to become alone at last. What people hear from others they don't heed. Where there is no communication, interest dies.

These two sad ships cannot be said to have passed in the night. There is no momentary elation when lights are beheld, or a horn is heard, or the faint strains of a gay dance band on a faraway deck. The vessels are too far apart, each lying beneath the other's horizon. The radio is turned off. They don't appear on TV.

The passengers are bewitched by satellite, dreaming of luxury liners which plow the waves proudly a thousand miles away. Self-interest does not allow them to value what is at hand. For them, there can only be the best!

THE DATE

He was not, frankly, looking for romance. She would have accepted romance, but was indifferent about it. So, here they were, out together.

He was sixty and admitted it, and needed someone to listen to him. She was sixty, but would not say so. She needed to cling to her fantasies.

She said she was fifty one. He didn't care.

He escorted her into the restaurant, not really knowing if he did it right or not. Self-consciously, he helped her with her chair. He knew that she was more socially accomplished than he, knew his own deficiencies.

"I'm not one of your movie heroes," he said. "I used to watch them, every week, when I was a young kid. They could all ride horses, and swim, and sing, and talk entertainingly, and kiss girls, and I couldn't do any of these things. I hope you aren't looking for a man like one of them. I can't even shuffle cards the way they could. I loved to see Tony Curtis shuffle cards in 'Mister Cory.' I hope you'll have a good time tonight. Even so."

He was being self-deprecating. She wouldn't hear him. It made her positively ill for a man to efface himself. All the time he was talking, she was thinking to herself.

What she wanted in a man was one who could take her out to a perfect place and act perfectly when they got there. There she could see herself the perfect companion, mistress of all social graces.

She looked around at the restaurant they were in. Small lamps, specked and dim, at each table, gave off a browning orange glow. Plastic coated paper lampshades had darkened with time. A chill of depression made her shiver.

When their food came, she scarcely looked at it. She knew it had been cooked and was being served all wrong, but this was not the kind of place where it would do any good to say this. She had, in the past, gone to places where a complaint from a diner would make the management aware that the guest was a lady; a lady when the title meant something, before the term had been made universal and consequently meaningless. Back then, she had felt if she did not send anything back to the kitchen, she would not appear truly socially knowing, or show she had proper control of the situation. She had to show that she knew what was what in this world she lived in. She knew how to be a hostess - to run a tight dinner party.

"I never learned to do all those things movie stars do," he said. "I grew up and learned how to work and I take pride in it. Where I work, with the other workers, we've built an institution, a monument in our work, that's a good thing for those that work there, and the town, and will be good in years to come, for the ones now young. I've done pretty good with my life. Don't you think?"

Good. Good. Good. She didn't answer him. There could be nothing more tiresome than "good." She was thinking about one time when a man she thought of as having impeccable manners, had taken her to a perfectly appointed place where everything had been beyond complaint. While she was serving them, a waitress had dropped a fork and the man instinctively bent to pick it up.

"I screamed," she thought, remembering, verbalizing silently, living again through the utter dismay of that moment. "I screamed at him, 'Don't pick up that fork!' Well, he straightened in his chair and let the fork alone, but the evening was ruined anyhow."

"I don't guess you noticed Tyrone Power's hands in 'Mississippi Gambler'?" he said, making it a question to her. He hoped for an answer. There was none. "I don't see how they learn to handle cards like that. I don't see how they do anything they do. The only pictures where I ever felt equal to or better than the actors were work pictures like Clark Gable and Spencer Tracy in 'Boom Town.' When a picture was about work, I knew something about what they were doing."

She was silent.

He continued to sit there in front of her, and he kept on talking. She didn't see him any more or hear him. The restaurant had changed, merging with her dream. It had become a fabulous place. She had changed too, inside, playing out a role of her own imagining. She was director and star. The set was closed to everyone. She remained, aloof to everything, thinking her own thoughts.

Soon he didn't talk any more. He sat, thinking about his memories - memories of movies he had seen long ago. And, he thought about his work life.

It was nearly still in the restaurant. Finally, he observed to her that the building was well-insulated. The street sounds could not find a way in. He knew from his years of experience with the crafts that the contractor who raised the building had done a good job. The floor was substantial and level and bore a deep shine.

She would have liked a small orchestra - perhaps four pieces - several soft strings. A woodwind. No piano. Keyboards were actually obscenities. The Classical Period! That's what she would like to hear. Nothing later. She classified music from the Romantic Period as being "treacle."

Behind the swinging door to the kitchen droned a tired exhaust fan. Its concert was gruff and monotonous. Neither of them heard it.

This self-appointed social arbiter dreamed of galas and fetes, she chomped at the bit to be off to the races. She wanted her life to gallop.

The steady plowhorse remembered how hard and faithfully he had worked, how obedient he had always been. Now he would be rewarded in a good pasture. He had no aspirations. He would stand behind his fence and look out across the land.

Neither found validation in the other. She fidgeted. He fought off sleep. And so, the evening went.

They didn't date again.

GEORGETOWN, SOUTH CAROLINA

"An Evening At Jolly Pierre's" was written in Georgetown in 1990. A man feels himself trapped in his job at a manufacturing plant, and in his marriage to a possessive woman. For this man, life is a saddened pep rally, which is about to go dark. The bonfire is ready to be quenched.

He has been reinforced in his shallow battling against societal conformity by a devil-may-care work chum - a fishing buddy - a philosophical boozer - a one-man cheering squad. But, the restraints holding him back dampen the caravan of delights his friend parades before his eyes. The cost to his self-concept is high.

The protagonist, in spite of himself, is shedding his Titanism. To attempt to overthrow the established gods is tiresome and slow, and doubtful of success. The cards are stacked. It is time not to try to be an American Existentialist any more.

If this protagonist is able to reform his life-style, everyone will be happy except his factotum, and Jolly Pierre, of course, who will lose the business.

AN EVENING AT JOLLY PIERRE'S

Thin Ratchel had a bumper sticker on his big pickup which was made up of the capital letter "I" followed by a depiction of a red heart, followed by the words "My Truck." No one would have known he loved his truck based on the way he treated it. His philosophy was that "a truck is to drive." When he drove into his yard that day, the rear wheels of the mean-looking orange truck churned furiously as he bounced out of the ruts of the dirt street which ran in front of his house.

He ground his teeth. His skin prickled. He had just finished his day's work at the air filter factory. He showered down on the accelerator. His hands clenched on the steering wheel. He drove the hell out of that truck. When he got ready to trade a truck in, it was worn out. Anyone buying a truck which had belonged to Thin Ratchel was buying trouble.

"They manufacture these things to run," he'd say.

He lurched across his yard, heedless of the damage his tires might do, and slammed on his brakes. The truck slid for a few feet and stopped. The wheels smoked.

"The more grass I kill with truck tires," he said aloud, defying whatever gods might be listening, "the less I have left to mow."

His wife, Callie, was pissed off. He was late cutting the grass. She'd let him know about it. She had become like her dog, Fema, always yapping. She wanted the floor of the screened side porch painted, and the steps to the porch, and the steps to the front and back doors.

She wanted the television antenna straightened. It had stood at a rakish angle, on the roof, since the hurricane. Reception was good. It made no sense to Thin to straighten the antenna.

305

"A television is to play," he'd said when she mentioned it. "Ours is working.

He could already hear Fema barking, with her high-pitched, hysterical style of delivery. Callie would be right behind her.

"Attica!" he muttered, leaping out of the truck. "Welcome to Attica."

He had his own dogs, but they stayed in dog pens out at his hunting club. He didn't have a house dog. Callie would have Fema sleeping in bed with her when he came in late. He had to move the dog out of his own bed before he could get in it.

"Any day she'll come out with a 'I Luv My Dog' sticker on her bumper."

He bounded up the steps on his long, thin, basketball player's legs, heavy work shoes clumping, his strong arms stretching out to grasp the door handle, so he could quickly let himself in, while being careful not to let Fema out. No use to upset Callie by letting her dog out.

"The house dog is to stay in and watch the house," he told the air. He pushed Fema out of his way with his foot.

He knew he was acting like a horse's ass. He'd settle down as soon as he could get a shower. There was some demonic thing, which he worked with at the air filter factory, which crawled about under his clothes, causing him to itch and burn all over. He couldn't wait, each day, for work to end so that he could come home and wash himself off.

Until he got a shower, he wanted everyone to leave him alone. He put on a terrible scowl in case Callie came near him and wanted to talk. He had a lean, tanned face, clean-shaven, with grey eyes and thin, slightly cruel looking lips. He looked twenty five and this was about right. He was twenty seven years old. He was a laboratory supervisor at the air filter factory. He had eight men who worked under him. He had machines to keep up, and he knew what every machine was to do. His men, and his machines, did what they were supposed to do. He had no problem with any of them. His work life was the way he wanted it. He was, if not happy, satisfied on the job.

"Is that you, Baby?" Callie called from somewhere in the house. Thin grunted. Then he said silently, "The woman is to cook. The woman is to wash dishes, the woman is to fuck. The woman is to keep quiet."

He sat momentarily on the sofa and pulled his work shoes off. Then he jumped up and whipped off his shirt. He had the same hard, slender body he had when he was a star athlete in college. He kept himself in good shape by spending time in the woods, as much as work and home chores allowed, never enough.

He ran behind deer dogs and poled his boat in the old rice fields and sometimes he pulled a shrimp net. He coached a softball team.

Callie came to the door as he dropped his pants in a heap by the door to the hall. She was thin, a little stooped. She was the same age as Thin, but she looked older. Her eyes darted about, harried.

"I heard your grunt," she said. She didn't smile. "I knew it was you."

Thin grunted again.

"Haven't you got a kiss for me?" she asked.

Thin pecked at her cheek.

"It was a chore, wasn't it?"

He knew he'd made her unhappy. He could feel how tired she was. He never gave her any emotional support. She had to fight for everything she got from him. Someday, she'd get tired of fighting him. She'd quit. He'd lose her.

"I hate it when you ask for it," he said. "If you wouldn't ask, I'd give you kisses and compliments. I'd do and say things you like. It'd be like it used to be."

"I've tried it that way. It didn't work. You didn't even notice what I was trying to do."

He threw his t-shirt on a chair. She began picking up after him.

"You could wait 'til we stop talking to do that."

"I can't wait." Her hands were nervous. They clutched the soiled clothing, twisting it. "I've got to be doing something."

"I'm sorry if I messed up your house," he said.

As soon as he was in the bathroom he tore off his jockey shorts and kicked them in a corner. He turned on the water in the shower, letting it run very hot. Callie tapped on the door. "Don't use all the hot water," she cried, "I have to wash dishes after a while." Thin pretended he couldn't hear her.

He stood under the shower and let the hot water run down his neck and through the hair on his chest and down around his lower body. He soaped himself with a kind of soap he had discovered which seemed to be the only thing that counteracted the itching material which he picked up each day at the air filter factory.

He allowed himself to engage in fantasy. He played out the same fantasy role that he entertained himself with every afternoon. He saw himself, not in the friendly shower in his own home, with its little towels appliqued with Dutch children wilting in the steam from his bath, but he was a Jew in a Nazi concentration camp, with deadly gas blowing out of the shower nozzle. An oppressive dictatorship was exterminating him.

He enjoyed playing the game. Naked, he cowered in the bathtub, away from the shower, pressing back against the cold tile which was just above the tub. He put his arms up over his head, bent at the elbows, so that his hands covered his face. He clutched his throat. He gasped for breath. He lifted a shuddering cry.

In his mind's eye, he could see Callie, moving quick and quiet as a panther to the bathroom door. It was the same every day.

"Are you all right?" he heard her call out. "God, Thin, I hate it when you do that!"

He ignored her.

He knew it totally wiped Callie out when he hollered like that and then remained silent when she called to see if he was all right. He pictured her stooped down, her ear against the wood of the door, her breath held so that she might hear what he was doing. Furtively, he kept himself from making a sound.

The fantasy was real to him. He was in a death camp and the gas was pouring in. Soon he would be smothering under a stack of piled up bodies, ready as the rest of them to be transported to the trenches and buried. He shook his head violently, trying to rid himself of the dream.

In a few moments, he straightened up and turned the shower off. He stepped out of the tub and picked up I bath towel and began to dry himself. He looked at himself in the long bathroom mirror. He took the towel and wiped the moisture off the mirror so that he could see his reflection better.

"If I was any better looking, I couldn't stand it," he said.

"Are you all right?" Callie called out to him.

He told her that he was. He draped a towel around himself and went to their bedroom where he put on clean underwear. He put on one of his company t-shirts and his denim pants. He put on his white socks and his penny loafers. He didn't have to comb his hair because it was cut short and it stood up on its own, but he put on some of his cologne that Callie's sister had given him for Christmas. When he went out, he would wear one of his jackets. He had four or five, most of them advertising different products.

As soon as he went into the living room, Callie asked him if he was going out that evening.

"I hope not," he said. "I'm tired."

"I just want to know so that I'll know whether or not to fix something to eat. I get tired of fixing supper for you, so's you run off with Rhodus Powl to Jolly Pierre's and me and the dog have to eat it."

Thin settled into the sofa and turned on the TV with the remote control. He was careful to put it back in the drawer he had taken it from, because Fema had chewed one up a few weeks before. That had cost him fifteen dollars.

"I'll just sit here and look at TV," he said.

"I feel like all you have me for is to go and look for your dogs, the day after you lose them hunting," Callie complained. "You hunt deer one day and I hunt dogs the next."

"That hasn't happened but twice this year," Thin told her. "What else have you got to do?"

Callie gave the floor a hopeless glance. "You can see what I do around here," she said.

They sat in brooding silence until Callie decided to get up and go to the kitchen and begin to cook supper. Thin could hear her rattling pans, making more noise than was necessary. He tiptoed into their room and took his jacket, which was Clemson orange, out of the closet. He wasn't sure Rhodus would come by, although he did every night. If Rhodus didn't come, he would eat supper. If Rhodus did come, he would eat the cold food when he got home.

He sat on the sofa with the jacket beside him. Fema came near him, trying to be friendly, and he picked her up and scratched behind her ears and under her chin. "I could take every bit of this dog's affection away from Callie if I wanted to," he thought to himself. He shifted for the first time since he had come home.

A truck horn sounded out in front of the house. Callie heard it. She came to the door of the living room. "That's Rhodus Powl," she said. "I guess you'll go off with him." She spotted the orange jacket. Thin dropped Fema to the floor.

He picked up the jacket. "I'll just go out and see what Rhodus wants," he said.

Rhodus worked at the air filter factory. He had an hourly job on the assembly line. At work, Thin was defensive about his friendship with Rhodus. Some of the men wondered why a supervisor and an hourly man hung around together as the two of them did. He knew that Callie hated Rhodus because Rhodus was single. He got blamed for encouraging Thin to do single things, like sitting at Jolly Pierre's evenings instead of staying at home, and spending his money on hunting and fishing.

Thin had a boat behind the house, which he had bought, even though Callie had begged him to use the money to get them a big luxury car such as she felt his position at the air filter factory demanded. Thin knew she knew Rhodus backed him in his plans to get the boat. Thin never drove the car, so the car was not a big priority with him. He went everywhere in his truck. Now, when he and Rhodus took the boat out, Callie would bitch all day.

Thin had to admit Rhodus didn't keep himself up. He had let himself get paunchy, and his clothes never looked neat. He wore his hair long. It just hung, untended, down the sides of his head and in back. He was forever pushing it back out of his face. They made him tuck it up under his hard hat, in the plant, for safety's sake. He had a black pickup truck which was never waxed and shined. He rinsed it off once in a while in the company's free carwash. Usually, he forgot.

Thin stepped lightly down the steps and went up to the window on the passenger side of the truck. Callie stood in the door and looked at him.

Rhodus' face lit up in a big smile. "Let's go get a couple of Bulls," he shouted. Thin felt his spirits rise in an instant. He had to smile back. He flung his left arm out and dragged his jacket on.

While he was putting his other arm in the right sleeve, he turned and looked at Callie. "I'm going and ride around a few minutes with Rhodus," he shouted.

Callie didn't answer. She backed away from the door and closed it.

"That fucking woman makes me feel like I'm in jail," Thin said. He settled back in Rhodus' truck, putting his foot up against the dash. Rhodus was trying to find something on the radio. They drove the few blocks to Jolly Pierre's.

Jolly Pierre came Out of the bayou country of Louisiana. He left the running of his place to Sweet Delight, who lived with him.

When they got to Jolly Pierre's, Thin saw immediately that there was only one other customer in the place, a nondescript, small fellow, perhaps thirty. The place was dark and it smelled of beer and disinfectant. Sweet Delight was always mopping. She kept a mop bucket and mop close at hand. These always smelled of pine oil. The air was redolent with the sweet odor which is emitted when the top of a can of beer is popped.

Just seeing the familiar bar with its bar stools and the tables, each with four chairs, and the booths, which filled the wall, gave Thin a feeling of peace. Above the bar was a TV, which was turned on. The sound was cut down so that it couldn't be heard.

"Bring us a couple of Bulls," Rhodus bellowed. He jerked a chair back and sat at one of the tables. Thin sat across from him. The nondescript little man was looking at them from his place in one of the booths.

Sweet Delight was all skin and bone. She had hardly any flesh on her. Her hair was dyed jet black. It was thin. She combed it so that it looked as if there was more than there was. She wore a lacy cap like French maids wear. She wore a short, little skirt like she had seen actresses in the movies who played French maids wear. She wore hard heels and her feet made a noise when she walked. This was good because the customers always knew where she was. If they were talking man-talk she shouldn't hear, and she came up behind them, they would stop talking.

Sweet Delight set two Bulls on the table. Rhodus grabbed his at once, and popped the top of it. Thin paid for the beer. Sweet Delight started to walk away, but Rhodus grabbed her arm. "Get something on the jukebox," he told her. He gave her a couple of bills. Jolly Pierre's had the best music anywhere around. Jolly Pierre's music was even better than the local country and western radio station.

Sweet Delight smiled and changed the bills into quarters and went and stood in front of the jukebox. The jukebox had colored lights which revolved and these lit up Sweet Delight's legs, each in turn. Sweet Delight liked sad songs sung by women. She would play such songs and sit and stare into space. Thin thought they would all be crying soon.

"How was your trip?" Rhodus asked.

Thin had been sent by the air filter factory to Kansas City to look at some equipment which they might buy for the lab. Thin was not used to going to places outside the southeast, but he had gone and he had a good time. He had a rented car and a fine motel room and everything all paid for by the company. He asked one of the men at the plant of the vendor he was visiting, where there was a place where they played country music and he was told about a bar with a country and western format, so he went there and met a lot of friends.

"I was drunked-up," he told Rhodus. "And, there was a woman there that wanted me to fuck her. I didn't really want to, but she kept on after me. I didn't know how to say no. I got drunker and drunker and the music was loud and people was talking shit. I was feeling pretty good. I didn't take the woman to my motel room. I went and hired another room in a real run-down looking place and I had to fuck her."

Thin stopped talking so Rhodus asked him, "Well, was that all there was to it?"

"I dozed off and went to sleep," Thin told him. "When I woke up in about thirty minutes, she was still there. She hadn't had the decency to leave. She wanted me to fuck her again. She was dirty. I should have gone out in my rental car and got my gun and gone back in there and shot her."

"For what?" Rhodus asked.

"She made me fuck her and she was dirty."

"Was she really dirty?"

Thin looked at Rhodus for a long time before he answered. He took his thumb and fingers and turned his beer can around and around. Finally, he said, as though Rhodus should already know, "All women are dirty, except my wife. When I go with any woman other than my wife, they make me feel dirty. I don't feel dirty when I go with my wife, but I feel dirty when I go with any other woman. I'd like to kill them when they make me feel like that."

"Every woman you pick up can't be dirty," Rhodus said. "There's some beautiful, clean women out there in the world."

"They're all dirty. I'd like to take my gun and shoot them."

"You let your fucking worry you too much," Rhodus told him. "I fuck just like a dog eats meat."

"Yeah? How's that?" Thin asked him. "With your mouth?"

Rhodus half rose from his chair and struck Thin a solid blow on the shoulder. It was in fun.

Rhodus had finished his beer. He broke the spell which the sad music had brought on Sweet Delight and asked her for another one. Thin said he wasn't ready for any more. Rhodus paid.

"I went fishing while you were gone," Rhodus told Thin. "The damnedest thing happened. I went with Jet and Herbert and Jet took an old guy with us, about in the late sixties, been a fisherman all his life. That old man could fish rings around any of us. We pulled the boat up beside the bank after a while and Pops, as they called him, was washing the fish we had caught and the rest of us was drinking Bulls. He'd take a fish in his right hand and, graceful as anything, he'd lower his arm in an arc and dip the fish in the river water and bring it back up just as gentle and smooth and put it in the cooler. It was just a pleasure to watch him. All at once a moccasin swam up beside the boat. He must have smelled the fish and he wanted some. He went straight for Pop's hand and bit him. We about fell through our assholes. It scared me so bad I thought they'd have to take me to the hospital. Pops just shook the snake off and slapped the water a few times to scare him away. The snake swam off and Pops just started washing the fish again, for all the world like nothing had happened."

An eighteen wheeler pulled up in front of Jolly Pierre's and a black man came inside. He was the driver of the truck. He sat on a stool at the bar and gave Sweet Delight his order.

"Look at the size of that Boo," Rhodus whispered to Thin. "Look at the hands on him and those boots. What size do you reckon those boots are?"

"He probably has them special made," Thin said. "Didn't you all take Pops to the hospital?"

"He wouldn't go," Rhodus explained incredulously. "He said the snake was feeding and there was no venom in his venom pockets. He said the bite wouldn't hurt him."

"Well, did it?" Thin asked.

"Not the last I heard," Rhodus said.

"When was that?"

"Today."

"Then, it's not going to hurt him," Thin said. "I mean, if it hasn't by now."

"I told Pops if that snake had bit me, it would have scared me so bad they would probably have had to take me to the funeral home, much less to the hospital."

"Most of us would have been that worried," Thin said. "Around here a moccasin bite is considered a dangerous thing. Most people start getting scared when they first smell a snake."

Sweet Delight came to the table on her loud shoes, carrying two Bulls.

"We didn't order any," Thin said.

"That man over in the booth sent them to you," Sweet Delight told them. "He wants to know if he can come over here and sit at your table with you."

"I don't see anything wrong with that," Rhodus said. "If he's nice enough to buy us a couple of Bulls, I guess he can come and sit with us."

"We can always get up and leave if we decide to," Thin agreed.

Sweet Delight went and told the man that he could come and sit at the table with Thin and Rhodus.

The man shuffled over to sit with them and slit down at the side of the table most distant from the bar.

"My name's Marvin," he said. "I believe that black man is after me. That's why I wanted to come and sit with you. I want to thank you for letting me."

Thin and Rhodus told him who they were. "What are you doing in Baytown?" Rhodus asked.

"I just drift around mostly," Marvin said. "I mostly just drift about from place to place. I just drifted into town."

"We're working men," Thin told him.

"I was intended to be a working man," Marvin said. "My folks was farmers."

"Where're you from?" Rhodus asked.

"Georgia," Marvin answered. "I'm from Georgia. I grew up on a farm and part of it would have belonged to me one day, if I hadn't messed up. I really messed up bad."

Thin and Rhodus looked at each other. They knew that a story was coming. They silently agreed with each other to settle back and listen to it. They both looked at Marvin with rapt attention.

Marvin was born in Lillian, Georgia. He had gone to school, and worked with his brothers and his father on the family farm. He was raised to be a church-going man and he was saved and baptized when he was fifteen and he went to church every Sunday. He sang with the choir.

When Marvin was a little older, he fell in love with a girl called Priscilla. Her mama had named her for the kind of curtains, called Priscilla, that were advertised in the Sears & Roebuck catalog.

Priscilla was a year younger than Marvin and the gentlest, sweetest little girl that anyone could ever have imagined anywhere. She seemed too fragile and innocent for this world. She had brothers and a father and uncles to look out for her. They didn't let her out much, but they let her go out with Marvin.

One night, when Marvin was eighteen and Priscilla was seventeen, he raped her.

"She was just beautiful," Marvin told Thin and Rhodus. "She was beautiful but she aggravated me, too. She didn't want me to touch her or kiss her or anything. I wanted to do everything with her. I wanted her to belong to me so that I could do anything I wanted with her. I didn't mean to hurt her, but one night, we were sitting out under a grape arbor that her daddy had fixed, the grapes up on poles and benches under it, and she got me shittin' with her standoffishness so I just fucked her. I hadn't fucked anyone before, but I knew what to do. I just laid it to her without any conscience."

Marvin paused for several minutes.

"Wasn't you going to marry her anyhow?" Rhodus asked.

"She wouldn't have me after that," Marvin said. "She took sick. She was sick for a long time after that night. She wouldn't come outside the house. I tried to see her, but they told me she wouldn't see me. Her brothers told me I hadn't heard the end of it."

"These things is best handled without the law," Rhodus said. "Did they call the law on you'"

"No. The two families met. Just the men. My brothers and my father never said a word. They just sat, grim-faced. I was scared of what Priscilla's family was going to do to me. I could see my family was going to let them do it, whatever they wanted to do. Priscilla's father told me that they were not going to call the law on me and none of them would ever lay a finger on me, but he said that they were going to hire someone, someday, in some place, to cruelly do to me what I done to Priscilla. They said I'd know him when I seen him. They said he'd find me wherever I went in the world, no matter how many years it was. I've been running, ever since."

"Maybe they've forgot about it by now," Thin said. "How many years has it been?"

"It's been more than ten years. I've seen a thousand men, on hundreds of streets, in hundreds of bars, on the railroads, big men, ugly men. I thought every one of them was the one that had come after me. I can't hold a job. I can't settle down in one place. I can't have any friends. I just drift. I drift, hoping not to see him, but hoping to see him so that it can be over. I want it to be over. I believe that black man sitting at the bar is the man."

Thin and Rhodus looked at the man called "the Boo." The man was sitting, patiently, evidently waiting for Sweet Delight to cook up some food for him.

He wasn't even drinking.

"I don't believe that's him," Thin said. "I believe those folks back in Georgia was shittin' you. I don't believe they intended to send anyone to find you and rape you. They just wanted you to spend your life being afraid."

"Well, they got that right. I been afraid. They haven't forgotten. It's coming. I know I deserve it. I've deserved all these years, to get cruelly and brutally fucked, for what I did to Priscilla. Now, you fellows know what I done. I wouldn't blame you if you took me and you both gave me what I deserve to get."

"Man! Watch your mouth!" Rhodus cried.

"It has happened. I've let men do anything they wanted with me because I've felt like I deserve it, I've been through a whole string of men, while I've been waiting for the real one to come along. It makes me feel better. I wish you men would take me somewhere, out of here, and hurt and humiliate me. It would do me a lot of good."

"That son of a bitch," Rhodus whispered to Thin, "both of us ought to fuck him."

"We'd both wind up with AIDS if we did," Thin said bluntly.

Rhodus crushed his beer can violently, bent it every which way, and tossed it toward the trash container. It went to the floor.

"I hope I didn't make you fellows mad," Marvin said.

"Don't worry about it. We're just two guys, friends, that happen to work at the same place. We just came out for a couple of beers," Thin told him.

"I guess I'd better go," marvin told them. "If that black man gets up and follows me after I leave, would you follow along too, and stay at a distance, but see that he doesn't hurt me too bad or kill me or something."

"Sure," Rhodus said. "Sure. We'll do that."

"The Boo is eating right now," Rhodus said. "He doesn't look like he's thinking about raping somebody."

Marvin looked at him with a sidelong glance. It was obvious to Thin that Marvin was really frightened. "We'll try to look out for you," he said.

Sweet Delight brought the black man some more food in boxes. She set these on the bar beside his plate. "I'm going," Marvin said. "I want to thank you again." He got up and quickly shuffled out the door.

Almost at once, the black man stood up and paid for his food and left, carrying the packages. "Let's go see what the hell is going on," Rhodus said. He and Thin went outside. Marvin was nowhere to be seen. The black man was standing beside the tractor to his rig. Rhodus and Thin walked over and spoke to him.

"I've got a woman and a child traveling with me," the black man told them. "She got stranded up north. I needed to bring her back south where her home people can help her. The child gets sick when she rides too long. I have to keep stopping. They needed food, too. They're eating now. I'll be able to make up some time. I'm way behind schedule, but maybe the good Lord will help me to catch up. I couldn't do this without His help."

"Yeah," Thin said, "the Lord will help you."

"I had to help this woman," the black man said. "If we don't look out for our women folks, who will?"

"That's right. Who will?" Thin echoed.

The black man swung his huge body up into the truck. Thin and Rhodus saw a little black girl peering down at them curiously. Thin smiled and lifted his hand.

When the door of the truck closed, Thin said, "Isn't all this some kind of shit?"

They stood back out of the way when the truck pulled away. "I believe that Marvin made up the whole story he told just so he could try to get us to go off with him," Rhodus told Thin. "We both of us should have fucked him!"

"Rhodus," Thin said. "You don't know anything."

They went and got in Rhodus' pickup. "I don't see why you would say I don't know anything," Rhodus said. "I believe Marvin was shittin' us."

"I'm sorry," Thin told him. "I'm thinking about all this. To Marvin, that black truck driver was the one sent after him, because Marvin saw him to be that. It 's like the woman I fucked in Kansas City was dirty because I perceived her to be. You believed the snake that bit Pops was a deadly reptile, so to you it was. All this is telling me something. I'm trying to read what it's telling me. It's like a quality test run in the lab. I input the data and there's a result."

"I'm getting sick," Rhodus said. "I should have eaten. I'll drop you off at your house, and I'm going home."

"Callie is like a jailer to me," Thin said. "Because I perceive her to be a jailer. That's the answer to the equation. I've got to see her in a new light. If we don't look out for our women folks, who's going to do it?" He talked as if he talked to himself. "I'm going to be busy a lot of the time. I'm going to an allergy specialist. There's something in the plant that I'm allergic to. It drives me crazy."

Rhodus looked at him with a stricken look in his eyes. Thin knew that Rhodus knew that he would not be going out to Jolly Pierre's with Rhodus any more.

He'd tried to let Rhodus down easy. That episode in his life was over. Thin knew that Rhodus was inexpressibly sad.

Rhodus stopped in front of Thin's house and Thin got out of the truck.

"I enjoyed being with you," Thin said.

He went inside the house.

GEORGETOWN, SOUTH CAROLINA

"The West Virginia Hunch" was written in Georgetown in 1990. Two aging former high school athletes remain competitive with each other.

This story is not about revolutionaries and messiahs. It is about the all-too-common disposition in rival males to entertain ambivalent feelings of need and hate or one another. It is also about the lack of awareness the women seem to possess about their husbands' inner lives.

There are many worlds here. They don't communicate very well.

THE WEST VIRGINIA HUNCH

When Horace Hiram Wade woke up that morning, the first thing he did was go outside. He did this every morning. He couldn't stand staying inside a house. The house he shared with his wife, Shelby Jean Winforth Wade, wasn't much. It sat under a couple of old trees in a little clearing in the woods and there were even shabbier buildings there used as cow shed, chicken roost and privy. The chickens were up and outside, too.

Horace Hiram, for sure, didn't feel proud of much he had. He wasn't even proud any more of Shelby Jean. He was proud of what he knew. He knew how to work with cattle and now, he knew how to handle women.

Today, right off, Horace Hiram noticed that the gate to the cow lot was ajar and his cow, Doris, had evidently wondered off. She was not there. He ran and looked in the cow shed to make sure, but she was gone. Horace Hiram went and threw himself down on an old bench that stood near the pump against the chicken yard fence. He leaned back against a fence post.

"I believe I can't stand it if anything happened to Doris," he said. He walked over and saw that her water bucket was full of clean water and he knew he had fed her the night before when he milked her. "I can't figure how come she would leave."

Shelby Jean was up. She had coffee made. She called Horace Hiram to come in the house. Horace Hiram went inside.

"Doris is run off," he told Shelby Jean.

"You going to look for her?" Shelby Jean had made biscuits and she had eggs fried and fatback pork. She asked Horace Hiram how much grits he wanted. He usually wanted a lot.

"I don't care," he said.

Shelby Jean was skinny and pale and her forehead was always puckered in a worried little frown. There was no color in her. Her hair was mouse brown and her lips were almost as pale as her face. Her eyes were grey and lusterless. She was dull looking. But, she loved Horace Hiram. Since the time in New Orleans when he had found out how to really make her happy, he was sure that she truly loved him.

Horace Hiram knew that he was a fine looking man and had always been. Back in high school there hadn't been but one other boy who could touch him

317

for looks and that was Beau Carl Middleton. As the two best looking and most athletic boys in their class, Horace Hiram and Beau Carl had been natural rivals and had hated each other. Horace Hiram had ended up marrying plain Shelby Jean and Beau Carl had married Mikki Jo, who was as precious looking as something handed down. Horace Hiram had always been sweet on Mikki Jo. One time during school, he had taken her out and he hadn't been able to give her what she wanted. He had always felt as if he should have a chance for a rematch. He thought about his life in this house with Shelby Jean, and the missing Doris, and he didn't care if he ate anything at all. There was one bright side to his life. Shelby Jean was not the kind of girl other men would come after. Horace Hiram felt very safe about leaving her alone. Having her run around on him was one thing he didn't have to worry about.

He ate what he could and went back out in the yard. Doris was a small muley-headed brindle cow, about two and a half years old. She'd already had her first calf. She was the best natured, gentlest little cow Horace Hiram had ever seen.

He could remember when he'd brought her home. He'd taught her how to drink milk out of a bucket. He'd submerge his hand in the milk and get her to suck his finger and then he'd pull her mouth down into the milk so she'd take some of it while she sucked his finger and she learned that this was the way she'd have to drink milk after this, now that they had taken her away from her mother. She trusted Horace Hiram for everything. When it was time, he taught her to eat feed and then she learned by herself how to eat grass. Horace Hiram led her to her visit to the bull when she came in heat and he helped her when her calf was born. He grieved with her when they took her calf away. She forgot it quickly. He milked her and fed her and lots of times he just sat against the fence near her stall and kept her company. Now, she was gone.

A ragged old Buick drove up in front of Horace Hiram's house and he knew that it was his brothers-in-law, Quincy and Pete Winforth, come to see Shelby Jean. Quincy and Pete Were both skinny like their sister and they had black hair and black hair grew on their faces. Neither of them had a habit of shaving more often than once a week. They were the kind of men who turned slightly to one side while walking, and spit. Horace Hiram knew that Shelby Jean would get mad with him if he didn't go in and speak to them, so he did, but he didn't stay but for a minute. He said he had to go to the woods and look for Doris.

Horace Hiram walked all over the woods. About a mile from his own house, he came up on a rise of ground and stood looking down at the house belonging to Beau Carl Middleton. Mikki Jo would be inside the house. Horace Hiram thought about how pretty she was with her red lips and bright blue eyes and blond hair and he knew that he would give his left nut for the chance to go out with her.

There was no sign of Doris, but he did find a place where someone had backed a pickup truck into a ditch so that the tailgate rested against the ditch bank, so's the floor of the truck would have been level with the ground at the top of the bank, and there were cow tracks leading up to the place. The cow tracks looked as if the cow had been dragged protesting toward the truck. There were long scuffmarks on the ground. Someone had loaded a cow into a truck at this spot. "Some son of a bitch has stole her," Horace Hiram muttered. "By now, she's probably at the slaughterhouse." Horace Hiram could hardly make his feet drag him home.

Quincy and Pete had brought some whiskey with them, and they invited Horace Hiram to have a drink and he felt like he needed one about as bad as he ever had. Shelby Jean was going to fix supper for them so they went outside to sit around in the yard drinking until she had everything ready.

Quincy and Pete did not have steady jobs, but they picked up a little work sometimes. They were always remembering the times when they had picked satsumas for fifty cents a day and how bad everything had been, then, after the sawmill shut down. No matter how bad things became, they could never be that bad again. They worked on the WPA. "Roosevelt came along and saved this country," they would say.

"John L. Lewis and President Roosevelt will look out for the working man," Pete Winforth said in a positive tone of voice.

Horace Hiram rested his head with its dark curly hair in his muscular arms. His eyes were dark and sorrowful. He clenched his strong, rather square hands into fists and felt that he was going to break down and cry right in front of his brothers-in-law. A sweat broke out on his tanned face.

Quincy and Pete were still talking when they heard a crashing in the underbrush as if some large creature was about to burst out of the woods. It was almost dark now, but the three men saw Doris come rapidly across the clearing, heading for her cow pen. There was a rope around her neck, and she was dragging something behind her. "Oh, thank God! It's her." Horace Hiram cried out. "Shelby Jean! Shelby Jean! Come out here and see about this cow!"

He ran to Doris and threw his arms about her neck, pulling at the rope that held her, tears running down his face. "There is more rejoicing for the lamb that was lost and is found than for all the other lambs in the farmer's flock," he shouted. He got the rope off. "Come and get some water and some food," he said, coaxing his cow.

Shelby was wiping her hands on her apron. "I know he thinks more of that critter than he does of me," she told her brothers.

Quincy and Pete were looking at what was attached to the other end of the rope from where Doris' head had been.

"It's a wooden side panel that somebody was using on their pickup truck to turn it into a cattle truck," Quincy said. He dragged it into the light. The board slats that made up the panel were painted a distinctive yellow color.

"Where you saw that somebody had backed a truck up against the ditch bank in order to load a cow into it, they tried dragging Doris into the truck," Pete said. "But, they couldn't get her to jump across the space to get in the truck, so they tied the rope to the side panel, intending to go around behind Doris and drive her in. But, Doris pulled the panel loose and ran off into the woods dragging it behind her."

"Now," Quincy said, "all we have to do is find the pickup truck that this panel belongs to and we'll know who has been stealing all the cows around here for the last couple of years."

"I know already," Horace Hiram said. "That yellow paint is the paint that was left over when Beau Carl painted John Bascum's store building. Beau Carl Middleton is the cattle thief."

"Well, let's go get the sheriff," Quincy shouted. He began straightening his clothing, which had twisted on him while he was lying on the ground drinking.

But Horace Hiram had another idea. "I'll go over and talk with Beau Carl tomorrow morning," he said. "I hope both of you will stay here with us until this is settled." Usually, he couldn't wait for Quincy and Pete to leave when they came to see their sister.

Horace Hiram was so excited he hardly slept any all night. The next morning, he got up even earlier than usual and went outside and fed the chickens and fed Doris and milked her and checked her all over to see if she had hurt herself anywhere the day before. It would have been easy for the side panel out of Beau Carl's truck to have tangled in the bushes, causing the rope to drag Doris down. Horace Hiram looked carefully, but he didn't see any cuts on Doris' hide or any knicks in her hair. "It's a darn good thing he didn't hurt my cow," Horace Hiram said.

He knew that Beau Carl did not like to get up early in the morning. Beau Carl picked up jobs painting around and about and he did most of his work in the late morning and early afternoon. During the late afternoons and evenings, he would get drunk. Horace Hiram knew that he had kept better care of himself than Beau Carl had. "If he gives me any shit, I'll beat his ass," Horace Hiram said.

When he got to Beau Carl's house, he beat heavily on the door and called out to Beau Carl in a deep voice. After a while, Beau Carl came and opened the door. He was buttoning his pants. His shirt was open down the front. Horace Hiram noted the paunch Beau Carl was developing. "It'd be a sorry woman would go with him now," Horace Hiram thought. "Although he was a great looking stud in high school." Horace Hiram could recall how Beau Carl had looked on the basketball court in his uniform with his legs and arms and chest all hairy.

"I come to see you because you tried to steal my cow," Horace Hiram said.

Beau Carl's insides heaved upwards, but he didn't vomit. "I don't know what you're talking about," he said.

"Doris!" Horace Hiram said. "I'm talking about my cow, Doris." He turned and looked with a steady stare toward Beau Carl's pickup truck. One of the slat side panels was missing. The odd shade of yellow paint showed under a coating of dew. "I see you're missing part of your truck."

"That panel's around here someplace." Beau Carl said. He had stepped outside and closed the door.

"It ain't. Doris drug it home. Me and my two brothers-in-law seen her do it, and I got it," Horace Hiram told him.

"I just don't see how she could have done that," Beau Carl said. He turned to the side and spit.

"I'm going to take my two brothers-in-law as witnesses to the sheriff and get him to come look at that side panel, and he is going to know you tried to steal Doris, and he is going to know that you have stole all the cows that have been missing around here in the past couple of years."

"Horace Hiram," Beau Carl said pleadingly, "we have always been friends since we were in school. We started out together in the first grade. Me and Mikki Jo is having a hard time here. I don't get much work, and I drink too much. My drinking money takes half or two thirds of all I make. I figure I'll just lose everything if you turn me in about this."

"You're right about one thing," Horace Hiram said. "You're going to lose everything. You're wrong about us being friends in school. The way I remember it, I always hated your guts."

"I was always jealous of you," Beau Carl said. "You were smarter than me. You always wore dress shirts to school. I didn't never have what you call polish or class."

"I was always jealous of you because girls thought you were such hot shit."

Horace Hiram smirked to himself. He knew that now, he had an ace that Beau Carl wasn't holding. He could drive girls crazy. He had the West Virginia Hunch, like he'd been taught In New Orleans. "What'll you give me if I don't turn you in?" he grinned.

"I'll try to get you some money," Beau Carl said weakly. "I done told you that I don't have any."

"I don't need any money," Horace Hiram told him. "I reckon me and Shelby Jean will get by on what I make. I was thinking more like maybe you'd fix it up where I could get to know Mikki Jo a little better. Me and Mikki Jo dated a time or two before you got married. She didn't think much of me. I think things might be different now. Do you think she'd let me come over in the afternoon and visit with her?"

"She would if I told her to," Beau Carl said.

"I want you to do that," Horace Hiram said, whirling around and looking him dead in the eye.

Beau Carl's face turned red. He looked at his hands, which were scarred and still had traces of paint on them. His nails were dirty. "When do you want to do this?" he asked.

"This afternoon," Horace Hiram said, "and I ain't coming to play. I'm coming to woo Dogpatch style. " When he said the last, his voice rose with excitement and he shouted so loud the trees at the end of the clearing echoed.

"You ain't going to do no good," Beau Carl said. "I've heard about the time before when Mikki Jo gave you a chance with her. She laughed at you then, and she'll laugh at you now."

"She won't laugh," Horace Hiram said confidently.

"Everything will go all right and then she won't never want to have nothing to do with you again. She'll let me come over here any time I want to. She'll be begging me to come. If you want me to, I'll give you some children, Beau Carl, seeing's you ain't got none."

"I ain't never seen none at your house either," Beau Carl told him, with some of his bravado coming back. He felt a lot better knowing he wasn't going to jail.

"I'll be back over here this afternoon." Horace Hiram said. "In the early part of the afternoon. After it's over, I'll let you come and get your truck panel and your rope."

At home, Horace Hiram told Shelby Jean and her brothers that he had talked with Beau Carl and that he was going back that afternoon to talk with him some more. Quincy and Pete were enjoying getting to visit so long with Shelby Jean. She was cooking for them and they had their whiskey so they could lay out under Horace Hiram's shade tree drinking.

Horace Hiram got his gun down and cleaned it and loaded it and stood it against the wall by the door to his and Shelby Jean's bedroom. He made Shelby Jean heat a kettle of water and brought the tub inside and fixed to take a bath. He got all cleaned up and put on clean clothes from the skin out. He decided that he really looked good and should make a hit anywhere, especially if he were being compared to Beau Carl. Beau Carl had lost it.

After he shaved very carefully and combed his hair, Horace Hiram picked up his gun and went jauntily out past where his family was sitting in the yard under the tree. "I might have some trouble with Beau Carl," he said. "If he gives me any trouble, I'll use my gun to bring him in. Alive or dead, I don't care."

"You be careful," Shelby Jean said. "Beau Carl's much of a man."

"Not that much."

When Horace Hiram got into the woods, he became very excited. He was remembering the time when he had gone to New Orleans to deliver a truckload of poles, and a man that was hanging around started talking to him and taught him a special way of fucking that was guaranteed to put a woman in such a fit of joy she'd most pass out. He paid the man five dollars, but it was worth it more than anything else he had ever paid for. He didn't know the man's name,

but he was from West Virginia, so Horace Hiram called the maneuver the West

Virginia Hunch after the man's home state. Horace Hiram figured no one in Mississippi knew about the technique and after he mastered it completely, he felt his ego all built up, and he felt as if he were more of a man than he had ever been, even when he was just getting out of high school, when he used to stay horny as hell.

Today, his ego got a real boost when he saw Beau Carl and realized his old rival was over the hill, while Horace Hiram was coming into a new prime. "I can just see him setting out there by his woodpile," Horace Hiram thought to himself. "When he sees me go into his house, he'll know that Mikki Jo is going to like what she sees and she's going to get excited right off. He's going to know just how she's going to act, and he's going to hurt inside. He's going to know what a miserable cuss he has become. He's going to imagine Mikki Jo slipping out of her dress and standing there all beautiful in her silk slip and she'll lift up her arms and throw her hair back and then she'll kick off one slipper and then she'll kick off the other slipper, and she'll lay back on the bed." Horace Hiram delighted in knowing how Beau Carl would feel thinking about this. "She'll make a little motion for me to come on over and I'll sit down beside her and she'll raise her hips up and I'll slide her slip up over her belly button and then I'll jump up and rip my shirt off and pull my shoes off and then lower my pants. She'll start begging me to get out of my shorts. Beau Carl will know that's the way she acts. He'll know when she's doing that. I'll be wishing he could see. Then, with one hand, I'll pull her panties off of her and rip her slip the rest of the way off and then I'll take my shorts off and when she sees my dick she'll start gasping and panting and then come after me just the way Doris would come after my finger when I was reaching her how to drink milk. Then, I'll jump on top of her and show her the old West Virginia Hunch, and outside Beau Carl will know that I'm rocking his bedroom, causing it to buzz, and he will cry out in agony, 'He's doing it! He's wooing her Dogpatch style!'"

When Horace Hiram arrived outside Beau Carl's house, it was just like he had imagined. Beau Carl was sitting out by the woodpile. He looked as if he had been crying. His nose was running and he wiped the snot off his face with the sleeve of his shirt. He wouldn't look up at Horace Hiram, but he knew that Horace Hiram had his gun with him. He just sat perfectly still staring at the ground.

Horace Hiram went up to the door and Mikki Jo opened it before he even had time to knock. She was wearing slippers and a sleeveless, tight-fitting dress. Her bare legs were smooth and white. Horace Hiram closed the door quickly.

"Horace Hiram," Mikki Jo said. "I'da went with you plenty of times before this if you'da said you wanted to. You didn't have to go to Beau Carl for me to go with you. I forgot all about that time at school when you couldn't do nothing. You won't be like that now."

Horace stared at her. "You're still pretty as a new calf racing in the sunshine," he told her.

"You look mighty good yourself, Horace Hiram," she said. "To tell the truth, for a long time I've wanted to be the only girl as has fucked both of the best-looking men in the county. That'll make me feel like I'm still desirable."

"You're still desirable," Horace Hiram said excitedly.

"You want some coffee?"

"No, I don't want any coffee."

They went into Beau Carl and Mikki Jo's bedroom, and Mikki Jo pulled off her dress and kicked off her shoes. Horace almost lost his breath when he saw her standing there in her rayon slip.

"We're going to have a lot of fun," she told him. "I'm going to do something real special for you."

"Like what?"

"I'm going to show you a new way of fucking. It'll get you more excited than anything else you've ever done."

"I believe I'll be able to show you something, too," Horace Hiram said

323

proudly.

"Beau Carl showed me this new way of doing it that he learned off somebody's wife. He didn't say who it was, but this woman's husband learned about it in New Orleans and he come home and showed her, and she showed Beau Carl and Beau Carl showed me, and I'm going to show you and you'll say it's the grandest thing you ever seen."

Horace Hiram took a step back from her and felt all his passion go cold and instead of the heat of anticipation, he was overcome with fear and an aching dread. "Did Beau Carl happen to say what this way of doing it was called?" he asked.

"The West Virginia Hunch," she told him.

"I've got to go," Horace Hiram said.

She ran and grabbed hold of him, pulled him up against herself. "You can't leave when I'm all hot and bothered like this," Nikki Jo screamed. "It's just like it was ten years ago when we were in high school. Man," she shouted, "you ain't shit."

Horace Hiram had jerked his clothes on and he ran out the door. Mikki Jo came after him in her slip.

"You can come and get your truck panel and your rope," Horace Hiram hollered at Beau Carl, who was still sitting in the sun beside the woodpile. "I'm not going to do anything to you."

When he got home, he didn't go inside where Shelby Jean and Quincy and Pete were. He'd left his gun at Beau Carl's. They'd notice how he looked and miss his gun. It was better not to face them.

He sat in Doris' lot, wiping away tears, talking to Doris softly.

"All that matters is I got you back," he said. Doris chewed her cud. Now and then, she swept away fly with her tail.

Except for Horace Hiram's inaudible, frantic talking, it was quiet. Horace Hiram figured he'd stay there with Doris at least until it was dark.

GEORGETOWN, SOUTH CAROLINA

"Roy and Enid" was written in Georgetown in 1990. A desperate woman seeking to escape an unwise marriage finds the biggest escape of all.
The story is based on an actual incident which took place forty years before the writing.

ROY AND ENID

Guns had always meant a lot at Enid's daddy's house. When she would be going with a boy out on the creek bank to fish and eat a picnic lunch, her daddy would look the boy over and if he felt like the boy couldn't properly protect Enid he would give Enid the rifle to carry so she could protect herself. "All kinds of people are liable to come up on you out on that river," he would say.

When Enid got a little older, she started going with men from the Air Force Base and didn't see so much of the boys she went to school with. Enid's daddy didn't give her the rifle to take with her when she went out with airmen. Maybe he should have, but doubtless he knew the gun wouldn't protect her from the wiles of her dates or from herself. Enid went too far with one of her dates, perhaps many of them. She became pregnant.

"I never could ask nice boys over to the house," she cried to her daddy. "Like as not you'd be sitting in the front room washing your feet in the hand basin when they came in," she complained. She also told him about how he'd start cussing and low-rating everyone, in a loud voice, if they all went out of a room and left the light on. Enid's daddy was very particular about not wasting electricity.

Anyway, she went off and had her baby. She brought it back with her and she and her mama and daddy were going to raise it.

Roy Miller fought the Second World War working on the pipes, stationed in the Aleutians. The cold weather toughened him up good. He was a rounder, a hard drinker, and he went out with girls for one thing. He made good money because he had learned a trade in the service and could work as a pipefitter anywhere he cared to. He loved to work. He felt at home in holes in the ground, bending his back above the shovel and throwing the dirt out, locating buried pipes, fixing what was wrong with them.

Enid never did get along with her parents after the baby was born. She was determined to get married. She advertised herself as able and her baby as "boot."

Roy Miller started taking her out right off and in no time they got married. Enid's parents had objected, but it had happened anyhow. Once Enid's mama had met Roy in the woods and he was drunk and smarted off at her, but she was on the horse, riding, looking for the cows, and he was on the ground and she had her pistol. She held it in Roy's face and told him she'd kill him if he made any trouble for her.

Now that they were married, Enid found out that Roy only married her because she was damaged goods that he could have contempt for and treat meanly.

After they had been married for a couple of years, and had two children, they moved to town. Every day she had to cook him a hot meal and ride on the city bus to the site of his job and give it to him so he could eat what he wanted and not a prepared lunch like most men had. He had warned her not ever to speak to another man on the bus. She didn't either. She believed he knew the bus driver and the bus driver would tell on her if she did.

This life was bad enough, but now they were going to California. Roy told her they would be taking the children and they would get into his old car and drive to California where they could make a new start. He could get a good job making plenty of money working for Kaiser.

Enid knew that he was really taking her so far away so that she would be completely removed from any friends she had and her family.

"You just want me completely under your hand," she had said to him. He hit her.

"There's my hand," Roy growled. "A man's wife and his children are his chattels. Ask any lawyer in Mississippi."

"Lawyers are men, too," she said. "I've got something to say about where we go," she told him.

"Where a man takes his family, following work, is his business," Roy said finally. "The woman belongs somewhere with her tits throwed over a rub-board. The woman don't belong in men's business."

What Enid decided to do seemed completely natural to her. Now, she was going to put a gun to the best use she had ever put one to. She kept her mouth shut and acted as though she would be going with Roy to California without a complaint. She told all her family, all her friends, they were going. She played out the scenario right up until the morning they were to leave. Roy was loading the car for traveling.

When he went inside the house for a last look around, she ran to the car and got his pistol out of the glove compartment. She went to the corner of the house and waited for him to come outside and go to the car. Then she stepped from behind the corner of the house and held the pistol out in front of her. She aimed it straight at Roy's muscular body, at his midsection, where she couldn't miss him. Her daddy had always told her if she was going to shoot a man she should aim at his body, not at his head. "The target is better," her daddy always said.

"Look here, Roy, at what I have for you," she said.

She looked up from his shirt front to the area of black hair above the top button of his shirt, and then to his face. She saw the unbelief and fear. She hesitated. He was a beautiful animal, hot blooded, full of life, ready to live for a long time more. This was the way she thought of him. She didn't want, all of a sudden, to destroy all this virility, this magnetism, this beauty, this will to live on. She lowered the gun to her side.

Roy's expression changed from that look of fear and unbelief to one of un-reasoning rage. He took one step toward her.

There was only one thing to do, then. She turned the gun and shot herself.

GEORGETOWN, SOUTH CAROLINA

"The Present" was written in Georgetown in 1990. A bored wife finds ex-citement in department store and is left with stimulating memories of her time there.

Husband and wife know little meaningful communication with each other.

Thank you, Mary, for telling me about the incident which occurred on the down escalator. This happened in a Sears store in Kansas City, MO. The rest of the story is a fabrication.

THE PRESENT

Lena and Rudolph were shopping together. Almost. Lena had gotten her husband to treat her to a visit to a department store. This did not happen often. Even with the novelty of the situation, it was a ho-hum thing.

It was not exactly accurate to say they shopped together, since Rudolph was in office supplies and she was in ladies' hats. They weren't sharing shopping. She was selecting a hat, spending the one hundred dollars he had given her, telling her to buy herself a present.

It was so like Rudolph to think that anything could be fixed with a gift of money. He was always giving Lena a cash gift and telling her to "buy yourself something." They had everything, so there was nothing which Lena needed. She would usually spend the money on some useless thing to further clutter their cluttered house. She was looking for a frivolous, ridiculous hat. Picking it out would be fun, even if she never wore it.

"This is what I am reduced to," she thought. "Selecting a hat is the biggest thrill I can expect to get today."

Sometimes he would send her to shop for their children. Lena liked to do this, but she was afraid they bought them too much. Children, these days, were already more materialistic than they should be. It was asking for trouble to indulge them. Lena was hard line. Rudolph was soft. They did not see eye to eye concerning what children should have.

They had gotten away from their sixteen year old daughter and their eleven year old son, for the afternoon and evening, and after shopping they would have dinner with wine, and after that they would listen to sensuous music in bed, and it would be endlessly tiresome.

That morning, they had quarreled. That, at least, had broken the monotony, and the quarrel was actually the reason they had decided to give themselves this afternoon and evening together. Barring the most extreme emergency, Rudolph was compelled from within to go to his work, no matter what needs of others were there to be filled. Sick or well, family obligations demanding otherwise, or whatever, Rudolph would not stay away from his office.

Lena had pointed this out to him in the heat of the argument. "I wish that, just one time, you'd put my feelings ahead of your job and do something I want you to do with your time." But, he was a workaholic, so who could talk to him?

All his working didn't keep him slim. The last trousers she had bought for him were forty six inches in the waist, and he had outgrown all his coats. Today he looked completely disarrayed, Lena despaired, shirt buttons gaping open in front and his pants appearing too short because they were bunched up at the top where they were too small. He had to lean over the counters to get close enough to see the merchandise, and this would make his face get all red and he would huff and puff as if he would blow the house away. His body was made to sit in a chair in an office, and that was what he did, for the most part. He worked when he was at home, the same as he did at his place of business.

During the quarrel, that morning, Lena had burst into tears, which she almost never did, and the outcome of the argument was Rudolph gave her one hundred dollars and said he would forego work that afternoon in order to take her shopping. In the evening they would go out and have dinner where there was entertainment, he said.

The quarrel was forgotten. Lena browsed among the hats. She could not recall what the quarrel was about. There should be no quarrel between herself and Rudolph. She tried not to fight with him. Her dissatisfaction was her own fault, since she had decided long ago to marry this boring husband, because he had prospects. All their problems would evaporate if only, somehow, she could find a way to bring a little excitement into their marriage. She had attempted fantasizing during sex, but she needed fuel to ignite her phantasms, which were as dull as her life. It was wrong of her to take out her frustrations on Rudolph. Her own hard, practical head had led her to where she was.

Lena had brown hair. At high school, she was often told it was the color of molasses candy. Boys wanted to lick it to see if it was sweet. It curled loosely, and these days a touch of gray could be found in it. She told her cosmetologist to leave it alone. A little gray wouldn't hurt anything. She was an expert with makeup and she was still shirt. She knew that she was attractive.

Lena and Rudolph had been married eighteen years. She was thirty nine. Her approaching fortieth birthday depressed her slightly, but there was nothing she could do about it, just as there was nothing she could do about the many boring aspects of her life. She told herself that it was not that she was older which depressed her, but that she had missed something.

Now, she set all her attention on the hats. She seldom wore one. But today, she simply wanted to get something memorable with the money Rudolph had given her, She was looking for a hat so individual, so impudent, so attention getting, that she would never forget it. It's personality would be stamped on her memory forever, and this, at least, would make the day live for her, always.

When she spied an off-the-face feathered royal blue felt (just a touch of dark fur), that was just over a hundred dollars, she knew this was it. She would comb her hair straight back and let her soft curls hang out behind, and the pert way it would turn up in front would give her a youthful sauciness. She could see herself even before she tried it on. The mirror confirmed the thought she had about it. So, it was a done deal.

She hoped the feathers and the fur were artificial, but she wouldn't dwell on that.

The saleslady had come, and she said Lena and the hat were made for each other, and she put the hat in the box. Lena went with the hat to the checkout counter. With tax, it would be a hundred and twenty dollars. Lena remembered that she had a twenty dollar bill of her own in addition to the hundred dollars Rudolph had given her.

When the cashier had rung up the sale, Lena discovered that she had failed to put her twenty dollar bill in her blue purse, which she had with her, and it was still in her brown purse at home, and her credit cards and checks were there too. "I'll just go and find my husband and come right back," Lena said. She was embarrassed to death. Several other customers were approaching and Lena knew she would hold them up, keeping the cashier from clearing her register. The cashier would have to call the assistant manager in order to void the transaction. It was easier to make the other customers wait until Lena could get back with the rest of the money.

In a moment, the cashier was relieved when a dark, handsome man hurried up to her register and said, "Didn't my wife have enough to pay for her purchase?" He appeared to be someone in his late thirties. He spoke with an accent. "She's gone to look for me, surely. I'll pay the difference myself."

There were sighs of relief from the others who were waiting. The man paid the twenty dollars and took the sales receipt and the hat. He walked slowly toward the escalator, a blank expression on his face.

Lena returned and the cashier told her her husband had paid for and taken the hat.

"I just left my husband in office supplies," Lena said. She saw the tall, dark man, a stranger to her, carrying the box. He was almost to the escalator. She walked after him, taken long strides, her heels clicking on the much polished floor. "What in hell do you think you're doing?" she asked him loudly when she was in earshot. She had read somewhere never to show fear in this type of situation. She wanted to sound as if she could take care of herself.

He turned around and looked at her with inquiring innocence. "Are you addressing me?" he asked.

"That's my hat," she said.

"No," he said. "This is my package. I have the sales slip." He spoke slowly, turning all his vowels into diphthongs, accenting his final syllables. Lena couldn't recognize the accent.

"What are you?" she asked. "Some miserable spick that paddled over from Cuba?"

"I am Juleo," he said in an aggrieved tone. "I am Basque."

Lena recalled a movie about sheep raising that Anthony Franciosa was in with Anthony Quinn. Her life had been made up of going to movies, and watching old movies at home with Rudolph's VCR, and looking at soap operas.

Anthony Franciosa had been supposed to be Basque, but of course, everyone knew he wasn't. She didn't believe the man was named Juleo and she didn't believe he was Basque. "You're lying," she said. "I guess I know my package, and that's my package."

"I'm sorry you think that," Juleo said. "This is a gift for my wife."

"It is a gift," she retorted. "For this wife."

" You stain my good name," he said. "What you are saying affects my honor."

"You have no honor. I can see that you are wicked. We can settle this in short order. I'm going to call a store official." She would show him what a lady, such as herself, was. A word from her to the right person would settle him. She and her husband counted for something here. She was not above tossing her weight around. After all, what was he?

They were standing at the foot of the down escalator where everyone riding down from the floors above disembarked. In that store, the up escalator and the down escalator were not side by side, but a little way removed from each other. A few people got off the escalator from time to time, while Lena and Juleo continued to argue. His accent still puzzled her. Then, she remembered how Al Pacino sounded playing Scarface, an actor at home with one accent trying to adopt another, less familiar one. It sounded false. She had put her finger on it. Juleo was a fake. "You're trying to shit me. You're a liar and a thief," she said. "I'm going to get the store detective. You stand your tail right there until I come back." This was the way she had talked when she was in high school. Now, she let twenty years of carefully nurtured poise and charm fall away and she became the feisty girl she had been before graduation from high school, before college, before all the civilizing years with Rudolph.

Juleo showed no sign of leaving.

At this particular time, a young man looking as if had stepped from the pages of James Agee. and his plain wife, and their two blank-eyed children came across the much polished floor to the foot of the escalator, walking with purpose, as though they knew what they were doing. They stood a few feet away from Juleo and Lena, staring at the escalator with identically sober expressions. Lena could not ascertain at first why they stood as they did, but then she understood that they wanted to go up, while the escalator was obviously transporting people down. The standing family, and Juleo and Lena, remained transfixed and silent for a long, strained minute and a half. Then, the man told his plain wife reassuringly, "It's bound to change in just a minute. We'll wait for it."

Lena realized he thought there was only one escalator, and that it reversed itself periodically, running up for a while and then down for a spell. The little family was waiting for it to reverse. Lena was put out of sorts with Juleo even more than before. If he were an American, he would take charge of the situation, as John Wayne would, tactfully explaining the workings of escalators to the man and his wife, painting out to them where they might board the up escalator. But Juleo said nothing. If he really were Basque and strange to the country, his failure to act might be excused, but Lena believed he was a native citizen of America, born and bred, who would not drop the mask he had assumed trying to delude her about himself because he had stolen her blue hat, which even now he was holding in his strong, long hands with their suntanned skin and crisp black hair, against his flat, flat stomach. Lena told herself he was probably what you call a Black German.

The young husband studied the escalator intently. "It's not going to change," he said. "You tote one of these young-uns, and I'll carry the other and we'll run against it and go up that way." He sat the boy, who was the older child on his hip, holding him with a hand under his chest and the legs sticking out behind. The wife took the smaller girl-child up in her arms and they began to run up the down escalator. Lena wanted to laugh and cry and Juleo stared at the scene with heavy Mediterranean regret. An assistant manager became aware of what was going on. He called the couple, who were making little headway against the fast-moving escalator, to give up and come down, and he took them around to the other escalator and saw them on their way to the mezzanine. He came back to where Lena and Juleo stood, and gave them a quizzical look. "They'll be all right, now," he said. Neither Lena nor Juleo said anything, so he walked away.

"You didn't accuse me to him," Juleo said. "Why as that?"

"I don't know," Lena told him. She wasn't angry anymore. The black comedy they had just witnessed had her laughing inside. "I should have accused," she said.

Lena knew her husband, Rudolph, was still in office supplies. He would buy little plastic recipe boxes which were made to hold three by five ruled index cards, and a supply of cards, Direct the divider cards which were lettered "A" through "Z" and, perhaps other plastic file boxes and maybe loose-leaf binders and the fillers. Rudolph had card files at home on his books, catalogued three or four different ways, and his compact discs, and his audio tapes, and his video tapes and he kept all these cards in little recipe boxes. He had so many boxes of three by five index cards that he kept these boxes in bigger boxes and had one master box that had cards telling where all the other boxes and cards were. Now, he was copying all the information from the cards in the boxes to his computer. Rudolph had a lot of anxiety about his files. He was afraid that, somehow, something would happen to them. Then he wouldn't know what he had. Before he left the store, he would go to the large table where the sale books were and go through them, one by one, buying many of them. When he got home he would catalog the books he bought by title, author, and one or more subjects. This was his life. He liked sex in the morning, while Lena preferred it at night.

Lena began to walk slowly around to the up escalator. A determination began to be born in her mind. "I have got to learn to feel excitement again, before I can expect Rudolph to give me excitement."

Juleo followed her, a short distance behind . He walked on the sides of his feet, graceful, like some feathered and beaded Cherokee. His shoulders he carried back. His head was high. He held the package with the hat against his hip with his right hand. His left arm swung free. Lena could smell his hair tonic, the fabric of his clothes, leather, the outdoors, something else - perhaps, chewing gum, by the cinnamon odor. She walked as though she knew what she was doing. She knew she was an intuitive person. Now, her intuition took over. She rode the escalator up to the fourth floor where the furniture department was. Juleo rode behind her. They rode in silence. Together, but not together. Rising and rising again.

They stood, at last, in the showroom. It was made to look like a bedroom. The furniture was in place. The panels, which simulated walls, were hung with draperies in front of false windows, and there were pictures, a nice bedroom clock, and a door leading to nowhere. Across a wide room packed with furniture, they could see a salesman showing items to a young couple. "Yuppies," Lena thought. "They've never seen a hard day." She knew the salesman would be coming to wait on them in a few minutes.

"This is like a theatre set," she said. "It reminds me of the stage in the auditorium at my high school. We used to go there during free periods. It was a place to go where no one would spy on us. Boys and girls went there. We thought the teachers didn't know, but they knew. We thought we were bad. We were defiant. We imagined we did wicked things. It was thrilling."

"You had fun there," Juleo said, with a comprehending smile. He could share with her the feeling she had about this memory of long ago. She felt his empathy. "Did you have plays?" he asked. "Were you in them?"

"Sometimes," Lena told him. She could remember a play when she was a junior, in which she played a very foolish young woman who had to choose between true love and possible wealth, who chose to strive for riches which it might or might not have been possible to realize. She walked across the showroom with its shiny furniture, her head high, affecting to be haughty, remembering, "I must have money," she said, "lots of it." She emphasized the word "it." That was the way she had said it, then. They had coached her tirelessly trying to get her to place the emphasis on "lots" but she couldn't master it. "I must have money," she practiced now. "Lots of it." She got it right at last. Some part of herself exerted a great will to be that high school girl again, unencumbered, receptacle of seething lava, eager. But the sober side of her wanted to believe that the girl in the play had made the right choice, those many years ago, and Lena had made the right choice too. That sober side of Lena screamed in her brain that she must run from Juleo or she would ruin everything for herself.

"Did you get money?" Juleo laughed and clapped his left hand against his thigh in delight.

"Enough," she said. She fought with herself, trying to decide whether to remain or to go. She knew that Juleo was watching her with discerning eyes, seeing how her breasts rose and fell, as her deep and rapid breathing came faster and faster.

A salesman passed near them. Lena pretended to be testing the mirror on the dresser. She turned to Juleo as if to ask him how he liked it.

"It frames you perfectly," he said. "You are a beautiful woman. You make the things around you beautiful."

Just these things, the interval when the salesman passed near, and Juleo's loving her with words removed the conflict from her mind. "I have never been unfaithful to my husband," she said, not as though it pertained to anything but as a simple statement of fact. She was caught up now, in the rhythm of high school. This was the stage. The false walls were the scenery. She was someone else, a school girl with a beautiful boy again, hiding from the teacher, feeling no guilt for having what she must have.

"What's behind the wall?" he asked.

"A space," she said, "an empty space with a potential for being filled with anything anyone can dream. It can be a Garden of Eden." She smelled the dry cleaning fluid in Juleo's clothes. She smelled the odor of crafty smoke. Mephistophelian. She reached out and touched him, the first time they had made bodily contact, She moved toward an opening between the wall panels. She was that girl in the play, only she wasn't calculating and mercenary now. She was seeking true love. She wouldn't make the mistake she had made then. "I must have love," she said, "lots of it." She said it perfectly.

"And you shall have it!" Juleo followed her into the space behind the panels and set the package on the floor. He pulled her up against himself and kissed her. His hands were sure . He was the rider, familiar with the reins, the horse-man who knows how to tease, to stroke, to fondle the mare, winning her acceptance.

"He's like a young man lusting for a young woman," Lena thought.

He knew how to manage women's clothes, and he disarrayed hers now, only slightly, but enough. Lena realized that she didn't have to manage things between them as she had to do with Rudolph. She gave up to Juleo. He could handle it.

"Take it easy," he told her. "Take it easy."

They stayed behind the panels for a long time. Lena found a deep contentment in letting someone strong take control. She could have stayed there forever. Eventually, however, like Adam and Eve, they had to leave this Garden.

They parted in front of the showroom and walked away from each other, as if they were strangers, which Lena acknowledged was what they were.

Lena took the elevator down. She thought Juleo rode down on the escalator.

Rudolph was looking through the audio tapes. He had bought books, blank video tapes, compact discs, post cards, index cards and a lot of supplies for his computer.

"Did you get your shopping done?" he asked. "Did you get a nice present?"

"I got the nicest present I've ever had." she told him.

"Well, what is it? When can I see it?"

"It's being engraved," she said, "I'll come back and get it tomorrow." She would select something then, which could be engraved and charged on one of her charge cards.

She realized that Juleo had been empty handed when they left the furniture showroom. They had both forgotten the package with the hat. They left it on the floor where Juleo had set it down. She burst out laughing.

"You are in a good humor," Rudolph said. "We must shop together more often."

Lena felt more maternal toward him than she did the children. "I haven't done anything to hurt him," she told herself. "We'll benefit. The present I got will be his present, too. Tomorrow morning, I'll wake up thinking about Juleo, and the enchantment will be there, and I will lift Rudolph up into the enchantment." In the future, Lena would make love to Rudolph, but she would be thinking of Juleo. Juleo said she made the things around her beautiful. This would be his present, every day.

"I wonder if Juleo remembered the hat and went back for it," she mused. "I hope he did. I hope he did."

She offered to help Rudolph carry his packages. Together, they left the store.

GEORGETOWN, SOUTH CAROLINA

"Matilda of God" was written in Georgetown 1990. Can a man find the way to relate properly to mule and his broader life at a Methodist camp meeting?

The writer was very sick after this and there was a break in his output. One long story was written in 1992, two stories in 1995, and two in 1996.

After the writer's serious illness, he spent much time working on novels.

MATILDA OF GOD

Beauramus walked with sauntering steps, sometimes kicking at a particular piece of gravel which lay on the road . A bit of rock with special individuality would catch his eye and he would kick it. He liked to see how high in the air he could make it rise, and how it would sail before it landed. He liked best to catch up to a piece of rock he had already kicked and kick it again.

At other times, he would stop kicking the gravel and would compare the red color of the clay of the ditch bank with the lighter color clay of the roadbed. He was not hurrying, and he was not out walking for enjoyment. In fact, he felt a solemnity, a gnawing unhappiness, about the trip up the road he was taking.

Now and then, he turned his face, which was too young to be wizened, too pinched to give an appearance of youth, up toward the sun. His cheeks were wrinkled and hairy. His forehead was high and white. His mouth was wide and his lips were thin, above a wide but short chin. When he looked upward, he squinted at the dazzling Mississippi sky and the spike trees which pierced it. Such trees were what remained of the piney woods, which was gone. The sky, he had learned in church, would remain until the end of time, when there would be a new heaven and a new earth. Ambling along in the spring sunshine, he shaded his eyes with the back of his simian hand.

Matilda walked behind him taking long swinging strides. He held in his fingers, almost absently, the short rope which dangled from her halter. She was such a good mule that she didn't have to wear a bit or have reins to guide her.

Beauramus was taking Matilda up to Kristeen and Et's house to see if he could sell her to Et. He wasn't hurrying because he faced his parting from Matilda with a feeling of sickness in his heart. Matilda was his friend. However, he had thought everything through and he felt it was best for Matilda and for him, too, that he sell her and close out his affairs and leave Hovie Junction. He would proceed to do this unless a way might be shown him that would change his mind.

One truth about Beauramus was he didn't want to be shut of his mule. He had come to rely on her. He would be plucking out his eye, but he had to break away from her.

Beauramus had decided to leave Hovie and to live in New Orleans, but he would settle Matilda in a good place before he went. It was not her fault he was going, so she must not suffer for it.

335

Beauramus stood with Matilda beside the road while a car passed which was filled with people who were dressed up, wearing suitcoats and white shirts and ties and Sunday dresses. He was careful that Matilda was out of harm's way. The people were going up to the Methodist Campground which was located just beyond Kristeen's daddy's place. The Methodists were having camp meeting this week. That night there would be scores of cars parked in the muddy field in front of the preaching shed and the sound of the preaching and the shouting would be heard, all the way down to Et and Kristeen's house, and the singing.

Beauramus had talked with Et a few days before about Matilda. He wanted to sell Matilda to Et because Et was a good boy who had come up from Wide Beach to marry Kristeen and since he had been living in Hovie Junction he had been like someone that had lived there all his life. His mother had money and property back in Wide Beach and she didn't like for her son to be married to Kristeen, but any man could see why Et had been bound to marry like he had when he got the chance.

Beauramus had decided to leave Mississippi and go to live in New Orleans. This move would eliminate some of the things about his life which were unsatisfactory. He worked for Mr. Myron Johnson cleaning up, picking up and hauling away the slabs from Mr. Johnson's two-man sawmill, and it was hardly any living at all. He would hitch Matilda to the wagon and they would hang around all day, with Matilda nodding and dozing and Beauramus tossing the slabs into the wagon, until finally when the mail shut down they would go home. Beauramus would store the slabs at his aunt's house, where he lived. He had a large pile of the wood piled against the rusty fence behind the house. Later he would saw the slabs up into lengths with the one-man crosscut saw. The wood would then fit in a wood stove and he and Matilda would go around and try to sell it for firewood.

People had told him about New Orleans. He had made up his mind that he was going. He would get a job as a stevedore. He would join the union. He would get a job unloading the banana boats and have plenty of money. Then, he would get an apartment, such as city people live in, and have a car too.

He never told himself, even if he knew them, all the reasons why he was going. One reason was, he acknowledged to himself, he was going to the city because he had been told that he could meet women there who'd go out with him, and who'd come stay with him at his apartment. Women around Hovie Junction made fun of him. They'd call, " Beauramus, Beauramus, come cram us! Come cram us!" When he'd make a move toward them, they'd begin to screech with laughter in their high-pitched voices and run away.

Women in New Orleans, when he had a good on the docks and his own money in his pocket, would not act like this.

Beauramus carefully explained to himself that the reason he was going to New Orleans was to make money. He was too ashamed to face the truth about himself in the light of women at home. It wasn't just that he was ugly. Lots of men were ugly, but Beauramus looked like a monkey. He was skinny and hairy, and he moved like a monkey. His posture and his stance were like a monkey's.

He had a monkey's eyes. Women were disgusted or amused by him.

He said he was going to the city so he could accumulate something for himself. In Hovie Junction, people were always saying that a person should work and save and accumulate something. Like Et and Kristeen.

Ed and Kristeen had built a house on her daddy's land after they got married. Kristeen had been Et's childhood sweetheart when she had gone down to Wide Beach as a school girl. She'd run around with a lot of men when Et was off in the service but none of them suited her. When Et came back, she married him and she had been satisfied ever since. She didn't run around any more, but people remembered when she did.

Et was built light, but strong as a steel guitar string, lean and angular. He had tanned skin and dark hair. His face was thin and his smile was slow. It took a while for his smile to get to his eyes. When it did, people could see he was a right pleasant fellow. Kristeen watched him all the time, liking to see him move. She liked most to watch him when he worked. He handled himself real well and Kristeen would sit, as still as a snake charming a bird, smiling and staring at him.

When Beauramus came up in Et's yard, he tied Matilda to a sapling that grew near the fence, and Matilda backed around so that the tail part of her was against the fence and then she lifted up her back foot and began swinging it slowly backward and forward. Her left foot was tender and she would find something to lean on and hold it up and let it sway that way because it seemed this made her easy.

Beauramus patted her on her neck and rubbed her nose with the palm of his hand. Matilda was with him all the time. When they weren't working, he would go out to her stall and stand beside her. He would put his arm up on her shoulders and rest his face against her neck. Sometimes, he would just be so lonesome and unhappy he would start to cry, and the tears would stand on Matilda's reddish brown hair and smile in the sunlight, 'til they rolled along and dropped off the ends. He would shake with sobs and make a strange groaning noise and Matilda would stand perfectly still and once in a while she would twitch one of her ears.

Beauramus hated going to New Orleans because he would have to get shut of Matilda before he could go. Matilda couldn't live in New Orleans. It would be all right for Matilda and Beauramus to be together in New Orleans, Beauramus being busy with the banana boats and the women and all, but there wouldn't be a place fixed for her.

Et and Kristeen only had one room in their house. The house was built of wood scarcely better than the slabs that Beauramus hauled away from the mill. They had put black builders' felt on part of it but they ran out before they got the south side done. The winter wind from the south didn't bother them much. It was the north wind that cut.

Mississippi had been a lot warmer before the piney woods had been cut away. Now, the wind could come, without interference, blasting straight down the right of way of the Illinois Central all the way from Chicago.

Kristeen and Et asked Beauramus inside and Kristeen watched how Et shook hands with Beauramus and listened to everything he said.

"I'm thinking about doing some farming next year," Et said. Kristeen's daddy had a lot of land that he didn't grow anything on. Everyone knew that he ran a still. Et worked with him running the still. That was the only work they did. Most of their time was spent chopping wood to fire the still. Once or twice a month, Kristeen would go to the big store to buy supplies. "If I can get her cheap enough, I'll buy your old mule. Since I hear you're going out of the state to live."

"How much do you call cheap?" Beauramus asked. "Matilda is a fine mule."

"I know she is," Et said. "You work her every day and she works good for you, but she is getting old. I reckon a few more years is all she's got."

Et didn't own anything. The land his house was built on belonged to Kristeen's daddy and so the house did, too, although Et had built it mostly with his two hands. Kristeen's car was outside. It was a two-seated Model A Ford. Back before Et came home and married Kristeen, she had found this car parked beside the road near her daddy's house. She had brought it up to her daddy's house and called the sheriff about it. He had told her that if no one claimed it she could have it. No one did claim the car and, after a while, the sheriff got her a title to the car fixed up. The car was grey, not black like most A-Model Fords.

"I don't know what to say," Beauramus said. "I can't just let Matilda go for little of nothing. She's just too fine of a mule."

"I'll fix some coffee," Kristeen said, jumping up. She was a beautiful red-head. She had a white skin without the freckles that marred so many redheaded people. Her eyes were blue and she had learned, herself, how to use makeup. But her figure was the thing that stopped men in their tracks and started them sniffing around like hungry hound dogs. Now, Beauramus watched her walk to the coal oil stove and lift the coffee pot and he forgot what it was that he and Et were talking about.

Gossip had it that the way Kristeen was stacked was what had got her the grey Ford and she hadn't really found it. Some man had given it to her and she had been afraid to carry it home, so she made up the story about finding it.

"I've got to get Kristeen to carry me down to the store in a little bit," Et said. "She won't let nobody drive her car but her," he added, explaining things.

"Matilda is good at hauling wood," Beauramus said. "She'd be good to haul up your wood for you."

"I figure she'd be worth what I'd give you for her. I'm not saying she ain't worth a good bit. It's just, I don't have it."

Kristeen had poured the coffee in cups and she brought Beauramus a cup, and the mayonnaise jar they used as a sugar bowl. They were out of cream until she went to the store. Her daddy didn't have a cow that was milking right then, so they had to use canned cream.

Beauramus put sugar in the coffee absentmindedly, wanting, but afraid, to look down Kristeen's dress front when she leaned over him.

Kristeen sat down and crossed her legs. She pulled her skirt down a little.

She knew Beauramus was looking at her. "I'm going to take a bath before we go to the store," she said. She got up and poured water from their drinking bucket into the kettle and set it on the stove, moving the coffee pot to another burner. "You're going to have to draw me the water," she told Et.

"If you leave that fire burning much longer on that stove, it's going to get hotter in here than it is already," Et said. He got up and went outside to where the washtub hung on a large nail, which was driven into the side of the house, and brought the tub inside. He set it down in the middle of the floor. Then, he made three trips out to the bucket well, with the drinking bucket, and returned and poured the water into the tub. It was cold, just coming up out of the ground. They sat in silence for a few minutes until the kettle began to sing on the stove. Kristeen dropped a bar of soap into the tub and then poured the hot water from the kettle into it.

"We have to go outside while my wife takes a bath," Et said.

As soon as Beauramus and Et were outside, Et put his foot up on an old sawhorse that had been standing there since they built the house. He spit on the ground, deliberately, so as not to get any on anything that might ever be useful. There was some lumber standing against the house and some broken bricks lying on the ground. "I can't give you more than eight dollars for Matilda," Et said.

Beauramus felt his skin growing hot all over his body. There was a rushing sound in his ears. He almost could not hear Et. He was thinking that, inside the house, Kristeen was getting ready to take her bath. In his mind's eye, he could see her, graceful as she was, reach down and lift the hem of her skirt, pulling the dress up so that more and more of her leg was revealed. Her dress was a cotton one, a print with light blue flowers on a white background. It might have been made out of a couple of those feed sacks they had down at the store, where the feed was put up in printed cotton. The material of the dress looked rough. Whatever it was made of, the dress covered Kristeen's delicious curves, the smooth, easy sweep of her hips and thighs. By now, Beauramus envisioned, she would have the dress hiked up above her waist and she'd be taking it with both hands to raise it over her head.

"If eight dollars is not enough," Et said, "I can't do no better. Eight dollars is a lot if you stop and think about it." Beauramus could see, in his imagination, Kristeen standing in her panties and her big bra and he could hardly stand it. "Matilda is getting mighty old for a mule," Et said.

Beauramus sat down on the sawhorse and leaned forward with his fingers pushed into his overalls pockets. He could hardly breathe. To him, it seemed hot as August. He could see Kristeen unsnapping her big bra and throwing it down and then he could see her stepping out of her panties. He could see her big breasts and the smooth skin on her waist and he could see the red hair... "Et, I didn't hear what you said," Beauramus said.

"I said eight dollars," Et looked at Beauramus strangely. "Man," he said, "are you all right?"

By now, Kristeen would have her feet in the water and, Oh, God! She would sit right down into the water with her knees all drawn up under her chin and she would take the washcloth and take the soap and begin to wash herself.

A surge of love for Matilda went through Beauramus and he wanted to go and put his arm around her neck and sing to her for a minute and maybe he'd cry because Kristeen was so beautiful.

He could imagine Kristeen with her knees spread out so they touched the top rim of the tub on each side of her and maybe she would lean forward so that the tips of her breasts would touch the water under the soapsuds. He could imagine how the soap bubbles would be popping next to her breasts, showering her skin with tiny sprays as each one broke. He hoped it would send a sensation through her that would delight her and maybe make her passionate. Maybe she'd start breathing short and she'd pick water up with her hands and let it pour back into the tub, rolling down her breasts.

"If I'd be that soap," Beauramus said out loud, "I know just where I'd sliiiide."

Beauramus realized he was thinking like this about Et's wife with Et standing there right in front of him and he became afraid and, turning, ran to Matilda and untied her bridle and dragged her away, out of Et's yard, into the red-clay road. For a moment, he thought he would lead her home, running, excited, needing to be there with her, needing something from her, needing relief.

But, he didn't run toward his home. He went the other way, up the clay road to where the Methodists were holding camp meeting. They were having afternoon preaching, but not many were in the tin-roofed shed listening to the preacher. Most of the Methodists who were there, were asleep in the cabins. They would stay up late that night and the preaching would go on in earnest.

Beauramus tied Matilda to a pine sapling and went inside the shed with its rough benches and sawdust floor and sat down.

"We are all tempted"' the preacher shouted. He was a short man with a round stomach. His sermon was just gathering momentum like a train taking a long uphill grade, gathering speed, gathering power. Beauramus didn't think much of the preacher'S looks, but he knew he was a man of God. He had a large bald spot on top of his head with a circle of dark hair running around it. "All of us have to fight temptation!" he roared. "None of us is free from it. It's no use to run from weakness, like Jonah ran when God called him to go to Ninevah. We need to stay and face our temptations. We need to battle them like men!"

A few people were scattered about on the benches. There was an elderly man sitting on the second row bench at the far right-hand side and he shouted, "Temptation! Oh Lord, help us to fight it!"

Beauramus sat on a bench near the back and put his head down on his knees. "I can't stay and fight," he thought. "My temptation is too strong." He was breathing hard and shaking. He saw an ant walking in the shavings on the floor. "As small as that ant is to me, that's how insignificant I am to God." His nose began to tickle like it always did when he smelled the sawdust down at the sawmill. He knew that in a few minutes he would begin to sneeze.

"One thing you better guard against," the preacher shouted, turning angry, "you better not say when you're tempted, You're tempted of God. God does not tempt men to do evil." He said this last sentence, not loudly, but with dreadful intensity and the old man on the right shouted, "Amen!" Beauramus put his hands up beside his face.

"You are tempted by your own lust, which is stirred up by the Devil," the preacher fairly bellowed out, and the old man shouted, "Amen!"

Beauramus jumped up and ran down the sawdust aisle, stumbling and tripping. He threw himself against the podium of rough pine boards at the preacher's feet. "I am lusting mightily," he cried out.

The preacher, more agile than his build would have proclaimed, leapt down beside Beauramus and put his arms about him. "Here, boy, you're taking it mighty hard. Jesus can forgive you. He can cleanse you of your lust. He can do it easy. You don't have to strain so."

"I don't see how He's going to do it," Beauramus groaned. "I've got a secret sin. The lust is big. Just a few minutes ago it happened," he said. "I was lusting after a man's wife with the man standing right in of me."

"Oh, that's bad," the preacher told him. His face reddened. "I'm Brother Hartsell," he said. He extended Beauramus his hand. "What's your name?"

"My name is Beauramus. I don't know if it's my real name or not. It don't seem like it could be. But, that's what folks call me."

"Beauramus, we are going to pray together and Jesus is going to heal you of your lust." Brother Hartsell made Beauramus kneel down in the sawdust and shavings and the old man got up and came over with them. Brother Hartsell knelt down and began to pray. "This brother is lusting," he prayed in a loud voice. "This brother is greatly afflicted by his lust. This brother wants this evil, dirty, degrading, unmanly lust taken away from him. He wants his heart to be cleansed of his terrible sin. He has confessed to me his lust is monumental."

Beauramus sneezed. "It is monumental," he cried. He burst into tears and his body shook. "It's not just for women," he said. "I lust after about everything. I'd even lust for the golden calf if there was such a thing." He was about to tell what was really troubling him, he trusted Brother Hartzell that much. Fortunately, he sneezed again.

Then, Beauramus felt removed from the space at the foot of the rough altar in the Methodist Campgrounds shed. He felt himself lifted up to a place he had never been before, where it was clean.

All at once, Jesus let him know what he should do. "Brother Hartzell," he said, "I want you to come outside with me and dedicate Matilda to God."

"Who's Matilda," Brother Hartzell asked.

"Matilda's my old mule. She's standing outside, probably swinging her tender foot right now, kind of holding it up and swinging it."

"Is that why you want your mule blessed?" Brother Hartzell asked, "because she's got a sore foot?"

"No. It's more important than that. It's very important."

"Well, I'm going to do it for you," Brother Hartzell said. He wheezed when he was getting to his feet. He walked slowly and with great dignity. The old man came alone, to witness the sight. The others in the shed sat looking blankly ahead, acting as though they had seen and heard nothing. When they got outside, Brother Hartsell went right up to Matilda's head and blessed her and dedicated her to God just as serious as anything. He touched her on her nose and took her bridle and handed it to Beauramus. "Your mule's all right now," he said.

Beauramus felt ecstatic. Tears flowed from his eyes. He put his head against Matilda's long head and put his hands on her neck up behind her ears. "You're safe now, Matilda," he said. "You're safe."

Some of the people who had been sitting inside had come outside and they were standing apart from Beauramus when lie spoke so they misunderstood him and thought he said to Matilda, "You're saved now." Well, they knew the mule was not saved. They would speak to Brother Hartsell about it later. Now, they began to drift away and go inside and pretty soon no one was outside but Matilda and Beauramus.

Et came striding across the rutted ground where so many cars would park again that night for the service. The field in front of the preaching shed was muddy. The cars' tires had cut deep the night before.

"Where'd you run off to?" Et asked. "Kristeen is all ready to go to town, but I wanted to find you before we went. What do you want to do about selling Matilda for the eight dollars I offered you?"

"I'm not going to New Orleans," Beauramus said. "I was just going over there because I thought I could get women in the big city. I'm going to stay here. Maybe I can get a woman here, pretty and nice like you've got. If I can't, I'll get by. I'm going to keep my job at the sawmill and I'm going to keep Matilda."

"All right," Et said. "You know what you want to do."

"I've had Matilda dedicated to God," Beauramus said.

"What'd you do that for," Et asked. "Do you think people will treat her nicer now that she's dedicated to God?"

"Being dedicated to God will protect her ," Beauramus explained.

"Matilda didn't need no protection," Et said. "Nobody has ever been mean to Matilda. Everybody around knows her and knows she's your mule."

"It will protect her from me," Beauramus said. "it will protect her from what I might have done to her."

"Oh," Et said. His smile started and spread over his face in understanding. "You go ahead on," he said. "You and Matilda will be all right."

GEORGETOWN, SOUTH CAROLINA

"The Unkindest Cut" was rewritten in Georgetown in 1992. The time and place of the writing of the first draft is not known. The first draft was written when the writer was still under the father fixation, probably in Charlotte in the '60s.

A middle-aged, blue-collar worker is disturbed by the influence upon himself of his dead father. He is haunted as surely as Hamlet was. He doesn't attack the problem with any more wisdom than Hamlet did. The ghost of his father is within himself. He is also haunted by the apparition of the boy which he once was. His hauntings result in his committing an irreversible act of violence.

The writer used much true detailed autobiographical data in this story, which was not his usual way of proceeding. His stories are usually more subtle and symbolic, sub rosa. This must have been the last of "the father stories" where the writer finally takes in hand the root of the chancre, blasts the festering father and the bleeding crippled child our of his system.

The story was originally written straight out, but vas later placed in a picture frame in order to make it more understandable and to add the contrast of the protagonist and ghosts with normal police officers. The cops are of a different breed. They bring a different air. Their careful, scientific approach to things makes the beguiled protagonist seem even more loony than he is.

Throw papa from the train!

THE UNKINDEST CUT

Frank Galley had never before entered the Baytown police station by the back door. He had come in by the front door several times, into the waiting room with its cheap, plastic furniture, where he spoke through the glass to give or get information. Once or twice, he had spoken to the desk sergeant or the dispatcher. This had been when he had business to transact, such as any everyday citizen on occasion have, with the police.

However, what was happening now was entirely different. This time they had brought him here in a police car, and he had been led in through the back door to the large interrogation room where the machine for establishing the fact of or extent of intoxication in an individual, stood. Back here there was none of the cheer of the exterior of the building, with its neat-cut grass and its flags, or the little waiting room, with its potted plants. This room had no windows, grey cement walls, and a floor like dark water where a culprit might tumble in and drown.

He was just an everyday citizen, and he had not been drinking. That was patent.

Everyone ignored the machine for determining the degree of intoxication in people suspected of being drunk, but the machine dominated the room. It seemed to say that modern technology would defeat the wrongdoer no matter how clever he might be. It could ferret out the truth, no matter what lies, what subterfuges, what artifices or motives were employed. Frank sat on one of the steel chairs and looked at it. His head was confused. His hand shook. This interlocking mechanism of men and machines, this small bureaucracy, he suddenly found himself in conflict with, was strong. He knew its might, that it could be devastating and overwhelming.

"I've got to take a piss," he said. They let a uniformed officer take him to the bathroom.

They apologized to him because he had to wait. Two detectives were coming out to talk with him. When he got back to his chair, he immediately felt as though he needed to go back to the bathroom. "God, I'm nervous!" he said.

The arresting officers looked at him knowingly, and then let their eyes meet. "He's flipped," one of them whispered. The other one thought it too.

It was 10:36 on Halloween night when he was brought in. He didn't know the time. He didn't hear what the officers whispered. He should have listened to everything, but he didn't try to hear anything. He wanted to disappear. He stared at the breathalyzer, hardly blinking, hardly taking a breath, bating his breath. "If I can keep from breathing, nothing will happen to me," he thought. He would keep as quiet as a mouse licking cotton.

The detectives arrived. "I'm Don Hart, Mr. Galley. Don't get up." Don Hart smiled, leaned over and shook Frank's sweating hand. He was a young person. Frank could see that he was sharp, alert, ready for whatever might come up. In a few minutes, he would enter information about Frank into a computer. Frank would suspect the officer had been familiar with computers since an early age. When he worked with the computer, his strong hands would caress its keys. His hands were tanned, with an even coating of dark hair, moving with firm command, a college ring, another ring which could have been a wedding ring, well-tended nails. Surgeon's hands, Frank thought. In a crowd of men, Frank would have dubbed Don Hart a physician, never a law enforcement officer. He had the firm, reassuring manner of a family practice doctor, a person to believe in.

Ken Cayuse stood by, perfectly still, hiding behind an inscrutable expression, slightly disdainful of cast. He was a muscular man, lean and powerful, with sensuous big-cat movement. "He must work out an hour a day," Frank thought. "Probably an airtight schedule which nothing is allowed to derail, his life running like the trains." A great roaring locomotive, that was Ken Cayuse.

"We might as well get on with this," Ken Cayuse said, gruffly. Frank saw through his pose, staged to deliberately show an attitude of impatience and irritation, bearing the implied threat of a more violent reaction to come. Frank knew he was being intimidated. Yet, he could not fight back. He was afraid. The entire scene, the unwelcoming room, the uniformed officers, the detectives, the terrible machine, all of it robbed him of his power to resist. Ken Cayuse's Cherokee eyes in his white man's face bored into Frank as if he could read Frank's soul. "This looks pretty cut and dried to me." He imagined he saw some little speck of lint on his trouser leg at the outside of his right ankle. He bent down, so that all the muscles in his back stretched under his shirt, and he slapped the cuff of his pants with violent swats which made Frank cringe away from him. He stood erect and looked down on Frank. "We might as well take it upstairs and get it over with." His disposition was manifestly unpleasant, Frank comprehended.

Frank had taken business management courses at the air filter plant. He had supervised men. He knew the trick, which could be employed to get and maintain an advantage in a confrontation. He knew the meaning of the maneuvers of Ken Cayuse. In spite of this, he was afraid of him.

Frank found that, ingratiating as Don Hart was, Ken Cayuse was equally terrifying. It was a game for children. He wanted to sob and run away. He rose to his feet, struggling to find his lost equilibrium, something steady to grasp and hang on to. He was only an everyday citizen who worked at the air filter plant. He spent every day in the laboratory, and he didn't bother anyone. Anyone at the plant would be willing to put in a good word for him. Everybody liked him. He wished now that just one of his many friends could be here with him, but of course none of them knew about what had happened.

Frank was taken up a flight of stairs, across the courtroom where city court was held, and into a small room which was furnished sparsely with a table and three chairs. "We want you to sit over there," Hart said. Frank sat down in a chair behind a table, facing the door. The detectives sat in two chairs, side by side, across from him. "We want you to make a statement."

Frank decided not to make it too easy. "I will," he said, "if I can be allowed to tell the whole story from beginning to end. I don't think I can make myself understood if I tell only part of it." He kept watching his hands, grasping at each other, twisting. "I wouldn't want to tell just the end of it."

"We know the end of it." Cayuse said, his voice hard. "A little boy came to your upstairs apartment with his pathetic paper bag, to beg trick-or-treat candy from you, and somehow he fell off the stairs and onto the front of your parked vehicle. Among other things, his neck was broken. The child is dead."

Frank lifted his hands and placed them over his ears. He looked wordlessly from one to the other of the detectives. A moan, which was almost inaudible, escaped from him but he did half-moan, half-sob from the pain of it.

"You can tell the story any way you want to," Hart told him. "We would like to record what you say."

"You waived your right to a lawyer and you waived your right to be silent before," Cayuse said. "Do you remember doing that out at your house when the officer put you under arrest?"

"Yes, I remember that."

"You said you wanted to talk. So now, talk."

"Let me kind of lay the groundwork," Hart said. The recorder was running. "Your name is Frank Galley. Fifty years of age. You live at 517 1/2 Castle Street. It's an upstairs apartment above a coin-operated laundry. You've lived at this address for about fifteen years. You work for Klean Air Filter Corporation, also for about fifteen years. You've never been in any trouble. Everybody says you're a fine fellow, everyone you work with. You don't mix with many people except those who work at the air filter plant. You stay to yourself. I believe you take care of your aged mother. Who's taking care of her tonight?"

"I don't know," Frank told him.

"We'll check it out," Cayuse said. "Let's get to last night. You left your outside light on. You wanted trick-or-treaters to feel welcome to come to your door. You had candy to give them. It looks pretty bad to me that you invited someone to your house, put on an open invitation to one and all, and then got mad with one who came so that you shoved him down the stairs. What did the boy do to cause you to do that?"

"Was it an accident?" Hart asked. "Did he accidentally trip and fall?"

"It wasn't exactly an accident," Frank admitted.

"You pushed him," Cayuse stated.

"I have to tell it from the beginning," Frank said.

"Let him." Hart said to Cayuse. "We told him he could. Maybe that's the only way he can explain it."

* * * *

The first time I saw the boy was in 1989 on Halloween, at about eight thirty or nine o'clock at night. I never fail to buy candy for the children at Halloween. My mother favors it. She says it is a thoughtful and kindly thing to do. I turn on my outside light so the trick-or-treaters will come. I want them to come. I want to do my part. They get a special fright coming to my apartment because they have to climb the outside stairs. The darkened windows of the laundry are spooky. The wind whines through the chinaberry tree, deep below in the darkness. I simply try to be a part of what the community is doing.

Lots of kids had come that night, most of them with parents hovering in the background, all of them dressed up in scary outfits, faces painted or masked, making their horrible noises, stretching out their hungry hands for treats. After a while, they stopped coming. I was about to turn off the outside light when the boy we're talking about came. He was in his everyday clothes. No one was with him. He looked too old to be out on Halloween night, but he came straight upstairs and knocked on the screen door and asked if he could have some candy. His blond hair was curly and tangled, damp with sweat where it lay on his forehead, it needed cutting, and ragged ringlets in back lay on his neck, which was none too clean. His sweatshirt was grey and not sufficient to keep him warm, but was all he had with him. His trousers had spots and tears. His shoes were badly scuffed. The boy's hands were chubby and lined in the creases with dirt, and I knew before I touched one of them in passing the candy they were clammy, cold but sweaty. He was pinch-faced. He looked as though a great finger and thumb had pressed the sides of his face, beginning at the forehead, squeezing ever harder in descent until the face, drained of color, ended in a weak, pointed chin under a pouting mouth. I both pitied and was repulsed by the miserable child. He grabbed greedily for the candy, stuffing it clumsily into a crumpled sack which he carried.

"Aren't you too old to be out trick-or-treating?" I asked. He must have been ten years old or older, but he had the solemn, appraising, wise eyes of someone limitlessly aged, such as some fearfully deprived children do. I hated him then. I hated him on that first visit. I remembered myself when we first lived back in the piney woods, when I was a towheaded kid, before my hair turned dark. I didn't want to remember this. The boy made another grab at the candy bowl. He managed to take another handful. He stood a few steps from me, on the porch, and seemed to sneer at my discomfiture. His whole attitude was one of scorn. His appraising eyes had become judgmental.

"Why don't you get you a better car than that piece of shit sitting down there?" he asked.

"I don't care about having a nice car," I said. I realized I was on the defensive. I couldn't simply tell him it was none of his business. I had, in 1989, a 1977 Ford station wagon which had been wrecked before I had it. It had a very bad body, but a powerful engine. It served my purposes.

"I think you reckon you're not supposed to have a car any better than that," the boy said.

"It's a lot better than my mother ever had," I muttered, not caring if he heard me or not, but he heard. He raised his head in a gesture bespeaking his wisdom and my stupidity and then went slowly down the long straight stair, looking back over his shoulder now and again, his every movement revealing the contempt he felt for me.

I went inside and flipped off the outside light so no one else would come. The boy had opened up a train of thought that seemed to obsess me. I don't like to get upset, because I believe that when I get upset it upsets my mother, but I couldn't help it, The boy had a curious and sinister effect on me.

I began to talk about the old days before we had come up out of the piney woods and the car we had, the '29 A-Model Ford, which my mother always drove.

My father never drove a car.

"Remember," I said, "remember Mother, how much anxiety you felt for all of us? Remember the years that you constantly felt sick, your stomach bothering you, day in and day out, because of the insecure position we were in? It was fear made you sick. You were forced to worry. No one else did. R e m e m b e r the car? We never knew when it would break down, stop running, die completely. The family would be lost without it. We had farm produce to take to town and sell. We had groceries to buy. We had business to transact.

"Night after night, you'd have the same dream. We were in town and you couldn't remember where you'd parked the car. You said it was we two you'd dream about. We'd walk and walk, frantic, searching and searching and searching, and we'd never find that car before you'd wake up?

"You told that dream so often, it seemed that I had dreamed it too, or we dreamed it together."

I knew I didn't have a good car, but the old station wagon suited me. I didn't see why that kid had to disparage it and start me to thinking about things which are best forgotten. In my position, maybe I should have a better car. Maybe people expect it. Maybe they whisper and chuckle about it. But, it was none of that arrogant kid's business. What he did was cause me to upset my whole house. It wounded me. Then, through days and evenings, and through weeks, it cost me time and trying to get over the hurt which happened to me that Hallow-een night.

* * * *

I did not see the boy for a year. I saw other children on the streets, as I went to and from work, in stores or at fast-food restaurants. Sometimes, I would sit on my porch, high up above the sound of them, watching as they ran along the sidewalk. Some of then, I recognized as children who had come to my door at Halloween, growing from year to year, too old to trick-or-treat any more. Win-ter turned to spring. Summer changed to fall. However, I never, during that time, caught a glimpse of the dirty, haughty boy.

Even so, on Halloween night in 1990, after the other children had come and gone, he came. It was about nine o'clock. He was wearing a grubby sweatshirt again. The wind was penetratingly cold, around the corner of the building. It wailed like an abandoned infant, half animal and half man, pleading for the return of its mother. It must have cut him cruelly, but he didn't seem to notice. His face was splotched with sticky dirt and his light hair was uncut, tangled, lying in disarray on his chubby neck. I held my bowl of candy out to him. He grabbed greedily for it, scooping up most of the contents in his first plunge. His pinched white face grimaced in triumph. He backed away, smirking at me, inso-lent or rather, as he had done the year before, he seemed able by his bearing, his facial expression, the slight movement of his hands, to convey his total disdain of me.

I had left the wooden door open part way, but the screen was closed. He sniffed.

"It smells like you've been cooking hamburgers," he said.

I didn't see how he could distinguish an odor apart from his own, since he himself bore an overpowering aroma such as that which reeks from squash be-ing boiled with onions.

"Couldn't you all have something better than that to eat?"

"My mother likes hamburger," I said. "She doesn't have good teeth. I never fix steaks or chops."

The boy smiled, but his smile mocked me. "Why don't you get your mother some better teeth?" He showed a hideous mouthful of blackened and broken teeth of his own. He was no bigger than he had been the year before.

He grabbed again for my candy bowl and got for his crumpled bag the re-mainder of the candy. His hand touched mine and it was cold and clammy. His growth was obviously stunted. He hadn't grown from one year's end to the next. This lay forth a dreary picture of what sort of food he'd had at his home. Alto-gether, he walked in manifest poverty, yet he smirked once again his disdain before making his deliberate, slow-paced descent of the stairs.

Inside, I was distraught. I began to rant and rave. This sort of thing was never good for my mother. She had always been afraid of violence. When I was a child, she had kept hammers and wrenches and anything else which might be used as a weapon picked up and put away to keep my father from killing someone. She was terrified that he had guns in the house. But now, I couldn't suppress what I felt. I was recalling when I was about ten or eleven when my mother had been able to draw some money (a few hundred dollars) from a trust fund of family money that had been left to her. The check had come in the mail and was deposited in the bank. We were in the car, the A-Model Ford, me in the middle, with my mother on the driver's side and my father on the other. My mother seemed happy. Elated.

"I'm going right in the store and buy a pound and a half of hamburger," she said. We hadn't had meat in weeks. We lived on eggs from our chickens, milk from our cow, vegetables we grew, either fresh or canned, bought bread.

"Damn that," my father shouted with great violence. "Damn that! Damn that! We won't touch that money. The money is to he kept for improvements to the farm."

My mother sagged. Next to me, her body touching mine, I felt the joy go out of her. "A pound and a half of hamburger will cost less than two dollars. I like to have a few things that I was always used to." I thought she was going to cry. My father was pale. I could feel him shaking.

He gestured with his hands, which were work worn and trembling. "That's the way people fail in this life. They get the chance to do something better. They get a little money, and instead of keeping it in one piece so they can accomplish something, they piss it away, spending it little by little until it's gone. I'm going to put a stop to this right now." My father chewed a chewing tobacco which was cured with apples. He always smelled of a mixture of tobacco and apple juice. Now, the apple odor seemed to be driven out of all his pores by the heat which was in him. He burned with inappropriate wrath, but his face was cold, paled to a grey color, moisture forming on his cheeks and upper lip. I could see each individual black stubble of beard, each red sprig of beard, each white, sickly strand of beard, standing out against the grey skin, swirled about by the flowing sweat. I felt my mother stiffen.

"It is my money," she said.

My father became self-pitying. He decried his own failure in life, the fact that nothing was his, that he had nothing, gave nothing, was unwanted and unloved. Then, my mother did cry, and he was angry again and shouted at her across me to shut up her blubbering. Finally, he told her to buy the meat. She did and cooked it, but eating it in stony silence, the three of us at the table, the ground beef stuck in our throats.

My home was a shambles again. The boy had caused me to remember many painful things which I didn't want to remember. My house was in turmoil.
I cursed him, wherever he was. Hatred and bitterness, from me, followed him wherever he had gone. I almost believed he had gone to live in Hell until the following year would come. That year, it took me a long time to get over his

abominable Halloween visit.

* * * *

In 1991, I had an uncanny dread of Halloween, a stifling uneasiness which began even before October. I bought my candy and swept my porch and the stairs. Although I had not seen the boy all year, I knew that on Halloween night he would come, and he did, about nine o'clock. I could have escaped him if I had left the light turned off and stayed inside. I had merely not to answer the door, to make myself take no part in Halloween that year. However, I felt some power compelling me to do everything as usual, to be factotum to custom, what the community expected me to be. I recalled an old phrase I had heard. Someone was said to have a "rendezvous with destiny." These words took on significant meaning with me. Could my life be hurtling on toward some ghoulish denouement with fate?

When he came, dressed no differently than before, looking no older, smirking and self-assured. He immediately grabbed for my candy howl with both hands. I snatched it away in anger. He read my look.

"You don't want to do this, do you?" he asked.

"I try to be a good citizen," I said, sounding defensive and very stuffy. "I try to be part of the community. I believe it is the duty of the old to help the young."

"What do you live on, a cloud?" he asked, "You sound like a beautiful dream. This is not a pretty night like Christmas. We're out here to get all we can get. You're a fool." I felt a blind, mindless rage push its way up from the pit of my stomach. I snatched his crumpled paper bag away from him and dumped all my candy into it and handed it back to him.

"Just go and leave me alone," I said.

In a flash, I knew something. I went inside. I could think of nothing else. I knew that, almost, I had acted exactly like my father. I had almost demonstrated a tantrum. I felt so disappointed in myself that I talked rapidly, incoherently, wildly, trying to express how I ached, how things inside of me tore at one another, sending drum rolls of anguish up to my brain. I felt a hammering pulse at the base of my skull, and all the time I was trying to convince myself that I was not like my father.

My mother didn't need for this to happen. It seems, looking back on it, the scene lasted for hours. I began to remember   the time I had been at the big store with my father and one of my friends. The son of one of my school teachers was working behind the counter. His mother was like a father and a mother to me, my mentor, my leader, my morality, my dream for the future, my patron saint. Her son, the young man working as a clerk, was only filling in during vacation, trying to make some money for college. Somehow, he failed to wait on my father when his turn came. No one was aware that anything was wrong until my father said loudly and hoarsely, "You don't have to wait on me, Sonny Biggs!" Sonny immediately began to apologize for having overlooked my father and he said he would wait on him at once. Not good enough. My father had started, and his rage had to run its course. He turned grey-faced, shook, his voice became so hoarse that part of the time he could hardly be heard. Then, he would regain his voice and shout out his protest. He leaned close to me and I could smell the strong apple odor of his breath. The odor of the apples and tobacco hung on his clothes. The owners of the store came running. Customers stood open mouthed. "I know you and your mother think you're better than me, Sonny Biggs! You think you're too good to wait on me! I keep my bill paid in here! I conduct myself as an honorable gentleman." I felt disapproval of my father from everyone there, and it centered most deeply in my friend, my peer, who stood beside me. I determined that never would I, in my life, be anything like my father. But, I knew that night in 1991, that I had been, time after time after time, just like him, and this apocalyptic Halloween night almost revealed an example again of how easy it would be for me to give way and rave and scream and push young people around saying things to them that would break them down to smaller size.

My house that night finally became quiet, but the carnage wrought by the boy's visit that Halloween was never to go away. I had experienced the shame of my father's public outbursts all over again, and the knowledge had grown within me, from that spark, just an irritating inkling, to a full-blown awareness that the same rage and defensiveness and sense of having been weighed in the scales and found wanting was in me, ready to burst out in full conflagration. I became scrupulous. A feeling of anxiety at what he had been and what I was made me become watchful of myself. For an entire year, I was soft spoken, kind and understanding of everyone, burying my head, wearing the cloak of righteousness, striking myself blind so that I would not see that thing which dismayed me.

* * * *

And so, Halloween in 1992 came. I knew he'd come. At about nine o'clock he knocked on the door. His knock was imperious, as though he knew that it had been mandated that I go to the door, that I must fulfill some diabolic contract which I had nothing to do with drawing, that I had to do what he wanted. I stepped outside. There was a misty rain. I shuddered with a chill which took hold of me as soon as I stood outside. I handed the boy the whole bowl of wrapped Halloween candy. He emptied it into his bag. A look of satisfaction was on his pinched face. It was the crowing smirk of ownership. He grinned as though he knew that I belonged to him. His will had been stronger than mine. He pushed the empty bowl back into my hands, his hands touching mine. They were colder and clammier than ever, and the odor of him was like a fresh cut squash, a squash that had grown under the big screening leaves of its parent plant, untouched by sunlight, musky, like something that had spread under bricks, mildew.

"You don't ever get any bigger," I said. "You've come here for four years, now. You wear the same clothes, and you don't grow. You don't get any manners either. You don't develop in any way. You're a cretin." The boy stuck his coated tongue out at me and made an obscene gesture with his stubby hand. I backed into the house. I needed to do anything to get out of that cold drizzle. I felt that my bones were rotting in the cold. I needed to do anything to get away from him.

I could hear my father railing at me, hoarse, his voice filled with the sorrow he felt in is disappointment in me. He was talking as though he was making general statements and meaning me. This was one of his favorite ploys. We all, he and I and my mother, knew he was talking about me, but he pretended he was not.

"There is nothing worse than a high-grade moron," he said. "You can take a low-grade moron and teach him how to do something, to work, to operate a simple machine, work in the field and use his hands, but a high-grade moron is just high enough on the scale so that he won't learn these things. At the same time, he is not smart enough to do anything worthwhile. You can't do anything with him, make anything out of him. You might as well take him out and cut his head off, like a chicken when you are getting ready to cook it and eat it." I could see him, ax in hand, grey-faced, lopping off some frightened bird's head. He turned his attack upon me directly. "You can't do anything. Most boys of your age can plow two or three acres before breakfast, or if the car breaks down they can fix it. You can't change a tire." He turned angrily on my mother. "This is what you've made out your beautiful boy," he shouted, scorn and disdain in his voice. "The two of you sit around with your aspirations and your visions, convinced you are so high and mighty. You plan the great things he will do. Well, I can see it written on his face, like a road map to desolation, he hasn't anything to give anyone. All he has to give the world is a handful of shit." My father's voice was fading out like a radio that was losing its signal. "He's just a high-grade moron and you won't believe it. He never will amount to anything. You can mark my words, and when what I say comes true I guess you'll be satisfied."

"Mother," I would cry out. "Don't let him talk about me this way!" But, she would never say anything, and he would accuse me of hiding behind her skirts.

She just let him cut me up. He was the one who should have lifted me up, guided me to be strong, protected me, but instead he slashed at me and slashed at me and slashed at me, dealing me the unkindest cut, that wider castration, that severed my chances to communicate with anyone.

"I put you lower than whale shit," his voice echoed in my small living room. "And, that's at the bottom of the ocean."

I wanted to scream, "Mother! Mother!" But it was no use. It was no use to call Mother.

I smelled the apples.

After that Halloween, I had a very good year. I knew my place in things. I got along with everyone. I knew that I would get along fine if I didn't bother anyone. I did my work and I went home. I was almost invisible. I scarcely breathed. Everybody liked me. If I had any fault at all, it was that I was too good, too helpful, and too kind.

* * * *

I felt that if the boy came on Halloween night that year, it would stretch me to the breaking point. I had done what he wanted. I had become what he wanted me to become. I had lived in the manner he wanted me to live. Was there a covenant, a bond between us, which we were both a party to? Why should there be such an arrangement, one which called only for me to be good, with no return for me? In a worldly contract,   both sides must benefit or there is no contract. Was Satan the third party to this unearthly agreement? If a pledge existed, why was I (the most affected party) not there at its inception?

I had fulfilled the bargain, if there was a bargain. The boy should leave me alone. I had not earned any more of his poisonous mischief. He had made me good. That was good. He had changed me, in my native essence, taken away my self. He had no right to do that. I hated him for that.

I hoped he would let me go in peace to redefine myself, get my identity back. But, even as I bought candy at the supermarket and got prepared for the trick-or-treaters to come, I knew there would be no truce between us. He would come and he would show me what else was to he exacted from me.

He was late this year.

I had begun to feel elated, thinking prayerfully he would not appear. Then, in a paralyzing moment, I heard him stomping up the stairs. I went outside and we faced each other. It was he, looking ten or eleven years old, needing a hair-cut, grimy fisted, rings of dirt on his neck, the fetid, musty odor. Suddenly, I wasn't amiable and gentle and kind. I was enraged. He went over to the screen door and put his hands up at the sides of his eyes and peered inside.

"It sure looks funny in there," he said. "It smells like rotten apples."

That was the way he worked, with seemingly ignorant and innocent remarks. He knew how to put things in motion inside of me. Dark things. Things I daren't speak of, which I could only act out.

I grabbed him by his shoulders and pulled him away from the door. He had upset my mother. His treatment of my mother was his crime. I pushed him toward the stairs. I had to get him away from me, banish him. I couldn't take it. I couldn't stand, this year, to go through what I had put up with for the past four years. I pushed him, and pushed him, and then gave him a well-placed kick.

He fell down the stairs halfway, and then rolled under the railing and dropped. He landed on my station wagon. All that I could think of was that at last, I was rid of him. He was gone.

* * * *

Cayuse and Hart shifted in their chairs. They lived active lives. Sitting so long had made them ache. They were silent for a few moments.

"We'd better get a copy made of that tape," Hart said. "We don't want to lose any of it."

They got up and went and stood outside the door of the room.

"We'll have to arrange to send him up to Columbia for psychiatric evaluation," Cayuse whispered. He seemed more angry than usual. "You stay with him. I'll take the tape downstairs. We've made a night of it."

"We have," he agreed.

* * * *

The next morning the sun shone brightly on Baytown. It was a crisp, invigorating day. It should have been a joyous day, alive with the honking of ducks and the sounds of harbor traffic, the energy of nature and men. Din. It was All Saints' Day. Neither Cayuse nor Hart came down to the station until after lunch. Hart, at once, spoke of troubled sleep. By afternoon, the sunshine was so bright Cayuse had put on his shades. His Cherokee eyes were hidden when he met Dr. John Phar. He would show Dr. Phar only his white man's face. That was enough for the doctor to see.

Dr. Phar was there ahead of them. He had been called in to make a psychological appraisal. This was usually done in cases where someone suffered a violent death administered at the hands of another. If they decided to send Frank Galley to the state hospital, Dr. Phar would draw up the papers. He had already been given the information which was in the arresting officers' report and he heard the tape. He was tamping tobacco in his pipe when the detectives came in. He studied them carefully through dark-rimmed glasses. He looked back into the bowl of his pipe with an air of indifference for the detectives.

Investigators had been busy. And Cayuse and Hart had received information. They leaned toward Dr. Phar, getting closer to him. He did not light his pipe. Carefully, he put it in his pocket.

"We'll give you what we have," Cayuse said. He paused because this was a dramatic moment. "In the first place, there is no mother. Frank Galley lived there alone. He had told people, when he came to Baytown about eighteen years ago, that he would be living with his mother, but no mother ever materialized. However, a lot of the people he worked with at the air filter plant thought he had a mother. He talked about her many times, but none of his fellow workers have ever seen her. They never went to his apartment, or if they did they didn't get inside the door. His friends say he's been known to turn down invitations on his mother's account and things like that, but there was no mother. There never was in Baytown."

"Okay," Phar said. "Okay." He scribbled some notes on a piece of his notepad.

"We got a report from Hungerford, Mississippi, where he grew up," Cayuse continued. "His father, Daniel Galley, killed Frank's mother when Frank was eleven years old. He tried to kill Frank, but Frank got away. Frank was raised by relatives. He never gave them a moment's trouble. It seemed to his kin the murder and violence didn't have any effect on him."

He gave Phar a copy of the report to read.

"Okay," Phar said, looking it over. "I see the mother's name was Eris. Homer's Eris indirectly caused the Trojan War. I wonder if the Galleys knew that about her."

Cayuse and Hart looked at him blankly.

"The first Eris," Phar explained.

"We interviewed the boy's parents," Hart said. "They're completely over-come. It was their only child. The mother won't talk at all. The father can talk. He's a pathetic man, broken. He didn't have anything but his son. But, he's carrying it better than his wife. He gave me the information we needed. They're new people in town. They came from Georgia. They got here about two weeks ago. The father said their boy didn't know anyone in town. He went out trick-or-treating because he was lonely and hoped he'd meet some other kids from his school he could talk to."

Phar sat up straight looked at Hart's face. "Did you verify this? Did they really just come here two weeks ago? That would mean the boy that came to Galley's this year was not the boy that came there on the other Halloween nights."

"We'll have to find out who that boy way, who came in the other years," Cayuse stated in a determined voice. "We'll find out who he was."

"Or what he was," Phar said.

He took the report of the interview with the parents from Hart and glanced over it quickly. "We'll have to get him over to see the judge and make arrange-ments for him to be taken up to Columbia. That's all I can recommend."

"Let's go back to the cell," Cayuse said. "You can see Frank. You can see if you can get any more out of him. That is, if you want to." He took Phar's arm and the three of them went back and were let into the holding cell.

* * * *

"Mr. Galley, I am John Phar," Phar said. "Do you know what has hap-pened?"

"I killed the boy," Frank said in a soft, level voice. Then, he paled and began to tremble. His hands shook. His beard, black and red and white, stood out, stubble by stubble, against his grey face. His voice grew hoarse and harsh. "I've tried to kill him for years," he shouted. He stood up and paced heavily around the cell. "I finally accomplished it. You know, he was ruined."

"Who ruined him, Mr. Galley?"

"Eris," Frank laughed loudly. "I killed the boy and he's dead. He was no good. He deserved to die."

"I don't believe he deserved to die," Phar said. "Please sit down, sir. We can be gentlemen, can't we? You are an honorable gentleman, aren't you?"

"I've always tried to be," Frank said. He sat down.

Phar took out his pipe, but he didn't light it. "Sir, I've told you who I am. I wonder if you will tell me who you are?"

The man sitting in front of Phar put his shoulders back and lifted his head. He looked Phar fiercely in the eye. "Why sir," he answered, "I'm Daniel Gal-ley." His eyes bored into Phar's, conspiratorial, confiding. "I know you knew that."

"Yes, I did know that," Phar said.

Cayuse noticed it first and then the other two did. There was suddenly a strong odor of apples in the room.

GEORGETOWN, SOUTH CAROLINA

"Cedarbird" was written in Georgetown in 1992. A friendly, needy ghost helps two generations of a family.

The ghost here is presented as benevolent and helpful, but also as having a certain self-interest in things. All of this writer's ghosts have the desire to put things in order, attach blame where due, and tie up loose ends.

The writer, when writing this story, had retired from the steel mill. His thoughts drifted back to Mississippi, that sad, barren, cutover land of his youth.

CEDARBIRD

When Miriam Ord strolled outdoors, after dark, she scanned the trees near her house to see if there might be a ghostly figure roosting in one of them. Everyone knew that ghosts hang out at night in cedar trees. That's their favorite kind. There was one phantom Miriam had seen often, swaying white and luminous, with a pale, full moon shining through her ectoplasm; the delicate branches of the cedar, hairy as spiders' legs, almost concealing her.

Sibley said it was only a cedar waxwing, bathed in moonlight, its brown-gray feathers shining like a silver mirror, reflecting the stars. That's the sort of imagery Sibley thought of.

"We sure came through some high old times to get here," Miriam had babbled to Sibley over and over. She was still breathless in the awareness that they had been able to buy this farm. She couldn't stop talking about it.

The Ords were approaching fifty. Already, they had realized their lifelong dream of settling on farm land, on a small tributary of the Wolf River, in what had been a part of the old piney woods of Mississippi.

They were proud of their land, and the old house, which was built of cypress and heart pine before the turn of the century.

For the first time in their lives, they could have as many animals to live with them as they wanted.

Sibley Ord, close-shaven, always wearing dark-rimmed glasses, pale, had begun as a bookkeeper at a naval stores company, upon arriving at home from the Second World War. He had risen in the company, and here they were, owning their own farm. It was cause for excitement.

The Ord daughter, Marcia, stated defiantly that she was thinking of marriage. Miriam hoped to have the wedding in their new farm home, but her heart sank when she thought of what her child was about to do.

"Pete Posey is so nondescript," Miriam told Sibley. "And, not only colorless, but, I think, untrustworthy." Of course, Marcia was twenty-four. Miriam still wanted to smother her under the blanket of her protection.

"I wouldn't hire him," Sibley agreed. "He'd never pass the drug test." At the plant, he had had the power to hire and fire. He saw all man as potential employees. "To Marcia he's as sweet as the scent of pine. She doesn't realize, the first firm, Southern breeze may waft him away."

On this particular night, the moon was full. So splendid for ghosts! Miriam walked about in what would, come next season, be an impressive flower garden. Now, the area was bare, except for clumps of sedge, and thickets of gall berries. Dewberry vines and blackberry bushes grew a little farther along the sandy path. They would reach out raking fingers, to pull at Miriam's hose and dresses when she walked too far that way.

Beyond the blackberries was the wood, with its dwarf pines, its poplars, the lone magnolia tree, and the cedar. Miriam had come out to ponder alone, because the night before she had had a dream.

Once, while Sibley was in North Africa, during the war, when Miriam was still not quite a woman, but almost still an adolescent girl, she had had sleeping dreams. She had burned with a fever, and she had had dreams.

Married to Sibley, she was not given to night dreaming. But, now, after settling into the new place; being excited; she had dreamed again, about a black man, whom she had seen in dreams before. He always had a perplexed and sorrowful expression on his face; his eyes hopeful, pleading. He wanted something from her. Based on what she knew about such things, Miriam supposed that the man bore about him some terrible secret, which he wanted Miriam to find the answer to, so that a great wrong might be righted.

She knew that the name of the black man was Powell. He came from a bygone age. He wore a striped shirt with no collar, a neckerchief, and brogan shoes. His hair was close cropped to his head. He was a powerful man, a working man, a man whose face would have been benevolent if it were not so sad.

After Miriam was sick, that time when Sibley was overseas, the family told her that she had talked in her delirium about people no one had ever heard of. She called for Cord, and Barth, and Powell; and, especially, Minna. She did not call out the name of Sibley even once.

Rumor had it that there was someone other than Sibley in Miriam's life, at that time. People looked across Miriam's bed, the sheets wet with her sweating, and at her reddened face, and their eyes met in silent titillation in their shared knowledge that Miriam had strayed. They fanned the poor prone sick girl, and bathed her head, but they looked, one to the other, accusing her.

But, now it was 1969. Miriam went as near to the cedar tree as the briars would allow her. There was no chalky apparition sitting among the bows. The moon shone through the tree unimpeded.

Since she had dreamed of Powell the night before, she thought that, perhaps, the cedar tree would not be empty. She thought that tonight Minna might visit there.

Miriam knew that she had been a strange one. At the time of her illness, there had been much head shaking over her.

"Miriam has only just now gone through the change from a girl into a woman," someone would wisely say. "Things happen inside a girl's body at a time like that."

Miriam's family did not concern themselves about her dreams. They were part of her growing up.

But, now, she had had a dream once more, and Miriam's body was going through a change again.

Back in the house, where Sibley tried unsuccessfully to make his television set play, Miriam kicked off her flats and sat in a deep chair, the one she always sat in at their old house near the coast.

"What were you doing out there in the dark?"

"Walking."

"Walking?"

"I was nervous."

"Here?"

"Even here. I love this place, but I'm worried sick about Marcia."

"There's little we can do about that."

"Everything we have will be hers someday. Do you want Pete Posey to have everything we've worked for? This house? This land, with all its memories?"

"What memories? We just moved here. We haven't made any memories yet." Sibley leered at her. "Perhaps, we could make a memory tonight?" Hopeful.

Miriam turned to one side, ignoring the overture.

"The house has memories," she said.

When Miriam and Sibley had gone to close the deal with the real estate agent for the farm, the agent, a busty, loudmouthed painted peahen, had talked endlessly, but Miriam didn't hear the barrage of blather.

She was subdued and contemplative. She felt that she had been to this house, on-this somber meander of the river, near this ruined cypress forest before.

"The house is sound." The peahen's delivery was pedantic. "It was built by a businessman-farmer, about 1895, of the best materials to be obtained, most of them from right on the acreage, cut in his own mill. He did quite well; a lumberman, the owner of a waterwheel, which straddled the creek, and powered a sawmill and a cotton gin. One night, the gate to the millpond gave way and the water rushed through, destroying the entire operation. The worst of it was, during the excitement of the gate breaking and the flooding, the lady of the house ran away from her husband with a one-armed man. It's said, they went to Texas."

"I don't think that's right," Miriam said. She had begun to listen.

The peahen looked at her strangely.

"You mean you don't think it was right of them to run off to Texas together?"

"No. I mean I don't think what you've told is correct about what happened. I don't think they went to Texas."

"It seems to be what the husband believed, even into his old age. That's what he always said. There are people here who knew him. He died at ninety-five. It doesn't matter, now." The peahen continued. "That old man never hurt that house any. He stayed there alone. He should have married again, had children, brought the normal wear and tear to the house. He did none of that. He didn't reestablish his business. He was seldom seen. I recall, from when I was a child, there used to be rumors once in awhile that he had died, and was lying dead up there in that house. We kids, frightened to death, would go there and peep in the windows, hoping to see his mouldering body, but the rumors about his death were never true. He'd chase us away, waving a shotgun. He never shot any of us, thank the Lord.

"At last, he did die. He wasn't alone. He knew what was coming. He sent for some people. He died in the hospital down in Hancock County."

"I've had the title checked," Sibley said dryly, "That's what I'm concerned about. I don't care about past tenants."

"Oh, I do," Miriam said. "I think it's sort of nice having a house with a history."

"You go ahead and live in your cobwebs of the past," Sibley told her. "Surrounded by gossipy whisperings. It appeals to me that the roof has never leaked."

The next day, after they signed the papers for the farm, Miriam and Sibley walked down to where the dribbling creek ran through the property. Miriam stooped and picked up a large spike; a nail which had almost rusted through, eaten up by sixty-five years of exposure.

"This is from the old mill," Miriam -told Sibley. "See how high the banks are there? The mill was like a dogtrot house, gabled on each end. It sat astride the river, which was much larger then. Why was that? The waterwheel was beside it, and the mill pond backed up for two-thirds of a mile. The water here dropped for eight feet, over the wheel. I can almost hear the squeaks and grinding noises the wheel made, and the splashing of the water."

"Miriam," Sibley said. "Please don't begin to talk about things you know very little about. How do you know all this?"

"I just know. When I was lying sick, and you were in North Africa, I saw this place, the way it was. There was another war. Touching this old rusty nail brought it all back to me."

The stream might have been larger, as you say. When the forest was cut away, erosion of the land set in, and the little streams like this tended to silt over. It may have been larger, then."

"Oh, Sibley, you do understand!" Miriam cried. "See, the ford was here, near the mill. You can tell where the road was. The stream on this side of the mill must have been small. All the water was retained in the millpond. Only what spilled over the wheel came along here."

"If it was like you say," Sibley said. "There was a mountain of water backed up behind that dam. The sawmill here could have been a big one."

"Let's go to the house. I want to talk with you about Marcia."

Sibley had always left the rearing of Marcia to Miriam. What had he ever understood about girl children? His life had been taken up with the figures on ledger sheets, pens and inks, adding machines and typewriters. Lately, computers.

They sat on the wide front porch in rocking chairs which Miriam had bought. They had had no porch at the old home. Here there were two.

They did not like Pete Posey, period. He was a wormy, bestial sensualist, without an abstract thought in his brain. That was part of the problem. But, the worst of it was that Marcia, attending college, down on the coast, had shared an apartment, at Biloxi, with an airman, for over a year. His name was Chat Westcott, and he was flying over Vietnam. Any day, they might receive word that he was captured or dead.

Chet was a much nicer boy than Pete, and since it was he Marcia had already lived with, her parents felt she should marry him.

Marcia continued to write Chet letters, not wanting to tell him she had had a change of heart about him until he could come home.

"He might get desperate and do something silly. He might put himself into danger and die," Marcia told them. "It would be my fault."

"If you marry Pete, he'll have to know that," Sibley told her.

"Why?" she asked, innocently. "I'd continue to write."

"That's not the way it's done."

"That's how I do it," Marcia said, defiantly. "What would it hurt? Everybody would be happy."

"Your father means it wouldn't be ethical."

Marcia stared at them with wide uncomprehending eyes. Sibley did not try to talk to Marcia after that.

Now, she was coming, with Pate Posey, with plans for getting married during spring break.

Marcia imagined herself a flower child. She was vociferous in her opposition to the war in Vietnam. When Chet received his orders to ship out from Keesler, Marcia had begged him to go AWOL and run away with her to Canada. Chet would not do it. Marcia reasoned that he did not love her, so she began to look about among other young men.

"I'm glad I didn't have the problem Chet Westcott has," Sibley told Miriam. "When I was overseas, during the war, I couldn't have survived in Africa, if I'd had that sort of sword hanging over my head." Sibley reached across between the chairs and touched his wife. "I know that you were absolutely true to me. You never looked at another man while I was gone. I'm afraid you're a much better woman than our daughter. It must be the way we raised her."

"That's not exactly true," Miriam responded. "There was someone. I never told. I think I should tell, now.

Perhaps, you won't think so hard of Marcia. If I tell you my story, it may help you to see what a woman goes through when the man she loves has been taken away from her."

Sibley was aghast. After almost thirty years of marriage, was he to find that things had not always been as secure for him with Miriam as he thought? As pat?

Under African skies, he had dreamed bedouin dreams of gallant, adventurous men, and demure, virtuous women. The continent of Africa had cast a spell upon him. He had been enchanted. He heard in the running feet of horse, across the sand, romantic drumrolls, stirring his blood. He had not talked about this when he came home, but in Africa he had seen himself an audacious rider on a white stallion, who would sweep the exquisite Miriam away to his castle on the desert. He was sure none had ever intruded into that land of miracle he shared with Miriam, and none ever would. Touching Miriam's hand, Sibley lived these old dreams once more, felt his love for Miriam reinforced.

"There was one," Miriam said. "Besides you. Before I had the fever. They wrote to you about the fever. I met a man named Tredan Slean. He was a man of property. He was in his forties. He was not drafted to go to the war."

"I never heard of him."

"He moved away from the coast before you came home. He wanted me to go with him. I was tempted."

When Sibley came back from Africa he went to school under the G.I. Bill. Now, Miriam was proud of him, an accountant, and a retired officer of a large company, and very distinguished looking.

But, then, she had not known if Sibley would have any future at all. He might never come home from the war. Tredan Slean could offer her proof. He had a future. She was too friendly with him; wanted to go away with him. She almost forgot good, right-motivated, visionary Sibley, who should have been her own soldier and her hero. Yet she wrote to Sibley, keeping the door open. She had not made her decision yet.

"I went into the fever at this time," she told Sibley. "I was out of my head. I entered an old world which no longer exists. I met people named Minna, and Barth, and Cord, and Powell. I touched them. I talked with them. It was more real to me than my own bed, and house, and family. The dreams came daily. I saw Minna, a girl of my age, only voluptuous, raven-haired, pale-skinned, lissome and supple. She was so unlike me. Yet, like me. I know she was rebellious. She loved a young man, Barth Withy, and there was a war then, too. It was the time of the Spanish-American war, and Barth went away to Cuba."

Minna Bettencourt was an apprentice in a dressmaking shop, where she was paid fifty cents for each twelve-hour day of a six-day week. She was seventeen, and she knew she was beautiful. Squinting at the tiny stitches she was forced to sew, her bosom seethed with a rage to have something better. She would never be a dressmaker!

But, if she married Barth, she would find herself lucky for having a trade. Barth had been an ox-driver since the age of thirteen. Minna had first seen him stalking through town with his team, pulling great pine logs on a cart to the sawmill. He cracked his whip, not to move his oxen faster, but to entertain himself, and for the enjoyment of all who were within earshot. People came to the doors of cabins and houses to smile and wave to him when he strutted past. His back and shoulders were strong. He carried himself like a prince. Minna gazed out of the window of the dressmaker's sawing room and fell in love with him.

She saw Barth, with his oxen, many times before she met him. The cracking of his whip made her jerk in response. Sometimes a chill moved over her when she heard the whip's outcry, but sometimes there was joy. The sound always brought her a smoldering excitement. She felt all hot and weak, and her breath came quickly.

Minna would hide her face behind her falling black hair at these times so that no one in the shop would observe her heightened color, her trembling fingers on the needle.

Barth loved to surprise the people who lived near the mill. He could make his whip sound sometimes like the crack of a rifle. At other times he could make it boom like a cannon. People roundabout would think the Spanish had invaded. They would run for their guns.

At last, she contrived to meet him. He saw that she was healthy and lovely; a fit match for himself. The first time he crushed her in his arms, Minna almost fell in a swoon. She felt oceanic tides course through her body, and she heard the sound of the sea in her ears, ringing, the surf pounding like a savage drum.

Soon, they were engaged.

The Piney Woods, in Mississippi, and Alabama, and Louisiana has always given more than its share of sons to America when there has been a war. Barth Withy had to go away.

He left, proud in his overalls and his brogan shoes. Minna wondered when she would see him again.

Cord Breland was older. He claimed to be twenty-five, but he was thirty. He had been watching the romance which blossomed between Barth and Minna. Everyone about knew everything about each other. There were no secrets near the waterwheel and the mill. Cord figured that Minna "was broke into pleasing a man." Barth had not been going with her just to pass the time of day. That bubbling yearling had, without doubt, mounted the heifer!

Cord was a farmer. He had made the millpond, and built the waterwheel, and the mill to saw his own logs when he cleared more land. He ginned cotton for himself and his neighbors. Before his sawmill came, people must drag their logs with oxen to the river, and float them down to Delisle. Then, they would walk back home. Cord had blessed his neighbors by building the mill. But, he had no wife and no children. He had been too busy working the forest, turning it into a farm, to think about such things.

Now, he saw that Minna was the most beautiful woman in the east part of the county.

Cord's millpond was eight feet deep. There was enough water in it, so that its fall would power the circular saw and the gin machinery in his mill.

Birds, circling and diving, gratefully ate trout from the pond. Their sharp eyes were able to see any errant fish which swam near the pond's smooth surface.

Cord would be like an old bird. He would circle Minna, and when she didn't suspect, he'd dive on her, and she would be his catch. He'd take her home, like a string of fish, a trophy to mount on the wall.

Cord had built a fine house of cypress and heart pine, figuring held be getting married. He had lots of rooms to fill with children. A man's wife and children were his chattel, and he wanted to increase his holdings, before he was older.

In his house were four fireplaces, including the large one in the kitchen. He kept the house warm in winter with fires started with lightwood.

Minna was dazzled. When he asked her, she married Cord Breland. Her eyes told her that Cord was a very rich man, and she lusted after his riches.

Cord's mill was small, as mills go. Where the big mills were, life was ordered by the mill whistles, and the smoke from the boilers always drifted into the pure Mississippi sky. The whine of circular saws, and gang saws, and sash saws could be heard blending, all day, and sometimes all night. There were electric lights in the mills. The odor of pine was everywhere.

Minna was happy and exhilarated in her house, which Cord said belonged to her. With Cord, in bed at night, she did not receive the fiery rush she had felt when kissing Barth. Cord was not everything she wanted, but she would have children soon, and they would fill her life. In the meantime, she had beautiful dresses, and a black woman to dress her and do her hair. Soon, she would make Cord take her on trips to New Orleans, and Natchez; even Memphis. She would be planning for a good school to send her sons to.

Barth came home from the war, his right arm shot off and buried in Cuba. When Minna saw him, hot tears came to her eyes.

"You can't drive the oxen anymore," she said. "What will you do?"

Cord arranged with a friend for Barth to have a job in a mill office down on Bayou Bernard. Barth set out, on foot, to go there.

But, he did not go. In a few days, he was back.

He had found an old dog on the road, and named him Howard, and brought him back with him. He came to see Minna in her house when Cord was working in the woods.

"I can't be everywhere," Cord said to himself, but it worried him that Barth was not at Handsboro. "There's only one thing Barth is hanging around here for. I know that flat out. But, Minna's not going to get shut of me to have that cripple. Barth's got nothing to his name except the pants he stands up in." Cord did not worry unduly.

Barth said that he would learn how to handle the whip and the oxen with his left hand, but all the men shook their heads knowing it was impossible.

"I'll be an ox-driver again," Barth said. But, his whip was silent.

Barth spent his time with his gun, walking knee-deep in a bog near the ford, at the foot of the waterwheel. He shot squirrels. He would bring them to Cord's house for cooking in Cord's kitchen. Howard would not enter the water, but sat at the edge of the bog, an anxious expression on his face, afraid that Barth was in danger. Barth could recall when he had driven his oxen through that bog. A horse would have floundered and been lost in there, but the oxen, with Barth driving them, made it through.

Barth was bitter. He could only sit, now, with the old men, exchanging tales of how logs had been hauled out of bottomless hollows, and over perilous grades. Barth would remind them of how he had been able to snake any log out of the woods to the river.

Never again would these things be.

Minna was touched by malaria. Cord was frantic. He ordered the cypress swamp behind the house cut down and drained to discourage the mosquitoes. He wanted to take Minna away from the swamp fevers to Natchez, away from Barth, and away from a growing dissatisfaction which seemed to overtake her. But, he could not leave his business. He would lose everything!

The cypress trees were girdled and allowed to die. When they were dry, Cord sent men with crosscut saws into the swamp, to saw the trees down some six or eight feet above the earth. Only a dried out cypress tree would float down the river. A green cypress log would sink. Cork had a sale for the cypress. It would be put on a ship at the Bay of St. Louis.

The destruction of the cypress forest was complete and Cork set black men with shovels to digging ditches to drain the hazard to his wife's health which he believed this ravished woodland to be.

Next year, Cord would plant the land in cotton. Cotton would grow sky high in that rich alluvial soil.

Cord was clearing land on a hillside. One day he used dynamite to blow a hole in the hardpan which was only inches beneath the orange surface of the land. With holes dynamited in the hardpan, the land could drain, and rancid water would not stand preventing things to grow. He blew four holes that day.

At the house, Minna heard the explosions, and for a moment she believed that it was Barth with his whip, making the sound of a cannon, ready to drive his oxen again, ready to be a man, ready to love her. But, it was not Barth. it was her husband.

Minna was feverish and pregnant. When she heard the booms, she started up, and she lost the child she was carrying. While gentle black hands tended her, she called out for Barth. And, Cord arrived home in time to hear.

Minna still loved Barth. She was touched by his predicament. She was all passion and sympathy for Barth. He came to her house almost every day, while Cord was at work at his many ventures.

Cord had great energy because he loved his young wife. Yet, Minna might not ever have another child.

One day Cord came home and he saw Howard sleeping on the wide front porch. Howard raised his head and growled at Cord. The dog looked upon this turf as his territory, and he looked upon Cord as an intruder. He rose up and bared his teeth at Cord.

Cord knew that Barth Withy was inside the house with his wife. He had known, since the day of the miscarriage, that Minna still cared for Barth, but he had not believed she was unfaithful. Finding that she was, Cord was not happy any more.

He did not beat Minna, or remind her that he owned her. He merely asked her to stay with him, live in his house, sleep in his bed sometimes, if possible give him a child.

Cord did not have a friend to confide in. The closest thing he had to a friend was a black man named Powell, who operated the mill and gin. Powell seldom spoke. He never spoke about what the white people did. He merely looked on, with sad and anxious eyes, knowing that there would be trouble in the end.

One day Barth brought his whip to Minna's house and threatened to beat her with it. He was bitter and angry that she had not waited for him when he was gone to war. He was irreconcilable that she could not be his; that she had placed herself outside his reach, while he was away losing an arm for Theodore Roosevelt. All his hope for a livelihood and home, in this place, was gone.

Barth slept in the woods. He ate what the cook would give him from Cord's kitchen. His few belongings were stashed at a black family's cabin. Cord must never know where. He might bring reprisal on these people who were employees of his.

Minna saw how miserable Barth was. She knew that in cities, away from the log-woods, Barth could find work, even with one arm. She agreed to go away with him.

"You'd leave all this for me?"

"Yes. I did this to you. We can go down on the coast, perhaps to Pascagoula. I'll get a job sewing."

Under a full moon, early, when Cord usually read, Minna and Barth raced for the ford. Barth had a rowboat on the river. He and Minna could drift down to Delisle and go over land to Pascagoula. They would start a new life, using other names.

But, Cord was aware of what they were doing. He had been told of their plans by servants who eavesdropped.

On that fatal night, there were two disasters. The gate to the millpond was raised up, or burst, and Minna and Barth ran away.

Cord's business ventures and his home were ruined. He was a broken man after this, suspicious, paranoid, thinking that everyone was against him.

He told people that Powell had helped the pair escape, that Powell had opened the gate to the pond to divert attention from the fleeing lovers. Cork brought charges against this helper, who had so long been faithful, and Powell was sent to prison.

Without Minna and without Powell, Cord retreated into his own self-imposed loneliness, seldom being seen outside his house, except when he had to transact some item of business in the town. The farm languished. The forest began to grow again, unchallenged by sawyers' saws.

An atmosphere of despair clouded the area. The black people moved away. The town disappeared. The mill pond was never remade. The saws and gin machinery were sold. Cord walked in and out of his house for sixty years, an embittered recluse, already old when the tribulation began. He became dried up inside at thirty-five, a hypochondriac at forty. His timber was cut by others. He saw the land become a domain of stumps, and then saw the hardwoods tentatively spout again, with a sparse growth of pines intermingled. He saw the bog where the cypress forest had been decreased to an area the size of a large room. He saw all his diligently created farmland revert to shrubs. Everywhere there was ruin. He sat, often reading his Bible, railing to empty rooms about the faithlessness of women and the treachery of virile men.

In 1900, the pioneer phase of lumbering in the piney woods was about to end. Big things were coming. Pine trees would lift the Mississippi Gulf Coast to heights it had never dared hope it might achieve. From its ports, the world would be supplied with a share in the greatest windfall of virgin timber which God has ever supplied to an area, until it was gone.

But, Cord would not be a part of all that. He sat on the sidelines, until 1965, when he died.

And then, in 1969, the Ords came, to make the lovely, abandoned old house their home.

"You see," Miriam said. "I know all about this farm. Minna came to me, over and over, when I was in that terrible fever, and she told me every bit of her story."

"I don't think she told you all," Sibley said. "I think there is still some part missing."

"I might have gone with Tredan Slean," Miriam said. "If not for her. Her story made me see that it is wrong to desert a true love and marry another, lesser man. That was Minna's mistake. If she had not deserted Barth, everything would have been all right."

"I know I'm your true love, and always have been," Sibley told her, smiling. "You didn't have to tell me this silly story. You didn't have to tell me about Trenholm Snead, or whatever his name was." He deprecated his old rival.

"I wanted to tell you. I wanted you to see that Marcia is not the first woman who has become confused and wanted to run away after an available man, when the man she loves is not available."

"I know the song. If a girl can't be near to the man whom she cares for, she'll care for the man who is near."

"I'm afraid that's it. Are we a miserable sex?"

"You're all princesses, dazzling the gardens of men. We'd never do without you. Do you think Marcia will make it?"

"I was young and impressionable when I knew Tradan. I was seventeen. Marcia is almost twenty-five. She's been to college, lived in her own apartment. Lived with a man. She should know better."

"I guess it's time to have a little faith."

"Something saved me from making an awful mistake in 1942. Maybe that something will save Marcia now. I give Minna Bettencourt credit for restoring my whole life to me. She came to me with her story and saved me from making a grave error. Aren't we both glad?" She slapped her husband's knee.

"It was something inside yourself that saved you,"

Sibley told her. "You just couldn't do what you started to, Let's hope that same something is in Marcia. If it's there, it will save her, too."

Marcia arrived, in her car. She was slender, with a puckishness gone sour. She was almost boyish looking. There was a slightly sullen air about her, which she took few pains to hide. It was plain to all that the mother, a late bloomer, was more attractive than the daughter. Perhaps, this was at the root of Marcia's perpetual rebellion.

Sibley and Miriam were barely settled in their new home.

Painters and electricians were about. There was a room for Marcia to sleep in. Sibley had given up trying to make his television play. The antenna was not tall enough. A new one could be brought. A new floor was being laid in the kitchen.

"I miss the TV. I'd like to see Dan Rather. I like to keep up with what's going on in Washington and Vietnam," Sibley said.

"You must call for someone to fix it."

He played his albums.

The day after Marcia came, Pete Posey arrived. He was driving a frayed, red Dart.

"Why are you here?" Marcia asked, testily.

"I go where you go," he said, gallantly.

"I see." Marcia did not smile. She had come to help her parents get settled into the new home, and to use her public relations arts on them to get them to accept Pete. His being there, breathing down their backs was not going to help.

The Ords looked at Pete, standing grinning in the sunshine, his hair uncut and wild, his jeans on his ridiculously short legs too loose. There was a button off his fading shirt. He had drooled chocolate on that grimy garment.

"You evidently left in a hurry this morning," Marcia said. "I see you didn't shave."

"I woke up and got right in the car."

"You may visit Marcia here," Sibley told him. "But, there will be no smoking pot in the house, and there will be no lovemaking in any of the bedrooms. We will give you a room separate from hers. If you want to smoke or make love, you'll do that outside. And, don't use any filthy language in front of me or my wife. We are not used to it."

"I'll sleep in the car," Pete said, cheerfully, scratching himself in private places.

"You look as though you slept in the car last night," Marcia said.

"How'd you guess?"

"Let's go inside."

In front of her parents, as something to be added to the family circle, Pete looked out of place. Marcia was embarrassed by him, but he was, figuratively, climbing all over everybody, happy as a wet puppy. "This is a swell place," he said. "You do any hunting?" This was directed to Sibley.

"Not yet."

"Do you guess old bear is living back there in the woods? I hear people's seen panthers on Wolf River."

"I've heard that, too," Sibley said.

Marcia went with Pete to bring in several packages he had in his car. When she leaned into the Dart, she saw a bra on the floor.

"What's this?"

"You must have left that."

"It's not mine."

"I don't know where it came from."

"That's a lie," Marcia said, angrily. "I'll tell you one thing, I take a lot off of you, but if I find out you're running after other women, you're out of my life. That, I won't put up with. If you're going with me, I'm going to be the only one you go with. That's that."

"I haven't even looked at another girl since we starting dating."

Marcia could only think of Chet Westcott, flying over Vietnam, risking his life every day. He could be shot down, and it would be weeks before she'd know it. She had never had to worry about his running after other women. They had lived as though married, although not married. It had been comfortable.

"I want to do right," Pete said. "I don't want to live the life I've lived in the past."

"Don't you even think of embarrassing me in front of my parents," Marcia said.

Miriam draw Marcia aside and talked with her, insistently.

"I don't like that boy. I hate to see you mixed up with him." But, Pete Posey was a lady's man, and Marcia couldn't resist him. "We went along with it when you were living with Chat Westcott, because he was a nice person, but this is different. If you're thinking of living with Pete Posey, you can forget about your daddy and me until you come to your senses."

Marcia told Pete that night, when they lay on a blanket on a patch of grass behind the house, that her parents were not going to tolerate Pete unless the two of them were married.

Pete happily agreed that they would wed. He had noted that Sibley had retired with savings, and a good pension, and Sibley owned this fine farm in Pearl River County. If Pete and Marcia were married, her parents would help them, which translated, they would help him.

Pete wanted to make love, right there on the ground, but Marcia pushed him away.

"I'm going inside," she said. "You go do whatever you want to do."

Pete was cursing and angry, high on pot and alcohol, and he leaped up and went to his car and drove away. Marcia lingered on the back porch of the house.

In the moonlight, she saw a woman standing under a magnolia tree at the edge of the wood. The woman seemed to emit her own light. She was perfectly plain to Marcia; a beautiful woman; she had long, curling black hair and her face was creamy white. But, sad in the eyes.

The woman wore a long dress which reached her ankles. She must be sorrowful. She was looking at Marcia with a long penetrating gaze.

The woman's form was perfect. She held up her hands, seeming to entreat Marcia about something. She lifted her head and looked Marcia in the eyes. The eyes of this woman burned into Marcia's.

Marcia took a step toward her.

"Hello, there," Marcia called out, thinking the woman must be a neighbor who had ventured over to meet them. The woman did not reply. Marcia looked away for a second, and when she looked back the woman was gone.

"There was a woman outside," Marcia told Miriam, as soon as she entered the house. Miriam was immediately alert.

"Who?"

"I don't know." Marcia described the woman. "She was lovely."

"I'm sure she was."

Miriam made arrangements for Marcia and Pete to be married.

"If you're going to do this, I want to see to it that you do it right." Perhaps, a nice religious ceremony would sober them. Miriam wanted them to see what a serious step marriage is.

Marcia lectured Pete again about his becoming faithless.

"Just because we're married doesn't mean I won't drop you like a hot potato. Any time I catch you stepping around on me, I'll kick your scrawny behind out!"

The marriage license was obtained and people were found to take part in the ceremony. It would be in the afternoon. They would drive to Poplarville in Marcia's car and stay overnight in a motel. Pete knew of a good one that was a kind of a truck stop.

"I'd hoped for more than this for you," Miriam said. "This is a different day. I know you smoke pot. I've heard stories about LSD. You've marched in opposition to the war. Your father was ready to go in 1940, to fight for his country. I hoped you'd get a man who would do as much. I admire Chet for his service to the country."

"Poor square Chat Westcott! B-o-o-or-ing!"

"You didn't think so at first."

"I was in love with the uniform; the fact he could fly."

"Well, he may be well rid of you. I hate to say that about my own daughter."

"I don't see how you can speak to me like that," Marcia said, really aggrieved. "And, on my wedding day!"

Pete was out walking about, looking over Sibley's holdings. On his short legs, he looked, to Marcia, like a striped-tailed raccoon. He was scrounging for something he could eat, wanting to fill his belly with roots and nuts, wanting to find bright things he could take home to his burrow. She thought of the bra in the car. What girl had he stolen that treasure from?

Marcia left her mother. Miriam's words led Marcia to think demeaning things about Pete, to see ugly pictures of him in her mind. She was so angry with Miriam's lecturing, she would not stay in the house. She saw Pete walking through the sedge, kicking at the gall berries, holding his shining face up to the sun.

Marcia started to hail him.

Then, she saw the woman. It was the same woman she had seen outside the house a few nights before. The woman's dress was mauve, but the sunshine made it look richly textured, like expensive fur. It danced on her body.

The skirt was split up the side, and the woman had opened it and was showing Pete her leg. She wore high-heeled, buttoned shoes. Marcia had never seen a woman like this before.

Apparently, Pete liked what he saw. He approached the woman. She walked away from him a few steps. He approached again. She sidled, swaying her skirt with her left hand, moving easily on the rough ground. Pete tried to come closer to her. She began to run; not in fear, but enticingly. Pete ran after her.

Marcia was furious. The woman was tempting Pate, and Pete was falling for it. He would probably lay with her right there on a cleared, sandy place which had once been part of an old cypress swamp. A fallen log lay in the woman's path. She was quick to get around it.

Marcia saw everything. The woman ran faster, and Pete ran faster. The woman seemed almost to float. Blackberry briars tore at Pete, scratching his bare arms, cutting his ankles. He ran blindly, panting, like a randy dog after its female, like a rutting goat. And, this was to be his wedding deny!

The woman ran into a space where water stood. Her feet did not seem to touch the water. She sailed above it. She looked back at Pete and smiled, her teeth flashing like knives, beckoning him on.

Pete floundered in the water. He ran to the very center of the wet place, which was a bog, and he began to sink. Marcia came to the edge of the pool when he was up to his armpits, about to breath water.

"Help me!" Pete cried. He must rat yellow before her. This was his nature. He cried and flailed his arms about. The flies settled on his face.

Marcia ran to her father's house. Workmen went to help. Others were called. They were able to pull Pete out of the bog before he drowned. The muck sucked his pants off. He stood before a dozen people in his jockey shorts, his legs like those of a goat, encased in mud.

"This satyr has about had it," Sibley said. "Listen to him neigh."

Pete was bawling. He babbled hysterically. Marcia turned and walked away.

"Daddy," she said. "When Pete gets settled down, will you help him get ready, so he can go back to the coast?"

"I can do that," Sibley said, pleased as punch.

Marcia told Miriam about the woman she had seen.

"Did Pete see her, too?"

"He must have ... based on the way he was acting."

"It's strange," Miriam said.

Marcia left the day after Pete. She had sat up the night before and written Chet Westcott a long letter.

Miriam walked in the cleared area behind the house. She hoped she might see Minna. She knew that it was Minna who came to save Marcia from making a terrible mistake, just as she had saved Miriam from making a mistake in 1942. She wished she could thank Minna, but Minna did not appear.

She talked with Sibley about it.

"It can all be explained logically," Sibley told her. "You didn't have a case of precognition, seeing this farm long before we came here. In your dreams, you imagined the people and the happenings you say occurred here. When we came here, you saw certain similarities to the dreams you had in '42. It suggested things to you. I don't think any of this is really supernatural."

"Marcia saw her. I think Pete saw her. It was Minna. How did they see her if it is not real?"

"I don't think Pete saw anything. I think he just went off his nut from all the dope he's been snorting, and he ran through the brush, and he fell in the bog."

"Even if Pete didn't see her, Marcia saw her."

"Okay., for the sake of argument, I'll grant that you and Marcia saw the same ghost. Somehow, by some telepathy between mother and daughter, you transmitted the image of Minna to her. You wanted Marcia to see Minna so damned bad that she did. All I can say is, it worked out for the best. It was a bountiful day when we saw the last of Pete Posey."

"I have seen Minna Bettencourt in dreams," Miriam said, adamantly. "And, Marcia has seen her while she was awake. Twice."

"Okay."

"And, Pete saw her, too."

"We'll ask him, if we ever see him again."

Miriam laughed.

"We'll have a good life here. Our resident ghost will see to it."

"Let me ask one more question. Why would she do it? A ghost must have a reason for doing what it does. Is this just a caprice for her? Is it all a lark? I don't think so. If you've really seen a ghost, there is a reason for it, something that is to the ghost's self-interest. Ghosts don't just get up and walk around at night for the pleasure of it."

A dreamy, thoughtful look came to Miriam's face.

"It all has something to do with that terrible night when Minna and Barth were running away and the dam broke. I have a feeling that Barth's cant hook and his peavey are somewhere down there beside the creek, buried in the sand. He wouldn't have left here without taking them. Them and his ox-whip. I don't know why, but I have the feeling they're there beside the creek, buried in sand." she gave a little shiver. "And, perhaps, bones."

"Well, I won't dig and look for them."

That night, when Miriam slept, she saw the sad black face of Powell, entreating her, hopeful that she would understand some need he had and help him. It had been Powell's face she saw first of all her dream faces, back during the war, when Sibley was away. She had been in a terrible fever. That might explain what happened then, but she was healthy now.

She found herself standing in the dogtrot, at the mill which straddled the river, the mill pond behind her, the ford across the creek before. It was night. The waterwheel was not turning. The whole world was silent.

Miriam became afraid. With her, standing and looking out over the rivulet was a presence. It materialized and became a man. She knew it was Cord Breland. He was in a fury. His face was black with rage. Empty veins stood out on his neck. His hands gripped a railing, the skin drawn so white the knuckles seemed ready to burst through it. His manic white hands were bloodless. Lightning seemed to leap from his silvered eyes. His chest rose and fall, but there was no rasp of air. Cord Breland did not breathe.

Miriam looked where Cord was looking and she saw a man and woman come running from the house toward the ford. Lithe as a cat, Cord manipulated levers and wheels so that, just as the running pair entered the ford, the gate to the millpond burst open and the flood overwhelmed Minna and Barth and they drowned, their bodies swept along who knew how far down the raging river. Miriam began to gasp and cry. Then, she saw the face of Powell again. He had been a witness to it all.

The time was the present. On the sandy bank of the creek, the two ghosts stood before Miriam. There was great contention between them. It was over her. Miriam knew that Powell wanted her to live and tell what she had seen of the past. Cord Breland wanted her to die.

Terror gripped her last Cord should get the upper hand and be free to do something to her so that she could not tell and ruin his memory. She knew that he could not touch her, but he could drive her mad. She rooted for Powell, fighting for her sanity.

The two ghosts fought to exhaustion, until at last Powell pinned Cord to the ground. Then, Cord suddenly disappeared. Powell stood up, and ran away.

The story which Cord first had told, that the dam had broken by accident, so that in the turmoil which followed Minna and Barth might escape together to Texas was not true. In fact, Cord had murdered them.

Cord knew that Powell knew, but he trusted Powell to keep silent. Whenever he told his original version of what happened, Powell would look at him silently, with brooding eyes, his face drawn into a grimace of outrage.

Powell became hag-ridden. Minna knew how to come out of her skin and ride on Powell's back. She came to him every night and rode Powell all night long so that he woke in the morning with his face all lathered in sweat.

Minna wanted Powell to tell that Cord had murdered her, and her lover, Barth.

Powell had purchased a jo-mo from a witchdoctor who chanced by, and he used it to protect himself from Minna, but Minna, after a few nights was able to get a cook to steal the jo-mo, so Powell was at her mercy again.

Cord did not know about Minna's haunting Powell, but he sensed that Powell was going to tell.

Cord told a new story. He accused Powell in court of having wrecked Cord's millpond as a diversion to aid Minna and Barth in their escape.

Powell was found guilty. He was sent away to prison. He died in jail.

Miriam sat bolt upright in bed beside Sibley.

"Powell was innocent," she cried. "Minna and Barth were horribly murdered. Powell went to prison because Cord took a lying oath. There were great wrongs. Minna only wanted for someone to know. She only wanted the wrongs righted."

"That's why she came to see you," Sibley said, sleepily.

"In 1942, she knew we would marry, and have a daughter, and buy this farm. She started trying to tell me what happened to them. That's all she wanted. She did it for herself, and Barth, and Powell. Now, their story is known. They can all rest."

"You go and tell everyone you see. Especially, you tell that old peahen that sells real estate out of her home."

"You're laughing at me. You do see that I'm right about all this, don't you?"

"If you'll move over here, close beside me, I'll go and begin digging, in the morning, in the sand, by the creek for Barth's cant hook and his peavey. When I've found those, I'll believe you."

Miriam saw Minna many times after that, when the moon was rising all silver and round; when there were black shadows under the trees in the wood Minna would rise, floating to perch on a limb of the cedar tree. She'd smile at Miriam, sit for a moment, and then wave good-bye.

One night she came and sat longer than usual. Somehow, Miriam knew this would be her final visit. Minna waved her last good-bye, and began to fade slowly away.

"Oh, thank you, forever, dear friend," Miriam breathed, feeling hot tears in her eyes. "Thank you, my Cedarbird."

The cant hook and the peavey have never been found.

But, this does not mean they are not there.

GEORGETOWN, SOUTH CAROLINA

"Like Mother Like Son" was written in Georgetown in 1995. In this story self-destructive behaviors practiced in a family over several generations become woven into a sorry fabric of extinction. The scene is New York City. This writer had never been there. This was his perception of New York City under Mayor Dinkins. The wanton mother and the deviate son are fixtures in this writer's novels, one of which also is laid in New York City.

This story does not judge the rightness or wrongness of homosexual sex, as compared to any other sex outside of marriage, or to a complete absence of sex. This story says it is very wrong to knowingly place someone in danger of contracting AIDS.

Inciting another to acts which will almost of a certainty lead to that person's infection with the AIDS virus is the height of criminal irresponsibility — abandoned reckless endangerment. Period!

LIKE MOTHER, LIKE SON

The room George Goodin occupied in New York City was, eerily, like every room he had lived in in his short life. The same stains of spattered grease were on the walls. There was the same broken furniture set sparsely about. The same busy roaches and water-bugs bustled in and out of the trash pail.

George had always noticed how sprightly and happy roaches were when they were working. George didn't work. He never had, and he had not seen many people who did.

Every house his mother had gotten for them to live in, back in hidebound, small-town Pennsylvania where he was born, had had the same noisy, hard-to-operate, leaking plumbing, and the same odors which George now encountered, of garbage, and standing water, and mildew, and dust.

George felt right at home. He pulled a sheet, which was too small for the bed, up over the striped ticking of the thin mattress, and stretched back upon it. He tapped a small radio with his fingers to make it play. The radio had a caved plastic case. It crackled noisily, picking up interference. The radio had never played right in the city. George was made for the city.

George fixed his eyes on the door to the hall. It always reminded him of another particular door, in one particular house, at one particular time. That was the time Megabob Wesley had done things to him which were good and bad. The bad part was that Megabob hurt him. The good part was that Megabob taught him that he had something men wanted. That was the beginning of his career, his waxing power over other men.

George's mother, Darlene Goodin, had got all dressed up that day, and the room all around her reeked of what Megabob called "nigger perfume."

"No white woman should smell like that," he told her gruffly, laughing. He was loving the scent. It was exciting him.

She had made out as if to hit him, and walked out the front door laughing back at him.

"You make enough out there to bring us back a couple of pizzas," Megabob called, as she went down the steps.

"I'll bring you back something better than pizza. The johns will have it all warmed up for you."

"You won't bring me nothing," Megabob shouted.

"You'd never dream what I can give you," George's mother had said.

George stood that day with his ear to the door from the hallway listening to the exchange between his mother and this live-in daddy of his. He felt that when six months had passed, he wouldn't be able to remember how Megabob looked. Megabob would be gone like all the others, and his memory would be gone with him.

But, George did not yet know that this live-in daddy would be different. This daddy would be the one who would hurt him, and teach him valuable lessons.

Megabob jerked the door open. George almost fell into the front room, with its rattan furniture, and its odor of stale pizza and beer.

"What do you mean by prying?" Megabob asked.

"I wasn't prying."

"You were prying." Megabob studied George, who was twelve years old, carefully, sizing up his skinny ass and reading his pitiful, eager-to-please white face.

Megabob's great gut hung over his belt. His face was florid. He was sweating.

"It's fucking hot today," he said. "How much do you know about what me and your mother was talking about? Do you understand what goes on around here?"

"I know my mother has gone to get some money, downtown, like she always does when she dresses up like that."

"Where do you think she gets the money?"

George lied.

"From the bank."

"The bank between her legs?"

"I don't think I know what you mean."

"I mean your mama has got a bank between her legs and it belongs to me. She's downtown selling off pieces of it. She'll bring the money back to me."

"I don't know about that."

"Your mama better be selling. Sometimes she gives. It ain't right for your mama to be giving away what's mine. How do you think someone could make that up to me?"

"I don't know, sir." George was getting scared.

"I think you've got a bank between your legs. It would just be right for you to give me a piece of that, to make up for my property that your mama might be downtown giving away."

"I don't know how to do what you say."

"I can easy show you," Megabob said. "I'll be nice. I'll just make a little deposit in your bank."

George could still recall every detail of the fear, the pain, the embarrassment that he felt. Megabob had taken him into Darlene's bedroom and undressed him. He spread newspapers all up under George so they wouldn't get anything on the bed. He got on top of George. George could recall the way Megabob grunted and gasped, how he finally fell on the papers beside George with a look of happy contentment on his fleshy face.

Megabob pinched George's ass.

"I like young stuff like this. You did good," he turned on his side and looked at George's face, almost with affection. "You go get cleaned up and put your clothes on. We don't want your mama to know about this."

George felt a sense of triumph, of power over this clumsy, lumbering man. Megabob wanted him not to tell, that was a card he could play. But, the trump card was, Megabob would surely want to do what he had done again. George had a hold over this live-in daddy, like held never had over one before.

The blood he lost was worth it.

George's brothers and sisters were over at his aunt's house. There were five of them, all younger than he. Darlene was a bastard, and George was a bastard, and all his little brothers and sisters were bastards.

"It's a bastard world," George told himself, listening to the honking of horns and the squeal of brakes on the busy New York street outside his building. He turned off the radio.

He was dressed in jeans and a T-shirt. He sat up and put on run-over loafers. He took a comb out of his pocket and swept his hair back. His complexion was sallow, his hair dishwater blond. His father must have been a stocky Pennsylvania German or a Polack. George was short. He was not much taller than he had been at age twelve, during those few months Megabob had fooled with him, before Megabob went away.

Megabob had been just like all the rest of George's daddies. One night he and Darlene had had a terrible fight and he was gone.

"Your boy's a better piece of ass than you," Megabob told Darlene. "He's the only thing I've been hanging around here for. I'll bet you didn't know that."

"No. I didn't know it," Darlene said, and she cried, which was something she never did.

Later she had looked at George with stricken eyes and clutched him close to her.

"I want you to forget all about anything Megabob did to you," she told George, a desperate tone in her voice. "I want you to put it out of your mind, and never think of it again."

But, George had thought of it. With Megabob gone, he started doing things with his little brother, Wiley, and then with boys at school, and then with men he met on the streets of their middle-sized farm town.

"I just love it!" he'd say. "I love all of it. I love the fucking, and the sucking, and the being fucked!"

George hid his fuck-books under his mattress, and went out in the hall and locked his door. He went down in the elevator to the street.

He went and stood on the corner for a while, sizing up the men who walked past, thinking which ones were cute, and which would do in a pinch, and which ones he would reject. He saw one monstrously gorgeous brute come by. The sight of him made George reel with dizziness and prickle with heat.

"If I could sit up on top of that," he said. "For just twenty minutes. I'd be better than Queen Elizabeth! Who could be better than me, then?"

The hairy, muscled, tanned, arrogant man did not look to the right or the left. He was oblivious that George existed. George felt the hurt and the excitement which he found in this man's contempt of everything around him.

"Oh, God! I'd like for him to fuck me. I'd like for him to just tear me up."

In a few moments, George saw Eben. He didn't know Eben yet, but he saw a slender, neat man of about thirty looking at him. Eben was the sort of man that George would not refuse to go to bed with, but one he could not get really excited about either. George looked at him boldly, sizing him up from head to toe.

"West Virginia," George thought. "He's too seedy to be from Pennsylvania. Farther south. I'd say, West Virginia. He looks hungry."

Eben came straight up to George and held out his hand.

"Name's Eben," he said. "I thought you wouldn't mind talking with me a few minutes. I get pretty lonesome in New York."

"Many people do," George said, in a breathless, husky tone. He didn't let his full voice out.

"I'm not originally from here."

"West Virginia," George guessed. "You're from West Virginia."

Eben was startled. "How'd you know? I am from West Virginia."

"The best-looking men in the world come from West Virginia," George told him.

"Oh, I'm not good-looking," Eben said, shyly.

"You'll do."

"I don't guess I'll be staying for very long in this city. I just wanted to see it, once."

"It's a city of thrills. Are you looking for a thrill?"

"I've already done what I came here to do," Eben said. "I went to the top of the Empire State Building."

"Oh," George trilled. "That was a delight."

Neither of them knew that the Empire State Building was long ago called, "Al Smith's last erection." This would have titillated George and shocked Eben. The Empire State Building was the ultimate phallus.

"That's what I came here to do," Eben said. "To go to the top of the Empire State Building. I memorized one verse of Scripture, so that I could stand up on top of the Empire State, and tell it to New York." Eben's eyes stared, and his fingers grasped at something in the air in front of him, which only he could see. "'O Jerusalem, Jerusalem, thou that killest the prophets, and stonest them which are sent unto thee, how often would I have gathered thy children together, even as a hen gathereth her chickens under her wings, and ye would not!'"

George liked the part about the hen. He imagined that all the men of the world were his chicks, and he just wanted to put his arms out and grasp them all against his chest. He loved them every one.

"Not many people could hear you, if you stood on top of a tall building to say it. I don't think that saying it up there did much good."

"It was merely symbolic," Eben said. "I see that, now. God has used you to show me that. I need to tell it in the streets. I believe God is calling me to stay in New York awhile longer. The curse upon this city is that they do not scourge the evildoer, but they slay the ones who stand and cry out against evil."

George looked at the indifferent crowd which thronged the sidewalk. Eben could never get the attention of these people. It was hard enough for George to, even at night when he came out in drag.

"Good luck," George said.

Eben walked slowly away, as one who has beheld a heavenly vision, one who is transfixed by a compelling dream.

George turned his attention to a sailor, who was standing against a storefront, hiking his pants from time to time and watching the hemlines of women. George decided to go up and speak to him.

It didn't work out.

The days came and went and George could not have counted the tricks he dragged up to his sordid room. The room, as it stood, was a link to his past, when his mother had been known in town as a woman who knew how to give it to any man, any way he wanted it. But, the presence of a man in the room, transformed it, made it golden and bright, a chamber for the courtesan of Dumas fils, the doctor's wife of Flaubert, the noble whore of Guy de Maupassant, Zola's evil sex-goddess, Nana. How they had wondered at his choice of reading, in high school!

He didn't read these things, anymore. He lived them! This great Paris on the Hudson was all he could have longed for, the city of his carved alabastrine dreams. He could just go out and pick men off the canyon streets, like so many flowers from within a twilight glade, and bring them home, and the lovemaking and sex never ended. It was what he lived for: the lusty presence of men, and the lingering odor men left when they were gone.

The summer went. Fall was in the air, but it was still warm. George dressed carefully. He put on long, dark pantyhose which would hide the ugly ulcers which had come to his legs, and his soft green, long-sleeved crushed velvet blouse, which hid the strange blue sores on his left arm. He put on his forest-green miniskirt, which was ever so short, and made his face up patiently, and donned his orange wig. He got up on heels and put his costume jewelry in place, a garish pendant around his neck, and bracelets and finger rings which flashed fires of all colors.

He was going out for money. When he tricked in jeans and T-shirt in the afternoon, it was for pleasure. When he tricked in drag, it was for cash. He had his own special alley where he serviced the men. If they paid him, he gave them suckie-poo, or he would even bend over and let them have it that way for a little more.

George knew how to give it to a man, any way he wanted it. Like mother, like son.

On this fall night, George was given pause on his pell-mell journey to his place on the street, by sight of

Eben, the wild-eyed man from West Virginia, who had quoted from the Bible. George hardly knew him, at first. Eben had changed. He was no longer neat and bandbox clean. His hair and beard had grown out, ragged and long. His clothes were dirty. He was red-eyed and drooling. He did not wear his glasses. He shook his fists in the air. He was talking loud; causing there to surge about him, a mocking and jeering crowd.

George went and stood behind a stout man in a business suit who was listening. He could not believe that this was the same man he had spoken to, only several months before. Of course, Eben would not have recognized him either, walking about in miniskirt and heels.

"'Behold, your house is left unto you desolate,'" Eben was saying, passionately.

"Yeah, yeah," the crowd amened, derisively.

"It's the niggers and queers that are doing this. Niggers bring drugs, and bastards, and violence with them, wherever they go, and queers bring AIDS. Every bad thing in the world comes out of Africa, in one great tidal wave after another. Niggers have flooded these shores, as much a pestilence as any named hurricane, and the AIDS virus has followed them from Africa, borne upon the unspeakable lusts of perverts. Hurricanes! Hurricanes originate in Africa. The heart of the dark continent is where they come from."

"Zarathustra has come down from his mountain for sure," a thin-chested youth in tight jeans and an open shirt shouted. "You better go back where you come from, Red-neck, before somebody kills you, talking that way."

"People from Africa bring tribal violence with them. They boast about its pyramids, but what good are they? Nobody's ever found the use for them. God did not need them to stand as a monument to Him. 'The heavens declare the glory of God.' The pyramids just stand, thumping demonstrations of the egotistic ambitions of a group of earthly kings. Millions died to create them, just as millions die today to make some drug-lord rich, and to sow further violence in this country." Someone threw a peeled, overripe banana at Eben. He clawed the mess from his face and threw it on the sidewalk. He looked at it for a moment where it lay. "I guess some nigger did that," he said. "We had a good country here before the niggers came."

"Who do you think brought us?" a black guy shouted, in a good-natured African voice. "It ain't our fault we're here, bothering you so much."

"Everywhere I look, I see niggers and queers. They're the reason New York City is desolate."

"We're not all that desolate, motherfucker."

People were pushing against Eben, bumping up against him. He was about to lose his footing. His eyes grew wilder.

"You better go see a shrink," someone shouted.

"A man got to be crazy, talking that shit, with all us different kinds of people standing around."

"I am sent to stand among the perpetrators, to reveal to them their sinfulness."

"Man, we know we sin," someone near George said, in a world-weary voice. George felt himself akin to this voice. He, too, knew that he sinned. But, it was so much fun, and it felt so good! He wouldn't want to become a miserable man like Eben.

The crowd had grown larger. George was excited by it all. He saw a sleazy, wizened and gray drug-pusher he knew, who was called Little Rat, because of his diminutive size and his ways, standing at the edge of the seething, angry mass of humanity. Little Rat was looking at Eben like, for him, Eben was money in the bank, or a plane ticket to paradise.

A burly black cop hurried along the street, wheezing, with his cuffs rattling at his side. He was sweating in the cool fall night. Little Rat made a sign to him.

Burly Cop did not look toward George, although he was aware that George was standing there in drag. George knew Burly Cop knew George was a male hooker.

Somehow, Burly Cop seemed to be satisfied that Little Rat was there. Little Rat was Burly Cop's stoolie. It was as if it had been prearranged for him to be there. But, primarily, the cop's mind was not on Little Rat or George. He went straight to Eben.

"Sir, you have incited a riot here. I'm going to run you in."

"I'm not inciting a riot. I'm preaching against evil. I'm preaching against violence, tribal warfare, and drugs, and sex outside of marriage in this city. God has told me to bring this message to New York."

Someone spoke up in the voice of outrage.

"He's been doing it for weeks. You've seen him before. He's put down the pyramids."

"He's been using the word, 'nigger.' He's been saying, 'queer.' Those words will easily incite a riot," a middle-aged black woman said, in a cultured voice.

"I got a complaint about this man from this citizen over here," the cop said, pointing to Little Rat. "He give me a call about him, said he was inflaming the people. I've got to run him in."

"Perhaps, you can get help for him," the woman said. "If there is anything I can do, I will appear."

Another cop had joined the group.

"Get her name and address," Burly Cop said to the other officer.

"We know you," a white man said. "You're a racist cop. You're out to get this man because he talks against black people. He's got First Amendment Rights."

"I'm taking him in. They'll decide about his rights down there. He can talk to the ACLU."

"Why don't you take in some of these other guys that's out here committing crimes? Why don't you spend your time picking on real lawbreakers?"

"I don't see any of these other people breaking the law. This man," Burly Cop said, pointing to Eben. "I seen. I seen him standing up here inciting people to riot. He's disturbed the peace. He's blocking the sidewalk. We can't have this."

Eben had been emboldened by that stranger's intercession for him.

"I do have First Amendment Rights," he said. He planted his feet mulelike on the pavement. Burly Cop could see that Eben was not going to go anywhere willingly.

"You won't come along peaceable? I see."

"I don't have to go with you for exercising my right of free speech. I am preaching the Word of God."

Burly Cop took hold of him, and he gave Burly Cop a little push backward.

"You're resisting arrest," Burly Cop said. He began to beat Eben with his cudgel, first on one side of his head, and then on the other. Eben made a move to strike him. "You just tried again to strike a police officer during the performance of his duty! I hope everyone witnessed that." Burly Cop was sweating and gasping. "I'll tell the truth, I've been waiting for the chance to throw the book at you. I don't like the things you say!"

Burly Cop held his chest with one hand and beat Eben with the other. His heart was pounding. His fat girth would bounce with every stroke of his mighty cudgel against Eben's head and shoulders.

Blood from Eben's scalp and face poured in a flood to the sidewalk. In a moment, Eben fell and lay still.

"You better call an ambulance," Burly Cop told the other officer. "We don't want to haul him in the police car. He'll get blood all over it."

"You've made dog-meat out of him," one black guy said. "He didn't do anything that bad."

"You move on, or I'll lock you up, too. You care to ride along to the station with this racist bigot?"

"Which one?" the black guy mumbled under his breath. He shuffled away.

The woman, who had given her name, had disappeared. George felt it was time for him to move on, too. He could not see any sign of life from Eben.

Eben had told George when they had met, that time before, that this city would always kill the messenger, those called to attempt to save; and not those creating the need for the message, those known to prowl about wantonly to slay, in people, both the body and the soul.

As George walked away, he saw Little Rat making a sale on the corner.

George hurried on to the place on the street where he always stood to hustle.

After a while, a curious young man stood looking at George. He thought George was a woman. George spoke in falsetto to the young man.

"I'm Octavia. You looking for a good time?"

"My name's Sim."

"That sounds like the West. Are you from the West?"

"Nebraska."

"You look real corn-fed. They tell me men from Nebraska have got big things."

Sim reddened.

"I don't know about that."

"We could go back there in the alley, and I could find out if that's true."

Sim was cautious. He was beginning to sense that there was something strange about this woman. He was looking at George's big hands, and his Adam's apple.

"I believe you're a man," Sim said, incredulously.

"I wish you could see your face," George said, laughing in his natural voice. "You're really surprised." This young man was blond, and clean, and pretty. George would have done him for nothing. He kept looking at Sim's broad, farm-boy shoulders, and his strong thighs, used to gripping the sides of horses.

"I'd like to go with you," George said, anxiously.

"I believe you'd take me back in there and rob me," Sim said. "I didn't come to New York to get robbed."

"I don't rob people," George said, with honest indignation. "I show a man a good time and then he pays me. It's strictly business."

"I don't know," Sim said, doubtfully. "How much?"

"You look so fresh, so milk-fed. You'd never dream what I can give you."

"I'm not sure what you mean."

"I mean," George said, firmly grasping Sim's yielding arm. "Do you want a blow, or don't you? Come with me, and you'll see what you'll get."

GEORGETOWN, SOUTH CAROLINA

"One-Zero-Two Point Eight" was written in Georgetown in 1995.
Reincarnation can miscarry. A blue-collar worker in New York City slowly
becomes aware of the complex nature of his wife.
Police officers are there to protect and serve you.

ONE-ZERO-TWO POINT EIGHT

Bundled in the back seat of the big police cruiser, with his lady at his side, Duke spoke only once during the ride to the hospital. The brights on an oncoming vehicle blinded the officer driving, so that he almost struck the curb. The heavy car rocked when the cop jerked it back into its proper lane. Had there been a car parked out there in the dark, at the side of the puddled street, the cop car would have given it a stiff wallop. Bet your sweet ass!

"That fucker should try dimming his lights once in awhile," Duke said, aggrieved. He shouted in his blue-collar voice; talking loud, a man used to speaking in conflict with the noise of working machinery at the plant where he was employed.

Inside himself, he had to laugh. He could see the officers sweating.

"That tightened my asshole a screw or two," he observed, closing his remarks. "And theirs, too," he thought with satisfaction.

"There's rain on the windshield," the fat cop said. The skinny cop was driving.

Duke's mouth had gone dry. His throat and lungs were telling him shit, desiring smoke. He had a softpack of Camels in the pocket of his shirt, but he didn't light up. The two mismatched cops who owned the front seat could be prone to get right pissed if a passenger smoked.

There was no need to talk in the car, so far as Duke could see, when he had already told his story, back at his house, where he'd telephoned for the two officers.

They had performed like the city's finest, which was what they called themselves, and it was a good thing because Duke and his lady were highly agitated by what had occurred to them earlier that night. They had had quick need of the law.

It had all begun because of this fucking rain. It had rained so hard all the litter that people had dropped on the sidewalks had been carried down into the gutters, clogging the drains. Along with the dog shit. Columbus Avenue was awash.

Duke held his head down and walked rapidly, skipping actually, through puddles, trying to get home. A real gulley-washer came again, and the water hit him in the face like Niagara herself spewing out her mighty torrent.

Duke spotted the quivering neon sign in front of Mr. Rabinowitz's liquor store, so he decided to cop a few minutes' relief from the storm by going inside. He never bought anything from Mr. Rabinowitz any more. He had stopped drinking when his lady came. But, the store clerk wouldn't charge a man for standing in out of the rain a moment, although Mr. Rabinowitz was that tight.

When Duke got inside and was dripping on Mr. Rabinowitz's scuffed tile floor, the clerk eyed him suspiciously.

"Can I help you with something?"

"Man, I can't cut this downpour. I got to get in out of the rain," Duke said, taking out his Camels. He shook the pack. It had not got wet, thank God. "I hope it won't offend you if I stand here a minute 'til it stops." He lit a cigarette. He hadn't noticed the 'no smoking' sign which Mr. Rabinowitz had taped to the wall at the end of the counter.

The clerk looked down at the wet floor.

"Be my guest," he said, in a flat tone of voice.

Duke knew the clerk was pissed. outside, the rain was slacking. Duke was about to leave, when the door burst open and a sickly-looking little punk, with his right hand thrust deep into his coat pocket and his cap pulled down over his eyes, came in. This denizen looked all around; at the stock on the shelves and the clerk, and at Duke. His eyes just swept the whole store in one nervous circling motion.

Duke read the signs. This was bad news.

Duke was a medium-sized man who lifted heavy things and worked with reluctant machines. He had a couple of side hustles. He wasn't that afraid of trouble. He kept himself in good shape. But, he looked like no impediment to anyone who was focused on doing something rotten. Plenty of guys wouldn't be scared to jump in his shit, in one skinny minute, if they felt inclined. Duke was always careful not to offend anyone.

The clerk was pimply-faced youthful and always wore either an angry or a frightened look on his face.

Neither Duke nor the clerk would be good for much in an emergency that might result in physical confrontation. Duke looked too nonthreatening to arouse fear, a necessary skill for fighting; and the clerk was obviously too ill-equipped and incapable for the rough stuff to put up his gloves.

The punk whipped out a vicious-looking snub-nosed pistol and motioned it at Duke. Duke saw the rust on the barrel and the grime on the punk's hand. The hand had nails which were split and eaten away by the bandit's ferreting teeth.

"You stand back out of my way," the young man ordered. His hard little eyes then rested on the clerk's face. "You give me everything out of that fat till, or I'll blow your balls away. You'll sing falsetto, and men will fuck you."

Duke reasoned the clerk would give the punk all the money, and the punk would split.

But, the clerk was already in a fury, inside, because Duke had wet his floor and he was going to have to mop it up.

"Fuck you!" he said, defiant and surly, like a petulant and stubborn child.

There was a tremendous explosion which reverberated in the close quarters of the small liquor store. Duke saw the astonished clerk grasp his chest and begin to fall. Blood gushed over the clerk's hands and spattered the countertop.

The gunman turned and attempted to fire his gun at Duke, taking deadly aim, but the weapon emitted only a gentle click, the most pleasing sound Duke had ever heard. It was some kind of cheap oriental crap. Duke would recommend it in the future.

While the gunman tried to open the cash register, beating it with the useless pistol, Duke just about tore the street door down getting outside into the pelting rain.

He ran to a house that had Chinese ginkgos growing all around it, and squatted against the wall in deep shadow, holding his breath.

An old man heard him and stuck his thin, silver head outside.

"Call the cops," Duke shouted. "There's been a shooting at Rabinowitz's!" So he had done his duty. The cops were informed. He was not one of those New Yorkers who refused to get involved. He wanted to do what was right by the city and its citizens.

Just when he wanted it to rain for at least forty days and forty nights, the rain stopped. He saw the gunman come out of the liquor store looking all around. The punk was carrying Mr. Rabinowitz's cash register. He threw it down on the sidewalk, and it burst open. He picked up the coins and bills with hungry hands and crammed them into his jeans. He took a turn in the other direction, so Duke crawled out of his hiding place and ran all the way home. He didn't wait for the cops or look back.

When Duke went in his house, he ran and rested his face between the voluptuous breasts of his lady. She had leaped up from her chair, and she threw her arms about him, ecstatic at the sight of him. She let him stroke her hair and she kissed him under each eye, before he went to put on dry clothing.

The lady was tall; and her arms, thighs, midriff, and buttocks were firm. Her skin was smooth. Irregular freckles showed dimly through the tanned skin of her face. Her nose wrinkled when she smiled. This was all fine, but what really made Duke understand that he possessed a jewel was the heat of her. In her pubic region, she seethed like a furnace. All of the time.

Duke was coming back from the bedroom when he and his lady heard a series of sharp sounds outside. Duke knew at once that it was the sound of his rose trellis being broken down. The thin laths being trampled underfoot made the snapping noise which they heard. Someone was walking about under the ailanthus trees!

A furtive look had come into the lady's gray eyes. She stole into the kitchen and Duke followed her. Outside they could see the shadowy figure of a small man.

"It's the punk," Duke said. "He seen which way I come. When I ran, he ran after me. He's come to kill me so that I won't be able to finger him to the cops."

The killer was on the stoop, kicking in the aluminum kitchen door. Duke and his lady cowered against the cabinets. Duke's face had become ghastly white, so that each strand of his black, day's growth of beard could be separately seen. The lady stood tense and trembling, her head slightly raised.

The killer burst in. He didn't look to the right or the left, but walked straight toward Duke in the dimly lit kitchen, pointing his gun. He would have unjammed it, or there was no cow in Texas. It would fire this time. Bet your ass!

Duke's lady moved as swift as a clap of lightning. Duke had never seen a human being move so fast. She caught the punk's gun hand and his forearm, and sank her teeth into his wrist. Duke heard the bone snap and he saw the blood. The punk dropped his gun.

"Now, you get the fuck out of here," Duke said, coming on strong and loud. He was king in his castle again. The killer turned and ran past the damaged door. It swayed for a moment, disconsolate, and then it closed behind him.

It was raining shithooks again. Duke called for the police to come.

"You sure saved my shriveled ass," Duke told his lady, admiringly. "I'll say for you: You've got a set of teeth hung on you."

It had been a lucky day when Duke had found his lady. He was coming back from the Rockaways on the subway when he saw her standing, looking at him, grey-eyed with her sensual breasts rising and falling, just swinging her ass and smiling. He had brought her home and she had never left him since.

Duke was proud of her. She spent much of her time reading improving books. Tonight, when Duke came in, she had been reading a heavy tome concerning the transmigration of souls. This could be a good thing if the transfer worked right; but Duke knew, any system can fuck up. It happened every day at the plant. Nothing was foolproof. In this reincarnation thing: What if the switch made from one life to another was incomplete? It could happen in New York City!

The lady picked up the book again, while they waited for the police, and a mystic smile spread over her face, as she read. She was a fucking Mona Lisa!

It was like a heroin high must be for a junkie for Duke to just look at her.

She did not reproach him for being out on the streets so late on a stormy night. Duke had been out to pick up a few bucks. His lady understood about these things. Later, he would be nervous and he wouldn't be able to sleep, and she would sit up with him, reading her book and dreaming of the way it was in India a million years ago.

When the cops came, the fat one and the skinny one, they spent half the night writing up reports of what had transpired at the liquor store and what had happened in Duke's kitchen. They put the punk's gun in a plastic bag and the towel which Duke had used to wipe up his blood in another one.

" I want this lady to go to the emergency room and get checked out," the fat one said.

"He didn't hurt her. She's all right."

"What Officer Ricks is trying to say," the skinny one intervened. "is, this lady bit some low-life, scumbag, street rat, and his blood went into her mouth and we want to be sure that she doesn't catch any kind of a disease."

"She's not some fucking vampire Dracula," Duke defended her. "She didn't drink his blood."

Absolute terror struck him. He could imagine his lady coming down with some leprous disease. He could see her lying in a hospital bed, her firm body turning soft, her lovely skin becoming wrinkled, the treat of her turning off. He could imagine the great fire she carried about in her loins gradually cooling until she was cold and white as marble. They hastened to get ready to go.

So, this was how Duke and his lady came to be riding in the big police cruiser to the hospital, where the lady would be carefully checked by a doctor to see that she was all right.

The doctor was named Dr. Dave. Duke found out right away that he was from Indonesia. Dr. Dave was assisted by Nurse Hildebreath.

Duke's lady looked down upon Nurse Hildebreath with frozen indifference, seeming to have an organic dislike of her.

Nurse Hildebreath was given to arching her back and humming under her breath. She had great moon eyes, yellow and round. When she moved, it was without a sound, and when she spoke she hissed.

Dr. Dave was nondescript.

"He should be somewhere, dressed in a breechclout, poling some goddamned narrow-assed boat through reeds," Duke told himself. Duke could see Dr. Dave sucking innocent shellfish out of their shells, making delighted noises. A fucking pig!

The fat cop had disappeared, but the skinny cop stood against the wall. He would not sit down on one of the orange plastic chairs which were furnished by the hospital. Duke did not sit down. He paced.

Emotion welled up inside him. He felt his cheeks burn. His chest ached as though it would explode. He was afraid that he was going to cry in front of the skinny cop and Nurse Hildebreath.

"I love my lady very much," he said. They had been looking at him, strangely.

"We know you do," the nurse said, in her professional voice. Who gave a fuck?

"That woman had a life before I met her. She had a good life. She gave it up for me. She gave up her freedom to do anything she wanted, to come to my house and look after me. She has the patience to sit and listen to my cares and worries. But, I can tell you something else about her; if you want to hear." His voice trailed off doubtfully.

The skinny cop looked at Nurse Hildebreath. Her face was impassive.

"We want to hear," he said.

"It's like something magic," Duke told them. "She knows by instinct when there's something wrong. She'll smile and touch me on the arm, and look me dead in the eyes. It's the deepest gaze you've ever seen. I can read the love she has for me. I know how much that woman loves me!"

"You're very lucky," Nurse Hildebreath commented. There was a trace of bitterness in her voice. She had always held herself apart from people, at arm's length, expecting them to love her, in spite of her curious tendency toward aloofness, but people didn't love her.

Duke wondered what his lady and that foreign doctor were doing for so long in the examining room. He felt that she was somehow in peril. He worried about her now, as he knew she always worried for him when he was out on the streets, trying to pick up a few dollars and putting himself at risk. He knew that if he should die, there was one loyal soul that would grieve for him.

"That young murderer won't be back out there to bother you or your wife for a long time," the skinny cop promised. "Officer Ricks has gone to take the weapon to the station. It will be checked for fingerprints to match against those on the broke cash register. Later, when we capture a suspect, his fingerprints and your identification will lock him into the crime. We're making a careful investigation. The captured suspect won't find any loophole to escape through."

"What happened to the clerk?"

"He was DOA."

A chill passed over Duke's shoulders and ran along both sides of his rib cage; icy fingers sliding down to freeze his crotch. This was reality. He had escaped the killer's gun twice. The first time, it must have been God who intervened. The second time, he was saved by his lady. There must not be a third time. The third time was always the charm, everyone said. If there were another time, the punk would surely succeed.

"I hope you catch him soon. That motherfucker aims to kill me."

"There are police officers who have been out looking for him since that citizen called. They'll catch him before long, or we'll soon identify him through his prints and pick him up."

"This is a busy night," Nurse Hildebreath spit, thankful there was another nurse on duty.

The woman was sly. She acted as though she knew some secret about Duke's lady which Duke did not know. She acted as if there were something which she and Duke's lady had in common, like two people from the same place who meet in the city, and are civil to each other, but who would rather not have met.

"We appreciate your being here," the skinny cop told her.

"It's a pleasure when people are as nice as you," she mewed, looking as if she would like to jump in his lap. But, he had continued to stand. She swished about and found her purse. She dug some coins from it. She got an ice cream bar from the machine.

Duke could see that she hungered for that police officer's trim little uniformed body. But, the skinny cop knew how to maintain a wall erected about himself. The skinny cop's mind was all on business.

Duke laughed inside himself over Nurse Hildebreath's frustration.

At last, Duke's lady and Dr. Dave returned from the examining room.

"That didn't take long, did it?" Dr. Dave asked, a phrase he used often, so he could be successful with saying it. "She's A-OK," he continued, with his accent. "Not to worry. Not to have concern. Should come back in one month for tests. To be sure."

Dr. Dave and Nurse Hildebreath chattered together over some reports. They wrote down bits of information about Duke's lady. Nurse Hildebreath, smiled and giggled a lot, purring and rubbing against Dr. Dave's shoulder, and he was inscrutable.

The skinny cop's beeper told him that Officer Ricks was outside the emergency room area, in the black and white. He led Duke and his lady to the car.

"They've picked up a suspect," Ricks said. "I'll be back for you in the morning so that you can go and pick him out of the lineup. I'll call and let you know what time. Now, we'll take you home."

Duke could see he'd lose a day's work.

Home. That was what Duke wanted. To go home. He wanted to lie in his own bed, with his lady, warm and safe, with the lights off, where he could forget the killer eyes of the murderous, jerk-off degenerate that tried twice to kill his ass.

When they were there, Duke's lady curled up beside him in a ball, and touched his forearm with her lips. The hair on his arm and his chest bristled in response to her tongue and her fingertips. She gave a deep satisfied moan.

It had been quite an evening! But, everything was satisfactory now. It had stopped raining. Duke tried to erase everything pertaining to the past eight hours from his mind.

But, one thing worried him. When Dr. Dave had been filling out papers and Nurse Hildebreath had been trying to get his pants down, Dr. Dave had said, the only alarming thing about Duke's lady was the fact that her temperature was 102.8 degrees.

Nurse Hildebreath had then offered the smug, catty observation that 102.8 is normal temperature for a dog.

That stung.

GEORGETOWN, SOUTH CAROLINA

"Triad Lost" was written in Georgetown in 1996. School Days! The writer recalls his time at Horry-Georgetown Technical College, where he liked a teacher so much he named his dog after her. The dog's name is Karen.

How to tell the sheep from the goats? That is the problem! The story is about six young people. Which three comprise the unholy three? Which are indeed the lost triad? How can we ever say who are the saved, and who are the lost? Do all vulnerable young people wear a necklace of figs, ready to be destroyed by loup-garou? Does some lurking evil demand daily sacrifices? Does the werewolf really walk? Is this the way the world is? Sometimes it seems so. But, the writer is an optimist, unrepentantly, unchangeably optimistic. He is always up.

The writer knew happy days at this college. A fellow student told him he should write lyrics for country music. "You have the subject matter for it," she told him. This remark hit a solemn and sweet chord in the writer. He never forgot what the lady said. This was the only time this woman ever spoke to him. It was an anointing — at least a validation. He was not for kings and tycoons, but for guys and ladies who work in the Air Filter Plant in Baytown, SC. Now he knows what his voice is and who it is for. He has found that he is today what he had always known himself to be.

Through Mississippi summers and winters, through years of wearing "Travelin' Shoes", through years of working in the steel mill (with activities in the union), with a father who would crush and a mother who would smother, he had sought out the people, in their churches, their schools, their workplaces, and the streets. It was the plain stories heard in barber shops and doctors' waiting rooms, the touch of ordinary people that was his "subject matter." He wants nothing more than to be the teller of their tales, like they have been shown to him.

The name of this book is "Out Of The Iron Furnace." The stories belong as much to all the people that the scribe has come into contact with as they do to him. The stories are the wealth of the people who have lived them. They are given to those that will care to read them. Such as that poor girl who has just turned a trick and is hitchhiking her way home where she will be able to feed her hungry children.

It is true "I Never Left Home." I have been at home everywhere I have ever been.

TRIAD LOST

Otios!!! Darling Ruck wrote the word in her composition book. She underlined it and followed it with four exclamation points. Otiose so perfectly described her fellow classmates, Billy Boohan, Ward Tully, and Sofia Weems ... vain... empty ... hollow. And, idle!

Darling did not let her eyes rest on these three for long, in her survey of the sunny classroom at Apple Technical College. There were better things for her to look at.

Like Jarvis Rad Rand!

Darling studied the way her fellow student Jarvis Rad's light shirt stretched across the muscles of his back, and the smooth, tanned skin of his bare arms and the nape of his neck, and the moist swirl of his dark hair.

He seemed daily, at school, to carry with him the quiet energy and pent-up purpose he exhibited on the basketball court. Jarvis Rad usually wore a serious, almost sleepy expression on his face. He could, however, on a moment's notice, alter to a state of frenetic animation, much to everyone's startled surprise and awed delight.

On the basketball court, he would move with marvelous control, until the moment came when he would become like a madman, a wolverine, galvanizing himself and his team to action.

Darling had often heard people screaming their cheers, stamping their feet, pounding each other's shoulders, when Jarvis Rad would become berserk and take possession of a game.

Every girl on campus looked at Jarvis Rad the way Darling Ruck was looking at him. With adoration!

Except Sofia Weems.

Sofia had what she wanted elsewhere, in Billy and Ward, her loyal henchmen. The three were inseparable.

Darling's Aunt Delph, who was more than an aunt ... she was a friend ... made acrid comments about the way Sofia flaunted her "love bubbles."

Darling was simple and plain. Freckles hid just beneath the pale skin of her face, wanting to pop out ... to darken... a sorrow to Darling Ruck. Her hair was the color of the fur on a useless yard dog her father had once had, whom he called "Ol' Yalla," and loved. She kept her hair cut short, pushed back out of the way. Darling was small, short, almost flat-chested.

But, she did well in school.

She wondered, now, if she might aver be as delighted with anyone as Sofia, and Billy and Ward were with each other. Of course, if that someone were Jarvis Rad, Darling knew she would be.

But, would a boy like Jarvis Rad be delighted with Darling? He never seemed to notice her.

Darling called Sofia and her friends "The Lost Triad." She wrote these words, now, in her composition book.

Darling felt Joe Dipple's pale gray eyes upon herself. Joe Dipple was a pink-faced boy, slight of build. His wrists were always dirty. When he washed his hands, he did not wash that high. The tops of his socks hung limp about his hairy ankles. He wore khaki pants, and a pale yellow shirt open over a white T-shirt.

Darling's father, Rodney Ruck, and Joe's father worked at the same plant. The families liked and respected each other.

"I'd hate to see you give Joe the go-by," Aunt Delph had said to Darling...

often. "You let him get a little more age on him. He'll make a fine man. You wait and see. That boy were raised right. He weren't snatched up."

"He's not very smart," Darling said, thoughtfully. "His grades at school are atrocious."

"Atrocious, as you say," Aunt Delph said, warming to her subject. "Joe Dipple is a hardworking, steady young man."

Darling never pursued the subject of Joe with Aunt Delph, or her mother or father.

Joe had a ragged, old Chevrolet, which he kept running like a trooper. He came to get Darling every day to give her a ride to school. Sometimes he came to her house in the evenings, smelling of gasoline and sweat, and they studied together.

"Joe Dipple is like a younger brother to me," Darling was always explaining. She felt herself to be older and more experienced than Joe, but they were the same age. "He doesn't act nearly as mature as Jarvis Rad Rand."

"I know you think Jarvis Rad is the cream of the pot," Aunt Delph often answered. "In the first place, he doesn't even look at you." This made Darling's cheeks burn. "In the second place, you give both these boys a little time and see which one goes the farthest. You may be surprised."

Looking at Joe in the pleasant large classroom, Darling thought of how Joe sat in church every Sunday; inattentive, feeling uncomfortable in his Sunday clothes. He showed the same inattention to Mr. Shadid, their eager and earnest instructor in English Literature.

Darling took her attention from Joe Dipple and returned it to Mr. Shadid. Her thoughts had drifted completely away from the dark-skinned teacher. She was drifting. But, in the sunlit room, which was bright and warm, all the students looked bored and sleepy.

Except Jarvis Rad.

Jarvis Rad was a perfect student. He listened to every word that Mr. Shadid said, and he took notes.

For days they had been studying the major English poets. Today, as always, Mr. Shadid's dark face was very solemn, businesslike. His language was very broken.

The students were being lad through Byron's "The Bride of Abydos." Darling identified with the lovely Zuleika, the heroine of the poem, who was under parental pressure to wed the undesirable Bey of Carasman. She had started to read the poem the night before. She had found it difficult. She had fallen asleep. So, today she did not know the ending. She was curious to see what would happen to Zuleika.

Darling dreamed of a platonic friendship with Jarvis Rad. She didn't know anything about any other kind. She was prepared to stand modestly at his side; a worshipping, loyal sister ... ready to encourage him in all that he did - cheer him on.

Jarvis Rad's family owned a business, and he had a fine car. When he graduated from high school his parents had bought him a Pontiac Grand Am automobile, which was red, with a gray interior. Jarvis Rad had had it for two years and had never put a scratch on it, save one.

The students at Apple Tech had seen this scratch. It was a mystery to them.

The car was just right for an athlete, and the "bon vivant" which Darling felt ha surely must be when he was not at school. Actually she meant, a boulevardier. Jarvis Rad cut himself a figure of romance, adventure, and excitement for Darling. He had been a grade ahead of Joe and herself at high school.. There, he had reigned a basketball king. Now, she looked at Joe Dipple. He was slumped in his seat, toying with a pen. The death of Salim, dramatically told in Byron's poem, did not move him. This was the boy Aunt Delph treasured as though he were "something handed down!"

Mr. Shadid talked on in his strange English, which was perfect and without flaw, but hard to understand. His inflections and accents were those of India. His speech sounded like a song. He was enthusiastic, forthright. His large, dark eyes pleaded that the students be interested and learn. In his country, students were famished to be educated. It this place, a despondent apathy hung over the classroom.

Darling could see Joe Dipple's wide, run-over, dusty shoes. She looked at him from head to toe. He needed a haircut. His hair was short. It should be trimmed regularly to keep it neat.

Darling almost forgot herself ... nearly allowed herself to make a "tsking" sound. She took her eyes away from Joe. In a moment, he might turn and smile at her. She didn't want that. In front of all the other students!

But, Joe Dipple was not smiling today. The rumors Darling had heard of him were true. He was about to be kicked out of school because of poor grades. They would give him only one more chance.

"I just don't care about all this shit they hand us," he said. "I can't get interested in it."

"I really don't know how we can motivate you," the counselor had told him. "It concerns me a lot, because I care about you."

"Yeah. Tell me more," Joe had thought.

Darling chided him for his attitude.

If Darling Ruck would encourage him, help him nights with his lessons, he would try harder ... that's what he told her ... but she just couldn't see spending all her evenings with him. He knew that. She wanted something else. Better.

Joe seized every opportunity to talk with Darling; at school, at church, when they did rarely study together, but she looked right through him, seemed always to be thinking about somewhere ... or someone ... else.

Joe knew she had a crush on Jarvis Rad. if she ever got one-half a chance with him, she'd drop her tepid friendship with Joe forever. He knew how devotedly she would sit at Jarvis Rad's knee, helping HIM with his studies, if he needed help, which seemed unlikely.

The only thing which kept hope alive in Joe was the fact that Jarvis Rad had never paid the slightest attention to Darling.

Sometimes, Joe would get his dad's permission to use the good family car at night, instead of his old heap, and he would ask Darling to go out with him, but she wouldn't go. If she went, he might take it to mean there was something between them.

Mr. Shadid stopped talking.

Joe put up his hand, wanting to take part. Wanting to seem to be working in this class.

"Did Zuleika die?" he asked.

Mr. Shadid looked at him strangely.

"That's the tragedy of the poem," he said.

So, Darling thought, Zuleika did die! She grieved herself to death rather than worry the man her family wanted to force upon her, after the noble Selim was killed. It was a very sad poem..

Many in the class were not saddened. There were twitters of laughter in the room because of Joe's question and Mr. Shadid's reaction.

"Shi . . .it!" someone said, in the area of the room where the Lost Triad sat. Mr. Shadid looked hurt and angry. When Mr. Shadid felt pain, his whole soul came up into his face and eyes. It was a torment to him that English Literature was not taken seriously.

Joe Dipple blushed. His pink cheeks became ever redder.

Darling looked upon Jarvis Rad as a rock of strength.

He was oblivious to everyone else in the room. He edited his notes, waited to give Mr. Shadid his undivided attention when the teacher would speak again.

"I simply DIE over Jarvis Rad," Darling thought to herself.

She studied his feet. Jarvis Rad wore trousers which were cut long enough so that the cuffs covered the top of his neat cotton .. with a touch of nylon for stretch .. blue ... houndstooth patterned ... imported socks. There was no expanse of hairy skin revealed between his pants and his socks, as was the case with Joe Dipple. His narrow shoes were expensive loafers, polished to a mellow brown... almost golden... subdued shine.

Jarvis Rad's shirt was a delicate glory; short-sleeved, band-collared, ivory and marine and earth. It was silk and cotton. Darling studied the geometric pattern.

"I simply wish that I could reach out my hand and caress that fabric," she thought, imparting to herself a breathless secret. " I wish I could just rub my hands all over it. I'd like to bury my face in it, drown in the scent of that heady cologne he always wears."

Darling wished she could have wallpaper at home in her room with that pattern and those colors ... marvelous sheen!

But, Darling had to admit to herself that Jarvis Rad had never even looked at her.

Suddenly, the bell rang to end the class. Mr. Shadid hastily gave them an assignment for preparation for the next day. Darling stacked her books and cradled them in her arm. She started for the door.

Billy and Ward and Sofia blocked her way for a moment. She had to stand very close to them, waiting for them to move on.

"Let's go smoke a little weed," Billy said, ignoring the presence of Darling. She was no rat.

"I feel like I could blast a joint," Ward agreed, "after all that shit Shadid just put us through. A few times I thought I was going to puke. That Indian acts like he really eats up that stuff."

"He must- be some kind of a fucking fruit fairy."

"We've got a class coming up," Sofia said.

Billy looked at her with mock seriousness.

"So?" he inquired, at last.

They all three burst out laughing. Darling followed them out into the open air. It was good to breath the grassy, pine-scented atmosphere of the back campus. She heard a bird sing from the "skraggily" oleander bushes. She saw the Lost Triad skipping toward Billy Boohan's dilapidated old black Ford pickup.

"Let's don't sit in the truck," Ward said. "You've got a broke window. It'll let the smoke out."

"Where'll we sit?"

Darling saw them go toward and then enter Jarvis Rad's Grand Am. He had left it unlocked. Sofie sat in the back. Billy and Ward settled into the deep bucket seats.

"I wonder if I should go and tell Jarvis Rad?" Darling thought. "He might not like it for them to be sitting in his car."

She felt backward about approaching Jarvis Rad. He might think she was running after him. And, what the Lost Triad did was none of her business.

Her mind was diverted. Joe Dipple came up to her.

"I've got to go to the office," he said. "They've sent for me."

"For what? Your bill is paid, isn't it?"

"It's about my grades," Joe told her, a desperate expression on his face, which was sickly white. Now, his face was not pink at all.

Darling hurried to her class. She was taking instruction in a word-processor program. The class was small, because neither the Lost Triad nor Joe Dipple were there. There was only Jarvis Rad, herself, and a few others. Jarvis Rad sat at a computer which was far from hers. She could see only the top of his head.

The hour dragged. The Lost Triad did not return, and Joe Dipple did not come back. When the hour was over, Darling want to the office to find Joe. He was supposed to give her a ride home.

"Joe left a long time ago," the girl in the front office said. Darling knew her as Johnetta. "They had him back in there and talked with him very hard. They told him if he didn't catch his grades up right away he was out of here."

"Where'd he go?"

Johnetta shrugged and smiled, white teeth flashing in a black face. It was her "sorry I can't help you" look.

"I'll look around outside," Darling said. "I way need to come back in here and call my Aunt Delph to come get me. I don't have a way to go home."

"Any time," Johnetta said.

Outside, Darling saw the Lost Triad tumbling out of the red Grand Am, laughing and slapping each other on relaxed shoulders. Jarvis Rad had not come out yet. He was talking with the computer instructor. It was important for him to learn all about computers. He was already using them at his father's business. Someday, business would be his.

Darling was about to go back to the office to phone when Jarvis Rad came out the door from the classroom.

"You still here?" he asked.

"Joe Dipple went home early. I was supposed to ride with him." There was no one about. The Lost Triad had gotten in Billy's old truck and ridden away, laying a trail of smoke. Darling was not thinking about them.

"I'll give you a lift," Jarvis Rad told her. "You need any help with your books?"

"No," Darling said. "That's o.k. I will accept a ride."

Her heart was burning. She could not believe her good fortune. Jarvis Rad Rand was actually going to give her a ride home! She could not let anything spoil this moment, the culmination of all her longing.

He opened the door on the passenger side for her. At once, a pungent odor blew out of the car, into her face. It diminished after a minute. They stood with the door open. They looked at the ugly scratch on the side of his car.

"One night, they had me penned in the parking lot. I couldn't get out. I just went crazy. I wanted to tear up every car on the lot. I scratched my car trying to go through a place that was too narrow. I can't stand to be restrained. I've got to be free. I've got to be able to move! I had to get out of there. That's why that scratch is on my car." Jarvis Rad could recall the frustration and rage he had felt that night all over again. A demon had come up inside him. Something utterly destructive. Sometimes, he got the same feeling ... the compulsion to bust free ... when a player guarded him too closely on the basketball court. He wanted to break that player's face. "I can't stand anyone breathing down my back," he said.

By the time Jarvis Rad went around the car and got in, the odor if marijuana was almost gone from the car.

"I'm going to have to use some air-freshener in here," ha said. "Something stinks."

Darling did not tell him that the Lost Triad had used his car as a place to smoke. That might create a discordant note in the symphony of this perfect afternoon. She leaned back against the pearly seat, put her books beside her next the console.

"I love this car," she said. "It's very comfortable."

Jarvis Rad forgot the smell. Darling was glad. If she told him what had transpired, he might tear off looking for Billy Boohan's old truck. He might overtake them, and make trouble.

They sped along the highway. Everyone always exceeded the speed Jarvis Rad was no exception. But, the road was four-laned and wide. There was a grassy median between the northbound and the southbound lanes. Darling watched as the small business establishments seemed to fly by on sparkling wings. She felt like a queen at her coronation.

"Did you like the poem by Byron?" Darling asked. "Did you like 'The Bride of Abydos?' I thought it was sad."

"You could say that," Jarvis Rad said, teasingly. "Selim. was killed. Zuleika died. So, the Bey didn't get Zuleika. No one got what they wanted."

"It was a lost triad," Darling told him, very seriously. "The Lost Triad is a secret name I have for Billy and Ward and Sofia. I have it written in my composition book."

Jarvis laughed.

"You've got a sharp mind there," he said. "It's funny I never noticed before. Maybe we could get together some time. We could go out for a cheeseburger."

"I'd like to."

Darling felt light. She felt incredibly lighter than she had ever felt, as though she could sail into space, as straight and as sure as a rocket. She would rise to float among the stars, hearing them twinkle all about her, sprinkling her with their dust, so that she would feel like the most beautiful luminary in the heavens.

"Maybe we could plan to go tomorrow night," he said.

Darling felt herself lifted upon a magic swing, whizzing back and forth, seeing the earth beneath her grow small on the outswing and larger on the swing back.

Darling returned to the world to notice that they passed the Dipple house. It was right on the highway. Joe Dipple was out in the front yard, mowing the grass. He saw them.

Darling smiled her broadest smile for Joe Dipple. She lifted her head, showed him the pride and happiness she felt sitting at Jarvis Rad's side. She waved her hand .. the way Queen Elizabeth always waved when she went out on the streets in her carriage.

Jarvis Rad switched on his stereo. The beat of the bass in the rock music he played caused Darling to vibrate.

"Uh, oh!" Jarvis Rad said, turning off the music. "There's a roadblock ahead. No sweat though. It will only take a minute." He began to fumble in his back pocket with his left hand to find his wallet with his driver's license. He stopped easily and smiled up at the officer. Cool.

There were four officers from different law enforcement agencies and the sniffer dog was there. The sniffer dog was named Stormin' Norman.

The moment Jarvis Rad rolled down the window, Stormin' Norman, smiling and lifting his head high, told the officer there was dope in the car.

Officers made Jarvis Rad pull over onto the grassy median, and he and Darling had to get out of the car. They were patted down, books looked into, the dog sniffed them. Jarvis Rad could see that this dog was grinning, but he knew Stormin' Norman could be lethal. The dog went into the car and sniffed it out thoroughly. Jarvis Rad had to open the trunk. Stormin' Norman got right up inside.

No drugs were found.

Jarvis Rad was livid.

"You held me!" he told the officer. "You restrained me and messed up my car. You had no cause to search me. There's no drugs here."

"There has been," the officer said. "We just didn't catch you while you was holding. You just go along and be glad you got away this time. And.... You be careful in the future."

The officer wasn't apologetic. He was stern and accusing.

Darling's effervescent spirits had fizzed away. The scintillating ride with Jarvis Rad had gone flat.

"I guess I ought to tell you. I saw Sofie and Billy and Ward in your car. They were smoking pot. That's what you swelled when we came out and got in the car."

Jarvis Rad's knuckles on the steering wheel want white. Ha blazed up with the same fury that Darling had seen him display once in awhile on the basketball court. Then, it was glorious to behold. Now, it was frightening.

"You scare me," she said. "I thought you were a different person than you are. There's something animal and violent in you. You're like a bull in a pasture, content to graze peacefully until someone comes too near you. Then, you go mad!"

"You don't sit there and criticize me," Jarvis Rad told her. "You don't know shit about me! I fucking well don't have to take anything from you. You could have told me they'd been in my car."

"It's just that I'm disappointed. I thought you were such a nice boy...."

"I'll show you nice," Jarvis Rad said, gnashing his teeth.

He made the Grand Am career onto the dirt road which ran past the dumpsters. Behind the dumpsters, he stopped. He seized upon Darling, roughly.

Before she could think what was happening, he was up on his knees on the console, his head over the back seat. He held onto her with a grip of iron with his left hand, while with his right he undid his blue suede belt, and opened his dark blue cuffed dress trousers. He was already pushing down his pants - matching lapis, mesh thong with the natural lift support, when Darling broke free of him and leaped out of the car. Jarvis Rad cursed at her, slamming the car door shut. He spun around in the area behind the dumpsters, the Grand Am's wheels throwing filthy dirt into the air. He came past Darling, his back wheels spinning. He rolled down the window and threw her books onto the ground!

Darling saw him turn onto the highway, almost hitting a truck. He sped away. She stooped to pick up her books...crying.

Darling walked slowly to the highway. It was not far for her to walk home. She would be there in just a few minutes, with Mother, and Father, and Aunt Delph, the people who loved her. But, she could not possibly tell them what had happened.

She wiped her eyes with a tissue.

She could forget about Jarvis Rad. That silly schoolgirl crush was over. Now, she saw the world as it really was. To her, Jarvis Rad was dead!

Darling's shoes were thin. She was walking on gravel. She was very relieved in a few minutes when she was overtaken by wasp-waisted Aunt Delph driving her sensible Plymouth.

Aunt Delph's sharp eyes, in her sharp face, saw immediately something was wrong.

"Why are you walking home?" she asked.

"Joe Dipple went home early. He had to go to the office. There was something bad about his grades. I don't know."

"He's a good boy," Aunt Delph said. "If he had someone to work with him. He doesn't get the support at home he should. You should help him."

"I don't want to help Joe Dipple," Darling said, miserably. Her face wore a stricken look.

"He's ruffled your tail feathers, I suppose."

"No. Not Joe. It was someone else. I don't feel like talking."

"You be nice to Joe."

Darling thought about Joe. If she could get him to pull his socks up and get his hair trimmed, he wouldn't be so bad. If only he weren't so pink-faced. He might be facing his very last chance to stay in school. Perhaps, she would help him. A shudder ran through her as she thought of Jarvis Rad.

"I'll call Joe later. We could study together. He could come over to my house. We could start tonight."

"I think that would be the right thing to do," Aunt Delph told her, with satisfaction.

At home, Darling thought of calling Joe, but she felt low, too unhappy to do it. She was grieving for something inside herself which had died. It was the belief that there could be a perfect boy. She had thought Jarvis Rad was this.

There was no perfect boy in this world. Darling said good-bye to the girl she had been. She looked at her plain little face in the mirror of her dresser. Joe Dipple was right for her. She would just see what she could make out of him.

Darling stared out of her window, watched shadows lengthen across the mown back yard. A bird rested on her mother's clothesline. A cat walked by. The jay squawked at the cat. In a few minutes, she heard her father drive up.

She joined him in the kitchen. They sat down at the kitchen table, after she fixed him a cold glass of soda.

"How was your day?" she asked.

"A usual day," Rodney Ruck told her. "Oh! Something unusual did happen. I just saw Joe Dipple. He had a duffel bag with his clothes in it, and he was thumbing a ride on the highway. He said he was leaving."

"Leaving?"

"Going away. He said he knew he was going to flunk out of school. He had given up. He said a funny thing...."

"What was that?"

"He told me to tell you he hoped you'd be very happy. He said he saw you riding around with Jarvis Rad Rand in his Pontiac. Were you in the car with Jarvis Rad?"

"Yes," Darling said weakly.

"I didn't know you went around with him."

"He just gave me a ride."

"Anyhow, Joe said he is leaving home. I left him standing there. In a few minutes, he got a ride in an eighteen-wheeler. I caught it in the rearview mirror. The truck went barreling up the road toward North Carolina."

Darling leaped up, excited.

"Where's he gone? I've got to get him back!"

"He's lit a shuck out of here," Rodney Ruck said, finally. "That truck will take him straight into Richmond city. I recognized the truck. It's one comes to the mill. "

"Oh, Dad! I'm swimming in stormy water .... All of us are."

"All who?"

"Triad Lost...Jarvis Rad, Joe, and me. Oh, see what has become of us......"

"I'm sorry," Rodney said, "I don't think I know what you mean. I'm sorry you're upset."

"It's all right," Darling said, touching her father's hand with her fingertips. She smiled. Her smile radiated no heat and no light. She slumped in the wooden chair.

"I've lost both of them," she thought. "What now will I dream. about?"

She went to her room and opened her composition book.

She wrote down the date, and the time, and penned ...

"When Love, who sent, forgot to save

The young, the beautiful, the brave ....

— Byron."

And...

"Finis. "

GEORGETOWN, SOUTH CAROLINA

"Groundhog Day" was written in Georgetown in 1996. This story shows that even though one steps in dog shit early on, one can remain an optimist, still daring to believe that there will unexpectedly come in life an opportunity to reach out and grasp happiness. Many are those who are rewarded, after they have entertained angels unawares.

GROUNDHOG DAY

"You ain't shit," Egan Tipley annunciated to his wife Vel, as they pushed their way through the promiseless glass door into Dave Radlay's open 'til two country bar. The door had reflected but dimly the frugal lights of the parking lot, and from inside no warming eruption of cheer had beckoned, save the dull, Satanic, red glow of the jukebox.

And ... Vel Tipley had stepped in dog shit.

A finger of fog on icy air followed them inside, and for a moment the occupants of this dank Inferno heard the exigent twitter of raindrops ... ice droplets ... striking the broken pavement which lay begrimed before the door.

The jukebox had just stopped playing. Egan recognized the dying strains of a Marty Stuart recording, one of his favorites.

Egan's stentorian testimony regarding his companion's total dearth of value rang and echoed under the low ceiling of that sultry cell they had entered so clumsily.

At once, Egan began to sweat. He unbuttoned his mill jacket; crashed a broganned foot against a chair.

The only three occupants of the place showed calm acceptance of Egan and Vel. But, Egan had interrupted, in this primal haunt, a carefully-wrought rhythm which had been nurtured there. The thoughtful cigarette, the relished drink, the placid contemplation were upset.

Vel, biting her lip, walked... unsteadily to be sure ... but, she walked. That was the miracle.

Egan lumbered behind her, a great boar of a man, his gut rolling from under his open jacket, a thicket of stubble on his face. He wiped viscid mucus from his lips with the back of his scarred, blunt hand.

"You had to bring me out on this night from Hell!" he reproachfully spat at Vel.

"God knows, my chest cavity is already full of fucking phlegm!"

"I'm celebrating," Vel mumbled.

"Tell us Vel .... What are you celebrating ... ?" Egan asked, nastily. "Vel?"

"It's Groundhog Day today."

"It's a sad celebration," Egan told her. "Sit down here at this table," he directed. "Hopefully, this chair will be able to support the weight of your big ass." He tasted the Coca-Cola chair against the floor for strength. He slammed it down, all four feet together, and backed away, watching as Vel crouched low over it, hesitated, and at last sat down.

The chair was in no danger. Vel was a large woman. But not bigger than most. Her flat face was sallow, and her cornshuck hair was straight, pulled back in a partial bun. She took her handkerchief off and tossed it on the table.

"I've got to have a beer," she said.

"He's coming now, with a couple of cool ones in his hands," Egan said.

Radley, leaving his cigarette burning on the bar, approached them, bringing two cans of Egan's brand and two cold glasses. He limped. Radley had served in Vietnam... re-upped three times ... where there was nothing to do but fight a war and smoke. Ha had brought the smoking back with him. He had left the war in Asia.

"You better have cleaned your shoes good," Egan told Vel, hatefully. "If I catch a whiff of dog shit, while I'm trying to enjoy a cold beer, I'll puke."

Radley set the beers on the shaky table and walked away. Back to his cigarette.

Sitting near the table which Egan had chosen was Jake, a large-boned, spare, bearded truck driver, lovingly fingering a brew, savoring odor of beer which permeated the place.

When Egan and Vel had arrived in the parking lot, Egan had spent a minute eyeballing Jake's rig, while Vel washed her loafer in a freezing puddle of rain.

The eighteen-wheeler was ready to roll. The motor purred. A light steam arose from the hood. Jake was hauling a load of canned fish ... for cats.

"Jeez," Jake said to Egan, by way of being friendly. "This is a bone-chilling night."

There was a huge Confederate flag displayed on the front of Jake's tractor, but Egan picked up Jake's Northern accent at once. Egan made no move to be friendly. He knew this night would cut a man's ass, without some Yankee having to tell him.

Jake occupied a table by himself. He settled back and looked at Egan with cagey disapproval; drank his beer from the can. Now and then he put quarters in the jukebox and played Marty Stuart songs..."Hillybilly Rock"...things like that ... trying to liven up the place.

Vel loved Marty Stuart ... his cute and wiggling body... all that black hair ... that puckish expression he wore on his face. She smiled her approval whenever Jake fed more quarters into the jukebox.

"You sure know good music," she said.

"Anybody don't like Marty Stuart, don't know what's good," Jake said, mimicking the Southern accent he heard all around him. Vel did not know he was making fun of them. Egan knew.

A pale, blond youth, his eyes cobwebbed with dreams, sat like a pale ghost at the end of the bar, almost in darkness, yet shining. He did not seem to notice that Egan and Vel had come in.

But ... Jake looked at them brashly. He was his own man ... King of the Road. He did not need to be anything but what he was.

Vel attempted to pour beer into one of the glasses. Some sloshed on the table top.

Egan looked up at Radley, who only stared at them, waiting for a cue. Radley exhaled two jets of smoke through his nostrils. Ha lay his cigarette carefully down.

A glum expression shadowed Radley's suntanned features. His mustache was trimmed with precision. His appearance showed that he took time with his personal grooming; did his exercises each day in spite of his game leg. He kept up his clothes so that he always looked dogface fresh. He maintained his work area behind the bar with as much care as he gave to his body.

"Bring us a rag over here," Egan said. "My wife has made a mess."

Radley came with a white cloth. He would have wiped away the spilled beer, but Egan wanted to do it. He snatched the rag from Radley and swiped it around on the table top.

"You can keep the rag over here with you," Radley said, walking away, slow and deliberate, so that his limp was hardly noticeable.

Egan sat staring at the soggy rag; surly, and aloof. Vel raised her eyes to gaze at him. He did not return her look.

Vel turned clumsily in her seat so she could look at Jake. Jake looked back at her, his face freezing into a cold, 'possum grin. His lips were thin.

Jake's eyes sparkled. His face, except for his eyes and his lips, was hidden in heavy sideburns and a beard. Egan studiously avoided looking at him, except from the corner of his eye.

Egan hated the ponytail he saw hanging from under Jake's truck-driver hat.

To Jake, his ponytail and his beard were badges of his individuality. He wore them arrogantly.

"Any man don't like 'em can kiss my ass," he always said.

Without being invited, Vel rose to her feet and tottered to Jake's table, where she sat down heavily.

"You gonna bring your beer?" Jake asked.

"I meant to."

With an indifferent shrug, Egan pushed Vel's beer to the edge of the table nearest Jake and Vel.

Jake rose up, standing six-and-a-half-feet tall. He was about to pick up the beer, but a thought stopped him in his tracks.

"We don't need this," he said. "We'll get you a fresh glass of beer."

Jake told Radley to bring Vel a new beer.

"None of this cheap piss," he said. "Bring the lady a glass of good beer." He tossed a twenty dollar bill on the table. He would use his attentions to Vel to make Egan look bad.

"I just wanted to come out and celebrate Groundhog Day," Vel was saying, as justification for her presence in this place on this night. "I just wanted to get out of the house, for a change. Egan works all the time at the plant. We never go anyplace. I thought, tonight, we'd have a good time." Her hands clutched together...jerked ... almost tipping her beer. "Egan got mad with me in the parking lot, because of something I stepped in."

Egan could hear them, but he did not look up. He studied the cleaning rag, which Radley had given him, where it lay on the table before him, as if it had been a gilded fleece. All his journeyings and wanderings had led to this fleece; this stinking bit of cotton... for cleaning up behind Vel.

His life was a mess ... his wife a stumblebum, doddering across the Earth, stepping in things. He couldn't call himself much of a man.

Egan needed a charm ... a fetish ... Something like this limp rag; a talisman from that clean man, Radley.

He needed something to believe in.

Let Vel booze it up with that truck driver. At the present time, this didn't matter to Egan, any more than anything else which he might happen to think of would.

There was no way that he could believe in Vel.

"I'm like a groundhog," Vel was telling Jake. "I live in a dark hole, afraid to come out. What do you think I might be so scared of out there in the light?" Her lips drew together in a worried pout. "I've got to think it through."

"You do that," Jake said.

"It's not Egan I'm afraid of .... is it?"

"Tell me what kind of hole you're in."

"It's a hole shaped like a bottle."

The jukebox played. Jake had put a dollar's worth of quarters in. It was Marty Stuart again; lively, charismatic, teasing, frank. Marty was singing about Western girls.

Vel straightened her back and lifted her head.

"I can be a Western girl," she told Jake. "Are you from the West?" She snapped her fingers in time with the music. "I wish I had worn my cowgirl hat," she said.

Egan looked at her, contempt and embarrassed pity mingled in his face.

"You belong on a ranch," he said loudly. "Only you'd be a cow, if you was there. You ain't one of the cowgirls by no means."

Vel ignored Egan.

"My name's Vel," she said. "It don't stand for MarVEL, it stands for VELvet. Soft and sexy. Can you believe that?" She raised her hands limply, pointing to herself. "I guess that's Captain Marvel sitting over there at that table I just left."

Egan's eyes had become glazed. He stared at the rag.

"I can see that Groundhog Day is very important to you," Jake said.

Vel studied for a long time.

"I'll say this much .... I know how a groundhog feels, living in a hole in the ground, afraid to come out."

"I don't think you're afraid of your husband. I think you're afraid of something else. Maybe you better go in for counseling." Jake was not teasing her. He was really sincere. Whatever was bothering Vel .... Egan just wasn't getting it. Someone should.

Pere, that lissome youth, ray of light in this darkling den, who sat at the bar, had remained staring straight ahead, as though he were not aware of the others in the room. Now, he turned on his barstool and looked at them.

Jake was already bored. The fun was not in Vel. The fun was in provoking Egan, and Egan would not be provoked. Jake wished now that Vel would go away.

Egan was too tired to be angry with Jake. What Jake was doing just didn't matter to him. He knew Jake would like to confront him directly, make him stand up, make him mad enough to fight. But, Jake was careful. This was not his turf.

So, for the time, Jake's hormonal cravings had to go unsatisfied. The room was silent accept for the jukebox.

Then, Pere left his barstool, and came offering to sit down at Egan's table. Radley tried to warn him away.

Radley was, as Egan was, able to read Jake like an open and spread-out road map to Combat City. He knew Egan feared Jake's shoulders and his great hands. Egan swallowed his bile. Radley was afraid Egan might try to vent his pent-up anger and his frustration upon the inexperienced Pere.

"Don't...." Radley began.

But, Egan looked up at Pere with a smile.

"Sit down, Bubba," he said.

"I want to thank you for letting me sit here with you," Pere said. "I was feeling pretty lonesome, sitting over there by myself." Pere's voice was deep, but muted. His shyness led him to speak softly.

"Christ," Egan said.

"I wanted to talk to someone a little bit about my mother."

"Oh, Christ!"

"My mother died just two weeks ago," Pere said. The sad strains of his voice blended with low chords on the jukebox. Pere's jacket was too light. His body was wiry and strong, but slight. "I had to make a sad pilgrimage to Georgia for the funeral. The death of that sweet soul was a great loss to me and my family, but we know there is another star in Heaven today. "

"I'm sorry to hear of your family's sorrow."

Pere's manner was formal. He talked as if he were presenting a speech. The tone, the words, the way the sentences rolled off Pere's tongue ... almost like poetry... reminded Egan of something; something he didn't yet have a handle on.

"I wish you could have seen the funeral." Pere spoke dreamily, seeming almost unaware of Egan. "In that field, behind our church, grayed with the chill of winter, there must have been four hundred cars, which brought people to pay tribute. People came from the four corners of the county. And, relatives from as far as Aiken. My mother bore the greatest respect a community could offer. Everybody loved her."

"My mother was like that," Egan said. But, he knew that his mother wasn't. His mother was nothing like that at all. Not such a drunk as Vel, but a slob like Vel. Egan had never had a good woman of his own.

"The flowers were piled so high at my mother's funeral that it took three vans to haul them to the cemetery. She was herself the Rose of Sharon, a Lily of the Valley. We had to leave her body and the other flowers at the gravesite to face a cutting wind, under sorrowing, cruel, overcast sky, but I knew my mother was jubilant in a land of unclouded day."

"That was a big funeral."

"There were three preachers sitting on the rostrum in the church. Two preached and the other prayed."

"I've been to big funerals like that."

"There was soft weeping among the women," Pere said, a glow of satisfaction on his pale face. He was caught up again in the wonder of that most solemn moment, in the sanctuary, at his mother's last service. "Outside, people acted like they couldn't say enough good about her, commend her enough for the life she'd led."

Now, Egan grasped what it was that was familiar to him about this boy. This boy smelled of the church, an odor like Egan had smelled, suffering through preaching as a boy; the fresh wax on the pews, the scent of open hymnals, the sickening fragrance of altar flowers. The perfume of all those women!

Pere sounded like the church; the sonorous intonations of the minister, the familiar cadence of the congregation singing hymns, and especially the majestic rhythms of King James ... being read slowly ... exaltedly!

Pere was saturated with the church. Egan had known boys like this ... almost become one of them... once.

"Preachers taught you how to talk," Egan commented. He twisted uneasily in his seat.

Radley stood near. He had come from behind the bar. He polished table-tops.

Vel and Jake were silent.

"There was a reason for your mother's funeral to be like it was," Egan said.

"Things like that don't just happen."

"I've thought about it a lot, these past two weeks with nobody to talk to. It was because of my father. My father treated my mother as if she was a saint, the Queen of England! He thanked her when she cooked for us, and complimented what she had done, even when the food was pretty poor. He walked beside her in public, striding tall ... so much taller than me ... showing he was proud to have her at his side. I've seen him a thousand times helping her put on her coat. He held the car door for her, every time, like they ware still courting. My father is a quiet, Christian man. But, he dared any man to disrespect my mother."

"Did he get in many fights because of this?" Egan asked him.

"I never heard of him having to fight one time. Other man saw how he honored her ... her price was above rubies ... and they honored her, too."

"I see how that could happen, when those involved was a good man and a good woman."

"There was six of us boys. Daddy would have whipped any one of us with a plowline would have disrespected her. Every one of us learned early to keep a civil tongue in our mouths around her. All the sons sat together at the funeral ... our father there with us. He was strong in his grief. He knew where Mother was. That day, we all did what we should have done ... remembering Mother."

"You was raised right," Egan said.

"My mama raised us. My daddy and us boys treated her like a queen, and everyone else found the grace to do so, too. I can't remember anything in my life, connected with her, but things to be proud about, to cherish, and honor."

"What are you doing here?"

"I'm working a construction job. I just came in here because it's sort of cold ... the place where I'm staying."

It was warm in Radley's bar, Egan noted gratefully. Vel looked sleepy. Her head nodded a bit. Jake stared at the revolving lights of the jukebox.

"I want to thank you for letting me sit here and talk to you," Pere said. "I hadn't talked to anyone about my mother, since she died. I don't talk around the man I work with. I needed to tell about it ... that day when our family circle was broken for the first time. It will be mended by and by."

"Yes," Egan said. "It will."

Pere got up and returned to his barstool.

"I hope Vel don't fall and bust her ass," Egan thought. Vel was going to sleep. "She has consumed enough beer to float a trawler containing a full catch of shrimp"

Jake began shaking his head, and a great upheaval took place in his insides. He pushed himself roughly away from the table. He hurdled several Coca-Cola chairs and bounded into the men's room,.

In a moment, everyone in the bar could hear Jake puking.

A desolate look washed over Vel's stolid features. She had thought Jake was Burt Reynolds .... And, already this dream was lost. Jake, it turned out, was no big man, for all his height, and breadth, and his cocky Northern manner.

Vel dared not look at Egan. Her large shoulders hunched in upon herself, pushing her downward. Her chin rested upon her chest.

Egan got unsteadily up from his chair. He went and stood over Vel.

"Let's go home," he said, softly. "Let me help you get into your coat. We'll go, get in the truck, and go home."

Vel, afraid to trust ... afraid to hope ... raised her head to look at Egan's chest. She could not meet his eye.

"It's a trick," she said, "you talking that soft way."

"It's no trick." Egan could hear the wracking spasms of Jake's vomiting. "I just want you to come home with me. We can fry some bacon and eggs."

Jake came out of the men's room. He stood, uncertainly, looking at Egan and Vel.

"This lady is my wife," Egan said. "I hope you'll make a note of that. In case we ever meet again."

He picked up Vel's poor wrinkled coat off the chair and helped her put her arms into it. He brushed it carefully with his hands, knocking off lint and crumbs which had accumulated on it. There was a cleaning job due here. Vel stood... a little proudly... smiling weakly.

"I'm scared," Vel said. "If you bring me out into the light too fast, I'll run back in my hole and stay there for twenty-eight more days." A look of weak triumph spread across her face. "It's just come to me what I'm afraid of. The light will make me sea my own shadow. I'm afraid of my shadow. If I see my shadow, I'll know what I look like."

"I'll bring your ass out into the light," Egan said, grimly. "You won't run back into the dark. I won't let you." He grasped her arm, steadying her.

The jukebox played Marty Stuart's great anthem, "That's Country."

"You're goddamned right we're Country," Egan shouted. "And proud of it!"

Outside, they sloshed through the terrible night to get to Egan's truck. Egan opened the door on the passenger side so Vel could climb in. He helped her boost herself up the high step into the pickup.

Vel settled back against the icy cushion, beneath the gun rack, kicking empty beer cans away from her feet, feeling like a queen.

The grizzled woodchuck herself had always been was not there.

"I hope I can always feel this good," she said. "And, that ain't just the beer talking."

ACKNOWLEDGEMENTS

1.   Carrie Brown who paid when the truck brought the manuscripts and books and household things to Georgetown from Charlotte; Who always stepped into the breach; Who was loyal, loving, believing and able; A friend forever to me and to my work.

2.   Tim Chatman who saved much of this material from the dumpster; who read these works tirelessly over the years; and who commented in depth upon things his sharp inner eye was able to see there; A man of special vision.

3.   Mike Daugherty who was a great stabilizing influence in my life, who was ever interested in my writing, and who was ever encouraging about it.

4.   Amy Faggart - my mother - the source of my eternal optimism. She packed up much of this material in Mississippi and mailed it to North Carolina so that it was not lost.

5.   Ted Gagliano who was patient in helping me through the bad times — who read and listened, and hoped for me and with me.

6.   Bill Moorman - my friend since 1938 - someone who can always see my points of view whether he agrees with them or not. He has carefully read almost everything I ever wrote and.acts as custodian of much of it. No one else has done more for me.

7.   Roy Nicholas who held me in higher regard than he held himself; Made me believe in my talent; Hoped for so much for me; All for such a short time.

8.   Robbie Tindall, who is ever "Like a Prince."

Would You Like To Be Published?

JMT Publications can help! Write us for more information about our unique subsidy publishing program. We can help you go from writer to published author in less than a year.

YES! I want to know more about how I can become a published author in less than one year!

Name _____

Mailing Address _____

City _____

State _____   Zip _____

❏ I have a manuscript completed now

❏ I am currently working on a manuscript

❏ I am planning to write a manuscript

Mail to: JMT Publications, PO Box 64, Shirley, IN 47384, or scan & e-mail to: jeantype@excite.com

---

Additional copies of *Out Of The Iron Furnace* can be obtained from the author or through our online bookstore: **http://jmtpubs.hypermart.net**